Copyright 2019 © Amore Publishing

Cover by Robin Harper of Wicked By Design

Photo: © Regina Wamba

Models: Alexander Denning and Cherry

All rights reserved.

No part of this book may be reproduced in any form or by any electronic or mechanical means, including information storage and retrieval systems, without written permission from the author, except for the use of brief quotations in a book review.

THE COMPLETE SERIES

PLAY WITH ME

DIAMOND IN THE ROUGH 1

1
———

RAELYNN

"No! Please! Somebody, help!"

The car skidded out of control and tires burned their rubbered tracks into the road. I gripped the 'oh shit' handle in the car, feeling us careening out of control. I screamed for help as I saw a car going over the edge. Sounds of metal crunching against metal sounded helplessly in my ears as I cried out a name I didn't recognize. A name that sounded unfamiliar, even as it fell from my lips.

Then the world muted itself around me.

Our car came to a stop just beyond the impact point. The mangled guard rail in front of us ignited into flames as I pushed out of the car. I stumbled around, feeling my stomach upheaving its contents onto the road. I couldn't regain control. I couldn't see straight. Between motion sickness and worry bubbling in my gut, my dinner didn't stand a chance of staying down.

"Help!" I roared.

I stumbled to the guard rail and peered over the edge. I gazed into the darkness below, watching it undulate, as if it were laughing at me. I looked around for the car I knew had plummeted over the edge. I tried to gaze beyond the darkness. Beyond the movement. Beyond the endless expanse of nothing that seemed to cloak the fall downward.

"Are you down there?" I exclaimed.

I heard someone calling my name. Someone off in the

distance. I whipped my head up, surveying the world around me. All it did was fall into darkness. Slowly, the creeping nothingness swallowed up colors. Shapes. Sounds. My eyes widened as the road disappeared. I looked up, watching the stars get swallowed whole by the hellish expanse of Vantablack around me. I kept backing up until my legs touched the mangled guard rail. I felt the piercing, heated shards dig into my skin while the flames themselves were put out by the nothingness that surrounded me.

Then a piercing sound ricocheted through my ears.

I stumbled back, falling off the edge and into the darkness below. I reached up for the world above me, but it quickly fell away. Everything got swallowed up. I felt myself falling. Panicking. Breathing harder and harder. I flailed my arms, turning myself around until I was facing what I thought was the ground.

And it was then I saw it.

"No," I gasped.

I bolted upright in my bed, feeling sweat trickling down the nape of my neck. I wiped at my brow, listening as my alarm for school went off. I licked my chapped lips, wincing at how dry they were as I tossed the covers off my bare legs. I closed my eyes as my feet touched down onto the dirty carpet of my floor, burying my face in my hands.

"Not again," I murmured.

That damn dream never ceased to haunt me. For as long as I could remember, it started off every fucking school year. Without fail. The night before my first day of school, I'd have that dream. It didn't matter what I did, what I ate before bed, whether or not I took something to help me sleep, or what I watched in order to fall asleep. For years, that same dream ushered in my years of school.

And it seemed as if my senior year of high school was no different.

"I need a shower," I murmured.

The cold sweats always made me feel gross. Especially when they soaked through the T-shirts I wore at night. I pulled it all off, even my soaked panties, before tossing them into the hamper. Even from beyond my bedroom door, I heard the snores of a man. Some man my mother had probably dragged home from the bar last night. I rolled my eyes as I walked into my bathroom. I turned the water on and let it run for five minutes before I sighed.

Apparently, I'd have to take a cold shower this morning.

"Great," I whispered.

It was the shortest shower of my life. But I did what I had to do. I washed my body, ran some shampoo through my hair, then decided to forgo conditioner so I could fucking get warm. I hopped out and reached for a towel, slipping and sliding everywhere in the process. I still didn't have my legs underneath me. This summer had been enough of a hell-binding, torturous state. What with my terrible ongoing job at the grocery store and Mom sucking down half of whatever I made at the bar every night. I got the job my freshman year to start helping out. I got the damn job in the first place so we wouldn't have to keep picking and choosing which bills to pay every month.

But when I went to turn on my bedroom light, I realized the only thing my money did was help my mother bring home more men.

Because our electricity had been shut off.

"Fucking great," I sighed.

I focused on getting ready for school, because the sooner I got out of the house the sooner I could let this entire summer fall from my mind. I tied my hair back into a low ponytail, then brushed my teeth. I pulled on the first outfit my hands found, since I couldn't see what the hell I was doing. And after rummaging around in the change jar for lunch money, I grabbed my backpack and an apple to have for breakfast. I even grabbed a water from the pantry, just to splurge on myself a little bit.

The relief I felt as I stepped out onto the porch almost knocked me off my feet.

I saw the foreign car in the driveway and shook my head. It sure as hell wasn't her boyfriend's car. Nor was it hers. I snickered as I walked up the driveway, making my way to school. My mother was notorious for bringing home random one-night stands. Even if she did have a steady boyfriend who gave her whatever the hell she wanted.

You know, in exchange for knocking her around a little.

"And yet, we still can't pay our bills," I muttered.

I took a large bite of my apple before cracking open the bottled water. I knew I'd catch hell for it after school, since my mother practically had a counter on the food in our home. But I didn't care. I was thirsty as hell after sweating through the night. After dealing with that stupid nightmare.

I shivered at the thought of it.

"There she is!" Michael exclaimed.

I smiled as I tossed my apple core down a drain pipe. Allison came barreling for me, her long blond hair billowing in the summer breeze behind her. I held my arms out, catching her as she ran into me, almost knocking me clear off my damn feet. I hugged her tightly as the collar of her Ralph Lauren shirt tickled my neck. And before I could even let go to take a look at her parents' traditional 'first day of school' outfit for her, Michael had his arms around both of us.

Squeezing the ever blessed-fuck out of our bodies.

"Michael, I can't breathe," Allison choked out.

"Mike. Are you high?" I croaked.

"Oh, I missed the two of you. I didn't see you guys at all this summer," Michael said.

"Stop. Please. I beg of you," Allison said breathlessly.

"I'll kill you in your sleep," I hissed.

Michael released us and we both dropped to our feet. Allison and I heaved for air, then I stood back and surveyed her outfit. Typical, for her parents. A bright pink collared shirt with a pale blue emblazoned Ralph Lauren logo against her chest. A khaki skirt with boat shoes that were, somehow, the same color as her khakis. I giggled at the laces matching the pink hue of her shirt and the pale blue earrings twinkling in her ears. I shook my head in fascination, never ceasing to be amazed at the outfits her parents could conjure.

I snickered. "Your parents single-handedly keep Ralph Lauren in business."

Allison held out her arms. "What? They're good clothes. You mean you don't like this outfit? I wore the blue just for you."

Michael grinned. "Well, by the looks of Rae, black and brown are in this year."

I rolled my eyes. "Says the boy wearing eggshell-colored shorts that come two inches above his knees."

Allison nodded. "I'm just impressed you know what shade 'eggshell' is."

Michael faked a tear. "Mom would be so proud of you."

I looked down at my outfit and shook my head. I looked like a maniac. My hair was frizzy from no conditioner. My black shirt had lint and dust all over it. And my brown pants were so baggy my inner thighs rubbed together when I walked. None of which took into account my bright green flip-flops Mom had purchased for me this summer on a whim to apologize for some fight she had with her boyfriend.

A fight that wound up destroying my hand-me-down iPod because it got thrown against the wall.

"You guys ready for school?" I asked.

But my two best friends in the entire world were giving me 'the look.'

I sighed. "Guys, not now. Please."

Allison quirked an eyebrow. "Did you have that nightmare again?"

Michael narrowed his eyes. "Or did your mother do something?"

I shrugged. "Why can't it be both?"

Michael shook his head as Allison let out a string of curses under her breath.

I giggled. "Don't let your mom hear you talk like that."

Michael wrapped his arm around my shoulders. "Anything I can do?"

"Yeah. You can stop dwelling on it and help me get to school faster."

The three of us fell in line, abandoning my rundown neighborhood in exchange for perfectly-manicured lawns and sprawling homes. That was the Riverbend High area I knew. Not the rundown shacks in the shadows of the town I lived in, but the massive homes Allison and Michael lived in. They lived perfect lives. They had perfect families. Michael with his adoptive parents that loved him as if he were their own. And Allison with her biological parents that were still very much in love. It seemed that with the nicer suburbs came nicer lives. Nicer parents. Nicer homes to be raised in and nicer food to eat. I envied them for the lives they had. I envied the relationships they had with their parents.

I'd kill to have that relationship with my *one* parent.

Allison cleared her throat. "So what are you two doing this weekend?"

Michael smiled. "Please, oh please tell me this is leading into another weekend visit at your place. I love your basement, and girl talk is always fun to listen to."

I laughed. "You know I'm not doing anything. I only work

every other weekend at the grocery store even though I beg for more hours. You know how it goes. Why?"

Allison linked her arm with mine. "Well, my parents are going to Palm Springs Thursday evening for a spa retreat. Won't be back until Monday afternoon."

Michael thrust his fist into the air. "Yes! Girl time! Nailed it!"

I threw my head back in laughter as Allison shook her head.

"Seriously, though. You guys should come over. The both of you. We can watch girly movies and eat shitty food," she said.

Michael smiled brightly. "And I can finally get you two to watch Top Gun."

I sighed. "Are you really still on that tangent? You haven't gotten us to watch it for two years. What makes you think this weekend is gonna be any different?"

Allison snickered. "We'll watch Top Gun if you paint our toes."

Michael pointed at the two of us. "Deal."

My jaw dropped. "Wait, don't I get a say in this?"

Michael shook his head. "Already made the deal. Sorry, guys!"

Allison whispered, "I mean, he's going to paint our toenails. Make the most of it, okay?"

I shook my head, watching as Michael grinned. I knew there wasn't a damn thing that boy wouldn't do for Allison. He had it bad for her, and she knew it. It was cute, though. They'd been going back and forth for damn near two years with one another. Flirting, but neither of them making a move.

I mean, they'd make cute preppy little babies. With his above-the-knee shorts and her collared shirts.

The child would come out wearing boat shoes, if they had anything to do with it.

Allison furrowed her brow. "What's so funny?"

I giggled. "Nothing. Just thinking about this weekend."

Michael paused. "You better wash your feet. I'm not painting grody toenails."

I shrugged. "You already agreed. No toenails, no Top Gun."

He shook his head. "You're gross, you know that?"

Allison winked. "I'll wash mine, don't worry."

Michael stared down at me. "If you don't wash your feet, I'm painting your toenails purple."

I gasped. "You wouldn't dare."

Allison butted in. "Or pink!"

My eyes narrowed. "I'd kill you both in your sleep."

Allison moved from my arm to Michael's as the three of us stepped onto the school's sidewalk. We kept talking about our weekend, making plans for food and drinks and what time we'd be over. I knew it wouldn't be an issue, either. Mom never gave a shit what I was doing on the weekends. She was nowhere to be found, which gave me free rein of the house and whatever was in it.

Then the three of us came to a stop in front of the high school doors.

"You guys ready for our last year?" Michael asked.

Allison nodded. "I already know where I'm applying for college. Just gotta make the grades to get me there."

Michael looked down at me. "What about you, Rae?"

I shrugged. "Could be worse."

Allison peeked over. "Do you know where you're going to be applying for college?"

I didn't know how to answer her. I was a C-plus student, at best. Which meant my future included community college, a technical degree, and a prayer to somehow get the hell away from my mother for good.

Michael knocked against me. "Earth to Rae. You there?"

I shook my head. "Sorry. Allison's question dazed me there. Because for the life of me, I don't know how a sane person can be standing in front of school and be thinking about *more* school."

And as Allison playfully stormed away from us, Michael ran after her. Like he'd always done.

Leaving me to stand there and smile at them as dread slowly filled my gut.

2

CLINTON

I groaned and rolled over, burying my face into the pillow. It reeked of booze and regret, just how I liked it. My jeans rubbed against my legs and I groaned, then wiggled my toes. I felt my bike boots on my feet over the sweaty socks creating blisters against my heels. I rolled over, flopping onto my back as I sprawled out in my king-size bed.

And I lay there in the pitch black room, reliving the fantastic party the other night.

I grinned as the sun tried its hardest to stream around my blackout curtains. I cracked my neck, then toed off my boots. I needed to get these damn socks off. I needed to change my pants. I needed to get washed up for the first day of school.

Then again, I didn't really want to.

"Fuck school," I murmured.

I rolled back over, reaching for my cellphone. And when I clicked the harsh white light on, I chuckled. Of course it was almost lunch time. I'd slept through my first two periods. What a great way to start my senior year. The smell of alcohol followed me as I sat up. I burped, and the taste was rancid. I was damn near the puking stage, but I refused to do that.

I refused to pussy out after the best party of the summer.

I slipped to the edge of my bed, groaning. I felt like utter shit. One too many beers, and it was hard to move. Hard to think straight. Hard to even fathom getting myself cleaned up so I could get to school. I mean, if my parents figured out I was late for my first day, all hell might break loose.

They might video chat me from their safari trip and really give me a good tongue lashing.

"Idiots," I said, snickering.

I pulled myself out of bed and stumbled into the wall. I caught myself with my hands, but the glaring rays of the sun made me cower away. Fuck, that sun was bright. Did it have a dimmer dial of some sort? I sighed as I stumbled my way around my darkened room, running my knees into furniture and jamming my pinky toe against my bed frame.

"Fuck!" I roared.

Why the hell did I need so much mahogany furniture in my fucking bedroom?

Oh, yeah. Because my parents had more money than sense.

"Fucking bullshit," I murmured.

I stripped my clothes off, leaving a trail from the foot of my bed all the way to the shower. I turned on the hot water and got in, allowing the burps to work their way up with ease. I refused to puke, though. And as I leaned my head against the tiles of the shower wall, I drew in a deep breath.

If I got to school right at lunch time, I could fill my stomach with enough bread to get me through the rest of the day.

"Or you could just not go," I whispered.

Nope. The last time I missed a day of school like this, my parents actually flew back from their vacation, taking the time out of their busy recreational flight schedule to be decent parents for once. And it ended up with them selling off my fucking bike. I wasn't losing another bike over this. That thing was my peace. My solace. It made me feel powerful and on top of the world.

Plus, it got me laid more times than I cared to count.

"Nope. Get your ass to school," I murmured.

The summer had been great, but it was time to get back to reality. I cleaned myself up, slowly sobering as my vision cleared. I sighed as I got out of the shower, feeling the steam wrap around me. It was nice waking up in an empty house, kicking around streamers and empty beer cans and wiping red Dixie cups off my bathroom counter.

Yeah. It felt nice to always fucking be alone.

"If someone fucked in my bathroom, they're never invited back," I said, sighing.

Getting ready for school was a pain in my ass. But it had to happen. I didn't give a damn, though. I'd show up for lunch break and find Roy. Screw chemistry and English class. I didn't need any of that shit in my life. I had no plans to go to college. I had no plans to continue education past high school. Despite my parents constantly nagging the fuck out of me for it, I had other plans. Other wants. Other wishes. I wanted to work on bikes and write my fucking books. I wanted people to leave me the fuck alone so I could indulge the only two things on this planet I loved.

Motorcycles and writing.

"Fuck my parents," I growled.

And as I reached for my toothbrush, I settled into my morning routine. A lonely routine I'd crafted over the years to deal with my parents never being around.

Hell, it wasn't my fucking fault they wanted to enjoy their money rather than their son.

The revving of my motorcycle engine was my second favorite thing about my damn bike. The first being how it vibrated underneath my ass. I pulled into the backyard parking lot of the school, where all the juniors and seniors were allowed to park their shit. I found myself a spot in back, next to the woods where I knew no one would fuck with my shit. Not that they dared do it anyway. The last person to touch my bike without permission ended up with a broken nose and blood on their shirt.

So what if I got suspended for the rest of the month for it?

Don't fucking touch my stuff.

I turned my bike off and put the kickstand down. And after sliding my helmet off, I hung it off the handlebars. No one had even come toward my bike since that incident last year, so I knew my shit was safe. I slipped my bike keys into the pocket of my jeans, then straightened out my leather coat. People stared at me. Those who ate lunch at their cars so they could listen to music followed me with their eyes. Girls giggled off in the distance, causing me to wink at them from beyond my sunglasses. I loved it when the girls swooned. There was no bigger turn-on to high school girls than a senior who rode a bike. I licked my lips as I walked by a gaggle of cheerleaders, their eyes sweeping over my body with lust.

I winked at the head cheerleader. By the end of the semester, I'd have her right where I wanted her.

On my lap, riding my cock, with my bike vibrating underneath her ass cheeks.

I pushed my way through the back doors of the school, making my way to the cafeteria. My eyes scanned the room as I slid off my sunglasses in search of Roy. My best bud. My closest friend. I mean, Roy was a fucking kiss-ass. He wanted nothing more than to be exactly like me. Which was outstanding, until he wore my same fucking outfits. I hated it when he did that shit. I couldn't stand it when we turned up in the same clothes. Thank God his parents had refused to let him get tattoos that matched mine. But he was a pushover. Someone to boss around and laugh at whenever he ended up doing the stupid shit I asked him to do.

Roy was good entertainment.

I spotted him from across the room.

"There's the big guy!" Roy exclaimed.

I grinned as I started across the cafeteria, feeling teachers and vice principals alike stare me down. I walked with my shoulders rolled back and confidence in my step. They hated me because they wanted to be like me. Carefree, with enough friends and money to run circles around the town of Riverbend twelve times over. That was how Roy and I knew one another. Our parents constantly competed with their wealth and ran in many of the same circles. Hell, Roy already had his college years planned out by his father. One well-timed donation to any Ivy League school of Roy's choosing, and he could coast through the damn place on his father's dime.

I didn't want anything from my parents, though.

I didn't want any reason for them to keep meddling in my fucking life after I graduated.

Roy grinned. "I was wondering when the hell you'd show up."

I sat down beside him and he passed me a tray of food. Pizza, two rolls, two massive cookies, and a soda.

I smiled. "Oh, hell yeah. Pizza day's the best around here."

"Figured you'd need it after keg-standing through half the damn party last night."

I snickered. "How much of it did I get down?"

"Looked to be about seven beers' worth, I'd say," Roy said.

"Eh, looks more like six to me."

"I thought it was ten."

"It was a smaller keg. Pretty sure he fucking chugged half of it."

Roy chuckled. "Either way, you were sloshed. And it was incredible. That sloppy makeout session with Honkers? Priceless."

I paused. "You mean the new head cheerleader?"

He raised his eyebrows. "Who the fuck else is Honkers? You seen the tits on that girl?"

I grinned to myself before I took a bite of my pizza. So that's why she had her eyes on me coming into the school. Already trying to claim something that wasn't hers.

That'll make fucking her easier.

I nodded. "Speaking of honkers, here comes your girl."

Marina walked up, all smiles. "Hey, guys. Clint. And hi there, handsome."

Roy scoffed. "The fuck am I last for? You got the hots for my friend over here?"

She giggled. "Never. But rumor has it our new lead cheerleader does."

"You better lock that shit down, Clint."

"Trust me, I have plans."

Roy swiveled himself around and she flopped right down into his lap. I grinned as he ground up into her, making all the teachers shake their heads at him. He didn't give a shit, though. Just like me. And as I wolfed down my slice of pizza, I snuck his off his tray while he sucked face with his current piece of ass.

Who had nothing to eat but a banana for lunch.

Girl's got an eating problem.

It sure as hell didn't affect her tits, though. Because Roy was definitely a tit kinda guy.

Not my thing, but whatever. Tits were just tits. Nothing special about them. Now, an ass on the other hand? Fucking hell. It was clear these guys hadn't gone near a decent one yet in their lives. Because if they had? They wouldn't give a second fucking thought to tits on a girl.

Ever.

Marina took a small bite of her banana. "So how was your summer, Roy? I didn't see as much of you as I'd like."

Roy smiled. "You saw plenty of me last night."

"Roy."

"What? Did you not like it? Because I can certainly give it another shot if you didn't."

She giggled. "You're something else, you know that?"

I swallowed hard. "Did he fuck you well enough?"

Roy grimaced. "The fuck, dude? I don't go around asking if you fucked your girls well enough."

Marina laughed. "You know damn good and well he did."

Roy paused. "Hey, now. I don't like dirty mouths on my women. Tone the language down, or you're gonna have problems."

"Sorry, handsome."

She kissed Roy's cheek and I rolled my eyes. I didn't get the point of having a girlfriend. I mean, why the hell would I only want to fuck one girl at a time? Sounded boring to me. Marina started gabbing Roy's ear off about shit I didn't care about, which caused me to practically inhale my lunch. Anything to get away from her tinny voice and her boisterous giggle. Roy needed to bring less annoying girlfriends around if they wanted to sit with us at lunch. Because I couldn't handle that shit one bit.

Then Marina snickered. "Speaking of losers."

Roy laughed. "Holy fuck. Look who it is."

"Is that Rae?"

"Holy shit, she filled out over the summer."

"The fuck's she wearing, though?"

Marina rolled her eyes. "Why can't someone teach that poor girl some decent fashion sense?"

I cracked open my soda and swiveled around in my chair. And when my eyes fell onto her, I grinned. Rae Cleaver. Loser extraordinaire. Came from the wrong side of the tracks, and her clothes boasted of it every single fucking day. She was the pet project of the school. Well, one of them. For some reason, the county felt the need to draw redistricting lines among the suburbs in order to get some of the city scum into better schools. And the only reason I knew that was because my parents rallied hard not to let that happen. I mean, why the fuck did our education have to be ruined simply because we had money and they didn't?

Sucked to be them, but life wasn't always fair.

Even I knew that much.

Marina sighed. "She looks pathetic. Can someone go over there and tell her brown doesn't go with black like that?"

Roy slapped her ass. "Why don't you do the honors, sexy?"

Marina yelped, then playfully swatted Roy's shoulder. Yet another gesture that made my eyes roll before they went back to sucking on one another's faces. I didn't know how the hell they breathed through all that. Or how he tolerated that girl's wide-ass tongue filling up his face.

To each their own, I guess.

And as I picked up my tray to carry over to the trash can, Rae brushed through my peripheral. I turned my head, watching her a little too long as she sat off in the corner. She was sitting there, waiting for those two dinky little friends of hers. The preppy, uptight bitch and the boy who probably sucked dick with his butt-hole. She had a pathetic excuse for a lunch, too. Soup and a bottled water. What the fuck was up with these girls and not eating? Did they think that shit was attractive? Because if Rae thought that was her selling point, then she obviously didn't understand the appeal of decent clothes. I mean, with her dirty black shirt and her faded brown pants, she looked like something out of a horror novel. Surrounded by us, she looked completely out of her league. Tease her hair out and she'd look like actual white trash. Like someone from an actual horror film. Like that creature underneath a child's bed that only came out to play if the child's foot slipped over the edge.

Looks like I found my fun for the semester.

Then again, Rae Cleaver was always entertaining. Especially because she didn't take jokes very well.

3

RAELYNN

I sighed as I sat down at the corner table where we always sat. The first couple days of school were always stupidly long and boring. We went over the syllabus for every class the first day, then the second day was used to recap things we learned last year. They were the only two days of school where I never felt bad for zoning out. Where I never worried about falling asleep or missing something the teacher was saying.

"Only three more periods to go," I murmured.

I looked down at my lunch and sighed. It was all I could afford until I got paid this weekend by the grocery store. Soup and a bottled water. Even though I was fucking starving. I slipped the top off the soup and picked up my spoon. Thankfully, it came with a mound of crackers. I crunched them up and poured them over the top of the soup, making the liquid mess a little more solid. It didn't look appealing to the eye, but it sure as hell would feel good once it got to my stomach.

I saw something move in my peripheral and was relieved to have my friends show up.

It wasn't until I looked over, however, that I saw it wasn't them at all.

"You know, we really should have coordinated our schedules more so we could've…"

I traced my eyes up those faded jeans. Up that worn leather

jacket. The figure plopped down into the seat next to me, where Allison usually sat. I wrinkled my nose as his face came into view. Clinton Clarke. The high school asshole and overall 'pump and dump' station.

The boy was a regular manwhore, and he owned every bit of it. *Barf.*

Clint grinned. "We really should have coordinated our schedules. I'm gonna miss having you in English."

I wrinkled my nose. "What do you want?"

I put my spoon down, refusing to eat in front of him. I watched his eyes follow my movements, and something crossed his face. Disgust? Confusion? Neither of those would've shocked me. If Clint wasn't absolutely freaked out by the way I ran my life on a daily basis, my general presence was probably confusing to him. I mean, really? A girl that didn't want to jump his bones at the drop of a hat?

It probably confused the hell out of him.

And the thought made me giggle.

"Got something you wanna share with the class?" he asked.

I shrugged. "Nope."

"You got another outfit you can change into so you don't keep hurting my eyes?"

I grinned. "Don't like it? Don't look."

"Kinda hard not to look."

"Is that a crack at my weight? Or a crack at the fact that you secretly think I'm sexy and don't want to admit it?"

He snickered. "You wish I saw you that way."

"Trust me, you're not my type."

His eyebrows rose. "Oh? And what is your type? The monster in the closet?"

"I feel like that's a joke that probably requires some explanation. And ever since I had English with you last year, we both know you're not the best at those."

His face fell. "Fuck you."

I sighed. "What do you want, Clint?"

I heard high-pitched laughter come from across the cafeteria and rolled my eyes. Marina Lancaster's laughter was the loudest, most piercing thing I'd ever heard. It was the most recognizable laugh, too. I saw Clint's eye flinch, but then a grin appeared on his face. I didn't like that grin, either. It made me shift in my seat, uncomfortable in his presence. That was the grin of Satan himself. Who had a plan to do something to destroy me in front of a cafeteria full of people.

Where the fuck are Allison and Michael?

"I just wanted to say hi," Clint said.

I licked my lips. "Yeah. Right."

He feigned shock. "What? Do you really not believe me, Miss Cleaver?"

"Not a fucking chance."

"You really should watch that little mouth of yours. Boys don't like women with dirty words in their vocabulary."

"I'm just shocked you know the word 'vocabulary.'"

Clint's eyes boiled with anger. "Unlike some fat-ass idiots in this school, I don't have to pay attention in class to pass mine."

"No. You just need Mommy and Daddy's money to help you do that."

He leaned his forearm against the table. "How's your mom doing, Rae? I heard she had quite a time this past weekend."

I rolled my eyes. "Clever, Clinton. A mom joke. We're all impressed. Such original material."

He narrowed his eyes. "It's Clint."

I started slow-clapping, which caused Marina to laugh even harder. And while her laugh was the most annoying thing on the face of this planet, it only served to piss Clint off more. Which was a marvelous sight.

I stopped clapping. "I don't care what you want to be called. If you're going to come over here and harass me with your idiotic tactics, at least be prepared to take your own damn medication, asshole."

Clint snarled. "At least my mother's not a filthy cum-dumpster like yours is."

"Nope. She's just an absent, rich, tottie little woman who's addicted to painkillers and plastic surgery. Which would be the reason why your father left her, right? Traded her in for a newer model. Also known as your stepmother?"

"At least she wants to look decent for my father. You don't even want to look decent for yourself. What, you hate yourself that much? Or do you just hate the attention you know I'd love to pay you if you wore decent clothes?"

I scoffed. "I'd never give a second thought to the likes of you."

He grinned. "Why? Scared I'd make you a sexaholic, like your mother?"

"No. I'd only be scared of the multiple STDs you'd pass on, seeing as you're nothing but a useless manwhore."

"The last thing I am is useless, sweet cheeks. You just don't like admitting that because it means I might just be better than you. When really, this entire school is better than you."

"Why? Because most everyone in this school has more money than me? Why don't you harp on something you haven't already beaten and shot out back?"

He smiled widely. "Maybe I'll just pay your mother some attention this coming weekend, then. What's the bar she likes to frequent? Bar None's?"

I tried not to let the comment get under my skin because I understood how boys like Clint worked. I had no patience for him, and I wanted to waste no more energy on this asshole or anything he had to say. He was only trying to look tough for his friends, to come into his senior year with a bang. Like he did every fucking school year. Only this time, he'd chosen me to sink his teeth into.

And he was about to get a very rude awakening.

I sighed. "Look, Clinton. I get it. Really, I do. You come over here and you tease me and push my buttons because you want a reaction. Because your parents are never around to pay you any attention. I understand, completely. My mother pays me no attention, so we're more alike than you think."

He snarled. "I'll never be like you."

"Why? Because you have money, or because you lack class?"

"You don't know the first fucking thing about having class."

"I do know the first fucking thing about ruffling your feathers, though, Mr. Peacock."

He narrowed his eyes. "Don't you dare."

I giggled. "What, Mr. Peacock? Don't like the name?"

"It's Clint, you useless little bitch."

"Mr. Peacock it is. I knew you'd come to enjoy it."

I watched his fists ball up, and for a split second I thought he was going to slug me. I braced myself. Prepared my body to fight its way out of this corner he'd backed me into. The cafeteria became eerily silent. I felt everyone watching us. I felt my hands trembling from a lack of nourishment. I felt the room tilting as my blood sugar plummeted. I had to eat. Despite what I knew was coming if I tried, I had to get something in my stomach.

I worked up the courage to pick up my spoon and dip it into my soup. As Clint's eyes became engulfed in rage at my words, I puckered my lips and blew a stream of cool air across the steaming hot soup before clearing my throat.

"Are you done? Because if you are, my friends are here and I'd like to eat in peace."

I saw Michael and Allison standing behind him holding their trays of food, ready to sit down with me. I put the spoonful of soup between my lips, and I could've sworn I saw his eyes follow the movement. But it was a fleeting motion and I wasn't sure if I'd caught it right. He turned around, surveying my friends, and it was then I saw it.

I watched his posture relax as that wild smile came back into view.

It was as if everything played out in slow motion. Michael's food tray fell from his hands as he lunged toward Clint. Allison jerked her tray up toward her own face, tossing food all over her chest as Clint quickly got up. He threw himself forward, his hand making its way underneath the table. I heard Allison squealing as food poured over her and I heard Michael yelling at Clint to get away from me. And as Clint's hand slammed underneath the table, I watched my only food for the rest of the day jostle. My water bottle turned over, flooding my brown pants as the piping hot soup tumbled against my chest. I felt it soaking my outfit as I stood up, my jaw dropped open as the spoon fell from my hand.

Clint's chuckle dawned on my ears, causing the world to move at regular speed as I snapped my face over toward his.

I licked my lips. "You're going to regret that."

His eyes fell down my body. "Trust me, I already do. No one wants to see those clothes clinging to a body like yours. You should probably go home and change."

Allison hissed. "You're a fucking loser, Clint."

Michael stepped in front of her. "Get the heck out of here."

Clint lunged at him, causing Michael and Allison to flinch. He laughed at the two of them, then turned back to me. I looked down at the mess my clothes had become. The soup that was on my stomach instead of in it. The searing hot pain forced tears to my eyes as he snickered, then walked away. I shook my hands off. I saw teachers rushing up to him and me. I saw the principal already pulling Clint aside, which only garnered him more respect from his bullshit friends.

And it was then I tuned in to the rest of the cafeteria.

It was then I tuned into the raucous laughter as everyone stared at me.

A teacher came over to talk to me, but I gathered up my things and raced out of the room, leaving the laughing behind. I felt Allison hot on my heels as I threw myself into the bathroom. I heard the door close and lock. And as I brushed tears away from my eyes, I clenched my teeth tight.

"He's just a dick, Rae. Don't let him get to you," Allison said.

I clenched my fists. "It's not him I'm angry at. It's the rest of those dickweeds."

Allison pulled at some paper towels and ran them underneath some water. I didn't have a chance in hell of cleaning up these clothes enough to look respectable throughout the rest of the day. Not that I'd looked respectable beforehand. But at least I'd looked better than this. She handed me a soaked paper towel before getting one for herself. Together, we wiped the soup off my shirt.

She shrugged. "I mean, at least it's a black shirt. Sit in the right lighting and people won't even know it's there."

I sighed. "Yeah, well, they'll still smell it coming from a mile away."

"Good thing tomato soup smells good?"

Somehow—like she always did—Allison got me to laugh. My grimace became a grin, and soon we were gabbing while trying to clean off our clothes. I sighed as I racked my brain, trying to figure out what the hell I was going to do for the rest of the day.

Then it dawned on me.

"We need to go to my locker," I said.

Allison paused. "Do you have a change of clothes there?"

I nodded. "I mean, they're not the best clothes. But look at what I'm already wearing. I have P.E. this year because I skipped it my freshman year."

She smiled. "Your gym clothes are in your locker?"

"Will you come with me?"

"I'll do you one better. Give me your locker number and combination. I'll go get it for you."

"You're a lifesaver, you know that?"

She winked. "I have a tendency to have good ideas every once in a while."

And as I rattled off what she needed to know, she slipped out of the bathroom. Leaving me to stand in the mirror and take a good, hard look at myself.

Something I hated doing.

Especially if I was alone.

4
____

CLINTON

With my sunglasses sinking down the bridge of my nose, I tossed my jacket over my shoulder. History. I hated history class. Any history class, really. But especially world history. The fuck did I care what happened on the other side of the planet over a hundred years ago? Didn't affect me now. But, for some reason, it was required of me to know.

I didn't mind being late to class, though.

The teacher pursed her lips. "How nice of you to join us, Mr. Clarke."

I grinned. "Pleasure's all mine, Mrs. Christ."

"Take a seat, and know it's your spot for the rest of the semester."

I scanned the room, taking in the pathetic crowd of losers that had already been in class for damn near twenty minutes. And as my eyes gravitated toward the front corner desk, there she sat. Rae Cleaver. In a pair of bright orange shorts, a white tank top, and some random jacket tossed over her shoulders. My smile grew positively out of control. She'd changed into her gym clothes. And oh, was it a sight to behold. I didn't think I'd ever seen Rae in anything other than pants. I mean, did the idiot not take P.E. her freshman year to get it out of the way?

Figures. Stupid as hell, just like her mother.

I snorted as I made my way toward the back row. I sure as hell wasn't taking the seat behind Rae. I mean, I didn't want to smell the musty stench of her house all damn period. I flopped myself in the back corner desk, where I pushed my sunglasses up my face. And as that stuck up, preppy little Allison leaned in toward Rae, I saw the two of them whisper to one another. Exchanging secrets about me.

I mean, it was painfully obvious they were talking about me.

Thanks for making me the center of your world, ladies.

The teacher clapped her hands. "All right. Now that our daily distraction is over, let's get back to the syllabus."

I raised my hand. "Mrs. Christ?"

"You can get a syllabus at the end of class. Take notes while you're here, and don't be late to my class again."

I heard giggles rising up from the front corner of the classroom. Allison, with her bright blond hair, and Rae. With her plain brown hair, her annoying little freckles, and her dark eyes. Like blackened pits of despair that reeked of the desolate wasteland called 'her neighborhood.'

I watched her throughout class. I watched Rae tuck her foot up under her thigh, splaying it out more against her seat. The teacher rambled on about shit I didn't care about as Rae's frizzy ponytail swung against her back. That jacket slipped from her shoulders, revealing a softly-toned strength underneath them that called for a second glance.

Or a really fucking long stare.

Maybe she's not all pig fat, after all.

"Mr. Clarke?"

I whipped my head to the front of the classroom as Mrs. Christ called my name.

"Yep?"

The teacher sighed. "Can you answer for the class why world history is so important?"

I licked my lips. "Uh, because it's important to know thine enemy?"

Some of the class giggled, but all Rae did was stare at the whiteboard, studiously ignoring me, even though I knew she felt me staring. I knew she felt my presence. I knew she wanted to look back, too. Allison kept peeking. Snickering. Shaking her head at me, like some disapproving mother. I guessed she was preparing for her future role as a stay-at-home soccer mom, ready to punish her kids with a swift blow of her angry gaze.

If her future husband was lucky enough, she'd put out a decent blowjob every once in a while.

"Mr. Clarke," the teacher said curtly.

I sighed. "What?"

She narrowed her eyes. "Tuck in the attitude and consider this a reflection of your daily grade. What's the importance of world history?"

"I take it my answer wasn't an acceptable one."

Allison scoffed. "Obviously, idiot."

The teacher frowned. "Miss Denver, let me handle it."

I grinned. "Then handle it a little better this time around."

The class oohed, and it caused me to smile widely. I loved getting underneath my teachers' skin. Why they kept promoting me up grades, I'd never understand. Why they kept giving me grades I never earned, I'd never get. Maybe they didn't want to put up with me anymore. Or maybe my parents had given so much money to this damn place that they felt they couldn't fail me. Either way, it wasn't as if my parents were in town to do anything about it.

I mean, they had at least a day's worth of flights ahead of them before they could even think about popping me upside my head.

Mrs. Christ nodded curtly. "Is there anyone else that wants to join Mr. Clarke in a daily failing grade?"

I shrugged. "Not my fault you don't care about your enemies."

"That's enough, Clinton."

Rae giggled. "Be careful, he doesn't like that name very much."

The class laughed along with her and I shot her a death glare. I wanted to wrap my hand up in that damn ponytail of hers and tug until she cried for me to stop. Who the fuck did she think she was, embarrassing me like that?

Oh, she'd get what was coming to her soon enough.

"Miss Cleaver, one more outburst from you and you'll be heading to the principal's office."

I snickered. "I don't think she's ever been there before. Might be a fun field trip."

Allison turned around. "Your parents around to sign your permission slip, Clint?"

I glared. "I don't know. Why don't you ask your mother when she's getting home from my father's bed later?"

"That's enough!" Mrs. Christ exclaimed.

And then Rae turned around. "Put a fucking sock in it, asshole."

Part of the class was dying with laughter, and the other part stared in horror. I smiled deviously at her as our history teacher walked over to her desk, tapping on it twice. I knew that signal all too well. It was practically my mantra during my high school years. One tap means a warning, two taps means the principal's office. And when Mrs. Christ leveled her eyes with me, I held up my hands.

"I'm going. I'm going. I know how this works," I said.

The teacher sighed. "And you'd do well to try and straighten yourself out. Because unlike the rest of your teachers, I'm not afraid of your parents. I've got no issues failing you right out of my class and holding you back a year if that's what it takes to straighten you out."

Rae scoffed. "Good luck with that."

I feigned shock. "Why, Miss Cleaver. You're already in hot water. Whatever did you say that for?"

"I'll put my fist through your face if you don't stop."

"I'd love to see you try."

Mrs. Christ raised her voice. "Principal's office. Now!"

Rae bit down on the inside of her cheek in frustration and I blew her a kiss. I slid my sunglasses down on my face, watching her boil over with anger as I tossed her a playful wink. Oh, having history together was going to be fun. Especially right after our lunch break. Back-to-back moments where I got to pick and poke and prod until she finally exploded.

And maybe, I could get her in the principal's office a few more times with me.

I walked over to the classroom door and held it open for her. I bowed deeply as she walked through, and I felt her bump my forehead with her hip. Hard. The motion made the class cackle with laughter again, but it stunned me for a split second. The softness of her skin. The warmth of her hip. The strength behind it as I stumbled back a bit.

Rae definitely had some secrets underneath those clothes.

And I want to uncover all of them.

I shot up at the thought and shook my head. I let the door bang closed as I trotted to catch up with Rae. She was striding, trying to get away from me as we made our way for the stairs. I shoved the door open, forcing it to swing back before letting go. And as I turned around, I watched Rae hold out her hands. The door slammed back into her, knocking her clear off her feet as curses left her lips.

"Fucking hell, are you serious?"

I puckered my lips. "Oh, baby. You kiss your momma with that mouth?"

She bounced down the stairs. "Get the hell away from me."

I caught up to her, slinging my arm around her shoulders. "And here I thought we were becoming best buds."

Then, out of nowhere, she gripped my wrist. She wrangled me away from her body, twisting my arm around my back. She bent my wrist up, causing me to growl out as she shoved me into the wall. And as we stood there on the platform between the staircases, she shoved her knee into the back of my thigh.

"If you ever touch me again, be prepared to lose your hand. Understood?"

I snickered. "Feisty little one, aren't you?"

She shoved me one last time, then released my wrist. I turned around, rubbing at my shoulder as she made her way quickly down the steps. Well, well, well. Rae Cleaver was just full of surprises, wasn't she?

It only spurred me on, made me want to rush to her side. I got there just in time to open the bottom stairwell door for her, then ushered her through. She glared at me, causing me to chuckle as her face scrunched up. Those insane freckles on her face always moved at the slightest twitch of her muscles, causing her eyes to ignite. She reacted more than anyone I'd ever picked on. And I enjoyed the way she attempted to defend herself.

Especially when she put her hands on me.

I like them a little spicy.

I strode after her, shouldering her as we made our way for the principal's office. She scoffed and moved away from me, but I brushed against her again, trying to see how angry I could make her before we got to our final destination. And when she shoved me with her hands, the strength behind her push damn near knocked me off my feet.

I stumbled. "Wow. Got some power behind that push."

"And don't you forget it."

I grinned. "Never thought a goody-good like you would get sent to the principal's office. That's usually my forte."

And while she ignored me, I knew she couldn't for long.

"Those shorts look good on you. Though your legs could use a fresh shave."

"Do your bras always look this terrible on you?"

"Why the hell didn't you just take P.E. our freshman year? You look ridiculous in that getup."

"Whose jacket is that anyway? Let me see."

I pulled the jacket off her shoulders and that's when it happened. She spun around, ripped it clear from my hand, and pressed her fingertips against my chest. She backed me all the way into the wall as I held up my hands, playfully grinning at her as she glared up at me. Her brown eyes went from black tar pits of desolation to glowing amber gems. Lit up by an exploding sky and pulsating with the anger of a thousand rabid dogs.

I'd never seen this side of her before. And it was intriguing.

"Listen here, you waste of space. You're pathetic. You get underneath people's skin because you can't stand your own life, so you have to make everyone else miserable just like you are. I know how you operate, because my mother's the same way. The two of you are no different, which means I'll treat you no different. So keep being a manwhore and keep putting out and keep trying to deflect from the sadness you feel inside. And while I'm reaching for the stars, enjoying my life, you'll be struggling to climb out of the hell hole you've dug for yourself. Got it?"

Her nostrils flared. Her eyes grew wider. Her cheeks flushed with a deep red tint, accenting the freckles they backdropped. I almost couldn't take my eyes off her. I almost couldn't slip away from her grasp. But when she shoved my chest one last time, it shocked me back into reality.

"Did you just call your mother a whore?" I asked.

"Ugh!"

She stormed through the front foyer of the school, and I watched as she left. Just… left. She didn't pass go. She didn't collect her two hundred dollars. And she sure as hell didn't follow me to the principal's office. Oh, that would get her detention. The goody-good who tried her best to be as rich as her best friends would sit her ass in some lonely room for the rest of the week. Which made me salivate with excitement. I mean, there was nothing more fun than ruining someone's day.

But when I watched those same people ruin their week just to get away from me?

I mean, it was practically a fucking Christmas gift.

5

RAELYNN

I sucked air through my teeth as my pencil doodled along the edges of my notebook. After completely bailing school a couple of days ago, I'd been called into the principal's office first thing yesterday morning. I mean, I didn't even get through the damn front doors with Michael and Allison before the principal beckoned me with his crooked finger. It made me irate that I was having to pay a price by simply standing up to Clinton Clarke. It was sickening to me that I was being punished after saying what I knew the *teacher* even wanted to say to him!

And now, here I sat, doodling in my notebook and waiting for the time to pass.

The principal gave me detention after school for an hour for the rest of the week. As recompense for my outburst, for shoving him into a wall—which was wonderfully caught on camera for people to behold—and for storming out of school without a note. Great. Fucking grand. It was me, the nose picker, the born-again meth head, and the drug dealer.

The only good thing about detention was the fact that Clint hadn't actually showed up. He wasn't there after school yesterday, nor was he there today. And while I knew he'd pay a hefty price for it, it wasn't like he cared. Kids like him never cared about that kind of shit. The only thing he cared about was his image, the pussy he wanted to slay, and how he looked riding his bike.

Which was pretty pathetic, if someone asked me.

I sighed as I kept sketching in the margins of my notes from class. I drew little characters to act out scenes from world history we'd already learned about. I drew a bobblehead of Clint with his tongue hanging out and his eyes crossed. I smiled as I made a little speech bubble. I giggled as I wrote out all sorts of jokes that made him look like the knuckle-dragging, drooling idiot he was.

Then the detention teacher shushed me.

I peeked up at him, watching as he went back to reading his book. I rolled my eyes and propped my chin against my hand, continuing to sketch little bobbleheads. I had one of Clint with his ripped leather jacket tossed over his face. I had one of him bent over, with his ass crack showing. I had one of him drunk, with his eyes rolled back and vomit sliding down his chin. I quickly felt the therapeutic effects taking hold, and before I knew it there were four entire blank pages filled to the brim with comedic, insulting doodles of this asshole.

Soon, the bobbleheads became extensive drawings. I created an entire character around this guy. A character that went around trying to pick on people before getting his ass beat. The pages of my notebook became comic book blocks. And soon, dialogue flowed from my fingertips. I licked my lips, focusing on the way my pencil markings flowed across the paper. And I thanked my stars I had mechanical pencils. I got them for free at the grocery store, along with the lead. Which meant never having to get up and sharpen my pencil.

So my creative flow was never interrupted.

Serves him right.

I drew him in all sorts of scenarios. Falling into a volcano after being shoved out of a helicopter by Allison. Being tossed to the alligators by Michael after he made an unsavory joke about her. Me, shoving him off a cliff and watching as he plummeted to the water, crying like the gigantic baby he was as his arms flailed around in the air.

An image from my dream bombarded my mind. My own arms flailing as I fell, deeper and deeper into the darkness.

Not even Clint deserves to know what that feels like.

I ripped the page out of my notebook and crumpled it up. Which earned me a hearty shush from the teacher at the front of the classroom. I decided to draw me putting Clint into the wall instead. Shoving him so hard into the wall his nose bled. Pulling at his wrist so much it dislocated. I let my imagination run away with me, concocting all sorts of scenarios where Clint got exactly what was coming to him.

Then I closed my notebook with a sigh.

I looked up at the clock and saw I still had thirty more minutes. Great. Thirty fucking minutes to sit here and contemplate my life. I pulled my ponytail out of its holder and re-did it. Put it up higher on my head to get it off the nape of my neck. I wasn't sure why the room was so hot, but for some reason I kept sweating down my back. It made my shirt stick to my skin and caused the seat underneath me to grow damp.

And the only thing it made me think about was how relentlessly Clint would be teasing me right now if he were here.

Thank fuck, he isn't.

I gazed out the window and let my mind wander. I replayed one of the many conversations Allison had already spewed over lunch about her future plans. College, and all that. It didn't shock me that, miraculously, Michael wanted to go to the same college as her. He pretended that it was because their sports management program was the best in this part of the country. Allison, of course, was clueless about what he was doing. She was clueless about how Michael felt about her, and it was almost comedic. It was so juicy and delicious that I could've written an entire comic book series on their interactions. On the way Michael drooled over her and how absolutely brain dead she was to the entire thing.

It was sweet.

In a weird sort of way.

Allison's conversations had me thinking, though. I mean, regular college would never be for me. But I also didn't want to work at the grocery store for the rest of my life. If I wanted to really chase a dream, I'd chase character design. I'd apply for schools that cared more about artistic talent than grades, and I'd submit a portfolio. Granted, it wouldn't be a professional portfolio. Just shit I'd done in my art electives. But the thought made me smile.

Being able to do graphic and character design for the rest of my life genuinely made me smile.

Or maybe I could start my own comic book line.

I sighed as I slid down into my chair. Unlike Allison and Michael, however, I'd have to work full time in order to save up the money. I didn't have the grades for scholarships, and being poor only got someone like me so far with federal grants and shit like that. I sure as hell wasn't taking out loans, either. Not without some sort of guaranteed way to pay them back. Which meant me working in the grocery store full-time—or working another job full-time—until I saved up the money for my first few semesters.

Which meant Mom couldn't drink my money away.

Which meant I'd have to move out.

Which would cost money for rent and bills and shit like that.

Which I wouldn't be able to afford on an hourly paycheck of minimum wage.

Fuck.

I didn't want to let those things stop me, though. Because every time I walked into my house, it reminded me of the kind of life I didn't want. It reminded me of the kind of legacy I didn't want to leave behind. Every time I went over to Allison's house or Michael's place, the kind of life I wanted slapped me in the face. And not just the money, either. It was the happiness. Having a loving family that gave a damn about each other. Having mouth-watering food on the table for every meal. Having every kind of drink I could have ever possibly wanted spilling out of the fridge at any given moment.

I didn't want to just survive, like my mother.

I wanted to thrive, like Allison and Michael.

Shit takes money, though.

Why the fuck did good things always take money?

"Detention dismissed."

The teacher's voice caught my ear and I gathered up my things as quickly as I could. I had to work from seven to close at the grocery store tonight. But Michael said he was treating Allison and me to soup and sandwiches. I dashed out of the room, heading straight for the front doors of the high school. I shoved myself out of them, ready to race home to find my bike so I could get to the bistro quicker.

Until a horn honking caught my ear.

"Come on, Rae! Get in!" Allison exclaimed.

She waved her arm out the window to catch my attention and I smiled. I trotted over to the SUV Michael's parents had bought him and climbed in back, happy to be with my friends. He blazed a trail away from the school, heading into town as Allison craned her neck to look back at me.

"So, how's the time you're doing? What's it like? Does it remind you of prison?"

I rolled my eyes. "It's not jail time. It's just detention."

Michael snickered. "And we've never had detention. You have to fill us in on everything that's happening. What's it like? Does it smell? How's Clint been?"

I sighed. "You know damn good and well Clint Clarke doesn't show up to things like detention."

Allison paused. "Wait, he's not showing up?"

Michael chuckled. "Doesn't shock me one bit. What do you think they'll do to him if he doesn't go?"

Allison scoffed. "The nerve of that jerk. Sticking you in detention by ruffling your feathers, then skipping out on the punishment he deserves. Selfish little—"

I grinned. "Careful, now. You might ruin that pristine outfit of yours."

Michael sighed. "I mean, he'll probably get expelled. Which would give us all a nice break."

Allison fell back into her seat. "Well, I for one hope it happens. Everyone's tired of that knucklehead."

I smiled. "Allison, your insults give me life. You know that?"

Michael grumbled, "I can't stand that guy. Someone needs to beat some sense into him."

Allison gasped. "Michael. I've never known you to be a violent person."

I snickered. "He's not, until he is. I've seen him come close to punching someone in the face. Remember that guy that kept teasing you sophomore year?"

Allison thought about it. "Oh, my gosh. I completely forgot about that. The foreign exchange student from Germany that we had. Timmy?"

Michael frowned. "Tommy."

Allison patted his shoulder. "That's right. Tommy. He was teasing me about my braces, and you stepped in to shut him down. What was it you said to him?"

I shook my head. "I can't believe you don't remember this. He said—"

"—If you ever decide to look her way again with anything but admiration in your eyes, be prepared to lose them," Michael supplied.

Allison giggled. "Aww, my hero. We can always count on you, can't we?"

The pride in Michael's face warmed my heart.

We rode in silence until he pulled the vehicle into the parking lot of the bistro. I looked across the road and sighed, already dreading my four or so hours of work. But it was necessary if I wanted to eat lunch. Or put away any money for my future. Or generally not piss my mother off with not having any money she could mooch off me.

Michael craned his head back. "You ready to go eat? It's on me."

I smiled. "I appreciate it, but you know I can—"

Allison cleared her throat. "Let the man pay, Rae. Sometimes, paying makes them feel powerful. Right?"

Michael smiled brightly. "Right."

I rolled my eyes and giggled as I got out of the car. The three of us walked into the sandwich shop and I ordered as much food as I could without seeming selfish. A full-size sandwich, since Michael got himself one. A bowl of soup, since Allison got herself one. A dessert, since all of us wanted one, and a large drink. Which I could refill and take with me to work.

"I'm proud of you, you know."

I whipped my head around, staring up into Michael's face.

"What was that?" I asked.

He grinned down at me. "For standing up to Clint. I'm proud of you. People don't do that with him, and they should. Someone needs to teach his arrogant ass a lesson one of these days. Maybe they'll be inspired by how you stand up to him and actually do it."

Allison slipped between the two of us. "Oh, yeah? And who do you think is going to put the school bully in his place?"

He shrugged. "Anyone, really."

I sighed. "He's not worth it, guys. Trust me. Bullies like him feed on the rise he gets out of people. For all we know, he'll go home and orgasm to it later."

Allison gasped. "Rae!"

Michael threw his head back, laughing. "She's got a point."

And as our food got handed to us, I debated whether or not to save half of my sandwich. After all, it would make a very good breakfast.

If Mom didn't steal it from the refrigerator first.

6

CLINTON

I smashed the buttons. "Come on, you can't go faster than that? He's getting away!"

Roy tilted to the side. "You're the one who decided to modify your car at the last second. I would've been fine had you not pulled some shady shit."

"Shady shit! It's not shady when I'm making last minute tweaks to my car. The fuck's wrong with you?"

"Well, how about we agree to disagree and smoke the asswipes?"

Our cars raced around the track on the projection screen television. I'd decided to have Roy over instead of going to detention. Playing Forza 4 sounded a hell of a lot better than sitting in some smelly, nasty, stinky room with Rae fucking Cleaver. And we had a good race going, too. I shot up from my chair, walking closer to the projector screen as we came upon our competition.

I pointed. "Go off the track. See that ditch? Fly over it and meet me on the other side."

Roy snickered. "The fuck? Are you trying to get me thrown—"

"Just do it, dickweed! I'm trying not to cost us our rank in this damn game!"

I kept pressing buttons and fiddling with the modifications I'd made to my car. This damn thing was my pride and joy. I'd been grinding until the early hours of the morning over the summer, winning races and getting enough in-game cash to buy what I wanted to for it. Its speed was unmatched. The engine horsepower was out of this world. The car fucking screamed around the track, smoking these newbies like it was a fish fry.

Then the front door slammed out.

"What the—?"

My eyes peeled away from the screen, and I watched in shock as my father walked through the front doors. He was followed by my stepmother, who looked like her head was about to explode with fury. The horrific sound of my car crashing into a tree caused Roy to groan.

Roy stood up quickly. "Mr. Clarke. Mrs. Clarke. How was the safari?"

My father leveled his eyes with me. "Roy. Go home."

"Right away, sir. See you tomorrow, Clint."

Pussy.

I tossed my controller onto the couch as the race came to a close. We almost had it. We almost had those idiots! And now our ranking would fall. We wouldn't have the money we needed to fix our cars. And I'd have to deal with my parents ranting and screaming for a while so they could make themselves feel like decent people.

It wasn't until Roy closed the front door behind him that my father spoke.

"What's this I hear about you getting into it with your teacher and a female student on Monday?"

My stepmother came and stood beside my father, trying to present some sort of bullshit united front, even though the two of us never talked. I wanted nothing to do with her—or my real mother, for that matter. I was glad that bitch came in and ruined my father's marriage. I was glad to be rid of my drug-addicted mother who wanted to do nothing more than spend my father's money until we were out on the fucking street.

But that didn't mean I had to be all buddy-buddy with his new, hot piece of ass.

I sighed. "They pissed me off. The hell was I supposed to do?"

Dad narrowed his eyes. "First of all, you watch that language in this house. And second of all, you man up. A man never allows his emotions to rage out of control like that. You need to learn how to keep it on a leash."

"Like you do Cecilia over there?"

"What did you say?"

Her eyes stayed pinned on me, but she didn't move. She didn't say a word, and she sure as hell didn't come to my defense. Figures, since she'd always been far removed from the situation. Just another plastic-surgery woman who simply knew how to take her place next to Dad. As my father came into the living room, I prepared myself to buck against it. It wouldn't be the first time I'd physically fought him. It would just be the first time he had the balls to start a fist fight like that in front of someone.

Dad gripped my leather jacket. "You'd do well to remember your manners and mind them in the presence of adults."

I grinned. "Do adults manhandle their children in their own home?"

"Take it easy, Howard. You're toeing a line."

My eyebrows rose at hearing Cecilia's voice. But it did nothing to harness my father's rage. His anger. It did nothing but remind me exactly where I got my anger issues from. Exactly why I'd always felt like a burden. Exactly why I'd always hated my fucking father, no matter what he felt he'd done for me.

Dad shoved me against a wall. "How many times am I going to have to bail your pathetic ass out of these situations?"

I shrugged. "I don't know. How much money you got on you nowadays?"

He growled. "I'm sick and tired of that school calling us, Clinton. Don't you know we have better things to do than worry about our fully-grown son who seems incapable of doing anything right? How the fuck do you expect to have any future?"

"Howard."

Hearing Cecilia's voice was so foreign to me. And yet, it was nice. Actually having someone step up to my defense.

Sort of.

I licked my lips. "Fully grown because I just turned eighteen? Or fully grown because you started your first business at eighteen?"

Dad scoffed. "You're a fucking joke."

Cecilia cleared her throat. "Howard. That's enough."

I smiled at my father, wondering if he'd actually listen to the tits with a voice. My father didn't give a shit about anything but himself. And his new hot wife. He didn't give a damn when my mother first got addicted to painkillers because of her cesarean with me. He didn't give a shit when she slipped into postpartum depression and threw herself off the roof. He certainly didn't give a shit when she stopped taking care of the house and started spending all his money. Leaving me home alone to stew in my own waste and starve.

Oh, no. He only gave a shit when he couldn't keep up with the credit cards she kept taking out in his name. He only gave a shit when it impacted his finances. Not me, or my well-being. So it didn't shock me one bit when I felt his hand tighten against my leather jacket instead of releasing it.

Because my father never gave a shit about me for a fucking day in his pathetic life.

"You get your shit together, you hear me? Or you're out on your ass. Plain and simple."

I scoffed. "You gonna throw me out while you're in Bora Bora? Or before you two jet off to Australia for Christmas?"

Dad chuckled. "You've got balls, I'll give you that."

"Howard. Cut it out!"

"Shut up, Cecilia!"

I chuckled. "Wow. You really know how to treat the ladies."

Dad shoved my chest. "You've got one last chance to keep your ass out of trouble until I can stick you somewhere after you graduate. One chance, you hear me?"

I glared at him. "Or what?"

Dad smiled. "Or you're really not going to like our next conversation."

I watched my stepmother stride over with her thin legs and her high heels. She grabbed my father's arm, yanking it away from my leather coat. I dusted off his touch as she forcefully pulled him away from me, giving me some space to slip away from the wall. I wasn't staying here another fucking second. Not with that asshole in the house. I walked into the kitchen and grabbed a beer from the fridge, sticking it in the inside pocket of my jacket.

"And don't you dare think about going anywhere tonight!" Dad roared.

I shrugged. "Too late."

I slipped into the garage and stormed for my bike. I jammed my fist into the garage door button on the wall, watching it roll up. I threw my leg over my motorcycle as Dad appeared in the doorway. I cranked the engine up too quickly to hear whatever the hell it was he was screaming at me.

"What was that? I can't hear you!"

I pointed to my ears, watching as my father's face reddened with frustration. Cecilia appeared behind him, rubbing his back and trying to calm him down. Fucking hell, that woman was too good for him. They were all too good for him, including my mother. I knew, deep down, my father was the reason why my mother got ruined. Putting up with his bullshit and always bending to his ways and dealing with his anger all the fucking time. It made me sick. And soon enough, he'd destroy Cecilia, too. Cast her out into the backyard like a piece of used furniture to burn before finding another trophy wife to stand at his side.

Another woman to burn with the rest of them.

I backed my bike out of the garage and swung it around. I heard my father rushing after me, but I took off down the driveway. I looked in my rearview mirror, watching him run until he had to bend over to catch his breath. That's what he got, with all the traveling and car riding and not enough time spent in the gym.

"Fat ass," I murmured.

I drove into town, setting my sights on the park. It was the one place where I could always go, get cheap food, and sit. Possibly write. I always kept my notebooks and pens in the back compartment of my bike, just in case inspiration hit me.

I also kept it hidden as much as I could. I never wrote when people were around. Because holy fuck, if my friends knew I wrote poetry and short stories as a hobby? My reputation would be shot. I'd be just like every other asshole I gave swirlies to on a regular basis.

And the idea of Roy stepping into my position practically made me cackle.

Because he'd only ever be half the man I was.

7

RAELYNN

I shoved some things into a backpack on Friday morning, readying myself for this fun little weekend. I was ready to get out of here. Especially since I wasn't working. Ready to get through the last hour of detention so I could be on my way to my best friend's house for another wonderful sleepover. But, for once, I came downstairs to my mother already down there. I walked into the living room, skirting their makeout session while I waited in the wings. The lip-smacking made my stomach turn, and I breathed a sigh of relief when D.J. finally left. The smell of coffee filled the foyer as I tried to erase those sights and sounds from my mind, silently feeling sorry for the asshole she was cheating on.

Then again, there was a big chance he knew it. Why he continued to pay some of her bills and keep her around if she was, I'd never understand.

Then again, I also didn't want to understand.

With my clothes and my phone charger in a bag, I made my way into the kitchen. I heard D.J. race out of our driveway, peeling out like he thought he was hot shit. I knew announcing to my mother I was going away for the weekend could go one of two ways. She'd either wave me out the door while she nursed her hangover with another beer, or she'd chew me out until I got fed up enough to slip out the door myself.

But after an entire week of detention, I didn't care if the

woman tried strapping me down to keep me home. I was fucking going to this sleepover.

I peeked around the corner. "I'm going to spend the weekend at Allison's."

Mom sighed. "That's fine, honey. You'll be home Sunday?"

"Yep."

"All right. Well, maybe next week you and I can have an old-fashioned girls' night? Like how we used to?"

I studied my mother and how rough she looked. The hickeys on her neck. Her knotted, disheveled hair. The way her shoulders slouched as she sat at the kitchen table, pouring beer into her fucking coffee. I came around the corner and went to sit beside her. Something was off. Something didn't feel right. And while I wanted to turn down the invite to her version of a girls' night, I also didn't want to leave her like this.

"Mom?"

She slowly looked over at me and I saw how tired she looked. The bags underneath her eyes. The pallor of her skin. Her trembling hand brought her mug of coffee to her lips, where she chugged a little too hard and a little too long. I placed my hand on her shoulder and she flinched, which told me everything I needed to know.

And when she finally faced me, I saw the blackened expanse of her right eye.

I sighed. "Oh, Mom."

She patted my hand. "Yeah, an old-fashioned girls' night soon. Okay?"

"Promise you won't invite D.J.?"

And even though she nodded, I knew she was lying. It didn't matter how many times her boyfriend smacked her around. Or made her cry. Or made her feel worthless. Whenever she wanted to spend time with me, he inevitably showed up. She always broke down and called him back. Begged for him to come over so she could 'make things right.'

Which was the reason I always kept earplugs on my bedside table.

I stood up, kissing her cheek as a shudder left her lips. She was holding back tears, and it broke my heart. Because no matter what kind of shit my mother got herself into, she was still my mother. And she'd been through hell all her life. Starting with her own parents, who'd routinely slapped her around. Followed by my father, who proposed when they got pregnant with me, only to jump ship when I was only three years old. The string of boyfriends she'd had over the years were varying degrees of the same. A cokehead that got her addicted before she finally let him go. A rehab facility coordinator who ended up being the reason she got clean. And who ended up being married. A string of one-night stands that introduced me to so many sexual things a teenager should never have been exposed to.

And now? D.J.

The man who paid some of our bills in exchange for my mother's soul.

"Please take care of yourself," I whispered against her ear.

She nodded. "You know I always do. No matter what, I'll always do my best to take care of you."

"You're important too, Mom. Always remember that."

"I miss you, you know."

"Well, then maybe we'll have that girls' night soon."

Mom smiled softly. "You know, D.J.'s not really that bad."

I sighed. "I'm sure he isn't, Mom."

"And he takes care of us. He's the reason why we only have to choose one bill to ignore a month. Not the multiple ones, like we used to do."

I nodded. "I know, Mom. I know. And I miss you, too. But I have to go. I'm going to be late for school."

I rubbed her back as I tried to process everything. I never could tell my mother how much I missed her without getting angry with her. And I felt myself growing very upset very quickly. Without trying to hold her accountable for her actions throughout the years. While the rational part of me knew she kept trying her hardest, the other part of me wondered why the fuck she always had to try it with guys. Why not get a job on her own? It wasn't like I couldn't fend for myself. Why not take out some loans? Get a technical degree? Make something of herself instead of hopping from man to man, hoping he'd swoop in and free us from this bondage?

I mean, I was familiar with the books my mother read. Books that were passed down to her through trash cans and bags dropped all around our street. Our neighborhood was practically a rich person's dump, and I'd caught my mother many times opening up trash bags to dig around and see what was inside.

Mom cleared her throat. "You need any lunch money, beautiful?"

I shook my head. "Nope. I've got my own."

"Good girl. Make sure to always do that. Provide for yourself."

I bit my tongue on what I wanted to say. Because no matter what I wanted to do, I'd never kick a person when they were down.

Unlike D.J.

Even though my heart didn't want to, my gut told me to leave. So I did. I left my mother to chug back her beer-laced coffee and I headed straight for school. With every step I took, I grew infuriated with D.J. With every step I took, comics unfolded in my mind. Graphic novels with curt colors, dripping with blood from D.J.'s veins. I shook with fury as I walked out of the neighborhood, trying to focus on where I was going.

Why the hell did men like D.J. and Clint have to exist in this world?

That was exactly who my mother's boyfriend reminded me of, too. Clinton fucking Clarke. The two of them were cocky. Arrogant. Angry. Entitled. Rude.

Flat-out mean.

As the mouth of my neighborhood dumped me onto the curb, I made my way for Allison and Michael. They flagged me down with their arms, and I gave them both a thumbs-up, letting them know I was cleared to come over this weekend. The two of them high-fived as I picked up the pace, letting my dark, dank neighborhood fall into the background as the green grass and rolling white picket fences of our quaint area in Riverbend fill my view.

Then something whooshed by me.

The roaring of the motorcycle engine caught me off-guard, and I flinched. I knew it was Clint, and my only hope was that he hadn't seen me. I picked up the pace, jogging down the sidewalk to try and get to Allison and Michael. But when I saw his brake lights flash, I grumbled to myself.

Especially when it pulled over to the curb. Blocking my path to my friends.

Great. Just great.

He pulled off his helmet. "Well, well, well. Good morning, detention rat."

I ignored him and kept walking, watching as Michael bolted for me. Allison trailed behind him, trying to get to me before Clint could do any sort of damage to my morning.

Then I heard him whistle. "Nice ass, Cleaver."

Michael linked his arm with mine. "Put a sock in it, Clinton."

Allison snickered. "Yeah. Go terrorize someone your own size."

Clint chuckled. "Trust me, that ass is big enough for me."

Allison scoffed. "Disgusting pig."

"I like watching you walk away, Cleaver! You should wear skinny jeans more often!"

I went to swirl around, but Michael tightened his grip on me. Allison's hand fell to the small of my back as the two of them escorted me across the street. I wanted to smack that fucking grin right off Clint's face. I wanted to ball-stomp him into the curb until he was crying out for his drug-addled mommy. Yes, Clint was D.J. The younger, more pompous version. What I wouldn't give to put the two of them in a room and give Clint the rude awakening that was coming to him.

Maybe he'd turn into a decent human being if he knew being a womanizing, abusive asshole was his future.

We got across the road and I heard Clint rev the engine of his bike. I spun around, ripping away from my two best friends as I glared hotly at him. He puckered his lips, blowing me a kiss before he wiggled his tongue around in the air. And as he slid his helmet back onto his head, I stuck my middle finger up. Just for him. For his eyes only to take in.

And as he rushed by us on his bike, I heard him laughing at me.

"Come on, let's get you inside," Allison said softly.

The burning sensation on the backs of my eyes made me feel weak, frustrated, incompetent. I was tired of that asshole, and I didn't know why he wouldn't stop torturing me. I'd watched my mother bend to these men her entire life. And I knew if I simply stood up to them as they came into my life, I'd be fine. They'd go away. They'd find some other woman to torture and I'd be free of them.

But I was standing up to Clint. And he kept coming back. If I ignored Clint, he'd only come at me harder. Why couldn't he leave me alone? Why couldn't he go pick on someone else?

I didn't understand it anymore.

"So what color do you want your toes painted tonight?" Michael asked.

I cleared my throat. "Red sounds nice."

Allison opened the doors. "Oh, spicy. I like it. Matches your personality."

Michael smiled. "You know, you could rock a head full of red hair, too. I mean, with those freckles and this beautiful skin you've got."

Allison gasped. "That's it! We should dye your hair, too!"

I shook my head. "Oh, no."

She pouted. "Oh, come on. It'll be fun. Your hair can match your toes, and you can take some of my shirts that probably match, too."

I grinned. "You mean you have shirts that aren't pastel colors?"

Allison's face fell. "Ha. Ha. Ha. Jerk."

Michael chuckled. "Maybe just some under-the-hair highlights, then? You know, so when you wear it down, you can't see them. But when you wear your ponytails, you can?"

I furrowed my brow. "How do you know so much about all this shit?"

He groaned. "Mom."

Allison giggled. "Well, if you don't want to you don't have to. But you'd look hot with them."

I sighed. "Why don't we dye your hair, then?"

Allison's eyes widened. "And deal with the wrath of my mother? Not a chance. You know how she feels about hair dye. Ever since she had that reaction a few years back, she's been on that all-natural healthy-everything kick. If she came back to me with dyed hair, she'd probably disown me."

Michael scoffed. "I hate to admit I even know this, but there are all-natural hair dyes out there."

I threw my head back, laughing. "Your mom is fantastic, you know that?"

He smiled. "I was adopted by some good ones, yes."

Allison took my hand. "So you'll think about it?"

And as I sighed, I ended up nodding my head.

"Okay. I'll think about it."

8

———

CLINTON

I swung my bike into the parking stall in front of the school. It was open, for once, and I wanted to make sure I took full advantage of it. All the best girls in this high school hung out in front. And it was those same girls that took to the back parking lot during lunch. Oh, the mischief they got into. It practically made me salivate. I felt their eyes on me as I revved my engine. I turned it off and put the kickstand down. I felt them scanning my long legs and the breadth of my shoulders as I kicked my leg over my bike. I slipped my helmet off, then slipped my sunglasses on quickly. They all watched the powerful man on campus with googly eyes, hoping to get a slice of me.

And I enjoyed putting on a show for them.

"Ladies," I said, grinning.

The head cheerleader walked up. "Hi there, Clint."

I licked my lips. "Hello there, beautiful."

"Nice ride you've got. Been meaning to let you know. It's much better than the one you had last year."

"That'll teach my father to sell it out from underneath me. Bought and paid for with my own money, too."

She smiled. "Your own money, huh? So, uh, when you taking me out, then? With that money of yours?"

I grinned. "Whenever you let me take a peek underneath that skirt of yours. You know you can't do that to my heart, beautiful.

High-kicking those legs at practice without letting me get a close-up look."

"Oh, you're bad, Clint."

I winked from beyond my sunglasses. "And you love it, gorgeous."

She giggled as she turned on her heels in her pristine white tennis shoes. Her barely-there hips sauntered back over to her friends, where I knew she'd boast about talking to the bad boy on campus. They always did. The girls around here thought cozying up to me would boost their status in this school. That they could somehow unravel the mysterious bad boy that didn't give a fuck what anyone else thought.

And I most certainly used that to my advantage.

"I see you're already locking things down with tits over there."

I chuckled as Roy walked up to me, his arm slung around Marina's shoulders. She swayed those thin hips of hers in the skirt she wore, chewing on her bubblegum like her fucking life depended on it. I still didn't know what he saw in those women. Girls with bony arms, gangly legs, and horse faces. But he didn't understand why I enjoyed my women with a little more meat on their bones. It evened out.

Gave us more to gawk at without getting jealous, too.

I shrugged. "She's nice enough."

Roy quirked an eyebrow. "Nice enough? A few days ago, you were ready to get it on with her. You feelin' okay?"

I snickered. "You might want to envision me getting it on with her, but I haven't even started that rat race."

Marina giggled. "And here I thought leather jacket over here was the kinky one of the group."

Roy rolled his eyes. "What the fuck have we talked about with that mouth of yours?"

"Sorry, Roy."

"You're so nasty. All the time. That talk is meant for only me, when we're alone. Got it?"

I chuckled as Roy gripped Marina's chin. But, once they started sucking face again, I turned away. I didn't want to watch that shit. Gross as fuck. The way they swapped that chewing gum around like it was a shared snack made my stomach turn. Roy was a nasty one, though. He enjoyed things with women I'd never indulge in a million years. Like passing them around and jerking off on their faces with other men surrounding her, too.

I mean, come on. I had some fucking standards.

And I sure as hell wasn't jerking off in front of a crowd of dudes.

A small crowd gathered and I pushed off my bike. I hung my helmet off the handlebars of my bike, like I did every morning. We all started shooting the shit while those of us taken within the group practically dry-humped one another in front of the school. Roy pinned Marina to the front wall, kissing down her neck while she made sounds that would haunt me in my damn nightmares.

Then the main show arrived.

I saw Rae walking up with Michael and Allison. And I knew they were giving her a pep talk. She looked on the verge of tears, and it was priceless. Oh, if I made Rae cry this semester, it would be the icing on the cake. She prided herself in being tough. Strong. Different than the rest of us. But she wouldn't be so different if the big, bad Clint made her cry.

I made everyone cry.

Even my own damn mother.

"I hate to see her go, boys," I said, chuckling.

Rae scoffed. "Do you ever know when to stop?"

Michael piped up. "Don't pay him any mind, Rae. Keep walking."

And as her friend Allison started rubbing her back, I found my 'in.'

"Hey, Allison," I called out.

She shook her head. "Whatever it is, I don't care about it. Come on, Rae. Let's get to homeroom."

The crowd parted for me. "Have you and Michael fucked yet? Or is the jury still out on whether or not he'd rather partner up with me?"

The three of them stopped and that brightly-colored twat whipped around. Allison clung to Rae as he stormed me, taking long strides with those chicken legs of his. I shot up, rolling my shoulders back as he approached me. There wasn't a damn kid in this school that towered over me. Not when I stood at over six fucking feet tall. Michael craned his neck back to keep my eyes in view. His nostrils flared with anger as a grin spread like wildfire across my face.

"Oh look," I said, "I poked the bear."

Michael's eye twitched. "You leave them out of this. You wanna pick on me? That's fine. But, only a pussy little prick like you picks on girls."

I circled around him. "Oh, yeah? Trying to be the big, tough guy so we don't figure out you suck dicks with your butthole?"

He grimaced. "Could you be any more crass? I mean, really. Come on."

I shrugged. "All I'm saying is own up to who you are and what you like. If dudes are your thing, why hide it? Only embarrasses you more."

I blew against his ear, causing my friends to laugh when he jumped. Michael's eyes bubbled with rage and I heard Rae calling out for me. Telling me to stop. Her friend held her back, though. Kept her from storming over. And as Michael stood toe-to-toe with me, I smiled.

"Let me guess. Her pussy's not tight enough for you."

Michael growled. "That's it."

The beast snapped, and I saw his fist coming around from the corner of my vision. I heard Rae and Allison shriek, calling out for him as I wrapped my hand around his wrist. I brought my knee into his stomach, buckling him as he gasped for air. And as the girls came charging for me, my friends closed the circle. They pumped their fists in the air. They pushed Rae and Allison away as I watched Michael gasp on his hands and knees.

"I mean, really. If you're going to be a man's man, at least man up a little bit. You of all people should know gay dudes don't like pussies."

He lunged off the concrete and wrapped his arms around me. He barreled through the crowd behind me, knocking me clear over my bike. I heard him cursing. I heard him shouting. I heard the pitter patter of footsteps as my bike went tumbling to the ground. The second I heard metal and paint scraping against the concrete, my vision dripped red. I lost all sense of time and space, of what I was doing.

Because no one fucked with my bike.

"You're dead meat," I grunted.

I brought my elbow down into Michael's back and he pulled away from me. He kicked my shins, then reached down and grabbed my ankles. He flipped me clear over my fucking bike before stepping over it as a crowd of kids gathered. They chanted, "Fight! Fight! Fight!" And as I scrambled to my feet, I saw him coming for me again.

Only this time, I was ready.

I hit him with a right hook that sent him stumbling back. I heard the girls crying out, but it was no use. Their voices faded into the background. Michael's face slowly morphed into my father's. I hit him with a blow to his gut, taking him back down again. And as my knee came up to connect with his chin, I felt anger swelling my veins, blood rushing through my ears. I heard nothing but the sound of my own racing heart as steam came barreling out of my ears.

I had some anger to dispel. And Michael's face always irritated the fuck out of me.

Time to make a statement.

I reached down and grabbed Michael's shirt. I pulled him off the ground, holding him in midair before I dropped him to his feet. I threw a few punches he dodged while he tried to get his bearings. Then he came for me again. He ran straight into my stomach, taking me to the fucking ground again. But as I wrapped my legs around him, I rolled him over. I forced him to look up at the sky before my face came into view. I smiled broadly down at him as I saw my father, pinned underneath my legs.

"You're gonna regret that move, asshole," I glowered.

His arms came up in defense of his face as blow after blow landed on his arms. I heard sirens wailing off in the distance and I knew I had to wrap it up. But not before I broke this fucker's nose. I felt him bucking underneath me. I felt him trying to get away. And just as I went to pry his arms away from his face like the coward he was, I felt someone tugging at my leather jacket.

"Get. The fuck. Off him!"

Rae's voice took me back. I felt her hands wrapping into my leather jacket, pulling me away from her friend. And for a second, it stunned me. Her knuckles dragged across the nape of my neck, shooting electricity down my spine. I heard teachers calling out in the distance, rushing toward us as she pried me off her friend.

Then she tossed me to the side. Like I was a fucking rag doll.

I wiped at my mouth as Michael scrambled off the ground. His eyes bulged with anger as he tried coming at me again. Rae placed her hands against his chest, and for some reason I didn't like that. I didn't like her touching him like that. Fuck, I didn't like her touching me like that.

I spat. "Get the hell out of my way."

Rae whipped around. "Not a chance in hell, you womanizing, abusive dickwad."

Everyone cheered as the three of them scampered off. But her words cut deep. I watched them rush off as someone tugged at my arm, trying to get me inside the school. Girls kept looking on, smiling and cheering my victory. I shook myself away from whoever the hell had a grip on my elbow before I scurried into school. The last fucking thing I needed to be caught doing after seeing my father yesterday was fighting. Because I knew damn good and well that selfish asshole would toss me out on my ass the second he got the chance. The second he found any reason to deem me a threat to his new wife, or to him, or to that bullshit prison I called home.

But I couldn't shake the way Rae handled herself. The way she handled me. It was reminiscent of her putting me into that damn stairwell wall.

And for a split second, I wondered where she learned how to handle herself like that.

9

RAELYNN

The second I heard Clint's words, I saw Michael snap. I saw it in his eyes, and his fist flew like wildfire. I didn't even know Michael knew how to throw a punch like that. But when I saw Clint wrap his hand around Michael's wrist, I knew he was in trouble.

I shrieked. "Michael, no!"

Allison kept screaming as the fight continued. Clint's fucking goonies closed in the fight, and I struggled to get through the crowd. I heard them tussling around, punches being landed and grunts filling the air. Someone gasped and I heard something drop to the ground. And as Roy physically shoved me back, I jammed the heel of my hand directly into his ballsack.

Marina gawked. "What the fuck?"

I shook my hand out as I stepped around Roy. He could die, as far as I was concerned. I started charging Clint, with Allison hot on my heels before the sea of people closed again. I leapt into the air, feeling them catch me and hold me back. And that was when I realized Michael was the one gasping for air.

Shit. Shit shit shit shit shit.

"I mean, really. If you're going to be a man's man, at least man up a little bit. You of all people should know gay dudes don't like pussies."

Clint's words fired me up like nothing I'd ever experienced before. And I found a renewed sense of vigor to tear through that damn crowd. I saw Michael practically toss him over his bike and I heard Allison cheering him on from behind me. I scrapped with a few people in front of me, trying to get them out of my way. And the more people I tossed to the side, the more adrenaline I felt rushing through my system. My vision bounced between Clint and Michael and D.J. and my mother. It was hard to focus. Hard to see straight. Hard to keep things in line as faces morphed and changed right before my eyes.

Then Allison's voice pierced my hazy thoughts.

"No! Stop it! You're going to kill him!"

I looked up, only to see Clint hoisting Michael in the air. I gawked at the scene as kids cheered and clapped, chanting for Clint to slam him into the ground. Michael had his hands around Clint's forearm, and fear gripped my chest. And the second Michael went plummeting to the ground, I knew I had to get to him.

Otherwise, we'd be in a hospital later.

Everything happened so quickly after that. First, Michael was in the air. Then he was punching Clint. Then Clint was somehow on top of him on the ground. I took one last charge through the crowd, physically shoving girls and guys alike to the concrete. Sirens wailed in the distance as teachers rushed over to see what was going on. The last thing Michael needed was to get caught fighting, and the last thing any of us needed was to be seen as cohorts in the matter.

"Get. The fuck. Off him!"

My hands came down on to Clint's leather jacket and I tugged. I wrapped my hands up in the worn material and felt something akin to a god take over my body. I tugged at him once. Twice. Three times, before I felt his body move. I tightened my grip into his jacket so tightly I felt my knuckles dragging across his skin. I gnashed my teeth together as Allison rushed around us. I growled out like a wild animal as I felt his body budge. I pried him off Michael, watching as Allison helped the poor boy to his feet.

Then I tossed Clint to the side.

Like some discarded paper plate of useless food.

I rushed to Michael, who was foaming at the mouth with anger. His eyes bulged and his nose was bleeding, but overall, he looked good for going a few rounds with Clint Clarke. Which was always a bad idea, given how massive Clint was in the first place. I placed my hands against his chest while Allison tugged at his wrist, trying to pull him away from the fight as I tapped my hands against him.

"Come on. Let's get out of here. We need to get you cleaned up."

Clint growled, "Get the hell out of my way."

And when I whipped around, I leveled my eyes directly with his.

"Not a chance in hell, you womanizing, abusive dickwad."

Allison grunted. "Come. On. Michael. It's done. Enough is enough. Walk away. Just walk away from him."

I turned around and kept pushing at his chest, trying to get him away from all this chaos. Fighting Clint Clarke was a bad fucking idea because the boy was practically made for scrapping. Built for schoolyard fights and drawing blood from his enemies. The kids around us booed as Allison and I physically dragged Michael away from that fucking fight. Clint kept yelling after us, but I wasn't paying attention to what he was saying. Michael kept hollering back, too. And the only thing I did was reach up and place my hand over his mouth.

"Stop it. He's not worth the energy, I promise you that," I said.

Some of Clint's friends followed us, trying to block us in again. But Allison kept stepping on their toes. She jammed her heel into their feet, causing them to buckle and cry out. I was very proud of her. It made me smile as she backed up, clearing a pathway for us to get away from the chaos. The teachers were on their way, and I had a sneaking suspicion that siren call off in the distance was for us. And if Michael got caught fighting in any way, that blemish on his record might override his good grades and keep him from getting into college.

Michael grumbled, "I'm gonna bury that fucker."

Allison sighed. "You're making me break a sweat. Can't you tuck it in?"

I giggled. "You're going to be in deep shit if you're caught. Why don't we get this sleepover started early?"

With our backpacks practically hanging off our bodies, we dashed across the front lawn of the schoolyard. Michael had Allison's hand tightly in his, and I brought up the rear. Just in case anyone else tried coming after us. The last thing we needed was to deal with the fallout from this bullshit drama. Because as far as I was concerned? Clint could take the brunt of it all. By himself. Since he was the asshole that started it in the first place.

But I had to work not to give him the satisfaction of looking back.

I don't know why I wanted to look back and check on him, but I fought that urge. He didn't deserve someone making sure he was all right like that. We rushed across the street just before the schoolyard bell tolled, signaling the beginning of the day.

The day we'd all skip in order to get this party started.

We didn't stop running until we got to Allison's house. She pulled out her keys, and Michael's hand instinctively fell to the small of her back. I smiled at their connection. At how this had somehow bonded them. And since Allison wasn't brushing him off, I figured that was as good a sign as any.

That Allison returned Michael's affections.

We all walked inside and I stood there, marveling at the grandeur of Allison's home. It never ceased to amaze me. I slowly closed the front door behind me, taking in the beautiful staircase. The wooden banisters that glistened in the sunlight streaming through the multiple windows of the home. The hardwood floors that matched those banisters, covered intricately with plush rugs that sat underneath cushioned, comfy furniture. No matter how many times I went over to Allison's or Michael's homes, I was always amazed at how they looked. Large, with vaulted ceilings. Beautiful stainless steel appliances that always looked brand new every time I came over. Massive flatscreen televisions mounted on walls and expansive decorations that added a classy sort of flair to the entire place.

I sighed. "Wow."

"I'm going to grab some things to bring down into the basement. Rae, can you take Michael down there?"

Allison's voice ripped me from my trance and I nodded.

"Yep. Come on, Michael. Let's go get you cleaned up. You look like hell."

He snickered. "I feel like it."

I shrugged. "That's what you get for trying to take on Clint Clarke first thing in the morning."

While Allison rummaged around in the kitchen, I took Michael's hand. I led him down into the basement, where I clicked the light on, illuminating the beautiful expanse of one of the most perfect spaces I'd ever seen. It was practically its own apartment down here, complete with a little kitchenette area, a mounted flatscreen television, every single streaming service known to man loaded on the smart television, and bedrooms as far as the eye could see. There were bookshelves lining the walls, filled with books I wanted to read. The plush microfiber furniture was broken up with bean bags we always flopped onto when coming downstairs. The soft carpet underneath my feet caused me to toe off my shoes, just so I could feel the material tickle my toes.

But, when Michael sat down with a grunt, it pulled me back to reality again.

"I'll be right back. We need to get you cleaned up," I said.

Michael sighed. "I don't plan on moving until lunch."

I giggled as I walked into the bathroom. I fished out the first aid kit from underneath the sink, then walked back into the main room. I sat down by Michael before I opened the kit, preparing myself to clean him up. He had caked blood on his nose and a scrape just above his left eye. Not to mention the massive amount of spit he had dripping down his neck. I ripped open an alcohol wipe and gripped his chin softly. I turned his face toward me, tilting his head in order to clean him a little better.

Then I gave him a knowing smile. "For the record, I'm never going to forget that you leapt to defend Allison's honor instead of mine."

Michael's eyes widened. "Rae, I'm so sorry. I didn't mean t—"

I shook my head. "It's fine, Michael. It's all right. I know you like her."

He paused. "Is it that obvious?"

"Oh, yeah. Very. But she's doing a good job hiding the fact that she likes that you went to bat for her. Against Clint, of all people."

"You don't think she's upset with me?"

"Did you see the way she let you take her hand? The way she let you usher her into her own house? Come on, Michael. You're not that dumb."

He hissed. "That hurt. Ah."

I shrugged. "Don't go up against Clint again and it won't hurt."

"I'd do it again in a heartbeat for her, though."

I nodded. "I know you would. Just know I see things you don't. She feels the same way. But you know how Allison is."

"She's perfect the way she is."

His words warmed my heart. "Bravo to you, by the way."

"For what?"

I winked. "For taking on hell itself to defend your woman. We like those kinds of gestures."

10

CLINTON

I sat there during after-school detention, wrapping yet another cold washcloth around my fucking split knuckles. They hurt like hell, but they didn't hurt as much as my pride. I wanted to beat that fucker into the ground. I wanted to split his damn face open and let people see Michael for the hoity-toity bullshit of a human being he really was. I licked my lips as I gazed out the window. My entire body hurt, if I was being honest. He put up a damn good fight, though I'd never admit it to anyone.

But Rae? She fucking threw me off him like it was nothing.

Why are you still thinking about her?

The question was a good one. And one that overtook my mind as I sat there after school in the dank, sweaty, smelly classroom. I dabbed at my knuckles, which had been bleeding on and off all day. The school nurse literally did the bare minimum needed to get me cleaned up before sending me back to class. She couldn't have given less of a shit about me if she'd actively tried. Then again, she'd cleaned up a lot of my messes over the years.

She was probably just as tired of me as I was of her.

Why the hell was Rae on my mind so much lately? I mean, she was a pain in the ass. Nothing more than that, either. She came from a shitty family. From a shitty part of town. She was nothing more than mere entertainment during these boring-ass school days. And her snark made me want to spit in her general direction. Her snarky remarks every time I said something to her got underneath my skin.

Who the hell did she think she was anyway?

While she might be the only chick in this school who didn't turn red in the cheeks and get all tongue-tied around me, that didn't make her special. It only made me work harder to make sure she understood she really wasn't all that different after all. She wasn't as strong as she thought she was. She wasn't as 'neat-o' as her mother probably told her she was. In the end, she was exactly like us. Exactly like the rich bitches she snubbed her nose at every time she walked into the damn school.

I mean, we even let her walk into this school. With her ratty clothes and her on-time homework and her hard-earned money for lunch. Did she think she was better than us? Because that wasn't the truth. Not by a longshot. She should've been praising us for letting her walk through those doors. She should've been thanking her lucky stars she didn't get it any worse around here, coming from the part of town she did.

The fuck's her problem?

I scoffed as I sat back in my chair. I was done wondering about her. I was done with the unanswered questions I had regarding this stupid little girl. By the time this semester was over, I'd know what her deal was. I'd know what made her tick. I'd know why she felt she could waltz around here, buck up to me, and pull me out of my own damn fights.

You fucked up this time, povo.

"Mr. Clarke?"

The teacher's voice pulled me from my trance and I slowly looked over at him.

"Yep?"

"The nurse wants to see you one last time. Then you're free to go."

I snickered. "She miss me already?"

The teacher rolled his eyes. "Keep up that attitude and I'll make you stay here another hour for shits and giggles."

"Ah, cursing. Such a bigshot move."

He glared at me as I stood up. I picked up my things and winked at him, then headed out the door. I unwrapped my knuckles and tossed the bloodied rag into the nearest trash can, then headed for the front doors. I sure as hell wasn't seeing that fat-ass nurse again, nor was I going to walk anywhere near the principal's office.

Because I had plans for my weekend.

"Not so fast, Clint."

I paused just beyond the front doors as I held them open. The nurse's voice caught me off-guard, and I sighed as I closed my eyes. I turned around, watching as she beckoned for me to come inside. I snickered as I moved toward her, watching her point to the front office door.

"My office. Now."

I rolled my eyes as she took my backpack off my arm. I sauntered through the door, puffing my chest out for the receptionist still at the desk. She shook her head at me, but all it did was make me grin. If these people thought they could put a damper on my parade, they had another thing coming. I had plans with Roy this weekend. There was a massive party I was going to, whether they liked it or not.

But when I rounded the corner into the nurse's office, I groaned.

"Seriously?" I asked.

The nurse closed the door behind us. "Seriously. Sit."

"I'm fine, Mrs. Abernathy."

"Get up there, or I'm calling your father to come down here and deal with you his way."

"Pretty sure he's on a plane somewhere else."

She snickered. "And I'm sure telling him his son has a possible concussion would get him to turn around in a heartbeat."

I hopped up onto the paper-covered seat and the nurse began her evaluation. She shined lights in my eyes and made me open my mouth. She checked my knuckles before covering them in this goopy substance. She wrapped them up with gauze and poked around in places an overweight married woman shouldn't have been touching on a high school student. She felt along my ribcage and squeezed my shoulders. She shoved some sort of wooden implement down my throat, causing me to gag. I smacked her hand away, watching as she leveled her eyes with me.

Then she slid her fingertips around my neck. Causing me to wince.

"And there it is," she said.

I paused. "What?"

She sighed. "Well, you don't have a concussion. But you've given yourself whiplash."

"How the fuck did I get—"

"Language."

I rolled my eyes. "How does one get whiplash without a car accident?"

"Whiplash is just a term for when the neck snaps back and forth too quickly. I guess when you were pushed over your bike this morning, you tensed. Right?"

I shrugged. "So?"

"When you tense, it makes it worse. You have whiplash, which means you'll have to take it easy. No riding fast. No more fights. Because if you injure your neck further, you'll be in the hospital with an actual concussion."

"Sounds better than this place."

She sighed. "All you need to do is keep it in line this year. Then you can graduate and go fight other adults on your own time. But, so long as you're fighting on this campus you're my responsibility."

I chuckled. "If I didn't know any better, I'd say it sounds like you care, Mrs. Abernathy."

"You make it hard to care, Clint. But I do."

Her words disarmed me, and the only thing I could do was laugh. I brushed off her comment as I slipped off the paper-covered table or whatever the hell I was on. But her words stuck with me as I grabbed my backpack.

"Not too fast on that bike, Clarke!"

I grinned. "I'll go as slow as possible. Promise!"

"Yeah, yeah, yeah."

I finally made it out of the school and walked over to my bike. Seeing how scratched up it had become made me seethe all over again. That fucker had no right to throw me over my bike. He had no right to ruin the paint job that took me painstaking hours over the summer to perfect. I grumbled to myself as I shoved my backpack into the compartment on the back of my bike. I slipped my helmet over my head, wincing as it clamped down around my neck. I'd have to watch that. Because it definitely didn't feel pretty.

And as I tossed my leg over my bike, I saw Mrs. Abernathy standing at the front doors of the school.

Really?

I shook my head as I cranked up my bike. I put on a nice show for her, inching my way out of there as slowly as I could. Going the speed limit, and nothing more than that. But once the school was out of view, I cranked it up. I blazed a trail down the main stretch of our little slice of Riverbend, weaving my way through town. I pulled over for a snack, running my ass through my favorite fast food place, then pulled over to eat. I took a long bike ride, trying to clear my thoughts. Trying to prepare myself for the bomb-ass pool party that didn't start until tonight.

Courtesy of Marina's parents' empty house.

After stuffing my face full of greasy food, I cranked up my bike. I sped back to my place, charging through the front doors of my empty house. I snickered as I turned on lights. A massive mansion my father owned, and I was the only one that occupied it on a regular basis. While he and my fake-titted stepmother were jetting off to beautiful places, I was here. Being parented over Skype and only seeing them whenever I really got my ass into trouble.

Not like I give a shit about them, either.

After changing into my swimsuit, I pulled my jeans back over my legs. I grabbed my stuff for the night, including a towel, then made my way back out to my bike. I sped over to Marina's place, where Roy stood out front to greet me. I parked my bike in the driveway, inching it off to the side. Because I sure as hell wasn't keeping it on the road after the scrapes and bumps it had taken that morning.

Fucking Michael.

"Figured you could use a drink."

I smiled at Roy. "Please tell me that's—"

"Jungle juice? Hell yeah, it is. You know Marina makes the good stuff."

I hung up my helmet and grabbed my towel. Taking the drink from Roy's hand, I sloshed it back. I mean, I chugged it down. I felt the alcohol working its way through my veins as girls giggled off in the distance and water splashed around the corners of the house. I clapped Roy's hand, bringing him in for a shoulder tap before we made our way around the house. I handed my empty glass off to a girl by the jugs of jungle juice, flashing her a devious smile. One well-timed smile and the silent promise of a kiss goodnight and my drink was full as the line continued to grow beside me.

I winked. "Thanks, hot stuff. Love the suit, by the way."

She giggled. "Thanks, Clint."

Roy held out his arms. "Welcome to the party. I think it's the biggest one yet."

I grinned. "Which means the girls are in their smallest bikinis yet."

"Hell yeah, they are."

"Good. Now, where's that damn hot tub?"

Roy pointed, and I saw a gaggle of beautiful girls in it. Their string bikinis barely clung to their bodies as I made my way over. I tossed my towel off to the side, chugging back my second drink before ridding myself of my clothes. I felt their eyes on me, gazing over my muscles and marveling at my tall form. Ladies love the tall ones, and I was the tallest guy out of all these fuckers at this party.

Which gave me a very unfair advantage.

"Ready to make way, ladies?" I asked.

They all giggled as I stepped into the tub, sinking into the hot water. Bubbles raged around us as I swam between a couple of them, allowing my arms to settle on the outside rim. A beautifully-tanned girl swam over, sitting directly onto my lap. And as she wrapped her arms around my neck, I tried my best not to wince.

"I heard you were in a fight this morning," she purred. "Are you okay, Clint?"

I grinned. "A few bumps and bruises. But you should see the other guy."

"Is there anything I can do?"

I smiled. "Why don't you kiss me and make it all better, beautiful?"

And the pain in my neck quickly dissipated as her pillowy soft lips inched closer to mine.

11

RAELYNN

"Are you sure you have to cancel? I mean, I'm sure Dad's work will understand."

Michael and I sat on the couch, listening as Allison bartered with her parents. We looked at one another with knowing looks. Our weekend was about to be flushed down the toilet.

"I get it. I understand. No, no, no, I'm not disappointed. I just know how much you were looking forward to this. Are you okay?"

I sighed as I pushed myself off the couch. I gathered up the snacks Allison had handed to me earlier and pressed them into my backpack. No use sitting on the couch if we had to get out of here before her parents got back.

"An hour out? Gotcha. Want me to order a pizza or something? I know that always makes you feel better."

Michael grumbled. "Better get a move on."

The two of us began packing ourselves up as Allison hung up the call. She came back into the room with a sorrowful look on her face. I held up my hand. I didn't want her feeling bad for this. It wasn't her fault. I mean, her mother was a stay-at-home mom, sure. But her father owned his own business. A few of them, in fact. And that always made for a very volatile schedule. This wasn't the first weekend extravaganza his work had impeded, and it wouldn't be the last.

Allison sighed. "Well, I guess this is as good a time as any to tell you guys."

I paused. "What do you mean?"

She shrugged. "I was hoping to celebrate this weekend. But since my parents are on their way back from the airport…"

Michael paused. "You got in somewhere, didn't you?"

Allison smiled softly. "I got into UCLA. My first pick. I just got the acceptance letter a couple days ago. I'm officially in their architecture program."

"Oh. My. Gosh!"

I squealed with delight as I rushed toward my best friend. I picked her up, swinging her around as laughter fell from her lips. Michael pulled her away from me and hugged her close. The two of them shared a long embrace as I watched, smiling from ear to ear. I walked up behind Allison and rubbed her back. Michael tucked her head underneath his chin while he held her close.

And for a split second, I was jealous of the relationship blooming between them.

Michael murmured. "I'm so proud of you."

I smiled. "So am I, Allison. Really."

She sighed. "That really takes a load off my shoulders, you know?"

"So what does that mean for your senior year? Can you coast it now?"

He chuckled. "She'll have to submit her final report cards at the end of every semester. Just to make sure she keeps her grades up."

"Well, that's bullshit."

Allison giggled. "I'm just so glad I got in, you know? I didn't want to leave California in order to study, and now I don't have to."

"Which means we can see each other all we want."

She turned around, facing me. "Exactly."

I embraced her again, hugging her close and swinging her from side to side. Michael wrapped his arms around both of us, trying to get back in on the action. I looked up at him, giving him a knowing wink. And after he was done blushing furiously, we all stepped away from one another.

"Ice cream. Sunday afternoon. That's what we'll do to celebrate," I said.

Michael nodded. "And it's on me."

Allison rolled her eyes. "Not everything has to be on you."

Michael scoffed. "Why don't you two let me spoil you every now and again? I don't get it."

I laughed. "Because you're always doing it."

He rolled his eyes. "Fine. But I'm picking you up. Be ready by three? That sound good?"

And after Allison and I nodded, the three of us headed upstairs.

It was almost painful, walking away from our planned weekend. But I understood why we had to do it. I walked myself home, watching the sun set over the horizon as the smell of garbage and darkness filled my nostrils. I thought back on the conversation I'd had with my mother this morning. Maybe this would be a good time for our girls' night in. I mean, with it being so last-minute and all that, she wouldn't have enough time to invite her bullshit boyfriend over.

Or so I thought.

"Hey, Mom. You here?"

She poked her head down the stairs. "Rae? I thought you were at Allison's for the weekend."

I set my bag down. "Her parents' spa retreat or whatever had to be canceled because of her father's work. So I'm home."

"Oh, that's nice."

"Want to do our girls' night tonight? I've even got some snacks in my bag. Some chips, some cookies. There's a sandwich or two, too."

Instead of seeing my mother smile, I saw her wince.

"What?" I asked.

She sighed. "I didn't think you were going to be home until Sunday. So I invited D.J. over for the night."

"Ah."

"I'm sorry, honey. It's just that—"

I waved it off. "It's fine. Don't worry about it. It was a last-minute thing anyway."

"You can have dinner with us. He's picking up something nice from that Italian place up the road. I could give him a call really quickly. You want some lasagna?"

I shook my head. "No, it's fine. I've got plenty of food in my bag."

"We could throw a movie in after dinner?"

"Mom, it's fine. I promise. I have some homework I need to get done anyway if I have any chance of actually enjoying my weekend. You two have fun, okay?"

I carried my things up the stairs, brushing quickly by my mother. Of course she'd take this time to invite D.J. over. What the hell else did I expect? I made my way into my bedroom and closed the door, ready to tear into my reading for English while I munched on some cookies. I flopped onto my bed and pulled out my books. I spread out my snacks as my mouth began salivating. I didn't know what it was about the on-brand cookies that tasted so good. But they were always better than the off-brand ones my mother bought.

However, I didn't even get halfway through my reading before the fighting started.

"I'm sorry, D.J. I didn't realize you wanted me to get wine."

He sighed. "Beer doesn't go with Italian food. Are you that thick-headed?"

Mom scoffed. "Well, I'm not a wine connoisseur. I wouldn't even know what kind to get with noodles and shit."

"No, you just know how to open your throat and chug it back so you can get drunk all the time. Right?"

"You're the one always dragging me off to parties when I'm completely content hanging around here with you. Just you. In your arms."

"Well, maybe if you weren't such a boring little fuck, I wouldn't always have to drag you to parties to get you to loosen up!"

I rolled my eyes as I reached for my headphones. Then I remembered that D.J. had thrown my iPod full of music against a fucking wall. Great. I hunkered down in my bed, pulling the covers over my ears. I tried blocking out their fighting as I struggled to get through my reading. But finally I couldn't take it any longer. It had taken me two hours to do what should have only taken forty-five minutes, and I couldn't take their arguing any longer.

Homework can wait.

Mom cursed. "Fuck, D.J.! I just wanted to have a nice night with you. Why did you have to come in here and blow a gasket first thing?"

D.J. snarled. "You cuss at me one more time and I'm going to show you exactly what dirty mouths like yours deserve."

"Oh, really. A threat to hit me? Like you don't do that enough as it is. You keep slapping me around enough and I just might hit back!'

"I'd like to see you try, you pathetic excuse for a woman."

I shook my head as I slipped out of bed. I stored my snacks underneath my bed for a rainy day, then changed my clothes. I put myself in the only sundress I had. I wanted to feel the cool summer air on my legs as I walked around. Because being anywhere right now was better than being here. D.J. was hot, then cold. Good, then bad. One week, he brought over flowers and money and gifts. And the next week, they were fighting downstairs until he decided to beat on my mom. I felt it coming, too. The beatdown. The cold to his hot.

And if I was here for it, I wasn't too sure I wouldn't try to kill him.

"Just get out!" Mom yelled.

Something crashed against the wall before D.J.'s voice sounded.

"You're lucky that didn't land, you little bitch."

I heard my mother on the verge of tears as I slipped into my tennis shoes. I pried open my window, feeling the cool summer breeze against my legs as I slipped out onto the roof. I shimmied down the drain pipe, dropping to my feet. And after smoothing my dress down over my knees, I took off for the road.

I couldn't stand it any longer.

I had to get the hell away from this place.

12

———

CLINTON

I pulled into the driveway of my father's mansion and sighed. Ten o'clock at night, with the party just getting started, and Marina's parents had to ruin the whole fucking thing. I mean, come on. Women were practically fighting over me. I was teasing them to the high heavens, too. Acting like I'd kiss them, only to turn my head and start flirting with another. Chicks loved that shit. Loved working hard for a man they wanted. And I was working them in the hot tub like magic.

Until Marina's parents busted the damn thing up.

Roy got to stay, though. I watched the way he sucked up to her parents. The way he started rattling on about trying to keep everyone safe and keep Marina away from the 'ruckus.' Oh, he sucked up well to them. Kissed their asses so much they actually let him stay. Roy! Of all fucking people! The boy who was fucking their daughter in the middle of the damn football field after school, and they let him stay. All because he knew how to put on a good show. All because he knew how to appear like the good boy before seducing his girlfriend.

I wish I had a girl to have some quality time with.

I shook the thought from my head. I got laid enough as it was. Quality time with a girl would only dampen shit like that. Once a guy started cuddling with a chick, that's all she wanted to do. Cuddle. I'd have to start begging for blowjobs after that. And fuck that nonsense. Clint Clarke didn't beg. If anything, women got down on their knees and begged to give me one. Just to say they had the pleasure of tasting my cock in their mouth.

The thought made me grin as I swung my leg over my bike.

Nope, there was no point in going steady with a girl. I hadn't done it before now, and I had no intention of doing it later on in life. I didn't see the point in it. Fucking around with one girl and her getting pissed off if I saw a nice ass walking by me. What was the point in that? Why spend my time begging to get fucked when I could go out any night and be guaranteed a fuck? Relationships were pointless. They destroyed people. Turned them into shadows of their former selves.

I should know, too.

I watched it happen with my mother.

I opened the garage door to get inside and paused. Seeing my father's cherry red convertible in the garage made me groan. What the fuck now? Why the hell was he home? What the fuck did he want to shove up my ass this time?

I braced myself for whatever I was walking into as I approached the side garage door.

"About damn time you showed up."

His voice hit my ears as I walked through the door. I stood in the sprawling kitchen, seeing him and Cecilia sitting at the table. There was food out. A plate set for me. Their plates were clear of any food they might have been eating and everything had grown cold. I snickered as I closed the door behind me. I shrugged as I slid my bike keys into my pocket.

Then I licked my lips. "Didn't know family dinners were our thing."

Dad narrowed his eyes. "Where have you been?"

"Marina's. Hanging out with Roy."

"Why the fuck did I get a call from the school saying you'd been in a fight this morning?"

You're dead, Mrs. Abernathy.

I shook my head. "It was nothing. Some pathetic boy came at me and I defended myself."

Dad stood up. "Not what I heard."

"Well, I don't care what you heard. That's not what happened. He crossed a line, so I defended myself."

"Does that crossed line happen to be something he did to that bike of yours? Because I've got every intention of taking that away from you right now."

"You aren't taking that from me again."

Dad charged from around the kitchen table and I puffed out my chest. Cecilia stood up, hollering for him to stop as he barreled directly into me. I winced as the pain in my neck grew. He shoved me against the wall, then pinned me with his hands wrapped up in my shirt. Apparently, all he heard was I'd been in a fight. He didn't give a shit about the injuries I'd suffered during the event.

Typical, for my father.

Cecilia slammed her hand on the table. "You know that nurse said he's only a few steps away from a concussion. Let him go."

Dad growled. "You're so full of shit. Thinking you can walk around here like you own the place. Don't forget who bought you that bike."

I grinned. "You bought my first bike. I dipped into my trust fund with your permission to buy the second one."

"And don't you dare forget who can take that away from you."

I snickered. "If you did, you'd be stuck with me. Which is something I know you don't want."

"Not when you're a piece of trash."

"Like father, like son."

I gnashed my teeth at him before I saw his hand come into view. And before I could even blink, I felt his knuckles crack against my cheekbone. My neck felt as if it were on fire, and I stumbled on my feet. I felt my father grip my shirt again and bring me back into the wall, only to come down against my face again.

He hit me three solid times before Cecilia's shrieks caused him to pause.

"Howard! Stop it! You're going to put him in the hospital!"

I felt my father release my shirt and I slipped back down to my feet. But my father spun around and I heard him yelling at her. I knew he was probably spitting on her. I watched him stick his finger in her face, but she stood her ground, her small frame enveloped in the most expensive of fabrics. The two of them yelled back and forth at one another, but I had no idea what they were saying. I didn't care, either. All I knew was I had to get out.

I had to get away from this place.

I reached for the garage door and ripped it open. I stumbled out, my vision slowly coming into focus. I saw the garage door closing and I made a break for it. I heard my father screaming my name as I ducked underneath the moving metal door. I dug my keys out and slung my leg over my bike. My father's voice approached me from behind as I quickly struck up my engine.

"Get back here, you son of a bitch. That bike is mine!"

And just as I felt his hands on the back of my leather jacket, I tore off.

Cecilia's cries faded into the background. My father's cursing fell away from my ears. The engine of my bike roared underneath me, vibrating as it carried me away from that fucking hellhole. The wind rushed through my hair. I sped out of the neighborhood, making my way for the high school. I didn't know where the fuck I was going, but I sure as hell wasn't going home.

Ever, if I could swing it.

I hope you rot in hell, Dad.

I drove around town, feeling my wallet burning a hole against my ass cheek. I stopped off at a diner, where my stomach started growling at the smells of food. I walked inside and slid my helmet off, watching as people gave me strange looks. I made my way for the bathroom and scoffed when I saw myself, finally realizing why people kept giving me awkward glances.

One of my father's slaps had actually bruised my face.

"Just great."

I sighed as I splashed some water on it. I ran some through my hair, watching as it glistened. The bruise was faint. But with the pale skin I'd inherited from the fucker himself, it was easy to see. I licked my lips and dried off my hands, then ran the paper towel over my face. I winced at the pain. My neck felt stiff. My cheeks were on fire. My ears were ringing from how loud my father had been yelling at me.

Then my stomach kicked in again.

"I need some food."

I tossed the paper towel away and slammed out of the bathroom. I took a seat in a corner booth, where the biggest waiter in the diner came up to me. I peeked over at the girls, watching as they cowered away. Fucking figured. I'd gone from the man every woman wanted to flock around, to the man people feared. And all because of some fucking bruise that wasn't even my damn fault.

Note to self, girlfriends and bruises from my father ruin my mojo.

The waiter sighed. "Can I get you anything?"

I leaned back. "Got anything on special?"

"Ten percent off our chicken and waffles."

I wrinkled my nose. "Odd combination."

"Drench it all in syrup and it's fantastic."

I sighed. "Sure. That's fine, then. An order of that, a slice of German chocolate cake, and coffee."

"Cream and sugar?"

"Yep."

He paused. "It might not be my place, but you need to talk to someone?"

I snickered. "Nah, I'm good."

"You sure? That's a pretty decent shiner."

"It only looks bad because I'm pale as fuck in the middle of California."

And even though the two of us shared a small moment of laughter, I still saw the nervousness in his eyes.

"That's all. Thanks," I said.

He left to place my order while everyone continued to stare at me. The freak in the leather jacket with the blackened cheek.

13

RAELYNN

I stared off into the darkness as I sat on the park bench. A ratty park, on the outskirts of the suburb where our small little area was stashed. The metal monkey bars were rusted through. Half of the swings were broken. The plastic of the slides had been cracked for years. Even the sandbox had been infested with bugs and fleas and all sorts of things, driving the families around here to abandon it. But I found solace in this place. In the crispy grass that had been fried by the sun. In the dead trees that surrounded this little patch of land. I sipped my green tea, reveling in its taste. Just another thing that separated me from the coffee-guzzling masses of those that surrounded me.

I sighed as I dwelled in my moment of turmoil.

I'd never been good at brushing things off. I had to pick through it. Tear it apart before piecing it back together. If I didn't, I'd be stuck in a never-ending cycle of untapped emotion and swirling memories. I had to delve deep into it so I understood how to talk about it intelligently. Or, at the very least, build a fucking bridge and get over it.

I needed to pick through the chaos of my home. The insanity of my mother. The decrepit state of her good-for-nothing boyfriend. I closed my eyes, listening as her shrieks filled my mind. Sipping on my tea as the sound of D.J.'s hand cracking against her jaw made me wince. Grimace.

Wish I was anywhere other than here.

"Deep breaths," I whispered to myself.

I continued sipping my tea until there was nothing left. I felt my mind slowing down. And, for once, I relaxed. A cool summer breeze kicked up, pulling the last of my hair out of its ponytail. I reached for the band before it fell to the ground. I ran my fingers through my hair, trying to work out the knots. I smoothed it over my shoulders, fluffing it in the wind. My dress kicked up around my shins, cooling off my thighs as I sat on the wooden park bench that still held the heat of the day within its bones.

Then I heard it.

The rumble of a motorcycle.

I can't be that unlucky. Please tell me I'm not that unlucky.

I sighed as I opened my eyes and set my empty tea container on the ground. I drew in a deep breath, listening as the bike crept closer, rumbling up the road behind me and finally turning off.

And moments later, I found myself staring at Clint Clarke's torso.

I sighed. "What do you want?"

"Is anyone sitting here?"

I snickered. "Nope. And neither are you."

I glared up at him, but all I saw was that snarky little grin of his. That stupid smirk I wanted to slap right off his fucking face. Only it didn't reach his eyes like it normally did in school. There was a sadness to his features that I knew all too well. I watched him carefully as he moved off to the side. Despite what I'd told him, he sat down beside me, hissing as the heat of the bench came into contact with his ass. I stared at him, watching as his eyes connected with something off in the distance. And as his guard came down, so did his grin.

It sank into a frown that had become the physical mantra of my life. A frown that constantly looked back at me in the mirror every morning.

Clint cleared his throat. "Sorry I kicked your friend's ass."

I shook my head. "He got in a few punches, too."

"Doesn't mean he didn't get his ass beat."

"And you deserved every punch he landed."

He shrugged. "Maybe so."

"Really? You're trying to be the good guy now?"

"I'll never be the good guy. Not my thing."

I turned my eyes out toward the playground. "Why are you such a dick all the time? Isn't it enough that we can't stand you?"

I saw Clint turn his head as he stared at me. And even though I felt him burning a hole in the side of my face, I refused to look over at him. I refused to give him the satisfaction of gazing into my eyes. He stared at me for a long time, and I wondered what he was thinking. I found myself wanting to have a peek inside his mind, just to know why the hell he was staring for so long.

Then his voice filled the space around us.

"I don't know. I guess 'cause it's easy. And it's something I'm actually good at."

I rolled my eyes. "The pity card won't get you far with me."

"Not looking for any."

"Good."

He shrugged. "It's true. I'm good at making people hate me. I'm good at being a dick. That's what I do."

I arched an eyebrow. "Wow. Deep motivations, bro."

"Hey, you're the one that asked a dumb question."

"Just didn't expect the answer to be dumber."

"Why do you always do that?"

I snickered. "Do what?"

"Fire back with such animosity?"

I whipped my eyes over to him. "You're asking me—the boy who's bullied me on and off for years—why I address you with a burning hatred? Are you fucking kidding me right now?"

He shrugged. "Maybe if you were nicer, like your friend Allison, people wouldn't be so standoffish to you."

"Is that before or after you made overt sexual jokes about her to Michael?"

"I mean, at least they weren't directed at her."

"Oh. Yeah. Right. Because that makes it all better."

I scoffed and shook my head. I leaned back against the park bench, wishing and praying and hoping he'd go away. I just wanted some peace. Some quiet. Some fucking clarity. I didn't want to deal with his bullshit.

I didn't want to deal with Clint.

"So what are you doing out on a night like this?"

I closed my eyes. "You aren't going to leave me alone, are you?"

He scoffed. "I mean, I figured you'd be with goody two shoes Allison or some shit like that."

"I was, until our plans got canceled."

"Ah, she busy kissing Michael's booboos?"

I bit down on the inside of my cheek. "If you don't leave, I'm leaving."

"Have a safe trip home."

I crossed my arms over my chest, irate at his ability to completely spoil whatever moment of happiness I found for myself. But I wasn't leaving. I had been here first, and he was the one that wasn't wanted in this scenario. If he wanted to be rid of me, then he could leave the same way he came. And if he didn't want to leave, then I'd annoy the hell out of him until he did.

Clint chuckled. "Stubborn, I see."

I shrugged. "You're the one making this more difficult than it needs to be."

"Not really. You don't want to be around me, then leave."

"I'm not the one who obliterated the moment with my presence in the first place."

"Big word for a small girl."

"Well, if you paid attention in English class at all, you might have a few to throw around yourself."

"Kind of a non-sequitur, if you think about it."

I furrowed my brow. "What?"

"A non-sequitur. A phrase that doesn't—"

I held up my hand. "I know what a non-sequitur is, you dick. I'm just not sure how—"

I looked over at him and found him smiling at me. And not the kind of smile I was used to seeing on his face. It wasn't malicious. It didn't shiver me to my core. It was… just a smile. A genuine, eye-reaching, illuminating smile. I'd never seen Clint smile like that before. Hell, I'd never seen him smile at all. But something like this?

It made him look almost boyish.

"Shocked I know the term? Or shocked that I used it correctly?"

I drew in a sharp breath. "What I said was only partially—I mean, if you twist it—I—you know what that word means?"

He chuckled. "English is my strong suit. That's why I don't pay attention in class."

"Didn't you almost fail, though?"

He shrugged. "C-minus. Not bad for never turning in homework."

"That means you would've had to ace all your tests, though. Read the material?"

"What? You think I can't read?"

"Not that you can't. Just that you don't."

He grinned. "Maybe I have a few tricks up my sleeve every now and again."

I quickly turned away from him and tightened my arms across my chest. I wasn't going to let him disarm me. I wasn't going to let him in. I wasn't going to let him closer, or talk to him about anything, or even tell him why the hell I was out here. I wasn't going to indulge my personal life with the school bully. No matter how he tried to woo me into it.

But, I had to admit, he'd officially shocked me.

He snickered. "Still not gonna talk?"

I shook my head. "Nope."

"Even though you now know I'm not just a bully?"

"No one is ever 'just' anything. Being a bully is your domi-nating trait. So it is what it is."

"But, if it wasn't, you'd talk to me. Wouldn't you?"

"Doesn't matter now, does it?"

He chuckled. "Answering a question with a question is never a good thing, Cleaver."

And even though I tried keeping my guard up, I felt it slowly slipping down with him.

Something I didn't even think to be possible.

14

——————

CLINTON

I mean, I got it. I understood why Rae didn't want to talk with me. I just found it crazy that we both ended up here at the same time. I mean, fuck. She was sitting on my bench! A bench I'd practically claimed back in eighth grade. I came to this damn park whenever I needed to clear my head. Whenever I needed to fuck some shit up without getting into trouble with the town of Riverbend. Most of the cracks in these slides were from me. The broken, rusted-through metal monkey bars had been broken through in the first place because of me terrorizing this damn place. I mean, parents and families alike had abandoned it years and years ago. The second the sandbox became infested and sent kids to the hospital, they shunned this place. Making it the perfect park for angsty teenagers and homeless people alike to find whatever fucking piece of solace they could in this decrepit park. And with Rae sitting on my damn bench?

I didn't believe in coincidences that much.

Especially since you can't stop thinking about the girl, asshole.

I licked my lips. "I come here sometimes, too."

I heard Rae snicker to herself, but she didn't say anything.

"It's true. I've come here regularly ever since eighth grade. I sit on this exact bench, right where you're sitting, and I stare between those two dying trees."

I pointed off into the distance as she drew in a deep breath.

"It's not going to work. I know you're making this shit up."

I shrugged. "Think what you want, but it's true. I come here at night, sit where you are so I can look between those trees, and I get the perfect view of the north star."

I looked over at her, watching as her eyes lifted. I saw her gazing through the trees before they widened a bit. She looked over at me, shock pouring over her features. Then she went back to staring at the ground. She scooted over a bit, closer to the edge of the bench. Away from me, like I was the plague. Like I was some sort of virus. Like I was a piece of trash she wanted nothing to do with.

And I don't know what the fuck spurred my mouth to start running. But once it started, I couldn't stop it.

"I came here the first time my father ever hit me. I had a teacher threatening to hold me back in eighth grade because I never turned in my homework, of all things. And the fight that ensued with my father was rough. It was the first time I'd ever yelled at him. The first time I'd ever stood up to him. And when he saw I wasn't backing down, he hit me. He hit me so hard it threw me clean across the damn room. I ran out of the house, got on my pedal bike, and didn't stop until I collapsed with exhaustion in this park. Slept on this bench until morning, before Roy's parents found me laying out on this thing."

I felt Rae's eyes slowly panning over to me as I sighed heavily.

"At school, it's easy to forget about all that shit. It's easy to forget about home. About my mother. About my father and how aggressive he is. I get to be a different version of me there. A stronger version of me."

Rae scoffed. "You think you're stronger because people are afraid of you?"

I shrugged. "I guess."

She paused. "You know, that's actually pretty typical. Guys like you don't have power at home, so you take it out on others in a place where you feel powerful."

"I take it you have a point here?"

"I do. It means your sob story isn't so special. Or sob-worthy."

The laughter that bubbled up my throat spewed out of my mouth before I could catch it. I tucked my arms over my chest, letting my head fall back. My eyes closed as laughter took over me. My shoulders shook and my stomach jumped, and for the first time in a long time I felt free of the chains of my home. Without having to be at school.

Which was a miracle in and of itself.

"What's wrong with you, Clint?"

I sighed, trying to rein in my laughter. "Oh, ho ho. Holy fuck. So much, Rae. So much is wrong with me. But let's be real for a second. You're just as screwed up as I am, at the end of the day."

She didn't answer, and that caused me to look over at her. I saw her curl even more into herself, and something inside me wanted to reach out to her. Physically. I forced it back, though. I tucked my arms tighter underneath my arm pits, trying my best to make her feel comfortable.

Because I wanted her to be comfortable around me, for some reason.

I sighed. "Look, I get it. You don't have a good home life. You look at all those big houses we have and the fancy clothes Michael and Allison wear, and you think it's a better life. But it isn't. We all have our issues. My dad slaps me around more than I care to admit. I'm sure your mom has some equally fucked-up shit she does to you."

Rae spat. "Which is none of your business."

"Maybe. Maybe not. But it does you no good not to talk about it."

"Oh, like you talk about it with everyone?"

"I just did, didn't I?"

And then, as if the heavens decided to actually play in my favor, Rae sighed.

"Mom's got this boyfriend. D.J. And he's such a shitbag of a guy, you know? I mean, I know it broke my mother down when my dad left. I was only three, so I don't remember shit about him or anything. But, she just filtered through so many stupid men before landing on, what? D.J.? Some dude that pays some of her bills sometimes and slaps her around a bit? Fucking hell, I can't stand it when they start arguing. One minute, he's bringing over Italian dinner for a nice meal, bringing her flowers. Bringing me gifts. And the next minute? Mom's got a black eye and she's out drinking at bars all weekend before dragging nameless men home to try and make herself feel less alone. I don't get it. Why can't she just… survive without them? Why can't she just put in the effort to thrive? Why does some guy have to be the miraculous answer to all her problems? It's exhausting after a while. Trying to keep up and deal with it all in the background." Then, after a pause, "But not as exhausting as being around you. You really do me in. I'd take D.J. over you any day."

I chuckled and shook my head. Ever the strong one. Trying to keep up that icy demeanor when all she wanted to do was drop her guard. Nevertheless, the need to reach out and hug her was so great I felt myself shaking. I wanted to punch whoever this D.J. guy was until his eyes fucking bulged. How dare he treat a woman like that? How dare he think he could put his hands on a woman and get away with it? I watched Rae's cheeks blush deeply. Even in the darkness, I saw her skin redden. And as she flickered her eyes toward mine, she scoffed.

"What?" I asked.

She shook her head. "I can't believe I just told you all that."

"Why?"

"You mean, other than the fact that you're the biggest asshole at our school?"

I sighed. "Don't be like that, Rae."

"Be like what?"

"So moody."

She leered. "I'm not moody."

"So that bubbling rage in your eye is a reaction to something else? Maybe the pollen? Possibly the fleas infesting the sandbox over there? Did you get bit by a raccoon? I hear the Riverbend raccoons have rabies."

She scoffed and shook her head. But soon, that scoff turned to a giggle. Which morphed into laughter that tilted her head off to the side. The beautiful sound wrapped around us, and I couldn't help but smile. Her arms fell away from her chest and she placed her face in her hands, shaking her head as more laughter fell from her lips.

"What is even happening, Clint?"

I smiled. "You're growing weak for me. Just like all girls do."

Her laughter paused. "Don't do that."

"Do what?"

"If I'm not going to be moody, then you're not going to be a pompous windbag manwhore."

My eyebrows rose. "How long have you had that one tucked away?"

"Not as long as you'd think. I'm quick-witted in some moments."

"I see that."

She looked over at me and her eyes fell to my lips. My smile made her smile, and for the first time I saw her eyes ignite. With the moon above reflecting in her amber pools, it reminded me of the strength of a tree. The rungs of a redwood covered in sappy bark, cloaked in the effervescent darkness California had to offer. I found myself swimming in them. Falling into them and never wanting to return.

The writer in me wanted to pen a poem devoted to the swirling rungs of her brown eyes.

Rae cleared her throat. "What are you looking at?"

I cocked my head. "You."

"What about me?"

"I like this side of you."

She blushed. "Oh, come on. Cut the shit and get to the punch line."

"What punch line?"

"Whatever it is that made you come over and sit down on this bench."

"Is it really so hard to imagine that you're the reason I felt compelled to sit down?"

She snickered. "Felt compelled? Who are you again?"

I turned my body toward her. "I'm the Clint you've always seen."

"I've never seen this side of you."

"Do you want to see more?"

My hand gravitated to her cheek and I cupped her soft skin. My thumb brushed against it as her eyes searched mine. Wild, and curious, and a bit mysterious. And as a grin settled across my face, she smiled up at me. I felt her nod against my hand before she nuzzled my palm. I felt myself being pulled into her atmospheric orbit. Stanzas of poems not yet penned regarding her beauty rushed through my mind. I felt her face getting closer as her body heat encompassed me. And when our lips touched, fireworks went off in my mind.

This was the kind of girl wars were started over.

My elbows tingled. My toes curled. I felt electricity sizzle down my spine. Her tongue pressed against my lips and I was all too eager to let her inside. All too eager to wrap her up in my arms. I pulled her close, heaving her into my lap, and she straddled me with effortless perfection. An entire epic poem spilled forth in my mind, encompassing the whole of Rae. From the soft touch of her fingertips against my jaw to the searing heat of her lips against my own.

Even the way her body fell against me constituted its own story of praise.

I pulled back softly. "Ever been on a bike?"

Rae shook her head. "No. I haven't."

"Want to ride on one?"

When she didn't answer me, I stood up. I picked her up in my arms with ease as she squealed and clung to me. I set her down on her feet, taking her hand and tugging her toward my motorcycle. She resisted at first. But then she gave way to me. Gave way to my silent command as we headed for our escape.

"Come on. I'll take you for a ride," I said.

And without a second thought, I handed off my helmet to her.

15

RAELYNN

Clinging to Clint around his waist as we zoomed through the streets of our hometown wasn't something I ever thought I'd be doing. And yet, I found myself holding tighter to him with every passing mile. He took the long way around town, pointing out toward the ocean and slowing down so I could gawk at it. We stopped at a bakery that was in its closing hour and he picked us up some pastries at half price. We even stopped to get me one last green tea, while he chugged back a black coffee.

It was a side of him I would have never imagined existed in my wildest dreams.

I stopped questioning where we were going after a while. But once we pulled into the driveway of his home, I grew nervous. What the hell were we doing back here? I figured he'd take me home. Or back to the park. Or drop me off at the high school.

"Uh, Clint?"

He turned off his bike. "What?"

I slipped the helmet off. "What are we doing at your house?"

He put his kickstand down. "Well, you said you didn't wanna go home. But everything else around here's closed. We got these pastries. Figured you'd wanna go somewhere, drink something, and eat."

"So we're at your house? Where your father is right now?"

"Nah. Dad goes to the casino to blow off steam after we fight. He won't be back until tomorrow night at the earliest."

"And your stepmom?"

He scoffed. "She's always at his side. If he's not here, she's not either."

He helped me off the bike, catching me as I stumbled. I felt myself blushing underneath the strength of his arms, but I tried not to show it. I tried not to give in to it. This was madness. This was Clint Clarke, for fuck's sake. The boy that had swung on Michael this morning! There was no way the butterflies in my gut were for him. There was no way on God's green earth I felt the way I did because of him.

And yet, when he took my hand to lead me inside, I felt my stomach jump.

Turn around. Go home while you still can.

I watched Clint type in a password on a keypad that opened the garage. And with the bag of pastries in one hand, he led me straight through a door and into his kitchen. I gawked as I walked inside, too. His kitchen alone was bigger than Allison's entire fucking living room. Holy shit, if I thought Allison's and Michael's parents had massive homes, then I'd really been an ignorant little girl.

Because Clint's father didn't own a home.

He owned a damn mansion.

"You want the cinnamon or cheese danish?" Clint's voice pierced my shock.

"Um, cheese."

He nodded. "Cinnamon for me, then. Which is great, because I'm a cinnamon fanatic."

"Good to know."

"What do you want to drink?"

I didn't hear his question. I kept scanning the room with my eyes, wondering how big this place was.

"Rae."

I heard the chuckle in his voice and my eyes whipped over to his.

"What's up?"

He grinned. "Wanna see the rest of the house?"

I nodded with delight and he dropped the pastries. He scooped my hand into his, and together we started through the house. He showed me the living room, with a massive projection screen on an entire wall. He showed me something called a sitting room, which was literally just a room with a bar and some chairs. He took me into a library. A legitimate library with floor-to-ceiling bookshelves that lined every square inch of wall in the damn place.

Then he led me upstairs. To the middle of the three levels the house had.

"Who the hell needs this much house?"

Clint chuckled. "Dad, apparently. He bought this place before Mom even got pregnant with me. Only three people live here, but it's got six bedrooms. And all of them have their own bathrooms."

I scoffed. "Seems a bit like overkill."

He shrugged. "That's my father for you. Here, this is my room."

He reached through a doorway and turned on the light. And when his bedroom came into view, I stopped in my tracks. It was the size of mine and my mother's put together. And then some. I slowly walked into the room, taking in the blackout curtains over his windows. The beautiful wooden frame of his massive king-size bed. The carpet underneath my feet made me feel as if I were walking on memory foam pillows.

And yet, there was such a sinister presence within all of it.

"I'm so sorry," I whispered.

I slowly turned around, watching as Clint closed the door behind him.

"For what?"

I shook my head. "For… everything, I guess."

He nodded. "It's fine. I don't make it easy for people to see me."

I snickered. "This is the part where you apologize, too."

"I'm getting there."

He made his way to me. I felt his hands against my waist, and I didn't hate it. His green eyes sparkled as they danced with mine, and I felt him peering into my soul. His black hair fell into his face, prompting me to raise my fingertips in order to brush it away. Our skin touched. I felt my breath hitch in my throat. And even though I wanted to pull away from him, something inside me rooted me there. Grounded me, forcing me to stare into the eyes of a boy who understood me more than most.

More than anyone, really.

"I like this side of you," I whispered. I cupped his cheek, and he nuzzled into my palm.

"I'm sorry for always being a dick. It's just easier than anything else."

"Trust me, I get it."

He nodded. "I know."

Our foreheads fell together and his hands slipped to my hips. I felt him gathering up the fabric of my dress as our lips slowly moved together. Our eyes met. My heart slammed against my chest. And as the backs of my legs met the edge of his mattress, his hands slid my dress up to my thighs.

Just as our lips collided.

His tongue met mine and stars erupted behind my eyes. I felt my body pucker for him and places on me tingle I'd never paid attention to in my life. Like the slats between my toes as I wrapped my legs around him. Or the crooks of my knees as his hands slid down my legs. With every stroke of his tongue, my skin prickled. With every groan of his I swallowed down, my hairs stood on end. I felt electrified. I felt myself sizzling into a puddle of nothingness. And as his hands gravitated to my panties, I felt the rest of my walls crashing down.

Are you really about to do this?

I slid his leather jacket away from his shoulders and quickly gathered his shirt over his head. He wrapped his arm around me, hoisting me higher on the bed before he knelt against the mattress. His muscles came into view and I licked my lips, staring at the ink that adorned his arms and torso. He was beautiful. Every part of him. Angrily beautiful in ways I understood. My fingers slid through his hair as his lips came down against my neck. I felt my thighs warming and my panties wetting. He pushed my dress up as he kissed down my neck, exploring me with a kindness and a gentleness I would have never associated with him.

With every press of his lips against my skin, he rewrote what it meant to be Clint Clarke.

"Oh, yes," I whispered.

He groaned as his lips fell to my thighs. I toed my tennis shoes off, feeling him slip my panties down my legs. He rose up long enough to pull the fabric away from my body. And when my feet got tangled up in the fabric, he smiled down at me. He chuckled along with my giggles, making me feel comfortable in my own skin, even with the thick thighs and broad hips that didn't look very much like the girls he usually stared at.

Then I watched him unbuckle his jeans.

It happened so quickly, I almost didn't catch it. He crashed back down to me, our lips colliding as my legs spread for him. He reached down for something as his jeans fell to his knees and soon, something hard fell between my thighs. I felt him pulsing and dripping, his kisses becoming sloppy as his fingers explored my depths. I moaned for him, buckling underneath his touch. He nibbled at my neck as his fingers filled me, stroking my swollen walls.

Before his girth replaced those dexterous fingers.

"Clint," I gasped.

"Holy fuck, Rae."

"Yes. Oh, my—just yes."

He chuckled before his lips captured mine again. I felt his forearms press against the mattress on either side of my head. I wrapped myself around him, feeling his thickening length stroke against my walls with every thrust of his hips. I gasped for more. His bed bucked as he picked up the pace. I raked my nails down his back, listening to him growl into the crook of my neck. My toes ran down the backs of his legs. I locked onto him, feeling him growing thicker inside me. My eyes rolled back, my body shook and I quivered around him as my body began to tense.

"That's it. Come on, Rae. I feel you. Just let it go."

"Clint! Yes! Oh, Cli—"

My jaw unhinged and my back bowed so deeply I figured it would snap. My body shook for him. Quaked for him. And a darkness overcame me. I chanted his name like a shattered prayer, a choked, wanton sound falling from my lips. I felt him pumping into me, thrusting faster and faster. Harder and harder. Begging my body to hang on just a second longer.

Before he, too, burst.

"Rae," he growled.

When he collapsed against me, I felt full. With every thread of his arousal that touched my body, I felt blanketed in him. His sloppy kisses turned to soft nuzzles of his nose as his face found the crook of my neck again. He rested against me, his muscles cradling the curves of my body. And as my arms fell away from his back, I sighed with relief.

I smiled up at the ceiling.
All because of the bully from Riverbend High.

16

CLINTON

My eyes fell open and I groaned. The smell of her still lingered in the room with me, and it made me smile. I rolled over, half expecting to see her next to me, lying there with her dress bunched up over her hips and her legs spread. Ready to go another round as the two of us woke up together.

But when I rolled over, there was nothing but my bed to greet me.

"Figures," I murmured.

As I lay there, staring up at the ceiling, my mind fell back to last night. What had gone down between me and Rae. How good it felt. How right it seemed. I'd never experienced something that calm and collected with a girl before. Usually, they were eager to suck me off for a bit before poking their pretty little asses out for me. But this was something else, with Rae. Something slower. Deeper. More sensual than I'd experienced before.

"Fucking hell," I said, sighing.

I rolled over one last time, placing my face where her head had been. I drew her scent in deep as my mind pulled me back to those moments. How nice she had felt in my arms as I fell asleep. How soft her skin felt against mine. How much her body had enveloped me as we grew to fevered heights.

"I gotta write something," I said, groaning.

I sat up in bed and reached for my bedside table. I pulled out another notebook and pen I kept stashed there, and my muse ran wild. I scratched down rudimentary poems and premises for short stories. I cranked them out, one after another, until the sun pierced through my blackout curtains. I ran my hand through my hair, flipping through the pages of nonsense I'd written down simply because Rae had refueled something inside me.

"What the fuck?" I asked breathlessly.

My cell phone vibrating on my bedside table pulled me from my trance. And for a good reason, because I didn't want to think about shit like this anymore. I tossed my notebook and pen back into the bedside table, then reached for my phone. But my muse still hadn't calmed down. Words rattled through my mind that I hoped I'd be able to recall later. Words that could have only described the beauty and the appeal that had been Rae last night.

I opened up the text message I had and saw it was from Roy. And as I read it, a cold bucket of ice water got tossed onto my muse.

Roy: Get your ass over to my place. I had a great time with Marina last night. And you'll never guess what we did in her parents' bed.

For some reason, I felt the need to roll my eyes. I tossed my phone onto the mattress and slid out of bed, resolving myself to a shower. Though I was hesitant to wash Rae's scent off my body. I took an extra-long hot shower, allowing my mind to wander a little more one last time.

Then I got out and got ready to head to Roy's.

Dad still wasn't home when I got downstairs. Which didn't shock me one bit. He and Cecilia had probably gotten a hotel room somewhere, where he could bang out his anger toward me with her body. I shook my head. That poor fucking woman. What girls like her wouldn't do for money astounded me. Money was useless. Money was almost nothing, despite what people wanted to believe. I grabbed a banana from the fruit bowl and peeled it open, eating it as I walked out to my bike.

I tossed the peel off to the side, threw my leg over my bike, and started for Roy's.

With thoughts of Rae bombarding my mind.

Oh, Clint.

The way she said my name so sweetly made my skin tingle. Unlike the squeals and the whimpers from most girls, hers were soft sighs. Guttural groans. Less of a porn video and more of a religious experience. I didn't believe in God and all that shit. But I did believe in angels.

And Rae was one of them.

I need to write that down later.

I rode over to Roy's and found him on the porch, waiting for me. And the second I took a look at his neck, I knew I was in for a long story. He had hickeys everywhere. Bite marks. Nail marks down his arms. I mean, he was fucking covered in evidence of her. And while I usually would've been interested in a story like this, I found myself not caring about the topic at all.

"So after you assholes left, her parents stayed downstairs," Roy said.

I parked my bike in front of his porch and turned off the engine.

"Uh huh. I take it you two had sex in their bed?" I asked.

"Oh, not just their bed. Their shower. Their bathroom. Bent over their fucking dresser. It was hot, man. Marina was all like, 'Mom, my television isn't working. Can we watch a movie in your bedroom?' And the second she looked at me with those 'fuck me' eyes, I knew it was on. We didn't even get five minutes into the damn credits before she hopped on this dick."

"Sounds like you had a good time," I said, grinning.

"Oh, hell yeah. You know what she let me do?"

"I take it you convinced her to try anal."

"Fuck yeah, I did! She gripped those bedsheets like such a good girl for me, too. I'll never fucking go back. That was the tightest hole I'd ever experienced. I don't even want her pussy anymore."

I snickered. "Told you it was a great experience."

"Great? This was a miraculous experience. I've never come that hard in my life, dude."

While this would've been the part where I interjected with my nightly escapades, I found myself playing my cards close to my chest. I didn't want to tell Roy what I'd gotten up to last night. I didn't want to confide in him all the dirty, nasty secrets of the night. Usually, I did. The two of us went back and forth, until one of us outdid the other for the day. But I didn't feel like I could confide in him with what happened between me and Rae.

It felt wrong, for some reason.

"So, please tell me you left some marks behind on her body,

too. Because that's a pretty bitch-ass thing for you to be marked up and for her to not be," I said.

He snickered. "She was all over me, dude. I got my marks in, but make no mistake. She couldn't keep her paws and her lips off me. She gobbled my cock down with ease before we even got started. I didn't even have to warm her up."

"Hell yeah, Roy. That's the way to do it."

"Marina sure is a giver. And I think I'm gonna keep her around for a little while."

I grinned. "Sex really that good?"

"Have you been listening to me at all? The sex is fantastic. I mean, yeah, she's a bit thin. But I like 'em thin. Less to push away to get to the holes I really want."

I shook my head. "Nope. After I'm done, I want to fall against my girl and feel her catch me with her softness."

"You've always been attracted to fatties. I don't get that."

"Not fatties, Roy. Just those girls with a little more to give is all. Trust me, if you ever feel a pair of soft thighs wrapped around your waist, you'll never go back."

"No, thanks. If her thighs rub together, you can count me out. You know how badly pussy smells after thighs have been rubbing against it all damn day? Fucking hell, no thank you."

I chuckled. "Pussy stinks anyway. Get over it, or don't eat it."

He shrugged. "Marina's don't stink. I don't know what the fuck she does to it, but it smells like fucking candy and roses, man. Keeps it bare for me, too. I mean, every inch of her is just smooth as ice cream. When I do feel like going down on her, I'm there for a while. Especially since she lets me do practically whatever I want if I can make her come a few times with my tongue."

"A few times? Let's not overstate now."

"What? Okay, okay. Three times with my tongue. The most I've ever done."

"On Marina? Or in general?"

He grinned. "Not enough detail for you yet?"

As Roy launched into yet more stories about his girlfriend, my mind drifted back to Rae. I wondered if she'd gotten home okay last night. If I'd see her again, privately. I thought forward to Monday, and whether or not things might be weird at school. Would she acknowledge me? Would it be business as usual? Was she embarrassed that she'd slept with me?

I found myself hoping she wasn't embarrassed at all. In fact, I found myself hoping we could actually be civil.

Maybe even kind to one another.

"Earth to Clint, you there?"

I shook my head. "Sorry. I was drowning in the boring stories of your sexual escapades."

He gawked. "Boring? Boring!? You call fucking my girlfriend in her parents' bed four times boring?"

"No, I call it nasty. Because that's their marital bed. All they do is fuck in it. So now, technically, you've fucked Marina, her mother, and her father. Because you know their shit's all over that mattress."

He paused. "Holy fuck, I need to shower again."

And as I threw my head back with laughter, Roy scampered off into his house. Readying himself for the scrub-down of the century.

Which gave my mind more time to drift back to Rae.

17

RAELYNN

I drew in a deep breath before knocking on Allison's front door. I'd barely gotten any sleep last night, and I needed to talk with my best friend. But not Michael. Holy shit, Michael would kill me if he knew what had happened.

"Hey there, Rae! Come in, come in. You hungry? There's still some leftover breakfast."

Allison's mother was an absolute ray of sunshine. I smiled at her as I walked through the door she held open for me, feeling the cool air conditioning of their home envelop me. I had to hold back tears. I was more emotional than I'd ever felt in my life, and I sure as hell didn't want to be explaining to Mrs. Denver why I had come to her house crying.

"We've got biscuits, some eggs that are still warm, sausage I can reheat—"

"I'm actually not hungry. But thank you, Mrs. Denver," I said.

She quirked an eyebrow. "You? Not hungry? You feeling okay, Rae?"

I snickered. "Just had a big breakfast at my house is all."

She looked at me for a long time and I prayed she bought the lie. And even though I figured she knew I was lying, she didn't call me out on it. She simply nodded her head and walked off, calling for Allison as she got to the bottom of the staircase.

I shoved my hands into my pockets, hoping to conceal their trembling.

"Allison! Rae's here, honey!"

"Coming, Mom!"

"Thanks, Mrs. Denver. I appreciate it," I said.

She smiled. "Anytime. You know you're always welcome."

I nodded. "I know."

"And if there's anything you ever want to talk about, just know it stays between us. Okay?"

I smiled softly. "I really appreciate that. Thank you."

Allison came bounding down the steps with her blond hair up in a bun. She grabbed my hand and tugged me back upstairs, dragging me. Step by step. We stumbled into her room and she closed the door, and the smell of nail polish remover wafted heavily under my nose.

"I figured since we couldn't paint our nails last night, we could do it now. I mean, Michael isn't here. But we can still do it. Right?"

I furrowed my brow. "Did you set all this out before you came down?"

She snickered. "Not a chance. I just started to change out my own nail polish when Mom yelled that you were here. I figured it was a nice coincidence."

She flopped down onto the floor, then reached for my wrists. She dragged me with her, and together, we picked out our next nail color. She dropped her feet into my lap before she handed me the pale pink color she wanted on her toes. She'd already cleaned the nail polish off them once, leaving me a dry and alcohol-soaked canvas for which to do my shoddy work.

Which gave me some time to gather my thoughts.

"Did something happen with your mother?"

I shook my head. "No. Not at all. I mean, yes. But that's not why I came over."

Allison sighed. "D.J. again?"

I rolled my eyes. "When is it ever not D.J.?"

"What did he do?"

"The usual. Fighting. Mom threw something against the wall at him. Things got heated. I ended up sneaking out of my window and heading to the park last night."

"Why in the world didn't you come here? You could've stayed overnight instead of going back home after all that mess."

I paused. "I didn't go home until this morning."

"Oh?"

I bit my bottom lip. "I stayed with Clint last night."

Allison yanked her foot away. "You did what now?"

"It's not—"

"How in the world did you end up there?"

I sighed. "He found me at the park. Did you know his father slaps him around?"

"Who in the world cares what his father does? How did you end up at his house overnight? Wait a second. Did you—?"

I slowly looked up at her and her eyes bulged.

"You didn't."

"It just sort of happened, Allison. I'm still not completely sure what happened."

She scoffed. "An alien took over your body. That's what happened. Are you serious? You slept with Clint Clarke?"

My face fell. "Let's say that a little louder. I don't think the rest of the block heard."

"Does Michael know?"

"Hell no! Michael doesn't know, and he won't know."

Allison nodded. "Good. Because after that fight, he'd kill you if he found out."

"Yeah. I know."

I screwed the cap back onto the nail polish and tossed it to the ground. I put my head in my hands, trying to steady my breathing as tears rushed my eyes. Allison's hand came down against my back, drawing small circles with her palms. I drew in a deep breaths as my heartrate skyrocketed. Every time I thought back to last night, my hands trembled. My heart stuttered.

And I still didn't know if it was a good or bad thing.

Allison kissed the side of my head. "Tell me what happened."

I shrugged. "I don't know what happened. That's the issue. We talked for a little bit. I found out why he's such a dick all the time. He was kind enough to try and get my mind off D.J. and all that shit. And then, we were in his bedroom and I lost control of myself."

"There's gotta be more to this, Rae."

I shook my head. "There really isn't. One minute we were talking about our shitty parents, then the next minute he was kissing me and I didn't want him to stop. It was just—"

"Are you sure we're talking about the same Clint Clarke here? I mean, the boy who slugged away at our best friend?"

I nodded slowly, feeling so many emotions flood my stomach. Shock. Awe. Happiness. Confusion. But none of it was guilt.

Which confused me even more.

I looked up from my hands. "I really want to tell Michael about it."

Allison scoffed. "You can't. After taking the beating he did and stepping up for us—"

"For you."

I looked over and saw Allison blushing.

"Well, at any rate, after what happened Friday morning, Michael wouldn't speak to you for a while. He's awesome and all, but the boy can hold a grudge."

I groaned. "I don't like the idea of keeping secrets from my best friends, though."

She shook her head. "Trust me, it won't do him any good to know. Plus, you've got me. You've told me, and you can keep telling me until you come to terms with what's happened. Because I feel you shaking. I know you regret what happened."

"That's the thing. I don't. I'm not shaking because I regret it. I'm shaking because—"

I flopped down onto my back, staring up at her ceiling fan. How the hell did I explain any of this to her when I couldn't even explain it to myself?

Allison lay down next to me. "You don't need all the answers now. Just talk about what you can."

My hands covered my face. "What the actual fuck is happening with my life right now?"

She giggled. "I know one thing we have to figure out, though. And that's what to do about Clinton come Monday."

"I… I don't know, Allison."

"Well, let's start with what you want to do. What do you hope happens Monday?"

I shrugged. "I don't know that either."

"We should figure it out, then. Because something tells me he's not going to leave you alone. Nothing is ever that easy with him."

"I didn't fuck him so he'd leave me alone."

She paused. "Then why did you?"

I closed my eyes. "Because it felt like he understood me. And I liked that."

Allison took my hand as the two of us stared at the ceiling. The smell of nail polish remover slowly faded away, but the memories of last night didn't. I squeezed her hand, trying not to think about it. Trying not to root myself in last night. But I couldn't help it. The way I'd fallen asleep against Clint. The way his muscles felt cradling me last night. How I woke up at four in the morning only to realize I'd fallen asleep right beside him. Wrapped up in him. With my leg pressed between his and my head tucked underneath his chin.

It was so unlike the Clint Clarke I knew.

And yet, it made all the sense in the world.

Allison cleared her throat. "Penny for your thoughts."

I squeezed her hand again. "I fell asleep with him last night."

"What time did you get home?"

"About four-thirty in the morning."

"Did he take you home?"

I shook my head. "I didn't want to wake him up."

"Why not?"

Because I knew if he asked me to stay, I would have.

I sighed. "I don't know. I don't know much of anything right now. I just—needed to tell someone. And you were the only person I could think of that wouldn't completely alienate me for it."

The room fell silent as butterflies ignited in my gut. The same kind of butterflies I'd had last night. Why the fuck did I feel this way? It felt like I had a crush on the school's biggest asshole. Which was wrong on so many accounts I couldn't even begin to explain all of it to myself. I closed my eyes, trying to push all the memories away. It was a one-time moment I had the chance to write off as me being completely vulnerable. Not right in the head, what with everything going on between my mother and her bullshit boyfriend. And I knew people would believe me, too. If I told them it was a moment of absolute insanity due to my home life, they wouldn't question things.

But I'd know it wasn't the truth.

And Clint might pay a hefty price for it.

Why the fuck do I care what kind of price he pays for it? He beat up my best friend!

"Shit," I whispered.

Allison snickered. "Sounds like we need to find a distraction for you today."

"You mean we can't just lie here and debate on ways to erase my memory?"

She giggled. "I mean, it sounds fun in theory. But I wouldn't appreciate it if you forgot all about me."

"Not my entire life. Just the past forty-eight hours."

"How does getting lunch out somewhere sound? We can take the mind-erasing from there."

And as my stomach growled out, betraying my actual hunger, a smile crossed my face.

"Soup and sandwiches?" I asked.

Allison sat up. "Soup and sandwiches it is."

18

———

CLINTON

I heard my father storm through the door Sunday evening, much later than I figured he'd come back from that damn casino. He was muttering to himself, something about bananas and shoving them down someone's throat. I grinned to myself as I heard the trash can lid bang against the wall.

Good. He found it.

I heard Cecilia's soft voice cooing at him. Treating him like some damn child as she tried soothing away his worries and his anger. It was pathetic, really. Listening to a grown-ass woman coddle a grown-ass man like that. I didn't want to be in the house. Not with her, not with him, and not with the tension they brought with them.

If I was lucky, they'd be on another airplane in the morning. Heading off on yet another trip.

And out of my damn hair.

I picked up my cell phone and shoved it into my pocket. It was late, but I didn't care. I grabbed the keys to my bike and snuck down the stairs, bypassing the living room altogether. Stepmommy dearest and my bullshit father were curled up, watching a movie. And still, I heard him grumbling to himself. He was the most miserable asshole on the face of this planet, and I couldn't wait until I graduated.

Because I had all sorts of plans on how to get out from underneath him.

I opened the side garage door without a sound and rummaged around for the second bike helmet I knew I had stashed away somewhere. And just as I tucked it under my arm, I heard my father's voice.

"Clint? You out there? You know damn good and well what your curfew is on the weekends."

I threw my leg over my bike and cranked up the engine. I slipped my helmet over my head, then pinned the other one between myself and the bike. I zoomed out of the garage, leaving my house in the shadows as I tore out of the neighborhood. I didn't give a shit about my father or his rules. If he wanted to be a decent parent, he could stay home, stay away from the casino, and stop beating up on me whenever he didn't like something I was doing.

I cruised down the road until I came to the opening of the neighborhood. And instead of taking a right to head on into town, I took a left. I found myself at the mouth of Rae's neighborhood, and I slowed down to see if I could find her house. I only had a general idea of which one it was. It wasn't hard to spot once I came upon it.

I recognized that rusted-out bright green bike of hers she used to ride back in middle school.

I looked through the living room window and saw her mother watching television. She was leaned up against someone. Some dude that was snoring away with his head lobbed back. I shook my head as I walked the bike into the driveway. My eyes scanned the front of the house, coming upon one lone light that was on upstairs.

Hopefully that's Rae's bedroom.

I put the kickstand down, though I didn't turn off the engine. I set the extra helmet on the bike, then started picking up gravel rocks from her driveway. I tossed them at the window, missing the first couple of times. But, the third rock landed directly against the glass. Making a much louder sound than I had anticipated.

But it did draw Rae to the window.

"What the—Clint?"

I waved. "Come on down. I have a helmet for you."

She shook her head. "I can't. I'm about to go to bed."

I shrugged. "So?"

"Mom's downstairs with some guy, Clint."

"And I'm pretty sure they're both knocked out. Or in a trance. She hasn't looked out the window at me yet."

I watched her bite her lower lip, and the motion tugged at my gut. She looked so cute like that, with her hair in a bun. I preferred it down, like it had been the other night. I saw a smile creep across her face before she closed her window, then the light to her bedroom went off.

At first, I thought she was turning me down.

Until the front door opened.

"Come on. We have to hurry."

I smiled as I tossed her the helmet. She slid it over her head and I chuckled at her pajamas. She had on these flimsy pajama bottoms that had all sorts of stars and hearts and sparkles all over it. And the tank top she wore barely stayed on her body. She whipped some sort of woven jacket or whatever around her shoulders, then leapt onto the back of my bike.

And when I felt her arms wrap around me, my world slowly settled into place.

"I hope you're hungry. Because there's a diner I've got my eye on tonight."

Rae giggled. "And here I thought you had your eye on me tonight."

I grinned. "I have my eye on you tonight for dessert, that's for sure."

"You're so bad. But you better hurry. If there's a promise of food, I can't hold my stomach off for long."

"A girl that eats. I love it."

I backed out of her driveway and we tore off down the road. She squealed, clinging to me as I raced us into town. I adored the feeling of her wrapped around me. The way she fisted my jacket and buried her helmeted head against my back. I smiled brightly as we cruised through town. I took the long way to the diner, just so I had more time to savor the moment with her.

Eventually, though, we pulled into the parking lot. And I was all too eager to escort her inside with our hands tangled up together.

"You know, my mother would have a heart attack if she knew I got on the back of some guy's bike."

I slid into the booth. "Some guy?"

Rae nodded. "Well, you. But yes. To her? Some guy."

I chuckled. "I'm not just some guy, Rae."

"Oh, yeah? And what are you, then?"

I winked. "I'm *the* guy. You really should know this by now."

"Idiot."

The waitress brought us menus, but I was too busy staring at the flush in Rae's cheeks. Oh, she was so easily flustered. And I loved it. Her nose wrinkled up as she put the menu in front of her face. I reached out and slowly slid it down. She was too cute to cover up, with her freckles and her tinted cheeks and her wild hair.

Since when the hell did girls become 'cute'?

Rae cleared her throat. "Whatcha thinking about getting?"

I shrugged. "The usual."

"Care to fill me in on what that is?"

"A double cheeseburger with everything, a chocolate shake with extra cherries, and extra crispy fries. Two orders of them."

The waitress walked back up. "Well, now that I have his order, are you ready, hun?"

I grinned. "Yeah, hun. You ready?"

Rae shook her head. "His order actually sounds nice. Can you make two of those?"

My eyebrows rose. "That's a lot of food."

"And you apparently underestimate how much of it I can put away."

The waitress scribbled on her pad. "All right. Two double cheeseburgers with everything, two chocolate shakes with extra cherries, and two double orders of extra crispy fries. Anything else?"

A hotel room to properly work this meal off with the cutest girl alive.

Rae shook her head. "I'm good."

"Me, too. That'll be it, thanks."

The waitress gathered the menus. "I'll be back with your shakes in a few minutes, guys."

I sighed. "So is that guy I saw with your mother D.J.?"

Rae paused. "No, actually."

I leaned back. "That happen often?"

She nodded. "Every time they get into a fight. She rebounds with some guy, they fight again, D.J. showers her with gifts so she'll come back, then the cycle starts all over again."

"I'm sorry, Rae."

She shrugged. "Shit happens."

"Do you remember anything about your dad?"

"Wow. You really just wanna dive in there, don't you?"

"I mean, do you have anyone else to talk about it with?"

"Allison and Michael."

"Have you ever talked with them about it?"

She shrugged. "Doesn't mean I won't."

I quirked an eyebrow, listening to her sigh. "You know I'll understand."

"Why don't we start with what happened to your mother?"

I nodded. "All right. What do you want to know?"

"What really happened, Clint?"

I sighed. "I wish I knew. One day she was okay. And the next, she wasn't. Painkillers are a bitch, but when you put it together with postpartum depression, it becomes a big issue."

"Your mother struggled after having you?"

"My mother struggled all the time. I think the reason why Dad put up with it, too, was because of her looks. He's into the whole 'trophy wife' thing. And Mom didn't mind pumping out kids so long as she could shop and keep up with her plastic surgery addiction."

"I'm sorry, Clint."

I shook my head. "I truly do believe Dad ruined her. I mean, there are pictures I've come across of her from time to time, and the smile on her face is just—"

I got lost in my memories for a second. And I didn't get pulled from them until our milkshakes touched down. I nodded at the waitress and she left us be, then I felt something warm against my foot under the table.

And when I looked underneath, I found Rae wrapping her legs around mine. Trying to comfort me. Trying to cradle me. Trying to be there for me.

No one had ever done that for me before. I felt my heart leap to life.

"No, I don't have any memories of my dad. According to Mom, he wasn't even around much when they were together. I mean, they got engaged. Got married. Had me. But, for some reason, he jumped ship when I was three and that was that."

I sighed. "Did your mother ever tell you what happened?"

Rae shook her head. "I can't get her to talk about it. Like, ever.

I don't know that I'll ever know what really happened. Why Dad really left us. Why he really didn't want us."

"I'm sure it wasn't that."

"Are you, though? I mean, it's possible. Mom's not easy to deal with. My grandparents disowned us, practically, because of her erratic behavior. For all I know, Dad got fed up with it and was worried I'd turn out the same way. So he left to avoid all that."

I reached out, taking her hand. "You don't seem erratic to me."

She snickered. "Oh, yeah? And sleeping with the high school bully on a whim after he got into a fight with my best friend isn't erratic?"

"You make it sound like that's a bad thing. Was it really that bad of a thing?"

And as our plates of food settled in front of us, Rae shook her head.

"No. It really wasn't."

19

RAELYNN

C lint grinned at me from across the table before he let go of my hand. We dove into the food, sinking our teeth into fabulous, greasy burgers that made me moan with delight. There was an extravagant amount of food. But I knew I'd eat it all. In some ways, I forgot Clint was sitting there. Watching me. Staring at me. Taking in the way ketchup slid across my cheeks and how the lettuce slid away from my burger, dropping onto the plate.

"If you cut it in half, the vegetables will stay better."

I slowly looked over at him as I found myself mid-bite into my glorious burger.

"Oh, yeah?" I asked with my mouth full.

He chuckled. "Yep."

He held up half of his burger and I put mine down. I wiped off my face as his eyes danced along me, watching my every move. I wasn't sure what the hell he was staring at, but I didn't like it. I'd never been underneath someone's gaze so intently, and it made me squirm in my seat. I picked up my knife, cutting the burger in half before I picked up the part of it I had already been chewing on.

And I found that the vegetables didn't slip out as easily.

I smiled. "Genius."

"I've eaten many burgers in my lifetime. I've perfected the art."

I shook my head. "There's no art to eating them. There's only the art of cleaning yourself up after them."

"That an art you've perfected?"

"You making fun of the way I eat, Clarke?"

He winked. "Maybe just a bit."

I rolled my eyes. "A teaser, even on a date. How romantic."

"I mean, we could share our milkshakes if you wanted. Get two straws. Nuzzle our noses together and feed each other cherries."

"I'm not eating anything from your fingertips. I don't know where those things have been."

He grinned. "I could tell you where they will be later."

"You sound pretty sure of yourself there. I wouldn't get too cocky."

"But maybe just a little cocky. Right?"

I felt myself blushing as I shook my head. We went back and forth like that over our food, but it wasn't the kind of dickish banter I'd known him to have. It was playful. Flirtatious. Nice, even. He had a great sense of humor, and I found myself laughing and partially choking on my food every time he slid a joke in at the right time. Who would've thought Clint Clarke had a decent sense of humor?

Certainly not me.

Clint pointed to my shake. "You got enough room for that?"

I leaned back. "I have to admit, this was a lot more food than I realized."

He grinned. "Maybe try not to keep up with me next time."

"If you challenge me, I'll make myself sick proving you wrong."

"And that would be one of the many reasons why you're not like your mother."

The comment caught me off-guard, and it settled itself deep in the pit of my soul. It affected me in so many ways that it brought tears to my eyes. I looked down into my lap, playing with the loose fabric of my cardigan. I blinked rapidly, trying to keep myself together. Except the tears fell anyway.

And I felt my body being slid across the booth seat.

"Come here," he murmured.

He wrapped his arm around me and I leaned against him. I felt his strength as he comforted me. As he slid his hand up and down my arm. I tucked my head underneath his chin, feeling him lean back with me. And as I rested against him, I allowed the full force of that complimented truth barrel over me.

"You really think I'm not like her?" I whispered.

He shook his head. "Not one damn bit."

I sniffled. "Thank you."

"You have nothing to thank me for. You're not like your mother. End of story. You're strong. You're vibrant. You're resilient. And one of these days, you'll get out of this place. Just like me."

I paused. "You want to get out, too?"

"More than anything on this planet."

"What will you do once you leave?"

He shrugged. "Not go to school, if I can help it. Maybe I'll open up my own bike shop. Or become an apprentice somewhere and get some certs. Work on some writing or some bullshit like that while I'm at it. Anything's better than what I'm doing now, that's for sure."

I nodded. "I know what you mean."

He pulled me closer. "What about you? Any plans after high school?"

"I'd love to move out with Allison and get a place together. Maybe with Michael moving in with us or something. She's been accepted to UCLA's architecture program, and I imagine Michael will apply to go there just to be around her more."

"That boy's got it bad for her."

I giggled. "He does, and it's adorable. I love it. And I'm totally for it."

The two of us sat in silence for a little while before he reached for his milkshake. He held the straw up to my lips and I took a small sip. Then he followed it up with a sip of his own. He went back and forth like that for a while. Until we'd drained the first of two milkshakes.

But when he offered me a sip of the second one, I had to wave it away.

"I cave. I concede. You win. Holy shit, I'm so full I hurt."

Clint kissed the top of my head. "We'll sit here for a few minutes then, before we head out."

I nuzzled against him. "Are we headed anywhere specific? Or you just taking me back home?"

He shrugged. "I figured we could do whatever you wanted. Go to the park. Go on a ride. Go to the beach. Go back to my place…"

I gazed up into his face, watching him peer down at me. There was a hint of darkness in his eyes. A wanton, knowing flicker that made my heart slam against my chest. I nodded softly, silently answering the question he refused to put out there. And as a grin settled across his face, he raised his hand in the air.

Prompting the waitress to deliver our check.

Our exit was a blur. We moved so quickly as laughter fell from our lips that I had a hard time taking in the scenery. I rested my head against Clint's back as we rode back to his house, with it being well past one in the morning. We pulled silently into his driveway, parked his bike, and stowed our helmets away.

Before we stumbled up the steps.

"Mm, you taste like chocolate," he said, chuckling.

I slid his jacket off his shoulders as he pinned me against the wall.

"And you taste like french fries," I said, whispering.

He winked. "Wanna see what that combination tastes like?"

I reached up, gripping his hair as I tugged him back down to me. Our lips collided, and he picked me up effortlessly, with an ease and a grace that made my stomach flutter with a million different butterflies. He was good at giving me that reaction. That feeling of effortlessly floating. He walked us into his room and closed the door behind him with his foot. And when the door thudded, I giggled against his lips.

"Ssshhh, we're gonna wake up the house."

He chuckled. "You'd like that, wouldn't you?"

He tossed me to the bed and I squealed. I held myself up, watching him strip himself bare for me. His muscles came into view, causing me to lick my lips. I scrambled, kneeling against the mattress as I followed his motions, sliding my clothes off my body until my bare nakedness matched his.

And the way he ran his eyes over me made me shiver.

"Fucking hell, you're gorgeous."

He crashed against me and we fell to his bed. His lips kissed every inch of my skin as I bucked and rolled for him. He kissed down my neck. He raked his teeth along my shoulder. He even nibbled against the crook of my arms. My arms, of all places! I tingled in areas I'd never paid attention to before. Like the small of my back and the tip of my nose. I gasped and moaned. I fisted the sheets as he slid my legs over his shoulders. I leaned up, watching him disappear between my legs.

And as the moonlight streamed around his blackout curtains, his tongue pierced my folds.

"Oh, shit," I choked out.

My head fell to the pillow and the room spun. My hands twisted wildly in his hair as I lost control of my movements. I bucked ravenously against him. I pressed my heels into his back. His tongue slid along my slit, making me wetter by the second. I trembled against his lips as I felt him fill me with his fingers. My toes curled and my eyes rolled back, giving way to guttural sounds that forced their way up the back of my throat.

"That's it. That's it. That's it. Clint."

I spiraled, falling into an endless sea of pleasure as his tongue pressed heavily between my legs. I felt my arousal trickling down my skin as I locked out against him. His hands pinned my hips to the bed. I felt him licking me clean as I fell, weak against the mattress. I gasped for air, the room spinning around me as he kissed softly up my body, leaving behind a trail of wet-lipped outlines that made me smile.

That made me hungrier for him.

"You're fucking perfect," he growled.

He captured my lips with his and I tasted myself on him. It filled me with a desire I'd never experienced, and soon I lifted my hips to him in sacrifice. He guided his thick girth against my walls, filling me. Shaking me. Causing me to cling to him. My nails dug into his skin. I felt his muscles rolling underneath his taut skin, working desperately for my pleasure. His movements were stark. Our hips snapped together. His bed moved with our rocking as I gasped against his ear. Bit down into his shoulder. Marked him in any way I could so any girl at school would see and realize he was taken.

Taken by me.

"Clint. Yes. Yes. Yes. Don't stop."

"Never. I'm not fucking stopping, and neither are you."

His words gave me shivers. My skin prickled everywhere, from my toes to my nose. My gut tightened as the sounds of skin slapping skin ricocheted around his room. I kissed the shell of his ear and whispered how amazing he made me feel with every broken breath. Fire raged through my veins, spurring the electrical shocks that pulsed against my spine.

I felt him everywhere. In the crook of my waist. Behind my knees. In the nape of my neck as he growled against my skin.

"So close. So close. So fucking close, Rae. Come with me."

My back bowed into him and my body unleashed. I clamped down around his length, pulling him deeper as my body begged for his nourishment. I wrapped my arms and legs around him, curling into him as he took what he wanted. And as his hands dug into the mattress, I felt the beast within him finally unleash, rutting against me as he poured into me, marking me as his own. Sinking his teeth into my breasts. Growling how perfect I was as he pinned me to the bed, breathing raggedly through his nose.

I committed every sound to memory. Every smell. Every touch. Every kiss. Every stroke. And when he collapsed against me, I slid my hands up and down his back. I danced my fingertips against his muscles. I kissed his neck and his shoulder and his ear softly, feeling him quivering against me.

"Stay with me," he murmured.

And as a smile crossed my face, I nodded my head.

"Fine by me."

20

RAELYNN

$\mathbf{M}$y eyes fell open before I shot up in bed. The room smelled different. It looked different. The layout wasn't what I was used to.

"Shit."

I threw the covers off me as Clint groaned next to me. I had to practically tumble myself out of bed, since the damn thing was so big. I fell to the floor, scrambling up before I ran straight into the wall. And as I stumbled along, trying to find the damn bathroom, Clint chuckled.

"Need a light?"

The room filled with a blinding light and I shielded my eyes. I grumbled underneath my breath as I reached for the door handle. I threw the door open, ready to relieve myself and try to get ready for school. Because fuck only knew what time it really was.

Instead of the bathroom, though, I was met with Clint's fucking closet.

He chuckled. "On the other side of the room."

"I hate you," I murmured.

I rushed through the bedroom, trying the door on the other side of the room. And when it gave way to a toilet, I sighed with relief. I closed the door behind me, rushing for it. Rushing for the relief it would provide me. However, the light outside made me nervous. It was much too bright for first thing in the morning. I'd most certainly missed my first period. How much of second period I'd missed, I wasn't sure.

A knock came at the door. "Need anything in there?"

I swallowed. "Just some privacy would be nice."

"I mean, you did hit the wall pretty hard. You okay?"

"I'm not bleeding, if that's what you're asking."

I drowned out his voice with the sound of the toilet flushing. I splashed some water on my face, trying to remove the sleep from my eyes. I took the liberty of using what I had around me. Hand soap on my face. Toothpaste on my finger. I used a generous amount of mouthwash, gargling before spitting it out. I picked up the hair-filled brush and said a small prayer, then ran it underneath the water. And as Clint knocked softly on the door again, I groaned.

"Can you give a girl a second?"

"You aren't the only one that has to pee, sweet cheeks."

I murmured, "Call me that again and see what happens."

"You know, you could just skip class."

I ran the wet hairbrush through my hair. "Not a chance."

"You could spend some more time with me."

"Yeah, like that's a smart decision."

He snickered. "Your words would hurt if I thought for even a second you believed them."

I finished brushing my hair before piling it on top of my head. I secured it with my rubber band, then stormed over to the door. I ripped it open, taking stock of Clint's towering form and raven hair, mussed and hanging over his eyes. I watched as those green orbs peeked out from underneath that thick head of hair. I watched as his grin grew into a salacious smile. He slipped beside me, inching me out of the bathroom before he closed the door.

Then he called out to me again.

"We could go back to the diner for some lunch."

I scoffed. "In your dreams, Clint. I have to get to school. I'm not like you."

He chuckled. "We could go to the park. Walk around. Spend a day on the beach!"

"You're crazy. This has got to stop. And it stops now. I can't keep doing this."

The door ripped open. "Doing what?"

"Don't you take that innocent tone with me, Clinton Clarke. This has to be done between us. Me, doing you."

He grinned. "Come on. You don't really want to do that. Why deny yourself such a good thing?"

"You're trouble. That's why."

"Hell yeah, I am."

I felt his eyes on me as I walked around his bedroom. I scooped my clothes off the floor, trying to quickly pull them on. I slid my brastraps up my shoulders, only for him to remove them again. I batted him away before I finally got it on, only for him to steal my pants. I shook my head at his tactics. At how he held my tank top over his head. I'd look like an idiot going to school in pajama pants and my cardigan, but it was the only choice I had.

I scoffed. "Clint. Cut it out. Give me my shirt."

He shook his head. "I really don't know why you want to cover up such a beautiful body."

"Because I don't do trouble. I have plans. I have school, and you're a distraction from that."

He handed my shirt back. "I'll take that as a compliment."

I rolled my eyes. "Of course you would."

"Why are you so bent out of shape over this? It's just one day. We can head to school at lunch time."

"Like the fun little entrance you made on the first day of school? No thank you. All I need to do is get through our senior year, then I can focus on work."

"You sound so boring. Where's the fun Rae I had last night?"

I shook my head. "She's gone. Dead. You fucked her into the mattress then suffocated her with your muscles."

His eyebrows wiggled. "Will some CPR bring her back to life?"

I felt his hands fall against my waist and I batted him away. I slipped my cardigan over my shoulders, then looked around for my shoes.

"Aren't you going to get dressed?" I asked.

"Oh, I'm not going to class."

I paused. "Yes you are."

He snickered. "No, I'm really not."

I reached for his shirt, tossing it to him. "Yeah, you are. And you're going to get ready now, because you're my ride."

He stood tall. "Tell you what. I'll make you a deal."

"I'm not sucking your cock so you can take me to school, if that's what you're about to ask."

"If that didn't sound so tempting, I'd say your words wound me."

I sighed. "What is it, Clint? We don't have long before we have to leave."

He wrapped his arms around me and spun me around. I groaned with frustration before his fingertips started dancing along my sides. Giggles fell from my lips. I wiggled around, trying desperately to get away from his grasp. He picked me up, threw me over his shoulder, then spanked me on my ass. When I yelped, he did it again. And as I continued to yelp, he continued to do it.

"Clint, put me—ah!—down. What are you—ah!—doing?"

He laughed. "You're just adorable, you know that?"

He tossed me against the mattress and I felt myself jump. He pounced on my body, his lips falling hotly against my neck. I moaned as I pushed him away. I groaned as I tried to knock him off me. But I felt his girth growing, his body heating, his hands venturing along my body, pushing up my tank top. Pulling off my cardigan. Stripping me of the fabric I'd just gotten onto my body.

"Clint, I can't."

His lips found my ear. "A ride for a ride. That's my deal. Take it or leave it."

I snickered. "You're intolerable."

"Is that a yes?"

I grinned as I wrapped my legs around his naked waist. I rolled him over, feeling his cock settling hard against my thigh. My hands planted into his chest, and he looked at me with deviousness in his eyes. He licked his lips as his hands slid my cardigan off. I ripped my tank top over my head, bringing my clothed breasts into view. He slipped me back over, sliding my pants off with one motion of his hands. As he slid down my body, he rid me of the only barrier between us.

Then his eyes flickered up to mine.

"Ready to ride me off into the sunset, beautiful?"

And as I pulled him back up to my lips, I rolled him onto his back, straddling him as I kissed him and prepared myself to be filled with him.

21

RAELYNN

I panted for breath as I gazed up at the ceiling fan. Around and around it went, causing the room to tilt before I closed my eyes. I felt something flexing under my head. Something warm. Something strong. A heat rolled into me before something pressed against my ear. And the sounds it made sent chills down my entire body.

"It was worth it, wasn't it?"

I snickered and shook my head. I'd never give him the satisfaction of inflating that ego any more than it already was. But he was right. Missing second period had been worth that moment with him. Worth the torrential lust that poured over the two of us as he held me steady, rocking deep within me. I smiled thinking about it. I snuggled into him as he crooked himself against me, holding me with his arms. Cradling me with his legs. Allowing me to bury myself into the crook of his neck and hide away from the world.

"Hey there," he said, chuckling.

I smiled. "Hi."

He kissed the top of my head. "You doing okay down there?"

"I don't know. Depends. Does my hair look rough?"

"Are you asking me if you have sex hair? Really, Rae?"

I shrugged. "Don't have long to get to school now. We practically gotta get up and roll out."

He groaned as he rolled over and it made me laugh. I climbed on top of him, peppering his face with kisses. I settled my chin against his chest, watching as his eyes closed. Every movement he made entranced me. Every blink of his eye was a mystery I wanted to unravel. Every tick of his lips was a grin I wanted to question. Every stretch of his limbs was an opportunity I wanted to take to climb him like a fucking tree. And as his arms wrapped around me, I felt myself melting into him.

He sighed. "You're really thinking about school after all that? Because I can hardly see straight."

I snickered. "You didn't do your job as well as I did, then. Because my vision's just fine."

"Oh, you're gonna pay for that."

He rolled me over quickly as giggles fell from my lips. He muted them with his mouth, kissing me with a passion that sent my heart fluttering wildly. I slid my fingers through his hair, feeling him trying to wiggle between my legs. I moved my head side to side, and he tried to stop me as he deepened the kiss.

"Don't leave. Stay here with me," he whispered.

I giggled. "You can't keep distracting me with sex. It won't work after a while."

"I can spice it up enough to keep you here all day."

I winked. "Doubt it."

He scoffed and rolled over, gripping his chest, feigning a heart attack. It made me laugh. I slid out of bed, making my way for his bathroom. I needed one last check of my neck and my hair before I had any chance of covering shit up in school today. We were twenty minutes away from our lunch period. And us walking in together wasn't an option. He'd have to drop me off on the curb or something so the two of us could walk into the school at separate points.

Because I sure as hell wasn't ready for that firefight.

I pulled my hair out of its bun. "Are you sure my hair doesn't look bad?"

"It looks great, Rae."

"Are you just saying that to get me to shut up?"

"If I wanted to do that, I'd tell you what I really thought of your hair."

I grinned. "Now I'm intrigued."

I looked over at him, watching as he leaned against the bathroom doorway. He'd already gotten his pants on, but he still stood there shirtless. I let my eyes travel over the soft rings of his abs, my gaze lingering on the steady rise and fall of his chest. He crossed his arms over his body, flexing his biceps at me and causing me to lick my lips as he drew in a deep breath.

"If I wanted to get you to shut up, I'd tell you your hair doesn't mean shit to me. Because telling you that your hair is beautiful is like telling someone the sun's bright. It's obvious, trite, and overdone. If I really wanted to compliment you, I'd say how taken I am with the way your eyes match your hair. With the way your freckles undulate when you laugh. With the way your mind betrays an intelligence and maturity far beyond the high schoolers I have the privilege of spending time with. And if I really wanted to leave you speechless, I'd punctuate it with something like this."

He pushed off the doorway, crossing the threshold of the bathroom. His hand cupped my cheek, and as his thumb slid across my skin I felt my heart stop in my chest.

"I'd tell you the sun is jealous of the light you emit simply by being yourself. And that your hair has shit-all to do with it."

I drew in a ragged breath. "Stop it."

"I'm serious."

"I know you are, and I need you to stop it."

"Why?"

I blinked rapidly. "Because."

"Give me one damn good reason, and I'll stop."

Because you're not supposed to steal my heart.

"Because your long-winded compliments are going to make us late for lunch."

His eyes fell to my lips before his thumb ran along my skin. I shivered at his touch just before his lips pressed against mine. My head tilted back. He cradled the nape of my neck as he stepped forward, closing the gap between us. And as he slid his fingers through my hair, I whimpered against his lips.

"Your hair looks fine," he whispered.

I nodded quickly, then turned away from him. I cleared my throat and pulled my hair back into the traditional ponytail people were used to. I felt Clint's eyes on me, but I refused to look at him, because if I did I might just give in. I might just stay with him for the rest of the day instead of going to school and doing what I needed to do in order to get out of this hellhole.

He really does know how to own the English language.

The two of us got dressed, then he ushered me out of his room. With his hand on the small of my back, he guided me down the stairs, making a beeline straight for the front door. I knew why, too. Neither of us were sure whether or not his father was home. I mean, surely he'd be at work so close to lunch on a Monday. But things were always unpredictable. Schedules changed at the drop of a hat. Vacations got canceled at the last minute due to work. And sometimes, parents came home for lunch instead of eating out.

Clint reached for the doorknob. "I'll drop you off at the front curb on the road before I park behind the school."

I paused. "So we aren't walking in together?"

"Do you want to?"

"Does it matter?"

The two of us froze as his father's heavy voice sounded behind us. I slowly turned around, watching as Clint stepped in front of me. He reached behind me, slowly backing me toward the door. And as he opened it, I felt the heat of the day beat against my back.

I didn't let go of his leather jacket, though. He had to come with me. He was my ride.

Clint cleared his throat. "Morning, Dad."

"Who the fuck is that?" he asked gruffly.

"Hi. I'm—"

Clint cut me off. "None of your damn business."

His father narrowed his eyes. "You wanna try that again?"

"No. I really don't."

I drew in a sharp breath. "Clint, come on. We're gonna be late."

"Did she just come down from upstairs?"

Clint nodded. "Yes, sir."

"And is that fucking allowed in this house?"

"Probably not, sir."

His father charged him and I cried out. Clint shoved his ass out, knocking me outside before his father gripped his leather jacket. I reached out for him, watching as his father picked him up onto his tippy toes. And as his father barreled him back into the wall, I cupped my hands over my cheeks.

"I'm sick and tired of you thinking you run this house. Shut the damn door," he glowered.

I whimpered. "Clint."

He peeked back at me with nothing but sadness in his eyes. And as his hand reached out for the door, he nodded his head.

"Get outta here, Rae. Sorry for making you late and not being able to give you a ride."

"Mr. Clarke, this is all my fault. We just need to get to school. This won't happen again, I swear it. Please, Mr. Clarke."

His father gnashed his teeth at me. "Shut the hell up and get off my property."

Clint growled. "You talk to her like that again and you'll have to deal with me."

His father chuckled. "And you think you're what? Hot stuff? Because you can screw some poor girl from your high school in your own bed? You think that makes you hot stuff?"

And as Clint slammed the front door closed, I heard a resounding smack.

"No!" I exclaimed.

I heard his father yelling from behind the door, and it scared the living shit out of me. Holy fuck, his father made Clint's mean side look like Mary Poppins. I heard them fighting behind the door. It kept rattling with fury as I backed away from it. I stumbled down the porch steps, trying to get my feet underneath me as tears rushed down my face.

And as a woman's voice started yelling above all the ruckus, I made a mad dash for the road. I kept running and running. I ran until the yelling faded behind me and the sound of Clint's voice was but a distant memory. My lungs heaved for air. I felt my legs giving out as I got to the entrance of his neighborhood. I tore across the street, hearing horns honking as my cardigan wafted behind me. Sweat trickled down the nape of my neck. It grew hard to draw in air as I stumbled my way for the front doors of the school. I had to tell someone. I had to let them know what the hell was happening to Clint.

But, when I ripped the doors to the high school open, Allison appeared at my side.

"Girl. Holy mackerel. I've been looking for you all day. Michael! I found her!"

The sound of footsteps rushed beside me before someone else took my arm.

"She looks like hell. Come on. Bathroom time."

I shook my head. "No, no. I need to talk to someone. I need to—"

Michael rubbed my back. "We'll talk in a second. Right now, you need a brush to your hair, a wet paper towel to the back of your neck, and some water."

Allison sighed. "Did you oversleep?"

He scoffed. "The girl never oversleeps. You know damn good and well her mother did something."

I kept shaking my head, trying to get a word in edgewise. They dragged me down a hallway and into one of the unisex bathrooms our high school had. A new installment after our school system passed some law that required two of them to be in every school now. They tugged me in there and closed the door. I put my hands on my knees to try and catch my breath. A cool paper towel came down against my neck, and the temperature change made me heave.

Causing me to throw myself at the toilet.

"That's it. That's right. Get it all out," Allison said softly.

Michael sighed. "What should we do?"

"Is there anything we can do? Just be here for her?"

I couldn't speak. Couldn't talk. Between catching my breath and gagging into the toilet, I didn't have a chance in hell of telling them what had actually happened. Not that I could say anything in front of Michael without starting some sort of third world war between us all. No, I had to keep it to myself. Just until I could pull away from them long enough to talk to a counselor of some sort. Tell them what I'd witnessed. Tell them what was going on.

Maybe then, Clint could get the fucking help he'd needed all this time.

22

CLINTON

I punched mindlessly at the buttons on my controller. Roy kept yelling out, jumping out of his seat and trying to direct what I did with my car. But I didn't give a shit. I hadn't gone to school since my father blew his fucking cap through the roof and beat me to a bloody pulp. Well, practically. It felt like that for the past couple of days. My face ached. My nose kept bleeding at random times and my eye was swollen shut. The bruise on my jaw kept growing, and the more it grew the harder it got to eat.

Thank fuck, I like bananas.

Roy scoffed. "Come on, Clint. You mean to tell me that other eye still isn't good? You completely missed the guy on the left."

I snickered. "You put more mods on your car, didn't you?"

"Yeah. Cost me a shit ton, too. Trying to make back some of the money so I can get to modding this other car I won last night in a race. It's a sweet one, too."

"Well, get us ready for another one. I'm gonna go get something to drink."

I set the controller down and walked out as Roy continued cursing under his breath. I shook my head as I walked into the kitchen, then sighed as I opened the fridge. The only good thing about this school week was that Dad had jetted off with Cecilia again. She'd convinced him to whisk her away to the Philippines. Why the fuck she wanted to go there I had no idea. But the promise of beaches, cocktails, and landing tail for my father was too much for him to pass up.

Which got him the fuck away from me.

That man had knocked me around for a good half hour after I shoved Rae out the door. And my only hope was that she hadn't stuck around long enough to hear any of it. It was brutal. I felt myself fighting for my life as I dodged some of my father's punches. Even when Cecilia intervened, he knocked her to the ground with his elbow. My father didn't give a shit about anyone other than himself. And after that moment, I knew he wouldn't think twice before burning me to the ground if it benefited him.

I wrote him off completely, telling myself that once I got out, I sure as hell wasn't coming back.

Ever.

"Hey, can you grab me a soda?" Roy called out.

"Coke, Mountain Dew, or Dr. Pepper?" I asked.

"Whichever one you haven't held up to your face yet. Which makes you look badass, by the way. I don't know why you aren't coming to school. The ladies would be all over you with those bruises."

I rolled my eyes as I reached for the exact Coke I'd pressed against my eye the other day. I carried the food back out to the living room, tossing it right at Roy's fucking chest. He stumbled with it, dropping his controller and crashing his car into a ditch. I chuckled as he cursed under his breath. But there were more important things than fucking Forza 4.

Like figuring out what the hell I was going to do about Rae.

"So, how long's the dad gone now?" Roy asked as he cracked open his drink.

"For the next couple weeks, I hope. At the very least, the rest of this one," I said.

"I smell a party coming on."

I shook my head. "Maybe once I'm healed a little. But not this weekend. Marina's place is fine."

"Why the hell don't you wanna show off those bruises? You always did before."

I shrugged. "Just don't feel like it this time. The fuck you care about it so much for?"

"Damn. Fine. I'll put a sock in it."

"Thanks."

I flopped back down into my seat, refusing to talk about what happened with Roy. He'd poked and prodded when he first came over after lunch, skipping his last two periods in favor of hanging out here. He did it often, too. Just randomly came over, knocked on the door, and took up space in this house. My father couldn't stand Roy. And sometimes, neither could I. But he was my only friend that didn't pry about my bruises beyond making a few bullshit comments.

Some worse than others.

We continued our racing game in silence, stacking up the winnings and racing around the tracks. Forza was getting boring, though. We had plowed through all the car racing games over the years, and it was the most mindless game on the damn market. Around and around a racing track, racking up money to modify cars we'd never have. Playing the same racing game as some defunct twelve-year-old somewhere whose mother wanted to pawn him off on games so she could fuck her boyfriend in peace.

If only they knew the life that was headed straight for them, full speed ahead.

"Earth to Clint. You there, man?"

Roy's voice ripped me from my trance and my eyes fell against the projection screen. Shit, the race had started and I was still hanging out at the starting line. I sighed as I peeled away from the flashing lights, racing around some random city with some random obstacles and some random cars chasing after us. I cut through the town, running some cars over trying to get into first place. I lost myself in the mindless momentum of it all. I sank myself into the tens of thousands of dollars we racked up in this game.

"Just twenty grand more," I murmured to myself.

A knock came at the door.

I jumped at the sound. It shocked me so badly that Roy gave me a quizzical look. We finished up the race while the knocking continued, and I knew exactly who it was. I looked at my watch, clocking the time. School had gotten out thirty minutes ago. And not just anyone stood at someone's door, knocking for ten damn minutes.

Roy furrowed his brow. "Who the fuck isn't leaving you alone?"

I set my controller down after the race came to a close. Roy cursed the game, muttering under his breath about how we deserved more money from that win. I rolled my eyes as I made my way for the door, wondering if I should open it. Did she know I was here? Was my bike parked out front? I hadn't gotten on the damn thing in a couple days. For all I knew, Dad had sold this bike off as well.

But when she knocked at the door again, I opened it up just to get her to stop.

"You should go," I said.

Rae looked up at me, but she didn't say anything. Her jaw fell open in shock and her hand reached out to touch my bruises. I backed away from her touch. If Roy saw her out here, it'd be the end of both of us. He'd never let me live this down, and he'd tease her relentlessly about it in school.

Which meant I wasn't liable for the condition I left him in.

Rae gasped. "I've, uh… I've been worried about you."

I shrugged. "Well, here I am. Still alive and kicking."

"What did he do to you?"

"Who the hell's at the door, Clint?"

I rolled my eyes. "None of your damn business, Roy."

Rae tried reaching up for my bruises again, but I backed away. I closed the door a little more, trying to block her view of the inside of the house. It was a wreck. Shit was strewn everywhere, and I hadn't showered since Monday morning. But she didn't take the fucking hint.

"Let me come in. Let me help you clean up a bit."

I scoffed. "I'm fine. Get out of here, Rae."

"You need a doctor, Clint. Someone has to know what's going on."

I paused. "Did you tell anyone?"

"Tell anyone what?"

"Rae, don't you dare tell me you told someone at that fucking school what's happening."

"And what if I did?"

She tried reaching for my eye again, but I snatched her wrist. If she told anyone at that damn school what was going on and they started poking around, I wasn't sure I'd survive my father's assault. I'd kept it hidden from the school this long. And the last thing I needed was someone attempting to upend my life because it was their job to give a shit about me.

"Leave, Rae. I'm serio—"

"Cleaver!?"

I closed my eyes and quickly dropped her wrist. I stuck my tongue into the inside of my cheek as Roy pried the door away from my hand. I sighed as Rae's eyes flickered over to him, and he pushed his way beside me, chuckling. I'd tried to spare Rae from my best friend, but it had been her choice not to fucking listen.

Why the fuck did she never listen?

Roy laughed. "What the hell are you doing here, Cleaver Beaver?"

Rae rolled her eyes. "I could ask you the same thing, Roy Toy."

He shrugged. "I don't mind being a toy. Especially Marina's."

"Gross," she murmured.

I sighed. "I'm fine. Thanks for the homework, but it wasn't necessary. You've done your duty for the day. Let the school know I'll be back when I feel like it."

Roy scoffed. "Homework? This idiot thought you'd actually want homework?"

Rae grumbled, "I'm not an idiot."

"Goodbye, Rae."

"Wait a second. Rae?"

I saw her grow uncomfortable as Roy studied the two of us. She shuffled on her feet, her hands buried into the pockets of those faded brown pants of hers. I shoved Roy out of the way with my hip, going to close the door.

But it was too late.

"Hold up. Hold up, hold up, hold up. I know what's going on here."

Roy's voice filled my ears as panic flooded Rae's eyes.

I growled. "Roy. Cut the shit."

He barked with laughter. "Ho-lee shit. Are you fucking kidding me? You got it on… with *her*?"

Roy threw his head back with laughter as Rae turned bright pink. I looked over at her, trying to tell her how sorry I was with my eyes. But all she did was look down at her feet.

"Glad you're doing okay," she murmured. Then she turned on her heel and walked down the porch steps.

Roy slapped my back. "Holy fucking shit. That's a serious trophy, dude. Was she still a virgin? Does she shave? I feel like a girl with the last name 'Cleaver' either shaves everything, or shaves nothing. Come on, man, you can tell me. Wait a second, why the fuck didn't you tell me in the first damn place? We've got so much to talk about!"

I slammed the door closed and whipped around on him. I glared at him through my good eye, backing him slowly into the living room. He held up his hands in mock surrender, furrowing his brow deeply at me.

Then I licked my lips. "That was some bullshit you just pulled back there."

He scoffed. "And?"

"You were an ass. And you had no right to be."

"Oh, come on, Clint. There's plenty of bitches in the sea, dude. Don't waste another minute on the likes of that stuck-up snob. She'll end up like her mother, and you'll be glad you got rid of her when you could. You know they all end up like their parents."

I wanted to strangle him. I wanted to rip his tongue straight from his head. But I didn't. I drew in a few deep breaths before pushing by him, then scooped up my game controller. I fell against the couch and sighed, closing my eyes as a headache spread along the back of my skull. My mind conjured the face of Rae. The embarrassed look in her eyes. The bright pink tint of her cheeks. Maybe this was for the best. Maybe she was embarrassed, having been with me.

I mean, I was the school bully, after all. The big, bad, manwhore wolf. The man who couldn't even stand up to his father for fear of losing his own fucking life.

I certainly wasn't some prize to take home to Mommy.

"You ready for another race?"

My good eye flew open as Roy flopped down beside me. His Coke sloshed over the side, falling to my jeans with a cool splash. I slowly looked down at it, then glanced at him as he took a sip.

"You gonna cry over spilled Coke? Or are you gonna fill me in on the dirty, nasty details of the school slob?"

I quirked an eyebrow. "There a third option?"

Roy clicked his tongue. "Come on. Really? You're gonna hold out on me like that? I tell you every little fun detail with Marina, but you're not going to tell me about bagging the school sass-mouth? That's just wrong, dude. On so many levels."

"How is Marina doing, anyway?"

"Oh-ho-ho, she's fantastic. Really taking a liking to the taste of my dick after her lunch banana."

And as he launched into his latest escapades with his girlfriend, I started up a new race for us, hoping it was enough to distract him from the fact that I'd never divulge those details with him.

Because I sure as hell didn't need the questions that would conjure.

23

———

RAELYNN

I pulled my ponytail out and ran my fingers through my hair while Allison fixed her makeup beside me. I'd been spending lunches in here with her, especially since I hadn't been hungry. All this week, I'd been worried about Clint. Worried he was hurt, or in the hospital, or worse. And when I showed up at his house yesterday after school, I got shooed away and laughed at.

I wondered if he was embarrassed of me. It sure seemed like it, with how quickly he tried to get me to leave.

Allison sighed. "How are things with your mom?"

I rolled my eyes. "About as good as you can expect."

"Didn't D.J. show up last night? I think that's what you said before you hung up the phone."

"Yep. To apologize, like always. He brought flowers for Mom. A nice dinner I was forced to sit down and have."

Allison scoffed. "What was his present for you this time?"

I shook my head. "Money. Money I didn't want to take, but Mom made me. I've got it in my wallet, but I don't even know what to do with it. I'm thinking about slipping it in my mother's purse later."

"Why don't you use it to get ahead on your lunches? So you don't have to keep using your money from work."

I shrugged. "I might just put it in my savings account. Get me a hundred dollars closer to my goal."

She paused. "He gave you a hundred dollars? Just like that?"

I nodded. "Yep. Just like that. And now, it's simply a game of wait until they fight again. Which should be soon. They can't go more than a couple of weeks without repeating the cycle."

"You know you're always welcome to come over. My parents love you. For all they care, you could live with us."

I giggled. "Don't say shit like that. I might just take you up on it."

"How do my eyes look?"

I grinned. "Like Michael wants to get lost in them."

I watched her blush a bright shade of pink and I thought it was the cutest thing. This crush going back and forth between her and Michael was awesome to watch unfold. I mean, I knew he'd had the hots for her ever since eighth grade. All this time, I'd been telling him she might never return his affections. Allison had always been driven by her future. By school. By her architecture and her life's aspirations. As far as I knew, she hadn't even been kissed.

Because if she had been, I'd certainly know about it.

"Want some?" she asked, holding out her mascara.

I scoffed. "And who the fuck would I be wearing that for?"

"I don't know. Maybe Clint Clarke?"

Marina's voice wrapped around us as my eyes fell onto her reflection. I watched her walk out of one of the stalls as Allison's jaw dropped open. Holy shit, she'd been in there the entire time. Listening. Eavesdropping. Learning shit about my life I certainly didn't want her to know about.

Marina giggled. "Sucks about your mom. But money talks. And good dick."

Allison snarled. "What the heck do you want?"

Marina grinned. "Such harsh words. Might want to tone it down there."

"What, Marina?" I asked flatly.

She smiled sweetly before she came over to the sink beside me. She washed her hands with meticulous precision, cleaning underneath her fingernails. I slowly looked over at Allison, watching my best friend silently glower at this girl. Whatever was coming, it wasn't good. And with Roy finding out about my affair with Clint yesterday, it didn't shock me that I was now having a run-in with his girlfriend.

Marina reached for the paper towels. "So I heard a little rumor."

I rolled my eyes. "I'm sure you did."

Allison scoffed. "What rumor, Marina?"

She smiled brightly. "A rumor that says your friend is fucking the brains out of Clint Clarke himself."

I peeked over at Allison and watched her face pale.

I sighed. "I take it you heard this from Roy?"

Marina wiped her hands off. "Let's just say a little birdie told me."

"A little birdie you're fucking around with."

She threw the paper towel away. "What's it to you if we are?"

Allison went to say something, but I held up my hand. It would be nothing but wasted energy. And this was my fight, not hers. I didn't know what Marina had up her sleeve. I didn't know what she was trying to do. But I didn't want Allison caught up in it. I wanted her to enjoy her senior year.

Not be dragged down by a decision I'd made in a moment of weakness.

"What do you want, Marina?"

She giggled. "I just want to hear it from you. That's all."

"Well, then you're barking up the wrong tree."

She snickered. "Figures. You'll freely talk about your mother hoeing around. But you certainly don't want to talk about you doing it."

Allison took a step forward. "That's enough."

I turned around, pressing my hands against her shoulders. I leveled my gaze at her as Marina threw her head back with laughter. I shook my head. The last thing we needed was some girl fight where we pulled at each other's hair and eventually got expelled. Michael had almost blemished his perfect record with the fight against Clint. I wasn't about to let Allison throw her acceptance to UCLA away because she wanted to claw this bitch's eyes out.

"Let me handle this," I whispered.

Then I turned around to face Marina.

"I'll ask you again. What is it you want?"

Marina leapt for me, getting into my face. "I'll tell you what I want, you little slut. I want you to know your place. I want you to know exactly where you stand with a man like Clint. You're nothing compared to him. He's got the world at his feet, and you'll be drowning in squalor. Fucking men in an effort to pay your bills. Whoring around like your mother does. We already see you turning into her. You look like her. Smell like her. Talk like her. Walk like her. And soon, you'll fuck like her, too. The town mattress, ready for a good ride whenever you're drunk enough."

I shrugged. "Too bad I don't drink."

Marina scoffed. "Just like Clint beat the snot out of your friend, I've got no problems beating the snot out of you. Or your little friend behind you. You think you're tough, but you're nothing, Cleaver."

I grinned. "If I didn't know any better, I'd say this was coming from a place of jealousy."

She paused. "So the two of you are fucking."

I shrugged. "Why do you care if we are?"

Marina lunged at me and I heard Allison squeal. But I held my ground. I didn't flinch. I didn't blink. And I sure as hell didn't move. Marina ran her eyes down my body before moving along beside me, brushing her shoulder against mine.

"I'll be watching you, you piece of trailer trash," she said.

I snickered. "I'd have to live in a trailer for that title, Marina. Or do you not know the difference between a house and a trailer?"

"I don't know. Maybe I'll get Clint to educate me this weekend at my pool party. You know, once he's done making out with the girls in the hot tub. That's his favorite pastime. And it really is a treat to watch once those girls get to grinding in his lap."

I bristled at her words as she left. I heard her giggle fade down the hallway, her heels clicking against the tiled flooring. I slowly turned around to Allison, who was visibly trembling with anger. The embarrassed tinted blush of her cheeks had turned to a full-on crimson rage, her fists clenched at her sides.

"Allison, breathe. She's not worth the effort."

She shook her head. "She is an absolute, raging bitch."

My eyebrows rose. "I think that's the first time I've ever heard you use that word."

"Well, it's true. Marina's nothing but a—a sleazy, good for nothing rollercoaster boys can have a good ride on before bouncing to the next one!"

I giggled. "Wow."

"What?"

I paused. "I kind of like this side of you."

"I sucked down what happened with Michael. I mean, he's a guy. He can take care of himself. But watching it happen to you? That's completely different. I'm done with this… this stuff. I'm done with Clint and his cronies screwing around with you just because he's—"

I held my hand up. "Allison."

She sighed. "Sorry."

The two of us turned toward the bathroom exit.

"What the heck was that all about anyway?" she breathed.

And as my mind swirled with the encounter, my shock turned to rage. I knew exactly what it was about. I knew exactly where that information had come from. Though I didn't want to admit it —nor did I want to believe it—I knew what was happening. I knew what Clint was doing.

"It was a wake-up call, Allison. That's what it was. And it's time I finally listened to the alarm."

It was time for me to accept that my weakest moment would now be used against me. Especially if my suspicions regarding why were correct.

I turned to Allison. "Is Clint at school today?"

She paused. "Yes. He was in first period math today with Michael."

"Good."

I started out of the bathroom, feeling Allison trail behind as I turned my attention to him. That boy. The boy I had a strong feeling had been manipulating me from the beginning.

It was time for me to get some answers.

24

CLINTON

Marina choked down that damn banana like she probably choked down Roy's fucking dick. She sat on his lap, giggling and kissing the tip of his nose like the innocent girl Roy wanted her to be. He had a sick sense of humor, wanting to destroy innocence like that. I liked my women primed, though. Already knowing what they wanted, and ready to bestow their talents upon me.

Then again, I hadn't thought about any girl since my encounters with Rae.

"Oh, Clint. Where'd you get those bruises?"

"Here, let me help."

"Can I do anything for you?"

"Do you want me to get you some ice cream?"

I looked over at Roy and he winked. He was right. Women couldn't resist a guy with bruises on his fucking face. But if they knew how I'd gotten those bruises, it would be a different story. The line of girls coming up to me asked me where I got them, and each time my fight story became a little more dramatic. It went from some kid on the side of the road to some kid picking on a girl on the side of the road. Then, it morphed into some college kid on the side of the road picking on his fiancée before I offered to show her what a real man could provide.

It was the first time in my life I ever felt pathetic for it.

"Clint!"

Rae's voice pierced through the cafeteria and my eyes fell upon her. She strode with intensity in her movements and a sour expression on her face. The girl at my side, trying to practically spoon-feed me ice cream, got up and stepped off to the side. Roy chuckled and out of the corner of my eye I saw Marina's lips curve into a wide grin. I spread my arms out, letting my knees fall apart in the stance I was known for.

Spreading myself wide for all to see.

Gotta keep up appearances.

Rae stopped in front of me. "Fancy seeing you at school."

I shrugged. "Can't keep everything hidden forever."

She grinned. "No, you can't."

I flickered my eyes over to Allison and saw her staring at Marina. I didn't know what the fuck that bitch had done, but it had certainly pissed the two of them off. Rae had her hands balled up into fists. Hell, so did Allison. I narrowed my eyes softly—well, my good eye. The other one was still too swollen. I tried to read her, to figure out why the hell she was storming up to me in the cafeteria on a whim.

I mean, I had to give her props for her balls. Especially after the encounter with Roy the other day. But what was her problem?

I licked my lips. "Can I help you?"

Marina giggled. "Yeah, Rae. Can Clint help himself to you?"

Roy let out a bark of a laugh as the rest of the guys around us chuckled. But Rae didn't bat an eye. She kept staring at me. Glaring at me. With those fists balled up, ready to fly.

Then she pointed her trembling finger at me.

"I'm only going to tell you this once, because I'm done with your antics."

Marina smacked her lips. "Oooh, scary. Practically a haunted house."

Roy wrapped his arm around her waist. "I bet her house is one."

Everyone snickered again. But Rae didn't move. She stood strong, and I admired her for that. Because my friends could be ruthless when they chose to be.

I sighed. "What is it, Cleaver?"

Her eye twitched. "If this is the kind of bullshit I have to put up with to be friends with you, then it's not worth it. Do you hear me?

I'm not going to be cornered in a bathroom and teased relentlessly for shit I'm trying to do to help you. To befriend you. To see the decent fucking person beyond the shitstain that is the boy that walks into this school every day."

I watched her shoot a killer look at Marina before her eyes came back to mine.

"So if these are the lowlifes you're going to hang out with? These stubborn, ignorant, pig-headed, ugly people? Then we're through. You and me, and whatever this is, it's over."

I blinked at her, not knowing what to say. Did she really expect me to make a choice right now? In front of my friends? When our fuckable encounters were nothing more than rumor at this point? I looked over at Marina, watching her practically foaming at the mouth. What the hell had she done to these two girls?

I cast a glare at Roy before my eyes panned back to Rae.

She furrowed her brow. "I guess I have my answer then?"

What the fuck did she really expect me to do? I mean, I knew we had something special. A connection I'd never shared with anyone else. She got me, and I got her. And when I was with her, the rest of the world faded away. But when she wasn't around, when we weren't behind closed doors, the world existed. Sure, it was only high school. And yeah, I hung around shitty people. But I sure as hell wasn't going to spend my senior year—the last glory year of my life—fucking around in the shadows and having spit balls stuck to the back of my head.

She's the only person who doesn't make you feel like shit, Clint. Don't do this.

"Well?" Marina asked.

I kept staring at Rae as I answered her. "Put a cock in it and shut up."

Everyone snickered again behind me except Roy. He didn't stand up for her, but he sure as hell didn't buck up to me. He knew his place.

Like everyone else.

You don't have to put on a show with Rae.

"Well?" she asked.

I didn't know what to do. Things with her were so new. I mean, days old kind of new. And it was terrifying. What was I supposed to do? Toss the entirety of my reputation away on a girl I'd fucked around with for a few days? She wasn't just any girl, though. Even I knew that. But was I ready for a move like that? Was I ready to abandon my post as top dog of this school and attempt something else with her? Something that wasn't guaranteed?

For all I knew, this was a ploy of hers. A ploy to peel me away from my throne so she could wreak revenge and havoc on my life. I mean, we had a history, she and I. And not simply a sexual one. I'd made her life a living nightmare freshman year. And she'd been my target on and off for the rest of high school.

For all I knew, this was her revenge. Her plan. And with Allison at her side after what I did to Michael? It wouldn't have shocked me one bit.

I'm not ready to take that chance yet.

Rae sighed. "You did this on purpose, didn't you?"

Marina giggled. "You mean, did he do you on purpose?"

I grumbled, "Put a muzzle on that girl or get her the fuck away from this table."

Roy scoffed. "Say what now?"

Rae sighed. "It's fine. Just don't play stupid. I know they know. I've accepted that. But at least give me the satisfaction of confirming the nightmare I've already come to terms with."

I shrugged. "Not sure what you mean."

Roy chuckled. "She means, did you fuck her in order to use it against her? Because honestly, if you did? Fucking props to you. Because that's some lowdown shit and I love it."

Marina cackled. "Cleaver Beaver the Dick Eater. Has a nice ring to it."

Roy threw his head back in laughter and the gang behind me joined in. I sat there, staring up at Rae, and I saw Allison tearing up, getting emotional for her. It was the first time I'd ever felt guilty for teasing someone. For pushing someone around. I wanted to apologize to them for what happened with Michael. I wanted to apologize for the unhinged animals behind me, cackling and barking with laughter like feral fucking animals.

Rae nodded. "This was always going to be used against me, wasn't it?"

Her voice was so soft, it almost got swallowed up by the laughter around me. And yet I heard it. Loud and clear. Like a fucking bullhorn. How the fuck could she even think that? Did I come off as that terrible of a person? That much of an asshole?

Because that was some shit my father would have pulled in his younger years.

Holy shit, I'm turning into my father.

Allison sniffled. "Come on, Rae. Let's get out of here. None of them are worth it."

Marina snickered. "Not what Rae thought when she was spreading her legs."

"Can it!" I roared.

The entire fucking cafeteria came to a grinding halt as I looked over at that bitch.

"What the fuck has your boyfriend, on numerous occasions, told you about that disgusting mouth of yours? Either keep it closed or take Roy somewhere and stuff it full. Got it? Holy fuck, Marina."

Everyone's eyes went wide as I turned my attention back to Rae. But, try as I might, I couldn't bring myself to address the issue at hand. She shook her head side to side, then allowed Allison to turn her around. She peeked over her shoulder at me as a sadness filled her stare. Then she stopped and turned around to face me.

"Thank you for giving me the answer I needed," she said.

I paused, then sighed. "You're welcome, I guess."

The cafeteria returned to its dull roar as Allison shook her head. I saw Rae's chin trembling and it broke my fucking heart. I turned my eyes out toward the window, where some of the nerds sat on the back patio doing homework while eating their fucking lunch. I couldn't stand to look at her. I couldn't stand to look at myself.

You're a sorry excuse for a human, Clint. Just like your father.

"You all deserve each other, you know that?"

I snickered at Rae's voice. "Yeah, I guess so."

And I watched as Allison physically pulled her out of the cafeteria, leaving me surrounded by a bunch of brainless, nitwitted assholes I wanted nothing more to do with.

Fuck my life.

25

RAELYNN

I sat at my window as the thunder rolled. The snacks under my bed were long gone, but I wasn't hungry anyway. Not after my encounter with Clint at school today. I placed my elbow on the windowsill, resting my chin in my hand. I saw lightning crack the sky, illuminating the world around me. Black outlines of decrepit houses came into view. The rolling green hills of the rich beyond ignited, taunting me with what I'd never have. The storm rolled in, bringing the pitter-patter of rain. I watched it come, a shower of greatness. Here to wash away the stench of our garbage-laden street.

It didn't wash away the hurt in my heart, though.

"Fuck Clinton Clarke."

The rain battered against my window as lightning pierced the sky overhead. The clouds hung low, pregnant with rain. They were so close I imagined I was almost able to reach up and touch them. I placed my forehead against my window, the same window I'd crawled out of that night I first slept with Clint. I closed my eyes and reminisced about how much I'd hated the fact that he'd found me. How much I'd enjoyed opening up to him. How wonderful the bike ride had been and how kind he'd been.

How gentle he was.

"Stop it," I muttered. "You're torturing yourself."

Tears rolled down my cheeks with every flash of lightning. And as the thunder crashed, I let my sobs run free. All day, I'd kept them in check. Throughout history, where I felt Clint staring at me. Throughout P.E., where I saw him in the bleachers watching me from beyond his sunglasses. I dealt with the snickers and the names murmured under people's breath as I passed by. Cleaver Beaver the Dick Eater. How quickly shit like that worked its way around the school.

I wondered if I was turning into my mother.

"Shit."

I put my head in my hands and cried. I didn't try to hold it back any longer. The thunder covered up my sobs and the lightning heated my tears. And as the rain battered harder against my window, it was almost like the storm was trying to wash my sins away. Wash my tears away. Cheer me up with its furious might. I was envious of the storm. How strong it was. How it could rage, and people didn't bat an eye. If anything, they cowered away. Respecting it. Admiring it. Sitting out on the porch and watching it in a mesmerized sort of awe.

Now I know how Clint feels.

I didn't know which was worse, being invisible to the masses or being seen only for my greatest mistake. But the truth of the matter was that I still didn't regard Clint as a mistake. I never could. What we'd shared was tremendous, even if he didn't feel it. Even if it was faked on his end. Even if he completely fabricated his words and his actions and his emotions, I hadn't. I didn't. And I never would.

"That's what makes you better than him."

I sat up from my arms and dried my face. I sniffled until my nose was clear, then went back to watching the storm. I'd had my moment of weakness, and now it was time to press onward and forward, like nothing ever happened. It was all I had, and it was all I'd use. Because in the end, that made me better than them. They could flash their money around and ride in their expensive cars and wear their designer clothes to school. But, in the end, what made me better and stronger than them was my ability to persevere.

Whereas they broke down over a scuffed tennis shoe. Or a broken nail.

Except Clint.

I shook the thought from my head. He was like them. Just like them. He wasn't different. He showed me that today. There was no use in crying over him. He was nothing but a cup of spilled, spoiled milk.

I hated that I'd fallen for it, though. I was angry at myself for falling for his tricks. His ruse. Not seeing through the wolfish grin long enough to latch onto his plan. His ultimate plan to destroy me. His ultimate plan to play the best trick this fucking high school had ever seen.

Fucking around with the school charity case before exposing her to be like every other girl who wanted to ride Clint Clarke's cock.

It was genius. And simple. And I'd fallen for all of it.

I sighed. "You're such a fool, Rae. Holy shit."

A knock came at my door and I shot up from the windowsill. I dove back into my bed, covering myself up as I tried to make myself look presentable. The last thing I needed was my mother knowing any of this, for more shame to come down onto the people in this family. I called out for her to come in, hiding my reddened cheeks with my pillow.

When the door slowly swung open, she arched her brow at me.

"You okay in here?"

I sighed. "That obvious?"

She snickered. "I may or may not have been standing here for a few minutes now."

"Oh."

Mom walked into my room and closed the door behind her. She came and sat on the edge of my bed, patting my leg. I didn't like her seeing me like this. I had to take care of her. That was how this dynamic worked. That was how it always worked with us.

But I needed my mom, too.

"You wanna talk about it?" she asked.

I rolled my eyes. "Just some stupid boy at school."

Mom sighed. "I'm familiar with those."

I paused. "How far do you think a bully would go in order to get a rise out of someone?"

"Why do you ask?"

"I think a bully at my school has gone a little too far with some stuff."

"Would this be the stupid boy at school?"

I scoffed. "Aren't all stupid boys eventually bullies?"

She paused. "You have a good point."

The two of us shared a brief moment of laughter before Mom took my hand.

"Has he hurt you, sweetheart?"

I sighed. "Not physically."

She nodded. "Okay, good. I mean, not good with the hurt. But—"

My eyes widened. "Oh, no no no. Nothing—nothing like that. Nothing like what you're thinking."

"You'd tell me though? If it was?"

"I promise, everything that happened wa—"

Mom raised her eyebrows as I caught what I was about to say.

"I, uh…"

She giggled. "Sweetheart, I was much younger than eighteen when I started having sex with boys."

"Mom."

She smiled. "I'm not going to go into that. We had that talk when you were much younger. But let me see if I can piece this together. You fell for the school bully, had some romantic moments together, and now he wants nothing to do with you. Right?"

I paused. "Don't tell me you've experienced something like that, too."

She shrugged. "It happens sometimes. Maybe not quite like that, but it does happen. And it sucks. And I kind of want to wring his throat."

I giggled at her words as the pillow slowly slid away from my face.

"What do I do?"

She sighed. "There's nothing you can do. You can't change a man. So you can't let that man change you. Bad boys are just that. Bad. Bad for you. Bad for themselves. Bad for anyone who comes into their lives."

I nodded slowly. "People at school will know soon enough."

"And all you can do is stand up to them. Stand your ground and don't let them beat you into it. High school is relentless. There isn't a person on this planet—rich or poor—that would do it all over again. I'm here for you, no matter what. And you can talk to me about anything, okay?"

I smiled softly. "Thanks, Mom."

She tucked a strand of hair behind my ear. "I guess we both have a tendency to go for the wrong men."

I giggled. "Yeah. Fuck D.J."

Mom laughed, covering my mouth with her hand. "Fuck D.J."

"Did something happen?"

Her hand fell away from my face. "Isn't something always happening with him?"

"I thought you two just made up, though?"

She shrugged. "Maybe I didn't want to make up this time. Maybe I'm ready to let him go."

"Wait, seriously?"

"Seriously."

I paused. "You're done with him? I mean, for real this time?"

She nodded. "For real this time. I have to stop this cycle, Rae. I didn't realize the damage I was doing to myself. Or to you. Or to us. I'm sorry, sweetheart. I'm sorry I've set this kind of example for you. I'm sorry I raised you in all this. I'm so—please forgive me, honey."

"Of course, Mom. Of course I forgive you."

She started crying and I pulled her closely to me. I wrapped my arms around her, silently thanking any god that would listen. Maybe this was it. The breakthrough my mother needed in order to see the life she had carved out for herself. I cried along with her, burying my face into her hair as she scooped me into her lap. I hadn't been in my mother's lap for years. Since I was nothing but a child who stood tall enough to wrap my arms around her hips. She held me close, rocking me side to side as the two of us grieved with one another.

Grieved for our broken hearts and minds.

Mom kissed the top of my head. "I love you so much, sweetheart."

My breathing shuddered. "I love you, too."

"It's done. I promise you, it's over. He's never coming back around. You have my word."

"Thank you, Mommy. Thank you so much."

She whispered. "I've missed hearing you call me that."

Mom held me as the rain continued to batter against the window. Even though the thunder rolled away into the distance, the rain continued to flood our front lawn, drowning the grass seeds Mom and I always attempted to plant and grow during the summer months. I sighed as I pulled away, falling back to the mattress of the bed. And as Mom stood up, she reached for my hand.

"Want to watch a movie and make a pizza delivery guy drive out to us in this nonsense?"

I smiled. "Oh, hell yeah."

She leveled her eyes with me before soft laughter fell from her lips. I took my mother's hand, and together, we started down the hallways. We slipped down the stairs in our socks, laughing and picking at one another as we crash-landed into the foyer. Mom went to grab her cell phone while I picked out a movie, and the only thing that raced through my mind was how things felt normal again.

How things felt good again.

"Pepperoni and pineapple?" Mom called out.

"And mushroom!"

Mom barked with laughter. "Thanks for the afterthought, kid."

I giggled. "You're welcome. Especially after you see what I'm gonna make us watch."

"Please tell me it's not another Rocky movie."

And instead of answering her, I simply let the opening song do it for me.

Mom poked her head around the corner. "I'm ordering brownies instead of cinnamon bites for that one."

"Hey," I protested. "I like their cinnamon bites!"

She winked as she ducked back around the corner, wrapping up the order for our meal of the night. I sat down on the couch, watching my favorite Rocky movie make its entrance. But the second Mom came back into the room, a knock sounded at the door.

"Huh. Bit fast for a pizza guy, don't you think?"

I shook my head, smiling. "I'll get it. You sit down and watch this cinematic marvel."

Mom groaned. "We're watching The Notebook after this."

"If I can stay awake through it, I'll even promise to act like I'm paying attention."

"Ha. Ha. Ha."

I threw my head back with laughter as my mother's voice. I hadn't felt this carefree with her in a long time, and it felt wonderful. The last time we had a true girls' night like this, I was just starting seventh grade. We'd watched Beauty and the Beast while wolfing down pasta from her favorite Italian place up the street, and ended up falling asleep together on the couch halfway through the second movie.

I couldn't wait to do the same thing tonight.

I reached for the doorknob as the rain finally slowed to a trickle. I smiled brightly as I greeted whoever the hell was at the door at six in the evening on a Thursday night. I expected it to be a few people. Allison, coming over to check on me. Clint, coming to grovel at my feet before I curb-stomped his face. Even Marina, coming to take another jab at me before she went and got off with her boyfriend.

But, I sure as hell didn't expect to see Michael. Soaking wet. Dripping with venom from his lips and angry eyes that widened as I appeared at the doorway.

"You hooked up with Clinton Clarke? Are you fucking kidding me?"

And just like that, things were not-so-good again.

26

CLINTON

"**S**hot! Shot! Shot! Shot!"

The crowd chanted as another double shot got shoved into my hand. Girls reached out for me as Roy slapped me on the back, cheering me on yet another time. I'd lost count of how many of these I'd had. I didn't have a damn clue how full my stomach was of vodka. The only things I was aware of was the smell of Marina's backyard pool and the chanting, laughter and clapping as I drank all these assholes under the damn table.

I had numbed myself so I wouldn't feel the pain of losing Rae.

"Yeah, Clint! Get it!"

Everyone clapped as I threw back the clear liquid. I opened my throat, allowing it to slide directly into my stomach without so much as swallowing. Fucking hell, I'd gotten too good at that. And it felt marvelous. Kind of. In a way.

Why didn't this feel as good as it used to?

"Care for another one, big boy?"

"Eat some peanuts first."

"Want a sip of my margarita? Tequila always gets me ready for another round."

"Woo! Clint! Come jump in the pool with me!"

I felt someone tugging at me and I ripped back. I leaned against the bar counter with a smirk on my face, gazing at the horde of people around me. Girls in their bikinis and their barely-there tits. Girls with slim hips and tiny waists and long legs ready to wrap themselves around me. Dyed blond hair flashed, as the alcohol-soaked girls that had come to have a good time and be admired preened and strutted.

And yet, my mind still drifted back to Rae.

It's better this way.

"You can do one with me, right?" Roy asked.

I felt him shove another shot in my hand before he raised up his own. We clinked our shot glasses together before throwing them back, and I felt my world tilt in on itself. For a split second, I stood on the sky, looking down at the stars and the cloudy night before gazing up at the pool, the grass, the concrete and the people walking around.

You're gonna be sick tonight, jackass.

With a blink of my eye, the world righted itself. But my stomach didn't feel well. I drew in some deep breaths, trying to keep it all down and not get sick on myself. This crowd of assholes would spread it around school come Monday. I slumped against one of the bar stools as the girls walked away, jumping into the pool and shrieking in delight. Marina beckoned for Roy, swaying her hips and jiggling those small tits of hers, and Roy clapped me against the shoulder as he headed for his lay of the night. I sat there with thoughts of Rae floating around in the alcohol that swirled around my brain.

She deserves better than you, dickweed.

I scoffed as I closed my eyes. I swallowed hard a few times, trying to settle the bile creeping up the back of my damn throat. I mean, how long could I have expected us to last, anyway? Rae would have left me the second something better came along. I knew how women worked. What they wanted out of life. They were all the same, once I stripped back the clothes and the soft demeanors. And knowing my luck, something better would have come along sooner rather than later.

Just when I'd started to fall for her.

Get up, asshole. You need water.

But I didn't want to get up.

"And this is Clint," Roy said.

The giggle that filled my ear caused me to open my eyes, and I found myself staring at a very pretty girl. Short red hair. Freckles all across her face and bright brown eyes. A slim figure not at all concealed in a string bikini. She looked like the rest of the girls here. A bit too long-legged. A bit too buck-toothed. A bit too much waterproof makeup and absolutely no curves in sight.

I nodded. "Hey there."

The girl giggled. "Hi."

Roy smiled proudly. "This, my friend, is Lindsey."

I licked my lips. "Nice to meet you."

She nodded. "You, too. I, uh, saw you over here. With those shots."

I quirked an eyebrow. "You like what you see?"

And when she blushed, I had my answer.

Roy cleared his throat. "Well, I'll let you two get to know one another. Clint."

"Yep?"

"Don't do anything I wouldn't do."

I rolled my eyes as the girl let out another soft giggle. A forced one. One that probably got her into Roy's good graces in the first place. I appreciated the effort, but I wasn't into it. Lindsey was a pretty girl, but she wasn't Rae.

Still, though, she sat next to me at the bar.

"Do you come to these parties often?"

I slowly panned my eyes over to her. "Yep. You?"

She shook her head. "No. First time ever being invited."

"Is it everything you could have hoped for, and more?"

"That depends. What are you doing later on?"

My cockeyed grin spread across my face, but I didn't make a move for her. She wasn't my type. Wasn't my style. And I had no issues letting her know it. I lobbed my head over to see her and found her blushing again. Tainting that creamy skin of hers that, in any other world, would have had me on my knees ready to give her the attention she wanted.

Tonight, however, was different.

I chuckled. "I'm sleeping off this alcohol and trying not to wake up with a bleeding hangover in the morning."

Lindsey's face fell. "Oh."

"That's the price ya pay for shooting vodka all night."

"Guess it's rough being the entertainment."

And as she snickered, her words slapped me across the face.

Entertainment.

I was nothing but the entertainment?

I heard her say something, but I didn't catch it. I felt her kiss my cheek as her hand lingered against my thigh, but I hardly felt it. And as she walked away, I didn't even steal a glance at her barely-there ass. My mind had latched onto that word. That phrase. It parsed out every syllable and bounced around in my head. Taunting me. Lashing out at me. Encompassing the whole of my high school career.

Entertainment.

My eyes slowly focused on the crowd around me as images of a trained monkey rushed through my mind. Being slapped around and whipped by trainers before being put in front of a crowd and expected to obey. It was an apt description. One that made my stomach turn over on itself. And as I sat there on the sidelines watching everyone else party, I wondered how I'd gotten there.

Here.

At this dumbass party with these dumbass people.

Do I even like these people?

In a flash, I was unsure of everything in my life. As I slid off the barstool and made my way for the patio doors, I felt people clamoring for my attention. Women tugging me over to the hot tub and guys trying to get me into the pool. Roy tried sliding my leather jacket off, but I simply shook him off me.

"The fuck, man? I set you up with a good catch."

"You good? You need some water?"

"Give him some space. I think he's gonna puke."

"Hey! Clint! What gives?"

I ignored all of their comments and questions as I lumbered into Marina's parents' house. I slid the patio doors closed behind me, seeking solace in the ice cold air conditioning of their kitchen. I walked over to the fridge and pulled out a bottle of water, chugging it back as it filled my stomach. I backed it up with another. Then another. And slowly, I felt my veins being freed of the alcohol I'd pushed through them.

Which freed my mind up to roam even more.

"Clint! The fuck!"

Roy's muffled voice hit my ears and I turned around. I saw him banging his fist on the kitchen window before he shrugged at me with an attitude I didn't like. I held my bottle of water up to him before drinking the rest back, but Roy wasn't a fan of my actions. He looked pissed. Though I didn't know why.

I mean, did he sell his soul to Satan in order to get me that girl? *Terrible exchange.*

I tossed my third empty bottle of water into the trash can, then grabbed a fourth. And as I cracked it open, I started walking through the house. It was small, compared to my father's. But there was a lot of love in this place. I felt it. The walls bled with it. And it made me smile. The sounds of the party fell into the background as I walked down the small hallway. I stood in the living room, gazing out at the front lawn as whispers of happy secrets puffed up from the plush carpet I stood on.

You don't belong here.

My eyes fell onto my bike and I felt myself gravitating to the front door. I slid my bottled water into my leather jacket pocket, making my way outside. My feet carried me toward my bike as I drew in a deep breath. And as I slung my leg over the side, I reached for my helmet.

Drink the water first.

"The fuck are you doing!?"

Roy's voice caused my head to whip up as I held my helmet in my hands.

"You leaving already?"

And as my best friend came closer to me, something happened. Something changed. Something shifted.

For the first time since I'd started high school, I wanted as far away from Roy as I could get.

27

RAELYNN

"Now, class, make sure you read the labels on your beakers and bottles carefully. I understand we have a shower in the back, but that doesn't mean I want to use it today."

The class let out a soft titter, but I kept my eyes trained on my hands. I wrung them in circles, taking deep breaths as I kept reliving that moment. The look on Michael's face a few nights ago when he strolled up onto my porch during that thunderstorm. The anger in his eyes. The heat in his voice. The way he scoffed at me before stalking away, not giving me any time to craft any sort of a response.

Just an accusation and my guilty face staring back at him.

Allison nudged me "You listening?"

My head whipped up. "Sorry. Yeah."

"If you're listening, what did the teacher just say?"

"He doesn't want to use the shower today."

"That was seven statements ago. So you're not listening. Good. At least I know now."

"You know damn good and well why I'm not listening."

The teacher cleared his throat. "There something you want to share with the class, ladies?"

Allison shook her head. "No, sir. Nothing."

And when he looked at me, all I did was shake my head.

"Good. Now, one last thing. Once you document everything

you see from your experiment, I want you to keep your notes with you until tomorrow's class. We're going to be taking three sets of notes and comparing them for grades at the end of the week. So make sure not to get any liquids on them."

I sighed. "Great."

Allison giggled. "I'll help you out as much as I can. I know you're not the cleanest person around."

"Thanks? Maybe?"

"Hey, at least you were listening this time."

I shot her a look, but all she did was giggle. Our teacher released us to the hounds, allowing us to conduct the experiment in front of us with very minimal instruction. I hated chemistry. Science had been the bane of my existence ever since middle school. But it was required, and if I took it now I wouldn't have to take it in college.

Good for you, thinking about the future.

Allison and I worked in silence for a few minutes. We poured chemicals into beakers together and documented what we witnessed. We combined elements that made a sort of putty mixture before melting into a pile of goop. Which was weird and utterly unexpected. I was almost certain we'd done that particular facet wrong. But what really felt odd was standing with Allison in complete and utter silence.

So I took a leap of faith.

"You know, don't you?"

She sighed. "It's not hard to pinpoint. Especially since Michael didn't want to walk with us this morning."

"Has he talked with you about it?"

"No. He hasn't so much as looked my way."

I sighed. "I'm so sorry, Allison."

She shook her head. "Nothing to be sorry about. If anything, you should apologize to him for keeping it from him for so long."

"Thanks."

"Just trying to tell it like it is."

I paused. "He was so angry, Allison. I mean, just furious. Standing on my porch, drenched in water. Fists clenched. Teeth grinding together. I mean, I didn't even get a chance to respond before he stormed back off through my drowned front yard. I've never seen him like that before. I'm worried about him."

"He probably feels betrayed."

"And I feel like shit for that."

"How are we doing back there, ladies?" our teacher piped up from across the room.

I tried my best not to sigh. "Doing great, Mr. Abernathy."

He nodded. "Wonderful. Now get back to work."

Allison picked up her pencil. "Right away, Mr. Abernathy."

We kept our heads down with the experiments and the descriptions until his attention was off us. Then, Allison flickered her eyes over to me. I felt her studying me. Trying to figure out what the fuck to say next. And I hated it. I hated all of this. I wanted to talk with Michael. I wanted to explain what had happened, to tell him the kind of life Clint actually led, because I knew Michael well. I knew if *he* knew, he'd look at this differently. Despite the fight. Despite the blood. Despite the anger.

Then I felt my cheeks flush with red.

"I'm so embarrassed, Allison."

She rubbed my back. "He'll come around soon enough. He has to."

I scoffed. "Does he, though? Because right now, I'm the all-around shitty friend."

"He just doesn't get it right now. He needs to cool that hot head of his, and then yes. He'll come around. He always does."

"Have you ever seen him this upset before?"

And when I looked over at her, she shook her head.

"I haven't, no. But, I know what he's like when he gets frustrated with schoolwork. Or his parents. He loves you. Just like I do. And when he's done pitching his fit, he'll come around. Trust me."

I shrugged. "If you say so."

"Boys just don't understand this kind of thing."

I scoffed. "Well, add me to that bunch. Because I don't get it either."

She sighed. "Look, in the end, it doesn't matter. It's over, right? So just give Michael some time and he'll bounce back eventually. I'm sure of it."

"I really hope you're right."

"If you'd like to share with the class, I'm sure all of us could take a break to listen."

I bit down on the inside of my cheek as Mr. Abernathy's voice rose above the class. My eyes locked with his, and I saw him staring at me with a cool look on his face. He thought he was clever.

Smart. Observant. But all I did was smile politely at him before drawing in a deep breath.

"No, sir. Just talking about the experiments and how they relate to real life. You know, like how I'd enjoy melting a very specific boy I know into a puddle of goop just by pouring this blue substance over his head."

"Rae," Allison hissed.

Mr. Abernathy's eyes widened. "A boy?"

I nodded. "Mm-hmm. Boy troubles during science experiments. I think I've got a new podcast, don't you? That's what I was talking about, by the way. Podcasts and boys."

The classroom snickered and laughed as the teacher's face fell.

"Ah, well uh. Just—keep your head focused and in the game. You've only got fifteen minutes left in class and I expect the two of you to be through that list of experiments."

Allison sighed. "This is our last one, Mr. Abernathy."

He nodded curtly. "Well, good then."

I shook my head as our very uncomfortable teacher hunkered his way down into his chair. He crossed his arms over his chest, glaring at us from beyond his invisible-framed glasses. I wasn't convinced by Allison's reassuring words, but it didn't stop me from hoping she was right. I mean, I couldn't bear to lose one of my best friends over this stupid thing. This stupid, idiotic boy thing.

Stupid and idiotic. Sounds like something you'd get yourself into.

"You think I should go over to his house after school sometime this week?"

Allison poured the clear liquid into the beaker. "I don't think that's a good idea."

"Why not?"

"Look, it's bubbling up."

I watched the bubbles turn all sorts of fluorescent colors as it climbed up the neck of the glass beaker. It overflowed and we quickly moved our notes before jotting down what we'd witnessed. I kept stealing glances over at Allison. I watched her pen move quickly across her notepad. Something looked different about her. I couldn't place it, but I knew it.

She was hiding something from me.

"Allison."

"Hmmm?"

"What aren't you telling me?"

And when her pen faltered, I knew I had her.

"Rae, don't do this now. Okay?"

I scoffed. "So you have been talking to Michael."

"Rae—"

"Just tell me the damn truth, Allison."

I kept my voice at a hushed volume, but I still felt people's eyes on me and Mr. Abernathy lingering around us. I still felt as if the world was shining its great, big beacon directly into my fucking face.

And after Allison was done jotting down her notes, she turned her attention to me.

"No, Michael hasn't talked about the incident between you two. But yes. We've talked, a lot, over this past weekend. Which was the first reason I knew something was up. He called every day, multiple times a day. Came over a few times. He talked about anything and everything other than this one thing, and you know Michael. You know he's just not like that. He's not a chatterbox about his life."

I paused. "Is he okay?"

She nodded. "He's fine. He's angry. He's hurt. He's upset, clearly. But he's fine. So, when I tell you to give him time, that's what you need to do. From someone who spent practically all damn weekend with him? Give. Michael. Time."

Then the lunch bell rang, causing the class to scatter and rush for the hallways.

Just like the entire world seemed to rush around in my mind.

28

———

CLINTON

I sat in math class staring out the window onto the school lawn. The weekend had been rough. Solitary. Filled with a lot of sleeping and multiple hangover cures. Roy ended up pulling me back into that fucking party of Marina's, where I ended up getting so shitfaced that I passed out on the porch. The fucking concrete porch. I woke up the next morning to Marina shaking me like a damn blender, telling me to wake up and get out before her parents got home. I drove back to my place tipsy and tired, trying my hardest to keep my bike steady on the road as I chugged back the lukewarm bottle of water still stuffed down into my pocket somehow.

Only to be met with my father at the front door.

My neck still hurt from that encounter. But as far as brushes with my father went, this one was pretty tame. Cecilia pulled him off me, which was a first. And to punish her for it, my father left a few hours later for a business trip without her. Left her behind in the house to mope around in her heels and her perfectly-manicured fingernails.

Making me feel like a stranger in my own damn childhood house.

The rest of the weekend was spent in my room. I hoarded food there like a wild animal and didn't come out until it was time for school this morning. I skipped Monday. I didn't like Mondays, anyway. I called in for myself, actually. Made a few retching noises. Let loose a few burps. Talked to the school nurse. And in the span of ten minutes, I had a free day from school without a phone call to my father.

Which was the last thing I needed to happen right now.

I slept all day yesterday, and as I sat there in my boring as hell math class, I wished to be sleeping again. In the comfort of my own bed with music softly playing in the background. But no. I had to be here. Because the school breathed down our throats and sent out needless phone calls to parents if we didn't show up. Like I still wasn't some legal-ass adult at eighteen. I mean, everything happened at eighteen. I could buy cigarettes. Doctors didn't have to go through my parents anymore. I could schedule my own medical shit. Fill my own prescriptions. Buy fucking nose medicine over the counter with my I.D.

So why the fuck didn't schools stop calling parents when we turned eighteen?

If the doctor couldn't do it, why could they?

Makes no damn sense.

"Mr. Clarke?"

I whipped my eyes to the front of the classroom, where Miss Abigail was staring at me from beyond her black-framed glasses.

"Yeah?"

She pursed her lips. "What's the value of 'x'?"

I shrugged. "Depends on how you dumped them, I guess."

But, instead of the class laughing like they usually did, I watched them shake their heads and scowl at me. A couple of the girls from the party at Marina's rolled their eyes before passing notes to each another. I felt like that monkey again. Only now I was failing at my job. And if I wasn't here for entertainment and laughter, then what the fuck was I here for?

I suddenly felt out of place at school, too.

Like I had at home this past weekend.

"Very funny, Mr. Clarke. Explains why you haven't done your homework in a week, too."

And with that, Miss Abigail turned her attention away from me. A flippant response before paying attention to the students that were really important. The students that made teachers like her proud. The students teachers like her wanted to mentor. Wanted to remember. Wanted to mold and shape.

Just another retired circus monkey.

I felt something hot against the nape of my neck and turned around. And it didn't shock me one bit when I found Michael mean-mugging me from behind. He'd switched his seat in class to sit behind me instead of in front of me after that schoolyard fight. Why he'd done it was beyond me, but it wasn't something I cared about debating. Every time I saw that squirrelly little fucker, he made it a point to glare in my general direction.

Only his glares had gotten hotter with each passing day lately.

I blew him a kiss before turning around, then slumped into my seat. I let my eyes fall back out the window, gazing out at the green grass and bright blue sky as Miss Abigail's voice faded into the background. Classes changed and I gathered up my things. I went and flopped myself down in English class and saw Allison continuously stealing looks in my general direction. I didn't pay it any mind, though. I didn't give a shit about Michael or her. The only person I gave a damn about was Rae.

And I couldn't even get her to look at me.

I saw her in the hallways and tried to meet her eyes, but she always turned her back to me. I tried scanning the cafeteria at lunch time, trying to catch where her and her friends would park it. I wanted to hear her voice again. Even if it was in anger, cursing me out before slapping me across the face. Yelling at me was better than the whole barrel of 'nothing' she was tossing my way now.

And when I saw her walk into the cafeteria, hope ignited in my chest.

I stood up from my chair as Roy rattled on about some stupid-ass nonsense. Marina nibbled at her banana, keeping the trend of her starving herself going. I stood there, listening as voices faded into the background. And as Rae's eyes found mine, I saw her lips turn down at the sight of me.

Then she turned around and walked back out of the cafeteria.

"You good, Clint?"

Roy's voice pulled me back from the brink, as I felt my fists balling up, my arms shaking, every part of me tensing up as Allison and Michael appeared in the cafeteria doorway. Michael had a scowl on his face before he walked up to the lunch line. Allison rolled her eyes at me, the two of them moving in the opposite direction of Rae. That made me even more furious. Why the fuck weren't her friends with her during a time like this?

Roy tugged on my leather jacket. "Dude, sit down. I was getting to the best part. Marina did this new thing that—"

"I don't give a shit what your girlfriend does to your dick, dude!"

I whipped around, glaring at him as the cafeteria came to a grinding halt.

"I don't give a shit how she kisses you, or how she sucks you off. I don't care how much she puts out or the new shit you can get her to pull. I literally give no fucks about any of it. And you want to know why?"

Roy grimaced. "The hell's wrong with you?"

I chuckled bitterly. "I don't give a damn about it because I know you only do it to be cool. You do it to get attention and to try and be the big man, when you're not. It's pathetic. And you really need to stop, because you look like a shithead."

Roy slid Marina off his lap before he stood up, standing toe to toe with me. And despite the fact that I towered over him by almost five inches, he held his ground. Which was impressive, but stupid.

"You wanna run that by me again?"

I licked my lips. "I don't know. Were you dumb enough not to hear it the first time around?"

Marina hissed. "The two of you, shut up. Teachers are coming over."

I jumped at Roy, causing him to step back before I grinned at him. And as teachers in the cafeteria came to settle down the riff-raff, I strode to the cafeteria door. I wasn't hungry. I wasn't thirsty. The only thing I felt was anger. Frustration. Confusion. The three-course meal I'd been dining on for fucking days. I marched right out of that damn cafeteria, ignoring the teachers that called out after me. I got around the corner and charged for the glass double doors, slamming into them with a pop.

And when my eyes gazed down onto the football field, I saw three senior students from the school down the road laughing and joking around, and dumping shit onto the grass.

Perfect.

I made my way for the field, practically leaping down the stairs. I heard them laughing as one of them whipped out their cocks to literally piss on the painted outlines of our mascot on the green turf. I whistled to myself as my fists unclenched. I breathed a sigh of relief as their laughter came to a grinding halt. I hopped over the fence, touching down onto my feet as I smiled broadly at them.

"Afternoon, boys," I said.

And I chuckled as my victims cowered in their own fucking boots.

29

RAELYNN

I got halfway down the hallway before I rounded around the corner. I didn't want to come into contact with Clint. Not now. Not when things were so rough with, well, everything else. I waited for a few minutes, listening as Clint's voice boomed across the cafeteria. I didn't know what he was saying, but I knew he wasn't happy. I heard Roy's name tossed into everything, then I saw teachers getting up from the corner. Part of me wanted to rush to Clint, to help him calm down before he really got himself into some trouble.

But then his heavy footsteps faded away before the slamming of a door echoed in the distance.

I heard teachers fruitlessly calling out his name as a dull roar rose from the crowd of students in the cafeteria again. And after a few deep breaths, I made my way inside. I took my seat quickly in the corner, like I always did. The place where Michael, Allison, and I always sat. The place where Allison had kept me company yesterday while Michael strode past us, making his way for the outside patio.

Only this time, he slammed his tray down beside me just as Allison sat in front of me.

My eyes widened as I turned my body to face him. I peeked over at Allison, watching as she nodded toward Michael. I licked my lips, feeling the whole of my body lock up as my eyes met his.

This was the first time he'd so much as acknowledged my existence since his appearance on my doorstep. And I wasn't sure what to make of it all. He looked angry, but also tired. He looked frustrated, but also worn. Frazzled. Part of me wanted to reach out and hug him. But the rest of me knew better.

He sighed as he rested his elbow on the table.

"Look. I'm still pissed off. You hid this from me, and I don't get why you went for Clint of all the guys in this school. I don't get it, and I never will. But I want to put this behind us. Can we? Please?"

My jaw dropped open. "I, uh… don't know why you're asking me. I'm not the one to make that decision."

Michael snickered. "You have just as much of a choice about it as I do."

"I mean, not really. I'm not the one hurt. I'm the one doing the hurting."

"It's clear you're hurting, Rae. Just in a different way."

I paused. "Maybe so."

Allison darted her eyes between us. Michael sighed as his free hand settled against my knee. I looked down at it and smiled with tears in my eyes, then settled my hand on top of his. It felt good, having him back. Having him talk to me. Having him near me. I'd missed my friend, my confidant, my cheerleader and my guiding moral light.

I nodded as I held back tears. "I'd really like to put this behind us, yes."

Michael took my hand, ripping me out of my seat. And as he wrapped his long arms around me, I squeezed him around his waist. I giggled breathlessly as he nuzzled against me, trying to soothe my invisible wounds. I heard Allison get up before a soft pair of arms wrapped around both of us, causing Michael to chuckle to himself.

"Had to get in on the action, huh?"

Allison smiled. "I mean, I can never resist a good happily ever after."

I rolled my eyes. "You've been watching Disney movies again, haven't you?"

Allison scoffed. "Just let me say, 'And then everyone lived happily ever after, the end'."

Michael laughed. "Okay, but only this once."

All of us gave one last big squeeze, then we unraveled ourselves from one another. We sat down and started unpacking our lunches, smiling and talking like we used to do. It felt nice, having some semblance of normalcy around this table again. And it felt really good to hear Michael's lame jokes as I talked about Mom and D.J. I rehashed the conversation, telling them about my mother's decision. How I really felt she was serious this time. How it felt like things might actually be different.

But soon, I felt my eyes scanning the cafeteria.

"He left."

Michael's voice pulled my eyes back to him, and he gave me a knowing look.

"What?"

Allison giggled. "Oh, come on, Rae. Don't play that game."

Michael shook his head. "Lying's what got you into this mess, you know."

I sighed. "No, omitting information is what got me into this mess."

Allison smiled. "So, you admit you're lying now?"

I paused. "I plead the fifth."

Michael scoffed. "He left, and he hasn't come back yet."

I shrugged. "Oh, well. His loss. I was going to throw a Cheeto at him."

"Uh huh," Michael said as he spooned a bite of chicken pot pie into his mouth. "Sure, you don't."

I rolled my eyes at him before focusing on my peanut butter and jelly sandwich. Mom had actually packed me a lunch today. For the first time in years, I came downstairs to a brown paper bag that she handed off to me with a big smile on her face. And thinking about it made me smile with every bite. Mom looked radiant lately. Like a weight had been lifted off her shoulders. I mean, I knew she'd end up stressing herself out over money and bills. But being free of D.J. looked good on her.

I really hope it stays this way.

"So you actually told your mom about Clint?"

Allison's question made me nod as I swallowed my sandwich.

"Mm-hmm. I did. And I'm actually glad I did. It's been a long time since I've really been able to talk to her like that. And, despite the hiccup of that evening, we still enjoyed our pizza and movie marathon."

Michael grinned. "Shame you didn't invite me in for pizza."

I giggled. "You didn't stick around long enough for us to get to that point."

"You have a decent argument there."

"It's not an argument, it's just the truth. Nothing more, nothing less."

"Refreshing, coming from you."

I playfully glared at him. "That one feel good?"

Michael nodded. "Actually, it did."

"Good. Because it's the only one you'll get."

The three of us laughed again before a commotion started in the back of the cafeteria. Kids rushed to the windows and poured out onto the patio, their hands clapping and cupping over their mouths. I furrowed my brow deeply as I craned my neck, trying to figure out what the fuck was going on.

Then, I heard it. I heard what they were chanting.

"Fight! Fight! Fight! Fight!"

Allison's face fell. "Uh oh."

Michael shook his head. "Shit."

And as a sinking feeling filled my gut, I felt myself standing from my seat.

Clint.

I abandoned my lunch and pressed myself between Michael and the wall. I slipped away, listening to them yell at me as I headed for one of the windows. I pushed people out of the way, trying to catch a glimpse of what they were looking at. And when I saw a towering black mass dancing around on the football field, I felt my lunch creep up the back of my throat.

Shit.

I pushed away from the window and charged for the cafeteria exit. I had to navigate the masses, since they had already started rushing out the door. Teachers were trapped. The principal was stuck at the back of the hallway. It took all the effort I had to shove people to the concrete in order to get ahead of them.

And all the while, Allison and Michael yelled for me to come back.

30

CLINTON

I took a blow to the jaw and stumbled back. Actually stumbled. On my feet. That hadn't happened in a fight in quite some time. Usually, it was only my father that made me stumble backwards. These boys fought harder than I'd originally given them credit for. And I was happy for it. The pain gave me something to focus on. Their beady, disgusting little eyes gave me targets for the fury in my fists. I felt blood pumping through my veins and fire coursing through my bones. I felt alive. More alive than I ever had before.

Except with Rae.

"You're fucked, you little piece of shit."

I grinned. "Gotta take me down first."

I hooked my arm around his neck and bent him at the waist. Throwing my head back, I cracked the other guy in the nose behind me as he growled and cursed to himself. I laughed as I choked off the boy's air supply before an elbow came down into my back. And as I dropped to my hands and knees, it gave me the perfect angle to wrap my arm around some other boy's legs.

I didn't even know who was who. At this point, it was kill or be killed. Just like in my house.

And I sure as hell wasn't on the menu tonight.

"Fight! Fight! Fight! Fight!"

I heard chanting kids racing for the field. A crowd gathered as I shoved myself up off the ground. My jaw was swelling, my lip was busted, and one of my eyes was already swelling shut. More decorative scars and colors to go along with the ligature marks that took me for fucking ever to cover up this morning.

"You're dead," the kid snarled.

I simply smiled before I charged him.

"Clint! Clint! Clint! Clint!"

I yelled out as I tackled him to the ground. I straddled him, throwing punch after punch before his buddies dragged me off him. I slung my fists around like wildfire, feeling them connect as the crowd's chanting grew to a dull roar. I smelled their blood. Felt their fear. And it fueled me forward as I fisted a handful of hair and pulled some dude's head back.

"This is for fucking around with our field."

I punched him in the nose before someone tackled me to the ground. Kids cheered and girls cried out for me to stay safe as I rolled around on the turf with him. I smelled that piss growing closer. My eyes widened as we kept rolling around. I slid off his body, gripping his coat as I dragged him through the grass. Through the mud.

Right through that fucking urine stain his buddy left behind.

"What the—?"

I chuckled. "Tell Mommy Dearest that hot water really helps get out the stench of piss."

I tossed him off to the side before whipping around. One of the gangly boys charged me, and one knock of my fist had him on the ground. I clotheslined the other boy barreling for me, reveling in the glory as people chanted my name. This was where I excelled. This was my golden goose egg. I dabbed at the blood trickling down my chin as I turned toward the crowd, tossing my fists in the air.

Thankful for the distraction from all the misery that had been sinking me into the trenches.

"Watch out!"

The girl shrieked just before I got knocked to the ground. The asshole had me pinned, his fists flying in my general direction. And without thinking, I took a play out of Michael's book. I crossed my arms over my face, deflecting his pathetic attempts at being a man before I had the strength to roll him over.

Before someone gripped my jacket and pulled me off him.

"Clint! Stop it! Right now!"

A familiar voice rose from the crowd as the boy holding me tried tossing me to the ground. But, really, all he did was cause me to stumble around a bit. My eyes darted about, looking for that familiar voice. Listening out for the booming tones that echoed over the chants. Over the screams. Over the warnings from other girls that would surely pour themselves all over me to help clean up my cuts and scrapes.

"Stop this right now!"

Rae's voice pierced my fog of anger and helplessness as she appeared at the fence line. My eyes found hers, and I felt my heart leap in my chest. She was saying my name. Calling out for me. It was the first time I'd heard her voice in days.

"Rae," I whispered.

Then I got clocked. Right in the fucking jaw.

"Stop it! Please, Clint!"

Her voice spun around in my head as my back hit the ground. I felt my mouth pooling with blood as those three assholes danced around me. Swirling, like vultures, ready to strike the second I got up. I rolled over and planted on all fours as I spit out a mouthful of blood.

Then I felt someone drag me to my feet.

"That all you got, boy?"

"You're pathetic, you piece of shit."

"Looks like someone already got to him once, though. Serves him right, needing a reminder."

Those words lit my world on fire, and I wrenched away from the guy's grasp. I whipped around, clocking him with my fist straight into his gut. He doubled over and I threw my elbow back, connecting with someone's ribcage before I heard something fall to the ground. I turned around, bashing my head into the other guy's nose and watching blood pour down his face before I turned my attention back to the boy who was doubled over.

"Ready for the final countdown?" I asked.

I brought my knee up into the boy's forehead, watching him drop to his knees. The crowd erupted in applause as teachers tried pushing their way through, and then I heard it again. Rae's shrieking voice. Her words were muffled as adrenaline pumped through my veins. I twirled slowly, taking in the three boys who were flat on the ground at my feet.

I took a moment to revel in my victory before I felt someone tugging at my arm.

"Clint. That's enough. Stop this bullshit."

I looked over and saw Rae. Her voice pierced through my anger and my red-dripped vision slowly filtered back into regular color. Her eyes stared up at me. Her hands felt soft around my arm. She tugged me away from the circle of assholes I'd laid out on the football field, her eyes filled with frustration and fury.

And a bit of worry on the side.

"Rae," I said.

She huffed. "Come on. We have to get you out of here."

"What are you doing?"

She shook her head. "Keeping you from making anymore dumbass mistakes. Just leave those boys alone. Come with me. Please."

She tugged me a couple of steps away, but I heard the crowd gasp. I heard people calling out my name and it caused me to whip around. My arm wrenched away from Rae and I felt her trying to grab me. Her hands wrapped around my waist, trying to tug me off the field. I heard her pleading with me. Begging with me. Calling out my name just to get my attention. But all I saw were those three assholes charging me again. Stumbling on their feet and coming for more.

Which was something that made me smile.

"Give me a second, Rae."

"Clint, no!"

One of the guys attempted to sucker punch me in the gut, but I caught his wrist. I twisted his arm behind him before kicking him to the ground, then whirled around and trained my sights on the other two. I reached out for the next one that came for me, wrapping my large hand around his neck. I squeezed until he started beating his fist against my forearm, and I felt it again.

I felt Rae's hands fisting my leather jacket.

"We need to get the fuck out of here. Cut the shit, Clint!"

When I felt her hands fall away from me, I heard her yelp.

"Get the fuck out of my way, bitch."

My hand dropped the guy's neck as I slowly turned around. I vibrated with fury as I came into contact with the jock I had just kicked to the fucking ground. Rae lay there, gasping for air as she tried to roll over onto her stomach. And as my eyes slowly lifted to the jock that was standing beside her, he tossed me a wild grin.

"Getting your bitches to do your fighting now?"

I snarled. "You pathetic little fuck!"

I saw nothing. My vision tunneled, and the only thing I saw was his face busted into pieces on the ground. I snapped, lunging at him, wrapping my hands around his throat as I wrestled him back to the ground. I heard Rae whimpering, still telling me to stop, even as she gasped for her own air. I straddled the fat bastard and landed punch after punch, refusing to listen or stop. Refusing to cease my movements until this asshole stopped breathing.

I'd kill him for laying his hands on Rae.

He rolled me over and the fight changed. His blood dripped down onto my face as he punched my gut. I braced my abs, conserving my energy as he wore himself out. But, four punches in, he was ripped from my body. I saw him flying through the air like a bird in the sky before a familiar figure came into view. I looked over and saw Allison scooping Rae off the ground. I quickly got up, trying to figure out whether or not Rae was all right before I heard footsteps rushing up behind me.

"Oh, no you don't."

And as I turned around, I saw Michael land a punch straight on the fucker's nose.

Then he turned his anger onto the boy who'd put his hands on Rae.

31

RAELYNN

"Hey, Rae. You okay? Can you talk to me?"

I finally caught my breath as tears rushed down my cheeks. I nodded, but I didn't want to speak. I'd landed my back directly on a rock, and it knocked the wind clear out of me. Allison tilted me to the side, raising up my shirt to see if any damage had been done. I felt her fingertips against my skin as the fight raged on, making me angrier with every punch I heard landing in the distance.

"You're bleeding. Hold still."

I drew in a shuddering breath. "Make him stop."

Allison didn't answer me and it forced my eyes closed. I felt her wiping something across my skin as sirens sounded in the distance. Fucking hell, that was becoming the school song at this point. With Clint's fighting and Michael's temper, they probably had the damn police on speed dial. It seemed like the entire fucking high school had gathered for this fight. And why Clint was fighting them, I could only theorize at this point. My back hurt. My wrist hurt. My head felt swimmy, and I wanted to go home.

And finally, the fight drew to a close.

I heard grunts and groans of the three guys lying on the ground. I had no idea why the hell the teachers weren't intervening, but I figured they'd given up on this point. Given up on Clint.

On his fighting. On trying to rein him in. It made my heart sick for him, but I also couldn't blame them.

"Heads up," Allison murmured.

I felt her smooth my shirt down before a hand came into my watery view. I slowly raked my eyes up the arm, taking in the worn leather jacket before my eyes found his. Clint stood above me, concern filling his eyes. It was the only reason I took his hand, why I wanted to touch his bloody skin.

Because he genuinely looked worried.

"You're an absolute numbskull, Clint. You know that?"

Michael's voice filled my ears, but I was paying too much attention to Clint. His hands cupped my wrist, inspecting it before slowly turning me around. I felt him inching my shirt up before a smack resounded. I felt Clint's hand fall away from my body, and I closed my eyes, readying my ears for the punch I knew Clint would toss Michael's way.

But a punch didn't happen.

"I'm just making sure she's okay," Clint said.

Michael scoffed. "She would've been fine had you not gotten into the fight in the first damn place."

Allison sighed. "She didn't have to follow him on the field, though."

Michael's voice grew louder. "You know how she feels about this asshole! Of course she would!"

And then, Clint shocked us all into silence.

"You're right."

I slowly turned around, trying to make sense of what I'd just heard. I gazed up into his eyes, seeing nothing but remorse filling them. I peeked over at Michael and Allison, and even they were shocked. The kids fell silent behind us, waiting for something else to happen. Waiting for the sirens in the distance to come screaming into the parking lot behind the school.

"Principal! Scatter!"

Roy's voice boomed over everyone's heads and Clint reached out for me. Before I could even react, he took my good hand, tugging me alongside him as he ran off. I heard Michael yelling after me. I heard Allison calling out for me. But I didn't stop. I threaded my fingers with Clint's and ran alongside him, despite the pain in my back.

"Fine! I'll fucking cover for you assholes!"

I giggled and shook my head as Michael's voice filled my ears. Clint slammed through the gate at the end of the football field, pulling me behind him. We took off for the front of the school as the principal yelled after us. I knew teachers were running for us. But I also knew they wouldn't catch us.

"You're such an asshole, you know that? And stop pulling me, fucking hell, Clint. My wrist hurts."

He stopped in his tracks. "This is your bad wrist?"

I shook my head. "No. But that doesn't mean it doesn't fucking hurt."

"Then, come on and shut up before we're both in a hell of a lot of trouble."

I scoffed as he took my hand again. "We wouldn't be in this damn situation had you not fought in the first place!"

"No one asked you to intervene."

We started running again. "Yeah, well. Fuck me for caring, I guess."

We kept running until we got around the front of the building. Among the chaos and the insanity, the pain in my back and my wrist grew. I was pissed off at the entire world. For Clint and his bullshit fighting ways. At those boys for whatever the hell they'd been doing on the football field. For that asshole that actually knocked me down.

I'd never been knocked down before.

Clint makes you weak.

Ain't that the fucking truth.

We didn't stop running until we got to his bike. He tossed me a helmet and I slid behind him, wrapping my arms around his waist. I tried to ignore how wonderful it felt as he cranked up the engine. And just as the police were speeding into the back of the school, we sped out of the front.

"Hold on. We're gonna take these corners a bit sharp."

I wrapped my good hand into his leather jacket and let my hurt wrist fall between his legs. I closed my eyes, taking deep breaths of the wind as it swirled around our bodies. It felt like I was inches away from the asphalt as he careened out of the parking lot. It felt like we were breaking the sound barrier as we sped off into the distance. Even with my eyes closed, I knew where we were headed. I had the turns and directions memorized.

And when the stench of my neighborhood wafted under my nose, I felt my stomach clench.

I sighed as Clint pulled into my driveway. He put his kickstand down and turned off his engine, but he didn't move. I rested against the breadth of his strong back. I felt tired. Anxious. And yet, happy.

Happy to be against him again.

"Why are you such an idiot?" I whispered.

Clint cleared his throat. "Your mom home?"

I shook my head. "She's out putting in job applications."

"Good for her. Let's get you inside, then."

"You're coming with me?"

"I'm sure as hell not leaving you in this condition, no."

He slipped off the bike, then eased the helmet off my head. He smoothed my hair down around my face, then tucked some loose strands behind my ear. His touch ignited a fire in my gut. I didn't even understand how much I'd missed it until I felt it again. I let out a soft sigh, wishing for nothing more than his palm against my cheek.

But he pulled his hand away before he caved to the temptation.

"You need help?"

I scoffed. "I'm good. Thanks."

"Just a question, Rae."

"And a dumb one, at that. I can hold my own, Clint. Despite the fact that that douchebag knocked me off my feet."

"I should've killed him for that."

"And spend the rest of your life in jail? Nice."

"Does anything ever make you happy?"

I planted myself on my feet in the driveway before my eyes met his.

"Yeah. I've got plenty that makes me happy. But bullshit boys and their stupid fights don't happen to be one of them."

I turned on my heel and made my way for the porch, figuring he'd leave, drive off into the distance and never come back. So imagine my surprise when he stayed behind me, following me into the house. He closed the door behind us as I made my way to the couch. I watched as he found his way into the kitchen, and I wondered what he was doing. I started to stand up to go find out, but he must have heard me.

"Stay there, Rae. I'm coming with ice."

I leaned back into the couch with a sigh before I winced. I felt like utter shit. Clint came around the corner and sat down beside me. He reached for my wrist and slowly molded the ice pack to it. I watched him work, his bruised eye trained on my swelling skin. He helped me lean up before he slid my shirt up again, taking stock of the small wound on my back. And when his fingertips fell against the dried blood, I flinched.

But not because it hurt.

"You'll be bruised. The cut's only topical, though. We'll give the ice a few minutes on your wrist, then we'll move it to your back."

I nodded. "Okay."

He leaned me back into the couch before settling into the cushions beside me. I couldn't take my eyes off him. Couldn't stop looking at him as his hands fell between his legs. He stared hard at the wall, licking his lips, which were cracked open and bleeding. I wanted to lean against him, but wasn't sure if it was a good idea.

"I'm sorry."

Clint's words pulled me from my trance and I furrowed my brow.

"Wait, what? Why?"

He sighed. "I'm sorry for getting you hurt."

I shrugged. "Well, you didn't hurt me. So, yeah."

The pain that rose up in his eyes left me breathless.

"No, I didn't. But, I was reckless. And *that* got you hurt."

I had no rebuttal to that statement, either. Because he was technically right.

"How about we deal with one blow at a time, Clint. Okay?"

He nodded slowly. "Deal."

He moved the ice pack from my wrist to my back, leaning me up just enough to slide it between my skin and the couch cushions. I shivered at the cold as he leaned me back. Then he reached for my swollen wrists.

"Let me know if any of this hurts," he said.

And one by one, he began to softly massage the joints of my fingers.

32

CLINTON

I mindlessly massaged her fingers as she relaxed further into the couch. One of the few times Cecilia and I had ever interacted with one another was the one time my father ever did any real damage to my body. He had dislocated my wrist to teach me a lesson, then popped it back in once I agreed to clean up my bathroom. Cecilia had come in and help me clean it, then massaged my fingers before wrapping my wrist in an ace bandage to heal.

To this day, I can fully remember just how amazing that massage felt.

Rae sighed with relief as I slowly popped every knuckle. One by one, down her finger, until I'd traced all five of them. I massaged her palm slowly, being careful with the bones in the top of her hand. I worked my way toward her wrist, getting lighter and lighter until she flinched. Then I began backing up, making my way down the hand, back into the palm, and up to the tips of her fingers.

Giving myself time to process everything I thought. Everything I felt. Everything I wanted to do, but couldn't.

"You wanna tell me what this fight was all about now?"

I settled Rae's hand against my thigh, feeling her heat penetrate my jeans. Did I want to come clean? Did I want to open up to her? Did I want to let her in again?

Yes. Yes, I did.

I licked the blood off my lips. "This weekend was rough. Dad came home."

She paused. "What did he do, Clint?"

I shrugged. "The usual. Cecilia stepped in this time, though. And he wasn't happy about that."

"Is she okay?"

I snickered. "He punished me with a hand wrapped around my neck, and he punished her by leaving her behind while he jetted off on yet another business trip. Yeah. I think she's okay."

"So you lashed out at those guys because you needed… an outlet?"

"It's the only thing I know how to do when I'm confused and angry. It's the only way Dad ever taught me how to deal with shit."

"And you think that's productive?"

I shrugged. "Maybe not."

"I wouldn't think so either. Since you weren't doing a very good job of fighting."

I grinned as a soft chuckle bubbled up the back of my throat. I looked over at her, finding her smirking at me as her hand moved down to my knee. She squeezed it before moving it again, and I ached for her touch against my body again. I loved how she made me smile. How she had this ability to light up my world, even at a time like this.

"Don't be a smartass. It's not a good look."

She giggled. "And yet, it's in my blood."

I quirked an eyebrow. "I don't think it's genetic more so than a chromosomal defect."

"I'm shocked you even know what that is, considering you almost flunked out of sophomore science."

"And here I thought you never paid attention to me."

She snickered. "The only thing I paid attention to during that class was Mr. Blackman's ass. He had a nice one."

"And you weren't staring at my ass? How rude."

"Yours wasn't very nice back then."

"So you were looking."

And all at once, her face flushed red. It trickled down the nape of her neck, forcing me to swallow back a growl. I enjoyed bantering with her. I enjoyed making her flustered. The big, bad, tough girl from the wrong side of the tracks, melting into a puddle of embarrassment.

It looked spectacular on her.

"Well, Rae. The good news is that your wrist isn't broken."

She rolled her eyes. "I could've told you that."

"I'm sure. Can you tell me what it actually is, then?"

She glared playfully at me. "It's sprained, jackass."

I patted her head. "Good job, Rae. You get a gold star."

"You're a dick."

"And you love it."

Her eyes whipped up to mine and I saw something flash behind them. Something hot. Something passionate. Something way too fleeting for the moment. She looked away from me, casting her eyes down into her lap. So I decided not to back her into a corner over it.

I mean, I'd already gotten her to admit she enjoyed staring at my ass.

"Here. Let me get that ice pack real quick."

My hand pressed against the back of her shoulder and she leaned up. I heard her groaning a bit, which meant her muscles were already stiffening from the jarring impact. I stood up and took the ice pack back into the kitchen, tossing it into the freezer. Then I rummaged around for a washcloth.

"Time for some heat," I murmured to myself.

After drenching the washcloth in hot water, I wrung it out. I walked back into the living room, watching as Rae's eyes found mine again. I felt her studying me carefully. Trying to figure out her next move. I motioned for her to sit up and placed the washcloth against her bare skin, and the hiss that left her lips filled my ears.

"Does that hurt?" I asked.

She shook her head. "No. Just jarring, after the cold."

"Do you need a couple minutes?"

"No, no. I'm good. You can leave it."

"All right. Lean back for me. Like you did with the ice pack."

And after sliding her shirt down, she eased herself back into the cushions.

I sat down next to her. "You never should've charged that field, Rae. The hell were you thinking?"

"I was thinking about you, and how stupid you looked."

"You put yourself in harm's way for nothing. You know I can handle myself."

"And so can I, believe it or not."

"Says the girl who got knocked on her ass with one push."

She scoffed. "What? You saying I'm not tough?"

I growled. "No. I'm saying you could've gotten much worse, and I don't like the thought of you getting hurt."

"Well, I'm already hurt."

"I mean *more* hurt, Rae. Stop twisting my words and accept the fact that I give a shit."

She giggled. "How does that feel to admit?"

I grinned. "Probably more painful than that wrist of yours."

"You sure about that? Because it's a pretty gnarly sprain."

"Gnarly? You been surfing lately?"

She shrugged. "And if I have?"

I smiled. "I'd tell you I'd love to see you in that body suit sometime."

"And here I thought you liked me naked."

"I never said anything about not taking it off."

She blushed again, deepening that color against her beautifully-tanned body. I loved watching it. I adored everything about her reactions. The way she made her hair fall into her face to draw a sort of curtain between us. The way she shivered as I tucked that same piece of hair back behind her ear. The way she turned toward me, begging me silently with her eyes to touch her.

I especially liked the way she nuzzled against my palm, too. Once I offered it to her.

"I've missed you," I whispered.

Rae's eyes fell closed as I cupped her cheek softly. "I know."

"I'm sorry for not having the balls to choose you over Roy and the others. I should've had a different answer when you confronted me."

She nodded softly. "I know, Clint."

"You deserve better, you know."

She opened her eyes, locking them with my own. She lifted her head from my palm, leaving me wanting more of her heat. More of her skin. More of her body against mine. She scooted closer to me, letting her hurt hand settle against my thigh again. I swallowed hard, watching her face slowly gravitate to mine as the washcloth slid out from her shirt. Her eyes held me. Pinned me. Rooted me to the couch. And as her breath pulsed against my lips, she shook her head.

"Now *that* I don't believe."

I snickered. "You should. I'm not good."

She shrugged. "Neither am I."

"Don't you dare talk about yourself like that. You're the best, Rae."

"Then so are you."

"No, I'm not."

"Aren't you the one that pointed out just how much we have in common? You know, back when you stalked me at the park."

I chuckled. "I didn't stalk you."

She smirked. "You stalked me a little bit."

"I really didn't. I honestly found you by happenstance out there."

She shrugged. "It's fine. You don't have to admit it. But you're the one who said we were more alike than we seemed. So, if I'm worth it, you're worth it. Logic dictates it."

"Logic, huh? You a fan of all that nonsense?"

"Am I a fan of basic arguments and winning them? I mean, I am a girl."

My eyes fell to her lips before I licked my own again.

"Yes. You are a hell of a girl, Rae."

She scooted closer to me, our thighs pressed together. Heat crept up the nape of my neck as her hand slid up my thigh. Up my abs. Up my chest, until it settled against my shoulder. She had her arm almost around me. Almost giving me permission to wrap her up and pull her into my fucking lap.

Then her eyes fell to my lips.

"Do you have them now?"

I paused. "Do I have what?"

She giggled. "The balls, silly. Do you have the balls now to make the decision you should have made?"

"Depends. Are you giving me a second chance at the choice?"

And as she nodded, I wrapped my arms around her, pulling her into my lap as our noses nuzzled softly together.

"Yes," I whispered.

33

RAELYNN

I furrowed my brow. "Yes?"

Clint nodded. "Mm-hmm. Yes."

I grinned. "I mean, positive answer. But you might have to be a bit more specif—"

His lips crashed against mine and I slid my fingers through his hair. He tasted like metal and blood and sweat. The grass from the football field wafted up my nose as he tightened me against him. I felt his chest heaving, gasping for the air I robbed him of. And while I knew I needed to still be mad at him, I wasn't. I should have still been mad at him, but I couldn't be. He was an ass, yes. He had been an ass today, and he'd be an ass tomorrow. Starting a damn fight like that.

But…

"Oh, Rae," he growled.

Our lips kept connecting, cutting off our words. I wanted to taste more of him. Feel more of him. His tongue felt like silk and his body ignited an electrical storm in my mind. I couldn't think. Couldn't breathe. Couldn't process anything else other than the feel of his lips.

Which felt fantastic.

All at once, he whipped me around. My back lay against the couch cushions, my legs spreading to accommodate him. He fell against me, like a weighted blanket, comforting me as his hands explored what they wanted. He sucked on my lower lip and I arched into him, feeling fire rush through my veins as my legs began trembling. I slid his leather jacket away from his shoulders, not wanting any layers separating us any longer.

Even though I was still upset with him.

His words were punctuated with kisses. "I. Choose. You."

I sighed. "Say it again."

"I. Choose. You. Rae."

I moaned as his lips fell to my breasts. The way he stripped me of my clothes seemed effortless. The way our clothes mingled on the floor was like a song to our ever-uniting bodies. The warmth of his skin made me shiver. The heat of his tongue iced me over. I slid my hands down his back, feeling the pebbled muscles underneath his taut skin rolling for me as he sank in between my legs again. Our bodies clad in nothing.

Except one another.

He grinned. "And here I thought you hated my guts."

I scoffed. "Oh, don't get me wrong. I still hate your guts."

"Uh huh."

"I really do. You're a dick who pulled a dick move today. I hope you know that."

He nodded slowly. "I do. And you should hate me. You should always hate the kind of person I am."

"Now, get back down here and let me taste you again."

That cheeky little grin crawled across his face as I fisted his hair. I brought him back down to me, allowing his tongue to fill my mouth. I wrapped my arms around his neck and held him close, rolling my hips against him and feeling him growing against me. His hands ran over my waist, massaging my hips, exploring my thighs, cupping my breasts. I rolled us off the couch as my giggles filled the back of his throat. He held on tightly to me, catching me as I fell on top of him. And with a grunt, I straddled him. Placed my hands against his chest and leaned up to get a good look at him.

I smiled. "Wouldn't hurt so much if you hadn't gotten your ass beat."

He shot up, wrapping his arms around me. "You should see the other guys."

"Guys, huh? Sounds hot."

"You into that sort of thing?"

"Guess you'll never know."

He smiled before our lips collided again, only this time his hand slid through my hair. He pulled my head back, exposing my neck as he kissed down my skin. His teeth raked along my pulse point. I felt myself warming for him. Wetting for him. Ready for him. I whimpered as he kissed down the valley of my breasts, making his way to the pert peaks before he stopped.

I panted. "Clint."

He cupped the back of my head, slowly raising my head up until our eyes connected.

I paused. "What is it?"

His thumb smoothed along the tendrils of my hair. "You mean a lot to me."

I saw the sincerity in his eyes as he brought our foreheads together. I closed my eyes, feeling him slowly moving once more. He held tightly onto my body as he whipped me around, placing my back against the carpeted floor. I gazed into his eyes as he reached between our bodies. I licked my lips as I felt him seated against my entrance. I nodded softly, letting him know it was all right. And all at once, he filled me, shaking me against the carpet as our bodies became one.

"Clint, yes."

But he only shook his head before our lips fell together again.

I wrapped myself around him, holding on for dear life as he rolled against me. My legs locked around his waist. My arms went around his neck. I kissed his shoulder and nibbled his neck, allowing him the opportunity to take me to heights I'd never experienced before. He rolled faster, thrusting harder, stroking parts of me he hadn't touched yet. And as my eyes rolled back, I arched into him. I felt it coming, bubbling up. And the faster he moved, the more prone I was to succumbing to his assault.

His beautiful, salacious assault.

"Yes. Yes. Clint. Oh, shit. Clint, yes! Right there! Right there!"

"That's it, Rae. Let go. Do it for me, beautiful."

"Oh. Shit."

The words came out as whimpers. Broken syllables that fell from my lips. I felt myself vibrating around him, clamping down on him as the whole of my body lost control. He didn't stop, though. His face dropped to my neck and he kept on going. Kept on filling me. Kept on rolling and thrusting as I raked my nails up and down his arms, trying my best not to blow through the roof in ecstasy. I locked myself around him and managed to roll him over. I straddled him, my hands pressed once again into his chest. I gazed into his eyes as I swiveled my hips, feeling his hands grip them, guiding me. Teaching me with his movements how to please him. How to make him feel good.

How to make him soar.

"That's it, Rae. Perfect."

"Clint. I want you to feel good, too."

He reached up, cupping my cheek. "I always feel good when I'm around you."

I fell against his body, his hands cupping my ass cheeks. Our tongues twined together as I rested against him, feeling him hold me while he thrust. His hips rose, filling me and releasing me. Filling me and releasing me. And soon, I was on my back again, my legs in the air and tossed over his shoulder before he bent me in half.

"Oh, fuck!"

He grinned. "There's the spot you love so much."

"Shit. Shit. Shit. Shit."

"You'll say my name before it's all over."

The world slowly tunneled. All I saw was his face. All I felt was his body. All I knew was the scent and sounds and smells of him. My heart surged with delight. My soul welled with a happiness I'd never experienced before. And suddenly, I felt myself come alive. For the first time in my entire life, I knew what it felt like to be praised. Enjoyed. Cherished. Wanted. As my knees pressed into my chest and Clint drove himself deep into my body, I knew what it felt like to be prized.

I drew in a shuddering breath. "Thank you, Clint."

He ceased his movements and I opened my eyes. Well, the tunneling lifted as the electricity let go of its grip on my brain. His brow furrowed deeply as he rested there, on the backs of my legs. I smiled as I lifted my head to capture his lips softly before I nuzzled my nose against his.

"For what?" he asked.

I giggled. "For making me feel important."

My legs slid from his shoulders and his hands found mine. I lay there, our fingers threaded together as he pinned them above my head. Our eyes connected and didn't let go. Our hips moved in tandem and didn't let up. We breathed one another's air and shared one another's pleasure. I bucked when he rocked, and I jumped when he thrust.

And soon, we fell over the edge together.

With each other's names being chanted like breathless prayers on the cusp of the wind.

34

CLINTON

I stood on Rae's porch. "You sure this is something you wanna do?"

She shrugged. "Why not?"

"I mean, we could still take my bike. Ride in like a couple of badasses."

"Or we could park it here and walk to school. Giving us a little more time to spend with one another."

"Rae…"

"What?"

I sighed. "You know Allison and Michael aren't going to want to talk to me."

"We won't know until we give them a chance, you know."

"I know this. Michael doesn't like me."

"Michael fought alongside you yesterday."

"Yes, for you. Because you got hurt. Not because of me, or some brotherhood or some shit."

She rolled her eyes. "Come on. If we don't get started, we're going to be late. You can come home with me after school and get your bike."

I grinned. "Oh, really now? Will your mother be home?"

All she did was giggle, giving me an answer that suddenly made me want this entire school day to be over.

We walked hand in hand through her neighborhood, and I got

a good look at it. There was trash lying around in the streets. The lawns were filled with dirt and mud rather than freshly-trimmed grass. The homes had crooked porches and dilapidated roofs. Rae and her mother honestly lived in the best house on the block. Which still wasn't saying much. It gave me a glimpse into the life Rae led. The dark shadows that shrouded this place. The smell that hung in the air around the homes, no matter how hard the wind blew.

But, once we got to the exit of the neighborhood, I paused.

"What is it, Clint?"

I licked my lips. "This could ruin my image, you know? Walking to school with some girl. Not riding in on my bike waiting for all the girls to flock to me. It's hard work being a bad boy, you know."

She snickered. "Well, your image sucks and could do with some damaging."

But when I looked down into her eyes, I knew she understood how sincere my words were. This was a big step for me. Something different. Something I didn't know how to navigate. And she gave my hand a comforting squeeze before leading the way. We started out of her neighborhood, holding hands tightly as we walked up the block. Hell, even the sidewalk changed from a darker tinted, cracked concrete to the nice, white, smooth concrete I'd taken advantage of my entire life.

Then we stopped.

"Allison! Michael! Hey!"

Rae's voice filled the air and I looked up from the concrete, watching as confusion rolled over their faces. Allison trotted toward us, with that confusion morphing into surprise. Michael didn't seem the least bit entertained by the idea of seeing me.

I didn't blame him.

Allison stopped in front of Rae. "Hey there. What's going on?"

The two girls hugged one another, forcing Rae to drop my hand. Michael walked up and stood beside Allison, squaring off with me like he was ready for another fight. And what was worse was that he didn't look as if he'd been in a fight. He had no cuts. No scrapes. No bruising. Nothing. Whereas my eye was still swollen a bit, I had a black eye underneath it, and the cut on my lip had bruised up.

Michael scoffed. "Yeah. What's going on?"

Rae took my hand again. "Nothing. Just walking to school."

Michael darted his finger between the two of us. "He's walking you to school."

Allison shoved him with her shoulder. "Michael."

Rae shrugged. "He's walking with us to school. Got an issue with that?"

I looked over at her warily before I cleared my throat.

"Hey, Mike. I just wanna—"

He cut me off. "It's Michael, thanks."

I nodded slowly. "Michael. I'm sorry, you know, for the whole fight and everything. It happened at a time where I was angry at shit in my house, and I took it out on you."

He nodded. "Anything else?"

I paused. "Well, thank you for jumping in yesterday, too. You've got some serious fight, and I was impressed."

"Well, I didn't do it for you. I did it for Rae. But you're welcome. For not letting you get killed out there."

Allison swatted at his arm and I looked slowly over at Rae. But again, all she did was squeeze my hand. Like that was supposed to reassure me things would be all right. She stepped closer to me, leaning her cheek against my arm. And as I turned my head back to her two friends, I saw Michael's eyes ignite with anger.

While Allison's eyes filled with happiness.

Michael rolled his eyes. "Will he be walking with us every morning?"

Rae shrugged. "I don't know. Part of that is up to him. But I'd really like it if you two gave him a chance."

Michael scoffed. "He attacked me, Rae."

I nodded. "And I apologized for that. I got some shit going on at home and—"

He cut me off again. "We've all got shit going on at home."

Rae stepped in. "He's got my kinda shit going on, Michael."

And that quickly shut down the conversation. Though I wasn't completely happy with Rae blurting that out. Or equating my home situation to hers. Or talking about my home situation in general, like I was some fucking charity rehab project.

Rae sighed. "Anyway, please give him a chance. For my sake. I'll be spending more time with Clint now, and I'd like there to not always be this fighting and tension."

Michael grumbled. "Of course."

Allison linked her arm with his. "What he means is that of course, we'll give him a chance. For both of your sakes."

As the four of us walked to school, it was quiet. Rae didn't speak with them, and they didn't speak with us. Lines had been drawn in the sand, and we had our respective corners to stand in. And I didn't want it to be like this for Rae. She deserved better.

So I cleared my throat.

"Looks like you got out better from that fight yesterday than I did, Michael."

I looked over at him, but all he did was nod.

"Guess that's what happens when you don't run into a gaggle of guys without a plan."

I nodded. "Gaggle of guys. I like that. Especially since that one looked like a goose."

Allison giggled. "That's bad, Clint."

I shrugged. "Well, he did! And the way he announced his charges every time with that yell of his. I was waiting for him to fluff his feathers out and start chomping at me with his beak."

Rae laughed. "Have you ever been attacked by a goose? There's one that roams our neighborhood. I swear, it's hellbent on terrorizing every little kid in that cul-de-sac of ours."

Allison rolled her eyes. "I wake up to the honking of geese every morning, courtesy of the stupid pond Dad wanted to live beside when we first moved."

Michael chuckled. "Harsh words coming from you, Ali."

Rae paused. "Ali?"

We all stopped just outside of the school's front doors with Rae having a tight grip on my hand. While things had flowed in conversation well enough, now it came to a grinding halt. We all stared at one another, like four dumbasses all lost in the same math class. But as Allison's arm quickly fell from Michael's, I knew exactly what was happening.

And neither of them had told Rae yet.

Allison giggled nervously. "Um, we'll talk at lunch. Okay? When it's just the three of us?"

Rae's lips parted in shock. "I mean, I thought maybe—"

I butted in. "Of course. Just the three of you at lunch. Sure."

Michael snickered. "At least someone gets it."

I shot him a look as I squeezed Rae's hand. She nodded slowly, then the two of us ventured toward the doors. But as she pulled them open, I felt my nerves getting the best of me.

And I quickly dropped her hand.

She furrowed her brow. "What?"

I shook my head. "This isn't a good idea."

"Look, Clint. I'm not gonna force you to do something you don't want to do. But if you can't do this, that means you can't do us. I'm not your dirty little secret. I'm not just some rest stop you can park at sometimes. At least, that's not what I want to be."

"That's not what you are, Rae. Never. It's just all happening so—"

"Fast? Quick? Like lightning? Trust me, I get that. But I'm also not a slave to my image at school. I think we both know that. So, time to choose which one you want more. Your image or me."

I watched Michael and Allison slide past as Rae kept the door held open. Allison tossed me a wary look, but Michael could have killed me with the one he gave. Rae deserved better than this. She deserved better than me. But if I was the one she wanted, then I had to do my best. Right? I mean, I understood her position. I couldn't keep us in the shadows simply for the sake of some fucking high school bullshit.

So I squared my shoulders and stood tall.

"Fuck 'em, right?"

Rae smiled. "Yes. Fuck 'em. Now let's go before we're late for homeroom."

I reached for her and tugged her into the school. She giggled as she rested against me, her cheek pressed against my arm. We walked through the front foyer of the school together, in front of everyone. For all to see. I strutted my shit. I felt as if I were growing taller with every step I took. I walked down the main hallway before Rae took the lead, showing me where her locker was.

A locker I intended on walking her to every morning.

As she worked the lock, I started looking around. I took stock of the students. The teachers. Hell, even the principal. And while I assumed everyone's eyes would be on me, I didn't see a single soul looking in my direction. Not even in my general direction. I furrowed my brow as I found Roy slobbering all over Marina in a corner. I scanned the room and found the redhead from the party a couple weekends ago pressing herself against one of my other boys. No one had their eyes on me. No one gave a shit who I'd come into school with.

No one except me.

35

RAELYNN

Raelynn One Week Later

"Welcome to Grady's Groceries. May I interest you in a—?"

The man waved his hand in the air. "Just ring me up. I'm in a hurry."

I forced a smile. "Of course, sir."

I scanned the groceries as quickly as I could, then bagged them. Cold items in the blue bags, regular items in the yellow ones. Eggs went down first, then the loaf of bread sat on top. Chips in the same bag. Apple juice in another bag. With the frozen vegetables, ice cream, and pint of milk in the last one.

"That'll be $18.7—"

The man tossed a twenty-dollar bill at me. "Keep the change. I gotta go."

It bounced off my chest and fluttered to the belt as he scooped up his bags. He lumbered away, murmuring to himself as he walked straight out the doors into the pouring rain. I shook my head as I picked up the bill, cashing him out and setting the change aside. I slipped it into the manilla envelope I had at my register for the manager to collect. Extra money for the store without disrupting the balance of the registers at the end of the night.

I sighed. "I really hate this job sometimes."

Grady's Groceries was a small store in town that serviced a very specific group of people in the area. It wasn't a chain. It wasn't some big-box store. But it always had quality, fresh items. And it seemed as if people were always willing to pay for fresh and quality. Of course, there were items like frozen vegetables and things of that nature. However, that didn't stop the all-natural crowd from coming in and making my life a living nightmare.

Is this made with gluten?

Is this made near gluten?

Was someone thinking about gluten when they made this?

"Rae!"

My manager's voice ripped me from my trance. "What's up, Bryan?"

"We need help stocking. You up for a change of scenery? It'll be counted on your paycheck."

I smiled. "You know I'm always up to help."

"Great. Get back to aisle four. Dani's struggling with the lower shelves. Back's acting up again."

"Got it."

I logged out of my register and practically broke into a dead sprint for aisle four. Dani was the resident grandmother. Worked part-time in order to have more money to spoil the eight grandchildren she had. But sometimes she needed a bit of help. And I was more than willing to provide that help if it meant not having to interact with the pompous, arrogant customers that seemed to be out in full force today.

"Hey there, Dani."

She sighed. "Hey, Rae. Sorry for pulling you away."

"Now, you know good and well I don't mind. Whatcha stocking?"

"This damn cake icing. Why is it on the lower shelf? I keep telling Bryan cooking supplies need to be more accessible to people of my age because we're the ones that do most of the baking."

I took the icing from her hand. "And I'll make sure the suggestion is heard."

I crouched down and began unpacking the items while she took a break. I sat on the floor, divvying everything up and secretly wishing I could pop open a container of icing and start eating it. I unloaded one box before Dani scooted another toward me with her foot. Together we got the baking aisle restocked. Took about two hours, but we handled it.

Then it was back to my post and dealing with customers.

"Do you have this, but in blue?"

I paused. "You want a blue ice cream carton?"

"Yes. Everything has to be absolutely perfect for this party I'm throwing. Everything has to match. I like rocky road, but I can't find a rocky road in a blue carton."

"Sure, just give me—"

"Miss?"

I whipped my head around as Miss Blue Ice Cream scoffed. "Yes?"

"Is the bakery going to be making any more cakes? I need a freshly-baked carrot cake for something tonight."

I shook my head. "We stop producing cakes at seven."

"So no more cakes."

"No, ma'am."

"What if I pay for the cake?"

"There isn't anyone to make the cake right now. The bakery's completely shut down."

"What if I wait for a bit?"

I paused. "Waiting won't do you any good. There's no one here to make your cake."

"Well, can you call someone in?"

"To make your cake?"

"Yes. Aren't you listening?"

Miss Blue Ice Cream Spoke up. "I need help. This is melting, and I need you to help me."

I sighed. "Then go put it back so it won't melt. I can be there in a second to help you track down some rocky road in a blue container."

Mrs. Carrot spoke up. "Oh, a blue container? If you like non-dairy products, there's a rocky road in a nice light blue container at the end of the aisle, on the left. It's tucked beside the sherbets."

Were these people fucking serious right now?

Thankfully, Bryan came over and busted up the convention. Which enabled me to check out the three customers that had gathered around my register. I checked them out, moving as quickly as I could while Bryan dealt with the crazy that had been dumped into my lap. He checked them out personally, thank fuck. Before disappearing into his back office to take 'a breather.'

Like he'd put in some hard work for the day or some shit.

"And here I thought I'd find you smiling."

The second I heard Clint's voice, a massive smile did cross my face.

"Just like that one, actually."

I giggled. "What the hell are you doing here?"

He leaned against my kiosk. "Maybe I came to see a gorgeous girl. Or maybe I came to pick up an apple."

"Or maybe you came to distract yourself because your father's back home."

"Maybe you're smarter than you look."

I laughed as he leaned over, kissing me on the cheek. Thankfully, we were tanking into my last hour of work before the store had to close down. Which meant not many more people would come in. I leaned my hip against the register, gazing into Clint's eyes. I enjoyed having him there. He'd already popped in on me a couple of times to say 'hello' and grab something for Cecilia. But he hadn't ever stuck around.

Until now.

I licked my lips. "I take it you have nowhere else to be?"

He winked. "You mean, other than home? Come on, don't you remember? I reorganized my priorities. I'm a brand new man."

I rolled my eyes. "Until your father leaves to go back out of town."

He shrugged, and it made me shake my head. He was relentless in all the best ways. I reached out for his arm, patting it softly before his hand fell on top of mine. He brought my hand to his lips to kiss, sending goosebumps traveling up my arm.

And I watched his eyes follow their trail.

"It's okay, Clint. You can stay as late as you want. I won't tell anyone you hang out at Grady's Groceries in your spare time."

He chuckled. "Bless your heart."

"It needs some blessing. It's been having some inappropriate feelings lately."

He quirked an eyebrow. "Oh? Care to share with a curious ear?"

"That depends. What are you willing to do for them?"

"Oh, I like a good barter."

"You curious enough to do my homework for me?"

He smiled. "Not on your life. But, I can hold you close while you do your homework after your shift."

"And let your wandering hands distract me? Hardly. I'd end up flunking all my classes."

He shrugged. "I don't do my homework and I don't flunk classes."

"Because the teachers don't wanna hold you back and deal with you another year."

"Potato, po-tah-toe."

I snickered. "To answer your question, no. I don't have much homework to do after my shift. I usually get it done during my breaks on nights like this. Why?"

"Well, I was hoping I could sweep you away and steal some alone time with you. You know, if your attention doesn't have to be elsewhere."

"Oh, alone time. That sounds nice."

"I could make it real romantic for you. A shoulder massage. With some nice lotion."

"Can you make that a foot massage? My heels are killing me."

"Rae, I can make it a full body massage, if you want."

He winked at me and my stomach flipped over with desire. My heart skyrocketed to a rate that threatened to burst the blood vessels in my head. I licked my lips, watching his eyes rake over me before a soft chuckle fell from his lips. And while I still had a bit of history reading to do, I could also do with some one-on-one time with Clint.

Especially after this shift.

"Hey, Rae!"

I looked up. "Yes, Bryan?"

"Got a family emergency, I need to leave. Can you lock up the store? I sent Dani home to get some rest. She couldn't get back up on her feet after the incident in aisle four."

Clint quirked an eyebrow. "Incident?"

I nodded. "Yes, sir. I can do that."

"Good. I'll count the registers when I come in. Just wipe down your area, sweep up a bit, and make sure all returned groceries are back on the shelves."

"I hope everything's okay!"

"Me, too!"

I watched my manager zoom out of the grocery store, leaving me and Clint completely alone. I looked over at the clock, then groaned when I saw I still had forty-five minutes.

"So, what's the plan, Stan?"

I giggled. "If we don't get a customer in five minutes, I'll start shutting this place down."

Clint grinned. "Anything I can do to help?"

"You can keep your hands to yourself until we can get out of here."

"And here I thought grocery aisle sex sounded kinky."

"Not with video cameras recording us."

He shrugged. "I mean, I'm down for it."

I scoffed and swatted at him as giggles fell from my lips. And as we continued to talk, no one came in. Not a soul. With forty minutes left in my shift, I felt confident that if I shut things down, we wouldn't lose one single customer.

So I grabbed the paper towels and the cleaner fluid to start cleaning.

36

CLINTON

Despite Rae's protests, I jumped in and helped her. While she wiped down her register or whatever, I grabbed a broom and swept up some of the bigger dirt piles. I rolled the cart of returned groceries over to her, and together we started down the aisles. She handed me things and I placed them back on the shelves. And every once in a while, I stole a kiss for myself. The camera, too. But, mostly for myself.

Rae giggled. "You're gonna get me fired."

I grinned. "I mean, all I hear is more time with you."

"And what am I going to do when I graduate high school and don't have the money to move out on my own like I want?"

"Eh, we'll figure something out."

I stole one last kiss from her before I let her push me away. I chuckled as we continued walking up and down the aisles, putting back everything from all-natural peanut butter to gluten-free snack items. She gave me a kiss on the cheek before she shooed me outside, telling me she had to lock everything down from the inside out.

I headed over to my bike to wait for her.

Nighttime had settled over Riverbend. And in our little side of town, there were more stars in the sky than usual. I stared up at them, my arms crossed over my chest. I found myself discovering more things like this. Like the stars overhead. Or the beauty of a sunkissed horizon. I'd been writing more and more lately. For the first time in over a year, I had to go buy a new notepad. My muse attacked me at all times of the day and night, waking me from a dead sleep and forcing me to write things down so I didn't forget them.

And while I still struggled with this whole thing between Rae and me, I knew it was due to her.

She was my muse.

"You look lost in thought, handsome."

Rae's voice ripped me from my trance and I found her staring at me. Leaning against me. Sliding her arms around me with her lips only inches from mine.

"And what if I am?"

She smirked. "Well, I'd say 'penny for your thoughts,' but I think that price is a bit steep."

My lips puckered. "Oh, you're gonna pay for that one."

"Really? How—ah!"

I smiled as I slapped my hands down against her ass cheeks. The resounding crack made her jump closer to me, and I felt her chest pressing against mine. I captured her lips, swallowing her moans and protests as I massaged her butt. We leaned against my bike, our tongues intertwining, her soft whimpers of frustration turning into moans of pleasure.

I never wanted it to end, either.

"You really need to get a car."

I nuzzled my nose against hers. "A car? What on earth for?"

She kissed my lips softly. "They're much easier to make out in."

I chuckled. "Actually, that's the most convincing argument to buy a car I've ever heard."

"Does that mean you'll buy one?"

"That means I'll think about it. But only if you promise to break it in with me."

"Sounds like a good time."

"Sounds like a good promise."

She giggled before her lips captured mine again. Only this time, she stepped between my legs. Her body molded to me as I cloaked her back with my arms, trying to feel as much of her as I could at once. Her tongue slid across the roof of my mouth and I felt my cock aching for her beyond my jeans. My hands slid from her back to her ass, down her thighs and back again. I gripped her hair and pulled her head back softly. I licked down her pulse point, hearing her gasp softly as my name fell from her lips.

"Clint, oh."

That never ceased to make my heart skip a beat.

I buried my face in her chest. "What kind of trouble should we get into tonight?"

Her hands raked through my hair. "The kind of trouble that continues this saga."

I kissed her skin. "Mm, you had me at 'oh.'"

I hoisted her against my body and threw my leg over the bike. I settled her down against it, feeling her legs lock around me. Her hands clung to my leather jacket, pulling me closely against her. And as we sat in the shade of the trees planted specifically for this little shopping complex, I felt myself give way to her.

"Shit, Rae."

My hands slid up her shirt. I cupped her breasts, teasing her nipples through the padding of her bra. She rolled against me, my bike holding us steady as her tongue explored my mouth religiously. I wrapped my arms around her, running my palms along her bare skin, feeling her shake and shiver as goosebumps poured over her skin. I sucked on her lower lip and she kissed across my cheek. I felt her nibbling on my earlobe, causing me to growl out as my cock jumped with need for her.

Then she pressed her lips against the shell of my ear. "We really should get out of here."

"You don't have to tell me twice, beautiful."

It pained me to feel her slip away. But I knew it was headed toward something more pleasurable. More beautiful. More amazing than I could have ever expected from tonight. I handed her the helmet I'd dug out for her all those weeks ago, then slid my own over my head. I flipped up the visor, then reached out and flipped hers up. She gave me a massive smile as her cheeks flushed, then she inched her way onto the back of my bike. She was getting better at it. More steady, if that made any sense. Usually, she teetered, almost tripping over herself trying to get on.

But she'd gotten the hang of it.

I liked that.

I cranked up the engine. "Ready to get out of here?"

"What was that?"

"I said, are you ready to get out of here?"

Before she could answer, a set of headlights filled the parking lot, causing Rae to curse. They come straight for us, pulling up to my bike, blocking me in between the car and the tree that sat behind us.

Rae clung to me. "Who's that?"

I shook my head. "Probably Roy. But he can piss off. There's nothing to see here."

I slipped my helmet off and got off my bike. I kept my voice raised, hoping that Roy and the goons from school would buzz off and leave us the fuck alone. I hung the helmet on the handlebars, but felt Rae reach out for me. She pulled me back to her, so I wrapped my arm around her waist, trying to comfort her as she sat on the passenger's seat of my bike, pressing closer into me.

She was scared. And I couldn't blame her for it.

"I don't think that's Roy, Clint."

As the car door opened, I squinted my eyes, trying to figure out who the fuck was beaming us down with their high-beam headlights.

"Fucking cars," I murmured.

All at once, I saw the darkened outline of four guys. Two in the front, and two in the back. They leaned against the hood of the car, their silvery outlines looming over us. Once they stepped closer into the light, leaning against the hood of the car, I recognized them. Well, two of them.

From the football field last week.

Shit.

They stood there, looking at us. Like fucking goofballs with their arms crossed over their chests. They tried puffing out their muscles to look bigger, but I swear they were gangly little fucks. Rich bitch boys who didn't have a hope or a prayer in this world of stacking on muscle. And yet, I remembered the fight clearly. All three of those gangly assholes had a mean punch to them. They had been much stronger than they looked, and I'd be a damn fool to assume these other two fuckers would be any different.

"What do you want?"

My voice filled the space between us, but they didn't move. They didn't speak. They just stared at us with dumbass smirks on their faces. Rae pressed closer into me, and I felt her trembling. Shaking with fear. That pissed me off. No one scared my girl. No one rolled up on us and intimidated her like that.

She leaned into my ear. "Let's get out of here, okay? Speed away on your bike?"

I didn't answer her. I didn't want my answer to scare her. While motorcycles were fast, we didn't have time or space to get away from them. I wouldn't even get situated on my bike before they rammed into both of us, pinning us to the tree behind us. And I couldn't put Rae in danger like that. I couldn't let her get hurt again.

Which meant running wasn't an option.

"Please, Clint."

Hearing her beg made me sick to my stomach, but I shook my head. I felt her disappointment as she leaned her head against my shoulder, silently begging me to step down. But there was so much to this interaction she didn't understand. So many ways for her to get hurt that she didn't realize.

And if she had a chance to get hurt, it meant that option wasn't really an option at all.

37

RAELYNN

The more the men came into view, the more of them I saw. They were lean, but tall. Three of them as tall as Clint. Easily. They all had beer cans in their hands and the glossy look in their eyes told me they'd been drinking. Probably all night, up until this point. I felt sick to my stomach. The smiles on their faces were wicked. The palms of their hands dwarfed those regular-sized beer cans, and the way they looked at me was frightening.

Their eyes darted between Clint and me, but they kept resting their gazes on me.

I gasped. "Clint."

He pressed further back into me. "It's gonna be all right, Rae. Just do exactly as I ask."

I wasn't so sure about that, though.

Each of them leaned against the hood of the car, blocking out parts of the high beams that shone against us. And when the blind spots faded from my vision, I found all four of them licking their lips. Staring at me. Raking their eyes up and down the parts of me they could see. I slid off the bike, staying behind Clint. I fisted his leather jacket, drawing him closer as his arm wrapped around behind me. He tapped my waist, trying to comfort me as the boys started laughing to themselves.

Then one of them finally spoke up.

"You look scared."

I narrowed my eyes. "You think?"

Clint squeezed my side, telling me to stop. And for once, I listened. I didn't like the way they were looking at me. I didn't like the way they slowly boxed us in. They all pushed off the hood of the car, stalking toward us. Making their way for us. Eyeing me hotly as Clint tried obscuring their view. Clint stood his ground, despite the fact that I knew we needed to run. He locked eyes with the boy in front, who stood a little over an inch taller than him.

I still felt the other three boys staring me down. Looking at places on my body that made me want to punch them straight in their noses.

I snarled. "Fuck off."

Another boy snickered. "She's got spunk. I like spunk."

The boy staring at Clint grinned. "I hate spunk."

Clint grimaced. "Good thing it isn't up to you either way."

"Oh, yeah? And what makes you think that?"

I giggled bitterly. "Because you don't get to control me."

All four of the boys looked over at me and I clung tightly to Clint. I didn't know what to do. I didn't know what the right move was. Mom taught me to always stand up for myself. But what the hell was I supposed to do in a situation like this? I didn't want to run. I didn't want to abandon Clint. And yet, I knew I was the target. I knew if they got through Clint, I'd be in a hell of a lot of trouble.

I whispered. "What should we do?"

Clint peered over his shoulder. "Stay there and do as I ask."

One of the boys grinned. "An obedient girl. I like that in my women."

I scoffed. "Good thing I'm not your woman, then."

"I think we could change that. I hear you like bad boy dick."

"I guess that takes you out of the running, then."

The boy lunged at me and Clint jumped in the way. He stood toe to toe with him, staring him down as his chest puffed out. The other three guys started laughing, filling the air with the smell of beer. I rested my forehead against Clint's back, feeling him stiffening, tightening, shaking with fury. His fists balled up at his sides and the staredown began, each party waiting for the other to make a move.

Was it possible to stare them down until they sobered up? Until they got back into their car and left?

Where the hell is the patrol car that always comes through?

"Clint," I whispered.

One of the boys chuckled. "Think your girl's calling you."

Clint nodded. "And don't you forget who she belongs to."

"I don't think she belongs to anyone. She's a free-spirited girl, right? The one who ran to your defense?"

"And if I remember correctly, you're the asshole that knocked her down. Hurt her. And mark my words, you'll pay for that."

"Oh, she's got some fluff. She's good."

I felt Clint lunge and I gripped his leather jacket. I pulled him back to me as the boys erupted into laughter. He shrugged me off, whipping around and glaring at me. I glared right back, silently screaming at him, telling him there was no way on fuck's green earth he'd be able to take all four of them in a fight without them dragging me off in the process.

And when he drew in a deep breath, I watched his eyes soften.

"Look at that, boys! He's whipped already."

I heard the drunk assholes making whipping noises as they twirled their hands around in the air. Clint's face flushed with anger and he grew another two inches as fury filled his veins. He whipped back around and I tightened my grip on his leather jacket, trying desperately to keep a hold on this situation. I had my purse with me. It hung off my shoulder. And if I slipped my hand in there, I could press the emergency button on my phone, calling for help before this escalated.

Clint growled. "The four of you need to leave. Now."

Main Boy shook his head. "Eh, that doesn't sit well with me. I mean, what if the little lady's in trouble?"

I snickered. "I'm not. The only people I'd be in trouble with are the four of you."

"But it would be the best kind of trouble."

Clint grinned. "She gets plenty of that with me."

"And from the looks of her curves, there's plenty to go around. Sharing is caring, Clarke."

I wrangled Clint back again, feeling him trying to tug away from me. I slipped out from behind him and pressed my hands into his stomach, getting him to back up. I almost had him backed up, too. Until I felt a pair of hands on my hips. A pair of hands that weren't Clint's.

And he lost his fucking mind.

"What the fuck are you doing, touching my girl?"

"Clint! No!"

He lunged around me, slapping the boy's hands away. I whipped around with wide eyes, watching as Clint went straight for the boy's neck. His three goons wrapped their arms around Clint, dragging him back before tossing him onto the ground. And as I stood there, with a gasp falling from my lips, Main Boy looked straight at me.

"You ready to try a real man?"

Clint shot up from the ground. "You don't speak with her. At all."

"That right, sexy? You don't wanna talk to a man like me?"

I scoffed. "Hardly."

"Even if I know I can throw it down better than your measly little man here can?"

My eyes narrowed. "Sex isn't what I'm after."

The boys laughed at me as they leaned back against their car. Clint got in front of me again, blocking my body from their reach. I turned a little to the side, concealing my hand as it slipped into my purse, silently rummaging around for my phone.

Main Boy grinned. "So, entertain me. What is it you're after?"

I shrugged. "Not you four, that's for sure."

"And what about us do you not like?"

"Other than your overall assholeish nature, your ugly looks, your disgusting demeanors, and your pompous attitudes?"

He shrugged. "Yeah. Sure. Other than those."

I grinned. "I don't like small dicks."

Main Boy lunged off his car and Clint stepped in front of him, toe to toe again, though I knew he was upset with me. I pulled my hand out of my purse quickly, sliding my phone into my back pocket. Then I dropped my purse to the ground, trying to act like I was scared out of my mind to conceal what had just happened.

Just a few more shielded seconds, Clint. Work with me here.

I saw Clint's shoulders stiffen but his hands slowly unclenched. As he backed away from the guy, making his way back for me, I caught his eyes and saw the nervousness growing in them. His eyes darted around in the darkness, looking for a way out. He hugged me close and kissed the top of my head, then moved his lips to my ear.

"I'll pay for this statement later, but keep your fucking mouth shut, Rae."

I had a bad feeling about this. And so did Clint. He was nervous, which made me even more nervous. He turned back around, giving me darkness to stand in. And slowly, I slipped my hand around my back.

Main Boy's voice boomed. "You know what I think?"

Clint sighed. "What do you think, dickweed?"

"I think we've been chatting long enough. I came here for a good time, and I'm not leaving until I get one."

Then, as my finger found the red emergency button, I watched Main Boy rush for Clint.

38

CLINTON

I reached my arms out and fisted the guy's shirt as he came for me. I backed him all the way up to his car as Rae let out a yelp. I had to get these guys away from her. They were predatory, and they announced it well enough with their eyes. My bike was close. Really close. And the key was already in the ignition. I pinned that asshole to the hood of his car to give myself time to think. A well-placed knee to the groin turned his buddies' attention away from Rae and to me.

"Get him, guys."

As they ambushed me, I heard Rae calling out. The crunch of dead grass could be heard, and I hoped she was climbing into that fucking tree, doing her best to get away from these assholes. They ripped me away from the guy I had pinned to the hood of the car, tossing me back to my bike. And as I fell to the concrete, I gazed up at my getaway, hoping with all my might they'd follow me and leave Rae alone.

Piss them off first. They'll follow you then.

"That all you got?" I asked.

I leapt off the ground, poised for a fight as their main guy hunched over, grabbing his balls like a little bitch.

I grinned. "Because if that's all you got, there's no way in hell you'll please a girl like Rae. She needs something a little… thicker."

"Clint! Shut up and come on already!"

Her voice sounded far away, and I hoped that meant she was running. Another guy rushed toward me and I clotheslined him, preparing myself to throw another punch. The fight began and I hit them everywhere I could, making sure not to leave my bike. They kept coming at me with punches. With elbows. With snarky remarks about all the things they'd do to Rae once they got their hands on her.

I wasn't having any of it.

I ran myself into one guy's stomach, picking him up off the ground. I body-slammed him into the hood of the car, then moved just before another one kicked me. I heard the headlight shatter before the lighting dimmed around us. A yelp told me that glass had raked right across someone's skin. I chuckled to myself as I whipped around, lifting my legs to donkey kick the asshole headed for me.

And since I couldn't see Rae, I took that as a good sign.

"You guys really are pathetic!" I grunted. "This is easier than last week!"

"You're gonna die tonight, asshole."

The growling voice told me it was time. I bolted for my bike, praying to any god that might be listening for help in abating Rae's anger. Because I knew she'd be angry at me. Spitfire angry. But I had to get these assholes away from her. I had to keep her safe.

And whatever that took, I was willing to do it.

"Oh, no. You're not getting away. Get in the car, boys! We got ourselves an asshole to run down!"

"Clint!"

Her voice seemed so far away, but that was the point. Give her a chance to run before leading these guys off somewhere else. I threw my leg over my bike, not worrying about my helmet. I cranked up the engine and sped out of the parking lot, hearing my gear shifter groan and flailing my leg to get the kickstand up as I took off.

It worried me when I didn't see that headlight turning toward me in the rearview mirror.

"No!"

Rae's shriek told me everything I needed to know. I whipped around, revving my engine as I raced down the road. I saw the car hopping the curb, blowing past that fucking tree. I saw it racing up the street before the headlight illuminated Rae's form on the side of the road. She was climbing the chain-link fence around the elementary school playground, hopping it before the boys even got out of their fucking car.

I grabbed my helmet off my handlebars and pulled up behind their car, whipping the helmet at their rear windshield and shattering it into a million pieces.

That got their attention.

"You son of a bitch!"

Rae yelled, "Clint!"

"Get him!"

"You're dead tonight, fucker! I just replaced that damn thing!"

I laughed. "Gotta catch me first, assholes!"

Rae cupped her hands over her mouth. "Clint! Don't do this!"

"Get yourself safe, Rae. For fuck's sake, just stop fighting!"

I saw the car back away and turn around. It swerved, showing that the boys were more drunk than before. I turned and raced off, letting Rae's voice fade into the background as we peeled away from the grocery store, weaving in and out of the small parking lots. I didn't want to take this shit to the main roads. I didn't want anyone getting hurt. I just wanted to cause enough ruckus to get someone's attention. Anyone's. A police car driving by. Some innocent bystander who would call 9-1-1. I'd gladly go to jail and do time as the adult I was if it got these drunken, horny bastards away from my girl.

I wasn't sure if I'd ever be able to fix my relationship with Rae, though.

After something like this.

I felt an empty beer can clink against my bike and something wet sprayed my back. The car's engine revved, catching up with me. I throttled it through a parking lot and hopped another curb. My bike went airborne for a second before landing onto a small back road. I heard the car behind me practically falling apart in order to keep up with me. I knew if I looked back, I'd see something hanging off that piece of shit.

I tried looking around for Rae, but it was no use. I circled back to the grocery store but she wasn't near the elementary school or back inside the store. I didn't see her walking along the streets or heading into the gas station. I had no fucking clue where she'd gone, which meant I now had to solve the other issue on my hands.

"I see you!"

The four fucking maniacs chasing me in their rundown car.

The main roads were empty at this time of night. Half past ten, in the middle of the work week. I blazed a trail up the main roads, trying to get away from the goons. I soared through yellow lights and took sharp turns on red lights, hoping and praying to trigger a cop from out of nowhere. But, of course, there were none to be found tonight. Fucking hell, I'd torn through this town and gotten clocked by more cops than anyone else. Yet the one damn night I needed them to clock me, they weren't anywhere in sight.

That's some fucking karma, if I've ever witnessed it.

The closer they got to me, the more panicked I became. Rae was safe, and as long as they were tailing me, I knew she'd stay that way. They were drunk. They'd probably been to some dumbass party of hoes and gangly dickweeds from their high school. But I knew how volatile guys were when drunk. Roy and I had destroyed many lives while drunk. We'd wreaked many hours' worth of havoc with alcohol in our systems. And it seemed that no matter how hard I pushed my bike, they pushed their car just a tad bit harder.

The only way I stayed out of their reach was to take sharp turns.

Because their car couldn't handle them.

We blazed a trail through town before I took a sharp right. I rumbled over some abandoned railroad tracks and blazed into the darkness. A massive stretch of road that didn't have lamps hanging overhead. Nothing but dilapidated houses and abandoned parks where children used to get their kicks before growing up and moving away. I heard the car behind me sputtering as they continuously threw beer cans and bottles at my fucking wheels, trying to get me to career off the damn road. And when that didn't work, they moved over into the other lane in my rearview mirror, approaching me with their windows rolled down.

"Nice bike you got there!"

I peeked over at the guy who had tossed Rae to the ground last week.

"Think I could fuck your girl on it?"

I reached out with my hand and hooked my fingers up his nostrils, pulling at him until he was hanging halfway out of the car, screaming as the driver started swerving, trying to see what was happening. His hand wrapped around my wrist, clinging to me for dear life as he yelled in horror. I chuckled and smiled widely before releasing his nose, shoving him back into the car with my hand.

Then I slammed on the brakes of my bike, whipping a U-turn and kicking up burnt rubber before speeding off in the other direction. And for a while there, the car wasn't even in my rearview mirror. Did I shake them? Were they gone? I had enough time alone to breathe a sigh of relief.

Until I saw a light click on in the corner of my eye.

"Holy shit!"

"You motherfucker!"

I heard the boy behind the wheel of the car screaming as he careened out of the fucking woods. I slid my bike close to the asphalt, twisting away from him as he shot himself across the damn street. It took me a few seconds to get my bike back underneath me before I sped off again, and it was those few precious seconds that enabled them to catch right back up to me. On my tail again, like they had been.

And for the first time in my life, I had no idea what the fuck to do to shake these assholes.

39

RAELYNN

"Clint!"

I watched his bike speed off into the distance with the car behind him. I rushed across the elementary school playground, doing my best to try and figure out where the fuck he was headed. My lungs burned. My legs ached. I clutched my purse, wrapping it around my neck and shoulder before reaching for my phone. I pulled it out to see if anyone was listening.

But all I saw were a bunch of random numbers pressed into my phone.

"Shit," I hissed.

I could have sworn I'd pressed that damn red emergency button. Fucking hell, did I have to screw every little thing up? I kept running, feeling my purse slamming against me as the revving of Clint's engine started coming closer to me.

And as it barreled by the elementary school, I was still half a football field away from the road.

"Clint!" I roared.

I felt my voice growing hoarse. I saw the car rush by just as I got past the school building. I bent over, panting for air as I watched the car full of angry drunken idiots swerve down the road. Were there not any cops out tonight? At all? The hell was that about?

I had to get to Clint.

I fumbled with my phone as I stood up, throwing my head back, trying my hardest to catch my breath. Even for someone who enjoyed P.E. and sports, I still couldn't keep up. I grumbled to myself as I clutched my phone. I looked down, hovering my finger over the red emergency button. The dial-out to 9-1-1. The number that would surely bring people to help out this situation.

But then I heard laughing in the distance. I heard Clint's bike revving before the rickety sounds of the train tracks were heard.

If I called the police, would Clint get in trouble, too?

"I can't get him in trouble for this. It's not his fault," I murmured.

Instead, I dialed Michael's number. Hoping beyond all hope that he'd pick up the phone. I knew he was done with my shit. Done with me and the idiocy surrounding Clint and me. But Michael was the one with the car. Allison hadn't gotten her driver's license yet because of some weird fear of making herself motion sick, so her parents still carted her around.

I put my phone to my ear, listening to it ring as I started jogging toward the road that connected the parking lot of Grady's Groceries and the elementary school.

Michael chuckled, answering the phone. "Hey, Allison and I were just talking about you."

I panted for breath. "Michael. Please. I need your help."

"Wait, what? Rae, what's wrong?"

"Me. And Clint. It—I'm at the—"

"Clint? What the fuck has he done?"

I shook my head. "Nothing. He—he's in trouble and—"

"Why are you out of breath?"

I groaned. "Do you have your car at Allison's?"

He paused. "Uh, yeah?"

I drew in a deep breath. "Please. I need you to come get me. I'm standing outside of the elementary school. We have to go after Clint. It's important."

"And why should I give enough of a damn about him to do something like that?"

"Look, I know you're sick of his shit. And my shit. I know you're sick of me, despite the makeup session we kind of had in the cafeteria. But I need you to come get me. It's a very serious emergency, and explaining it only wastes time."

"You make it sound like he tossed himself off a bridge or something."

I yelled, "Damn it, Michael. I need you right now. My best fucking friend. Please. If you come get me, I'll leave you alone. For good. I won't talk to you. I won't approach you. I won't bother you with Clint shit ever again. Just please, this once, come get me and stop asking questions."

"I don't want that, and you know it."

"Well, you're sure as hell acting like it!"

I heard his bike revving off in the distance. Coming closer, only to fade back. And I could have sworn I heard the skidding of tires. The sound made me sick. So sick that I actually heaved. And when I did, Michael sighed.

"You said you're at the elementary school?"

I sniffled. "Yes."

"Are you crying?"

"Just shut the *fuck* up and get here."

"Fine. I'm on my way. But I'm leaving Allison behind. She doesn't need to get involved with his shit. Just like you shouldn't have."

"Spare me the lecture, please?"

"Stand on the curb so I can spot you. Bye."

I hung up the phone call and stood there like a damn idiot. The sounds faded into nothingness for a few seconds, and it forced tears down my cheeks. I knew the first question Michael would ask the second I got into his car. He'd want to know if I called the police. And if I didn't, he'd chastise me for it. He'd tell me I was turning into Clint, and I'd really risk losing my friend then.

So as I stood there waiting for him, I pressed that little red emergency button on my phone screen.

"9-1-1, what's your emergency?"

"Hi. Yes. I'd like to report an… ambush?"

"An ambush, ma'am?"

I cleared my throat. "Yes. An ambush. My boyfriend came to—"

Boyfriend? Is that what Clint was to me?

The word made me smile.

The operator cleared her throat. "Your boyfriend came where, ma'am?"

I shook my head. "Yes. Sorry. My boyfriend came to see me at work. We were standing in the parking lot after I locked up, and four drunk guys in a car pulled into the parking lot. Started harassing us. Calling us names. Throwing beer bottles and things at us. They were trying t—"

I heard the operator typing in the background as tears rushed to my eyes again.

"They were trying to what, ma'am? Where are you currently?"

I sighed. "I'm in Riverbend, in front of the elementary school beside a place called Grady's Groceries. I don't have any other address other than that. You guys have to hurry. My boyfriend started fighting with these guys so they wouldn't get to me. They were talking about things. Taking advantage of me and all that. He got on his bike and rode off, and a car full of drunk teenagers are following him. He's in a lot of trouble. Please."

"All right, ma'am. I want you to stay calm. About how old do you think the boys are?"

"No more than eighteen. They go to Lincoln High School."

The operator hummed. "Do you know what the car looked like?"

I searched around for Michael's SUV as I racked my brain.

"Uh… it was a low-riding car. Like, not like the usual way a car sits on its tires, if that makes any sense. And it was white. A white, low-riding car with tinted windows. I don't know anything other than that, though. I'm sorry."

"It's fine. It's okay. Just take some deep breaths for me. You're panting pretty hard."

Was I?

Shit, I was.

I drew in some deep breaths. "I don't want my boyfriend to get in trouble. He only fought against them and sped off to get them away from me. They were grabbing for me. There are parking lot cameras at Grady's Groceries. The footage should show—"

The operator cut me off. "It's okay. First we get everyone safe. Then we figure out who's at fault. But, from one woman to another, I believe you. Okay? Just stay where you are."

But just as she said that, Michael's SUV pulled up to the curb.

"I'm sorry, I have to go. Please. Send someone out here. Hurry. I think my boyfriend and those goons have raced across the railroad tracks. And there's a lot of trees and overpasses and things for them to get hurt on."

"Ma'am. Do not go after them. Please, stay on the line with me and wait for—"

I hung up the call and ripped Michael's door open. I climbed in, slamming the door closed as I buckled my seatbelt. I dropped my purse to the floorboard and slipped my phone into his cup holder. Then I looked him straight in his eyes as he waited for an explanation.

I sighed. "I've called the police. But we have to find Clint. He's in a lot of trouble. Serious trouble."

Michael scoffed. "Shouldn't shock you one bit."

"He's in trouble because he saved me from a group of drunk guys who wanted to take me, Michael."

"Take you? What the hell do you mean, ta—"

I leveled him with a stare that told him everything he needed to know. Finally, he pulled away from the curb and whipped a U-turn.

"I take it the revving engines beyond the railroad tracks are them?"

I nodded. "Yes. Please. Thank you."

"And you said you called the police?"

"I did. I told the 9-1-1 operator as much as I could remember. I just hope Clint doesn't get into too much trouble for helping me like that."

Michael paused. "What did he do, exactly?"

I shrugged. "What he always does. Harassed them to get their attention so I could run and hop the chain-link fence of the playground back there."

Michael nodded, but he didn't say anything. And for some reason, I wanted to know his thoughts. I wanted him to talk to me, even if it was in anger.

"Does he know the guys or anything? Or was it just a group of random guys?"

I winced, knowing how he'd react to the answer. "Two of the guys were from the football field fight the other day."

He scoffed. "See, Rae? That's what I'm telling you about this asshole of a dude. He's always in trouble. That's why you never should've gotten involved with him in the first place. You're a good girl. You're not the kind of girl who throws it all away on some dickhead with a nice face."

I gritted my teeth. "I know you're pissed off at me. And rightfully so. And yes, you're also probably right about Clint and this entire scenario. About a lot of things. But he did what he did tonight to protect me. I need you to trust me on that. So spare me the lecture and give it to me some other time. You know, when we figure out whether Clint is dead or not."

"Would do the world some good."

"Michael!"

"I don't like the dude, okay? He's an absolute maniac. Has been our entire high school career. Those comments he made about Allison? Absolutely unacceptable, whether he's screwing my friend or not."

I bit down on the inside of my cheek. "Just fucking drive."

"Fine by me."

40

CLINTON

At least they're far away from Rae.

It was the only thought that filled my head as I sped down the back roads. The further we got away from the railroad tracks, the worse the road conditions got. And suddenly, I understood where that phrase came from: 'The other side of the tracks.'

I'm not ever using that fucking phrase again.

I zoomed by crumbling neighborhoods with broken porch lights and cars propped up on cement blocks. I weaved in and out of abandoned neighborhoods, cursing how those assholes kept up with me. These guys were bad news. They had every intention of doing harm tonight. And with the endless supply of beer bottles and cans being tossed at the wheels of my fucking bike, they were still drinking.

Which meant this would only get worse for me if I couldn't shake them soon.

I whipped a U-turn and headed back for the railroad tracks. I felt my phone vibrating in my pocket, and I knew damn good and well who it was. Rae. Probably calling to see if I'd gotten away yet. Wanting to know if I was fine. If I was hurt. If I needed anything.

Fucking hell, she deserves better than all this.

"We're coming for you!"

"You won't get out of this alive!"

"You're an asswipe, and you'll stay an asswipe until we side-swipe your ass!"

They yelled at me. Taunted me. Actually made me fearful of what was to come. I turned back around, soaring away from the railroad tracks again as the car skidded to a stop behind me. I grinned as I threw it into gear. I felt my bike rumbling underneath me as my speed picked up. Sixty. Seventy. Eighty miles an hour. The wild whipped around me, cradling me and harboring the fugitive I'd become during this entire debacle.

God, if you get me out of this alive, I'll stop fucking around.

I was desperate. Because as I heard that bullshit white car gaining on me, I wondered if I'd ever shake them. If I'd ever get them off my damn tail. If there was anyone on this planet that wasn't in God's good graces, it was me. Well, my entire family. Because let's face it, my father needed to be included in that group. But, if he or she was listening—and he or she believed in mercy—I needed a massive chunk of it right about now.

"Come on," I growled.

As I soared over the Adderscape Bridge, I breathed a sigh of relief. The Riverbend outer city limits ended about a mile up the road. Which meant nothing but clear, straight roads for miles. I looked down at my gas tank and smiled. I still had three-fourths of a tank. And there was no way in hell those idiots would outdrive me in the gas-guzzling low-rider they had. If anything, I could keep traveling from city to city. Heading nothing but north until they ran out of gas or pulled over for some.

So, with that plan in mind, I set my cruise control to eighty-five.

Because even if I'm clocked for speeding, those fuckers will be, too.

I shook my head. "You never should have picked that fight, Clarke."

It never should have happened. The second we hit my bike, we should have been on it and headed somewhere else. I made us sitting ducks with my inability to do anything but devour Rae's body. Rae's presence. Rae's giggles and her curves. By sitting out there in an empty parking lot, I made us vulnerable to attacks. Attacks I was all too familiar with.

I sighed. "You're a fucking idiot."

And truthfully? The last thing I needed right now were more enemies. I had Roy and that asshole ex-posse back at the school. Because I knew damn good and well they weren't friends of mine anymore after my outburst. And while I didn't mind ditching those little bitches for something better, it'd make the rest of my senior year a pile of steaming shit. They'd torture me. Roy would take my place, so to speak, puff out his chest, and target me just to look like the big man on campus.

The question was, would I let him attack me? Or would I retaliate?

And outside of all that, Rae's friends hated me. Allison and Michael. Hell, my own father hated me. The only person right now other than Rae who put up with my presence was Cecilia. And that's only because she had to. My life was fucked, and I knew it. All because of some girl. Because of some night where my mouth started running and some girl started opening up and then my dick slipped and fell between the sweetest pair of legs to ever wrap around me.

Because you love her.

The thought startled me so badly I felt my bike wobbling. The motion snapped me from my trance, and I heard the car of idiots behind me laughing. I turned off the cruise control and swerved off the road, giving myself a second to catch my balance. Catch my breath.

Love?

Had I really fallen for Rae Cleaver?

"Get him, boys!"

I heard car doors open and I pushed off the grass. I got my bike back onto the road and took off, only I wasn't going in the right direction. I didn't care anymore, though. I'd stayed stationary long enough for those assholes to get out of their fucking car. That was something I could capitalize on.

"See you later, dickweeds."

I flew back in the opposite direction, approaching the bridge again. I forced my mind to concentrate, but it still had a tendency to wander. I mean, when the fuck was I going to catch a breath with people? When were the people in my life going to stop beating me up and start enjoying me? All I wanted was for my father to stop being such an asshole and my stepmother to actually give more a shit, instead of stepping in when she thought my father was hitting me a little *too* hard.

When would the school stop giving up on me and start trying to help me?

Gotta start helping yourself, Clarke.

I sighed as I felt the rumbling patches underneath my tires signaling the expanse of the bridge in front of me. I took a look in my rearview mirror, keeping an ear out for the sound of the car. But it was nowhere to be found. I didn't hear the guys yelling. I didn't feel them throwing bottles and cans at me. I even let off the gas, trying to see if I could hear them off in the distance.

There was nothing.

I sighed. "Holy shit, I think I actually lost them."

Relief washed over my body. I shook my head as the rumbling patches gave way to the reddened concrete that signaled bridges in our area. I slowed my pace down, giving my bike a chance to breathe as I drew in the nighttime air through my nose. Everything was silent. Everything felt peaceful. I pulled over on the side of the bridge, turning off my engine as the trees around us shaded me.

"Silence," I whispered.

There was nothing but the sound of the wind rustling the trees. Nothing but the sound of water rushing underneath the bridge. I peeked over the edge, seeing a great expanse of black with small caps of dark blue where the water rushed over smooth rocks at the bottom of the river. I'd completely forgotten this place existed. This small slice of country paradise on the outskirts of one of the biggest cities in the country.

I need to bring Rae here sometime. Have a picnic.

I smiled at the thought. The idea of bringing Rae here and sitting on the bank of the river. Our feet in the water. Our eyes, watching fish swim upstream, trying to fight the current. Our hands, interlaced as we looked out over the nature that surrounded us with full stomachs and a peaceful presence.

I let myself dream about it for a second before my mind took the helm again.

Sitting duck, Clarke.

Adrenaline rushed through my veins again. I cursed myself as I struck my bike's engine back up. It was happening again. Me letting the thought of Rae distract me. I had to keep moving. I had to get home. I had to get back to the school and the grocery store and see if Rae was all right. I needed to go by her house to make sure she'd gotten home. And if she wasn't home, I had to go out on a search for—

"Look who's the sucker now!"

My head whipped around as the blaring headlight of the car filled my vision. Their horn blared over the sound of their disgusting laughter. I felt a glass beer bottle slam directly between my eyes. And as my head fell back, the sound of screeching tires filled my ears. The smell of burning rubber wafted underneath my nostrils. I heard metal crunching against metal, alerting me to the imminent threat.

Get off the bike. Get off your fucking bike.

I moved my leg just before it got pinned. I lunged for the hood of the car, trying my best to avoid what was happening. I heard my bike slam against the metal railing of the bridge before the car backed up. I took off running, leaving my bike behind, darting for the trees. They were thick around these parts. No way in hell that car could navigate woods like that without being totaled.

But the throbbing in my forehead was too great.

"Geromino!"

It was the last thing I heard before I felt a searing pain waft up my side. I stumbled off my feet, hearing the laughter from those boys fill my ears. The car slammed into my side, shoving me toward the metal railing. And as I lost my balance, I felt myself teetering over the edge. Flailing my arms. Crying out for help. With tears threatening to burst from my eyes as the sky quickly came into view.

Before fading away into nothingness as my body slammed into the river.

41

RAELYNN

Michael white-knuckled his steering wheel. "Do you have any idea where the fuck they are?"

I shook my head. "No. Just keep driving."

"For all we know, he's back home. Safe and sound. While we're out here—"

"Just drive, damn it!"

I slid to the edge of the seat as Michael put on his high beams. We'd only just crossed the railroad tracks, and I already saw burnout marks on the asphalt of the road. There were patches of grass that had one-tire and two-tire streaks in them. I had Michael pull over on the side of the road. I hopped out and started looking around. I ran to the bridge, fearful that the worst had happened. I bent over the edge, looking for his bike. Looking for him. Looking for any signs of wreckage.

To my relief, there was none.

"Ready to keep going?"

I hopped back into his car. "Yes. Sorry. Thank you for stopping."

"Not a problem. Didn't think I'd actually see tire tracks out here."

"Do you believe me now?"

And when I shot him a look, all he did was purse his lips.

"How far out do you think they drove?"

I shrugged. "I figured we'd follow the tire tracks until they stop."

"Fine by me."

Every half-mile, we came upon them. Some of the tire tracks led into abandoned neighborhoods I'd only heard rumors about. But I kept my focus, not wanting to get off track. We had to find Clint before these guys did. Otherwise, he'd be in a lot of trouble.

Michael sighed. "You know the police won't find us all the way out here."

I nodded. "I know. If Clint and those boys are back there, they'll find them. Which is why we have to search back here. If there's any sign of them, I'll have to call 9-1-1 and update them. Or something."

"Yeah. Or something."

I ignored his remark. I was growing tired of Michael's attitude anyway. I mean, I wasn't pissed off at the fact that he wanted to fuck around with my best friend. The girl I'd known since elementary school. If anything, that should have pissed someone like me off. But it didn't. Because I wanted their happiness.

Why didn't they want mine?

Michael throttled it out of the neighborhood. "We're almost to the city limits."

I paused. "Adderscape Bridge?"

"That's the one, I think."

"Head there."

"Why?"

Worry filled my gut. "Please, just head there. I just… want to make sure."

"Whatever you say, Juliet."

I rolled my eyes at his comment as he blazed a trail down the road. There was no one back here. No lights. No animals. No people. No police. If Clint had raced himself into this territory, he didn't have any help at all. No hope of ever having someone come upon him to help. That was why I wanted to check every inch of this back road. Especially if the tire tracks were still fresh.

"How much further?"

Michael shrugged. "Two, three miles?"

"Can you go faster?"

"Just because Clint wants to break the sound barrier for you doesn't mean I do."

I scoffed. "You know what? Go ahead and stay angry with me. I don't care anymore."

"You sound more and more like him every day."

"I'm sorry that you don't like the fact that I'm dating some guy that punched you in the face. I'm sorry that you think he's an asshole. But when you take into account the fact that his father literally throws him around the house on a daily basis, and you take into account the fact that I should be pissed off that you're in love with my best friend, you don't have a leg to stand on."

"And why's that?"

"Because as Allison's girl, I should be pissed off that you want to screw with her. Fuck her. Or do whatever it is you want to do with her. But I'm not. I want you two to be happy together. I want her to see how you feel about her because I think you two would be great together. Because you're alike. Because you're similar. Because your lives mesh. Just like mine and Clint's do. So, if you expect me to be okay with the fact that you're slowly but surely macking on my best friend, get your fucking act together and suck it the hell up."

Michael put the pedal to the metal as we careened around the corner. The last turn before the straightaway over the bridge. His high beams pointed straight ahead, and I saw fresh tire tracks on the bridge.

As well as Clint's motorcycle crunched against the railing.

"Michael, stop!" I shrieked in his car. My voice filled the space around us as he came to a grinding halt. I ripped my seatbelt off and slammed out of the car, rushing toward the edge of the bridge. My heart leapt into my throat. Tears burned the backs of my eyes. I stumbled over to his bike, taking in the broken rearview mirror and the bent handlebar.

But, all things considered, it looked intact.

"Clint!"

My voice echoed off the trees and into the darkness of the water below. The metal barrier was bent. Fractured. Bowed, in some places. Then I saw the tire tracks right in front of the bike.

"They were here, Michael! They were here!"

Michael jogged up to me. "I'm checking the woods. Call the police."

"Michael, what if he's—"

"Just do as I'm telling you to do, Rae!"

I swallowed hard as I watched Michael rush for the woods. He darted into the trees before I turned my eyes back down toward the water. I didn't want to approach the edge. Flashes of the nightmare I always had before school came rushing back to me. My arms flailing as I fell over the edge. Darkness overcoming me just before I woke up. The smell of smoke. Of burnt rubber, singeing my nostril hairs.

Only this time, I wasn't sure if the smell was phantom, or real.

"Clint!"

My voice cracked before it gave out. I threw myself over the railing, gazing down into the darkened expanse below. I looked up at the sky, the starry sky that always permeated my worst nightmare. And as my eyes fell back down to the water, my stomach flipped over on itself.

A nightmare come true.

"Clint! Are you down there?"

My pathetic voice did nothing but hiss as I cupped my hands over my mouth. I heard Michael running around in the woods, calling out for Clint in the distance. Tears rushed down my cheeks. My hands shook. They gripped the edge with all their might, and I didn't know what to do. I knew he was down there. Had he been washed away by the current? His dead, lifeless body, floating down river until his jacket snagged onto something?

I heard Michael trotting up to me. "He's not in the woods. And if he is, he's not in a position to call out for me. I don't hear a car anywhere, either. Those guys must've buzzed off."

Yeah. After they ran him off the road.

"Did you call the police?"

Holy shit. My phone. The light on my phone.

I ripped my phone out of my pocket and turned on the flashlight. I heard Michael scoff as he shook his head, but his eyes fell over the railing, too. Down into the deep, dark abyss of the raging river. I turned the flashlight on my phone up as bright as I could get it, then shined it down onto the water.

Michael sighed. "It's at least a twenty-foot drop."

"You think that's enough to kill him?"

He paused. "I don't really know, Rae."

I flashed my light against the water as Michael stepped off to the side. I heard him talking into his phone. Saying something about 'a prior call' and 'needing an ambulance.' His voice faded away after that, though. Because the second my light fell onto Clint's body on the side of the river, my voice reached another fucking planet with the octave it leapt into.

"He's down there!"

I took off running, only for an arm to wrap around my waist. I felt Michael pulling me into him as he continued talking on his phone, trying to give directions to whoever the fuck was on the other end of the line. I heard him talking about tire tracks, and a car of guys. A bike on the bridge and a body in the river. I cried out for Clint, raking my nails against Michael's bare skin. But, despite the pain I knew he was in, he didn't release his grip.

"Rae, you can't go down there. It isn't—Rae!"

I growled. "Let me go."

"Not on your fucking life. I'm not losing you, too."

"He's not dead! Don't say shit like that!"

"The bank is too steep. You'll hurt yourself traversing it at night. The police are a few minutes out. When they get here—"

My nostrils flared. "Let—me—go, you asshole!"

I struggled against him as I heard his phone drop to the pavement. He wrapped both arms around me, hoisting me off my feet. I cried out for Clint as my voice left me completely. Tears rushed down my cheeks as I tried prying Michael's arms from around my waist. He carried me back to the car, away from the bike. Away from the bridge. Away from Clint's body lying on the edge of the riverbank.

"Clint!" I called breathlessly.

"Come on, Rae. Let's get in the car. This is a crime scene. The police are only a few minutes out."

"No, Clint. Please. Don't do this to me, please."

"I'm sorry, Rae. I'm so, so sorry."

Michael set me down onto my feet and pinned me against his car. I bashed my head against the glass, only to feel his hand wrap around it. I sobbed out into the night, gazing up at a nighttime sky I'd come to hate as images of my recurring nightmare continued to bombard me. The squealing of tires. The crunching of metal. That dumbass smell of burnt rubber that still lingered in the fucking air.

I drew in a shuddering breath. "It's my nightmare come true."

And when Michael didn't say anything, I knew he'd been thinking exactly that.

How could this have happened? Things were finally going smoothly. Things were finally going well for me and him. I knew what I wanted. I knew what I needed. I knew what I wanted to do with my life and who I wanted to do it with. I'd found someone who got me. Who understood me. A guy who made me feel on top of the world, and absolutely gorgeous in his arms. I found someone who didn't only leave his judgment of my life at the door, but he literally understood my life. Understood the judgment that came with my life. I finally had everything I could have ever asked for.

Him.

And now, I felt it all slipping through my fingertips.

Michael kept me pinned. "Do you want me to call Allison?"

I shook my head, unable to speak.

"Do you want to get out of here?"

I shook my head harder, trying to give my voice a few minutes to return.

"Do you want to talk about it?"

My eyes whipped open as tears streamed down my face. I glared at Michael, hating him for everything he was suggesting. Oh, he wanted to be here now? After being an absolute shitbag for the past couple of weeks? I could have spat in his face. I could have slapped him right across that dumbass, concerned little furrowed brow of his.

But I settled for shaking my head as I leveled him with a DEFCON-5 stare.

"Fair enough. I deserve that."

I nodded curtly, trying my hardest not to say anything. Trying my best to save my voice so I could keep calling out for Clint. I had to wake him up. As long as Michael was here, he wouldn't let me down that bank. Yelling was all I had to get him to wake the fuck up and get back here.

Because he couldn't leave me. Not now.

Not when I finally had all I wanted.

42

CLINTON

I felt my head pounding. I felt disoriented. For some reason, I felt water rushing over my legs. And I had no idea why. I sniffed the air, groaning as my head pounded with frustration. I felt something sharp underneath my side, prompting me to move. So many things bombarded my senses as I slowly came out of it.

Came out of what, though?

I swallowed hard, tasting the metallic essence of blood. I smelled smoke. And oil. And dirt. Why did I smell oil? What was going on?

I thought people smelled toast before they had strokes, or some shit.

I tried opening my eyes, but I couldn't. I tried rolling over, but it was all for nothing. It was like this massive disconnect with my soul and my body was taking place. Like that paralyzing sleep shit. I heard bats fluttering around me. Or a winged animal of some sort. Water dripped in the distance and continued rushing over my legs.

I started shivering from the cold, which only exacerbated the pain in my back.

Fuck.

I swallowed again, but the reflex was daunting. It made my nose hurt, of all things. I didn't know what the fuck that was about, either. Wind kicked up around me, causing me to shiver and hurt in places I hadn't realized. Like my nose again. My shoulder. My ankle.

Why the hell did I hurt in all these random places?

"Clint!"

I could have sworn I heard my name off in the distance, called in panic. I heard it again. And again. I heard it again before something popped, then the sound went away. I was probably imagining it. Dreaming it, because of the pain I was in. Holy shit, I'd never experienced pain like this before. The way my body felt was nothing compared to some of the beatings I'd taken from my father over the years. I drew in a deep breath, reeling from the pain in my nose and forcing myself to lick my lips.

The taste of blood was strong.

Fuck me, this hurts.

Even though I still couldn't open my eyes, I tried getting my bearings. I heard a fight going on in the distance. Scuffling of feet, and all that. I tried opening my eyes to figure out what was going on. Was someone in trouble? Did they need something?

I heard a whisper in the wind that sounded like my name, and I thought I might be losing it.

Pull yourself together. Where the fuck are you?

It was a good question. One I wasn't sure how to answer. I mean, I was obviously on the edge of a water source. Rushing water. A brook? Or a river? I mean, the water came all the way up to my hips. My feet were actually floating in it. So a deep river. I focused on the sounds around me, hoping anything would trigger a flood of memories. Something. Anything. A flash of a picture in order to give me context to the hellhole I'd woken up in.

I let my mind do the seeing for me.

There's wind rustling in leaves. Lots of trees. I'm in a forest, possibly. And it's cold. So there's no sun. A river, so there's water. Which means the droplets of water are coming from… an overhang? A tree?

A bridge.

Images bombarded my mind as the word 'bridge' soared through my mind. The car. My bike, crunched against a metal railing. A bridge, tumbling out of view. The sky above my head as my hands reached out for it. All of them still images. All of them, bringing into focus moving memories and images.

Rae.

"Clinton Clarke! Are you down there?"

"I see him! Clint!"

"Clinton!"

Fucking hell, I hate being called by my full name.

Just as quickly as the pictures started, they stopped, taking with them the moving images as I tried piecing together my night. The fuck was my brain doing? Why was it struggling like this so badly? I tried opening my eyes again as a light quickly illuminated my face. I felt the quick warmth and saw the light behind my eyelids before it disappeared. I heard people screaming out my name. I heard footsteps along something above me.

The bridge. That's the damn bridge.

That word started up another barrage of still images. A grocery store. My hand reaching out to push open the door. A girl, standing behind the register. With thick, beautiful dark hair and brooding brown eyes. I felt my heart leap in my chest. I felt my cold legs warming at the snippets of memories. I saw myself leaning against the counter, watching her smile and quirk an eyebrow at me. Feeling my eyes slowly inch down her body, taking in her toned curves.

Rae.

A pain ricocheted through my head and I groaned audibly. The first sound I'd forced my throat to make since I woke up. I tried drawing in a deep breath again, but the pain was too much. I stopped it midway, trying to open my jaw. Trying to part my lips. Trying anything to get more air into my lungs.

I couldn't open my jaw.

I'm gonna die here.

"Clint!"

"We're coming down for you. Stay put."

"Clinton Clarke! Can you hear us!?"

Their voices drifted away as my mind ripped me back into memories. The pain in my head was excruciating, and it seemed as if my body was hellbent on torturing me. The images began to move. Snippets of memories slowly became chunks of time. I felt Rae's lips against mine. The warmth and wetness of her tongue pressing against my own. My hands twitched, moving at the phantom feel of her ass cheeks in my palms. What I wouldn't give to be next to her. What I wouldn't give to feel her pressed against me, ridding me of my pain and warming me as this water threatened to drag me into the deep.

Into the cold, dark depths of its deadly stare.

I heard footsteps off in the distance. I wanted to cry out for them, but I couldn't. My mind kept interrupting my need to survive. It kept bombarding me with memories I no longer wanted. Because it wasn't thoughts of Rae any longer. I saw snippets of that car. Those headlights. Those assholes, and everything they'd said to Rae. What their eyes insinuated. What the licking of their lips foreshadowed. I felt anger blooming in my chest and rage coursing through my veins. A searing pain unlike anything I'd ever experienced trickled all the way down to my damn toes.

No one hurts Rae. Not on my watch.

Then it happened. The entire replay behind my eyelids. I saw myself riding my bike. I heard the screeching of those tires and the laughing of the boys behind me. My mind replayed it all. From the first time I rumbled over the railroad tracks to the neighborhoods we'd zoomed in and out of. The entire world fell silent to my ears as my mind took me down that dangerous path. Took me down memory lane, where I even remembered the plan I'd come up with.

Cruise out of town until they run out of gas.

It had been the perfect plan. Run them out of town. Get them away from Rae. And once they puttered over to the side of the road, speed off into the night. It was foolproof. It was perfection. So, how the hell did I fuck it up?

Because you're always a fuck-up, Clarke.

A fuck-up, Clarke.

A fuck-up, Clarke.

My voice morphed into my father's, and my mind held me hostage. I replayed the first time my father ever hit me. It was four months after he and my mother split up. We got into a fight because I wanted her to read me a bedtime story over the phone, like she used to read to me when she was still here. My father got angry with me. He thought I was accusing him of shitty stories. When really, all I wanted was my mother.

A small boy who wanted nothing but the comfort of his mother.

"Your mother's gone. She chose pills over us. So get used to it, or do without your stories."

Then he popped me on the side of the head.

A whimper bubbled up my throat. I begged my mind not to do

this. I fought with myself, trying to stop the reel playing out in my head. But it was no use. My mind had fully run away with me, and there was nothing I could do to stop it.

Hell, I couldn't even move. The fuck made me think I could control my own mind?

I'm dying. This is what it's like right before someone dies.

My mind replayed the last time I'd ever heard my mother's voice. It was two years after she'd left, and she called me on a whim. On my birthday. I remember crying into the phone, I was so happy to hear from her. An eleven-year-old kid, with his first-ever black eye from his father. That had been my father's birthday present to me. A black eye, because I wanted a chocolate birthday cake instead of a strawberry one.

"Hi, Mommy. When are you coming home? Please come home. Please come get me."

"Oh, honey. I'm gonna be coming soon, okay?"

I remember her slurred words. How they seemed like the most amazing thing at the time, until I grew older. Until I realized she'd called me in the middle of one of her pill highs. Probably out of guilt for abandoning us.

"Please, Mommy. Dad hits me. I just wanna be with you. Why can't I be with you?"

"Oh, honey. Your father knows what's best, okay?"

"No, he doesn't. I know why you left, okay? I know it's because he wanted you to live this life you didn't wanna live. Mom, just come get me, okay? Please?"

"That's enough, boy. Give me that phone."

So much truth for an eleven-year-old boy. And yet, it was true. After dealing with my father's beatings every time I didn't act the way he wanted me to, I knew why my mother left us. Why she started downing pills until she had the courage to leave. Her post-partum depression got the best of her after having me, and instead of Dad being supportive, he ignored her. Told her to suck it up. Forced her to continuously go out to parties and get dressed up and accompany him on trips and continue to please him and be his trophy wife because that was what he expected.

Despite my mother's suffering.

The pills were to find the courage to leave, weren't they, Mom?

It's the only question I'd ask her. If I ever saw my mother face to face again, it was the only thing I wanted to know. Because deep down, I knew that was the reason she started popping them. Why she let them take over her world. Why she let them ease down her throat.

It was so she could ease out of this life and go on to the next.

But why couldn't you take me with you?

My mind played one last reel in my head. One reel that made me feel more alone and more empty than ever before. It was the last time I ever heard from my mother. A card, in the mail. A card my father was reluctant to give me. It was my fourteenth birthday, and it got delivered to the house without a return address. Dad tossed it to me, grumbling something about his 'good for nothing ex.' And as I opened it with trembling hands, I found myself repeating the words.

Because I'd damn near memorized that letter.

Clint,

You're fourteen today, and I can't believe how much time has passed. I think about you every day, wondering if I made the right decision for you. And I guess I'll never know. But I want you to have something. It's coming in the mail for you in a few days. I saved up a lot of money for it, so I hope you like it.

I love you. Never forget that, no matter what.

- *Mom*

Two days later, a leather jacket arrived in the mail. Much too big for me at the time, but it was there. It arrived while my father was on a business trip. Probably the only reason it had gotten to me in the first place. Hell, my father paid me so little attention once I became a teenager that he didn't question the jacket at all until almost a year later.

Just before I turned fifteen.

And now, my fucking leather jacket is getting wet.

Sounds meshed in my mind. I felt the headlights in my face again. I saw light beyond my eyelids. The smell of smoke became too much and the cry of Rae's voice in my ear made me sick to my stomach. I heard those boys laughing. I heard the tires screeching. I heard the crunch of metal as my body jumped. Twitched. Shooting pain up and down my arms and legs before my eyes slowly opened, for the first time since I'd come to.

And I was staring up at that bullshit sky.

My jaw unlocked and I drew in lungfuls of air. My eyes darted around as my body slowly came to life, with my toes wiggling in my boots. I turned my head enough to take in the bank I was lying on. And yes, I was sprawled out on the river's edge. I centered my head again, with the edge of the bridge in view. Holy shit, I'd tumbled over the edge. Dropped at least twenty fucking feet down to this water.

How the fuck had I not ended up in the river?

Flashes of that came back, too. How I got off my bike. How I started running for the woods. How that damn car literally attempted to pin me to the metal railing.

Holy shit, those assholes had actually tried to kill me.

I need to call the cops.

"Clint!"

"Clinton!"

"Clinton Clarke!"

For some reason, I thought I heard Rae's voice. Among the foreign voices that somehow knew my name, I could have sworn I heard hers. But that wasn't possible. If this was the river-bridge combination I thought it was, I was damn near twenty miles away from her place of work. Where this shitshow kicked off.

She wouldn't have come that far down this road to find me.

Right?

I wondered what condition my bike was in. Fucking hell, it was probably totaled. Which Dad wouldn't be happy about. I'd get yet another beating for that shit before his guilt prompted him to buy me a newer one. A nicer one. That was how shit worked with Dad. He'd beat me, then feel guilty, then I'd wake up one morning to a nice-ass gift. And even then, it was only sometimes.

Only sometimes, he felt guilty for beating his son up.

I licked my lips again, tasting copper against my skin. I grimaced as the pain in my body slowly faded into the background. I felt myself growing used to it. Numb to the pain, like I'd become numb to my father. Numb to my home. Numb to the absence of my mother. Numb to the anger I always felt. Numb to the insecurities I kept buried deep in the pit of my soul.

"Clint!"

I tried bending my arms, but it was no use. I tried using my legs, but to no avail. Moving hurt too much. And part of me wanted this river to sweep me away and carry me off to somewhere else. Another place. Another time. A place where my mother existed and not my father. A place where school existed, but not Roy and those assholes. A place where my bike existed, but not the car chasing me.

A place where Rae existed, without her bullshit life and friends. *Rae.*

I closed my eyes, allowing her smell to wash over me. Allowing the feeling of her body pressed against mine to draw me back under. If this was it, dying with her memory on the tip of my brain was a nice way to go out. I felt myself accepting my death. Accepting how cold my body was growing. And while my father would surely call me a 'cop-out pussy' at my own damn funeral, it didn't matter.

So long as I had memories of Rae to keep me company.

I sighed as my jaw snapped shut again. Like my body had released itself, only to lock back up because it was easier to simply shut down. And all the while, I thought about how strange this was. How worried I'd been for Rae's safety. How worried I'd been that her friends wouldn't like me. How worried I'd been about some dumbass reputation being destroyed because she wanted to walk into school holding fucking hands.

None of that mattered anymore.

Because all that worrying had been for nothing, when this was how things were going to end.

I love you, Rae. And I hope you know that.

And as I felt myself slipping into the cold, dark expanse of the river, I could have sworn I heard Rae's voice ring out in the depths of my ears.

"Don't you die on me, Clinton Clarke!"

PROMISE ME

DIAMOND IN THE ROUGH 2

1

———

RAELYNN

"Rae, stop!"

I growled at him. "For the love of fuck, you'll let me go. Even if it kills me."

My phone stumbled out of my hand as I bit down into Michael's arm. But he released me. And I threw myself toward the edge of the bridge again. I felt him rushing for me, desperate to pull me back as I gazed over the twenty-foot drop. Sirens finally sounded in the distance. I flashed my light down there, catching yet another glimpse of where Clint was.

After slipping away from Michael's attempt to block me against the metal railing, I rushed for the tree line.

"Rae, are you thick-headed? You're going to get yourself killed!"

"I'm not leaving him down there by himself, Michael! Get over it or go home if you don't like it. I'll have an officer take me home."

I tripped over tree roots I couldn't see and forced myself to slow down. It was a very long drop to the river. A drop that would easily put me in Clint's position if I wasn't careful. But I knew he was alive. He had to be alive. Because no God in this universe was as cruel as that. I refused to believe that.

"I'm coming for you, Clint. Just hang on."

Sirens wailed as they rushed up the road. It felt like they were an eternity away. I heard the sirens, but I didn't see their head-lights. And I wondered how much longer until they actually got here. I pointed the flashlight on my camera down toward the ground. I heard Michael cursing my existence as I grabbed on to trees.

They inched me down, centimeter by centimeter, until I slipped.

"Rae!"

"Shit!"

I tumbled into a tree that caught me and I almost lost my phone. I lay against the tree, catching it as the steep ravine turned into damn-near the straightest drop I'd ever seen. Vines hung from the trees, dangling above the ground. And while I considered taking the chance, none of them dropped all the way to the river's bank.

Where Clint was sprawled out.

I groaned. "Come on, Rae. Think."

"Rae! Can you hear me?"

Michael's voice echoed off the trees and I rolled my eyes.

"Unfortunately!"

"Quit being a smartass and stay there. If you move and that tree gives—"

"Didn't I tell you to go home if you couldn't stop ordering me around?"

"Maybe I give too much of a shit to let my best friend kill herself over—"

The sirens swallowed his voice and I was thankful for it. Because I was damn near ready to toss *him* over the bridge's railing. I placed my phone inside my bra, with the flashlight facing outward. With the angle I was sitting at, it meant I had a clear shot of what the downslope had for me to cling to. Some rocks. A bunch of massive tree roots. If I was careful, I could still get down there.

So I shimmied down the tree and hung on tight.

"Damn it, Rae!"

I blocked out Michael's yelling as the sirens grew closer.

"Don't make me come down there after you!"

I rolled my eyes as I slipped over the edge, placing my foot on the first rock.

"Rae, Allison is going to kill you!"

"Shut! The fuck! Up!"

I heard Michael slam his hands against the metal guardrail as headlights slowly filtered through the trees, giving me more light to work with. I touched down on the first rock and let go of the tree, digging my nails into the dirt. I reached my foot out for the first tree root I saw and caught it, slipping my foot inside it.

And just as I stepped off the rock, the tree root moved.

"Ah!"

"Rae!"

I dug my hands into the dirt, feeling my fingernails scrape across rocks. I clung to the side of the earth, looking down at the fifteen-foot drop below me. I wasn't even halfway down, and already I was struggling.

He needs you, Rae. Don't force him to be alone like he's been all his life.

I panted. "I'm coming for you, Clint. Just hang on."

With some careful maneuvering, and lots of dirt caked under my fingernails, I finally hit the halfway point. If I dropped, it wouldn't kill me. But, it would hurt. I closed my eyes and breathed, allowing the rushing water to fill my ears. I plucked my phone out of my bra and shone it down, watching as the headlights through the trees poured light down onto us.

"They're here! They're here, Rae! Stop moving!"

I wanted to shove a damn sock down Michael's throat.

When I flashed my light down against the river, what I saw horrified me. The water was rising. The river rushed harder. And I saw Clint's legs floating. If I didn't hurry up, he'd be pulled away by the current. Swept away, without a trace.

And I couldn't let that happen.

I slipped my phone back into my bra and slowly made my way down. I slipped and yelped. I ripped my nails off my fingers as I clung to the side of the earth. Trees groaned as I stepped on their roots, making a staircase for myself. And just as I hit the last rock I needed, I drew in a deep breath.

"Clint, can you hear me?"

The sound of the rushing water grew behind me as I touched down onto the bank. My feet sank immediately into the mud. The silt. The thick of it all. Making it even harder to get to Clint. I lost a shoe prying my foot out of that shit. I heard tires squealing on the bridge as the smell of burnt rubber wafted up my nose.

Reminding me of that disgusting dream I hoped to never have again.

"Clint! Can you hear me?"

I kept repeating the phrase as I made my way for him. As his body kept rising. As his legs kept floating. I saw his hips leave the ground. Then his lower back. I saw his body tilted in the direction of the current, and I was still a few feet away from him.

"Clint!"

A wave came out of nowhere, jostling his body. And before I knew it, he sank underneath the river. I threw myself at him, reaching out for him as best as I could. But it was no use. His body swept itself away, dragged with the current as the water levels kept rising. Higher and higher, like some devil from below torturing me before he killed me, too.

"Clint! No!"

I sprinted as quickly as I could. It felt like I ran above the quicksand silt as my hand reached out for him. His leather jacket trailed behind him, fluttering on top of the water. And with one last lunge, I felt the fabric against my fingers. I clutched it, tugging as hard as I could. Tears rushed down my cheeks as my feet sank ankle-high into the silt and stuck, trapping me as the river rushed with a black fury.

I wouldn't let it take me tonight, though.

Because it wasn't allowed to have Clint.

"Come on. For fuck's sake."

I groaned and grunted as more sirens approached. As more tires squealed. As Michael continued to yell and scream at me. I got Clint above the surface of the water and pulled him up the embankment, holding on to him for dear life. I reached up for a tree root, tugging on it as a tree fell over the edge of the river. I screamed as it landed just beside me. Finally giving up because of the water erosion against its roots.

But it gave me something to cling to. Something to wrap my arm around as I held Clint against me.

I drew in a shaking breath. "Just hang on, okay? Help is here."

I kept pulling on the tree, getting us higher and higher. There was a small perch. A small indent in the side of the earth that provided the dream of relief. My arm cried out for mercy. It shook with a need for rest. But I wouldn't let my body give up now. I slid my arm up the tree, hanging on to Clint as I slowly made my way for that indented earth.

And when my back finally sat against it, I breathed a sigh of relief.

Finally, a patch of dirt that didn't try to swallow us whole.

"Come on. On your back. Let's go."

I rolled Clint off me and slid him to the ground. I put him on his back, gazing down into his face. The flashlight from my phone poking out of my bra gave me a hard glimpse at what he looked like. And it was hard to take in.

"Clint, can you hear me?"

I tapped his face softly, but I stopped soon after. His nose was broken. There was blood all over his cheeks and pooling in his mouth from the gash in his forehead. I reached out and checked his pulse. It was weak, but there. And as my eyes continued to roam over his body, I saw his shoulder was dislocated.

"Clint, please. You have to wake up for me, okay?"

I couldn't get over the blood. How much there was. How dark it looked against his skin. I didn't know where the hell it was all coming from and I felt panic grip my chest. I tapped his neck. I placed my hand over his heart. It seemed to be beating slower and slower. Like he was slowly fading away from me.

My tears dripped against his face. "Clint, please. You can't do this to me, okay?"

Memories flooded back. The first time he sat down next to me. The first time we kissed. That night in his room, where he stripped me of my clothes and made me feel things no other boy had. I remembered waking up to him in the middle of the night. Feeling his body wrapped around mine. And the only regret I had was that I hadn't stayed that first night. My only regret out of anything was sneaking out that first night and not cherishing the time we did have together.

"Clint, please!"

My shrieking voice echoed off the trees. Off the water. Off the caverns underneath the bridge. I heard people crying out my name. Telling me to stay put. But I didn't give them the time of day. I placed my forehead against Clint's chest, no longer feeling his heartbeat. No longer feeling life pumping through his veins. And as I sobbed against his chest, I lay down next to him.

"No, please. Clint."

I gripped his shirt. I cried until I heaved. My fingers slid down his arm, checking his pulse at his wrist. There was nothing. No beating. No rushing. No blood pumping through his veins. He felt cold as night. As cold as that fucking water that had almost whisked him away.

"You're a fighter, Clint. Fight for this. Fight for your life."

My words were nothing but a whisper in the wind. I kept repeating them, over and over. Hoping beyond all hope that he heard me. In the distance, I heard people coming down the ravine, headed for us as my sobs filled the space around us. The words kept tumbling from my lips like a prayer, reaching out to any God that was willing to look past my indiscretions and fulfill my only wish. I curled up next to his body. His dead, lifeless body. I clutched his chest, unable to make any sounds as my grief swallowed my voice whole.

Until...

"Holy shit."

The gasp startled me so badly I yelped. I shot up from Clint's side, gazing down into his eyes. Holy fuck, his eyes were open. Holy fuck, he was talking!

"Clint! Clint. Clint. Can you hear me, baby? Clint?"

"R-Rae?"

I cupped his cheek. "Holy shit. I—oh, my God. Clint! Don't close your eyes, okay? Don't close them again. The paramedics are coming. It's almost over. Just—Clint!"

I tapped his face as his eyes closed, and he groaned out in pain. I'd apologize later, but not right now. Because I sure as hell wasn't about to let this miracle slip through my fingers.

"That hurts."

"Because your nose is broken. Keep your eyes open, okay?"

His reddened eyes slowly rolled over to me as the voices and footsteps grew closer. I smiled down at him, my heart filling with joy and relief as he attempted a smile back. He winced, though. I knew his nose was giving him some trouble. And rightfully so.

Because it was practically flat against his face.

2

CLINTON

"Clint!"

"Mom?"

I whipped around, looking down as I saw myself clad in white. A white leather jacket, a white pair of jeans, and a white fucking turtleneck. Who the hell put me in a turtleneck? I looked up as I heard the sound of soft feet falling against a tile floor. I saw my mother running toward me, arms outstretched. And when I saw her, I smiled.

"Mom!"

I rushed for her, scooping her up into my arms. I twirled her around, hearing her giggle and laugh as my face fell against her bosom. That soft, glorious place I'd sought comfort in as a child. As a young boy, wanting nothing more than to seek shelter away from my father with her.

I spun her around for what seemed like an eternity before I put her down.

I buried my face into her shoulder. "It's so good to see you."

She ran her fingers through my hair. "I've missed you so much."

"Where the hell are we?"

"Language."

I snickered. "Thanks, Mom."

"Well, you and your father have always had such potty mouths."

I pulled back, gazing into her eyes. "Where are we?"

"Why don't you look around and see?"

As my eyes slowly gazed out over the white expanse of nothingness, I saw edges come into view. A couch. A hallway. A projector television sitting against the wall. I saw the edges of windows, looking out onto a great, big, blue sky. Clouds as white as my clothing floated high above, and the green grass of our front lawn sparkled in the sun.

I furrowed my brow. "We're home."

"We are, yes."

"But this doesn't look like home."

"Well, it's got a few changes."

"Why does it look so different?"

And when I turned around, I saw sorrow in my mother's eyes.

I paused. "What?"

Mom sighed. "Why don't we have a little talk?"

She reached her hand out for mine and I took it. She pulled me over to the couch. The one Roy and I always sat on. But it didn't feel like our couch. It didn't look like our space. It was a nice replica. Why the fuck was everything so white?

"Mom, what's going on?"

She paused. "It's complicated, sweetheart."

"I'm dreaming, aren't I?"

"In a way, yes."

"In a way?"

"Your body is giving out on you right now."

"So I'm dying."

"Do you remember much of anything?"

I nodded slowly. "I remember it all."

Mom patted my hand. "Who's the pretty girl coming for you?"

"Coming for me?"

She smiled. "Just answer the question, sweetheart. We don't have much time."

"I'm not following."

She cupped my cheek. "Who's this girl you've been spending time with?"

I felt so confused. And yet, this all still felt very natural. I nuzzled against my mother's palm, wanting nothing more than to stay here with her. Stay here, in her arms. Stay here, with her touch. Stay here, and feel her run her fingers through my hair for all eternity.

Maybe I'd get that, too. If I was really dying.

"Her name's Rae."

Mom smiled. "Pretty name. How'd you meet her?"

I snickered. "School, actually. I used to—"

And when I paused, Mom sighed.

"You used to pick on her."

I nodded. "Yes, ma'am."

"I still don't understand why in the world you run around with those kids. That Roy boy. They're such a bad influence on you."

I pulled away from her touch. "You don't understand, Mom. I can't expect you to."

"Then try. Try to explain it to me, while we have time."

"We'd have had time if you hadn't left me with Dad."

"I was in no condition to take care of you. I was hooked on so many things and—"

"And an abusive father seemed like the best route to take?"

Tears filled her eyes. "At least you would've been clothed. Fed. Had a roof over your head. I didn't have those things, after the divorce."

"You got a very nice settlement from Dad. He's still paying you alimony. What happened?"

She shook her head. "Can we try to focus on the good things? Please?"

"I want to know why you left me behind."

There was a long pause before a tear leaked down her cheek.

"Because I was selfish. Because I was thinking of only myself, in the moment. Between my depression and the medication I got hooked on, I fell into a dark hole. And I didn't want to take anyone with me. Pushing you away was the only rational fix I could come to in my pill-induced stupor, so you wouldn't fall into that hole with me. Just like divorcing me was your father's way of getting himself out of that hole. Because for a while, he was in it with me."

I chewed my lower lip. "I guess, in some ways, I already knew that."

"Because you're a smart boy, Clint. Even though you don't apply yourself in school and even though you run around with those hoodlums, you're a good kid. A smart kid. A fighter, with a strong spirit. Your father almost succeeded in dampening my strong spirit. Don't let him do that to you, okay?"

I paused. "If you're here with me, does this mean you're dead?"

She shook her head. "No, silly boy. I'm a manifestation. There isn't anything right now that we're talking about that you don't already know inside this funny little head of yours."

She tapped her finger softly against my temple and I caught her wrist with my hand. I pulled her palm to my lips and kissed it. Over, and over, and over again. I didn't care if it wasn't real. I didn't care if this wasn't really her. It felt like her. And smelled like her. Just like I remembered.

And I didn't want it to ever go away.

"You're a fighter, Clint. Fight for this. Fight for your life."

I shook my head. "I'm tired of fighting, Mom. I don't want to do it anymore."

"She's waiting for you, sweetheart."
"You're a fighter, Clint. Fight for this. Fight for your life."
I furrowed my brow as my mother's voice distorted itself.
"You're a fighter, Clint. Fight for this. Fight for your life."
"Mom?"
Her body started floating away, and I reached out for her.
"Mom!"
"She's waiting for you. Don't let her down like your father let me down."
"Mom! No!"
"You're a fighter, Clint. Fight for this. Fight for your life."
"You're a fighter, Clint. Fight for this. Fight for your life."
"You're a fighter, Clint. Fight for this. Fight for your life."
Then I drew in a deep, resounding breath.
"Holy shit."

A yelp hit my ears and made me flinch. All the white had faded away. The warmth of my mother's touch was gone. And for some reason, I was soaking fucking wet. I shivered as I gazed up at the night sky. A stark juxtaposition to my dream. Or my limbo. Or my purgatory.

Or whatever the fuck had just happened.

"Clint! Clint. Clint. Can you hear me, baby? Clint?"

I coughed. "R-Rae?"

Something warm cupped my cheek. "Holy shit. I—oh, my God. Clint! Don't close your eyes, okay? Don't close them again. The paramedics are coming. It's almost over. Just—Clint!"

I felt her tap my face and a blinding pain shot through my skin. I groaned and lobbed my head over toward her, taking in her blurry form. The blackened outline gave me comfort. Much like the comfort I'd just experienced with my mother.

Or the vision of my mother.

"That hurts."

Rae snickered. "Because your nose is broken. Keep your eyes open, okay?"

That explains a lot.

I heard footsteps off in the distance. I saw flashes of light and heard sirens above me. Rae settled against me, warming me with her presence as she gazed into my eyes. It was hard keeping my eyes open. My lungs felt like they were burning and drowning at the same time. She smiled at me. That tender, sweet, relieved smile she always had when she laid eyes on me.

And while I tried smiling back, my nose only let me go so far before I winced.

I groaned. "Yep. That's broken."

Rae sighed. "Your shoulder's dislocated, too."

"Explains the back pain."

"Well, lying on a rocky river bank will do that, too."

I snickered. "I suppose it will."

She whispered. "I'm so glad you're talking to me."

"I know you are."

"Because you—"

I nodded, ignoring the disorienting pain. "I know."

"You know?"

"I saw my mother."

"You… you did?"

I scoffed. "Yeah. Crazy, right?"

"Maybe when this is all done, you can tell me about it."

She cupped my cheek and I fell into the warmth. I lobbed my head over, trying to seek out as much of her comfort as I could. Holy hell, she felt fantastic. I almost didn't want the moment to end. Had it not been for the blinding pain that made me sick to my stomach, I would've cried out for everyone to leave us alone.

But I needed a damn hospital.

Before I died again.

"I promise you're gonna be okay."

Rae's lips pressed a kiss to my ear and I moaned. I didn't even try holding it back. Over and over, she pressed kisses against me, warming me from my toes to my nose. I felt my legs come back to life. I wiggled my toes as the sounds of sliding rock and dirt sounded above us. I felt sprinkles of the earth battering against my face, the smallest specks sending ricocheting pain signals all the way to my brain.

"It's okay. I'm right here. I'm going nowhere, okay?"

I sputtered. "How did you—? Are you okay?"

I couldn't speak through the pain anymore. It was excruciating. How the hell did Rae get down that steep cliff? Was she hurt? Had she fallen over, too? What the fuck was happening around me?

I couldn't crane my neck enough to see. All I felt were people gathering around us as Rae's lips left my ear.

"No, no, no. Come back."

"I'm right here, Clint. Just right here. Take my hand."

I felt her fingers curl around my wrist, but it wasn't enough. I needed her lips. Her body. Her warmth. Her presence. I needed more of her. All of her. I didn't want her to leave me like my mother had.

I drew in a shaking breath. "Please, don't leave."

"I swear to you, I'm going nowhere. I'm going straight to the hospital with you, all right? Just let the paramedics do what they do best."

I heard a count off before my body was lifted. I cried out in pain as the world around me flashed. In an instant, the dark world was gone. Replaced by the white of my dreams. Or my purgatory. I saw my mother's face smiling down at me. Clad in that beautiful white summer dress of hers.

"Don't let her down like your father let me down."

"Heave up!"

"Shit!"

"Clint, it's okay. I'm meeting you at the top, all right?"

"Heave up!"

"Fucking hell."

"Clint? Can you hear me?"

Every time someone called out 'heave up' my body jostled. I tilted my head off to the side, spitting up bile as the pain took over my body. I stopped fighting it. I stopped trying to make it better. And instead, I became one with it. The paramedics heaved me up from the ravine. A straight shot of absolute hell before pulling me over the edge of the bridge. I heard Rae scrambling for me. Telling me to keep my eyes open as lights flashed in them. I felt something prick the tops of my hands. I felt a mask come down over my face. I was overwhelmed. And scared.

Until I felt Rae's hand in mine again.

"I'm here. I'm back, baby. Okay? Can you hear me?"

I nodded my head, becoming one with the aching migraine as my eyes rolled her way. I saw her walking alongside me. Our fingers interlaced together. She was all I saw. Her dark outfit. Her dark hair. Her dark skin. Her dark eyes. Dark, like the night. Dark, like the water. Dark, like the abyss I'd fallen into. Dark, like my heart.

And somehow, I'd still fallen in love with her.

"Start a morphine drip. Get this kid some relief."

"Do it before you set his shoulder."

"Are you riding with us? Or him?"

Rae looked down at me before she kissed my cheek.

"See you at the hospital, okay? There's too many paramedics in the back to ride with you. They all need to work on you."

I nodded slowly, but I wasn't happy with the situation. But when her lips pressed against my forehead, I hung on to that feeling. That sensation. Those butterflies in my heart.

"See you soon," she whispered.

Then the morphine drip kicked on, causing my body to go limp as her hand slowly fell away from mine.

3

———

RAELYNN

Michael gripped my shoulders. "Come on. We can follow the ambulance. The paramedics have to work on him while driving, otherwise it's not going to be good."

My chest jumped as my hand fell from Clint's. I hated leaving him. I hated not being by his side. But Michael was right. They were all right. It was all hands on deck to save his life at this point. Especially since his heart had already stopped once. The second I told that to the paramedic, his eyes widened. They all leapt into action, like I'd just shot them to DEFCON-5 or some shit like that. I didn't like it. I didn't like how they reacted one damn bit.

But I let Michael guide me to his SUV so we could hop in.

"You have to breathe for me, Rae. Okay?"

I nodded. "I'm—trying. I'm—I-I-I-I—"

"It'll do us no good to have a panic attack. Take my hand. Here."

I slid my hand into his as we pulled off the bridge. We followed the speeding ambulance back through the woods, passing those neighborhoods and all those tire tracks. Which only served to make my panic worse. The world curled in on itself. I had to close my eyes to keep from getting sick. My chest felt as if it were caving in and my heartrate skyrocketed.

"Tell me five things you smell."

I furrowed my brow. "What?"

"Now, Rae. Five things you smell."

I tried sniffing the air in broken intakes of air. Trying to latch onto the world around me.

"Uh, I uh—I smell rubber. And—and oil."

"Three more. Hit me with 'em."

I snickered. "I smell your cologne."

"Good."

"And dirt."

"One more. You're doing great, Rae."

"And… and sweat."

"Okay. Give me four things you hear."

I trained my ears out onto the world, locking on to the sounds.

"I hear your car engine."

Michael snickered. "All right. Good one. Three more."

"I hear your classical music turned down. And your tires on the road."

"One more. You can do it."

I drew in my first steady breath as the sound hit my ears.

"I still hear the sirens behind us."

Michael paused. "Three things you taste."

"Taste?"

"Yep. Taste. Go. Now."

I drew in a deep lungful of air. "I taste dirt. Saliva. And…"

Michael squeezed my hand as he waited for my final answer.

"And metal."

"Okay, Rae. Open your eyes and tell me two things you see."

I slowly slid my eyes open and the world didn't tilt. It wasn't curling in on itself or spiraling outward. It was still, and the ambulance with its silent, flashing lights was still in front of us.

"I see the ambulance, and its flashing lights."

"Good. You need to do one more?"

I shook my head. "Nope. I think I'm grounded enough."

"You did good back there, Rae. You need to know that. Clint's alive because of you right now. And he's in capable hands."

"And to think you didn't want me down there."

Michael chuckled. "There's the Rae I know and love."

I turned my head toward him. "Love?"

He squeezed my hand again. "You know you're one of my best friends. Sometimes I hate you for things—but I'm never going to stop being your friend."

"Really?"

"Really, really."

I felt tears crest my eyes before another thought hit me.

"I should call Clint's parents."

"Do you have their number?"

"I've got Clint's home number, yes."

Michael nodded. "Then I'd give them a call. They need to know what's going on."

I reached down for my purse, shocked that I still had it. I smiled a thankful smile over at Michael and he nodded his head. And for the first time, I felt like things were finally resolved between us. I dug out my phone and scrolled through my contacts, coming upon Clint's home number. He'd given it to me in case of an emergency. But for the most part, he'd told me not to call it unless I absolutely had to.

And this was pretty much the biggest emergency on the planet.

I sighed. "Here goes nothing."

I dialed the number and the phone rang in my ear. It rang and it rang, and I almost hung up. Maybe his father and stepmother were out on another trip. Not even in town. Which wouldn't have shocked me a bit. Then, on the last ring, the phone picked up.

"Who's this?"

His father's gruff voice filled the phone and my mind pulled me back. Back to that morning where he found us leaving the house to go to school. That wild, empty smile. Those mean, villainous eyes. My stomach turned over as his voice filled my ear, and I almost couldn't speak.

Until Michael cleared his throat at me.

"Hi. Yes. Mr. Clarke?"

He paused. "This is he. Who is this? Why are you calling my phone so late at night?"

"This is Raelynn Cleaver. I don't know if you remember me, but—"

"Can you cut to the chase? I'm a bit busy with work over here."

"Clint's been in an accident. He's headed for the hospital."

The phone call fell silent before a sigh emanated over the phone.

"A crash on his bike?"

I paused. "More like someone ran him off the road and he fell over a bridge."

Michael quirked an eyebrow at me as my voice started to flatten. It sounded like his father was more annoyed than anything. There wasn't the slightest hint of worry in his tone.

"Well, that's what my son gets for pissing off half the city. What hospital are they headed to?"

My jaw dropped open. How the hell could he be so calloused?

"Um, they're headed to—"

I looked over at Michael as he mouthed the name of the hospital.

"—Dignity Health," I finished.

"How far out was he? That's clear across town."

"It was a bad wreck, Mr. Clarke. His heart stopped there for a while on the bank of the river. You really should get to the hospital."

And with a groan, his father hung up the phone.

"Son of a fucking bitch," I hissed.

I tossed my phone to the floorboard as my body vibrated with fury. I felt Michael staring at me as we came to a stop at a stoplight. I mean, the ambulance blew through it. But we weren't sure we could. Even if we were following it.

Then, he cleared his throat. "I take it the call didn't go well."

I snickered. "When I told him his son's heart stopped, he groaned and hung up on me."

"He what now?"

I nodded. "Yeah. I mean, I get that you don't like Clint because he's a dick. But his father makes him look like a saint."

"Sounds like it."

I leaned back against the leather seats of Michael's SUV and gazed out the window. Maybe I shouldn't have called his father at all. I didn't know. I wasn't sure if I'd made the right decision. So much had already happened tonight, and my head felt like it was still spinning. Michael took my hand again, holding it until we pulled into the hospital parking lot. I saw the ambulance crew hauling Clint out as we pulled into the parking garage, and I told Michael I'd pay for the ticket.

Then I shoved myself out of his car and took off.

"Rae! Wait up!"

I heard Michael racing after me as I kept my eyes trained on that ambulance. I hopped over railings and darted through medians. Car horns honked at me as I cut them off. I'd be damned if I let them stop me, though. I saw the ambulance pulling away from the hospital E.R. doors. Michael caught up with me, heaving for air as we charged through the automatic doors.

Just as they rolled Clint down the hallway, a nurse stopped us.

"You here with the crash victim?"

I nodded breathlessly. "Clint Clarke. Yes. I need to see him. I told him I wouldn't leave his—"

"He's being rushed into surgery. They prepped him in the ambulance. If you wait here—"

"Look, Nurse. I know. I get it. But I have to see him before that surgery. I told him he wouldn't do this alone, and I couldn't ride with him in the back."

The nurse sighed. "Girlfriend?"

I looked over at Michael before I nodded.

"Yes. Clint's my boyfriend."

She sighed. "I can only update you on so much since you aren't family. But what I can tell you is this: in less than two minutes, he's going to be on an operating table. And any time we waste, there's a higher chance he won't make it out of surgery. He'll understand once the surgery is over. Now, I need you to sit here and try to remain calm for us. Can you do that for me?"

I drew in a quick breath. "What do you mean, you can't update me on much? His family doesn't give a shit about him!"

Michael sighed. "Rae, take a breath for me."

"No! I'm done with the breathing. His father doesn't give a damn about that boy. And his stepmother is just some trophy at his side. And you're going to update them before you update me?"

"It's protocol. I'm sorry. I'll tell you what I can, but nothing more."

And with that, the nurse turned on her heels and went back to the intake desk.

I hissed to myself. "Bitch."

"All right. Let's sit you down before you get us thrown out of this place."

Michael guided me to a chair before he left. I watched him turn a corner, disappearing from sight, only to emerge with two bottles of water. He sat down beside me and handed me one, and I tossed him a thankful look. I didn't feel like talking anymore. I didn't feel like using my voice. It was going in and out already. Hoarse, before coming back mightier than ever. So the two of us sat in silence and sipped on our water.

Until Michael broke the silence.

"All we can do is wait. And in the meantime, maybe we can call Allison. Get her to bring us some food."

I shook my head. "I don't wanna bother her with this. Bothering you with it is enough."

"You're not bothering me. Okay?"

I nodded slowly, refusing to argue with him. "I still don't want to call her, though. I mean, if she gets in touch with you, don't lie to her. But I'm just…"

Michael rubbed my back. "I know. I know."

I nodded as I took another sip of my water before Michael spoke again.

"What about your mother?"

I snickered. "You mean the woman who's probably already made up with D.J. and is with him right now?"

He paused. "Wait, I thought they broke up for good."

"All I know is that Mom's still got money to pay bills even though she hadn't secured a new job yet. And the only place I know of where that money can come from is him."

"Shit. I'm so sorry, Rae."

I shrugged. "It's her life. Not mine. If that's how she wants to live it, then so be it. If anything, the fact that she hasn't called and asked me why I'm not home yet tells me all I need to know. She's making up with D.J., making plans with him, and doesn't have enough sense to realize I'm not home yet."

"I guess you and Clint do have some lifestyle similarities, then."

That statement said a lot, coming from Michael. Because I knew him well enough to know that was the first step in Clint being accepted into the fold. I mindlessly sipped on the water, refusing to break for the restroom just in case something with Clint popped up. I kept shifting us down, seat by seat, until we were stationed right beside the nurse's unit. This way, I could eavesdrop. Pick up bits and pieces of Clint's condition, hopefully.

Because apparently, being the girlfriend and the one to help him out in his most dire time wasn't enough merit to earn information on his condition.

Michael shifted. "When do you think his parents will show up?"

I shrugged. "Part of me isn't expecting them to show up at all."

"Seriously?"

"Seriously. His father's a damn nutcase. And his stepmother doesn't ever step in on anything until it's getting too violent. It's insane, what he puts up with."

"No wonder he's angry all the time."

I nodded. "You're telling me."

"Where's my son?"

The booming voice forced me to whip my head around. I looked at the emergency room doors, watching Clint's father barge straight through them. Cecilia was behind him, her hair fluttering down her back and her pristine heels clicking across the floor. Clint's father gripped her hand tightly, tugging her along as he bellowed for information.

"Clinton Clarke is here, and I want to know what the fuck is happening with my son!"

And as nurses rushed him, waiting on him hand and foot as they shoved information down his throat, I saw tears in Cecilia's eyes.

Tears I hoped were for Clint.

4

———

CLINTON

"*Clint!*"

"*Rae?*"

I turned around, taking in the bright blue color that surrounded us. I saw Rae in the most gorgeous dress. One that fell off her shoulders and fluttered just above her knees. She ran for me with the biggest smile on her face, and I held my arms out for her. She lunged at me, wrapping her entire body around me. And as her warmth encompassed me, I spun her around.

Around, and around, until we fell into the soft blue grass below us.

"Hi there, handsome."

She kissed my cheek and it shivered me to my toes.

"Hey there, beautiful."

"I'm glad you're okay."

I nodded. "Me, too. And I like this dress on you. You should wear stuff like this more often."

She giggled. "You mean you don't like my brown pants and my baggy black shirts?"

"I mean, they do nothing for your form, no. But, if you're comfortable wearing them, then it's fine."

"You just want to stare at my tits all day."

I grinned. "And you know you like it."

She laughed and snuggled next to me, using my arm as a pillow. Her leg slid between mine, and together, we stared up at the sky. The sky that matched our clothes. Matched my light blue leather jacket. Matched the light blue grass we lay on and the light blue trees swaying in the cool summer breeze. White clouds moved above us, dancing for us and morphing into shapes right before our very eyes.

Rae pointed. "Look. That one's dancing."

I smiled as the elephant got up on its hind legs and started shimmying.

"Holy shit, it is."

She giggled. "And that one looks like a heart. See it?"

I smiled. "I do see it, yes."

"Oh! The butterfly! It's flapping its wings!"

I scanned the clouds. "I don't see it."

"No, not the clouds. Over there, silly."

I turned my head to where she was pointing and I saw it. The biggest butterfly I'd ever seen in my life. Easily as big as my stomach, and it had the most beautiful wings I'd ever seen in my life. Intricate light blue and white patterns as it lifted off toward the sky. It sprinkled us with something. A sparkling dust of some sort. And as it floated toward the sky, covering us in this dust, I felt peace come over me. I felt Rae relax into me.

I felt my lips loosening.

"I love you, Rae."

Her hand cupped my cheek and she pulled my face toward hers, smiling brightly at me. As bright as the clouds hanging in the sky. Her thumb smoothed over my cheek and I leaned forward, capturing the sweetness of her lips. I rolled her over on the grass, kicking up more of that dust as we found ourselves smushed inside a patch of light blue and white wildflowers.

"I love you too, Clint."

I grinned. "You do, huh?"

She nodded. "I do, yes."

"Do you love me enough to stay by my side?"

"I do."

"Do you love me enough to deal with my shit?"

"I do."

"Do you love me enough to make love to me whenever I ask?"

She snickered, swatting at my chest. "You're about to lose brownie points here, handsome."

"Oooh, and what do these points get me?"

I slipped my hand underneath her dress as giggles fell from her lips. I captured them with mine, swallowing her sounds as her skin puckered underneath my fingertips. Her legs parted for me, allowing my body to sink between them. And as her womanly scent wafted up my nostrils, I felt my cock harden-

ing. I felt my body tightening. I felt her rolling against me, ready for my fingers to fill her as I danced over her bare pussy.

My eyebrows rose. "No underwear?"

And when that salacious little smile crossed her cheeks, I filled her pussy with my fingers.

"Oh, Clint."

"So wet for me."

She gasped. "Shit. Just like that."

"I've got you, Rae. I'll always have you. I'll never disappoint you like my father disappointed my mother."

"I know. I know. And it'll be all right, Clint."

I gazed down into her eyes, watching as a flash of darkness took over her face, muting her presence before bringing her back. My fingers stilled. My brow furrowed deeper. And as her hand cupped my cheek, I watched the light blue quickly fade into the darkest shade of navy I'd ever seen.

"It's going to be all right, Clint."

She disappeared from underneath me and my world tilted. The warmth of her pussy around my fingers were gone, and pain unlike any other raced up my spine. I cried out, watching as the world tilted me onto my back. I heard the rushing sounds of water. I smelled the scent of burning rubber. I heard someone calling my name in the distance as I gazed up at the navy blue sky. Dotted with stars that twinkled for my delight.

Trying to ease me through the pain.

"You're a fighter, Clint. Fight for this. Fight for your life."

As I lay there, a reel played out in the sky. Like the projector screen back inside the hellhole that was my father's mansion. I watched everything play out on screen. Like some kind of sick, twisted horror movie. As the water rushed over my legs, trying to carry me downstream, the movie played out. Those four drunk boys, rolling up on Rae and me in the parking lot. Them taunting her. Threatening her. Licking their lips at her and wanting to make her their meal for the night. I saw me harassing them, getting them to chase me while Rae hopped the fence to get away from them. I watched the car chase play out with horror filling my body. I felt my eyes widening as my nose ached. I felt my toes tingle as my shoulder slowly moved itself out of socket.

"Holy fuck!"

I roared out into the expanse of nothingness as the water lifted my body. I kept my eyes trained toward the sky as that damn phrase kept repeating itself. Over and over, from a disembodied voice that haunted me from the depths of the water.

"You're a fighter, Clint. Fight for this. Fight for your life."

I'm so fucking tired of fighting, though.

I saw the wreck. How the car slammed into my bike. I saw myself stumbling over toward the woods, trying to get away from the beer bottles those damn boys threw at me. I watched myself turn around. I watched that damn bottle clock me right between the eyes. I felt my head throbbing. Aching. Spilling with blood as the car rushed me again in my stunned stupor.

Before he ran into me completely, pushing me over the edge of the bridge.

"*No!*"

I saw my own body coming at me. I tried reaching out to catch myself, but I couldn't move. Just as my own body reached me, it turned into nothing. It felt like my soul had slipped into my body before the water whisked me away. I sank underneath, wrapped up in its cold nature. Sinking to the bottom as screaming filled my ears.

I felt the water dragging me away as my lungs refused to breathe.

"*You're a fighter, Clint. Fight for this. Fight for your life.*"

I felt my back fall against the rocks at the bottom of the river, my legs dangling helplessly in the water. My heart was giving out, my blood slowing. And as the world faded to black, I felt something snag against my coat.

My body stopped moving. But not soon enough.

"Holy shit."

My eyes ripped open and I panted for air. I stared up at a popcorn ceiling, listening as the sounds of beeping machines dawned on my ears. The smell of disinfectant filled my lungs. With every breath I took, it rooted me to the most uncomfortable bed I'd ever slept on. And as I licked my chapped lips, it confirmed my theories.

I was in a hospital. In a bed. Staring up at my room's ceiling.

It was silent. A silence I didn't expect to get. Where was Rae? She promised me she wouldn't leave me alone through all this. Wasn't she supposed to be here? Was she all right? Had something happened on the journey to the hospital?

Wait, what day was it? What time was it? Maybe she was simply at home, sleeping. I mean, I didn't know how long I'd been out. How long I'd been dreaming.

I reached my hand out, hoping Rae was there to take it. Maybe she was preoccupied. Or she was speaking and I simply couldn't hear it. I tried moving my neck, but couldn't. I tried darting my eyes around, but they moved too slowly. My body felt lighter than air. I wiggled my toes, and even tried bending my knees. There wasn't any pain. But there wasn't any feeling either.

And as my eyes fell onto the morphine drip, that answered my questions.

Shit. I was still drugged to the high heavens.

A hand slipped into mine, but I didn't recognize it. It was soft, but not necessarily warm. Not like Rae's. Or my mother's. I felt ring bands against my skin, nails softly scratching up my arm. I grimaced at the feeling and it quickly stopped, and that movement told me who it was.

"Welcome back, hun. How are you feeling?"

Cecilia.

My stepmother was in the room.

My eyes lobbed over as her chair scooted across the floor. She came into view, her hand still holding mine. I heard the clicking of her manicured nails, the scraping of her Louis Vuitton heels against the floor. Even in the hospital, her hair was perfect. The perfect face of makeup. Contoured with precision and glistening against the expensive diamonds my father showered her with. Her clothes were designer, in the middle of the fucking night. Just like my father always wanted with his women.

Wait, it was still the middle of the night, right?

Cecilia didn't say anything, so I didn't strike up a conversation. Because while it was nice having her there, I was still disappointed that she wasn't Rae. Where was she? Had my father scared her off? Holy fuck, if my father had scared that girl off, he'd be dead.

Once I could get out of this hospital bed.

My eyes slowly panned back up to the ceiling. Cecilia kept a grip on my hand, her grip growing stronger every minute that passed by. It didn't shock me one bit that my father hadn't surfaced yet. He was probably at work, doing some shit. Or taking work phone calls. Or booking their next vacation getaway.

You know, doing more important shit than tending to his son.

"Where's Rae?"

Cecilia sighed, and it gave me all the answer I needed. I felt my blood boiling. My fucking father with his fucking antics. The beeping machines around me began spiking. Cecilia gasped as she stood up from her chair. She leaned over me, her hair curtaining us off from the rest of the world. I heard something beeping close to my ear before something warm dripped through my system, making me feel like I was damn near peeing myself.

"Is everything okay in here?"

"What happened? Why did he spike?"

"Let me check his vitals."

Cecilia sighed. "I've already pressed the morphine button. Just give him a second. He's a strong boy. Stronger than he should be."

There was a sadness to the last part of that phrase. That last little sentence she tacked on there. I felt my eyes growing heavy as the drugs rushed my system. They settled my heartrate and my blood pressure back down. Nurses poked and prodded. They shone more lights in my eyes. One of them set themselves to the task of changing out my I.V. bag while another tugged on something that made my dick jump.

Shit. I had a catheter in.

Fucking grand.

"It's okay. I'm right here, sweetheart. Can you still hear me?"

I swallowed. "Yeah, Cecilia. I can hear you."

"Good. The nurses want you to stay awake through this morphine rush. So try to keep talking to me. What do you want to talk about?"

I want to talk about what the fuck my father said or did to Rae.

But, I settled on a better question. One that still required an answer.

"Where the hell is Dad?"

5

RAELYNN

Michael hissed. "Rae, we have to go."

I held up my hand as we crept through the hallways of the hospital. We dodged staff, racing around corners as I tried to get to Clint's ICU room. I sure as hell wasn't allowing his father to chase me off like that. I didn't give a damn how he felt about my being there or what he'd said to me to try and get me to leave. He didn't want to be here. He didn't give a shit about his son. The only thing he cared about was his businesses. How much money he pulled in.

How hard he could sock his son in the fucking jaw.

Michael grabbed my arm. "Rae, stop."

I ripped away from him. "If you don't want to be here, then go. I'll catch a ride back somehow. But I'm not leaving. Not until I know how Clint's doing."

"And if his father catches you sneaking about? If the doctors catch you?"

I shrugged. "What's he going to do? Hit a girl?"

Michael's face fell and I moved down the hallway again. Doctors had whisked them away to a room that had already been set aside for Clint after he came out of surgery. Which meant things didn't look very good. I wanted to know how the surgery had gone. Or was going. Or whatever his status was. I'd waited for almost two hours to find the opening I needed to sneak through those metal doors. To get back to

Clint. To see if I could pick up on any information I wanted. Anything to soothe my worried soul. I wanted to know exactly the kind of condition he was in. But when I saw Clint's father pacing up and down the hallway with his cell phone stuck in his ear, I paused. Taking in the scene. How apathetic and unapologetic the man looked.

And the kicker was that it didn't shock me one bit.

"No. No. I need you to do it the way I said for you to do it. You're costing us money. And a great deal of it. I won't be paying your paycheck if you don't do as I ask!"

His father's voice boomed down the hallway and I shook my head. I peeked back at Michael, watching his face fall. Then we hid around the corner of the empty hallways of the hospital as I tried my best to listen to what his father was saying.

"Is that man really doing work right now?" he asked.

I nodded. "Yep."

We tucked ourselves away, hiding as a doctor came around the corner. We pressed ourselves into a dark space, and I even held my breath so no one would hear us. The doctor passed, leaving the hallways bare and empty again. We clamored right back up to the corner. Right back to where we'd been.

I watched as the doctor approached Clint's father, and even I could see the frustration in the doctor's shoulders as they tensed.

I watched his father hold his fucking hand up to the doctor, telling him to hush while he continued working. I wanted to strangle the man myself. I wanted to beat him into oblivion so he could know exactly how he'd made Clint feel all these years.

Then his father finally put his phone away.

"What's going on with my son? Will he be okay?"

Michael murmured, "Like he cares."

"Shh!" I said curtly, turning my attention back down the hallway.

"Sir, your son is going to be okay. Surgery was touch and go there for a while, but we fixed him up and he should be coming out of it at any second. This is the room he'll recover in for a while. We wanted to go ahead and get him moved so we could hook him up to the pain medication he'll need. Your son will be in a great deal of pain for a few hours."

His father sighed. "How long will he have to be here? I've got a trip planned in a couple of days I really don't want to cancel."

Michael snickered. "He's really being serious, isn't he?"

I rolled my eyes. "If you don't shut u—"

The doctor shook his head. "I'm not sure if he'll be out of here in a couple of days. Three, maybe. If things go very well. But not under forty-eight hours. Your son sustained a great deal of trauma. And, there's a criminal investigation open right now, since it's pretty clear your son was run off the road."

Clint's father's eyes fell beyond the doctor and I knew he spotted me. Even as I tried to hide behind the corner, I heard his footsteps tearing toward me. Michael grabbed my arm, pulling me down the hallway as the footsteps came around the corner. And as his voice thundered down the hallway, all eyes were on us.

"What are you doing?"

Michael froze before I slowly turned around, watching Clint's doctor appear beside his father.

"I'd like to know the same thing, actually."

I sighed. "I just wanted to know how Clint was doing."

The doctor furrowed his brow. "And you are…?"

His father snickered. "No one important."

I glared at Clint's father. "I'm his girlfriend. I'm the one that found him. You said he's going to be okay, Doctor? Like, really okay?"

Clint's father stepped up to the plate. "He needs space. From you. Because I have a feeling you got him into this mess in the first place."

I shook my head. "That isn't what happened. Those boys approached us, sir. We had nothing to do with it."

The doctor held up his hand. "This sounds like a statement for the police in the E.R. waiting room. Where the two of you should be."

"Please," I begged, "I care about Clint. Deeply. And I'm worried about him. I don't have to see him. I just want to know what all he needed work on. I know his nose was broken. I think his shoulder was dislo—"

"Back off and let us handle this. Now. Before I have you escorted out."

I snapped back. "Or you'll what? Slug me like you enjoy slugging your son?"

His father lunged at me, causing Michael to step in front of me.

His father began ranting. Raving. Screaming down the hallway as the doctors and nurses held him back.

"You don't know shit about how this works! You don't know a damn thing! Get the hell out of here before I have you arrested and put in handcuffs and charged with attempted murder, you stupid little girl!"

Michael groaned. "Did you really have to spit that out?"

I pushed him away. "Maybe now someone will investigate it and arrest that man for all the things he should be thrown into jail for."

"Sir, calm down, or you'll be escorted off the premises."

"Sir, I'll have to sedate you if you don't stop."

"Get that girl out of here. She's not welcome around my son any longer!"

Tears rushed my eyes as a woman poked her head out of the recovery room. And when my eyes landed on Clint's stepmother, sorrow filled her face again. She mouthed how sorry she was to me. And for a moment, I thought maybe we understood one another.

Until someone grabbed my arm.

"You can't be back here if you're not family. I'm sorry, but romantic partners don't count. Come with me before you get into any more trouble."

I freely went with the nurse as she led me back out into the E.R. waiting room. And as Michael came up behind me, I started gathering my things. I'd lost my shoe along the way somewhere. Also, my phone. I picked it up and headed for the exit doors, not bothering to hear what Clint's father was still screaming down the hallways. People stared. Some gawked. Others eavesdropped in order to get their daily dose of gossip. I hopped out of the E.R. doors as I put my shoe on, then tucked my phone away in my bra.

As silent tears streaked my cheeks.

Michael placed his hand between my shoulder blades, silently leading me toward his car. But all I wanted to do was go and sit by Clint's bed. I couldn't stand this. I couldn't stand not knowing. What all did they have to do in surgery? How many stitches did he have? What kind of medication was he on? Would he fully recover? Would he be able to ride his bike again, if he wanted?

I needed to see him. Touch him. Place my ear against his heart and still hear it beating. I needed to know, without a shadow of a doubt, that he really was all right.

But his father wouldn't even give that to me.

I mean, what else did you expect, Rae?

Michael opened up his car door for me and helped me in. He closed the door, and I leaned my forehead against the cool glass. I let the sounds of the world fade into the background as I watched as the hospital disappeared in the rearview mirror while we drove away. I moved and weaved with the twists and turns Michael took. And after he pulled up to a drive-thru menu, his voice pierced the silence.

"You hungry?"

I shook my head, but my stomach betrayed me with a mighty growl.

"Medium Coke, large fry, and a chicken wrap?"

I shrugged. "Sure."

I didn't even bother moving to get my wallet. I knew Michael would insist he pay, so I didn't fight him. I didn't have the energy to, anyway. Part of me wanted to turn this car around and storm back into that hospital. Part of me wanted to spew everything I'd witnessed regarding Clint's father until that man was in fucking handcuffs.

The only thing that stopped me was Clint.

Because I wasn't sure if that was something he'd want me to do.

Michael paid for the food and handed me my bag. I sat up enough to reach for my drink before mindlessly sipping on it. The food stayed by my feet as he pulled into a parking space in the empty parking lot, pulling out his burger to devour.

Then I heaved a heavy sigh.

"None of this shit is fair."

Michael swallowed hard. "You just have to be patient. There's a reason why hospitals have rules like this. It's to protect the patient."

I scoffed. "And if the patient's father is an abusive dickweed?"

He shrugged. "Maybe the comment you made and how riled up his father got will prompt them to look into it. But, for right now, all you can do is hang tight and wait until Clint gets out of the hospital."

"Maybe his stepmom will reach out to me."

"By the sounds of it, she won't even be here in a couple of days."

"I mean, who's going to sign for Clint's discharge, then? Isn't that how that works?"

Michael shook his head. "At eighteen, a kid can sign for their own discharge. He's eighteen, right?"

I nodded. "He is, yeah."

"Then he'll check himself out. I guess."

"Such bullshit."

"I know. But you can't get so upset and frustrated over things you can't change. It is what it is, and even though it isn't good, it's also not in your control."

"And what was that thing about the doctor saying something about me talking to the police?"

"Oh, you were pretty out of it when we walked out of the E.R. When the police need your statement, they'll find you."

I sighed. "Great."

I didn't have the stomach to eat. Michael, however, inhaled his food. I wasn't even sure he tasted it. And as he backed out of the parking space, I clutched the food between my feet. My mom hadn't called me once. Not a single time to figure out where in the world I'd gotten off to. Which meant I was most certainly heading back to a house with D.J. in it. Michael made his way back to the school. And with each turn he made, I felt myself growing sicker and sicker in my stomach. Sipping on the Coke didn't help. Smelling the greasy food on the floorboard of his car didn't help, either.

"Stop the car."

Michael slammed on the brakes. "What? What's wrong?"

And as worry took hold, I threw open his SUV door. I leaned out, heaving in the middle of the road as we sat there in front of the high school.

Letting my body finally career itself out of control as my stomach leapt into my throat.

6

CLINTON

The question hung heavily in the room as Cecilia smoothed her thumb over my skin. I didn't know what day it was. What time it was. I felt disoriented. Drugged. And all I wanted to do was sleep.

Cecilia squeezed my hand. "Keep those eyes open."

"Then tell me where Dad is."

She sighed. "He stepped out for a little bit. Just… needed some air."

I snickered. "You're a terrible liar."

She giggled. "That obvious?"

I lobbed my eyes over to take her in. Even though I couldn't move my neck.

"I don't think I've ever heard you laugh."

She sighed. "To be honest, I don't do much of it nowadays, unless I'm with friends."

"Then why stay?"

"Hmmm?"

"If you aren't laughing, then you aren't happy. And if you aren't happy, then why are you still here?"

She shrugged. "I guess because it's familiar. Because I do love your father. And because I do love you."

"You don't have to tell me what I want to hear, Cecilia. Just tell me the truth."

"Why is that so hard for you to accept as truth?"

My eyes gravitated back toward the ceiling. The rush of warmth was gone, leaving me shivering, even though I was covered in blankets. Cecilia stood up, tucking the blankets along my legs as she spoke with the nurses. My eyes finally slid closed as their voices wafted around me. I felt Cecilia patting my leg, forcing me to stay awake through it all this time. Part of it was endearing, and part of it was annoying as fuck.

Then, once the nurses left the room, she sighed.

"Just tell me where Dad is. Because all you're really doing is confirming what I already know."

She sighed. "He's stepped out to make a few business calls."

I snickered. "Of course he has."

"Your father works hard. He's got four different businesses under his belt. Three of which are booming right now. He's got a lot on his—"

"I know, I know. His businesses are important. It's to provide the life I've got now. That's why he travels so much, because he loves me enough to provide for me. His love equates to money, and all that bullshit. You can spare me the lecture. I already know it."

"He does love you, Clint."

"Well, he's got a shit way of showing it."

My flat tone blanketed the room as Cecilia sat back down. I chewed on the inside of my lip as I lay there, practically trapped in this damn hospital bed. I didn't know when the hell I was getting out of here, but I had a feeling Dad wouldn't even be around to help me with it. At this point, I was more prone to the idea of my stepmother staying behind and helping rather than my own father.

Who I hated even calling 'Dad' at this point.

I sighed. "That man is a basket case."

Cecilia snickered. "I know."

"Then why the hell did you marry him?"

She shrugged. "Because he made me laugh. He made me feel special. It was easy to fall in love with him, though sometimes I wonder if I ended up falling in love with someone more like my own father."

I paused. "What do you mean?"

"Ah, we don't have to get into all that. Right now, we need to focus on—"

"Cecilia."

My curt tone shocked her into silence, and I heard why. I sounded like my father. My voice filled the room like my father. I closed my eyes, trying to swallow down the taste of my father's voice within my own.

"I'm sorry."

She took my hand. "It's okay."

I shook my head, ignoring the dull pain I still felt. "It's not."

"You just wanted me to—"

"I sounded just like him, and that's not okay. Because my father isn't an okay kind of man. You and I both know this."

Damn it, I wished I could fucking look at the woman. To read her face. To look in her eyes. To let her know she wasn't alone in all this.

I licked my lips. "What do you mean, he's like your father?"

Cecilia paused. "I'm not sure if I should really be talking about something like that with you."

"Why? Because Dad told you not to? Or because you don't want to?"

And when she fell silent, I knew the reason why.

"Don't let Dad be that control freak with you, okay? He gets it enough with me," I said.

She squeezed my hand. "Your father can be a bit off the wall, can't he?"

I snickered. "That's one way to describe it."

"My father was a bit off the wall, too."

"How so?"

"Oh, you know. Randomly yelling over things. Never quite sticking to the rules he set out. One day, my sisters and I couldn't wear dresses that came above our knees. And the next day, it was full-length dresses only. No boys' eyes should be on us. And if they were, it was somehow our fault."

"Yikes."

She giggled bitterly. "Yeah. It was a very traditional household. The women kept their heads down. Dressed modestly. Head to toe, if Dad preferred it that way. No makeup. No jewelry. No hair products. My father didn't believe in those kinds of things. Material possessions and all that."

"Were you raised Amish or something?"

Then the giggle was real. "We might as well have been.

Though that still might be an insult to the Amish people as a whole."

And that comment made me chuckle.

I squeezed her hand as the awkward conversation slowly started to flow. And in the back of my mind, I wondered why I hadn't taken the time to talk with Cecilia sooner than this. I mean, she and my father had been married for a few years. And in those years, there were things about her I'd never known. Like her laugh. Her bright smile. The way her touch felt against my own. I didn't know these things about her and she was my fucking stepmother.

Cecilia's sniffing ripped me from my mind.

"What's wrong?"

She swallowed hard. "I tried convincing your father to stay. I really did."

I paused. "He's not even at the hospital right now, is he?"

"I mean, I don't know for sure. But I do know your father. And it's been well over an hour since he's come back to the room."

"Yep. He's left for his office or something."

"I'm so sorry, Clint. I told him to put that damn phone away and pay attention to what was happening. Be present. But he just gets worse and worse with that work stuff of his."

"Cecilia, I hate to break it to you, but he's always been that way. There's no 'it' getting worse. It's just you figuring out that this isn't behavior that'll change."

She sighed. "I suppose you're right."

I paused. "Are you okay?"

She snickered. "I believe that's the question I should be asking you."

"Doesn't mean I can't ask you."

"You know, I don't know how to answer that question. I mean, your father and I have been together since you were fourteen years old. And now you're lying in this hospital and I'm sitting here holding your hand and I realize I don't know a thing about you."

The silence that followed that admission was deafening. Because she was right. She didn't know anything about me, and I sure as hell didn't know anything about her. I tugged her hand, pulling her up from her seat as she sat down on the edge of the bed. She leaned over me, placing one hand on one side of my body as I continued holding the one in my hand I already had.

"All right. Good to know," I said.

She furrowed her brow. "What?"

I snickered. "Your eyes. I didn't even know they were hazel."

"We're a sad bunch, aren't we?"

I shrugged. "We do the best we can."

Tears rushed her eyes. "I really did beg for him to stay."

"It's fine. I know the kind of man my father is. There's no use in begging with him, either. At least do yourself a favor and keep your dignity."

"There are so many times where I should have—"

"It's okay. There's no use dwelling on the past, either."

She wiped her tears away. "Again, isn't this the kind of thing I should be telling you?"

"Eh, I'm sure we'll get there."

That made her smile. Which made me smile. And slowly, the burden of the hospital room lifted from my shoulders. The two of us talked for a little bit. I found out more about her home life as a child. How drastically different it had been from mine. And yet, how similar our own fathers were. I told her about my mother. Every question she asked, I answered. Including why my leather jacket was so important to me. For the first time in years, we opened up to one another. Learned more about one another. And the more I learned, the more I wondered how the hell my pathetic excuse for a father had snagged such a bright, beautiful, candid woman for a second wife.

"You're way too good for my dad."

She giggled. "Maybe so. But he does have a softer side."

I rolled my eyes. "I'm sure he does."

"I know that sounds cliché and trite, but he does. At least, he did. I see it sometimes when we're on vacation."

"Well, tell him to send some of that softness my way. I could use some of it."

We stared at one another and my eyes lingered on her face. Her hazel eyes stared back at me from a full face of makeup that seemed almost luminescent. She didn't have a wrinkle on her face, courtesy of the botox I was sure Dad pumped into her skin. Her fake breasts were sky high, propped underneath her chin without any sort of effort. Her hair was pulled back in a modest fashion. Probably a habit she hadn't broken from her childhood. And as I lay there, studying her, I realized something.

She reminded me a bit of Mom.

Guess Dad has a type.

"Do you need anything?"

Cecilia's voice filled my mind and I shook my head.

"Nah. I'm good for now. Though I'd really like to see—"

A knock on the door interrupted my sentence, and I hoped it was Rae. Cecilia slid off the edge of the bed, whipping around to see who it was. I knew she wanted it to be Dad. While I wished it to be Rae. But instead, we were both disappointed as a man in a white coat came strolling in the door with a clipboard underneath his armpit.

My heart sank as he walked toward us. And I had a feeling Cecilia's heart was doing the same thing.

"Hey, Doc," I said.

Cecilia sat back down, quickly falling into 'her place.' She got out of the way of the man, making herself as small as possible as the doctor came to stand at my side. He silently checked my tubing. My I.V. My morphine drip. A few other things, before finally standing upright. I saw his eyes lingering on Cecilia for just a few seconds longer than was appropriate. Then he turned his attention back to me.

"All right. Since you've had an evening to rest and recuperate out of surgery, I think it's time we discuss what you're looking at in terms of your recovery."

I nodded. "Fair enough. How long do you think I'll be in the hospital?"

The doctor peeked back at Cecilia before answering. "Three days, at least. But the nurses have examined you all through the night and you seem very stable. If today goes well and we don't run into any issues, you'll be transferred out of ICU and into a regular room."

Cecilia sighed. "Thank the Lord."

"But your recovery is going to be daunting. You'll be on pain medication for a while. And there are police officers who are clamoring out here to speak with you once you're able to recall your side of events from last night."

I nodded. "You can send them in once we're done talking."

The doctor paused. "Do you want to wait for your father?"

Cecilia stood up before coming to my side. She found her voice as she reached for my hand, cradling it within hers. She looked that doctor straight in his eyes, even though I felt her hand trembling with nerves. Finding her place beside me when Dad should have been there himself.

"I'm here, and whatever you tell me I can relay to my husband," she said.

And damn it, I was proud of her for finding her voice.

7

RAELYNN

After I got sick on the side of the road, Michael made the executive decision to keep driving around. And I was thankful for it, because I couldn't go into my house like that. I'd still been too shaken up to deal with being alone. For all I knew, I'd walk right in on Mom and D.J. in the living room, and I'd erupt. Just completely unload all the stress and anxiety and worry on my shoulders off onto them. And they didn't deserve that.

I mean, D.J. did. But not Mom.

We drove around and Michael made me eat my food. Despite the fact that I was convinced it might make me sicker, he convinced me otherwise. And again, he'd been right. The saltiness of the fries settled my nausea, and eating the chicken wrap leveled out my blood sugar. For the most part, my trembling stopped. The shaking in my hands ceased. Some of the nausea in my stomach abated, giving me a bit of rest.

Then Michael drove me out to that park.

We sat there on the bench where Clint and I had sat a few weeks back. A few weeks. Holy shit, it felt like a few months. A few years. I ran my fingers through my hair and kept sighing. I gazed off at that bright star between the trees, wondering if Clint was all right. And the entire time, Michael stayed by my side. Even though Allison bombarded him with phone calls. Even though she begged him to tell her what was happening. He didn't tell her, and he didn't leave my side.

Which pushed even more tears down my face.

I cried on Michael's shoulder as we sat in that park. I ranted his ear off as I paced around in front of him. I regaled him with how Clint had found me out here. How much I wanted to shove his face into the dirt before he opened up randomly about his home life. Prompting me to talk about mine. I kept telling him story after story. How we made it back to Clint's house. What happened. How he made me feel. I spilled it all out to Michael and he listened while nodding his head, drinking it all in.

And not once did he criticize me for it.

As the remnants of the sun began blossoming over the tops of the trees, Michael finally took me home. I was shocked when I didn't see D.J.'s car in the driveway. But it didn't matter. Nothing mattered, at all. Nothing except Clint's health and happiness. His healing and what he'd have to do for his recovery time.

"See you at school?"

Michael's voice pulled me from my trance, but I shook my head.

"Not if I can help it."

I gathered up my garbage and slid out of his car. I closed the door behind me, listening as he backed out of my driveway. I'd have to find a way to thank him later. But not now. Right now, I couldn't focus on anything else. Especially after I threw my trash away in the trash can out front.

Because the second my hands came into view, I saw I still had Clint's blood on me.

"Shit."

I unlocked the front door and pushed my way inside. I closed it behind me, leaning my forehead against it. A sound pacing down the hallway made me jump. The footsteps grew closer, then they grew frantic. I whipped around, watching my mother rush me. Watching her robe flutter behind her with her hair wild and maniacal around the crown of her head.

Then her eyes fell to my clothes.

"What the—? Rae, where the hell have you been? Are you all right? What are you—is this your blood!?"

She ran toward me, her slippers sliding across the floor as she took my hands within hers. She tugged me into the kitchen, murmuring to herself in Spanish as she sat me down at the kitchen table. Her hands ran over me, checking for wounds or gashes. Anything to explain the blood I'd completely forgotten I was covered in.

"It's not mine," I whispered.

Mom paused. "Then whose is it? Where have you been? I've been up all night, worried sick about you."

I nodded slowly. "I'm sorry."

She pulled up a chair. "Rae, look at me."

I slowly turned my head to find her eyes, but I didn't try holding back my tears. Mom wiped them off my face, brushing away more crusted blood as she grimaced to herself.

"Talk to me, princess. What's going on?"

My lower lip quivered. "He's so hurt, Mom. He's in the hospital, and I can't know anything."

"Who's hurt? Michael?"

"No."

"Allison?"

I shook my head. "Clint."

She paused. "That the boy from school you talked to me about?"

I nodded. "We—it—happened so fast, Mom."

"Are you hurt, Raelynn?"

"I wish I was, instead of him."

"Oh, sweetheart."

She wrapped her arms around me and I sobbed against her. I heard myself wailing. I felt my chest heaving. It was almost like an out of body experience. My heart fluttered so wildly I thought I'd burst out from my chest and take off toward the rising sun. My legs locked up, shaking and trembling as my stomach slammed against my ribcage. It felt like my entire body was rebelling. Fighting back after years of being caged.

I shook against Mom, soaking her robe with tears as she stroked my back.

"I'm right here. It's okay. It's going to be okay."

"They ran him off the road, Mom. They wanted to kill him."

"Who did, sweetheart? Who wanted to kill him?"

"Those dumbass drunk boys!"

I shrieked it so loudly that Mom clung to me tighter. She stood up, pulling me against her as she slowly moved us from the kitchen to the living room. We fell to the couch and she pulled me into her lap, cradling me the way she used to do when I was a small girl.

She kissed the side of my head. "Tell me what happened."

I shook my head. "I can't—can't—can't ta—"

"Sh-sh-sh-sh-sh. It's okay. Deep breaths for me, princess. In through your nose, out through your mouth. Okay? Like this?"

I tried to do as Mom asked, but my breathing was choppy. Weak. I couldn't breathe out as much as she was and I had a hard time drawing in air. But she worked me through it. She counted softly in my ear as I sank against her. Sank into the warmth and comfort I'd always remembered about my mother. My tears slowly dried and my body quietly calmed down. And after a few minutes, my breathing evened out.

"There's a good girl. That's my princess. I'm right here, sweetheart. I'm not going anywhere."

I sniffled. "Clint came to hang out with me after work last night. He wanted to hang out before bringing me home on his bike."

She nodded. "Sounds like a good enough plan. What happened?"

I sighed. "Four boys drove up to us in some car. It was obvious they were drunk, too. A couple of the guys Clint knew from a fight that happened at school a couple days back or so. I don't know. I can't really remember the timeline anymore."

"It's okay. You can talk about whatever you want."

"It all happened so fast. It's such a blur. I just—they kept saying things to me. Looking at me. Licking their lips at me. Clint got them angry with him so they'd leave me alone. He told me to run, and I did. I hopped the fence to the elementary school playground and he took off on his bike."

"My God, princess."

"Next thing I know, I'm calling Michael to come get me. Calling 9-1-1 and telling them they have to get out there. We're driving up and down roads with tires squealing in the distance. And then we come upon Clint's bike."

I felt my voice catching in my throat as Mom tucked my head into the crook of her neck.

"Where was his bike?"

My chest jumped. "Crushed into the metal railing of a bridge. Momma, he fell into the river. Twenty feet, down onto the bank. It was terrible, Mom. He looked absolutely mangled. He stopped breathing. There was water. Michael kept screaming at me. There were sirens and I kept calling out his name, trying to get him to wake up. I just couldn't leave him down there like that, Mom. I couldn't let him be alone. Please don't be mad at me. Please."

"I could never be mad at you. Ever. I'm just so thankful you're okay."

"Please don't be mad. Please. Please, Mom. Please."

I cried into her, wrapping my arms around her neck. I clung to her tighter than I could ever remember, and she rocked me side to side. I heard her singing a song in my ear. A Spanish lullaby she'd always sung to me as a little girl. It calmed my soul and soothed my fears, quieting down my tears.

Then a knock came at the door.

"Raelynn Cleaver?"

The man's voice stunned both my mother and myself. Until it dawned on me.

The police.

The knock came again and Mom stood up with me. I slid to her side, walking with her toward the door as she cracked it open. I peeked around the corner with my tear-stained cheeks, studying the two officers standing on our porch.

Wow, Michael really wasn't joking.

"Can I help you?" Mom asked.

They brandished their badges. "I'm Officer Talbot. This here is Officer Williams. We need to speak with your daughter about an incident last night. A motorcycle wreck, supposedly involving a car full of boys?"

I piped up. "Not supposedly."

Mom held her hand up, signaling for me to be quiet.

"You are more than welcome to come inside and sit. I can make us some coffee. But before you speak with my daughter, she's going to get herself a hot shower."

The officer sighed. "Ma'am, I'm afraid this is urgent."

Mom stood her ground. "Well, so is her shower. She's covered in blood and still shaking from trauma. You can take it, or you can leave it. But if you take it, it comes with coffee, courtesy of me."

She held the door open, waiting for the officers to choose.

"Either way, I'm going to go run my daughter a hot shower before placing a call to her school. She's in no condition to go to classes today. Give us thirty minutes, and we'll be with you. Or find another time. I'm good either way."

And as my mother stood there, stronger than I'd ever seen her, I leaned my forehead against her shoulder. I kissed her robe, hoping she felt it through her clothing. Her hand came up, running through my hair as the officers murmured between themselves.

"All right, ma'am. We'd enjoy the cup of coffee."

Mom smiled. "Great. Let me get my daughter in a shower, then I'll brew a pot while placing that quick phone call."

8

CLINTON

"I already pushed back the trip, Cecilia. Just what exactly do you expect me to do about it?"

"I expect you to cancel it, Howard. Because your son is going to need you in the coming weeks."

I felt myself waking up, but I didn't open my eyes. The second I heard their voices, I stayed silent. I kept my breathing even. I wanted to listen in on their conversation. On what they were arguing about. And as their hushed whispers grew to faint growls, I wondered if my father would ever give a shit about me.

"I'm not canceling anything, Cecilia. This meeting is too important."

She scoffed. "Then do it via video conference. From your laptop, or your home office. My God, Howard, you've got one but you never use it."

"Because I have to be there in person. I'm the owner of the damn thing. I can't just not show up to a meeting everyone is expecting me to be at."

"Well, when you tell them your only child has gotten himself into a life-threatening accident. I'm sure they'll change their tune."

He snickered. "CeCe, we don't know the details of that crash. The police are still trying to sniff things out. For all we know, this was Clinton's fault!"

"And why does that matter?" she hissed.

"It matters because if he put himself in this situation, he can get himself out of it. It one hundred percent matters, if you knew anything about raising a boy like him!"

"So you think that even if he did cause this accident, he wouldn't need his father? Howard, he's staring down the barrel of weeks of physical therapy. Weeks of strenuous activity before he's walking normal and riding his bike and moving without assistance. He needs you at home. He's a boy, Howard."

"He's my boy, and don't you forget it. I know what I need to do in order to parent my son, Cecilia. You, of all people, don't need to educate me on that."

"Then step up and be the father he needs."

I waited for it. I braced for the cracking sound of his hand against her face. I mean, I knew it was coming. It would have been coming had I said something like that to him. Cecilia was brave. Braver than I could have ever been. I was proud of her for standing up for what she believed. And honored that she was standing up for me.

But I heard the door of my hospital room whip open, stalling out the moment in its tracks.

"Take it outside, if you have to fight. Clint needs his rest, and I won't have you two ruining it with your bickering. Understand?"

The doctor's voice was curt. Pierced. And I would have given anything to see my father's face. The argument halted in its tracks before Cecilia apologized. But all I heard from my father was the lumbering of footsteps, murmuring and stumbling. Cursing. I heard the clicking of Cecilia's heels as they left the room.

"Howard. Get back here!"

I let my eyes fall open as I stared at the ceiling. The doctor walked around me, checking vitals and shining that godforsaken light in my eyes. I wanted to rip that damn flashlight out of his hand and bash him over the head with it. Or shove it up his ass. One of the two.

"The talk with the police wear you out?"

I shrugged. "Got it over with."

"Sometimes that's the best course of action."

"What day is it?"

He chuckled. "Still Friday. Just after lunch. Almost two, I think? Have you eaten?"

"No."

"Well, I'll get the nurse to run down to the kitchen. The lunch trays have already gone by, but I'm sure she can pick you up something that is suitable for your current diet."

I sighed. "Ah, yes. The boring, no fun foods diet."

He snickered. "I've been on that diet before. It's more or less so nothing interacts with the medications you're on. Like food dyes and such."

"Just don't have anyone attempt to mix up white rice and a banana again. I don't know who decided that was a good thing, but it isn't."

The doctor took a few notes, then pressed my morphine button. I was on my last pump of it. After today, no more morphine. I wasn't sure how I'd take that. How my body would react to it. Or what kind of pain I'd be in. But any step down was a step closer to home. And a step closer to Rae.

Which was where I wanted to be.

I heard the doctor talking to Cecilia outside. But I didn't hear my father. No shocker there, of course. He probably stormed off and used this fight as an excuse to get more work done. And if it was up to me? He'd stay gone. He didn't help. He wasn't supportive. And, apparently, this accident was all my fault. At the very least, I didn't deserve an ounce of pity until it was proven that I didn't cause my almost-death.

He could fuck off with all that bullshit.

"Clint? Can you hear me?"

I nodded as I cleared my throat. Cecilia sat down beside me again, taking my hand like she had this morning.

"Dad's gone again, isn't he?"

"You know how he is."

I snickered. "Yeah, yeah. I know how he is."

That seemed to be the excuse for my father more days than not nowadays.

"How are you feeling, Clint?"

I sighed. "Better. But the doctor also just pressed my morphine button, so…"

"I was on morphine once, you know. A little ball drip thing fastened around my waist in a fanny pack."

"That when you got your boobs done?"

I didn't catch the question before it flew out of my mouth. But

I was kind of glad I didn't. Because it launched Cecilia into another story of her life I would have never expected from her.

"Actually, yes. It was a reconstructive surgery I got when I was twenty. Saved up almost my entire life for it."

I paused. "Reconstructive surgery?"

She giggled. "Yep. I left home when I was seventeen, after graduating high school early. And in between part-time classes at the local community college, I took on a job. Saved up as much as I could while living with three other girls in a two-bedroom apartment to save up enough money to have it corrected. And boy, was that a surgery."

"What was the defect?"

"Its technical name is 'tubular hypoplasia,' or something like that. It essentially means the base of a woman's breast is much narrower than it should be, causing a tissue deformity and nipple malformation during puberty."

"So much more than I ever needed to know about my stepmom."

"And yet, here we are."

The two of us laughed softly before she patted my arm.

"Hell of a surgery. Nine hours under, lots of sawing and suctioning and tugging about. And when I came out of it in recovery, I had this compression bra on and a fanny pack of morphine around my waist with tubes running into the tops of my chest."

"Yikes."

"Yep. I still don't remember those first two weeks of recuperation. Because morphine wasn't the only drug I was on during that recovery time."

I smiled. "Holy shit. I don't blame you on that one, then. This morphine's got me fucked up enough as it is."

"You know, part of me wants to tell you 'language.' But, here I am. Cursing up a storm along with you."

It almost felt surreal. Like this was simply another dream. The shy, timid, soft-spoken stepmother I'd become accustomed to was anything but. And it made me wonder why the absolute fuck she'd settled for someone like my father. Then again, I knew why. We both knew why. She'd grown up in a life of conservatism. And my father, well, wasn't. He gave her all the things she wanted. And even things she didn't want. That would be attractive to any woman. Even a woman with her head seemingly screwed on straight.

Money talked nowadays.

"So, weeks of physical therapy?"

She paused. "You heard that?"

I shrugged. "Bits and pieces. I was still waking up and falling back asleep."

"You're a shit liar, you know."

That made me laugh hard. "All right. All right. You caught me."

"I'm sorry, Clint."

"Don't be. You stuck up for me. No one's ever done that before."

"I should've started doing it sooner."

"Well, something tells me you've at least been trying."

"I'll get him to stay behind, though. Don't worry."

"At this point, I'd rather him go."

She paused. "Really?"

I nodded. "He's useless during shit like this. In his mind, this is my fault. So the medical bill will be my fault. For all I know, since I'm eighteen, he'll write me up some sort of an official loan document and expect me to pay him back for it. Either that, or he'll feel guilty after the fact and buy me a new bike to try and make things better."

"I'm sorry, Clint."

"Not your fault, Cecilia."

As I lay there, holding her hand within mine, I felt the crushing weight of an unwanted burden settle against my chest. I closed my eyes, hoping sleep would sweep me underneath its warm current again and rid me of the insanity of my mind. What in the world had I done to make my father hate me so much? Why couldn't he just love me? Accept me? I mean, I was his only child. It wasn't as if there was another child to play 'favorites' with.

Did he just not want me?

Had he ever wanted me?

"I'll be here with you, okay?"

Cecilia's voice pierced my thoughts, and my next question flew out faster than I could even process it.

"But why? You don't owe me anything. And I'm pretty sure you don't love Dad. So, you aren't sticking around for him."

And after a beat of silence, she sighed.

"I'll be here because I want to be here. And you'll just have to deal with it."

She didn't comment on my other insinuation. On the other comment I'd made. And I couldn't blame her.

I mean, how the hell could she love a man like that?

"I feel tired."

"Then get some rest. I've got a book I'm reading, and I'll let you know what the doctor says—if anything—once you wake back up."

I sighed. "What are you reading?"

She held up the book in front of my face. "Finding The Spouse You Married."

I would have laughed had my heart not randomly started aching for her. This beautiful woman, full of love and interesting stories and lessons to pass on, was reading some bullshit self-help book on how to make my dad treat her the way she wanted to be treated. It was sickening, and yet very telling of what my mother must've gone through with Dad.

I wondered if she'd ever tried reading books to fix what had become so broken.

"Want me to read you a page? The anecdotal stories are pretty funny."

I smiled, closing my eyes. "Sure. Go ahead."

"All right. This particular chapter is about getting the two spouses on the same page. Listen to this. There are two people in the story, Mary Margaret and James. And I'll let the story tell the rest."

I settled into bed as she launched into this story. A ridiculous story of some imaginary married couple that had drifted apart because James thought he wasn't getting enough sex. And Mary Margaret thought James had gotten lazy about sex. I chuckled as Cecilia giggled through the story, and before she could wrap it up the two of us fell apart in laughter. The story was so ridiculous, and had almost nothing to do with them getting on the same page. I mean, I'm sure it did, eventually. But Cecilia and I were laughing so hard we couldn't actually get to that part.

"It's so ridiculous. I still can't finish this chapter because of the story."

My chest jumped with laughter. "How the hell can you read shit like that?"

Cecilia kept giggling. "I don't know. It's so insane. And all the stories are like that. I guess I just…"

Her sentence trailed off and I coughed, trying to calm down my laughter. Because hers had shut down, like someone had flipped a switch inside her head.

"You just what?" I asked.

She sighed. "I guess I'm just desperate to get back the man I married, I guess. And maybe, if I read enough of these books, the answer will jump out at me and I can fix what's been so very broken for so long."

And in that moment, I didn't know which I hated more: my father, for putting her in this position, or the damn author of that book, for preying on women like her and draining them of their money, only to feed them shit I could sum up with one sentence.

It can't be fixed if the other person doesn't feel like they need fixing.

9
———

RAELYNN

"Why don't you come make brownies with me? We can have them for after dinner tonight."

"Want to try our hand at making fresh ice cream to go with them?"

"Let's go out to eat tonight. Come back to the brownies and have a movie night."

"Want to put on pajamas, too? We could go out to eat in our pajamas."

I knew my mother was trying the best she could to cheer me up. To get my mind off things. But all day yesterday had spiraled into my Saturday, and I still sat up in my room. By the window. Hoping someone might come over and give me information on how Clint was doing. His father, even if he yelled it at me. His stepmother, even if I had to pull it out of her. Hell, even the police officers, even if they had more questions for me to answer.

I'd take any update I could get.

I sighed, gazing out over the dirt we had for a front lawn. The rain drizzled down, creating a sheen of mist over everything as clouds rolled above. The sun hadn't peeked through once. So, apparently, it and I were on the same wavelength. The weather matched my mood perfectly, and I found myself brooding at my windowsill.

Until a knock came at my door.

"Hey there, sweetie."

I sighed. "Hey, Mom."

"I brought you some lunch. Leftovers from last night."

"Thanks."

"You mind if I eat in here with you? The breadsticks look tempting."

"You can have them, if you want."

I heard her sit on my bed, but I didn't move. I wasn't hungry. Even though eggplant parmesan was my favorite. I wanted to be at the hospital with Clint. By his side, assuring him I'd be there for him. I'd made him a promise. I'd told him I wouldn't leave his side. And yet I couldn't get past his fucking father.

At Clint's side was the only place I wanted to be.

And his father didn't give a shit about that.

Mom cleared her throat. "You sure you're not hungry?"

I nodded. "I'm sure."

"You want to come downstairs and watch Judge Judy with me?"

"Maybe later."

"It'll give you a chance to yell at the television for a while."

I shrugged. "Not really in a yelling mood."

She sighed. "Sweetheart, I know you're worried about him. But—"

"Mom, please. I just…"

I heard her stand up before her hand came down against my back. I closed my eyes, feeling my empty tear ducts try to churn out more salted tears. But there were no more for me to cry. My pillow had soaked all of them up last night. They burned without recompense as Mom rubbed my back, trying her best to continue distracting me.

I was tired of the distractions, though.

I wanted to know how Clint was doing.

"I made him a promise."

"I know you did, sweetie."

I sighed. "And I'm not there, like I promised."

"I'm sure he's a smart boy and has figured out why you aren't there. Especially if he doesn't have a good relationship with his father."

"I just don't get it. All I want to do is be there, and his father's being a—"

Mom sat down, wrapping her arms around me. She pulled me

against her and I felt my frustration growing. The more I thought about it, the angrier I became. I mean, why they fuck did his dad have to be such an absolute asshole? I'd confided in Mom with just about everything. The first time I ever met his father. What he did. The bruises Clint came to school with. The life he really led with his father behind those massive mansion doors.

Her party tricks were wearing thin as my worry for Clint grew.

"Maybe he's not at the hospital anymore," I murmured.

Mom kissed the top of my head. "At any rate, it's best if you stay here and wait for an update. The last thing you need to be doing is storming in there and getting yourself into trouble. Especially after already dealing with the police."

"It wasn't his fault, Mom."

"And I believe you. But, until things cool down, you know I'm right."

I hated that fact, too.

The doorbell rang downstairs and I scoffed. I didn't give a shit who it was, but I wanted them to leave. Mom kissed me one more time, then ventured downstairs. I heard her whistling to herself, like the sunshine poured out of her ass in that very moment. I rolled my eyes. I hunkered back down by the windowsill and watched the misty rainfall coat my window.

Until I heard familiar voices racing up the stairs.

"Hey! Girlie!"

"Your mom said you're up here!"

"Get dressed, we're heading out."

I whipped around at the sound of Allison and Michael's voices. They barged into my room, all smiles and dressed to the nines. Well, not really. But Michael stood there in a pair of khaki pants with a polo shirt tucked in and Allison was in one of her bright ensembles.

I furrowed my brow. "What are you guys doing here?"

Allison rolled her eyes. "Does that matter? Come on. Get cleaned up. We're heading out."

I stood. "Where are we going?"

Michael grinned. "Pretty sure there's someone in a hospital waiting to see you."

My eyes bulged before I started rushing around my room. I threw clothes around while Allison giggled at me, then I stumbled out of my pajamas. I heard Michael leave the room, leaving me to undress as Allison tossed me my clothes. And after I'd pulled on a fresh pair of jeans and a T-shirt, I rushed to the bathroom.

"Give me five minutes!"

I brushed my teeth and splashed some water in my face. I ran a brush through my hair before piling it on top of my head in a bun. I grabbed my chapstick and charged out of the bedroom, tucking it into my back pocket.

I found Allison and Michael at the bottom of the steps with my cell phone.

"Ready to go?" he asked.

I leapt down the steps, taking my phone from him. And as I tucked it away in my bra, I looked over at my mother. She smiled at me, blowing me a kiss as I stood there with my two best friends. My heart went out to her. I rushed over to her, giving her a massive hug before I pressed a kiss against her cheek.

"I love you," I whispered.

She patted my back. "I love you, too. Now, get going. I want to know how that boy's doing, too."

We rushed out toward Michael's car and hopped in. I crawled in back, anxious to get out of this driveway and on the road. I knew Mom had called Michael and Allison. Probably to try and pull me out of my funk.

But had she called the hospital as well?

I licked my lips. "Does anyone at the hospital know we're coming?"

Michael shrugged. "Does it matter? They can't expect you to just sit on your hands and wait without hearing a word. You were at the crash site."

Allison nodded. "It's absolutely ridiculous. You saved him. You're the one that found him. You deserve to know what's going on with him."

"He's got a bastard of a father, but that shouldn't stop him from updating you on his son's condition."

"If anything, he should be thanking you. Because you're the reason Clint is still alive."

I nodded slowly. "Thank you guys so much."

Allison reached back, taking my hand. "That's what friends are for."

I sniffled. "I take it Michael filled you in?"

She nodded. "On everything. Especially once you didn't show up at school yesterday."

"I'm sorry I didn't tell you. I just—"

She squeezed my hand. "No need to apologize, crazytown. I'm not upset. I'm just glad you guys are okay."

"Even Clint?"

Michael nodded. "Even Clint."

Allison had the bright idea of picking up fast food and sneaking it into the hospital for Clint. Which shocked me, because that was something she'd do for me. Was it possible they were finally considering Clint part of our group? A friend, even? I hoped so, in the pit of my soul. Allison stuffed the food into her purse after we were done eating, and even managed to prop up a soda in one of her pockets so it wouldn't tip over.

And after sneaking through the hospital corridors, we finally found Clint's room.

"Holy sh—"

I held up my hand, stopping Michael's sentence in its tracks. Clint was fast asleep, and no one was in his room. This couldn't have been planned any better. My eyes ran along him as I slowly walked into his room. His ICU room.

"Oh, Clint," I whispered.

I walked over to his bedside with my hands trembling. He was in rough shape. Even rougher than I remembered. Both of his eyes were blackened, along with his jaw. His nose had been set, so he had a brace around it, taped down to his face, which had red marks where it wasn't bruised. He had his right arm in a sling, and his neck was braced. Unable to move. He had tubes running in and out of his nose. In and out of his hands. His arms. Even from underneath the covers.

My lip quivered as I sat in a chair beside his bed.

I reached out for his hand, placing mine against his. I settled it softly, feeling how cold he was to the touch. The second I touched him, his eyes popped open. I yanked my hand back, but only partially. Because he moved with lightning speed, wrapping his hand around my wrist.

"Rae?"

I looked over at Michael and Allison as they stood at the foot of his bed, beckoning for me to talk to the boy.

"I can't move my neck. Please tell me that's you."

Tears rushed my eyes as I stood up. I slowly maneuvered myself into his view, listening as he breathed a sigh of relief. I sniffled and smiled, gazing into his bloodshot eyes.

"Hey there."

He grinned. "Hello, beautiful."

His fingers slipped between mine, our hands lacing themselves together. I wiped at my tears with my free hand as I sat on the edge of his bed. My eyes kept dancing over him. I knew there were probably injuries I couldn't see. And, as if he'd read my mind, he began rattling them off to me.

"I've got a concussion, too. Which is why my neck is braced like this."

I nodded slowly. "What else?"

He sighed. "Well, I broke my collarbone. Which didn't help my dislocated shoulder. My ribs are pretty bruised. But not broken, miraculously."

"Yeah."

"There was minor internal bleeding, though. They found it during surgery. I've got some stitches in places no one should have stitches. But it is what it is. If I have a good day today, I get moved out of ICU. They say the concussion is almost gone. So at least it wasn't a bad one."

"Oh, Clint."

Michael walked up beside me. "Jesus, man, you look rough."

Clint looked surprised, but didn't skip a beat. "I'd say I've had worse. But that would actually be a lie."

Allison walked around to his other side. "Can we get you anything?"

I smiled. "Are you able to eat?"

Michael nodded. "Because we brought you a burger and fries from a joint up the road."

Allison started pulling the food out. "With a Mountain Dew. Rae said it's your favorite."

Clint smiled. "That's my girl."

And my heart soared with delight.

Allison handed him the food as I navigated the controls for his hospital bed. I got him sitting up without moving his neck too much, then he took everything over. He seemed happy to see us. Having Allison and Michael with me didn't kick up too much tension. I kept smiling while Clint talked. While he chewed. While he swallowed. So many small things about him I'd taken for granted. Things no one ever thinks about enjoying on another person.

Until there's a fear of no longer having those things.

Michael cleared his throat. "Well, Allison and I should probably go stand guard."

Allison nodded. "Yeah. In case your parents come back."

Clint furrowed his brow. "My parents?"

I leaned in. "They don't exactly know we're here."

His eyes darkened. "What did my father say to you?"

I sighed. "We can talk about that later, okay? I promise I'll tell you why I haven't been here. I just wanted you to know I hadn't abandoned you. If I could have gotten to you, I would have."

He brought my hands to his lips to kiss. "I know. I know you would have. I know you better than that."

And as my two best friends slipped out into the hallway, I sighed at the touch of his lips against my skin.

A touch I hadn't been sure I'd ever feel again, thanks to the events of Thursday night.

10

CLINTON

I couldn't stop staring. I hadn't seen those eyes in what seemed like an eternity, and my blood boiled at the idea of my father robbing me of them. I heard my heart monitor ticking up. I felt my blood pressure rising. Rae's worried eyes darted to all the machines around me before dipping her lips down against my ear.

"Breathe for me. It's okay. I'm here. Just breathe."

I wrapped my arms around her, pulling her close to me. I didn't care what part of me hurt. I didn't care what part of me cried out for mercy. I needed to feel her. I needed to hold her. I needed to be close to her, just in case someone came to remove her. I closed my eyes, breathing along with her as she coached me through my breaths. I slid my left-hand fingers through her hair, trying to be ginger with my right arm in its sling. She curled up against me, snuggling into bed. Her warmth overcame me and the scent of her filled me with life.

I wanted nothing more than for her to stay here with me. Like this.

She drew in shuddered breaths and I wanted so badly to kiss her. To lean down and kiss the top of her head. She sniffled, wiped at her tears and snuggled deeper into me as I tried so hard to keep my groans of pain at bay. I wouldn't rob her of this. I wouldn't rob either of us of this moment.

Because it had been a long time coming.

"Thank you so much."

I furrowed my brow. "For what?"

She sniffled. "For doing what you did. For leading those assholes away. Had you not, they might've—"

I gripped her hair softly. "Never, on my life, would I have ever let something happen to you. Never. Not while you're around me. Do you hear me?"

She nodded softly. "I just can't help but think that this is all my fault."

"If I could shake my head fervently right now at you, I would. This isn't your fault. None of this would've taken place had those assholes just stayed at home. Passed right by us instead of coming into the parking lot. They started this. Not you, and certainly not me."

She paused. "The police came to talk to me yesterday morning."

"I've talked with them, too."

"Is everything going to be okay?"

"Once they find those dickweeds and arrest them, I'll feel even better. But, yes, beautiful. Everything is going to be okay. Thank you for talking with them. I'm sorry I couldn't have been there to support you through it."

She scoffed. "I'm sorry I haven't been here since the accident. I made you a promise and—"

"—and my father got in the way. Like he always does. This isn't your fault. I had a feeling my father had done something, even though my stepmother wouldn't tell me what he'd done."

"So they've been here for you? Through all this."

I sighed. "Eh, more or less. I've woken up to Cecilia instead of my father. The only time I woke up to the sound of Dad's voice, he was arguing with her."

"Arguing? About what?"

I scoffed. "A business trip Cecilia wanted him to cancel."

Rae rose up, looking into my eyes. "Are you fucking kidding me?"

I shrugged, groaning at the pain. "That's how he is. Work comes before everything. He thought he was doing everyone a favor by pushing the trip back once already."

"Your father's an absolute asshole."

I chuckled. "You don't have to tell me."

"You should tell the doctors what he does to you."

"By the sounds of it, someone already has."

Rae blushed, but all I did was laugh. I pulled her back down to my side, feeling her curl around me. Her leg slipped between mine, and it was the closest I'd felt to her in a long time. I drew in a deep breath as my fingertips stroked her arm, sending goosebumps puckering her skin for me to touch.

"It just kinda slipped out. I'm sorry."

I grinned. "Ah, worse things have happened. I'm eighteen, so there isn't much people can do now except look into my father. And he'll pay them off. Like he usually does. Then we'll go on about our lives and he'll buy me something out of guilt to make things okay again."

"So this has happened before? Someone reporting him?"

"Yep. I reported him once."

Rae sighed. "This is such shit."

"The way I see it, I've got less than a year. Then I graduate and I'm free to go and do as I please. Just need that high school diploma, even if it isn't enough to get me into a community college or whatever."

"Speaking of graduation, what does your recovery look like? You're going to walk and all that, right?"

"Well, I'm pretty beat up. I know Dad wants me out before he goes on this fun business trip. But just because my concussion is clearing up doesn't mean I'm out of here. If things go perfectly, I might get released in a couple days. But, realistically, I'm looking at another week in this hospital. At least, before they release me."

"What happens after they release you, Clint?"

"The usual. Physical therapy. Exercises. In home, and in an office somewhere. That will help fix my back and the movement in my arm, once my collarbone heals."

She paused. "Wait, your back? What happened to your back?"

I grinned. "I fell twenty feet down a ravine and landed on a bunch of rocks. My vertebrae have slipped out of place. My back's crooked from the impact."

Her eyes rose to meet mine. "You didn't tell me that."

"I'm sorry. I guess, in the grand scheme of things, it's easier if I tell you what's *not* wrong with me."

I laughed, but she didn't find that funny.

"Not a cool joke, Clint."

I cleared my throat. "Sorry, beautiful."

I watched her sit up, and already I missed her warmth. She placed one arm over me, propping herself up as her body hovered over mine. I gazed into her eyes as I sat there, staring at her. Propped up for the first time in days as I gazed upon the most beautiful face I'd ever come to know in my short life.

I smiled. "I'm really glad you're here."

Rae blushed. "I'm glad I'm here, too."

"You're eighteen, right?"

She paused. "Yeah. Why?"

"I'll have a talk with the doctor about putting you on my HIPAA form."

"Your what now?"

I chuckled. "It's a release form that designates who can know about my condition. Since you're technically a legal adult, I can put you on the list so the hospital can call and update you on how I'm doing."

"Or I could pick up your school work and bring it to you so we can study together. Which means your father looks like an absolute asshole if he stands in the way of your studies."

"I like the way you think, Cleaver."

She winked. "And here I thought you'd keep calling me 'beautiful.'"

My smile faded. "You'd really do that for me?"

"Do what?"

"Bring my schoolwork and help me study?"

"I mean, why wouldn't I? You're going to be here while school is still happening. You'll still have tests and shit like that. If you want to graduate, you have to at least not fail things. So, yeah. Of course I'd do that for you."

I felt overwhelmed by her words. This beautiful young girl really was willing to bend over backwards for me. Which was such a refreshing change of pace from my father. I blinked back tears, feeling like a great big pussy as a smile crossed Rae's face.

"We'll blame it on the pain you're in, okay?"

I snickered. "Yeah. Sure. Good thinking."

I looked up and saw Michael staring inside the room at us. And I could've sworn he and Allison were holding hands. He gave me a thumbs-up, I guess signaling to me that the coast was still clear. I reached my arm out for Rae again.

"Come here, gorgeous."

She smiled. "Oh, I like that one much better."

"I figured you would."

She lay back down in my arms and I closed my eyes. This was how I wanted things to be. Her, nestled against me, while I closed my eyes and slept. The food sat well in my stomach. Greasy, fatty food that helped me wake up a bit. All this healthy shit the hospital fed me—bland foods like rice and unbuttered toast—was getting old. And now that they had me off the morphine drip, why couldn't I have a nice burger?

Even if it came back up on me, it was still worth it to see Rae. To hold her again. To smell her again. To be next to her again.

"You saved me."

I snickered. "No, gorgeous. You saved me. And I owe you my life for it."

She kissed my chest. "You owe me nothing."

"I owe you everything, and you'll like it that way."

She giggled. "You're a mess, you know that?"

"A mess you like."

"A mess I—"

She paused, and my heart skipped a beat. Surely she hadn't been about to say something like that. What I wouldn't have given in that moment to look down at her. To read her face and gaze into her eyes. Fucking hell, this damn neck brace. I needed it off, and now.

But when she buried herself into my side, I knew. I knew what she almost said.

And I hoped one day, she knew I felt the same way.

"Get some rest, Clint. I'm sure you're exhausted."

I stroked my fingers up and down her back. "I don't want to miss a second with you."

She wrapped her arm around me. "I promise, I'll be back. I'm bringing your homework, remember? I've become your study buddy. Plus, you're putting me on that 'HIPPO' form."

"HIPAA."

"What?"

"HIPAA. With an 'A'."

"'HIPPO' sounds better."

I chuckled. "It does, doesn't it?"

"Yep. You can't get rid of me that easily, handsome."

I smiled. "Trust me, I don't want to."

She paused. "I like sappy you. It's very romantic."

"Don't give away all my secrets at school now. Can't have all the guys being as smooth as me. Someone might steal you away."

She snickered. "I'd like to see them try."

"I'll punch them in the throat if they try."

"You and what army?"

"Me and the left arm that can still move."

She giggled. "Let's not break the other arm, okay?"

"Technically, it's my collarbone. My right arm was just dislocated."

"Oh. Oh. Yeah. Totally better then, Mr. Internal Bleeding."

I laughed. "Are we really making jokes out of my injuries?"

She reached up, kissing my jawline. "Do we really have any other reaction to this situation?"

My face fell. "I guess you're right."

And as she tucked herself back against me, my eyes fell closed. Sleep began drawing me under. I felt myself succumbing to the darkness. And as my body relaxed, I hoped with all my might Rae would be here when I woke up. I hoped with all my might my father wouldn't give her any other trouble. But if he did, I hoped with all my might Cecilia would find her voice again.

Long enough to put him in his fucking place.

11

RAELYNN

Clint's soft sleeping sounds lulled me into my own sort of trance. I knew Michael and Allison wanted to get back on the road, since they'd been standing in the hallway for well over an hour. But I couldn't relinquish Clint. I kept wrapping myself around him. Clinging to him. Simply thankful to be in his presence again.

I have to go, though.

I sighed as I slowly untangled myself from his body. I reached up, pressing a soft kiss against his bruised cheek. His face looked like a mess. Every time I gazed up into it, there seemed to be a new bruise. Or a spreading bruise. Or another part of his face swelling. It made me sick to my stomach.

Let the boy sleep, Rae.

"I'll be back soon."

I whispered the words against the shell of his ear, then slipped off the bed. I peeked out into the hallway, watching as Michael and Allison stared at me. I sighed before nodding my head, signaling to him that I was ready to head out.

Until Clint jerked awake.

"Rae?"

I whipped around. "What is it? I'm right here."

"Rae? Where are you? Rae!"

I rushed back to his side, lunging myself into his face. I crawled back up onto the bed, straddling him as I blocked off his view of the rest of the room. Michael and Allison rushed in. I pressed my lips against Clint's, trying to stop his yelling. If he spooked the nurses or one of the doctors, we'd be thrown out.

"Sh-sh-sh-sh-sh. It's me. I'm right here."

His lip quivered. "I'm sorry. I—I felt you leave, and—"

I shook my head. "Your father isn't here. It's okay. I figured since you'd fallen asleep—"

"Dad's already gone."

He blurted out the words and I heard the hurt in his voice. I looked back at my two best friends, watching as they flicked their hands out at me. Telling me to stay as they made their leave again. His statement didn't shock me, but it hurt me. Mostly, because I saw how much it hurt Clint.

"What was that?" I asked.

He grimaced. "Dad's already gone."

I slid off to his side. "But, I thought you said—"

He sighed. "He and my stepmother got into another fight last night. I mean, a really good fight. The hospital threw them out. I haven't seen either of them since."

"Then maybe your father is still in town. Just not allowed back in the hospital."

"He called me to let me know he'd be back before I was released."

The flatness of Clint's voice turned my stomach. I took his hand, lacing our fingers together as I rested my head against his good shoulder. He drew in broken breaths, trying so hard to stay strong when I knew all he wanted to do was be weak.

I kissed his arm. "It's just me. You can let it out."

"He fucking left me, Rae. To rot in this hospital bed. And Cecilia isn't allowed back in the hospital. At least until tomorrow morning. And I have no one. Just the doctors and the nurse staff who come in here with their pitiful glances and their small talk."

"You have me."

He snickered. "Thank fuck for that."

I nuzzled against him. I watched his chest jump as his voice hiccuped. I gazed into his face, watching as tears rushed down his cheeks. I sat up, wiping at them softly with my fingertips. I grabbed his drink and put the straw to his lips, giving his trembling lip something to do.

"I'm right here. I won't go anywhere if you don't want me to."

He swallowed down the liquid. "I just—don't understand."

I rubbed his arm. "What don't you understand?"

He closed his eyes. "Why my father doesn't love me."

I didn't know how to answer him. I didn't know what to tell him. The only thing I could do was be there for him, so I settled deeper into his side. I watched him cry silent tears as he held his sounds back, his chest hiccupping with pain and anger and sadness.

"Clint, I—"

He sniffled. "For years, it's been this way. For years, my father has seen me as nothing. But, I mean, even the last time I was in the hospital, he was here. Present. Sure, typing away on his laptop and taking phone calls. I'd fallen out of a fucking tree and jammed my neck. And every time I woke up, he was at my bedside. Working, yes. But here. And now? He's nowhere to be found. On a jet somewhere, or chilling on some island with a cocktail in his hand while the only person who's been at my side since I was admitted to the hospital sits at home, by herself, because of him!"

I cupped his cheek. "I'm so sorry, Clint."

"My father is a good-for-nothing piece of shit. And he thinks that, for some reason, being back before I'm discharged is good enough. Like, sure. I'll leave you while you're in the hospital. While you're hooked up to tubes and in ICU. But, at least I'll be here by the time they take your fucking catheter out."

I leaned his bed back as he closed his eyes. Something in the pit of my gut told me he wanted to lean back, so I laid him down. I tucked the blankets around him tightly because I really didn't know what else to do.

Other than listen, of course.

He murmured, "Thanks."

I shook my head. "No thanks needed. I just wish I had something to tell you. Or advice to give."

He snickered. "There's no advice when it comes to my father. He treats me like a nuisance rather than a fucking son."

"I'd do anything to take your pain away, Clint. All of it. Physical. Emotional. Mental. All of it."

"I know you would. But I wouldn't let you. I've been dealing with this for a long time. I can do it for a few more months."

"If it makes you feel any better, you're right. He's a piece of shit human being who doesn't deserve the type of son you are in his life."

He scoffed. "I'm not anything special. It's not like I made things easy on him."

I nodded. "I'm sure that's true. But at one point in time, you were nothing but an innocent boy. A boy who missed his mother and didn't understand the world. Anger begets anger, Clint. You are this way and you act this way because you've learned to survive your father. Not thrive alongside him. And that's your father's fault."

His eyes found mine. "Since when did you become so smart?"

I smiled softly. "You forget we both have Daddy issues."

He chuckled. "How is it that you can make me smile, even in this kind of situation?"

I shrugged. "Consider it my superpower. Making people smile and laugh when they're on the brink of destruction."

"Says a lot about what you've been through."

"Yeah, well. I can cry on your shoulder about it a different time."

"Deal."

I squeezed his hand tightly. "I hope you know this isn't your fault."

"Rae, don't."

"I'm serious, Clint. None of this is your fault. It's got nothing do to with you. Some people just don't know how to be parents. Your father doesn't know how to be a parent. He only knows how to be a businessman, and everything else is a nuisance. Including your stepmother, I'm sure."

"I hope she comes back tomorrow. I've liked having her around."

I smiled. "That's good. I take it you guys have been talking a bit?"

"A bit, sure. I mean, it's been awkward. We don't really know each other, despite the fact that she's been around for a while. But, it's been nice waking up and having her around. She's helped a lot with the doctors. Relaying information. Shit like that."

"Sounds like she's finally figuring out how to step up as a parent."

"And she doesn't berate me for things like my father does."

I swallowed back my growl. "If I could get your father in a room for just a few minutes…"

Clint smirked. "I'd like to hear what you might do to him."

"For starters, I'd sneak in a baseball bat."

"Old school. I like it."

"His kneecaps wouldn't."

The two of us laughed softly as my eyes danced between his. Then Clint closed his eyes.

"I guess I just always wondered if he loved me or not. But now I guess I have my answer."

I snuggled against him, trying to be his rock while his foundation eroded from underneath him.

"And the funny thing now, Rae, is that I'm starting to regret ever wondering at all. I guess ignorance really is bliss, at times."

I looked back over my shoulder and saw Allison wiping at her tears. Even Michael's eyes were glistening. I didn't know what to say. As I looked to them for guidance, all they did was shrug their shoulders. None of us knew what to say. There were no words for the situation. I turned back around, finding Clint staring at me as I sighed.

"You can go, if they need to go," he said.

I nodded. "If they need to leave, they can come back around and get me. Or I'll catch a cab once a doctor kicks me out."

Allison piped up. "Actually, you've been okayed to stay in here for a bit."

I furrowed my brow. "Really?"

"Well, once we get you on this HIPAA form, yes."

I turned around at the sound of the strong voice. A man in a white coat came into the room with a clipboard and a pen. He handed it all to Clint before sitting him up in the hospital bed, using the controls that had taken me damn near ten minutes to figure out.

The doctor quirked an eyebrow. "While we're not fans of how you guys sneaked in—or brought him food—the truth of the matter is that neither his father nor his stepmother are allowed in here right now. So, as long as it's one person at a time, we can overlook some things for a few hours."

I smiled. "Thank you, Doctor. I really appreciate it."

Clint groaned. "What do I do, Doc?"

"Have this young woman put her name, address, and phone

number down. Then you sign at the bottom. That's all you need to do."

Clint handed me the clipboard. "Rae?"

And with a smile on my face, I took it from him to fill in.

Anything that got me one step closer to never being pushed away from his side again.

12

CLINTON

"All right, Mr. Clarke. It's that time again."

I smiled coyly. "Hello, Nurse Nina. Time for me to show you my nooks and crannies again?"

She giggled. "You better stop that flirtatious nonsense. My husband'll come in here and give you a piece of his mind."

"The more, the merrier."

"Hey, now! I saw that cutie patootie that came in here yesterday to visit. I also saw how she made your heartrate monitor rise and fall. You can't tell me there isn't something there."

I chuckled. "That's Rae. And she's a saint. Literally, my guardian angel. She's the one that found me in that ravine."

"Well, thank the Lord for that. Because without her, I wouldn't be accosted by you on a daily basis."

"And you know you'd miss it."

Nurse Nina was always a refreshing face on the ICU floor. An older lady with a spunky personality and a lovely meet-cute story she enjoyed telling people about. Everyone on the hall knew the story of how she and her husband met. And I had to admit, I didn't mind hearing it multiple times a day. She always had a smile on her face and a giggle on the tip of her tongue to offer someone. An infectious sound. One that reminded me a lot of Rae's giggle.

Thank fuck for Rae.

Nurse Nina sighed. "All right. Ready?"

I looked up at the ceiling. "Just be gentle with me. I'm tender, and sensitive."

She giggled. "You wish."

She pulled my blankets off, exposing me to the harsh cold of the room. And after she flipped up my hospital gown, she got to work. I had bandages covering stitches created during surgery. Multiple entry points where the surgeons had explored, cauterizing veins or whatever the fuck it was they did to stop the internal bleeding.

"All right. Things look nice."

I grinned. "Just nice, Nurse Nina?"

"Oh, stop it, you little hellion."

The humor detracted from the fact that she was literally raising my cock up to inspect me. Because out of everything else, my balls had also been bleeding when I came rolling into the E.R. She finished her inspection before changing my bandages. She ran this numbing salve over my wounds before covering them back up with new gauze. She taped everything down and flipped my gown over my hips. Then she changed my blankets out for these nice, warm sheets that made me moan as they hit my skin.

"Fresh out of the dryer. Why do you always flirt with me like this?"

Nurse Nina laughed. "I plucked them out just for you. It'll help you relax a bit."

But I knew the real reason she was doing it.

Does everyone on this damn hall know my father abandoned me?

I closed my eyes as she continued checking my vitals. I felt my tubes being finagled with, and I held my breath for it. I hated it when they shifted the ones going up my nose. It always pinched a bit more than I wanted. I listened as she whirled around the room, whistling to herself and trying to bring a bit of cheer into my life.

Then I heard the clicking of those heels.

"Uh oh. I think I hear someone coming down the hallway."

I opened my eyes as the nurse leaned up my hospital bed. And my heart exploded with delight when I saw Cecilia come into the room. Thank hell, the hospital had let her back in. Because this Sunday was creeping by slower than I wanted it to. She clutched a bag of food and it made me smile. Plus, she had some books in her hands. She pulled up a chair and sat down next to me, sitting the books in my lap.

"I found those on your bookshelf. They had various bookmarks in them, so I figured you might want to continue reading them to pass the time."

I grinned. "I appreciate that."

Cecilia unpacked the food. "I also brought lunch. There's this cute little cafe on the corner just a couple blocks down from here. Massive salads. And great soups. I got you a steak salad with extra meat, and then some thick tomato bisque soup and some of their freshly-baked bread to dip in it."

"Thank you, Cecilia."

"I also snagged you a lemon bar, if your sweet tooth starts acting up."

She said it as if she had some sort of dangerous secret she were carrying around. And the tone of her voice made me chuckle.

"That's more than enough food, thank you. Really. I'm glad you made it back today."

She sighed. "I'm sorry I let your father get to me like that. I couldn't stop thinking about you yesterday."

I reached out, taking her hand. "I'm glad you stood up for yourself against him. Even if it did get you tossed out."

"I should have kept a cooler head for you. You were here all alone yesterday. That isn't right. I shouldn't have been so selfish."

I squeezed her hand. "It's fine. Don't beat yourself up over it, okay?"

I wanted to tell her about Rae, but I figured… baby steps. I thanked her for the food and the books, then dug in while she ate beside me. I looked at the books in my lap and sighed with relief. I'd been painfully bored in this place. And while I usually would've been upset that she rifled through my room, she brought me four books I had been wanting to secretly devour for weeks now.

"I'm sure those books will help. And if there's anything you want from the house, just let me know. I'll do my best to find it."

I took a large bite of my salad. "Thank you. Really."

"Oh! I have exciting news, too."

I looked over at her as I chewed my food, watching as she set her salad down. She looked at me with pride in her eyes, and I wondered what had her so worked up in all the best ways.

"I talked with your father. And meetings are going well. He said he's going to video conference in tonight and hang around with us. I have the laptop in the car, I'll just have to go out and bring it up here once he tells me he's ready. He's going to text, I'll get the laptop, then boom! Howard's here with us."

She beamed with happiness, and I tried to give her the kindest smile I could. But I knew how my father worked. He'd get busy with something, or pissed off at something, and suddenly he'd forget all about me. I didn't have the slightest bit of hope he'd video conference in, much less remember to text Cecilia about it. But she looked so happy about it. So bright and vibrant with hope.

I didn't have the heart to destroy it.

"That sounds great. It'll be nice to see him."

She picked her salad back up. "He's been asking about you. Updates and such. I know he's worried, even though he isn't here right now. His flying out was a knee-jerk reaction to us fighting. Not you, Clint. I hope you know that."

Yeah, sure. "I know."

"Good. Very good. And to celebrate, I'll go out and get us something nice for dinner. You know, so you don't have to keep suffering through all this hospital food. This is going down easily enough, right?"

I nodded, taking another bite. "Like butter."

The two of us continued eating and her vibrance filled the room. I knew she'd take it harder than me when Dad faltered on his word. But I knew how things rolled around here. I didn't want to say any of this to my stepmother, though. She seemed so happy, and I wanted to enjoy that happiness for a while. So I chose to enjoy her company and eat with her instead of pin-pricking her happiness.

After all, my father did enough of that.

Ask her why.

I pushed the thought away from my mind. For days now, I'd been wondering why she loved my father. Why she was with my father. And while I could conjure a decent-enough answer, something about this entire situation I wanted to hear it from her mouth. Wanted to hear her open up and say it. Maybe it was all of our discussions, or somehow getting to know one another. But something inside me wanted to hear her admit why she was still with my father.

Then again, it also wasn't any of my business.

Plus, you don't want to piss her off and have her leave you alone in this place.

No. I really didn't want that. If Cecilia left, this hospital stay would be even more lonely than it had already become. No. It was better to keep the peace and let her be ignorant for a little while. Keep that blissful nature about her that filled up whatever space she might have occupied. She cured my loneliness. She made this stuffy ICU room more bearable.

Minus Rae, of course. Rae made this place shine. Hell, Rae made any place shine. Rae could've made the bowels of hell itself shine with her presence.

Thank fuck for Rae.

And maybe someday, I'd feel confident enough to indulge Cecilia with stories of my girlfriend.

13

RAELYNN

As I sat in my English class just before lunch, I felt everyone's eyes on me. I heard them whispering. I felt their minds wondering. I smelled their confusion and their questions. Their snickers made me upset. Their scoffs made me want to punch them. All day long, people had been staring. When Michael, Allison, and I walked through those school doors. Every time I walked to class and paused by Clint's locker. Every time I got up to do anything, everyone watched my every move.

It felt like even the teachers were out to get me.

"I heard he fell over."

"I heard he was pushed over."

"Do you think she pushed him over?"

"Maybe he jumped over because she won't leave him alone."

"I don't know, I heard there was a car involved."

"Her car?"

"No, no. I don't think she has a car."

"So she rides on the back of his bike? Lucky."

You're damn right I'm lucky.

As the day progressed on, I tried my best to keep my head above water. To stay out of the gossip and ignore the slivers of voices I heard wafting around me. Every transition to class made it a bit more difficult, though. Every bathroom break I took, the girls would stare at me. Silence themselves. Like they were talking about me before I walked up. I shook my head and made my way into the stalls, wanting a bit of peace and quiet. A safe space to breathe before going back out into the shark-infested waters of Valley High School.

I hated this fucking place.

I knew everyone was familiar with what happened. The crash. The boys. The car. Clint's bike. How he was in the hospital, and not due to return to school for a while. Everyone gossiped about it. I had to stop Allison from interjecting into their conversations. I had to hold Michael back a few times, seeing as he lunged at people trying to come up with asinine excuses as to why I was there.

"It's okay, Michael. Come on. We just need to get through the day."

In some ways, I was thankful for them. They wanted to leap to defend Clint. To defend me. And in other ways, I was upset. I was there. I brought Clint back to life. I was the one that got him into this situation, yet I was the one holding other people back?

Why did I always have to be the strong one for everyone else?

"No, for real, guys. Clint's really bad off."

"I heard he broke his collarbone."

"And a concussion? Poor guy. I don't know what Rae's doing here at school."

"Yeah, I'd be by his side every second if I was his girlfriend."

The only thing that made me smile was the school referring to me as 'his girlfriend.'

I didn't like anything else, though.

"Rae, can I ask you—?"

"Rae, what—?"

"Rae, do you have an update on—?"

"Rae, I heard you—"

Every time someone stopped to ask me a question—to actually own up to their curiosities—someone stepped in my way. Michael. Allison. A teacher. The principal. And I was thankful for it. I'd talked about it enough to the police. To the doctors. With Clint. With myself. I didn't want to talk about it with anyone else. I didn't want to keep reliving it. It happened, it was over, and all I wanted to do was focus on Clint's recovery.

And how to tap-dance around his father in the process.

The school lunch bell rang and I sighed. I gathered my things and rushed to my locker, exchanging one set of books for another. I held back tears as I twirled the dial to unlock it. At this point in my day, Clint would have come up and put his hand on my shoulder. Spun me around. Grinned down at me with that shit-eating grin of his before offering to carry my books. Yet his touch didn't come. That grin didn't appear. I stuffed my books into my locker and grabbed the ones I needed for the back half of my day, feeling my stomach growling out for food.

But I wasn't hungry.

I didn't have the energy to eat.

Michael walked up to me. "Ready for lunch?"

Allison giggled. "There you two are. I walked into the cafeteria and was like, 'Whoa, where is everyone?'"

She let out a forced giggle and I sighed. I closed my locker door and gave my best friend a polite smile, trying to thank her for her efforts. Then she put her hand on my shoulder. Much like Clint would have had he been there.

"He's going to be okay, Rae. I promise."

Michael took my books. "Yeah. He's strong as hell, and stubborn. He'll pull through this."

"I know. I know you guys are right. It just… hurts. The murmurs hurt. The rumors hurt. And make me angry. I just wish this school wasn't what it is, you know?"

Allison snickered. "You and me both. Now let's go get some food."

Michael sighed. "I'm starving. Is it pizza day yet?"

They managed to make me smile as we walked our way through the cafeteria. We got our food and sit down in our usual spot, with my books piled beside me. I only picked at a few things, though. Softly sipped my soda. What I wanted was to go back to the hospital. What I wanted was to be eating with Clint. What I wanted was to not be reminded constantly of what happened to him. What happened to us. What happened that night.

But every single student wanted a slice of the pie. A sliver of the drama all to themselves so they could feel important.

"Well. I wasn't sure if you'd show up today or not."

Roy's voice made the hairs on the back of my neck stand on end.

"Especially since you weren't here Friday."

And of course, there was Marina's voice. Right alongside his.

Allison scoffed. "You guys can just walk away."

Michael nodded. "Yeah. Leave her alone for now. This is serious."

I turned around, catching Roy's grin. "Oh, I know it's serious."

Marina giggled. "I hear he's busted up pretty badly."

I shrugged. "Then I don't know why you're smiling. Or laughing. Or even over here in the first place."

Roy chuckled. "Just wanna know, is his face busted up as badly as everyone says it is?"

Marina licked her lips. "There are a lot of rumors going around. Broken nose. Black eyes. Dislocated jaw. No teeth. Lost tongue."

"Guess he's not gonna be such a looker anymore, huh?"

I shot out of my seat. "You want to try running that by me again?"

"Rae, no."

"Rae, sit down. They aren't worth it."

Roy nodded. "You should listen to your posse."

Marina smiled brightly. "I heard he's on a liquid diet for the rest of the school year because his body got mangled with that drop."

Roy laughed. "You think he can still get it up, sweetheart?"

"I don't know, baby. I'm more curious to know if Rae will stay with him if he can't."

"That's it!"

I lunged at them, but Michael stood up. Marina took a step back and cradled into Roy's side, as he shot me a death glare. I swiped my hand out, catching my nails across Marina's face as she cried out in pain. And as the blood surfaced on her skin, Roy hissed at me.

"You'll pay for that, you freak."

Michael pressed his lips to my ear. "Calm down. Stop it. That's enough."

Allison stood up. "We need to get out of here. Teachers are coming."

Michael threw me over his shoulder as Allison gathered my books. They rushed me out of there as Marina whimpered like the bitch she was in some corner. Probably ready to suck Roy's dick to make herself feel better. Hot tears of anger raced down my cheeks as Michael jogged me down the hallway. Like I weighed nothing. Like I was nothing.

I am nothing.

I fell limp to his movements. I heard Allison huffing as she carried my books in her arms. They took me down to my history class before Michael put me back down on my feet, with Allison dropping my books to my desk.

And again, my eyes fell to the seat Clint sat in every class. Every day, after lunch.

"He's not here," I whispered.

Michael rubbed my back. "He'll be back before you know it."

Allison took my hands. "And until then, you have a promise to keep."

Holy shit, that's right.

I had to talk to Clint's teachers.

I spent the rest of my lunch break going around to his classes. I sat down with his teachers and told them exactly what was going on. Gave them the story everyone else wanted. And to my surprise, they listened with an open ear and were more than willing to help him.

"I want him to stay on track to graduate. I know if he applies himself, he can still get out of here with just shy of a 3.0 GPA. Which is still good enough to get him into most community colleges."

"Of course I'll give you his work. Let me send him a note, too. Let him know he's missed."

"Make sure he reads, too. I'm holding you accountable for the accuracy of his pop quizzes. Can you do that?"

Their generosity and understanding were overwhelming.

I gathered everything I needed from his first two periods and slipped it into my backpack. And while I usually kept that thing in my locker, I carried it around with me for the rest of the day. The principal allowed me access to his locker to get the books he needed for his classes. And the inside of his locker shocked me. I expected it to be in disarray. Filled with trash and disheveled with his books stacked on the small floor of it.

However, what I found gave me pause.

"Wow," the principal said.

I stared at a picture of myself. A yearbook picture of me from freshman year. It had obviously been torn out of a book, and it was taped to the inside of his locker. And beneath my face, a heart. A simple, black ink penned heart. I ran my fingertips along it. I felt tears cresting my eyes. I gazed along his organized locker, taking in his alphabetically-arranged textbooks and his notebooks neatly stacked and named.

I sniffled. "Oh, Clint."

"It's kind of you, you know. To help him stay on track with his grades."

The principal's voice caught me off-guard and I quickly wiped at my tears.

"I'd like to think he'd do the same for me."

He snickered. "You seem to bring out a different side of him. A side I've never seen before."

I nodded. "He's a good kid. He's just a bad home life."

"You'd be surprised how common that is."

The statement made me sick to my stomach.

"I mean, I know Clint isn't the most well-liked kid on campus or anything. But I'm really glad you guys are helping me out with this. I know he wants to graduate. If anything to get away from—"

I paused before I said anymore. And I watched as the principal nodded from the corner of my eye.

"Don't worry. I'll make sure his teachers work with you. And him. You know, to try and get him graduated."

I snickered. "And get him off your plate?"

"And get him going in the direction he needs to be in. A direction he deserves."

"You're right about that."

I finished gathering his books and the principal closed his locker. The bag was heavy, but I didn't care. A small price to pay for helping Clint recover and do what I know he wanted to do. My only regret was that I had to work tonight at the grocery store. Which came with its own set of worries and hesitations.

Like what the hell the manger would think—or say to me—once I walked through those doors.

I'll be there soon, Clint. I just have to get through work.

And I hoped with all my might I wouldn't be scared closing at work again after school.

14

CLINTON

C ecilia clicked her way into the room. "Guess who's calling!?"
Oh, goody.

I groaned as she sat on the edge of my bed, jostling me around. A laptop got flopped into my lap, and right there on the screen was the face of my father. Stoic. Cold. Still as stone. And I saw him analyzing me even from his laptop. Even though he'd overshot the video conference by an entire day, hey. At least he was calling, right?

"How's he feeling?" he asked.

I sighed. "He's feeling fine, Dad."

"Cece said you had physical therapy today. How'd that go?"

I shrugged. "My neck's out of that brace, so that's nice. Still hurts to move, though."

"Guess that's what happens when you throw yourself off a ravine."

I fluttered my eyes over to Cecilia, and she urged me to keep going with a nod of her head. I didn't want to do this. I didn't want to talk with my father. But it seemed like it made her happy. And out of all the people who had been the most supportive of me through this trying time, she'd been one of them.

So, why not make her happy?

"Yeah, well. I'll try not to do that next time."

Dad nodded. "What did they have you do in physical therapy?"

I licked my chapped lips. "Uh, some stretches with my back. Trying to get these vertebrae to straighten out on their own. Some leg work. Not really arm work, since my collarbone has to heal first."

"Can you see out of your eyes?"

"Yep. I can see your disapproving stare just fine."

Cecilia sighed. "Clint."

Dad's face fell. "Well, if you weren't always doing such disappointing things, there would be no need for the disapproving stare."

"Howard!"

I shook my head. "He's fine. It's whatever."

I felt myself still sweating from the physical therapy. And holy shit, that'd been rough. Walking around made me bust a sweat. But with all those exercises I felt like I was a young child again, relearning how to do everything. Moving my legs took effort. Propping myself up took time. I bent my back every which way, flexing my muscles like I hadn't moved them in years.

My body was damaged. My soul, weak. And I had a very long road of recovery ahead of me.

Cecilia cleared her throat. "Well, they said his first try at physical therapy went really well. They even gave him a few back stretches most people coming out of something like this can't even attempt. They think he's going to do really well."

Dad grunted. "How many weeks of physical therapy are we talking about?"

I mouthed to my stepmother, "He wants to know the money."

Cecilia shook me off. "They say six to eight weeks. Then, a re-evaluation to see if he needs another course of it."

Dad sighed. "Great. I'll get started on finding a home nurse or something. Which'll cost me an arm and a leg."

"Howard."

I shot Cecilia an 'I told you so' kind of look. For my father, it was all about money. How much I cost him. How much he spent on me. How much it took to apologize. What he had to dip into in order to cover the cost of something I'd done. I had no idea how to speak with my father. Well, scratch that. I knew exactly how to talk to my father. I just didn't care to. This entire time, all I'd wanted was for my father to come home and take care of me. Come home and visit. Field the doctors since he knew the bulk of my medical history.

But, now? Even just this video conference changed my mind.

He could stay wherever the hell he was for all I cared.

Cecilia whispered. "Howard, be kinder to your son. He's laid up in a hospital and you're nowhere to be found. I'll shut this laptop if you don't."

Dad snickered. "More time for me to work, then."

I shook my head. "Do you always have to win every fight?"

The room fell silent as my eyes fell to my father's on the computer screen.

"Because I really want to believe that you aren't the sorriest sack of shit I've ever known. That you say these things just to—"

"What did you say to me, boy?"

I raised my voice. "Any other half-decent father would be here with their child in the hospital. I almost died, Dad. Actually, I did die there for a little while. I've been resuscitated twice, and you act like I've stolen your last damn cookie from the fridge."

Cecilia took my hand. "Clint, take some breaths. Your heartrate is climbing."

"Yeah, because I'm talking with Dad. So now I'm done talking with Dad. You can take the laptop away."

My father glowered. "You're lucky I'm not there, son. Because a hospital bed doesn't protect you from the whooping you deserve."

"And I believe I've heard enough."

The doctor's voice rose from the corner of the room and I looked over. That man looked me square in my face before nodding his head softly. I wasn't sure what he was thinking, but damn did I ever want to know.

"Who's that?" my father asked.

Cecilia paused. "The doctor, honey. It's the doctor."

The man in the white coat walked over. "And this conversation is done."

"I'll let you know when I'm done speaking with my son."

I scoffed. "No worries. I'm done talking with him."

The doctor nodded. "You can remove the laptop now, Mrs. Clarke."

My father got in one last glare before Cecilia picked up the laptop. I heard him making remarks to himself as she carried the laptop out of the room. Typical remarks from my father. 'He's asking for something like this to happen.' 'How much did that doctor hear?' 'Maybe he needs something like this to teach him a lesson. He drives that bike much too recklessly for my tastes.'

I mean, did my stepmother have the damn volume turned up all the way on that thing?

I sighed as the doctor sat down on the edge of my bed. He patted my knee, holding his hand there as I stared at the wall. I heard him and my stepmother bickering. Again. Over the computer, out in the hallway. Pissing off people, including me.

"If your heartrate gets any higher, I have to sedate you."

I snickered. "Good."

The doctor paused. "You know, there are services for adults, too."

I slowly turned my head toward him. "What?"

He shrugged. "You don't fall under the protection of child services anymore. But there are adult services. You know, if it's always like this with your father."

"I'm good, thanks."

"I don't think you are."

I shrugged. "Then, that's what you think. But I know how to handle my dad. And in a few months, when I graduate, I won't have to at all."

"You know damn good and well that boy had a hand in what happened, Cecilia!"

"He's just a kid, Howard. Go easy on him. Your son almost died. Don't you have a heart anymore?"

"Right, of course it isn't his fault. It's never his fault when you're around. He had no hand in it at all, and it's all me. All the time."

"Yeah, well. Maybe you should heed my advice for once."

"He's my son. Not yours. Can it, or leave. You know the drill."

The conversation out in the hallway took me aback. I wasn't sure what to make of it but—but it sounded like Cecilia was standing up for me.

Like she had stood up for me in the past.

"I'll be right back," the doctor said.

With one last pat of his hand, he got up. He stormed out into the hallway, walked right up to that laptop, and closed it in the middle of my father's sentence. I snickered. Oh man, if there was a mushroom cloud in the distance, I knew why. I sighed with relief as

I eased myself back into the hospital bed, thankful to have some peace and quiet.

Then I felt Cecilia's hand fall against mine.

"I'm sorry, Clint."

I sighed. "Not your fault."

"I really thought he'd—"

"Give it a few more years. You'll stop expecting so much from him."

She squeezed my hand softly as a nurse came in and hooked me back up to a few things. She got my I.V. drip going again. Got the oxygen tubes seated in my nose. And as the nurse tucked me in, I felt my eyes flutter closed. Dad was partially right, though. I did have a hand in why I was run off the road. But not in the way my father thought. I hadn't instigated anything this time. I'd prevented it. I'd saved Rae from harm by throwing myself in harm's way. That shit was noble.

Right?

Don't second guess yourself because of that asshole.

Part of me wanted to tell my father. But I knew how he'd see it. If I told him it was to save some girl, he'd call me soft. He'd tell me Rae probably deserved whatever was coming to her, and that I needed to let her learn her lesson instead of babying her. And I wasn't sure I'd be able to keep myself from murdering him if I heard those words come out of his fucking face. Sure, I might have been able to tell Cecilia, but I knew if I told her she'd eventually tell my father. Because she was still in those years where she wanted to please him. Make him happy. Make him proud.

Whereas I'd abandoned those ideals around the time I was fifteen.

Dad won't understand the idea of defending a woman like that.

Cecilia patted my hand. "Get some rest. I'll be here when you wake up."

I nodded. "Sounds good."

"I'm really proud of what you accomplished today in PT."

"At least someone is."

"Your father's proud in his own way."

I snickered. "No, he's not. But, I'm glad you still think so. Means he hasn't gotten to you yet."

And when she didn't answer, I knew she knew I was right.

15

RAELYNN

I smiled as I walked through the hospital doors, not bothering to ask for Clint's room number. I knew where he was, and I was anxious to get to him. I tossed my shoulder pack around behind me, feeling it bounce against my legs. I moved as quickly as I could without running through the hallways, navigating the corridors before coming to his room.

I had a pep in my step and a giggle on my lips as I approached his door.

I looked around for his father. Or his stepmother. But there was no one except a nurse coming out of his room. I had all his homework. All his textbooks. And I was eager to dive into everything. I jogged down the hallway, slipping in my old tennis shoes along the freshly-waxed floors. The smell of disinfectant hung heavily in the air, but soon I stopped in my tracks.

When I saw some male nurses wheeling Clint out of his room.

"Where are you taking him?"

"Rae?"

I rushed to his side, taking his hand as he smiled at me.

"Hey, you're here."

I laced our fingers together. "Of course I'm here. What's wrong?"

He shook his head. "Nothing's wrong. I just get a normal room now."

"A normal roo—wait. Where's your neck brace?"

The nurse giggled. "Old handsome here's no longer got a concussion. Did well with his physical therapy today. So he gets a normal room and no more catheter."

Clint rolled his eyes. "She could've done without that part, Nurse Nina."

I furrowed my brow. "So you're doing okay? Nothing's wrong?"

"How could anything be wrong when you're here?"

I smiled at him, holding his hand as the nurses navigated his bed down the hallway. With this 'Nurse Nina' at the helm, directing traffic. She kept shamelessly flirting with Clint and he flirted right back. And while part of me was jealous, part of me was also thankful he had that kind of banter going on with someone here at the hospital.

Someone who made him smile whenever he didn't have anyone else.

"Wow. A regular room. I wonder what it's like. Does it have a cotton candy machine? Floor to ceiling windows? A nice tub for me to soak in?"

I giggled at Clint as we came to a stop in front of another hospital room.

Nurse Nina smiled. "Well, Cee, this isn't the DoubleTree. You get a private recuperation room with your own window, and a toilet that doesn't stink."

I quirked an eyebrow. "Cee?"

Clint winked. "That's what she calls me when her husband isn't around."

I nodded playfully. "Oh, okay. And here I thought I was supposed to be jealous."

"What? You mean you're not jealous, beautiful? I'm hurt."

And as the two of us laughed together, the male nurses got him situated into his new room.

I turned my back so the nurse could relieve him of his catheter. I took the time to set up our station for schoolwork, pulling out history, the one still fresh in my mind. I knew exactly what he'd missed and what he needed to get done before Friday. I flipped open to the page and things like that as the nurse walked beside me. She patted me on the back, causing me to look over at her. And with a friendly smile, she nodded.

"He's ready when you are, lucky girl."

"Thank you. For everything."

The nurse snickered. "Don't thank us yet. PT only gets harder from here. I'm sure he'll be cursing my name before too long."

Clint chuckled. "Never, Nurse Nina! How could I with that pretty face?"

I shook my head at the two of them as I turned around. And even after only a couple of days, Clint looked worlds better than he had. His neck wasn't braced. He didn't have oxygen tubes running up his nose. He only had one I.V. as opposed to two. And his face seemed a lot less swollen. I walked over to the edge of his bed and sat down, taking his hand within mine. And as I brought it to my lips to kiss, I felt him bend over. Freely.

To kiss me on top of the head.

I smiled. "You look amazing."

His lips lingered in my hair. "I feel amazing, now that you're here."

"Do you want to get started on history first? Or math?"

"First, I want to hear all about school. I'm sure there's been a circus act you've had to field."

I snickered. "I mean, whatever you're thinking is probably right. Roy and Marina have approached me a couple times, too."

"Oh, I'm sure they've had lots to say."

I rose up, looking into his eyes. "I think Roy has kind of become the schoolyard bully now. He's picking a great deal on Michael and Allison and me. Of course, with his girlfriend at his side. I mangled his face pretty badly, though."

He paused. "How so?"

I rolled my eyes. "She made a comment about how injured you were. That maybe you couldn't—"

I was hesitant to tell him. But he urged me on.

"You can tell me. Talk to me. It's okay."

I sighed. "Roy made a comment about you not having a nice face any longer. Then Marina backed it up with a comment about you not getting it up anymore. So, I lunged at her and raked my nails across her cheek."

He grinned. "That's my girl."

I blushed. "Well, she deserved it. Damn bitch."

"Are you okay, Rae?"

I shrugged. "I'm getting by. I'm really thankful the teachers and the principal are cooperating with me in terms of getting your schoolwork. Whatever it takes, you're going to graduate with us. Okay?"

"How are Aly and Mike?"

I paused. "Oh. Allison and Michael."

He nodded. "Yeah. How are they?"

Cute nicknames. I like them. "They're good. Worried about you. They're excited for the update when I see them tomorrow."

"We could call them, if you'd like."

"Oh, no, no. You're not getting out of schoolwork, sir."

"I mean, I've got other ways of getting out of schoolwork. But I think my heart monitor might give us away."

His hand slid slowly down my body and I shivered at his touch. I scooted closer to him, our foreheads falling together. Him joking around was a good sign. Moving a bit on his own. No longer chained to his bed. Our noses nuzzled together as his hand slipped to my lower back, inching me even closer to him.

And just as his lips hovered over mine…

"I think we should start with history."

He groaned. "Okay, okay. You win."

I smiled. "Great."

"What's up first?"

"Reading. There are three chapters we have to catch you up on. I can give you notes on the first one. Then, I actually have to read the other two. So try to stay with me. After that, two work- sheets. Then, we're done for the night. We can move on to math."

"Wonderful."

"I'll pretend that's a good exclamation."

I maneuvered myself in bed with him, staying above the covers. He wrapped his arm around me, leaning his head against my shoulder. And as I cracked open the textbook, I gave him the condensed version of chapter four. I talked him through the biggest points and told him I'd get him a copy of my notes. Then I turned to chapter five and began reading.

I read for a few pages before he sat up, groaning as he moved.

"Can you give me a second?"

I nodded. "Of course. Take your time. Do you need water?"

He sighed. "I just need a minute. The head hurts."

I leaned back in bed with him, watching as he closed his eyes. I took his hand, feeling him squeeze it as he breathed through what- ever he was experiencing. I kissed his cheek and whispered sweet nothings in his ear. The book soon fell to the floor, plopping open and crinkling the pages as he relaxed against me.

And five minutes later, the first snore erupted from his face.

Yikes.

I lay there with him for a little bit, staring at his face. His snores grew to exponential proportions, so I reached over and started finagling with some of the switches on his electronic bed. I finally got him going down, hitting that sweet spot where his snoring stopped.

And after I slowly inched away from him, I picked up the book off the floor.

"I'll just make some notes for him to go over."

A quick notation summary of Chapters Five and Six turned into me doing the worksheets for him. Quick answers that sounded like Clint before I moved onto his math homework. I intentionally got a few wrong, trying to make it look like I wasn't actually doing his work for him. And an hour later, I moved on to my own homework.

I stayed in that hospital room for almost three hours before Nurse Nina finally poked her head in.

"I hate to do this to you, honey. But, visiting hours wrapped up a few minutes ago."

I nodded. "Thanks. I'll get my things together."

"I can buy you maybe fifteen more minutes. But that's when the doctor comes back from his break."

I smiled, whispering, "I really appreciate it."

She crept in and took a quick look at Clint's vitals, then rushed back out. I quickly gathered my things, shoving our homework into my bag before I made my way back to his side. I took his hand, gazing into his sleeping face. The bruising from his broken nose was spreading. But the swelling had gone down a great deal. I smiled softly to myself, leaning forward to kiss his cheek. I let my lips linger, feeling him mindlessly press into my warmth before hunkering down further in bed.

And queuing up that damn snoring.

How did I ever sleep beside that?

"I'll see you soon," I murmured against his skin.

Then I picked up my things, threw the backpack strap across my back, and slowly made my way out of his room.

Wishing the entire time I could stay the night with him.

16

CLINTON

"Guess what day it is? Guess what. Day. It. Is."

I quirked an eyebrow. "Are you doing a parody of those commercials?"

Nurse Nina drew in a deep breath. "It's discharge day!"

My eyes widened. "Wait, what?"

"Surprise!"

Nurses and doctors jumped out of every orifice of my room. I had barely woken up. Just gotten out of the bathroom, literally hopped back into bed. And all of a sudden, my room was filled with people. I smiled as tears crested my eyes. Nurse Nina came over and hugged me, bending over my body. Her warm arms wrapped around me and I held her close, pressing my lips against her ear.

"Thank you so much. For everything."

She patted my back. "You did this yourself, Cee. We just came along for the ride."

The doctor walked up beside me. "Your official discharge paperwork. As well as a few other things you might need in your future. You know, just in case."

Nina backed up and the doctor looked me square in my eyes. I knew what he was talking about, too. I took the folder from him and peeked inside, taking in the paperwork. How to take care of my stitches. My body. How to schedule physical therapy and when to come see them next to get evaluated.

I also saw some brochures in there for adult assistance programs. And it made me sigh.

"Thanks, Doc. I really do appreciate it."

He patted my shoulder. "My number's in there. You call me anytime, day or night, if you need anything. And I mean anything. Okay?"

And without thinking, I reached out and wrapped my arm around his neck. I pulled him into a hug, feeling him brace himself against the bed. He chuckled against the side of my head before patting my back, and I sighed with relief.

"Thank you for everything you've done for me."

He shook his head. "Don't get it twisted. You did this. You fought, all week, to recuperate to this length. You're the fighter. We're simply the assistance in that fight."

Nurse Nina clapped her hands. "So, ready to get out of here? We have a few things to do, like gathering your prescriptions and scheduling your physical therapy. Then I get to wheel you out of here in a chair."

I smiled, pulling away from the doctor. "Does that mean races?"

"Do birds fly?"

I chuckled as they all helped me get out of bed. It seemed like it took a team of nurses to get me unhooked from all the tubes and machines. But, in reality, I was glad they were there. This staff had helped me around the clock for the past week and a half. They made Rae feel comfortable, they stood up for me with my father, and they encouraged my stepmother to keep speaking up for herself. It felt nice, having people in my corner.

Especially people like them.

"Your chariot awaits, Cee."

I grinned. "Oh, Nina. You really shouldn't have."

I flopped down into the wheelchair, clutching the folder of discharge paperwork in my lap. And away we went. I heard the doctor calling after us to slow down, but it only made me throw my hands in the air. Nina ran down the hallway with me, whooping and hollering as we careened around corners. She rushed me at that pace all the way down to their pharmacy, huffing and puffing as she sat with me. Waiting with me to get my medication.

"You got a ride home, kid?"

I nodded. "Stepmom's coming to get me."

She patted my knee. "She's one of the good ones. You make sure to keep her around."

I shrugged. "If my father stops being an asshole, she might actually stick around."

"What I wouldn't give for five minutes alone with that man."

We sat there, with her hand on my knee, and I settled my hand over hers. I squeezed it softly, reluctant to let it go. They called my name too soon for my prescriptions. She walked me through how to take them a little too fast. I had an entire support network in this hospital, and I wasn't ready to let them go.

They'd been so good to me.

And I wanted to find a way to thank them for that.

Nina rolled me out to the roundabout in the front of the hospital and I saw Cecilia drive up. Nina helped me out of the wheelchair as my stepmother parked the car, rushing around to help. I stood up and turned around. I saw my doctor as well as the rest of the staff standing there, softly clapping for me. I stood strong. I stood tall. And with a smile on my face, I cleared my throat.

"Thank you, guys. For saving my life. And I know you'll stand there, telling me I'm the one fighting. But, without your surgery and your I.V.s and your knowledge, I'd be dead and you know it."

Silence fell over everyone before I sighed.

"I'll never be able to fully thank you or ever pay you back for what you did for me. And my stepmom. But I'm going to find a way to try."

The doctor cleared his throat. "Take care of yourself. That's what you can do."

Nina smiled. "And keep up with your therapy."

I grinned. "Don't want me coming back to visit."

A resounding 'no' rose from the crowd.

All of us started laughing before everyone came to give me hugs. They clapped my back softly and murmured words of encouragement. Nina reminded me the order of my pills, then made me recite it back to her. Then, my doctor—once again—told me to call. Anytime. For anything.

And I hugged him a bit longer than I should have.

Climbing into the car was hard. Driving away from that

support system was even harder. But the second Cecelia took my hand, I felt at ease again. I relaxed against the leather interior of her car, my eyes fluttering closed as the car swerved softly with the roads. I didn't wake up until we'd pulled into the driveway of my home. I didn't say anything until Cecilia helped me inside. She settled me on the couch with a drink and a snack, then started writing out my medication schedule on a pad and a piece of paper as I rattled it off to her.

But the best part was that my father never came up in conversation.

Not once.

"All right. So, it's one of the painkillers in the morning, two of the anti-inflammatories after food at lunch. No later than two. Then another half a painkiller at night to help you sleep."

I nodded. "Right."

"Then, after one week, we add in the vitamin. Once the painkiller runs out."

I nodded. "Mm-hmm."

"And that vitamin is once in the morning up through the end of your first cycle of PT."

I grinned. "You got it."

"Perfect. I'll get this on the fridge so I can remember which ones to set out for you."

"You know you don't have to do that, right?"

She scoffed. "Nonsense. I'm going to help you out around here. I might not have to wipe your butt or anything. But that doesn't mean I can't get you your medication whenever you need it."

I smiled. "I appreciate it. Thanks."

"You need anything right now?"

"You mean other than a nap?"

She giggled. "Yep. Other than that."

I paused. "Oh! Yes, actually. A friend of mine is bringing my homework and stuff to me from school. She's helping me keep up with my studies."

"She, huh? Anything special about this… she?"

I snickered. "We're just studying."

She winked. "For now."

I chuckled. "Is that all right, though? If she comes by? I don't know if she will. She works sometimes. But I think this is her weekend off."

"If she pops by, she's more than welcome. I'm going to cook dinner tonight, so she can stay and eat with us."

"Dinner? I didn't know you cooked."

"What in the world do you think you've been eating for the past four years?"

"Uh, takeout?"

She cackled. "Well, glad to know my food tastes like takeout. I think."

"Wait a second, is that really your lasagna I've been eating?"

She nodded. "Oh, yeah. One of the many things my mother taught me was how to make most every traditional and popular recipe from scratch. That's my lasagna and breadsticks you've been eating."

My jaw dropped in shock. "Holy shit. I mean—"

She laughed. "You're fine. It's okay."

"Well, damn then. That's some insane cooking skills you've got."

"In another lifetime, maybe I would have done it professionally. But I'll settle for blowing you and your father's socks off."

A silence fell over us and she cleared her throat. She patted my leg before getting up, then made herself scarce. I heard her humming to herself in the kitchen, piddling around in there. Probably figuring out what to make for dinner. I pulled my phone out and crafted a text to Rae. Hoping she didn't have to work tonight.

Me: Hey. If you want to come over tonight, you can. Stepmom's cooking dinner, and you're more than welcome to come eat with us.

I stared down at the text message and paused. Had I ever invited a girl willingly over to my house before? I raised my head, staring off at the wall. Holy shit, this was a first for me. A first with a girl. Willingly inviting her into my world. I smiled as I looked back down at my phone. I sent the text message off with excitement rushing through my veins.

And a few minutes later, my phone vibrated.

Rae: I'd love to. Be over there after school?

Me: Sounds like a plan. I can't wait.

And I meant every word of it.

"Hey, Clint!"

"Yeah, Cecilia?"

"I'm about to make myself a little frozen banana milkshake. You want one?"

"Uh, yes please. That sounds fantastic."

She giggled. "I thought it'd go well with a movie. There's supposed to be an action movie marathon on this afternoon."

I paused. "You like action movies?"

"Are women not supposed to like those?"

"No, no, nothing like that. You just strike me as a—"

The whirring of the blender cut me off and I started laughing. I craned my neck back, peeking into the kitchen as her playful glare fell onto my face. I laughed harder than I had in a while with her. I clutched my ribs, coughing and laughing through the pain as the blender turned off.

Then, my stepmother's voice filled the room again.

"If you tell me I look like a romantic movie junkie, you'll get this milkshake down your shirt."

I chuckled. "That might actually feel good with how hot my ribs feel."

"Are you okay? Is your skin red or anything? Because that's supposed to be one of those things we look out for."

I lifted my shirt. "Nope. I don't see red. They just feel internally hot."

"Let me get a thermometer really quickly."

She whirled around me, bringing me the milkshake before jamming a thermometer under my tongue. She sat there, looking like a worried mother until the damn thing beeped. The relief on her face told me I wasn't running a fever. Which was a relief to me, too. Because after settling in on this couch, I sure as hell didn't want to move.

"Okay. Well, we'll keep an eye on that."

I nodded. "Sounds good to me."

She handed me the remote. "Find that marathon and I'm going to get my milkshake."

"And take off those heels?"

She paused. "I suppose I could do that."

"Are you not supposed to walk around without your heels on or something?"

The mere fact that she had to think about it told me all I had to know, too.

"Want a snack?" she asked.

I nodded slowly. "Whatever you want is fine with me."

"Wonderful. Because caramel popcorn goes great with a banana shake."

"Am I supposed to be having all this junk?"

"Don't worry. I'm cooking a healthy dinner, and there's no dessert. So we can just have dessert now."

I chuckled. "I don't know if it works like that."

She called out from the kitchen, "Hey! It's how I've kept my figure all these years. And it's not like you haven't been eating greasy burgers behind my back."

"Wait, how did you know about that?"

"You fart in your sleep, Clint. I know all things!"

I threw my head back in laughter as I turned on the projector television. Cecilia came in a few minutes later with a milkshake in one hand and a bowl of caramel popcorn for us to share in the other. I lifted my feet, watching her sit down before I settled my legs onto her lap. And as I flicked through the channels, trying to find this marathon, I felt at peace.

"Thank you, Cecilia."

"For what?"

"For looking out for me this past week and a half."

She smiled. "We look out for each other, right?"

I nodded. "Always."

"Oh! There it is. Fast and Furious 4. Not my favorite. But it's a good one."

As we settled into the movie, I found myself staring at her, not the television. I mindlessly sipped the most incredible milkshake I'd ever put in my face, and I gazed at the woman who'd had my back since the ambulance was called. This must be what it felt like to have a parent in my corner. An adult who looked out for me.

It felt refreshing. Nice. Supportive. Natural.

And I really hoped I didn't do anything to make her hate me like my father.

17

—————

RAELYNN

I rushed home after school, bursting through the front door. I ignored the car in the driveway. I ignored him calling out my name. I didn't want a damn thing to do with D.J. while he was over at the house. The only thing I wanted to do was quickly get ready for Clint's house and get the hell over there.

I was eager to spend time with him.

I closed myself off in my bedroom, blocking out the sounds of D.J. and my mother. Whether they were arguing or making out, I didn't know. And I sure as hell didn't care. I took my hair down from its ponytail and tried to find another way to fix it. I stripped down to nothing but my underwear, then rifled through my under-wear drawer. Did I have anything else that looked even remotely nice? Something other than morphed training bras and fucking cotton panties?

I dug to the bottom of my drawer before settling on a pair of panties that I'd technically outgrown. They were a bit tight around my hips, but showed off my ass cheeks nicely. I slipped them on, pairing them with a new bra Mom had managed to pick me up a few weeks ago. It wasn't a nice color or anything. Just a plain tan bra. But it had pretty little flower designs over the cups of them and lifted them off my chest a bit.

"Man, this thing is comfortable," I murmured.

I rifled through my drawers and pulled out my best pair of

jeans. A bit tight, a bit low-riding, and exactly what I was looking for. I hopped myself into them, jumping around before I fell to my bed. I wiggled my ass into those things and sucked it in, wanting nothing more than to get them buckled.

"Come on. You can do it. Just a little—there we go!"

I stood up and bent down, trying to stretch them out a bit. I swiveled my hips, feeling them loosen before I looped my fingers in the belt loops. I worked them up a bit higher. Just enough to cover the top of my panty line. Then I rifled through my T-shirts until I found my favorite one.

A bit too low cut and a bit too tight around my breasts.

"Perfect. Ha-ha!"

I slipped it over my head and fluffed out my hair. And I had to say, I looked great. I smiled at myself as I ran a brush through my hair, trying to figure out how to fix it. I usually wore it in a ponytail. Just a simple one. Nothing special. But, tonight? I wanted to do something special. This was the first evening I'd be spending with Clint in a while. And without him being in the hospital. I knew we had schoolwork to do. I knew we had things to catch up on.

But part of me hoped his hands might do a little exploring, as well.

"Rae?"

A soft knock came at my door as my mother's voice trailed in front of it. I debated on not opening it. Mostly because I didn't want to chance seeing D.J. behind her. She knocked on the door again, calling out my name as I ran my fingers through my hair again.

"D.J.'s still downstairs, honey."

Well, in that case…

I opened the door and let her in, watching as she walked through the threshold. And when she turned to face me, she grinned.

"Getting dolled up, I see."

I shrugged. "Maybe a bit."

She turned me back toward my mirror. "Know what you're going to do with your hair?"

"Not yet. I'm still trying to figure it out."

"Can I try something?"

I nodded and she started tracing her hands through my hair. I closed my eyes, feeling the comfort of her warmth I remembered from my childhood. For years, my mother had done my hair. Brushed it out after baths and put it up into pigtails during middle school. She always talked about how envious she was of my hair. How thick and shiny and luxurious it felt. I leaned into her a bit. I settled against her, drawing in a deep breath as she worked out the last of the knots.

"You've always had such gorgeous hair. I don't know why you keep it in that ponytail."

I shrugged. "Easier in the mornings, I guess."

"You're excited about tonight, aren't you?"

I nodded. "I am, yes. It's been a few days since I've seen him. You know, because of work and stuff."

"Well, you take your time tonight, okay? No need to rush back home."

"Thanks, Mom. I appreciate it."

I felt her hands pause. "He's a good boy, right?"

He's better than D.J. "Yes, ma'am. He's a good boy. The best of boys."

"Good. That's very good."

I opened my eyes and watched her in the mirror. I saw the worry in her face, but I didn't know what to say in order to get her to calm down. So, I didn't say anything at all. I let her put my hair up into a half ponytail, with my hair pouring down past my shoulders. She fluffed the remains of it out then hugged me from behind, settling her chin against my shoulder.

"You got a ride over there?"

I shrugged. "Figured I'd walk. Or ride my bike."

"Well, I can drive you. D.J. said I could borrow his car while he watches the game."

I nodded. "Thanks, Mom. I appreciate that."

"Let me just get my purse and we'll head out. I'm doing the food run while D.J. stays here."

The two of us made our way out of my bedroom and down the stairs. And even though I peered into our living room and saw that sorry sack of shit sitting on our couch, he didn't even acknowledge my presence. He didn't look at me. He didn't say 'hi' to me. He didn't say anything about my outfit or ask me where I was going. Not that I'd want to tell him anyway. But, still.

Dick.

Mom tapped me on my shoulder. "I'll be right back with food, D.J."

He nodded mindlessly. "Sounds good."

"I'm gonna drop Rae off for the night, then go get it."

"Uh huh."

"You want anything else tacked onto your regular order?"

"Not if it gets you out the door quicker."

I wanted to punch him in his nutsack. But Mom simply giggled. She laughed at him. Like he was making some sort of a joke.

"Be back soon, sweetheart."

D.J. nodded. "Uh huh."

What an absolute asshole.

We made our way out to D.J.'s car and I quickly slipped in. I wanted to get away from this house, and fast. Even if I couldn't stay over at Clint's for the night, I'd end up at Allison's. Because I sure as hell wasn't coming back home until D.J. left.

I pointed. "Take a right here."

"On it."

I talked to Mom all the way to Clint's house and she whistled lowly to herself. I saw her staring up at the massive mansion, her eyes widening as we parked in the roundabout driveway. I unbuckled my seatbelt. I leaned over and kissed her, thanking her for the ride.

Mom winked at me. "My daughter really knows how to snag 'em."

I snickered. "Have a good evening with D.J., Mom. Okay?"

My eyes found hers and she nodded slowly.

"I will. I promise."

I let myself out of the car and watched Mom drive away. I waved at her, wanting nothing more than to go right back to the house while she wasn't there and give that man a piece of my mind. I hated that she was back with him. I hated it, because I'd actually believed her the last time she told me it was over. I felt like we'd bonded over that moment. Bonded over our hurt and our pain. Yet, here she was, giving him another chance.

Then again, I'd given Clint a lot of chances, too.

I walked up to the front door and knocked. While I was nervous about meeting Clint's stepmother for the first time, formally, it didn't abate the butterflies in my stomach. I was anxious to see him. Anxious to hold him. Anxious to be in his presence again.

And when the front door opened, Clint smiled at me.

"Hey there, beau—oh!"

I threw myself into his arms, unable to contain my laughter. I wrapped my arms around his neck, holding him close as his body cloaked itself around mine. His arms hugged my back. He pulled me into the house, kicking the front door closed with his foot. I buried my face into the crook of his neck, feeling how much stronger he already was.

"You're upright."

Clint chuckled. "And you're here."

I giggled. "I am. Thank you for inviting me."

"Are we going to stay like this until we get to the kitchen?"

"Depends. Do we have to go to the kitchen right now?"

He snickered. "Nope. Not yet."

I drew in his scent, clinging to him as he held me tighter. His strength shocked me. Especially after such a terrible accident. I kissed his neck. His shoulder. His jawline. I nuzzled my nose against his as I slowly pulled away from him. His hand cupped the back of my head as his emerald eyes danced between mine.

And as he fisted my hair softly, I pressed my lips against his.

"Mmm, hello there, gorgeous."

I smiled. "Hi, handsome."

"I'm really glad you're here."

"Me, too."

"Ahem."

I jumped at the sound of the female voice, but Clint kept his arm wrapped around my waist. I saw his stepmother standing there, clad in a beautiful yellow dress and a crimson red apron. She smiled at the two of us before she came closer, her bare feet padding on the floor. She held her hand out to me, taking mine within hers. And I smiled at how warm and welcoming she became.

"It's nice to finally meet you, Rae. I'm Cecilia, Clint's stepmother. I've heard a great deal about you, too."

I paused. "You have?"

Clint chuckled. "Over the past few hours, at least."

I nodded. "That sounds about right."

Cecilia giggled. "Don't worry, he's not hiding you."

I shook my head. "I never would have thought that."

Clint squeezed my side and I leaned closer into him as Cecilia dropped my hand.

"Well, why don't you two come on into the kitchen? The lasagna just came out of the oven and the salad's ready. Plus, by the smells of it, the garlic bread is about to come out of the oven."

Clint chuckled. "You haven't lived until you've had her lasagna. Ready to eat?"

I shrugged. "I'm ready whenever the food's ready."

He kissed the side of my head. "A girl after my own stomach."

Cecilia laughed as she turned around, beckoning for us to follow her into the kitchen. And the smells that greeted me once we got there made my stomach growl out loud. It was a beautiful home-cooked meal, and the table was set with fine china and actual silverware. Not the plastic stuff we used, and not the fake silver stuff found in most stores. Genuine silver utensils.

"Rae, what would you like to drink?"

Cecilia's voice pulled me from my trance. "Um, soda or something is fine."

Clint pulled out my seat. "We've got Mountain Dew, Diet Dr. Pepper, and Coke."

"Um, Coke's fine. Thank you."

Cecilia was a brilliant host. She cracked open the can of Coke and poured it into the ice-filled crystal glass. Right in front of me. I'd never been treated this way before. Home-cooked meals in my house were microwaved meals and pre-cooked oven meals my mother slapped into the oven or something like that. With canned vegetables on the side. This was a spread. Lasagna. Fresh salad. Multiple dressings. Freshly-made garlic bread in actual loaf form.

Clint whispered in my ear, "And there's blueberry crumble for dessert."

And oh, the growl my stomach let out.

18

CLINTON

"Oh, holy sh—itake mushrooms."

I chuckled at the way Rae edited herself. "Good, huh?"

She groaned, taking another bite of the lasagna. "It's heaven. Where in the world did you learn to cook?"

Cecilia smiled. "My mother. She taught me a lot of homemade recipes. Macaroni and cheese. Basic noodles."

Rae's eyes widened. "You made these noodles?"

"Yes ma'am, I did."

Cecilia beamed with pride and my heart felt fuller than it had in a long time. Rae kept devouring the food like she hadn't eaten in weeks, and I loved it. I adored a girl that wasn't afraid to put carbs in her system. Not like the other girls at school, who walked around with fiber bars stuffed in their purses and ate nothing but fruit and yogurt for lunch.

"So, Rae. Are you a senior, too?"

Rae nodded. "Mm-hmm."

"Any plans after graduation?"

I waited with baited breath as Rae swallowed her food. For some reason, I was now wondering what her plans were. I mean, it hadn't been important before. But now that Cecilia had formally brought it up, I wanted to know the answer.

And quickly.

"Well, I've been saving back money from the grocery store.

And if I play my cards right, I'll have enough to share an apartment with Allison once we graduate."

Cecilia nodded. "And who's Allison?"

"Rae's best friend," I said.

She nodded. "Yep. Known her for years. She's been accepted into UCLA's architecture program early."

Cecilia smiled brightly. "Nice. So you'll still be close. You hear that, Clint?"

I snickered. "I do. Thanks."

"Are you wanting to go to UCLA, too?"

Rae shrugged. "I was thinking more of a community college. I don't want to get into loans or anything like that. Maybe work part-time, go to school part-time. Or work out something like where I work full time a year then go to school full time a year or something like that."

"That's noble. I admire you for that."

Rae paused. "You do?"

Cecilia nodded. "Mm-hmm. I graduated early from high school when I was seventeen and left home. I did part-time classes at a community college not too far from where I grew up and took on a job in between classes and such. Saved up as much as I could while living with three other girls in a two-bedroom apartment. It wasn't easy, but I wouldn't trade it for anything."

"What did you get your degree in?"

"Medical transcriptioning. A nice little work from home position that would have eventually paid an hourly wage equivalent to that of a full time job, plus benefits."

Rae nodded. "Then you got married?"

Cecilia smiled. "Well, a few other things happened in between there. I did work for a while. Struggled, but made it through. I met Howard about six years ago, so I lived a lot of life between that job and now."

"Is there a reason you graduated early?"

Cecilia looked at me from across the table and I shrugged. To be honest, I was simply excited they were getting along. Hitting it off. I was glad Cecilia didn't hate Rae, or vice versa. I was content with taking a backseat and letting them get to know one another. Because things felt calm this way. Peaceful. There was no tension or anger like there would have been had Dad been around for this dinner.

Then again, this dinner wouldn't have happened at all had Dad been here.

"I grew up in a very conservative home. And while I loved my parents, I knew there was a great deal more out there for me to experience. They did a lot of things while I was younger. Tried marrying me off at sixteen. Grounded me by locking me in my room and not letting me do things like to go school and have meals with the family."

Rae sighed. "I'm so sorry."

I furrowed my brow. "I didn't know that, Cecilia."

She giggled bitterly. "It's not really something you talk about. Especially with guests over. But she asked the question so I figured, why not answer it?"

Rae cleared her throat. "I mean, at least they taught you how to make awesome food. Plenty of grease pans to throw in their faces for later."

Cecilia snickered, almost blowing her water through her nose. Rae fell apart in a fit of giggles, and I quickly joined in, though it still hurt my ribs to laugh that much. Cecilia's head fell back as she barked with laughter, snorting and covering her mouth. Which only made us laugh harder. I'd never heard her laugh like this. Which meant I'd never heard her snort. And as we all leaned back into our chairs, I finally knew what it felt like.

Home.

I finally understood what the word meant.

"Oh, my gosh. I haven't laughed like that in ages."

Rae giggled. "You should hang around Clint more often, then. Some of the situations he can get himself into are hysterical."

I paused. "Hey, now. Sometimes a guy has to blow off steam."

Cecilia heaved for air. "You don't blow off steam. Otherwise you wouldn't be so full of hot air."

I playfully glared at her. "I think you're confusing me with Dad at this point."

And soon, the girls were falling over in their chairs with laughter.

The jokes continued through the night, even as we sat down with coffee and blueberry crumble. Tears crested our eyes from the hilarity of it all, and the worries of the accident quickly fell away from our memories. Cecilia looked comfortable in her own home. I felt comfortable in my own home. And Rae looked perfect in this home. With her red face and her silent laughter and her frazzled hair puffing out the redder her face got.

She was perfection in a bottle.

And I wanted to drink her down.

"All right, you two. I'm going to clean up. I'm assuming Clint has some homework to get done, so you guys might as well get to it."

I sighed. "Ready for torture hour?"

Rae got up, rolling her eyes. "You're such a drama queen when it comes to homework. Come on. It's not going to kill you to get caught up."

She took my hands within hers, helping me up from the chair. I playfully grunted, feigning absolute exhaustion and pain as I threw my arm around her shoulders.

"I can't make it. Rae, I just—say good things at my funeral. Tell them how loved I was. Make them remember!"

And as I fell with my body weight against her, she caught me in her arms. Giggled into my chest. Pulled me down the hallway before pushing me up the stairs. She grabbed a sack of books I didn't even realize she'd brought with her. An old, brown sack sitting in the corner by the stairs.

"Need me to get that?"

She shooed me away. "Come on. Up we go. I'm good. Let's go, Tiny."

I paused. "Tiny?"

But all she did was giggle to herself.

We found our way to my bedroom and I closed the door behind us. She hopped on the bed and started pulling out books. I couldn't stop staring at her. The way her hair poured down past her shoulders. The way it fell in her face. The way her breasts protruded from that tight T-shirt and the way her panties played peekaboo with me from the top of her jeans. I licked my lips as I made my way for her. I hopped onto the bed, watching the books and papers bounce.

"All right. English or math first?"

And as Rae looked up into my eyes, I grinned.

"What if we have dessert first?"

She rolled her eyes. "We've already had dessert."

I tucked a strand of hair behind her ear. "What about second dessert?"

"Clint, you're not using sex to get out of homework. Come on. I'm tired of doing it for you. Let's go."

I paused. "You've been doing my homework for me?"

She blushed, and my world came to a grinding halt. Had she actually been doing my homework for me? Why?

"We really should get started on this."

I smiled. "Didn't realize we'd made it to Guantanamo."

Rae rolled her eyes. "You done with the torture jokes? Because if we get started, it's less than an hour's worth of work."

"And then second dessert?"

"Math. Now."

She thrust the notebook and a pencil in my hands and away we went. She helped me through the problems I stumbled on and had some great explanations for me whenever I got hung up and frustrated. I'd always hated math. It was that course in school I almost always failed, even with tutoring and extra credit. It took me forty minutes alone just to stumble along through the one-page worksheet. And we hadn't even touched the history reading yet.

"Fucking hell."

Rae rubbed my back. "We'll take a break and then maybe I can read to you. Okay?"

I snickered. "I don't need you to read to me. I just need this shit to not exist."

"I know. But it's important. I know how much graduating means to you. So we'll get through it and then we can… do whatever else."

And when I caught her eye, she winked at me. Making fire surge through my veins.

I felt my strength coming back, so I pressed on. While the one-hour's worth of work took me almost three, Rae got me through it. Not once did she get upset or frustrated. Not once did she berate me for it or call me 'stupid' like my father used to. She didn't even comment on how long it took me to get all that shit done.

But, she did kiss me with triumphant desire when we finished.

"I'm proud of you, you know."

I smiled against her lips. "Thanks, beautiful."

Her forehead fell against my own. "When's your next appointment?"

"Uh… Monday. I think. Monday afternoon."

"You want me here for it?"

"I think it'll be during school. But you're more than welcome to come over afterward. You know, massage my aches and pains away."

She grinned. "Oh, really now?"

Rae pressed herself against me, lowering me to the mattress. I heard books and things falling to the ground, no doubt causing a ruckus of sound below us. I grunted as her weight settled against me, but not once did I move. I wanted her on top of me. I wanted the comfort of her weight pressing me into my mattress. I slid my fingers through her hair, working it out of that small ponytail she had until it curtained us off from the rest of the world.

"Hi," she said softly.

I grinned. "Hi there."

Then, her face fell. "They're still out there, you know. The guys who ran you off the road."

I wrapped my arms around her. "I know."

"I haven't had an update from the police. Have you?"

"I haven't, no."

"Do you think they'll find the guys?"

"I'm sure they will."

Rae nuzzled her nose against mine. "I'm scared about them still being out there."

I rolled her over, hovering above her as she stared back at me. With wide eyes and full lips that called to my cock, I captured them softly. She moaned against me. Rolled her body and parted her legs, opening herself up to me. We stripped one another of our clothes. Her touch against my skin ignited something in my chest. I kissed down her neck, trying to soothe away her worries as her body tensed underneath mine. And when my lips found hers again, I whispered against them.

"The worst is behind us. I promise."

19

RAELYNN

My hands slid up his back as soft sighs fell from my lips. I parted my thighs for him, feeling his rock steady girth fall against me. I rocked slowly, not wanting to hurt him. His kisses were soft. Light. Fluttering against my skin as he ran his nose down my pulse point.

"Clint," I whispered.

He groaned. "How I've missed that sound."

He kissed down my breasts. He wrapped his mouth around my puckered peaks. My body rose for him. Bucked for him. Ignited with goosebumps that rushed along my skin. His hands caressed me softly. I felt him creeping along, tracing me with his fingertips. His lips slid down my stomach. My muscles jumped for him at every turn.

"Clint, you should be on your—"

"No."

He kissed my folds. I moaned, pressing my head back into the pillows as his fingertips parted me. I gasped as his tongue fell between them, licking and sucking with wanton lust. I gripped my thighs around his face. He stroked softly, stoking the fire in my chest. I felt it consuming me. Like a forest fire raging through our mountains. I reached down for his hair. I gripped his tendrils. I pulled him closer to me as I rolled against his lips. His hands slid up my sides. I felt him massaging my breasts as my eyes rolled back.

And when my body popped, I trembled against the stubble on his cheeks.

"Oh—ye—Cli—yo—sh—fu—"

I couldn't speak. Couldn't catch my breath. He lapped me slowly, until my body collapsed after bowing itself out. I gasped for air as he pressed himself up. Wet kisses trailed behind his lips, leaving marks against my skin as he journeyed his way back up. His eyes found mine and he smiled down at me, glistening with my arousal against his skin.

"I want to taste."

Clapping my hand against the back of his head, I pulled him down to me and licked myself off his skin, moaning and consuming all of him I could. I felt his length pressing against my entrance. I bucked slowly, inching him deeper into my body. He growled down the back of my throat. He filled me to the brim. He stretched me and molded me, my body allowing him access to whatever he wanted.

Because I loved him.

Even if I didn't have the guts to admit it yet.

Grunts and growls fell from his lips as my hands slid down his back. I tightened my arms around his neck, letting my knees fall off to the side. Our bodies became one. I suckled on his lower lip as his girth grew against my walls. Colors sizzled and faded in my view as we rocked and bucked, slowly climbing a precipice we'd both been craving for days.

"Rae."

"Clint."

"I've missed you. So—so much."

"All of it. I—I need—oh, Clint."

"Tell me. Tell me what you need."

I crashed our lips together, grinding my hips against his own. My toes curled as I wrapped my feet behind his calves, hoping beyond all hope I wasn't hurting him. He picked up the pace, rolling and thrusting. Moving the bed on its frame as our kisses grew sloppy. He gripped my hair and pulled my head softly off to the side. He buried his face against my neck, breathing in my scent before sinking his teeth into me.

And as that coil in my gut snapped, my jaw unhinged in silent pleasure.

"Oh—yeah—"

He growled, digging his teeth deeper as his tongue traced my pulse point. The pain and pleasure, it was all too much. My entire body wrapped around him. I pulled him down against me, forcing him to collapse. His length jumped against my walls, pouring into me as my body massaged him. Milked him. Drank him all down. I wanted all of him. Every single piece of him.

So long as he'd let me have it.

He sighed. "Oh, Rae."

Clint kissed the teeth marks he'd left behind as our bodies stayed connected. I stroked his back, feeling him quiver against me as goosebumps rushed over his skin. It made me smile, feeling them. Feeling how his body reacted to my touch. I felt him pull back, slipping from between my thighs before something gushed between my legs.

I giggled. "Uh oh."

Clint shook his head. "We'll fix it tomorrow. Just—don't move."

"Trust me, I don't plan on it."

"Good."

He snuggled down against me before falling off to the side. He grunted with pain, pulling me into his arms and away from the mess we'd created. The covers came up and settled over my bare skin as my ass sank back into his pelvis. His arm wrapped around me, holding me steadily to him as he tucked us both in. This felt right. Good. Like things should have been. I wasn't sure of much, but I was sure of one thing.

Clint belonged in my world.

"Are you okay?"

My question pierced the silence before he followed it up with a kiss between my shoulder blades.

"I'm just fine, beautiful."

I paused. "Are you sure? I didn't hurt you?"

He chuckled. "You could never hurt me."

"You know what I mean."

I turned around, gazing into his eyes. He smoothed my hair away from my forehead before kissing it softly. My eyes fluttered closed and I melted into his touch. His arm wrapped back around me and I pressed my leg between his, seeking his warmth and his strength as the covers slipped over our heads.

"I promise, you didn't hurt me, Rae."

I smiled. "Good. Just making sure."

I lay there, gazing upon the bruising of his face. The nose brace was gone, but his eyes were still a soft black. His jaw was yellow, denoting the fading of his bruises. But it was still a painful reminder. I reached out and traced down his chest, my eyes following its contour. His lips fell against my forehead, kissing me over and over as my fingertips fluttered like feathers over the dark purple bruising of his ribs.

"Oh, Clint."

"I promise, I'm okay."

I sniffled. "My God, I'm so glad you are."

"Come here. I've got you, Rae."

I curled into him as much as he'd let me. And as I cried silent tears against his chest, I drifted off to sleep. With his fingers stroking through my hair and his lips peppering me with kisses, I gave in to him. I gave in to his warmth. His comfort. His strength. The beating of his heart lulled me to sleep. And the beating of his heart was the first thing I heard the next morning.

Before I slipped away from his grasp to go get us some coffee.

20

———

CLINTON

I groaned as I opened my eyes. A heavy weight felt like it was propped against me, keeping me rooted to the mattress. I reached out for Rae, expecting her to be there. Knowing damn good and well that was what I felt.

Instead, however, I felt the weight of the emptiness of the bed next to me.

"Fuck."

I sighed, lying there on my back as I stared up at the ceiling. I wished I'd woken up sooner to say goodbye to Rae. I sighed as I lay there, my arm slung over my eyes. I wanted to go back to sleep. In fact, I wanted to keep sleeping until she came back to visit. Until she came back again, so I could sit her on my lap, feel her straddle my body, and watch as she rode me off into the damn sunset.

"I need to write that down."

My hand fell off to the side, fumbling around for my phone. And when I picked it up, I saw it was a little past nine in the morning. On a Saturday. The fuck was I up so early for? I didn't have anything to do today. So I tossed my phone onto the bed where Rae had been and rolled over, face-planting into her pillow.

Sniffing in her scent.

I dreaded the lonely weekend ahead of me. I knew Cecilia had plans, and I had no idea when the hell my father was getting back into town. He'd already defaulted on many promises. Including the one where he said he'd be back in town before I got discharged from the hospital. I snickered into the pillow, wanting nothing more than to toss that man off a fucking cliff.

He should've taken the nose-dive off the bridge.

Not me.

I closed my eyes and envisioned Rae. What she'd look like if she were with me. Her hair mussed. Knotted. Tangled. Her eyes sparkling as she stared back at me with her sleepy orbs. Her smile, lopsided from the pleasure we'd both experienced. And her body, warm and comforting against my body. I lost myself in the vision. In how things could have panned out had she stayed. I wasn't sure when she'd slipped out last night. Or this morning. But I wanted to call and make sure she'd gotten home safely.

Then I heard the door open.

I furrowed my brow as I heard Rae's soft humming filtering through the door. The smell of coffee flooded my nose, filling the room with its presence. I smiled as my bedroom door closed, and then another scent caught my nose.

Were those pastries?

"What are you still doing here?"

I went to prop myself up on my elbow just as Rae yelped. And when I shot up from bed, I saw her stumble with the coffees. The brown paper bag from underneath her arm dropped to the ground, revealing several warm danishes and pastries. She cursed under her breath as the drink carrier tilted. Some of the coffee went spilling onto my carpet as she righted herself, refusing to let the drinks fall. I watched with a grin on my face, feeling bad that I'd scared her. But also incredibly happy she was still here.

"The hell's wrong with you? I almost peed myself!"

I chuckled. "I'm sorry. I just didn't know you were still here."

"I mean, I wasn't for a bit. But I didn't want to wake you up."

I watched her dip down, scooping the paper bag up under her arm again. I grunted as I sat myself up, trying to shake the morning stiffness so I could help her. By the time I got a pillow behind my back, she was already at my side. Sitting the coffees down, rearranging the food, then reaching for more pillows.

"Here, lean up."

"Rae, you don't—"

"I said, lean up, you stubborn boy."

She fluffed my pillows as I did what she asked. I couldn't take my eyes off her. She had her hair piled on top of her head and she had picked her way through my drawers. She had on a shirt of mine. And a pair of sweatpants. I looked over at my dresser drawer, seeing two of them pulled out and hanging on by a thread.

"Sorry, I was tired this morning."

I shook my head. "Don't you dare be sorry. You're welcome to anything in here."

She snickered. "Thanks."

I kept running my eyes over her, because she looked fucking fantastic in my clothes. They hung off her, completely covering her form. And yet, she'd never been sexier. She'd never been more beautiful. I licked my lips as she handed my coffee to me. The black liquid still steamed from the to-go lid, and I smelled hints of rosewater and caramel.

"I know it's a bit fancy, but trust me. I tried a sample of it. It's damn delicious."

I grinned. "I trust you. What'd you get?"

Rae shrugged. "The usual. Iced caramel macchiato with an extra shot."

"I'll have to remember that."

I took a sip of the coffee and was stunned at how good it tasted. I took another sip. Then another. And soon, I was chugging the damn thing down.

Rae giggled. "Good thing I got a large."

I nodded as I continued drinking, not wanting to let go of the lid. But the coffee burned my throat. So I slowed down in order to savor the taste a bit.

"What'd you say was in this again?"

Rae smiled. "Regular caffeinated coffee with a shot of rosewater and two pumps of caramel."

I grinned. "Damn, that's good."

"There's this cute little coffee shop not too far up the road. I got Michael to drive me up there."

"Buckheads Brews?"

"That's the one."

"You know, I always thought that place was a bar until I walked in there one day. I smelled lemon bars in the damn place and got confused."

She giggled. "I don't think you're the only one to make that assumption. They had an assortment of fresh pastries on sale because they didn't get the 'pastry to filling' ratio right. I don't know what the hell that means, but I got them half off. So I got a bunch of them."

"You didn't have to do that, you know."

"I don't have to do anything. But I wanted to."

I grinned. "Thank you, Rae."

She leaned over and kissed my cheek, letting her lips linger for a little bit. I scooted over, giving her enough room to sit on the edge of my bed. She didn't take the hint. Instead, she grabbed her coffee and leapt into bed with me, taking up the spot next to me she'd had last night. I reached for a cheese danish, handing it to her before digging out a lemon one for myself.

And when I took a bite out of the damn thing, I moaned.

"Holy shit."

Rae nodded. "Right?"

"So fucking good."

"Seriously. Their cheese ones are great. But I've got, like, four apple ones in there. You'd think that's gross. But it's not when they do it."

I took another bite. "How have I not known about these things? They're incredible."

"Have you ever actually been *in* there, tough stuff?"

I cast her a look that made her snicker. Of course I'd been in that damn place. Every fucking girl at our high school had been in that damn place. Which meant just about every guy in our school had been in there at least once. Doesn't mean I'd had their food, though. Just a plain coffee while the girl I was with got some hoity-toity soy-based milk-coffee concoction. Some girl I'd hooked up with wanted to go there for a date after skipping out on class sophomore year. Just after I'd gotten my bike license, and right before I totaled my first rusted-out motorcycle. I wasn't going to tell Rae that, of course. She didn't need to know those details.

But, yes. I'd been in the damn place before.

"Got any plans for your day?" I asked.

I peeked over at Rae and watched her shrug.

"I mean, they can wait."

I paused. "What's waiting?"

"Nothing much. Just a study session with Allison."

"Is it important?"

"Not as important as this."

"Are you sure?"

She rolled her eyes. "Yes, Clint. I'm sure. I don't actually need to study with Allison. It's just tradition for us before every major test with classes we share."

"What class?"

She paused. "History."

"Oh, goodie."

"Don't worry. I'll help you through the test."

I grinned. "Skipping study sessions for little old me, huh? What's next? Skipping classes? Skipping school days?"

"In your fucking dreams, hot stuff."

"That's more like it."

I leaned over and gave her a kiss, but she turned her lips toward mine. Instead of connecting with her cheek, her lips fell to mine. And I tasted that cheese danish against her skin. She moaned against me as my tongue pierced her lips. Her jaw dropped open, allowing me inside as I reached over to cup the back of her head. I contorted my body, swallowed my groans of pain as I tasted her breakfast upon her lips.

Then I pulled back. Because my ribs were screaming at me the more I moved toward her.

I winced. "I like that cheese danish."

Rae pushed me back. "Sit up. I know you're in pain."

"Never, when you're around."

"Clint—"

"Rae, it's okay. I pro—"

"Just let me take care of you, okay?"

I heard the frustration in her voice and it gave me pause.

"Just… just let me be here for you, all right?"

I nodded. "All right."

"You're important to me. You're worth this. You're worth skipping the study session and you're worth spending time with. I know you're used to being tough. Always doing it alone. But you're not alone right now. So, just… try to work with me, okay? It's okay to tell me when you're in pain."

"I'm just not used to it."

"Well, try to get used to it, please?"

I sighed. "I can give it my best shot."

"Here, let me fix your pillows."

I leaned forward for her again, letting her rearrange them

behind me. And as she doted on me, trying her best to make me feel comfortable, I felt cared about. For once. I felt loved, for once. It'd been a long time since I'd felt things like this before. Yet she and Cecilia were practically showering me with it. I had no idea what I'd done to deserve it. To warrant it.

But I hoped one day to find a way to pay them back for it.

Rae leaned me back. "There. How's that?"

I sighed with relief. "Much better."

"Good."

I grinned. "You think I'm worth skipping your study session for?"

"Don't you start."

"You want me more than school. You want me more than school."

"Well, there are times where I want torture more than school. So take it for what it's worth."

I shrugged. "I don't know. I've heard torture can be pleasurable at times. If you do it right."

She shot me a look. "You can keep all those thoughts to yourself."

"So my hands have free rein?"

She playfully shoved me. "You're insane, you know that?"

"Insane for you, sure."

Her eyes met mine and my heart grew two times in that moment. Two times bigger than what it usually was. Rae Cleaver —the outcast nerd of our school—was slowly filling a void I had ignored for a long time. A void I'd allowed to fester for much too long. A void I'd convinced myself didn't really exist.

I love you. Just say it. Tell her how you feel.

"Rae?"

"Yes?"

My hand moved to cup her cheek. "I—"

"Yeah, Clint?"

"You mean a lot to me. You know that, right?"

She nodded. "And you know you mean a lot to me, too. Right?"

I nodded. "I do."

"So then we mean a lot to each other."

"We do, yes."

She smiled softly. "Well, then…? Good."

But for some reason, that statement didn't seem good enough. Not for everything Rae had given me. Not for everything she'd done for me. Not for everything she'd filled within me.

One day, I'll show you. I'll write it down and shout it from the rooftops.

"Just like you deserve."

Rae furrowed her brow. "What was that?"

I paused. "What?"

"You murmured something. But I didn't understand you."

"Oh. I didn't realize I'd said anything."

"Are you feeling okay?"

She pressed her hand against my forehead, making me snicker. "I feel fine, Rae."

"You'd tell me if you didn't feel okay, right?"

I brought her hand to my lips to kiss. "I would."

"Promise?"

"Promise, promise."

And as I placed a kiss to the palm of her hand, I felt her snuggle against me.

A place that almost seemed to be carved out against my body just for hers to have.

21

RAELYNN

*Raelynn*One Week Later

I huffed to myself. "Come on, where the hell is it?"

Mom poked her head in my room. "Whatcha looking for, sweetheart?"

"Nothing. Nothing. I'm fine."

"Sure you don't need any help?"

I shook my head as I rushed around my room, listening as papers fluttered everywhere. I cursed myself, catching them out of thin air before piling them into a wrinkled ball within the palm of my hand. My eyes darted around the room. I had way too many things I needed to lug to school today. I had my homework and Clint's homework. My books *and* his books. Today was an exciting day, and I needed to make sure it all went off without a hitch.

"Sweetheart, sure you don't—"

I held up my hand. "Just give me a second to recuperate. I know it's in here somewhere."

"What's in here somewhere?"

"That damn history book," I murmured.

Mom let out a soft giggle and I looked over at her. She had her arms crossed around her chest and her head shook itself at me. The look in her eye was skeptical. But the smile on her face was telling. It made me blush underneath her gaze. It gave me pause as to just how much was rushing through my mind.

And on Clint's behalf, too.

"Have you checked under your bed?"

I sighed. "Nothing ever gets kicked under my bed, Mom. I'm not twelve anymore."

She shrugged. "Sometimes the one place where I find things are the last place I figured I'd find them."

I dropped down to my knees. "It's not going to be under my bed. I promise you, out of all the pla—"

Mom laughed as my words stopped in my tracks. I rolled my eyes as I reached under the bed, feeling my fingertips fall against the hardback cover of Clint's history textbook. I swallowed my grumbles and tried to find the hilarity in the situation. I grinned as my mother's laughter grew to almost fiendish volumes.

"Can you keep it down up there? I've only got one cup of coffee in me!"

Mom snickered. "Sorry, Deej!"

I rolled my eyes as I stood up. I hated that man. I hated him with every ounce of me I had. But there wasn't a damn thing I could do about his presence. I stood up with the book in my hand and slipped it into my shoulder satchel, then rifled through the papers on the bed.

"This goes with that. This goes here. Oh, that's mine. Yikes. And... where's the last page of this paper?"

I looked around the room before Mom cleared her throat.

"You mean this?"

I looked over at her and I found her clutching a sheet of paper. I walked over and saw the last little bit of typed information I needed for Clint's history paper. I took it from her with a thankful smile, then placed it with the rest of the sheets of paper. I clipped it, slipped it on top of his history book, then sandwiched it between that and his English book.

I needed to make sure I didn't accidentally turn in my homework as his.

Mom giggled. "Do you need a ride to school?"

I shook my head. "Nah, I've got it."

"Are you sure? That bag looks pretty—"

I heaved the shoulder strap over my body, grunting as I situated it. Yes, it was heavy. But I didn't want a ride to school from Mom. Because I knew what that entailed before she even said it.

"I'm fine, Mom. Really. I'll be good. Just need a bit of an earlier start."

She scoffed. "You're going to sweat through your clothes before you even get there. Come on, let us give you a ride. I can ride with you, and D.J. can drive us on his way to work."

"I'm good."

I hated the fact that Mom had officially gotten back together with D.J. It made me sick. It made me wonder if the things she'd said that night had ever been true. I wondered if she'd ever had plans to better her life. Or herself. Or her circumstance. I mean, in the back of my mind, I knew they hadn't been completely over. Someone was still paying the bills, since her applications had gone unanswered. According to her, at least. I wouldn't have been shocked one bit if they'd called for interviews and she had dodged the phone calls.

It was my mother, after all.

Mom shrugged. "Well, be careful, okay? I can tell that bag is heavy."

I nodded. "I promise I'll be careful. It's why I'm getting a bit of an earlier start. So I can take my time."

"You got any plans for after school? Maybe with this boy of yours?"

"His name's Clint. And I'm not sure."

"Did you have fun with him last weekend?"

Wow. Finally. After over a week of spending the night at Clint's place and meeting his stepmother, my own mother finally asked me about it. I tried not to let the pain and the hurt show on my face. I tried not to let it get to me too much. I mean, it had been nice, having my mother back. Having her fun banter and her attention and her love back. Not that she didn't love me. But she was a different type of mother whenever D.J. was around.

The type of mother that pretty much clocked out whenever I wasn't around.

I nodded. "We had a good time. Cecilia's really nice."

"His stepmother?"

"Mm-hmm. Very kind. She cooked this massive meal, too. Lasagna."

"Sounds like she's an amazing woman."

I heard the pain in Mom's voice. "She's amazing, just like you."

And when Mom smiled, I knew my words had at least soothed a temporary balm over whatever pain she was trying to cure with D.J. I didn't know much as a teenager, but I knew that much. I knew there was a good chance Mom had never gotten over my father leaving. Gotten over the way he abandoned us. So, being around D.J. and having D.J. always come back to her—like my father never had—sort of reassured her that she meant something to him. That she was worth something to this world.

At least, that's what the guidance counselor at my school said.

"Well, I need to get on to school."

Mom frowned. "You don't want to have some breakfast? Or some coffee with us?"

I don't want to deal with D.J., no. "Like I said, early start."

"Let me at least get you something to go. You can come down to the kitchen and I'll get you and D.J.—"

"Mom."

She paused, and I had to check myself. For whatever reason, she was pushing—hardcore—trying to get D.J. and myself into the same room. But it wouldn't happen. With all the shit happening with Clint and his schoolwork right now, I didn't have the energy to deal with my mother's abusive fucking boyfriend. I'd thrown in the towel with D.J. At least for now. If that was who my mother wanted to cuddle up with at night, then so be it. I was done putting my energy into her, trying to talk her out of this disgusting scenario.

I needed to focus my efforts on getting Clint healed and graduated.

Mom sighed. "D.J. just wants to see you, that's all."

I nodded. "Well, I don't want to see him."

"Come on, Raelynn. Just give him a chance."

"A chance?"

"Yes."

"A chance!"

"Rae, don't raise your voice like—"

I scoffed. "I've given him plenty of chances, Mom. Plenty. I gave him a chance after you came home with your first black eye. I gave him a chance after he stormed out of here one night after calling you a 'useless bitch.' I gave him a chance after he tried choking you out in the middle of the kitchen and I had to elbow him in his fucking lower back in order to get him to let go."

Mom's face hardened. "Raelynn Cleaver."

"I've given him plenty of chances. He doesn't get any more from me. I'm not you, Mom. I don't have to give him chances like you apparently feel like you need to. I don't want to have breakfast with him. I don't want to have coffee with him. I don't want a ride to school from him. And I don't want to see him. Ever."

"Raelynn!"

I shoved past my mother, feeling my satchel weighing me down. I flounced down the steps, listening as D.J.'s footsteps stormed down the hallway.

"The hell's all that ruckus in this house?"

And his question made me whip around to face him.

"You don't get to make demands in this house."

Mom paused in the middle of the steps. "Raelynn Cleaver. You shut that attitude down right now."

But I glared at D.J. "This isn't your home, this isn't your space, and that isn't your girlfriend. Because if you loved her, you wouldn't do half the things to her that you do."

"Rae! Stop!"

I took a step toward D.J. "I don't want to see you. I don't want to hear from you. And I sure as hell don't want you making demands in this house. And if my mother ever comes home with another bruise on her face? On her skin? I'm calling the damn police myself."

D.J. leveled me with a stare that could kill, but I didn't give a shit about it. I stormed out of the house, slamming the front door behind me as I made my way for the driveway. Already, I heard them fighting this morning. D.J. yelling in that house like he owned it. And Mom crying and trying to subdue him. The only good thing that might ever come from him striking Mom again is the fact that I'd live up to my promise. If Mom ever had another bruise on her skin I caught, the police would be at the house.

Getting my side of the story, despite what Mom wanted.

Sweat already trickled down the nape of my neck as I made my way for the edge of the neighborhood. I focused my mind on school. On the new week. On the excitement of the day. I smiled as Allison came into view, hopping out of Michael's car. She came rushing for me as Michael's trunk slowly eased itself open, her arms throwing themselves around me.

"Are you ready? I mean, really ready? You've probably been waiting for this for a while."

I smiled. "I'm ready for this, yes. I need to thank Michael for driving, too."

Michael leaned out his window. "You're welcome! Now, get your stuff in the back. We gotta go!"

Allison squealed as she helped me get my satchel from around my shoulder. We both grunted and groaned, heaving it into the trunk before the door closed automatically. I rushed around, watching Allison climb into the front seat. And as I slipped into the back seat, I set my eyes toward Clint's house.

Michael looked at me through the rearview mirror. "Ready?"

I nodded. "Ready, Freddy."

Allison giggled. "Let's do this."

Michael inched away from the curb and we took off down the road. We turned into Clint's neighborhood as I fed Michael directions. Down one street. Up another. A small U-turn because we took a left turn much too early. I smiled to myself as I saw Clint's house coming into view. My heart sang with delight when I saw him standing on his porch. Michael pulled into his roundabout driveway and I opened the door, watching as Clint lumbered over to the car.

It was his first day back at school, and I was ecstatic to have him there.

He smiled. "Morning, Rae."

And I smiled back. "Morning, Clint."

"Aly. Mike."

Allison rolled her window down. "Hey there, Brick. How you feeling?"

Clint paused. "Brick?"

She shrugged. "You're practically a brick wall to have survived what you did."

Michael chuckled. "She's not wrong."

Clint grinned. "Brick. I could get used to that."

Michael smiled. "All right. Hop in. Time for us to get to school."

I held out my hand. "Here, let me help."

I eased him into the car, thankful that Michael and Allison were willing to give Clint the support he needed. And the fact that they had agreed to help me almost immediately warmed my heart. It seemed as if they had accepted him. Drawn him into our little fold. I couldn't have been happier about it, too. I wanted the rest of the school year to be this way. Us, walking together to school hand in hand, with my two best friends who had come to accept Clint for who he was, what he was, and who he'd become.

Things finally felt as if they were falling into place.

I saw Michael peeking through his rearview mirror at Clint. And while I wasn't sure why, I had a feeling. I knew he was struggling to warm up to Clint. After all, Michael was the king of holding grudges. Still, I held Clint's hand tightly as we all rode to school, with Allison chattering her head off at us.

Then Michael pulled us into the back parking lot as he spoke up.

"You guys want to be dropped off at the curb?"

I looked over at Clint. "What do you want?"

He sighed. "While I don't like the idea of being catered to like that, it might help."

Michael nodded. "Say no more."

Allison turned around. "You need any help getting out?"

Clint shook his head. "You guys have done enough just picking me up. Thank you."

Michael shrugged. "Not a problem. Everyone needs help sometimes, you know?"

Clint nodded. "More than ever before, I know."

I leaned my cheek against his shoulder as Michael eased us up to the curb. I hopped out of the car, then wrapped around to Clint's side as his door opened. He was slow to get out of the car with his injuries. The bruises on his face were still a bit evident. Faded, but there. The bruise on his jawline had dissipated. His ribs still hurt him. That much I knew. But he was steadier on his hip. And his arm was finally out of that sling.

Though he still couldn't lift his arm beyond parallel with the ground.

I took his hand. "Easy does it. Take your time. We've got plenty of it."

Clint snickered. "I feel people staring."

"Fuck them. They got an issue with it, they can take it up with me."

"Oh, my hero."

I giggled and shook my head as Clint finally got himself out of the car. I wrapped my arm around his waist, feeling him inch his arm around my neck. I liked having him there. Wrapped around me. Claiming me in front of the entire school. However, I also felt him leaning against me a bit too much.

Which meant he was already tired from the moving he had to do.

"Come on, Brick. Let's get you to homeroom."

He chuckled. "I don't know if I'll get used to that kind of a nickname."

I shrugged. "Kinda suits you, though. With how big you are."

"You calling me fat, sweet cheeks?"

I grinned. "Maybe just a little."

"That's what happens when you're bedridden, I guess."

"Don't worry, I'll whip you right back into shape."

He growled softly. "That a promise, beautiful?"

And as I gazed up into his eyes, the world faded away for a split second.

"That's a definite promise, handsome."

22

CLINTON

All morning, I'd been apprehensive about going back to school. Because for once, I didn't want all the attention to be on me. I didn't want people asking me tons of questions and coming up to me wanting stories. I didn't want girls staring at me with their big doe eyes. I didn't want to tell them how I saved some girl's life by forcing drunk, bullshit assholes to chase me down. All I wanted to do was forget about everything that had happened, press the reset button, and try that entire night again.

Hell, try this entire year again so I could do right by Rae.

Dad came home for a short time this past week, making my life an absolute nightmare. I heard him and Cecilia fighting more than usual. Mostly because she kept standing up for me. Which, in my father's eyes, meant standing against him. I didn't understand that. I never would understand it. And though I was thankful for the times Rae came to visit, I hated the fact that things never quite felt like that dinner we'd shared. Just the three of us. Her, myself, and my stepmother.

Fucking hell, that man ruined everything good around him.

Through it all, though, I kept up with my physical therapy. Cecilia stayed at my side for every appointment, taking me to and from them like a parent should have. Hell, she stepped up to the plate more this past week than my father ever had in the entirety of my life! It felt great, to be honest. Having an adult in my corner for once. She cheered me on and worked me through my frustrations. She helped me stretch in the mornings, trying to work that bruised stiffness out of my muscles. After throwing down that beautiful lasagna dinner meal over a week ago, she got me back onto a strict diet. No overdoing it on the sodium, cutting back on the fatty foods, and getting rid of all the sodas in the house so I was forced to drink more water than I ever had in my entire life.

There were parts of me that didn't want to leave her care and come back to school.

But I knew I had to. Even though Rae had been a doll and come over every night she wasn't working to help me with school-work, it still wasn't enough. She was still doing about half of my work because I kept falling asleep. Or she kept jumping my bones. Or I kept jumping her bones.

Mmph, I want to take her home and jump her bones.

"Clint?"

Rae's voice ripped me from my trance and I found myself still looking down at her. She had this worried look on her face. How long had I zoned out? I knew I shouldn't have taken those damn painkillers before I left the house.

I cleared my throat. "Yeah, gorgeous?"

Rae blushed. "Are you sure you're okay to be at school today?"

I nodded. "I'm sure. Yep."

"You guys need anything?"

"Clint, you okay?"

Mike and Aly's voices pulled my head over to look at them. They were still at the curb, peering out of Aly's rolled-down window. Despite the fact that I knew Mike still had issues with me, I was thankful I'd had their support this morning. I nodded at them, hoping they understood how thankful I was for their support. Even with the way I'd treated them in the past.

Rae's hand slipped to my hip.

"We can do this, Clint. Okay?"

My eyes fell back to hers. "You sure about that?"

She smiled. "You've got the three of us. You'll be good."

Aly giggled. "Yep! The four amigos."

Mike snickered. "Let's not get ahead of ourselves just yet."

I rolled my eyes. "We need a much better nickname than that."

Rae grinned. "Brick and the gang?"

Mike scoffed. "Why does he get to be the frontrunner?"

Aly smiled brightly. "Because the three of us have to hold him up until he recuperates."

I paused. "That's… painfully accurate. Ouch. Thanks for the dose of reality."

Rae nudged me softly. "Don't worry. She's really good for that sometimes."

Mike nodded toward the school. "You two go inside. We'll meet you at Rae's locker."

And with that, he pulled away from the curb.

I walked into the school, leaning against Rae more than I wanted to. More than I wished I were. She held me against her with a firmness and a strength I'd come to admire. We walked into the school's back doors and I tried ignoring the looks. The gasps. The whispers and the attention. I hated it, which was something I never thought in a million years I'd hate. A month ago, I'd been strutting my shit. Playing up the bruises and the limping just to get the attention of the girls. And now? All I wanted to do was crawl into a hole and get away from their glances. Their whispers. Their unasked questions.

Rae kissed my chest. "Don't worry. They'll get over it."

I wasn't as hopeful about that as she sounded.

We finally got to Rae's locker and I leaned against it. I felt myself huffing for air, which was yet another thing I didn't like. Walking was still a chore, and I had no fucking clue how the hell I'd lug my books to my classes. I watched as Rae opened her locker. Her eyes scanned it quickly before they fell to her body. She groaned and rolled her eyes, then closed her locker with a bang.

My brow furrowed. "What is it?"

Aly yelled down the hallway. "She left this!"

I looked up, watching Mike and Aly walk down the hallway. And the two of them were clutching Rae's shoulder backpack thing she always had with her at school. The straps looked as if they were crying out for mercy. The bottom of the bag looked as if it were about to give way. I watched Rae as she scurried for it, allowing it to fall to the floor. She dragged it over to her locker and started sifting through things, pulling out not only her books, but mine as well.

And all I wanted to do was help her.

"Uh-uh-uh, not so fast."

Rae pressed her hand into my chest. She pushed me upright, abandoning her bag on the floor in front of her locker. She leveled me with a look as her hand slid down my torso. And when her fingertips rumbled over my ribs, my eye twitched.

Aly sighed. "We can help her. You need to rest when you can."

Mike nodded. "Trust me, the girls have it."

I bit down onto the inside of my cheek to keep from firing back. I didn't like this. Not one bit. I didn't like the sweat forming on Rae's brow. Or the soft groans falling from Aly's lips. I didn't like how hard they were working for me, because I had no idea how I'd repay them for their efforts. I mean, I could hardly bend the fuck over. How the hell was I supposed to repay their generosity to them when I was beat up like this?

I felt all eyes on me as we stood there, waiting for the morning bell to toll. We'd made it to school a little too early for my liking. Usually, I rode up on my bike just as the homeroom bell sounded. I never got here before that damn bell. And if I did, I was usually in the cafeteria, shooting the shit with Roy and the gang.

Speaking of, where the hell were those guys?

I sighed. "Thank you guys."

Rae gathered both my books and her books in her arms. "You're welcome. It's really not an issue."

Mike shrugged. "I mean, what were you going to do? Walk to school? Ride a bike?"

Aly nudged him. "Michael, be nice."

I snickered. "He is being nice."

Mike held out his hand. "See? Brick gets it."

I paused. "You guys are really gonna make that stick, aren't you?"

Aly giggled. "We really are."

Mike shrugged. "I mean, it fits. Brick walls don't cave easily. Simple as that."

I was taken aback by the compliment. Because that was what that was. A compliment. From Mike. The guy who, only a few weeks back, I'd punched directly in the face because of a comment I made about the very nice girl at his side. Thankfulness rushed through my veins. I grinned at him as I nodded my head. I reached my hand out, holding it there for him to shake.

And when Mike clapped his hand against mine, I smiled.

"Really. Thank you."

Mike nodded. "Whatever you need, dude. Just let us know."

Aly clapped her hands. "Finally! Yes. It's about time the two of you put things to rest."

Mike snickered. "I don't know what you're talking about."

I chuckled. "Not a damn clue."

The four of us stood by Rae's locker, shooting the shit and having a grand old time. I used to think that getting here before that homeroom bell was for losers and idiots. But this was a lot of fun. We stood around, making jokes and venting about classes. They put a smile on my face, and a few of my jokes put smiles on theirs. It felt nice, being around good people. Genuine people. People who didn't stand around, picking on those that walked by. People who minded their own damn business and had things to talk about other than the pussy they got over the weekend.

Fucking Roy.

Things felt different. In a good way. Laughing with Mike and Aly felt more carefree and less skeezy than it did with Roy and Marina. The past few weekends that I'd spent at home and in the hospital were actually better than the weekends I spent drinking and partying. Despite the pain and despite the hospital stay and despite the medication, I'd had more fun with Rae at my side than I did in a hot tub full of girls pouring shots down my damn throat.

Who the hell are you becoming?

Someone I wanted to become.

Aly laughed. "Oh, my gosh. Clint, you really missed it last week. Wedne—no, Thursday. Thursday morning, the principal came into his office with his robe still on. His robe, Clint."

My brow furrowed. "Why the hell did the principal come with—?"

Mike grinned. "He'd been out all day chasing down this new puppy they've gotten. His youngest let it out of the backyard, and he had to chase it down before he came into school."

Rae snickered. "Didn't have enough time to clean himself up much before he had to be in his office."

My jaw fell open. "And the man didn't just take a sick day?"

Aly shook her head. "I'm telling you, our principal is a workaholic!"

The four of us laughed at Rae's locker just before the bell

tolled. The screeching sound made me wince, and Rae was right there at my side. Rubbing my chest, kissing my arm, and trying to soothe me back down onto my toes. I wasn't sure why the bell startled me as much as it had. I wasn't sure why it made my entire body ache. But having Rae there helped. Having Aly and Mike there helped.

I like having people in my life who help.

I drew in a deep breath. "What classes do you guys have first this morning?"

Mike pointed behind him. "I've got chemistry first thing. I'm all the way back that way."

Aly nodded. "I've got biology with Rae before our English class together."

Rae gasped. "That's right! You two have English together before lunch. Here, Aly. Can you take this to class for him?"

Aly held out her hand. "Of course. I wasn't sure why you didn't give it to me sooner."

I watched the two girls exchange my books and homework as people filtered around us. And for a few seconds, I didn't pay attention to the snickering. To the stares. To the whispers and the gossip fluttering around us. The only thing I paid attention to was how willing these two girls were to help me. How they coordinated my schedule, right there. In front of me. Trying to figure out ways to make this day less painful on me. Trying to figure out ways to lighten the load I had to carry.

I slowly looked up at Mike and found him grinning at me. A knowing grin. One that said, 'welcome to my world.'

Holy shit, I liked his world.

Rae sighed. "All right. Let's get you to homeroom, big guy."

Aly pointed down the hallway. "I'm going to go turn in his prior English homework. Mike, I'll see you in homeroom?"

He smiled. "I'll save you a seat."

Rae looked up at me. "You ready to go?"

And as I lost myself in her eyes, I nodded.

"I'm ready to go."

The three of them walked with me until we had to go our separate ways. Despite people talking about us, they never wavered from my side until they had to. And it didn't take me long to understand why Rae had been friends with Mike and Aly for so many years. They were unwavering. Unfaltering. They didn't care about what those around them said. Or gossiped about. They were trust-worthy. Steadfast. Willing to help at the drop of a hat.

I could get used to this.

More than I had ever gotten used to being around Roy and Marina.

23

—————

RAELYNN

I sighed. "I wish I had homeroom with Clint."

Allison linked her arm with mine. "Well, homeroom with me will have to do."

"You know that's not what I meant."

"I know, I know. But I'm still trying to cheer you up."

"I'm just worried about him. I mean, what if he needs help?"

"He's a big boy. He'll get around on his own today."

My lips downturned. "He shouldn't have to."

Allison nodded. "I know. But it is what it is and you can't keep dwelling on things you can't change."

But I did.

All throughout homeroom, I wondered if Clint was all right. If kids were still whispering about him. Or, God forbid, picking on him. I wanted to be by his side, helping him through his classes. I wanted to be there, holding his hand and propping his arm around my shoulders. I kept imagining him lumbering down the hallways. Trying to get to his classes on time and still walking in late because he simply couldn't keep up with that kind of a pace from class to class.

At least we'd all have lunch together.

I leaned over. "Hey, Allison. Can I ask you something?"

She nodded. "What's up?"

"Is there any way you can help Clint get to lunch?"

"Oh, I already told him I'd help him."

I paused. "Wait, you did?"

"Well, yeah. We've got class together before our lunch break. Why wouldn't I?"

I smiled, leaning toward her to give her a hug. I wrapped my arms around her, thankful that my two best friends were finally opening up to Clint being around. I mean, I knew he'd been an ass. But I saw a change in him. A softer demeanor. A desire to do better for himself. It warmed my heart that I had Allison's support. It warmed my heart that she was willing to reach out and help Clint in such a manner.

I kissed her cheek. "I really appreciate it."

She rubbed my back. "Don't worry. Michael and I got this. We're here to help. Okay?"

"Okay. Yeah."

The bell tolled, signaling our first transition to class. Allison and I set off for our first period. Biology. Science, first thing in the fucking morning. Like, really? Who the hell made that schedule? Who in the world decided that biology at eight-thirty in the morning was a wonderful idea for anyone?

Then I felt Allison tapping me on the shoulder.

"Don't look now, but look at our two guys."

She pointed, and my heart warmed at the sight. I gazed down the hallway, watching as Michael walked alongside Clint. I smiled at them, watching Michael carry Clint's books. He had slowed his walking pace to stay by Clint's side, and kept him engaged in conversation. Hell, I even saw Michael reach out and steady his hand against Clint's shoulder when he stumbled over his own two feet in the hallway.

I smiled as my heart melted into a steaming puddle of thankfulness.

"Told you," Allison whispered.

I rolled my eyes as she linked her arm with mine. It was time for our morning torture session with one of the most boring teachers in this high school. I swear, his voice never wavered from its one monotone pitch. He wore the same five outfits every week. Every day, of every week. Like those outfits were specifically designated for those particular days of the week, and no other days.

I sighed. "Ready for the purple vest?"

Allison snickered. "You think he'd switch it up at some point in time, right?"

A small commotion at the end of the hallway ensued, and it caused us to pause in the doorway of the classroom. I looked down the hallway, squinting, as I tried to figure out what was going on. I saw Clint against the wall. At least, I thought it was Clint. When Michael came into view, I knew that had to be Clint.

I watched Michael place his hand on someone's chest. Backing them away from Clint. I didn't know what was going on, but it looked bad. I started down the hallway.

Until Allison pulled me back.

"They've got it."

I scoffed. "Something's wrong. I have to get to Clint real—"

"You're going to be late for class."

I whipped around. "I don't care if I'm late for class, Allison."

Kids started yelling and I turned back around. I saw Michael shoving a kid down the hallway before teachers began intervening. Only they didn't go after Michael and Clint. They went after the kid that had been pushed behind the corner. I didn't know what was going on. But what I saw warmed my heart even further. I saw my best friend wrap Clint's arm around his shoulder and help him into class.

Before running out of the room and sprinting down the stairs to his own.

Allison sighed. "Well, that's something I didn't think I'd ever see."

I smiled softly. "Right?"

"Do you think Michael will ask me to prom?"

I did a double-take. "Say what now?"

"Prom, Rae. Keep up. Do you think he'll ask me?"

"I mean—I—I don't—do you—do you want him to?"

She nodded. "Yes."

My eyebrows rose. Mostly because I'd never heard Allison be so blunt before.

"Well, then I'm sure he will."

"Girls."

The teacher's voice caught our ears and pulled us into the classroom. He held the door open for us and we made our way to the back. Where we always took our seats. I kept peeking over at Allison, trying to read her face. As we cracked our books open and focused on the lecture that would surely put us all to sleep, I wondered what was going through her head.

I didn't have to wonder long. Because once our teacher turned his back, she leaned toward me.

"Do you think I should drop hints?"

I kept my eyes on the teacher. "Yes."

"What kind? I'm not good with this kind of stuff."

We kept our voices low. Trying our hardest to make sure our conversation didn't interrupt the lecture. Or catch our teacher's attention.

"I mean, just start talking about things. You know, like prom dress shopping, or the fact that you don't have a date yet. Michael's smart. He'll eventually catch on."

Allison sighed. "I really hope so."

I grinned. "You really want this, don't you?"

She shrugged. "Yeah. I do."

"It's nice, seeing you admit it."

She looked over at me. "I don't really know when I started feeling this way, you know."

"I mean, sometimes you don't."

The girl in front of me turned around, giving me a mean-ass look. But I simply glared back at her. She needed to shut the hell up with that face of hers. Allison and I were having a very important conversation. My best friend of all these years was finally admitting that she wanted to be more than friends with Michael.

This was a monumental moment.

Allison held back her giggling. "He's been really sweet lately, you know. We've been spending a lot of time together."

I smiled brightly. "I feel a story coming on."

The girl in front of me whipped around. "Are you two serious?"

And even though our conversation had gone unnoticed, her harshly-whispered outburst caught our teacher's attention.

"Ashley. Turn around and pay attention, please."

She tossed me another glare, but I simply smiled at her. I wiggled my fingers at her, waving goodbye as she turned around in her seat. She slumped down, crossing her arms over her chest. And as our boring-ass teacher struck up his pointless lecture again, Allison pointed to her notebook.

I nodded my head.

I sat there, waiting for her note to be scrawled out. And while she wrote, I thought about how normal this all felt. Allison and I always talked away biology. Science was easy for me. Always had been. So long as I read the chapters, I'd be okay. Not once did I ever have to take notes in my science courses all throughout school. It just… clicked for me. Things made sense in the science world. Hypotheses and testing to figure something out? That resonated with me in an ethereal sort of way.

Hey, if video game design didn't work out for me, maybe I had a career in some science field somewhere.

Allison tapped my shoulder before passing me a note. And when I unraveled it, the smile on my face grew wide. My eyes flittered across the words, warming my soul and making me happier than I'd been in a long time.

Allison was totally smitten with Michael.

He's just been over at the house a lot. And my parents really like him. He gets along with my dad. Mom even lets us stay in the basement together. He'll come over and we'll watch movies. Or talk. Or do school work together. And a few days ago? He took my hand for the first time. His hand is so warm, Rae! I really hope he asks me to prom.

The great thing about writing notes back and forth was that it looked as if I were taking notes. All I had to do was look up every once in a while, nod at our teacher, then I was good to go to keep writing. I used my chicken scratch to write out what I wanted to say as quickly as possible. I erased a few words and tried writing them clearer, just to make sure Allison could actually read it. Because apparently, doodling and having a mind for graphic design didn't translate to good handwriting.

Allison, that's so awesome! I mean, I know Michael likes you. I see it in how he looks at you and wants to be around you and stuff. Trust me, if you drop those hints and make comments from time to time about how you don't have a date to prom? He'll pick up on the hints and ask. I mean, this is Michael we're talking about. Once he knows there's a good thing coming his way, he charges head-on to get it. Remember the deal he had with his parents about his car?

That had been a doozy of a school year. As I passed the note to Allison, the memory pulled me back. The three of us had taken driver's ed at the same time. Same after-school class. Same teacher. We even tripled up to take the same driving test together with our teacher in order to get some experience. And Michael wouldn't stop talking about the deal he'd made with his parents. If he passed his test the first time in the DMV with no questions missed on the written test and no points docked on the driving portion, they'd buy him his first car. But if he missed anything, he'd have to do what most kids did—ask permission to use their parents' car.

I mean, I'm sure they were banking on Michael getting at least one thing wrong. I mean, even the slightest thing! But when he aced that written test while we were all in the DMV, I grinned. And when he came back from that driving portion without a scratch on his record, I threw my head back in laughter.

A week later, his parents had anted up. They'd bought him the SUV he drives now, and he was damn proud of that car. That's Michael, though. That's always been his personality. When Michael wanted something he knew could be his, he went full-steam ahead in order to get it.

All Allison had to do was make it known that she wanted to be his.

"Pop quiz, everyone!"

Just as Allison passed her note back to me, the class groaned. I looked at her and quickly tucked the note away in my back pocket as our teacher passed out the worksheets. I saw the soft panic on Allison's face. But she didn't have to worry. During times like this, I let her cheat off my test. We had a code and everything down for it. And not once had we ever gotten caught.

But she didn't look over at me once during the quiz.

The bell to switch classes rang and we all rushed the teacher's desk. I tossed my pop quiz at him and waited for Allison, who was the last to get out of her chair. She had a confident smile on her face and a skip in her step as she handed our teacher her quiz. Then she came over and linked her arm with mine.

"That wasn't nearly as hard as I figured it would be. It was a recap quiz."

I smiled. "Ready to get going?"

"Let's see if we can catch Clint and Michael down the hallway where we saw them. I can help Clint into English, if he needs it."

"Thank you so much, Allison."

"What? We have the next class together."

"Can you just let me thank you without brushing it off and making me feel weird about it?"

She sighed. "I'm sorry. I just… every time you thank us, it reminds me that—at one time—you thought we might not help. And it makes me sad."

I shrugged. "Because at one time, I knew you guys wouldn't have. I'm really glad you've come around to him."

"He's changed a lot, you know. I already see it in him."

I nodded. "I see it, too."

"You think it'll stay that way once he's healed?"

"I don't know, Allison. I guess only time will tell with that one."

As Allison pulled away from my side to go help Clint out of his class, I pondered on that question. I thought about it as I made my way for my own class. I watched Allison walk off with Clint, but it didn't warm my heart like usual.

Would he stay this way after he was all healed?

Or would he go back to Roy and his gaggle of goons once he could hold his own again?

24

CLINTON

I groaned. "Thanks again, Aly. I really appreciate it."

She helped me into my seat. "Really, it's not a problem at all. I'm glad I can help."

"You wouldn't be willing to help an old man to lunch, too, would you?"

"Already planned on it. Don't worry."

She sat next to me, offering a kind smile in the process. It felt weird. One, because she usually sat at the front of the classroom. And two, because the smile she gave me was genuinely kind. Not the snide or berating kind of smiles I'd gotten used to with her. She set my books on top of my desk before situating her own, and I wondered what she was thinking. What was going on in her head? Was she helping me because she wanted to? Or because Rae kept putting her up to it?

Why did I want it to be the former?

"Oh. Great."

Aly's voice caught my attention and I looked over at her. As I followed her gaze, I saw what she was looking at. Roy and Marina had strolled into class, taking up their regular seats not too far away from us. Aly grimaced as she looked toward them, easing herself back into her seat.

I just hoped the pair didn't make a scene in the middle of class or something.

My eyes stared up at the clock, watching the minutes tick up to the top of the hour. And with every second that passed by, our English teacher didn't come into the room. Where the hell was that woman? Why was she so late this morning?

"You feel as bad as you look, dude?"

I saw Aly's head whip over toward me as I bit down onto the inside of my cheek. Roy's voice echoed in my ear as he leaned over, trying to close the space between us. I rolled my shoulders back, ignoring the pain in my collarbone. I slowly rolled my head around, trying to loosen myself up. All I had to do was ignore them. *Don't engage.* Because the second I engaged them, we were in trouble.

I let the comment roll off my back.

But I shouldn't have answered.

"I'm healing just fine. Thanks."

Roy scooted his desk a bit closer. "You got physical therapy or some shit you're doing?"

Had it not been for the grin on his girlfriend's face, I would've actually thought he cared.

"Yep. Three times a week right now. For the next few weeks."

Roy nodded. "Uh huh. Right. So you'll be back in shape soon enough?"

I licked my lips. "That's the plan."

"That's a shame. Really."

Aly scoffed. "Put a sock in it, Roy."

I slowly panned my gaze over to him, taking in the fire in his eyes. I shouldn't have asked, but he had me baited. Right there on his fucking hook.

"What's a shame?"

Roy snickered. "I mean, you getting back into shape. It's been nice not having you around."

Marina giggled. "Too bad that cliff was only twenty feet high."

I heard part of the class gasp at her comment. It was the top of the hour and the damn teacher still wasn't in the room. Where the fuck was she, anyway? I stared Roy down, trying my hardest to be the bigger man. There was no need for me to talk down to a woman. I certainly didn't want to become my father. I didn't want to let my anger take hold of me like it did him. That was Roy's bitch, so it was Roy's issue to handle.

My eyes held Roy's. "Yeah. Too bad, I guess."

Roy grinned. "I knew you were a depressed little shit."

Aly piped up. "That's enough, Roy."

Marina giggled. "Should've done us all a favor and finished what that bridge started."

Aly flew out of her chair. "The two of you are relentless. Can't you hear yourselves? Cut it the heck out."

Roy's eyebrows rose. "Wow. Strong language coming from you, Miss Priss."

I held my hand up, signaling for Aly to stop. "The two of you can talk to me. There's no need to involve her."

Marina scoffed. "Fucking around with her, too? Rae not enough for you anymore?"

I pointed my finger at her. "You keep my girl's name out of your mouth. It's not my fault you two have debased yourselves to absolutely nothing."

Roy smiled devilishly. "You mean, like you used to be?"

Marina frowned. "What, you think you're better than us now?"

"You think you've outgrown us?"

"Somehow leveled up in life?"

"You think this'll make Daddy love you more?"

"Or stop beating up on you? I've heard the stories. Roy tells me everything. Are you that open with Rae?"

"Does she know everything?"

"Or does she only know your cock size?"

"If you can still get it up, of course."

"Hey, asswipes!"

Aly's voice pierced through their banter and caught the attention of the entire class. My eyes widened as the curse fell from her lips, and I turned to face her. She had her fists clenched. She ground her teeth together. Her eyes bounced between Roy and Marina, her body vibrating in fear.

I leaned forward. "Aly, it's all right."

She leveled me with a quick look before turning her attention back to them.

"The only shame in this room is you two. The only people in this room who should throw themselves off anything are the pair of you. This entire school's sick of your shit. You hear me? Absolutely sick of it. Sick of you, Roy, for the bullshit you pull in the cafeteria. Trying to act like you're big stuff when all you want is for good ol' Mommy to pay you some attention. And you, Marina.

Everyone's sick and tired of coming around corners and catching you flirting with other guys when we all know you're still sucking Roy's—"

"Aly," I said curtly.

Her eyes flickered to me before she sighed. "All of us know that the only reason you two are still together is because nobody else can stand to hang out with either of you or listen to your asinine stories about getting prematurely drunk at parties before going off and doing God-knows-what to one another. So, shut the fuck up. Face forward. And leave Clint the hell alone with your shit."

The entire class fell silent. I sure as hell didn't know what to say. I'd never heard Aly curse. Much less that much in one fell swoop. I slowly panned my gaze over to Roy and Marina. Their eyes bounced between us as I gave them a punctuated head nod. Letting them know I agreed with everything that had just flown out of Aly's mouth.

With a few grumbles, they scooted back into their place. Faced the front of the classroom as everyone began whispering.

About them.

Not about me.

Aly sighed a soft sigh before sitting back down in her seat. I slowly turned my attention back to her, feeling a shocked smile cross my lips. She flipped her books open as our teacher finally made her presence known ten minutes after class was supposed to start. Aly leaned over, flipping open my own book to the page we needed to be on.

Then she looked up at me.

"What?"

I shook my head. "Thank you, Aly."

She shrugged. "We're all tired of their stuff."

"Oh, now you say 'stuff.'"

She smiled at me, and it caused me to chuckle. We muffled our laughter as the teacher started her lecture, rushing us through our homework so we could get to 'the good stuff,' as she called it. And while I loved my English class—mostly—this book we were reading could go kick rocks. It was the first book in all of high school I'd been forced to read that I didn't enjoy one damn bit.

Catch-22 could suck my—

"I really don't like this book."

Aly's murmur caught my ear and it made me grin.

"Me, neither. Don't worry."

She sighed. "Switching the points of view the entire time between, like, seventeen different characters is just a bit much."

I snickered. "Can we put that on Amazon somewhere? I feel like we should warn the masses."

"Is there something you'd like to share with the class, Clint?"

The teacher called me out and everyone turned to face me. Aly started giggling, hiding her face with her notebook as a grin trickled across my cheeks. I liked this. I liked talking with her in class. I had no idea how the fuck I'd ever stayed friends with the likes of Roy and Marina. But, I didn't see myself ever trading what I had now for what I'd had in the past.

The teacher cleared her throat. "Clint?"

I licked my lips. "I was just telling Aly here that we should write up a review on Amazon, warning people about the painful point of view changes in the book."

The teacher nodded. "What don't you like about them?"

I shrugged. "For one, it's distracting. By the time you come back around to a character's story, you have to flip back to their last chapter to see where their story left off. It's tedious."

Roy sniggered. "He's actually reading the book, for fuck's sake."

Marina murmured. "Guess loser pussy really changes you."

The teacher diverted her attention. "Roy. Marina. Anything to add?"

And when they shook their heads, Aly snickered.

"What's that for, bitch?"

Marina blurted out the statement and the teacher's jaw dropped open.

"Marina. Up here. Now."

She stood up. "No. I want to know why this goody-two-shoes thinks she can judge us just because we don't like reading these shit books."

Roy grabbed his girlfriend's arm. "Just get up to the front of the class."

"Hell, no! I'm tired of Allison and her judgmental glances. I'm tired of them thinking they're better than us. Just because the rest of us Sparknote this shit doesn't mean it makes her any better that she actually reads the books. And Clint, for that matter. Fucking loser after that fall of his. You're no better than—"

"Detention! Both of you! For the rest of the week!"

The teacher's exclamation caught our ears. Her words caused Aly to panic.

"Wait, who?"

The teacher crooked her finger. "Roy. Marina. Up here, now. And if you so much as make another peep, I'll move to have you both suspended from school. Until further notice."

Roy slammed out of his desk, scooting it across the floor. He jumped at a couple students staring him down, who all jerked back from him. I shook my head, watching as the dynamic duo made their way to the front of the class. Marina kept staring Aly down. Like she was about to do something drastic. I reached my hand out, placing it on Aly's desk. Marking my territory and letting them know that if they messed with her, they messed with me, too.

Then, watching as Marina and Roy shook their heads at me, I saw Aly turn her attention my way as well. I peeked over at her, watching as a sly grin crossed her face. A grin that said 'I got you.' A grin that said 'I'm on your side.'

And for once, I understood what it felt like to have a friend.

25

———

RAELYNN

Raelynn Three Weeks Later

I sat on the couch, waiting endlessly for Mom and D.J. to get out of the damn place. The two of them were going out for a date night. Which ultimately meant they'd be out until the break of dawn before they stumbled back in. Drunk, horny, and ready to make all sorts of noises until they finally passed out around breakfast time. It had been the same routine for the past couple of weeks, and it made me sick.

This time, however, I had a few plans in store for myself to keep my mind off things.

"So, how's your friend?"

D.J.'s voice filled the room and I tried my hardest not to roll my eyes. I was ready for them to leave. I wanted them to get out. Not because I didn't want to be around my mother, but because I was done entertaining D.J. I had no desire to get to know him. No passion to get close to him again. I didn't care about accepting him into some sort of fold or making him feel part of the family.

I just wanted him out of my space.

"Rae?"

I sighed. "Yeah?"

"Did you hear me?"

"I did."

"Well, is your friend doing all right?"

I shrugged. "He's fine."

"That's good."

"Yep."

"So, how's school?"

"It's school, I guess."

"What have you been up to lately? Anything fun with your friends? What are their names. Um… Mac and Dani?"

I rolled my eyes. "Michael and Allison."

"Right, right. How are things with them?"

"They're good."

"That's good."

I gazed out the window, wondering when Mom would get downstairs. I knew she wanted me to keep D.J. occupied because 'it upset him whenever he had to wait around' for her. Wow. What a fucking winner, Mom. But I didn't want to fight with her on it. She'd obviously made her choice, and in a few months I'd be graduated and out of here. Getting a place with Allison close to UCLA and rooming with my best friend ever.

And hopefully, finding myself a job or something not too long after that.

D.J. sighed. "You know how much longer your mom's going to be?"

I shrugged. "As long as it takes for her to feel confident walking down those stairs."

"We're going to be late."

"Then push back the reservations."

"We don't have reservations."

"Then there's no need for you to hop down her throat about it."

I whipped my head over, shooting D.J. a look. And as he rolled his eyes at me, I scoffed. I got up from the couch and left the room, refusing to be near him one second longer. Mom could take all the fucking time in the world she wanted to get ready. That was her right. And he had no right to get upset with her when all she wanted to do was look pretty for him.

Besides, I had to start getting ready myself.

Mom poked her head out. "That you, Rae?"

I walked down the hallway. "Yep."

She put her earrings in. "I thought you were talking with D.J. for me."

"Yeah, well. I'm done talking."

I walked into my bedroom and closed the door. I didn't want Mom talking me into going back down there. And not a minute later, D.J. was yelling up the stairs. Like it was his damn house.

"You coming, Lu? We don't have all night!"

"Come on. I'm sure you look fine."

"The restaurant won't have space for us if we don't leave now!"

"Lu!"

I almost opened my door and told him to shut the hell up. But I heard Mom finally call out for him. Telling him she was coming. I walked over to my window, listening as the two of them bickered downstairs. And as they left through the front door, I watched them walk to D.J.'s car. He looked up at me and paused. Right by his door. I pointed my fingers to my eyes before pointing back at him. Letting him know I was watching him. Always.

And after he shook his head at me, the two of them dipped into his car.

I scrambled out of my bedroom after that. I had to power clean some things. The kitchen sink was full of dishes, courtesy of the asshole that had just left. I wanted to vacuum the living room floor. Clint and I had a movie night on the books. One where we'd order pizza, curl up underneath some blankets, and watch movies until we passed out on the couch. Or upstairs in my bedroom. I grinned at the thought. Holy hell, Mom would shit bricks if Clint came down the stairs tomorrow morning.

Then again, she and D.J. would be snoring too loud to hear us doing anything in the morning, anyway.

I scrubbed at the dishes before rinsing them off in the sink. I stacked them neatly in the dish holder, letting them drip-dry on the counter. I pulled the vacuum out of the closet and struck it up, chastising myself for getting so sweaty. I had less than an hour to pull everything off. Especially since Clint was already halfway through his physical therapy appointment.

"Come on. You gotta get a shower still."

I ran the vacuum over the carpet as quickly as I could. Spot-treating it, really. Just to make it look a bit more decent. I shoved it into the closet and kicked the cord underneath the door, hoping it didn't come springing back out at the most inopportune moment. I ran up the steps, taking them two by two. Wanting nothing more than to barge into the bathroom and take the hottest shower alive.

But I settled for a cooler shower. Cold enough to get me to stop sweating without chilling me to the damn bone.

Out I hopped, ten minutes later, with a towel wrapped around my body. I rushed into my mother's bathroom, digging out her blow dryer. I didn't want my hair dripping wet for Clint once he got here. Especially if he wanted to play with it.

Oh, I loved it when he played with my hair.

I flipped my head over and felt the heat blast against my neck. I didn't know how to turn the heat down on the blow dryer, though. Was that even a function? So my neck began sweating. And my face. By the time my hair was dry, the rest of me was wet again. From the damn hair dryer being much too hot.

"Fuck."

I toweled myself off as I walked into my bedroom. I looked at the clock, groaning as my eyes read the time. Shit. It was already six o'clock. He was getting out of his appointment now, which meant he only had to cross town to get here.

"Gotta hurry, Rae," I murmured to myself as I rushed around with my fan on full blast. Trying to stop the sweating as I worked up yet another one. I pulled on some clothes and ran a brush through my hair. I fanned my face, trying to get the redness to stop pooling in my cheeks. I lay down on my bed, spread eagle, letting my damn crotch and my armpits air out.

I was so fucking nervous to have Clint over, it almost made me sick.

Why he insisted he come over after his last physical therapy appointment I wasn't sure. But who was I to say no? I wanted to spend time with him. I wanted to celebrate this moment with him. His first round of PT was over. And after a check-up tomorrow afternoon at the hospital, we'd know whether or not he needed another round. With every passing day for the past three weeks, he'd gotten stronger. He needed less and less help to get to classes. His bruises had faded into small, yellow patches of skin and his limping completely ceased.

Watching him heal had been an incredible journey.

But feeling how close we had become had been even better.

My phone ringing on my bedside table caught my ear. I reached over for the phone, hoping and praying it wasn't Clint.

Because I knew there was the slimmest chance that he'd be too tired to come over. I slapped my hand over my phone and pulled it up to my face. I saw Allison's name and smiled. Just who I wanted to talk to. She'd know how to calm my nerves down.

Until Allison blurted out what she wanted to say.

"Michael asked me to go to a movie tonight!"

I paused, my jaw falling open. "He did what?"

"Yes. Yes. I'm sorry. I wanted to call and see how you were doing and all because I know Clint's coming over but… Michael asked me out!"

"Ah!"

I squealed on the phone with her as I jumped up from my bed. I bounced around, shaking my hair out and pumping my fist in the air. Finally. Fucking finally! Michael had grown a pair of balls and asked Allison out on a date. I flopped back down onto the bed, my lungs panting softly for air as my hair splayed out along the comforter.

I smiled. "Oh, my gosh. I'm so fucking happy for you."

Allison giggled. "You think it's a date, right? This is a date?"

I paused. "Of course it's a damn date!"

"Because, you know, he didn't specifically use the word 'date.' I mean, he said, 'Do you want to go to a movie with me tonight?' Not 'Do you want to go on a date with me tonight?'"

"Allison."

"I know. I know. I just—I really don't want to read anymore into this than I should."

I grinned. "He's asked you out on a date. I promise you."

"So I'm not crazy? You know, getting dressed up and doing makeup and borrowing Mom's jewelry?"

I giggled. "Not crazy at all. I want you to have fun tonight. But make it easy for him to make a move on you during the movie."

"Wait, what?"

"Uh, yeah."

"What kind of move? You think he might…?"

I snickered as I sat up in bed, listening to Allison whisper the word. Like it was so dirty.

"Kiss me?"

I rolled my eyes. "You're seventeen years old, Allison. Pipe up."

She sighed. "What do I do if he tries to kiss me? Or hold my hand?"

"Do you want to kiss him or hold his hand?"

"I mean, maybe?"

"Allison."

She sighed. "Maybe a little bit."

I smiled. "You mean a lot a bit?"

"Shut up."

I laughed softly. "If he makes a move and you want it, then let it happen. You know how Michael is. If he wants something, he'll initiate it. And if you're not ready, tell him that. But, don't sit there with your arms crossed over your chest or some shit like that. Just be open. Be you, because that's all he wants."

She giggled. "I can do that."

"Promise?"

"Yep. I promise."

"Good. Now, I have to go. I still need to put myself together before Clint gets here. I expect a call in the morning telling me all about this movie!"

"If we watch it."

I gasped. "Allison!"

She laughed heartily into the phone. "Love you, mean it!"

My jaw fell open in shock as she hung up the phone. Did my little Allison just make a comment about not actually watching a movie with a guy? Holy hell, my little girl was becoming all grown up.

"Way to go, girl." I smiled to myself as I tossed the phone back onto my bedside table. Then I walked over to my mirror and ran my fingers through my hair, trying to tame some of the frizz. My cheeks were still red from rushing around, but the sweating had stopped. I made my way back into my mother's bathroom and found some of her body spray, so I decided to take some liberties.

And those liberties led into other trials. Other experiments. Other curiosities.

Soon, I smelled like something called 'cotton blossom' and looked like a damn clown. I turned on the hot water, splashing it in my face and trying to get it all off. Some of the makeup didn't actually come off. The mascara didn't run. The blush didn't budge. I gawked in the mirror as I scrubbed at my face, putting as much hand soap on my skin as I could manage.

Then, I looked down at the makeup I'd tried and groaned.

"Holy fuck, it's waterproof."

I searched around in the drawers for something to take this shit off. And through it all, I lost track of time. I finally found some makeup remover and doused it on a washcloth, hoping it was enough. I wiped it over my face and the makeup magically came off. Like a key slipped into just the right door. I breathed a sigh of relief as I scraped the putty off my face. Layer by layer, cursing myself for being so damn stupid.

Then, with my face redder and puffier than ever, a knock came at the door downstairs.

Just. Fuck.

26

CLINTON

"So, do you want to go ahead and do the evaluation? Or do it tomorrow?"

I paused, wiping the sweat off my brow. "I mean, if we can knock that shit out now, sure."

The therapist chuckled. "All right. Well, go ahead and stand up for me. I'm going to run you through a series of tests."

"You mean, more torture."

He grinned. "If you need a breather——"

I held up my hand. "No, no. I got it. Just… let me finish my water."

I'd be damned if I'd let this fucking accident get the best of me. I'd been going at this physical therapy hard. Harder than ever before. I did all these exercises when I wasn't in my therapy classes. Two, sometimes three times a fucking day. I refused to let it beat me. I refused to be crippled for the rest of my life. I refused to never feel the rumbling of a bike between my legs again. Or feel the wind wrapping around my body as I cruised down the highway.

I mean, Dad and Cecilia weren't on board for something like that yet. But I was trying.

"All right, Doc. Hit me with it."

My therapist laughed. "Hold your arms out. I'm going to press down on them, and you fight back."

I grinned. "You mean I can punch you in the face?"

"Not that kind of fighting back."

"Be more specific next time."

We laughed and bantered through the test. And while I still wasn't happy with how much work it took to get through those damn exercises, I proved a lot. I had most of my range of motion back in my arms. My collarbone was strong. All the bruises had healed up, leaving me with only the emotional and mental scarring of that night. My muscles felt better than they had in weeks. My ribcage no longer hurt. My back had straightened itself out and those vertebrae had slipped right back into place.

For once, I felt like myself again.

"All right, Doc. Give it to me straight. How did I do?"

I slumped down into my chair after the evaluation was over. Cecilia stood in the corner, clapping her hands softly and cheering me on. My therapist handed me another bottle of water, watching me as I cracked it open with ease.

And a smile slid across his face.

"You want my personal or professional opinion?"

I took a swig. "Why not both?"

He sat back. "Sounds good enough. Well, personally? You're doing fantastic. You're strong. You're stable. It's obvious you're not in any sizable amount of pain anymore. And the strength you've gotten back in your body is outstanding for only a month of in-and-out-patient therapy."

"So, what's your professional opinion?"

"In my professional opinion, you're clear to make a full recovery."

I leapt out of my chair, sending the water flying into the air. My therapist launched out of his, clapping me on the back as I hugged him tightly. I buried my face into the crook of his neck. I hopped around as Cecilia rejoiced in the corner. She came up and hugged me, pulling me away from my therapist. I picked her up and swung her around, still feeling the smallest twinge in my ribcage. But not much.

Not compared to what I'd gotten used to.

The therapist laughed. "Let's get you a follow-up appointment on the books for three months out. You know, just to check on you and make sure you're doing okay. I'll take the liberty of cancelling your appointment with the hospital tomorrow."

I set Cecilia down. "Thank you. So much. I really, really appreciate it."

"Not a problem, man. Come on. Let's get you checked out and I'll give you a formal list of exercises to keep up twice a day. Every day."

I felt like I'd been saying that a lot lately. That I was appreciative of people's efforts. But it was the truth. Cecilia, for sticking by me day in and day out with all this shit. For my therapist and the cursing he put up with to get me to this point. For Rae, and Mike, and Aly. Their support in school and huffing around my books when they didn't have to.

Rae, especially. For helping me keep my head above water with my grades.

I really have to thank her tonight.

Cecilia walked with me to the check-out desk. "What kinds of issues should we keep an eye out for?"

I snickered. "Already losing faith in me?"

My therapist grinned. "Honestly? I don't think there will be any trouble. He's strong. And he's only been getting stronger. But keep an eye out for the usual things. Unexplainable bruising around rehabilitation sights. Any sort of a fever spike. Redness, tenderness, or being swollen in these areas. Also, backsliding. If, for some reason, he backslides in pain or mobility, come back and see me immediately."

Cecilia nodded. "I'll make sure to keep an eye out."

I got myself checked out with my appointment. Scheduled just before we broke for Christmas break. I offered my arm to Cecilia, walking her out to her car instead of the other way around. It felt nice, escorting my stepmother to the car. For weeks, she'd been the one escorting me. Holding tightly to my waist in an attempt to get me to the car safely. And while I'd been appreciative of everyone's help over the past few weeks, it felt nice to help myself again.

Even if Dad wasn't here to witness any of it.

"So how are you feeling?"

I smiled at her question. "I'm feeling great. Really."

"Good. You still got plans with Rae tonight?"

I nodded. "At her place, yeah. Is it still okay if you drive me over there?"

"I mean, I'm certainly not going to make you walk."

"I'd drive myself if there was another car here for me to use.

But for some reason, Dad decided to park his at the airport this time around."

She sighed. "I know exactly why your father did it."

I snickered. "Well, I was going to play dumb, but…"

The two of us had a small laugh at his expense, but it was a tense sort of laughter. I knew convincing the two of them to let me have another bike would be almost impossible. That was definitely a purchase I'd have to save up for on my own down the road. After I graduated and got out from underneath my father's hawk-like eye. But having a regular car didn't seem completely unreasonable.

Until Dad randomly started outright refusing me access to his.

It wasn't as if I'd driven it much. I preferred my bike, mostly because I didn't have to ask his permission to use it. But there were a few occasions where I'd needed to use his car because my bike was in the shop or something. And he'd never been hesitant to give me his keys.

Now, though, he was actively keeping his car away from me. Getting it out from underneath my claws. Like hiding his keys. Or locking it down in the extra garage we had around back.

Or driving it to the fucking airport instead of having Cecilia take him so he could park his car in long-term parking.

My stepmom sighed. "I'm working with him on it. But you know how your father is."

I nodded. "I know. I know how he is. I know it'll take some time to convince him that I'll need a set of wheels again."

"You know he won't go for the bike, though. And neither do I."

"Trust me, I wasn't even dreaming of asking you guys about it."

She cranked up the car. "Good. Because I didn't want to fight with you about it."

I snickered. "I don't think we could fight if we wanted to."

"You think?"

And when I looked over at her, I shook my head. "Nope. I know."

She smiled at me as she backed the car out. Then we made our way out of the parking lot. She started heading toward home, getting out on the main roads and getting hooked up on every stoplight. It was frustrating, to say the least. I was ready to see Rae. Ready to hold her in my arms. Ready to give her the good news.

Ready to bend down and kiss her lips without it hurting so damn much.

"Well, let me work on your father a bit more about getting you a car. I think I know a sweet spot that'll work."

I chuckled. "Don't do anything you don't want to. That's all I'm saying."

She slapped my knee playfully. "Hey, now. I don't know what kind of woman you take me to be, but I can class it up when I want to."

"Which is why I still don't understand how you fell for Dad."

She sighed. "There is a side to your father you don't see much. A kind, romantic, and very caring side of him."

"Yeah, well. Let him know that sometimes it should come out to play with his son, too."

"What? You want him to send you two dozen white roses and some dark chocolates?"

I burst out laughing. "You're an absolute mess."

She giggled. "A mess that's trying to get you some wheels so you can have your independence back."

"Thank you for that, though. Seriously. I know I wouldn't even be able to have that conversation with Dad without him biting my head off."

"Well, I think you should have your freedom back. Especially now that this police investigation is winding down. It's becoming clearer and clearer to everyone involved that you weren't responsible for what happened. That should be enough to earn you your independence back."

I smiled. "Thanks."

"I mean, just look at it from a practical point of view. You shouldn't be relying on others to get around. You're eighteen years old. You're months away from graduating. And soon, you'll be off doing your own thing. You'll need a car to coordinate the life you want. Especially since your bike was completely totaled in the crash. There's no reason in this world why we can't take that insurance money and put a down payment on a car for you. It makes no sense."

"Take a left here."

"Got it."

"Cecilia?"

"Yeah?"

I placed my hand on her knee. "Thank you for being here for me."

She eased herself to a stop in the middle of the road. The middle of the dark, dank, smelly road that led us all the way to Rae's house. Lamp lights flickered in the distance, casting an eerie glow over the whole neighborhood. And as Cecilia's hand fell against mine, she squeezed it softly.

"You're welcome, Clint."

I sighed. "I just… not having Dad around for any of this hurt. Knowing how much he blamed me for all this hurt. Probably more than the physical pain I was in."

"I'm so sorry, Clint."

I shook my head. "No reason for you to be sorry. It is what it is. But I'm lucky I had you. I'm lucky you were on my side. Thank you for that, Cecilia. I'm glad this has given us a chance to get to know one another."

She blinked back tears as she brought my hand to her lips. She kissed it softly, leaving behind traces of her chapstick. She sniffled and I reached over toward her, wrapping her up in the most awkward hug I'd ever experienced.

It still felt wonderful, though. Feeling her hold me like that.

"I'm glad, too, Clint. I'm glad we got to spend some time together."

I snickered. "And you make an awesome as hell milkshake."

She giggled softly. "I'll make sure to make them more often for you."

I pulled back and watched her wipe at her tears. She settled into her seat, then I pointed out which house was Rae's. She eased us up to the driveway, dropping me off at the curb. But, before I got out, I leaned over and gave her a quick peck on the cheek.

"Thanks again."

She smiled. "Anytime, Clint. Now, go see your girl. I'm sure she's excited to see you."

And the woman didn't have to tell me twice.

27

RAELYNN

Shit. You look like a blown-up bobblehead, Rae.

The knock at the door startled me, causing me to toss myself out of my mother's bathroom. I scrambled for the steps, ready to throw myself into Clint's arms and drag him inside. My heart leapt into my throat. I heard a car driving away from the house as high beams filtered through the windows. Shadows pivoted along the walls, beckoning me further toward the front door as I jumped down the steps.

"Coming!"

Me and my red face are, at least.

With water droplets speckling the front of my shirt, I fluffed my hair back one last time, then unlocked the door. I threw it open, staring up into the eyes of the boy I'd come to adore. And the second his eyes laid themselves on me, he stepped forward.

"Holy fuck, I've missed you."

He breathed the words against my lips before he wrapped me in his arms. He picked me up against him, pulling me to my tiptoes as I gasped in shock. My arms slid around his neck. He barreled into my house, cloaking my back and pulling me close to him. His tongue filled my mouth. His essence overcame me. The smell of his cologne wafted up my nostrils, curling my toes and making me tremble against him.

He kept walking until my back was pinned against a wall. Any wall. I didn't give a shit which wall it was. He kicked his leg out, shutting the door closed with a crash as the world fell away.

And I took the time to melt into his kiss.

"Oh," I moaned down the back of his throat. He dipped down, gripping my thighs as he picked me clear up off my feet. My head fell off to the side as the kiss deepened, our tongues doing battle for the upper hand. I sucked on his lower lip and raked my teeth across his tongue. He fisted my hair, pulling my head off to the side as he dragged his warm, wet lips down my neck.

I gasped with desire in my bones.

Not once did he comment on how red my face was. Not once did he realize its puffiness. He kissed me. Devoured me. Ground his hips against me as he pinned me to the wall with his strength. I was taken aback by it all. By the way he effortlessly picked me up. I groaned as he pulled my shirt off to the side, sinking his teeth into my shoulder.

And when his face came back to meet mine, he cupped my cheek, causing me to smile as I drank him all in.

I giggled. "I take it things went well?"

He kissed me softly. "Better than 'well.'"

"Well. I suppose that's… good."

I grinned at him as he snickered. I laughed softly as he pressed a kiss to the tip of my nose. But when he captured my lips again, I sighed. Groaned. Rolled against him as I felt his cock pulse to life. The kiss was long. Sensual. His tongue lingered and his taste filled my mouth. My hands meandered into his hair, twirling up into its curls. He'd let it grow out a bit. Just enough for the ends to start flipping upward. Curling in on themselves and giving me just enough to hang on to.

I adored it.

"So are you going to tell me the good news, then?"

Clint paused. "Oh. Yeah. I should do that."

I snickered. "You really should, handsome."

He pulled back, seating me against the wall with his hips as his hands found mine. He threaded our fingers together. I placed my hands above my head. He pinned me to the damn wall, his eyes falling to my breasts. The way he licked his lips made me cast out all desire for our movie night. Replacing it with another desire.

"Clint?"

He shook his head. "My God, you're breathtaking."

I blushed. "You seem much better."

He smiled. "Because I am. They've cleared me, and expect me to make a full recovery."

"Wait, what?"

He nodded. "My therapist even cancelled my appointment with the hospital tomorrow. I don't have to see anyone for another three months."

"Wait, what!?"

He chuckled. "I'm free as a bird, and stronger than I've been in weeks."

"Clint! Holy shit!"

I bucked against him, freeing myself enough to wrap myself around his body. I hugged him close, burying my face into the crook of his neck. And as he held me tightly, our laughter filled the room. Tears of happiness rushed my eyes. Finally, this damn nightmare was over. Clint had been healed. He'd recuperated. And it seemed as if things were finally swaying back in our favor.

I kissed his neck. "I'm so happy for you."

"Mm, keep doing that and I'll show you just how happy you make me."

I kissed his skin again. "That a promise?"

Softly, deftly, I planted kisses against his skin. He pulled me away from the wall, carrying me into the living room as he made his way for the couch. I kissed up his pulse point, nibbling against his earlobe as I let my hands wander underneath the collar of his shirt, feeling his muscles rolling underneath that taut skin of his. He held me closely, his hands cupping my thighs tightly. He was back. My Clint. The old Clint. The strong, dexterous, confident Clint.

A new lease on life.

"You're mine."

The growl that left his lips made my eyes roll back. He dropped me to the couch, shedding his jacket and his shirt before falling to my body. I slid my hands down his back, memorizing the way his muscles rippled. My fingertips rumbled over their edges and fell into their divots. It was as if his body had been carved just for me. I molded to him, filling his empty spots as my legs spread for him. His tongue invaded my mouth. Pushed its way through as his hands shoved my shirt up. Ready, and waiting, to feel me.

"I. Need. You. Rae."

His kisses punctuated his words as he helped me lean up. Off came my shirt. And with a snap of his fingers, off came my bra. He groaned as it slid down my arms, casting itself off to the side like magic. I heard him toe his boots off as he laid me back down, the cushions catching my soft descent as his hands roamed my body. I arched and rolled against him. His lips kissed down my neck, causing goosebumps along my arms. The valley of my breasts welcomed his lips. My nipples stood up and applauded him as he journeyed his way down. I moaned for him. Groaned out his name. Bucked against him as the heat between my legs grew to searing temperatures.

"Clint, please. Now."

Off came my pants. My panties. My socks. My body, bared for him. Ready for his carnal taking. I watched his eyes roam over me. He stood up, hovering over me as his lean, chiseled abs came into view. The rings around them called to my eyes. My fingertips burned with a need to touch them. Clint grabbed my ankles, pulling my legs around until my back sat against the couch cushions.

Then he dropped to his knees.

"Clint, you don't—fuck!"

He hummed between my legs as he nibbled my thighs. He bit down into them, tasting them and raking his teeth across my dollops of excess. I spread myself for him, wanting nothing more than for him to devour me. And as I ran my hands through his hair, he kissed closer to where I wanted him. Lapped his tongue over where I needed him. Teased me relentlessly. Until I was a panting, sweating mess.

"I can't. Clint, you have t—oh!"

"Trust me, I'll get there, gorgeous."

His tongue sank into me and my eyes screwed shut. With every lick, I bucked against him. With every massage of his hands against my thighs, I rocked steadily against his lips. I shook uncontrollably, my legs giving way over his shoulders. My heels pressed into his muscles. I felt the whole of his body pulsating for my pleasure, and mine alone. My body ebbed endlessly, surging with electricity as it short-circuited my mind. All I knew was Clint. All I felt was Clint. All I smelled—and all I wanted to taste—was Clint.

"Yes. Yes. So clo—Cli—I—you—right there. Right there. Right there. Don't stop. Don't stop. Don't—stooo-ah!"

My body contracted as he threw me over the edge. His tongue pressed deeply, releasing me to the wolves as I plummeted through the stars. The world around me tilted. I felt things shifting and twirling in on themselves. My body contorted, trying to get away from the pleasurable assault as Clint fixed his grip around my legs. He pulled me closer, even as I tried backing away. Sweat dripped down the nape of my neck as my hands curled tightly into his hair. Nails raked across his scalp. His growls rattled my ribcage. I bucked wildly, losing all control of my body as he catapulted me to the heavens.

And as I crash-landed back against the couch, he rushed up my body.

"Now, I can take what I want."

His words made me weak in my knees as his lips fell against mine. I tasted myself on him, and it shut the rest of my body down. I was his, forever. For as long as he wanted. I'd weather any issue. Any trial. Any tribulation, just to keep him at my side. I had to have him now. There was no stopping for a movie. The only thing that mattered was being with Clint, in this moment.

"You're perfect, you know that?"

I whispered the words so softly I wasn't sure he'd heard me. But when he pulled back and gazed into my eyes, I knew. I knew he'd heard. He grinned down at me with that insolent little smirk of his, but his eyes twinkled like wildfire. He looked happy. Proud. Content. Satisfied. All the things he deserved to be.

And I wanted to make sure he experienced nothing else.

I helped him get his pants off. His boxers. His socks. Then, when the two of us were bared for one another, he slipped between my legs. I felt him press into me, our eyes never wavering. My jaw unhinged as grunts fell from his lips. But he didn't falter. He sank into me, my body swallowing him whole. I clung to him, my legs locking and my hands curling into the meat of his back. We fell to the couch cushions as he began pumping into me. In and out. With such a rhythmic pattern it left me breathless.

"Clint. Oh, yes. I've missed this. I've missed you. I'm so—so happy for—"

"Fucking hell, Rae. You're marvelous."

Our kisses grew sloppy. Our movements grew desperate. The couch moved with our efforts, scraping along the carpet as our bodies collided. The world faded away. Time and space had no existence between us. There was only me, Clint, and the loving look in his eye as he plunged deeper into my body.

Robbing both of us of our words.

He hooked his arms behind my legs, folding me in half. My jaw unhinged in silent pleasure, and I felt that coil tightening in my gut. He drove faster. Harder. Imprinting my body into the couch as our tongues intertwined. I swallowed his growls, matching them with my whimpers. My moans. My sighs of ecstasy. My heart beat for him. My body shook for him. I needed him, more than I'd ever needed anyone in my entire life. Tears of happiness sprang to my eyes as that coil tightened. As his body raked against my swollen nub. As his girth pressed against the whole of me, muting my world with the fire he pushed through my veins.

"Rae. Holy shit. Rae. I'm so close. I just—Rae. I need—"

"Oh, yes!"

My back arched and I fell over the edge. My back locked out and my jaw unhinged as unearthly sounds left my lips. He pounded relentlessly into me, snapping his hips against mine. The sounds of skin slapping skin filled my living room, drowning out the rest of the world around us. I felt him pulse once. Twice. Three times, before it happened.

He collapsed against me, our bodies spent against one another as evidence of our debauchery pooled between my legs. And as I laid there, watching the ceiling twist and turn, it became official.

Clint didn't know it yet, but I'd officially made love to him.

Because there was no other boy in this world for me, if not him.

28

CLINTON

I collapsed against her, completely spent as my body unleashed inside hers. I had no more strength left in me. After physical therapy. After recuperation. After fighting for weeks against my own body, it had finally worked in my favor. I promised myself that when I was finally strong again, I'd pick her up. Take her the way she deserved, and make love to her in ways she'd never experienced before.

Because, unbeknownst to her, I was making love to her.

I wonder if she feels the same way.

My face fell to the crook of her neck. Her arms wrapped sloppily around me as her pulsing pushed me out of her body. I lay there between her legs, soaking her in and memorizing everything about her. From the way her breasts felt against my chest to the way her heat cloaked my pelvis. The way my back burned with her raking nail marks and the way that sensation made me smile.

Even the way she clung to my hair. It made me want to keep growing it out. Because if that was something she liked, I sure as hell wasn't taking it from her.

She sighed. "Got a movie in mind you wanna watch?"

I snickered. "Pretty sure we just created our own."

"This is the part where I'd swat at you if I wasn't so drained."

"And that's the part where I'd catch your hand if you actually had the energy."

"I blame you for taking that energy away."

I grinned. "I'll gladly take that blame any day."

I kissed her skin as the two of us recuperated. Then, reluctantly, I peeled myself away from her body. I didn't know how long her mother would be gone. And the last thing I wanted us to do was get caught butt-ass naked on her mother's fucking couch. I chuckled as I slipped onto the floor, falling against my back. Rae giggled as she rolled off, softly falling into my arms.

"Come here, beautiful."

She kissed my shoulder. "I love it when you call me that."

She fell off to my side, her leg tossed between mine. Her arm lazily sat around my waist and I felt her cheek pressed against my arm. Finally, for the first time in weeks, I could hold her like I wanted. Without pain. Without fear. And without needing to shift. I slid my fingers through her hair, working out the knots we'd already created. I stared at the ceiling, keeping an ear out for any cars coming down the road.

And as Rae pulled a blanket over us, she gazed up into my face.

"What are you thinking about?"

Her voice snapped me from my trance. "What was that?"

"You had something on your mind. What were you thinking about?"

I paused. Mostly, because I wasn't sure if I should tell her. I mean, it wasn't really a good topic of conversation after what we'd just done. But, now that I didn't have physical therapy and rehabilitation occupying my mind, I found other things occupying it.

"You know you can tell me, Clint."

I nodded. "I know."

She kissed my jawline. "What's got you so distracted?"

I sighed, lowering my voice to a whisper. "I thought I was going to die, Rae."

She moved away from my side and I reached out for her. I didn't want her to move. Hell, I didn't even want to bring up the conversation. I didn't want to lie to her, though, either. I shot up like lightning, swallowing back a small groan. While the pain in my ribcage was mostly gone, it had its moments. Just like my physical therapist said it would. Rae held the blanket against her body as she covered her beauty from me. I reached out for her, pulling her back into me as I re-situated us. My back was against the couch while we sat on the floor, facing a blank television screen. One that should have been playing a movie, had we taken the time to actually indulge that whim.

Her cheek leaned against my shoulder. "You almost did."

I nodded. "You know, when I was bleeding out at the bottom of that hill, the only thing that kept me going was your voice."

"What?"

"Yeah. I think, even before I heard your voice, my body knew you were there. My heart did. And had it not been for you, that river would've dragged me off and I would've been done for."

She pressed deeply into me. "I wasn't going to let that happen. Not by a fucking long shot."

"I know. I wouldn't have pulled through had you not been there, Rae. Looking back on it now, I knew it was Mike calling out for you. I heard him. I heard him telling you to stop. And had you listened, I wouldn't be here."

"Michael was just trying t—"

I shook my head. "I'm not blaming him for anything. He was worried about you. And rightfully so. Just—thank you. For coming after me anyway."

"You're more than welcome, Clint."

"And thank you for coming to visit me, despite the dickhead my father can be. I'm glad that didn't keep you away, because I'm not sure I could've pulled through in that place had it not been for you."

She kissed my cheek. "Sure you would have. You're a fighter."

"Is it possible for a fighter to be tired of fighting, though?"

She cupped my cheek, turning my face toward hers. "Of course it's possible. But that doesn't mean a fighter loses his passion. It simply means he rests. This is your resting time, Clint. It's time for you to lean on those you can trust. But it doesn't mean you stop fighting. Not until you reach the top of wherever you want to be. And I'll be right there, fighting along with you. Every step of the way. Until you have everything you want out of your life."

I paused. "How the hell did I luck up with someone like you?"

She grinned. "You're good at sex."

I snickered before my lips found hers again. She giggled against my mouth as my tongue parted her lips. I cupped the nape of her neck. I held her to me as she moved against my body. I felt her straddle my lap, climbing against my body until she pressed against me once more. I slid my fingers through her hair, holding her tightly to me. And as her hands slid down my chest, they settled against my heart.

My rapidly-beating heart.

"Rae?"

"Yes, Clint?"

"There's something I need to tell you."

She pulled back, our eyes meeting while she studied me. My thumb stroked over her cheek as her fingertips danced along the outlines of my chest. The words were on the tip of my tongue. Sitting right there, percolating just for her. All I had to do was find the courage to say them. And I figured after almost dying, it'd be an easy thing to do.

But, it wasn't.

"Clint? What's wrong?"

I shook my head. "Nothing. I just—"

A flash of lights streamed through the living room windows and I'd never moved so fast in all my life. Rae rushed around, gathering her clothes as I stayed on the floor. I reached for my boxers, pulling them up so quickly I got my damn balls caught up in them. I moved my clothes to a corner, watching as Rae rushed into the kitchen. Never in my life had I gotten dressed so quickly. I didn't know I had that kind of speed built into me. I pulled my shirt over my head as the light faded down the road, not bothering to pull into the driveway.

And as Rae threw the front door open, she giggled breathlessly.

"Holy shit, that's the neighbors."

I panted. "So not your mom?"

She shook her head. "Not even a little bit."

She looked at me and the two of us threw our heads back in laughter. She closed the front door, then locked it to make sure we had enough time to piece ourselves together. Just in case the next time was her mother. I held my arms out for her and she fell into them, her body trembling from the adrenaline rush.

"I just knew it was them."

I chuckled. "Me too, sweetness. Me, too."

"So, want to actually watch that movie now?"

I kissed the top of her head. "Whatever you want to do."

We settled onto the couch and flipped through her television channels. There weren't many. At least, not as many as my father had on his package. And while it seemed like a simple thing, it illuminated a stark contrast between our worlds. Eventually, we settled on some sci-fi thriller. Rae clung to me as aliens did some things on screen I was only half-paying attention to. Because my mind kept ripping me back to the accident. Back to that embankment, to the moment my head slipped under water.

And the tug against my jacket as Rae pulled me out.

"Shit!"

"Fucking hell, warn a girl next time."

"Oh, come on. You're smarter than that. Be smarter than that."

"She's got heels on. She's not smarter than that."

I quirked an eyebrow. "What's wrong with heels?"

She shrugged. "I don't know. But the dumb girls in movies like these always wear heels. It's the stereotype."

"Odd."

"Right? You should change that in your writings. You know, make a new trend for women in pop culture, or something like that."

"Wow. I completely forgot I'd told you about my writing."

"Don't worry. I won't take offense this time."

She smiled up at me, and I felt my heart warm. It always felt warm with her. Whenever I was in her presence. I rubbed my hand up and down her arm, dancing my eyes between hers. She really was a beauty. A little button nose with wild hair framing her face. Deep pools of amber brown that gladly dragged me along their current. That was a river I'd happily drown myself in. The river of freckles that smattered themselves across her nose and her cheeks. The river of creaminess that dripped against her skin, accenting the dark features she possessed.

Rae snickered. "What are you staring at?"

The girl I love. "The most beautiful girl in the world."

The front door ripping open pulled us from our universe, and Rae immediately hopped back. I shot myself over to the other end of the couch, trying to look as natural as possible. With my legs spread and my hands settled against my thighs, I hooked my eyes to the television. I heard Rae panting softly, and the second her mother's eyes darted between the two of us, I knew we were caught.

"Oh. I'm, uh… you must be Clint."

I nodded. "Yes, ma'am."

She walked toward me. "Pleasure to meet you. How are you feeling?"

I shook her hand. "I'm feeling much better, thank you."

"I didn't know you were coming over, I'm sorry."

"It was kind of a last minute thing. My last therapy session ended and I guess I just wanted to see Rae. I hope that's okay?"

She smiled. "You're welcome here any—"

"Aren't you even gonna help me with these fucking food bags?"

A man's tinny voice resounded through the house as Rae's mother ripped her hand away from mine. I stole a glance at Rae, watching as her face fell. She shot me a look that I think was supposed to apologize. But it happened so quickly I almost didn't catch it.

"D.J., it's only two bags. Get over it."

Ah. The infamous D.J. The exact man I didn't want to meet. *Just great.*

I watched a spindly man walk through the door, carrying two food bags with him. There was an insignia of a restaurant emblazoned on them, but I didn't catch it. The first thing I caught was the angry look in D.J.'s eye. The argument seated on the tip of his tongue. The second thing I caught was how hard he stared me down before flickering his gaze over to Rae.

"This your friend?" he asked.

Rae nodded. "This is Clint."

He huffed. "Should be more space between you two."

Her mother balked. "Excuse me?"

Rae snickered. "You're not my father. You certainly don't get to dictate what's too close. Especially when you're in a house that isn't yours."

"Seems like your mother needs to teach you manners."

I cleared my throat. "Or, you need to simply learn your place."

D.J. dropped the bags. "What did you say to me?"

I stayed seated on the couch, keeping my cool. "I said, maybe you need to learn your place."

D.J. lunged at me, but Rae's mother stopped him from going any further. I, on the other hand, didn't even flinch. I was used to men like him. He reminded me a lot of my father. I heard both Rae and her mother murmuring, though I didn't take the time to figure out what they were saying.

Especially after Rae took my hand and pulled me up from the couch.

"You need to cool down."

"I'm gonna go get a beer."

"Yeah, you do that."

"Come on, Clint. Let's go upstairs."

"That boy shouldn't be taking her up anywhere."

"This is my house. You can it and get in there."

"I really hate that man."

"Rae, give me a second."

Voices swirled around me as Rae tugged me toward the stairs. She led me up them, her hand vibrating as it held mine tightly. I saw how tense her shoulders were, how angry she'd become. I took one last peek around the corner, glancing into the kitchen. Long enough to see that D.J. dickhead crack open a can of beer. He and Rae's mother were already arguing again. Lowly. And to themselves. Part of me wanted to stay behind to make sure he treated that woman with respect. But the other part of me gave in to Rae's tugging and pulling.

"Come on. We can hang out up here and not be disturbed."

I followed her all the way down the hallway.

Despite my inherent worry for her mother's safety.

29

RAELYNN

I pulled Clint into my bedroom and slammed the door closed. I leaned against it, watching as he took a seat on my bed. D.J.'s voice boomed up the stairs. "Don't you be slammin' doors in this house!" And when he did, I heard my mother start cursing him out.

"You bastard. Don't you dare talk to my daughter that way!"

"You're the one who told me she needed more structure. And apparently, manners!"

"Well, you sure as hell aren't the one to teach her about those. You barely have them yourself!"

"And now I see where she gets her wonderful tone. You think she's gonna end up a fucking doormat like her damn mother!?"

My lower lip trembled as I tried blocking it out. I felt something strong wrap around me, pulling me against something steady. I gripped the leather I felt against my skin and drew in a quivering breath. I buried myself against him, trying to mute the fighting as he walked me over to the bed.

"It's okay. I'm right here. Focus on my voice, Rae. I've got you."

I drew in a shuddered breath. "Fucking D.J."

"Let it out. Whatever you want to say, I'm here for you. I'm not going anywhere."

"He's such a fucking maniac. All the damn time! Especially the last time around. He used to not give a shit about what I did. He never used to think he owned this house until he just got back with my mother. I don't know what the fuck she told him, but I can't stand it."

He rubbed my back. "There we go. There it is. Let it all out."

He sat back down on my bed, pulling me into his lap. And I freely went along with him. It felt marvelous, having someone here with me. Not being alone while I listened to Mom and D.J. go back and forth at one another downstairs. Clint leaned back against my bed, drawing me deeper into him as I fell against his body. The bed bounced. But I stayed right there with him. Snuggling into him and wrapping myself around him, until our limbs were tangled up so tightly I wasn't sure where I ended and he began.

Clint kissed my forehead. "Is it always like this when he's around?"

I nodded slowly. "Practically. He's an absolute dickhole, too. Hits her. Uses her. And thinks he can get away with it because he pays some bills. I was so proud of my mother for putting in applications. For finally kicking him out and standing up for herself. I believed her, Clint. Really, truly believed her that it was over. That this nightmare of a man—"

"I want you to get one thing straight, Rae. That idiot down there? That's not a man."

"I know. I know."

"No, I don't think you do. Look at me."

I slowly panned my eyes to meet his. "Yeah?"

He gripped my chin. "D.J. isn't a man. He's a child, masquerading in the body of a man. He's got no clue what it means to be strong. To fight. To enjoy what he's got in front of him. The only thing he knows to do is take. Drain. And take advantage when he can. He's no better than my father. In fact, I'd easily put them in the same field together. They're one and the same. Understand this, Rae. He's not a man."

I sighed. "Why can't Mom leave him?"

"I don't know, Rae. Sometimes, women are raised to believe they don't have any other options. Or maybe she's got a hole of hurt she's trying to fill that she doesn't know how to fill any other way. What I want you to know is that D.J. isn't a man. And even if he was, what he's saying down there should have no bearing on who you are, or what you do with your life. Ever."

"He's just an absolute asshole. He charges in here and starts demanding shit from people like he owns the fucking place. I can't stand it. I told him the next time Mom came home with bruises on her skin, I'd be calling the damn police myself."

He grinned. "Good for you. I hope you keep your word on that."

"I plan on it."

"And Rae?"

I sighed. "Yeah, Clint?"

"At any point in time, you can call me. I know I don't have wheels right now, but my stepmom would have no issues coming to pick you up. Anytime, day or night. You call, and I'm here."

I smiled softly. "Thank you."

He kissed my forehead. "It's the least I can do for what you've done for me."

My eyes fluttered closed and I melted into him. I let the sound of his kisses drown out the sound of D.J. and Mom fighting. I curled into him, letting him hold me. I cried softly against him, allowing myself to be weak with him. Part of me still felt stupid. But the rest of me was thankful to have Clint there. It felt nice, having him support me like this. Having him weigh in on this issue and talk some real, solid sense into me.

Because some days, I wasn't capable of doing it myself.

I felt something vibrate against the bed and figured it was my phone. Until I peered over Clint's body and saw my phone still sitting on my bedside table. I furrowed my brow as the vibrations happened again. Only this time, Clint sat up. Taking me with him before his arms moved away from me.

"That's my phone."

I nodded. "Get it. It might be Cecilia."

He looked at me. "Are you sure?"

"Why wouldn't I be?"

"I don't want to interrupt what we've got going on right now. I mean, she's probably just calling to see when to pick me up. I can easily call her back."

I placed my hand on his knee. "Clint, pick up the phone. I won't take offense. It's fine, okay?"

"Are you sure?"

I cupped his cheek. "I promise. Thank you for listening to me. And for your reassurance."

He turned his face, kissing my palm. "Anytime, Rae. Anytime you need."

He pulled his phone out from his back pocket before his eyes widened. He picked it up in a hurry, and I wondered what was going on. Who was on the other line? It didn't sound like Cecilia when he picked it up. I scooted closer to him, trying to take stock of what the man's voice on the other end of the line was saying.

But, I couldn't understand a word coming from Clint's phone.

"Uh huh. Yes. I understand. Really? You found them? I—thank —I can't—thank you, Officer. Yes. Yes, I can. Just let me know what time and I'll be there. No, no. I'm good. I'll have a ride. My stepmom, yeah. I'll make sure of it. Yep. Eleven?"

He looked over at me like he was searching for something. All I could do, though, was shrug.

I mouthed to him. "Who is it?"

And when he mouthed back 'the police,' my jaw dropped open.

"Yes, Officer. Just—let me ask someone something really quickly. Uh huh. Hold on."

Then, he put his hand over the speaker of his phone. "They want me to come in at eleven in the morning tomorrow."

My eyes widened. "Did they find those boys? Did they catch them?"

He nodded. "That's what they're saying. They want me to come down to the station tomorrow and try to I.D. them."

"Holy shit, Clint. You have to go. You have to do this. Those boys deserve every ounce of justice the system can bring down on their fucking heads."

"Cecilia's probably going to take me."

I nodded. "Do you think she'd let me come along? You know, to help I.D. them, or something?"

He breathed with relief. "I'm glad you offered, because I was struggling with the words to ask."

"I'll be there, Clint. Just confirm with them the time. Okay?"

And with a nod, he returned to his phone call. "Officer? Yes, hey. I'm back. Sorry about that. Uh, eleven tomorrow in the morning works just fine. I'll be coming with my stepmother and the girl that was with me that night. Yes, the girl that found me. Uh huh. Yeah, she got a glimpse of them, too. A good one. Yep. I'll ask her if she can. But, either way, I'll I.D. them and answer your questions. Uh huh. I'm sure she will, too. Yep. I'll make sure she's prepared. Again, thank you so much."

He hung up the phone and tucked it away in his back pocket. I clamored on top of him, the argument raging downstairs already falling to the back of my mind. A massive smile crossed my face as Clint's hands fell to my hips. Holding me steady in his lap. Our foreheads fell together. I giggled as I touched his nose with mine. I slid my hand through his hair, silently wondering if he'd keep growing it out. Because it felt nice in between the slats of my fingers.

Clint sighed. "Thank you for coming with me in the morning."

I nodded. "Of course. I wouldn't have it any other way."

"They said they might want you to try and I.D. the guys if you got a good look at them."

"I'll never forget their faces."

"And they might have some questions for you. You know, to wrap things up and make sure all their letters are dotted and crossed."

I nodded. "If your stepmom can pick me up, we're good."

"I know she will. She likes you."

"Really?"

He snickered. "Yeah. She calls you 'my girl' already."

I shrugged. "I mean, I kind of am your girl."

He grinned. "I suppose, kind of. Sure."

I gasped, feigning shock. "Why, Clint. I never! How dare you betray me in such a way?"

"I have betrayed thee in no such fashion!"

I burst out in giggles and covered his face with kisses. His back fell to the mattress, and I went right along with him. I followed his every move as I peppered him with my lips. Kissing his cheeks. His forehead. His neck. His shoulders. He rolled me over, pinning me beneath his comforting weight. And as the argument finally died down below us, I smiled up into Clint's face.

"You're not going to get rid of me any time soon. So deal with it."

He kissed the tip of my nose. "Wouldn't dream of it, gorgeous."

"Plus, I'm ready to see those assholes get what's coming to them."

He chuckled. "And the truth really comes out."

"Hey, I can be supportive and vindictive at the same time. Girls are great multi-taskers."

"So, does that mean you can kiss. And. Hold. A. Conversation?"

He punctuated his words with fluttering kisses to my lips. Pulling me deeper into his atmosphere and refusing to let me go.

I giggled "Mm. I. Think. So."

He kissed me deeply. "Or, we could just do that."

And as I rolled him over, straddling his hips once more, I figured we could do a little more than that.

30

CLINTON

I saw Rae sitting on the front porch as we pulled up to her house. I sat in the front seat with Cecilia, but the second I caught a glimpse of Rae's face, I booked it to the back seat. I got out and slipped inside, leaning over to open Rae's door. And when she dropped down next to me, I saw the blank stare on her face. The way her lips were softly downturned. She had bags underneath her eyes and a tremble to her hand as she gripped the excess fabric of her jeans.

I reached over, settling my hand on top of hers. "You okay?"

But all she did was shrug.

"You guys ready to go?"

I nodded at Cecilia's question, then felt her ease us out of the driveway. I wanted to press the questions. I wanted to pull out of her what was wrong. But I didn't want to do it in front of my stepmother. Rae wasn't okay, though. And I had a feeling it had something to do with last night.

I watched as Rae gazed out the window. She watched the world pass us by as she sank heavier and heavier into the leather seats of the car. She didn't speak. Not one fucking word. And I desperately wanted to ask her what the hell happened after I left last night. I called Cecilia to come get me around midnight, and D.J. was still there. Her mother and D.J. had still been downstairs, going back and forth at one another. It was like they never stopped. She'd say one thing and he'd clap back. He'd say something wrong and she'd chew him out for it. It made me sick, leaving Rae in that kind of environment last night. I almost had a mind to ask Cecilia if she could come back with us.

But I figured that might've been crossing a line with Rae's mom.

Had D.J. done something to her? Said something to her? Because if he had, he was done. If he'd touched her, or berated her, or said anything to her that wasn't a compliment or asking her how she was, that asshole was dead meat. I didn't care that he was decades older than me. I didn't care that Rae's mother would probably hate me for it. The only thing I cared about right now was Rae's well-being.

And her being wasn't well at all.

Calm down, Clint. Focus.

I drew in deep breaths as I held Rae's hand. She didn't move. Didn't budge. She kept her eyes trained out the window and she didn't move her hand. She didn't flip it over so I could lace our fingers together. She didn't scoot closer to me so we could cuddle. She just leaned against the door. Heavily. Like she wanted to burst out and run away.

"All right, you two. We're here."

I softly squeezed Rae's hand. "Ready to get out?"

Rae ripped her hand away from mine and pressed out of the car. And after catching Cecilia's worried stare in the rearview mirror, I quickly followed behind her. The deal was for my stepmom to wait in the parking lot for us so we could make the quickest getaway possible. That, and I didn't want her worrying over my shoulder while I answered questions and did a lineup. If anything, I wanted to be there for Rae. I wanted to support her and help her through this. And I wasn't sure I'd be able to do that with my stepmother looming over my shoulder.

"Rae. Rae. Stop. You're walking—stop!"

I gripped her arm and spun her around just outside the precinct doors.

She sighed. "What?"

I furrowed my brow. "You haven't said a damn thing all morning. What's going on?"

"I just want to get this over with."

"You want to try not lying to me this time?"

She bit down on her lower lip. "Can we talk about it after we get this over with?"

I nodded. "I'll take that."

I slipped my hand into hers and away we went. We walked into the police station and checked in with the front desk. And I felt her holding my hand tighter than ever before. I slipped my arm around her as an officer came out, ushering us back into a room. There was a table with a photo album of pictures. A harsh light beamed down onto the laminated pages. I looked over at Rae before we walked over, my eyes fluttering over the pictures in front of us.

And before the officer could even tell us what the fuck was happening, I saw it.

Rae nodded. "That's the car."

The officer stepped up to the table. "Can you point to it?"

I pressed down onto the picture. "That one. That's the car that ran me off the road."

The officer nodded. "And you're sure of this?"

Rae snapped her eyes up. "I'll never forget what that car looked like."

I shook my head. "Neither will I. That's the car. Both of us are sure."

The officer grinned. "All right. Follow me. Time for the lineup before we ask you both some questions."

Rae clung to me as we were ushered into another room. Beside us was the officer who greeted us in the first room. And on the other side of us was a man who looked like a detective. We stood in front of a window that peered into a room, with something that looked like a height chart plastered onto the back wall.

I snickered. "Wow. It really does look like the TV shows."

And when Rae let out the softest giggle, it spread a wide smile across my face.

There she is.

The detective turned to us. "All right. It's simple. Some men will file in, and you two will point out the guys you recognize."

Rae finally spoke. "How many men are there going to be?"

The detective shook his head. "I'm not at liberty to discuss that. All you two have to do is point out the four boys from that night. Okay?"

I nodded. "Got it."

The first line of guys filed in, and I recognized none of them. I looked down at Rae to see if she had any opinions, but she shook her head, too. None of them looked familiar and I felt my stomach drop. Until another line of guys filtered in.

Rae perked up. "The one on the far right."

The officer nodded. "Number?"

I licked my lips. "Number One. Definitely. He was the one calling the shots that night. The one driving."

Rae scoffed. "He's the one that kept making the sexual jeers at me all night. He's one of those boys."

The detective sighed. "Any other ones look familiar?"

And when we both shook our heads, they sent the guys away.

We looked at five lines of guys before pointing out the four boys that had attacked us that night. I was confident in every single one we picked out. Rae was right there with me, too. Backing me up and even explaining what their roles had been. The leader. The driver. The one feeding everyone else opened beers. She even explained my relation to two of them, outlining the fight that had taken place at school. Her memory was fucking dead-on, and it was impressive.

But I knew it'd lead to a lot of uncomfortable questions with the officer later.

Anger radiated off her. With every line of guys that trudged in, she squeezed my hand harder. Her face grew redder. Seeing their faces brought back memories I wanted to forget. But Rae looked like she could practically kill over them. I smoothed my thumb over her knuckles as I pulled her close, trying to calm her down as much as I could.

Then, as we were ushered into a room for questioning, Rae turned around.

"What happens now?"

The detective cleared his throat. "Well, there are some questions the police will want to ask. All you have to do is answer them as honestly as you can. If you don't remember, say you don't. And whatever you do, don't lie. They'll write down your testimony, you'll sign it, and that'll be admitted into evidence when these boys go on trial. If they go on trial."

Rae bristled. "What do you mean 'if'?"

I sighed. "I have to press charges."

She paused. "Wait, you haven't done that already?"

The officer slipped into the room. "We haven't gotten to that point yet. But once you answer my questions, we can go over his options."

The detective nodded. "You're in good hands. Just answer the questions honestly, then we can go over what to charge these boys with. If you want to press them."

Rae scoffed. "Of course he's pressing charges. Right?"

She looked up at me, searching for an answer. But I didn't know what to say.

"Right. Clint?"

I sucked air through my teeth. "What would I even charge them with?"

The officer put a hand on my shoulder. "Once we get your signed testimony, we'll get you linked up with a lawyer. Because you're going to want to talk to one, kid."

Rae looked up at me. "You'll talk to one at least, right?"

I nodded. "Of course. Yeah."

But, deep down, I wasn't sure if I wanted to.

I mean, yeah. I'd almost died. But I'd had a hand in how this played out, too. The fight on the football field. And I didn't have the cleanest record with the police department in the first place. They'd broken up way too many parties I'd attended over the years. I'd gotten myself into plenty of trouble, speeding around on my bike and defacing public property with spray paint because I'd been an asshole as a freshman. Did a guy like me really stand a chance in court with something like this?

I wasn't sure. And Rae didn't like that.

"You have to press charges, Clint."

I sighed. "Let's get these questions answered first. One step at a time, okay?"

"Why in the world wouldn't you?"

The officer interrupted us. "If the two of you would take a seat, we don't have a lot of time."

The detective nodded. "Go on. I'll be in the hallway once you're done."

"Clint?"

The helplessness in Rae's voice punched me in the gut. I led her over to the table, trying my best to rip her away from the topic of conversation. My mind swirled with too many things, and it made it hard to concentrate. One step at a time. All I wanted to do was take it one step at a time. And after this sworn testimony or whatever the hell it was came to a close, we could discuss the next steps. Talk about what came after this.

Preferably with Cecilia.

31

RAELYNN

I sat at the table. "Thanks for having me over for dinner. I really appreciate it."

Allison's mom smiled at me. "You know you're always welcome, Rae. Anytime."

Allison's father nodded. "Especially after the day you had yesterday."

I peeked over at Allison. "My day."

My best friend nodded. "I told them about you and Clint heading to the police station. I hope that's okay."

I nodded slowly. "Yeah, yeah. That's fine."

Her mom slid the biscuits to me. "You know if you want to talk about it, we're here."

Her dad spooned me up some mashed potatoes. "Do you know if he's going to press charges at all?"

Allison scoffed. "I think he should, at least. Those boys need to get what's coming to them."

My eyebrows rose. "Wow. Harsh language coming from you."

Her mom murmured. "Well, it's true. The whole town is abuzz with it. Apparently, they almost killed him. Doesn't matter their age, they deserve to pay for their actions."

Her father grunted in approval. "And maybe their parents will learn a thing or two about actually keeping tabs on their kids from now on."

I didn't want to talk about it. Especially with her parents. But it was nice to know they were on my side. Especially since it took so much to convince Clint to press charges. I still didn't know why. I still didn't know why it had taken a lengthy conversation in the back of his stepmother's car in order to convince him to press charges against these assholes. I mean, they'd done so much to us that, apparently, I had a right to press charges as well.

I promised Clint that if I didn't press charges, he would.

Allison's mom filled my lemonade up and her father kept spooning food onto my plate. I loved coming over to eat with them. More because I enjoyed the family dynamic. They treated me like their own daughter, wanting to know about my life and giving me advice. Her father always stuffed me full of food, too. Which was outstanding, because he was an incredible cook.

I hummed. "This meatloaf is fantastic, Mr. Denver."

He smiled. "I'm glad you like it. I tried something a bit different with the spices and everything. Wasn't sure how it would turn out."

Allison's mom smiled. "It's great, honey. Really."

Allison piped up. "Does this mean Mom cooked dessert?"

I grinned. "Oh, was there a tag-team situation in the kitchen tonight?"

Her mom giggled. "I got the cobbler in the oven a bit late. So, dessert won't be for another hour or so. But, yes. There's cobbler in the oven cooking and fresh vanilla ice cream in the freezer."

I groaned. "You guys spoil me way too much."

Her dad chuckled. "And we'll make sure to send you home with some leftovers for you and your mom later on in the week."

I stuffed myself stupid before we were excused from the table. Which resulted in Allison and me lumbering up the stairs. I always ate too much whenever I came over for dinner. It just happened that way. We fell onto her bed and stared up at her ceiling fan, watching it go around and around and around. And as her door slowly shut itself because once the air conditioning kicked on, she rolled toward me.

"All right, Rae. Are we talking about the police station first, or my date?"

My eyes bulged. "Holy shit, your date!"

"Don't tell me you forgot."

"I didn't forget. I just... temporarily forgot it existed?"

She pursed her lips. "I'll forgive you this time, but only because I love you."

I lobbed my head over to see her. "How was the movie?"

"It. Was. Phenomenal! I met him there and he had the tickets and snacks already bought. Got my favorite, too. A small Dr. Pepper with those little crunch bite things, as well as some popcorn for us to split."

"Sounds like your kind of movie night."

"And guess what?"

I paused. "What?"

Allison scooted up to my ear. "He held my hand during the movie."

My jaw dropped open. "Allison! You scandalous little thing, you."

She playfully swatted at me. "Hey, now. Not all of us can have the hoppin' sex life you have."

"And it is hoppin'."

She giggled. "You're insane, you know that?"

I rolled over onto my stomach. "Okay, tell me. How did he do it, how far into the movie did he do it, and did you like it?"

"Okay. So, we weren't that far into the movie. I mean, maybe fifteen minutes before he tried. And he tried three times before he succeeded."

"Why? Did you keep pulling away or something?"

Her face flushed red. "I kept reaching for popcorn and things without paying attention to what he was doing."

"Allison!"

"I know! I know! It was terrible. I felt awful. But he did succeed."

"So… did you like it?"

She sighed. "I mean, it was a bit awkward at first. I've known Michael for years. It kind of felt like I was holding my brother's hand or something at first?"

"That's not good."

"No, no. It didn't feel like that the entire time. I think maybe he was nervous because he tried twice before and I moved and all that stuff. But once I relaxed into it and kind of leaned against him, it felt nice. You know, not completely awkward."

I nodded. "You think you'd do it again? Holding his hand?"

She paused. "I think I definitely would."

The two of us squealed together before we buried our faces into pillows. I was happy for her because I knew how much she wanted this. I knew how long she'd been crushing on Michael, and it was nice that the two of them were finally opening up that door between them. A door that practically everyone had seen, but no one was willing to admit existed.

Then Allison sighed. "All right. Your turn."

I groaned. "Do I have to?"

"Why don't we start with Clint pressing charges. You said he was?"

I nodded, tilting my head to the side. "Yeah, he is."

"How do you feel about that?"

I shrugged. "I don't like the fact that it took him so long to make that decision."

"What do you mean?"

"The entire police thing was just a mess. I mean, we picked out the car, picked those boys out of a lineup, then answered a barrage of questions that ended up being some written testimony we had to sign."

"Sounds pretty standard, actually."

I shrugged. "We talked in the back of his stepmom's car about the pros and cons of pressing charges. Pros and cons, Allison. Like he was planning to move into a home. Or changing up his wardrobe. Or choosing what college to apply for."

"Really?"

"Yeah. It was frustrating as hell, too. Apparently, I had the option to press charges, and when I blurted out that I'd be pressing charges, Clint changed his tune. Said if I didn't press charges, he promised he would."

"So he didn't really make the decision to press them."

"Nope. He did it so I wouldn't. And I still don't know why."

She furrowed her brow. "That's insane. He was severely injured."

I shrugged. "I know. Trust me, I get it. It boggles my mind, too. I'm just glad he's pressing them, one way or another. He needs to. Those boys need to rot."

"Do you know when he's talking to a lawyer?"

"Tomorrow, actually. After school. To see what steps he needs to take next."

"Do you know what they're going to charge those boys with?"

I sighed. "I don't have a clue."

"Do you want my opinion?"

"I'd love anything you've got for me right now."

Allison sat up. "Okay. Objectively speaking, here's what you've got. They approached you in the parking lot, right?"

"Right."

"And they said all this stuff to you before Clint distracted them, right?"

"Uh huh."

"Then, Clint drove off and they followed him. Pursued him, right?"

I nodded. "Yep."

"And even though Clint tried shaking them, they kept following him. Until they ran him off the road."

I swallowed hard. "Yeah."

"In my eyes? The only thing Clint has accountability for is getting their focus off you. That was his fault, and it had good intentions. Good motives. Everything else was spurred on by those boys. From pulling up to you guys in the first place to chasing him down, no matter what. To me? The charge should be attempted murder."

And after a brief pause, I nodded.

"You make a very good point about that."

Allison scoffed. "There's no point about it. Drunk or not, those boys knew what they were doing. If they had enough sense to keep in control of that car long enough to be able to ram Clint over the edge of that bridge, then they had enough sense to choose not to."

I grinned. "You sure you don't want to be a lawyer or something?"

She giggled. "Nah. I'm just really good at arguing. Dad hates it."

"Let me guess. You get it from your mother."

"We've chased Dad out of the house a few times. No joke."

The two of us fell apart in laughter, and it felt good to be laughing again. Especially with the whirlwind this weekend had been. Between listening to D.J. and my mother literally fight all Friday night to the police trip with Clint Saturday morning, I was exhausted. Deep in my bones. I was frustrated, I felt numb to the world, and all I wanted to do was crawl underneath a rock and stay there.

Yet, somehow, Allison had me laughing.

"You two ready for dessert?"

Her mother's voice filtered up the stairs and we scrambled off the bed. We raced back down the stairs, flopping onto the couch as her mother divvied out massive bowls of cobbler and ice cream. We all sat together, with Allison and me between her parents while we watched a movie and ate our fill. I laughed with them. I sniffled with them. We watched the sweetest little comedy that had us all roaring with laughter and holding back tears.

But all too soon, it was time to go.

"Here, there's plenty of leftovers. Take some to your mother."

"And some cobbler, too. We'll never eat all this I made."

"Want some lemonade?"

"I could pack some of this ice cream on ice for the trip back."

I snickered, holding the bags full of tupperware. "I promise, you guys, this is more than enough. Thank you. I really appreciate it."

After handing me one last bag of food, Allison got the keys to the car from her father. She drove me home, and I sat there for a second gathering the mental energy to walk into the house. I didn't see D.J.'s car, which was a massive relief. But something in the pit of my gut told me I was still walking into something bad.

Allison put her hand on my shoulder. "You okay?"

I nodded. "Yeah. I'm good. See you tomorrow morning?"

"See you then."

I pressed out of the car and made my way for the front door. And when I found it unlocked, my stomach dropped. Mom always locked the door. Even when she was home. Which meant someone had left and she hadn't bothered to lock it. The second I heard her sniffling, I knew. I knew exactly what had happened tonight.

"Rae? Is that you?"

I closed the door behind me. "Yeah, Mom. I'm home."

"What's that smell?"

"Cobbler and dinner from the Denvers' house."

"Can you bring it into the kitchen, please?"

I sighed as I made my way down the hallway. Shadows flashed across the walls as Allison backed out of the driveway, and I wanted nothing more than to chase her down. My home had become a living hell, and I didn't want to be here anymore. Especially when I saw my mother wiping at her eyes.

Because of fucking D.J.

"You hungry?"

She shook her head. "Just put it in the fridge."

I did as she asked, then walked over and put a hand on her shoulder. I squeezed it softly as I gazed blankly at the wall, wondering if it would ever stop. If my mother would ever notice her worth. If she'd ever pull herself out of this hole and move on with her life.

"I'm sorry for whatever he did to you tonight."

Then, without letting her explain, I showed myself off to my room.

32

CLINTON

I sat in the lawyer's office, hating the fact that my father was here. I knew this would happen, too. I told Cecilia not to tell him. I told her to just keep it between us. I didn't need Dad coming to this damn meeting with me. Cecilia would've been fine. Hell, I could've done this damn meeting myself! I mean, it took me a little bit to grasp the fact that I was about to press charges on four boys who tried killing me. But, all I had to do was digest that fact. Digest the —the realness of it all.

And of course, the second Cecilia updated my father, he was on the first plane ride home.

"Did we have to do this today? This couldn't have waited?"

Cecilia scoffed. "Howard, you didn't have to come. I told you I had this under control."

Dad shook his head. "The only thing you would've done is rack up a larger bill than necessary asking tons of unnecessary questions."

"So, you're only here to moderate your funds. Is that it? You don't care that we're here to prosecute the boys who almost killed our son?"

Dad paused. "You mean *my* son, Cece?"

I kept myself poised in my chair, even though I wanted to melt into a puddle on the floor. The second the lawyer's door opened, though, Dad shut his fucking face. Guess he'd learned his lesson with the doctor in the hospital. I peered over at Cecilia, watching as she crossed her leg over her knee, trying to keep her composure as much as possible, even though I saw the anger in her eyes.

Thank fuck, I'm sitting beside her.

"Afternoon. My name is Omar Littenberg."

The lawyer held his hand out for Dad and he stood to shake it. Cecilia stayed seated, but she shook his hand in kind. I stood, staring the man in the face with a grateful smile. And as I shook his hand, he held mine just a little longer than necessary.

Had he heard what had happened from the hallway?

Fuck. "It's really nice to meet you. Thank you for seeing us on such short notice."

He dropped my hand. "Of course. When I caught word of what happened from the police station, I immediately cleared my schedule."

Cecilia smiled. "You came highly recommended by the detective over there."

Dad scoffed. "I'll be the judge of whether or not you take my son's case."

Omar sat down. "Actually, you have no legal voice in this room."

Dad paused. "Excuse me?"

I sighed. "I'm eighteen, Dad. He doesn't need your consent. Only mine."

"Well, if he wants his check paid, he'll make sure he has my consent."

Cecilia hissed. "Howard, stop it. We're here for our son."

"My son."

I sighed. "Yes, you came recommended by the detective at the police station. He said something about you taking on these kinds of cases before?"

Omar nodded. "Mm-hmm. I specialize in juvie cases. Because they are usually presented to the court and judged in a much different fashion. You might be of legal age, but the boys who ran you down aren't. They're still seventeen, so their court proceedings will happen in a different light."

"Fair enough. So how much do you know about what happened?"

"I know as much as I need to know. Let me rattle it off and see if I've got it right."

Dad sighed. "Can we speed this up a bit?"

Omar darted his eyes over to my father. "This first meeting is free of charge. That's usually how it works with most lawyers."

Cecilia humped. "Now, will you hush?"

"Don't you talk to me that way."

"I'll talk to you however I want if it means you'll sit down and support your son for once."

I sat there with my eyes closed, waiting for them to stop bickering. And when Omar cleared his throat, I opened my eyes.

"The gist of it is you were approached by these boys, they chased you off, you tried to outrun them, and they ran you off the road and over a bridge. Correct?"

I nodded. "That's the gist of it, yes."

"Anything else you want me to know?"

I felt my father's eyes burrowing into me and I felt sick to my stomach. I wanted to tell the lawyer why they'd chased me off. I wanted to tell him I was defending the girl with me. Rae. And I saw he was waiting for me to bring her up. Cecilia reached over and took my hand, squeezing it for reassurance.

But I saw the look in my father's eye. Even from the corner of my own. If I didn't speed this up, there would be hell to pay.

He probably has a plane to get back to soon.

"Um, nothing I want to add for now. I'm really just looking for what we'd charge them with. I don't know how that all works."

Omar nodded. "Fair enough. I know this is probably pretty overwhelming. So I'll make it easy for you. Should you choose me for your case, I'd try the boys for attempted murder."

Cecilia gasped. "Murder?"

Dad scoffed. "They didn't try to kill my son. Come on."

Omar shot him a look. "I'm speaking with your son. I'd appreciate it if you didn't interject."

The two of them stared off with one another before the lawyer's attention fell back to me.

"They intentionally went after you. They intentionally ran you off the road. I've seen the crime photos. I've read the reports. The theories. And from the looks of the scene, you got off your bike and tried making a break for the woods. Didn't you?"

I felt my face pale as Cecilia squeezed my hand tighter.

"Is that true, honey?"

Dad murmured under his breath, but I didn't catch it.

"Uh, yeah. That's—that's true. You can see that from the pictures?"

Omar nodded. "Clear as day. Your bike is mangled in one place, but you went over the railing in another. There are separate sets of tire skid marks. Same tires, different areas. They intentionally pushed you over that railing. That's as much attempted murder as anything I've ever come across."

Holy shit. "Well, I appreciate your bluntness and honesty. Thank you."

"Mr. Clarke, these kids are lucky you're still breathing. Otherwise, they'd be staring down the barrel of a very unfortunate future. If it makes you feel any better, I can go easy on them. Suggest juvie for a spell, as well as a specialized schooling atmosphere and court-mandated therapy in exchange for no jail time and having their record expunged."

I paused. "I'm not sure if that makes me feel any better."

Cecilia butted in. "You have to do something, Clint. They really did a number on you. Even if you simply sue them for the hospital bills or something—"

Dad snickered. "Yeah. Pay me back some of that money."

"Howard!"

I rolled my eyes. "Please excuse him."

"Did you just excuse me for someone else?"

I looked over at my father. "I did. Because you're acting absolutely insane right now and I'm tired of it."

His eyes lit up with fire as he stood up from his chair. His eyes panned toward the lawyer as he buttoned his suit coat. Cecilia got up quickly and followed him out of the room, trying to talk some sense into him. And as the door closed behind them, I cleared my throat.

"I'm really sorry for that."

Omar shook his head. "Not your fault, Mr. Clarke."

I sighed. "So, if I wanted to press charges, what would we do?"

"We'd gather evidence and serve each of their families with a formal subpoena. The boys are being held right now, so there will be a bail hearing. In which case, I'll call for no bail since the charges are attempting to take your life from you. I'll pose that they're a threat for now, then suggest they be moved to a juvie facility where they can continue their studies while keeping you safe. Then a court date is set and we work on presenting the facts."

I nodded. "How long will this take?"

"I have a few questions."

Dad came barging back into the room and the lawyer shot out of his chair.

"Sir, you'll keep your voice down and keep it kosher. Or I'll have you removed from the premises."

Dad walked around the desk, standing toe to toe with the man. "My son needs to focus on his studies. Not fussing over putting four boys in prison."

"They tried killing your son."

"And he probably provoked them! Look, I know my son better than you. Better than anyone. He's a troublemaker, just like they are."

Cecilia yelped. "Howard! Stop it!"

"No! I'm done with you hopping all over my back and acting like my son is some wounded puppy. You said it yourself, Mr. Whatever Your Last Name Is, he's a legal adult. He doesn't conduct himself like one, though. Every single issue I've ever had with this boy has been brought on by prior actions. Did he tell you two of the boys that approached him that night had gotten into a fight with him earlier in the week?"

Omar shook his head. "No. But I read that in the report."

I stood up. "How do you know that, Dad?"

He glared at me. "Because I keep tabs on you. Everything you do. You got into a fight with two of those boys, didn't you? On the football field, at school. You stormed up to them and started wailing on them. For no reason. And you don't see them pressing charges on you, do you?"

Cecilia stepped to the forefront. "Are you saying Clint deserved to be run off the road?"

Dad rolled his eyes. "Hell, no! What I'm saying is that they came back for revenge. Like every single seventeen-year-old boy does when he's been wronged. My son isn't innocent in any of this. And the last thing he needs to be doing is batting off criminal charges of his own when he should be focusing on clawing himself out of high school. Because believe you me, his grades are barely there, at best."

I flopped back down into my chair. I didn't know what else to do. What else to say. I didn't have any more fight left in me, and I didn't care. I stared at the wall, listening as my father unleashed. He went on a damn rampage as my stepmother tried to calm him down. And all the while, the lawyer stood his ground. Took everything in. Listened to him with a nod of his head.

I just wanted to go home.

No, not home.

I wanted to go see Rae.

"Mr. Clarke?"

Omar's voice ripped me from my trance. "Yeah?"

Dad hissed. "You mean, 'yes, sir.'"

I nodded slowly. "I'm sorry. Yes, sir?"

"It sounds like your family has some things you need to discuss. Pros and cons, and all that."

Dad huffed. "You're damn right we do."

Omar pointed his finger. "One more outburst out of you and you're hauled away in handcuffs. Do you hear me?"

Cecilia stepped closer to him. "Howard, I'm begging you. Stop it."

He shrugged her off. "I'd like to see you try."

Omar shrugged. "Fair enough."

He pressed a button underneath his desk and two massive men appeared in the doorway. My eyes bulged as Cecilia stepped toward me, and I wrapped my arm around her shoulder. She gasped and squealed. We watched as Dad struggled against the two massive brutes. It felt like an out-of-body experience, watching him struggle like that. Watching him fight against them until they dragged him out of the office.

Then one of them reached over and closed the door.

"You aren't going to throw him in jail, are you?"

Cecilia's voice sounded frantic. But part of me hoped the lawyer did. I looked over just in time to see Omar shake his head, though. Which disappointed me a bit.

"No. He'll just be removed outside until he can calm down. But this meeting won't take much longer. I know you still have some things to mull over and discuss."

Cecilia nodded. "We do, but you've been very helpful. Thank you so much."

I watched the lawyer reach into his desk. He pulled out a small card, then scribbled something across the back. He didn't hand it to my stepmother, though. He handed it directly to me. I took the card from him and he shook my hand. But he held my gaze with a fervor that magnetized me to my spot.

"When you have a decision, you call me, okay? But, if you need anything—ever—reach out. I'm here to help. Always."

And as I read between the lines of his unspoken offering, I pocketed his card.

A warning much like the one the doctor in the hospital gave me.

33

RAELYNN

ichael smiled. "You look nice today, Allison."

I watched my best friend blush. "Thanks, Michael. You don't look half bad yourself."

"Is that a new shirt? I don't think I've seen it before."

"Nah, it's just been a while since I've worn it."

"Well, you should wear it more often. It really suits you. That color and everything."

I watched the way Allison smiled up at Michael. I saw the way he gazed down at her. I snickered to myself in the backseat, but the two of them didn't seem to hear me. Like we'd done for a while now, the three of us were in front of Clint's house. Picking him up for school. Even though he got stronger by the second, he still didn't have a set of wheels to get himself to and from campus. And by his words, he'd rather 'drop off that damn bridge again than ride a bus.'

Needless to say, he only cracked that joke once before I got on him about it.

I saw Michael go for Allison's hand again and I silently cheered him on. Allison was terrible about moving while Michael was making a move on her. I'd watched her do it twice this morning. I felt so bad for the guy! Because I knew she wasn't doing it on purpose. And when he finally got her hand within his, I mentally tossed my hands into the air. I didn't want to make a big deal out of it because I didn't want them to feel self conscious. Allison had always been easily embarrassed, and if Michael thought—for one second—he had embarrassed her, he'd stop everything he was doing immediately.

And none of us wanted that.

I watched their fingers intertwine before my gaze wandered out the window. I watched their reflection as the two of them talked softly amongst themselves. I liked the two of them together. They were cute. In my eyes, they were made for one another. But that kind of shit was also subjective. I tried to give them all the privacy I could afford. You know, with me being in the backseat and things like that.

Come on, Clint. We're gonna be late.

I pulled my phone out and looked at the time. We'd pulled into his driveway ten minutes ago, and part of me was growing worried. Had he hurt himself again? Was something wrong? I looked around at the windows upstairs, clocking his bedroom window. I didn't see the curtains fluttering. Nor did I see shadows passing by. The light was on, but no one was walking around. So he was obviously up.

Maybe I should send him another text.

I sent off my third text that morning, reminding him that we were outside. And if we didn't get a move on, we'd be late for class. I peeked back over at Michael and Allison, watching as they continued to smile and talk and gaze into one another's eyes. Allison had curled up into the passenger seat of the car, turning herself to face him completely. And Michael? Well, he was leaning well over the arm of his seat. Getting as close to Allison as he could before she pulled away from him.

Such an adorable couple.

A movement out from the corner of my eye caught my attention and I whipped my head back toward the window. My heart sang with delight as Clint walked out, his bag slung over his shoulder. But something was off about his movements. His eyes were downcast. He lumbered slower than usual. He wasn't walking with the same sort of confidence I usually saw in him, and I wondered what had happened.

Is his father home?

Michael cleared his throat. "Is Clint okay?"

Allison sighed. "So I'm not the only one that noticed. Good."

I shook my head. "I don't know. Don't say anything, okay?"

Michael nodded. "I had no intentions of it. He's been through enough lately. If he wants to talk, we're here."

Allison backed him up. "Uh huh. And if he doesn't want to talk, we're still going to be here."

I threw open the car door. "Thanks, guys. I really appreciate it."

I helped Clint into the car beside me, and not once did he look at me. He closed the door and flopped down next to me, sitting his bag between his legs. I ran my hand up and down this thigh and squeezed his knee softly, trying to get him to look at me. But even from behind his sunglasses, I saw him staring blankly out the window.

With his head turned away from me.

"Morning."

I said it as softly and evenly as I could. So the worry wasn't prevalent in my voice. But all he did was nod.

Michael looked at him in the rearview mirror. "How'd you sleep?"

Clint shrugged. "As good as I could."

Allison giggled. "I know how those nights are sometimes. Melatonin always helps me. I mean, I know it's technically to help kids and all that. But it helps me, too. Especially if I'm worried about a test. Are you worried ab… out a… test?"

The more Allison peered back at us, the more I shook my head. Too much. She was talking and saying way too much. Her nerves were getting the best of her, and Clint would sense that. She apologized with her eyes before turning back around, the car slowly bobbing and weaving as Michael drove us all to school.

And the entire time, Clint was silent.

On the one hand, I wanted to push it. I wanted to know what the fuck was going on. But I didn't want to do it in front of Michael and Allison. Because I knew that would make Clint very uncomfortable. So I kept massaging his knee and his thigh until Michael dropped us off. He pulled up to the back doors of the school and let us out, then went to go park the car with Allison. I had a feeling we wouldn't see them again this morning. So I pulled Clint off to the side. Into the shadows of the side of the school.

Where no one could see—or hear—us talk.

"Hey, are you okay?"

Clint shrugged. "I'm as good as I can be."

I snickered. "Which is apparently not very good. I know something's wrong. Do you want to talk about it?"

Clint dropped his bag. "Just—that shit with the lawyer yesterday."

I nodded. "What happened?"

He leaned against the brick wall of the school. "Dad's back in town."

"Oh, no."

"Oh, yeah. I told Cecilia time and time again not to tell Dad about the fucking lawyer. And of course, she didn't listen. She's awesome, but she never fucking listens. It's like she thinks Dad's actually gonna be this decent-as-fuck person one of these days. Then she gets shocked and hurt and scared when he loses his shit. She's been married to him for four years! The fuck is she thinking!?"

I placed my hands against his chest. "Deep breaths. Come on, take them with me. There we go."

I walked Clint through some even breathing. He was shaking against my hands, and I needed him to settle down. That explained everything. With his father back in town, shit always popped off. I smoothed my hands over his torso, trying to relax him. I watched him sink heavier and heavier into the brick wall as a cloud hovered over his head. His arms fell to his sides. He wrapped me up in his embrace and pulled me close. He kissed my forehead, sending electricity surging through my body as I closed my eyes. Tucked my head underneath his chin. And reveled in the way he stroked my back.

Clint sighed. "Dad doesn't want me pressing charges."

I scoffed. "Of. Fucking. Course."

"He still thinks I had something to do with it. And he's been keeping up with the police reports because he knew about the football field fight."

I sighed. "Shit."

"Yeah. To him, that's proof enough that I apparently deserved what I got. Because, to him, those seventeen-year old boys were just 'being boys and doing what boys do.'"

I pulled away a bit. "Did he actually say that?"

Clint nodded. "Right there in the fucking lawyer's office. I was so embarrassed I wanted to melt into the goddamn floor."

I gazed up into his eyes. "Clint? Your father's a piece of trash."

"Don't I know it."

"Clint, you need to press charges. They could have killed you. They almost did. Who the fuck does your dad think he is?"

He gave me a wary smile. "It's okay, Rae. There's no need for you to get worked up. I'll figure this all out. Especially once Cecilia can stop updating my dad every second of every fucking day."

"She just loves your dad. I get it. I mean, I don't know how she loves your dad. But she does."

He paused. "You get it?"

I felt my cheeks flush and I looked away from him. Fucking hell, I'd almost given myself away. Well, I'd practically given myself away, was more like it. Clint chuckled and pulled me back to him, placing a kiss to the top of my head. And as he rubbed my back with his large, strong hands, I felt my eyes fall closed.

"You keep doing that, I'm gonna fall asleep."

He kissed my head again. "My only wish is that we were in a bed somewhere so I could fall asleep with you."

I wrapped my arms around him. "Sore this morning?"

"A bit."

"Did you take your pain medication? Any of it?"

"Half a pill. It takes the edge off without making me loopy."

"Good. I wouldn't want you to be in too much pain today."

"Look at you, worrying about me like a good woman does."

I giggled. "Of course I'm going to worry about you. I care for you. I care about what happens to you. Unlike your fucking father, who I'd like to toss into a raging inferno."

He snickered. "Tell me how you really feel."

I kissed his chest. "Please don't let him make this decision for you. I'm here if you need to talk, but if you want my honest opinion, you have to press charges on these boys. They flagrantly came at you. They deserve what they're getting."

Clint nodded. "Okay."

The word was so soft. So timid. So… unlike Clint. It made me want to wring his father's fucking neck. I tilted my head back and stood on my tiptoes, placing a kiss against his lips. He paused for a split second before cupping my cheek. I felt his tongue sliding across my lips. I willfully opened up for him, wrapping my arms around his neck. And as our tongues fell together, the school bell rang in the background.

I groaned. "Fuck."

He chuckled. "Come on, beautiful. Let's get you to class before you experience what life is like on the other side of being on time."

"Does it have more kisses? Because I'd gladly experience it if it had more kisses."

"You're a mess, you know that?"

"A mess for you, Clint."

He gazed into my eyes before capturing my lips one last time. And then he picked me up off my feet. He tossed me over his shoulder, causing me to laugh out loud as he picked up his backpack. He spanked my ass cheeks, over and over. Until we got around the corner of the school.

Then he carried me inside, heading straight for my locker as laughter poured from my lips.

34

CLINTON

I watched Mike and Aly at lunch as I sat beside Rae. She leaned against me, falling between my legs and resting her weight against my chest. I'd missed holding her like this. I'd missed taking the whole of her against me and supporting her. As I wrapped my arms around her body, threading our fingers together, she pressed herself into me as close as she could get.

Thank fuck for that half a pain pill.

"So, Clint. How were classes this morning?"

Mike's voice ripped me from my trance and I nodded.

"Eh, they weren't too bad. English is getting interesting again, though. Now that we're finally onto another book."

Aly rolled her eyes. "Right? Catch-22 was the biggest drag alive. I still can't believe I forced myself to read that thing."

I snickered. "I didn't at all. I did the SparkNotes version and prayed a bit for the test."

"And let me guess, you still passed it."

I shrugged. "I mean, I felt confident about it today. Why? You hate me for it?"

"Hey, everyone's got their subject. Mine just isn't English."

Rae snickered. "Which is actually a shocker, since you love to read your textbooks."

Aly stuck her tongue out at Rae and it made me laugh. Mike, too. His eyes connected with mine and I nodded toward him, trying to get him to wrap his arm around the damn girl. I mean, Aly had practically leaned herself against him. Every chance she got, she tried touching him in some way. Her hand on his forearm whenever she was laughing at a joke of his. She paid attention intently every time he said something. She was throwing off signals more than any girl had ever thrown signals at me. And Mike seemed completely oblivious to it.

So I jiggled my arm at him before pulling Rae closer. Hoping he got the fucking point.

Aly looked over at him and blushed. *She* got the point. But Mike? He looked like he was about to puke. The poor kid had probably never put his arm around a girl before in his young adult life. I grinned as I watched Aly scoot closer to him, trying to make it as easy on him as possible.

And when he finally wrapped his arm around her, she placed her head against his shoulder.

"Hi there, Michael."

He grinned. "Hey there, Allison."

Rae giggled. "Awwww, how *cuuuuuute!*"

All of us started laughing, which caused Michael to pull Allison closer. She wrapped her arm around his waist, holding him while he held her. It was cute, really. The two of them made a fantastic couple. They looked the part. Talked the part. Thought in the same way, and had much of the same goals. I'd learned that over the multiple car rides we'd all had together over to the school. They talked about college. Career goals. Moving out and getting places of their own. They had the same sorts of ambitions with life, and in some ways I envied them.

You know, their ability to have options.

"You know, this day feels like it's crept by like a slug."

Rae's voice pulled me from my trance and I kissed the top of her head.

"I don't know. It's flown by for me," I said.

Mike shook his head. "Nope. I'm with Rae on this one. It's crept by painfully slow."

Aly shrugged. "I don't really care, to be honest."

Rae giggled. "If you could live here, you probably would."

"Hey, now. Hey. Just because I enjoy school doesn't mean I want to live here. I mean, cafeteria food for all three meals? I would rather d—"

She caught herself and everyone whipped their eyes over to me. Aly went to apologize, but I simply shook my head at her. This was exactly what I didn't want. I didn't want people tiptoeing around me. I didn't want people feeling they had to mute themselves in order to preserve my feelings. I didn't want things to change that drastically, simply because I wanted to try and keep things as normal as they could be. I wanted Rae leaning against me, I wanted my two new friends to joke around and poke fun at me, and I wanted to get through this school year with some sort of a future away from this place intact.

Aly stumbled over her words. "Clint—I'm—I'm so—"

I held up my hand. "Really, it's okay. This is exactly what I didn't want to happen. I don't want you guys feeling like you can't crack jokes or poke fun at things or generally have a laugh. I almost died. It happened. But it didn't kill me. It's going to take more than that. Okay?"

Aly nodded softly. "Okay."

Mike saluted me. "Loud and clear, General."

I snickered. "Rae. You good?"

She sighed. "Yeah, I'm okay. Just—don't like thinking about it."

I pulled her close. "I know you don't. I know."

Aly piped up. "So, what are you going to do now that you've identified the guys and whatnot?"

I paused. "What?"

Rae cringed. "I kind of told her about the trip to the police department."

Mike furrowed his brow. "Police department? Everything okay?"

I waved my hand in the air. "Yeah, yeah, things are good. Just had to identify the guys from that night. Pick out the car. Answer a few more questions. Shit like that."

Mike nodded. "How'd that go?"

I shrugged. "I mean, it came and it went. Rae was there to back me up on things. It was nice, having her there for support."

She tucked her head underneath my chin. "I'll go with you anytime, anywhere, if you need my support."

"Thanks, beautiful."

Aly sighed. "Awww, how cute."

Mike chuckled. "Now you know how Rae felt a few minutes ago."

I smiled as Mike pulled her closer, tucking her underneath his arm. I felt them staring at me, and I knew what they really wanted to know. I looked down at Rae, finding her eyes. I saw her shaking her head softly, silently telling me I didn't have to talk about it if I didn't want to. And while this isn't a conversation I wanted to have with many people, this was a conversation I could tolerate with Mike and Aly.

Which was more than I could have ever said for Roy and the gang.

"I mean, I had a talk with a lawyer yes—"

Rae interrupted me. "Seriously. If you don't want to talk about it, you don't have to."

Mike nodded. "That's true. If it's too much or something—"

I held my hand up. "You guys. It's fine. I promise, if I didn't want to talk about something, I wouldn't. Plain and simple. No matter how you guys felt about the matter."

Aly grinned. "I have my ways, trust me."

Mike nodded. "She really does. It's irritating, but endearing at the same time."

Aly shrugged. "All I heard was 'endearing.'"

Rae laughed. "Like the genuine woman she is."

We all had a laugh at that one before their eyes came back to me again. The laughter died down and the mood turned somber. I knew they wanted to know because they cared. Not because they wanted to exploit a weakness. But that was new to me. People genuinely caring instead of merely wanting to poke fun at some sort of a weakness I had within me.

It took me a second to get my feet underneath me for the story.

"Well, uh, I had an appointment after school yesterday with a lawyer. My stepmom went with me. And Dad. He was… well, he was himself."

Aly furrowed her brow. "What does that mean?"

Mike's face fell into stone. "What did he do to you?"

I shrugged. "What doesn't he do to me? Look, my father's a hard man. Always has been. And, if I'm being honest, he thinks that part of this whole issue is my fault."

Aly balked. "He thinks you being pushed over that bridge by a car is somehow your fault?"

I nodded. "That's how my dad is. I've always given him a hard time. Shit like that. So, in his eyes—once he found out about the fight on the football field—immediately I had as much of a hand in this as those other guys did."

Mike paused. "Football field fight?"

Rae sighed. "Two of the guys that night were from that fight."

Mike's lips downturned. "What the fuck?"

Aly gasped. "Michael!"

"What? I mean, seriously. Come on. Your dad can't actually think any of this was your fault. They almost killed you. They were drunk, from what I could gather from that night. They should be rotting away in jail. Or juvie. Or something."

I shrugged. "My father pretty much showed his ass in that office. Said things like I needed to be focusing on school instead of chasing down four guys I'd provoked."

Aly's jaw dropped open. "What!?"

"He also said I'd been a problem child my whole life. Essentially tried to paint me as some bad boy trying to get the one-up on someone before they got the one-up on me. He told the lawyer that he didn't see those boys pressing assault charges on me when I started the fight. So why should I press attempted murder charges on them simply because they were seeking out revenge like most young boys do?"

Mike's face turned red. "Is it always like this with your father?"

I sighed. "I mean, let's just say I've talked a big game in the past with bruises I've come to school with."

"Oh, Clint."

Aly reached across the table and offered her hand to me. And when I took it, I felt like I had a genuine friend in her. An ally, so to speak. It felt good, opening up to them. Leaning on them during a time like this. And before I knew it, my mouth ran away from me. I told them everything. When the hitting with my father started. The parties I went to on the weekends to get away from it all. The reasons why I came to school and bullied other people around. How I enjoyed it when my father was off on his trips and shit like that. I couldn't get my damn mouth to stop running until it had all come pouring out. And when I was done, Aly wiped tears away from her eyes while Mike placed his hand on my forearm.

"Clint, we're in your corner, man. You need to know that when I tell you this. Okay?"

I nodded. "Hit me with it."

Mike sighed. "You can't let these assholes off the hook. I'm serious. They deserve everything coming at them, and you can't let them get away with it. We're in your corner. The three of us. Backing you up if you need it. And if you need a place to come crash sometime, I'm sure my parents wouldn't mind one damn bit if you came and crashed at my place."

"I thought you hated my guts, Mike."

He shrugged. "I did."

"So... what's changed?"

He grinned. "You put your neck on the line for our girl. And that means more than anything that's happened in the past."

And when his eyes met Rae's, she snuggled against me. I wrapped my arms around her body and mindlessly kissed the top of her head as Mike pulled his hand away. I felt accepted by them. Loved by them. Respected by them in ways I'd never felt with anyone else in my life. For the first time, I understood what it meant to have genuine friends. I understood what it felt like to trust someone. I planted my nose into Rae's hair and breathed deeply as Mike pulled Aly closer into his side.

Then, Aly spoke up.

"So, who wants to come to my study party this weekend for midterms?"

And collectively, the three of us groaned together.

35

RAELYNN

"So, ready for the study party this weekend?"

Clint's voice sounded in my ear as I turned around, standing next to his locker. I leaned against it, watching as he placed his hand just beyond my shoulder. He was back. I loved it when he did this sort of thing. Cornered me and gazed down into my eyes with that knowing grin on his face. I licked my lips as my hand reached out for him. I slid my fingers along his chest. I let them settle against his heartbeat, reminding myself once more that he was still breathing. Still alive.

And that this wasn't a dream.

"You, Clint Clarke, want to go to a study session this weekend."

He shrugged. "Might be fun to watch Mike weirdly try to mack on Aly again."

I nodded. "Oh, oh. Gotcha. So, not about studying at all."

"Just about the drama. And the laughter. Nothing else. You know how it goes."

I winked. "I definitely know how it goes."

"But also maybe a bit of studying."

I quirked an eyebrow. "Actual studying?"

"Hey, that homework you aced for me has set a dangerous precedent I have to keep up with now."

I giggled. "Come here, you idiot."

I gripped his shirt and pulled him down to me, crashing our

lips together. As the last of the school bells tolled, signaling the end of the day and the departing of the busses, the ringing swallowed the world around us. My tongue found his, rushing goosebumps along my body. I felt students running by us, trying to get to their rides home before it was too late. Clint fell against me, pinning me to his locker. His hands fell to my hips as I slipped my arms around his neck. I giggled against him. His warmth surrounded me. And as he pulled me closer to him, his arms engulfed my back.

Making me feel safe, and reminding me of just how far he'd come with his recuperation.

"You know, that crash might actually be the best thing that's ever happened to my academic career."

I snickered against his lips. "You just like the fact that I did your homework."

He cupped my cheeks. "I mean, I'm also showing up to classes. Paying attention. Generally not being an ass."

I paused. "Maybe a little bit of an ass."

"Oh, now you're just asking to get punished."

"That obvious, huh?"

I smiled before I captured his lips again. His hands cradled my cheeks softly as the rest of the student body slowly trickled beyond us. I slid my hands through his hair, enjoying how he'd grown it out. The stubble on his jawline tickled my skin, sending shivers up and down my spine.

And as I groaned softly down the back of his throat, he broke the kiss. Nuzzled our noses together. Pressed his forehead against mine.

"Maybe we could go somewhere more private so I can dole out the punishment accordingly."

I giggled. "Only if you admit I had a little bit to do with how well school's going for you."

He paused, gazing into my eyes. "Don't you ever get it twisted. Rae. You're the sole reason why I'm doing so well."

I felt my heart skip a beat with his words. "Come on. Let's go back to my place."

"Your mom's not there?"

I shook my head. "Nope. Went out with D.J. last night, which means she won't be home for a day or two."

"I'm sorry, Rae."

"It is what it is. I mean, she made her choice. I can't do

anything to change her mind about that choice. She'll just have to deal with his shit, I guess."

"Do you want to talk about it?"

I shook my head. "Nope. But, I can think of other things I want to do."

I winked at him and that impudent little grin of his stretched across his face. I helped him exchange his books for the ones he needed out of his locker. Then, together, we started for the school doors. Our hands laced together as we started for my house. We walked across the school lawn as the summer sun beat down against our shoulders. His hand wiggled away from mine before he threaded his arm around my waist, pulling me close to him.

Then he kissed the top of my head. "I could do this after school every day, you know."

I grinned. "Come back to my place and punish me?"

He snickered. "Spending time with you, you numbskull. But, also yes, now that I think about it."

I swatted his chest. "You're relentless, you know that?"

"And you're gorgeous. Not my fault I can't stop staring at you."

"I'm pretty sure that is the billboard definition of a 'personal problem.'"

"You don't hate it, though. Do you?"

"Now hold on a second there, buddy. I never said anything about not enjoying it. You're just not going to blame that horny teenage mind of yours on me."

He chuckled. "You're a bit to blame. But in all the best ways."

I smiled. "Just know you aren't the only one that feels that way."

He growled playfully as he pulled me closer into his body. I worked my hand into his back pocket, feeling his strength rolling around against my palm. I leaned my head against his chest as we turned down my street, and the dirty, dingy smell of the place almost passed me by. I sighed with contentment as we made our way for the house. I saw it looming in the distance, like a darkly-smeared stain on a light blue canvas. Thunder rumbled in the distance, despite the sun hanging high in the sky. And as we walked all the way up to my porch, my mind began churning with all sorts of thoughts.

All sorts of nasty, wanton thoughts.

"Do you have to work tonight?"

Clint's voice caused me to focus. "Uh, no. I'm not on the schedule for a couple of days."

"I've noticed you haven't been working much lately."

I shrugged. "I think the manager is hesitant to schedule me. You know, since I was his main closer."

He paused. "Ah."

"It's fine, though. Really. Just means I get to spend more time with you."

"But I know you want the hours."

I reached for my keys. "I mean, I do. Yes. I need the money. But I've been saving money for a couple years now. I just have to shift around a few things and not spend so much of my money at once, and I'll be okay. You know, still on track for things."

"What kind of things?"

I slid the key into the lock. "You know, plans for after school."

"We've never really talked about those, you know."

I paused. "We haven't, actually."

"Want to talk about them now?"

I shrugged as I opened the door. "I mean, they aren't much. I want to move out and get a place with Allison. That'll probably put me near UCLA, since that's where she's headed for her architecture degree. I'll live off my savings for, hopefully, five months while I find a job. Then I can start saving money to go to a community college or something like that."

"What do you want to study?"

We walked inside. "Graphic design of some sort. You know, do something with all this doodling I do on a regular basis."

"Doodling?"

I nodded. "Yep. I enjoy drawing. Have we not talked about this?"

"Not enough for it to ingrain itself into my memory."

Huh. Odd. "Well, we can talk about it now, if you'd like."

I closed the door behind us and went to turn the lock. And as I did, I felt Clint's hands fall to my hips. His lips pressed against the shell of my ear, causing me to press back against him. Our bags dropped to the floor. My head fell back against his chest. I sighed as his hands traveled my body, massaging my excess and caressing my clothed breasts.

"How long have you been drawing?"

His voice was low. Rumbling. Sensuous. I moaned softly as he nibbled my ear, making my knees quake underneath me. He slowly walked me forward, pinning the front of my body to the door. He kissed down my neck, making me gasp as he pulled the collar of my T-shirt off to the side.

"Clint."

"Answer the question, Rae."

Then he spanked my ass softly, causing me to jump.

"Oh. I, uh… um… for as long as—I don't know. I just always have."

He nodded. "Kind of like my writing."

"Uh huh."

His fingers slid into the loops of my jeans. "Can you get a graphic design degree at a community college?"

He pulled me back into his rock hard girth and I moaned against the door.

"I don't—I don't know. I—I'm sure there are certificat—oh, Clint."

"Focus, Rae. I'm trying to get to know you better."

I groaned. "You're trying to torture me."

He chuckled. "Same difference."

"I don't—have it all quite planned. I guess I just—shit, Clint."

"You guess you just what, beautiful?"

His hands slipped underneath my shirt. "You can't do this to me. You're just—"

He bit into my shoulder with a growl. "Just what?"

I whipped around, no longer able to contain myself. My back fell against the door as I cupped his cheeks, pulling his lips to mine. But he stopped just mere centimeters from my lips. I felt his hands fisting my shirt. Ready to draw it over my head. My eyes found his and I saw a fire behind them. A fire I hadn't seen in weeks. I breathed the air he afforded me. I nuzzled my nose against his. And as his eyes closed, I heard emotion fill his voice.

"Whatever you want to do with your life, I'll always support it."

I love you. "Thank you, Clint."

His eyes opened. "I'm serious."

I love you. "I know."

"Wherever you go and whatever you do, I'll be cheering you on. From wherever I am."

I love you so much. "Thank you, handsome."

"And when I'm done with this beautiful body of yours, I want to talk through what your plans are. So we can get you progressing down a road you want to be on."

I love you to the moon and back. "Sounds good to me."

Our lips fell together and his hands gripped behind my thighs. He hoisted me against him, pinning me to the front door as his tongue fell down the back of my throat. He pulled me away, effortlessly carrying me up the steps and to my bedroom. I reached out with my hand to slam the door closed. I sucked on his lower lip as growls bubbled up his throat. My back fell to the mattress as he freed my hands from around his neck. He threaded our fingers together and pinned them above my head. He kissed down my cheek. My neck. My clothed chest and my stomach. I rocked against him as my thighs heated, waiting for him to strip me of my clothes.

And it took us no time to get one another naked.

He filled me with his girth and rocked against my body. He tossed my legs over his shoulders and pounded into me. My jaw unhinged, crying out in ecstasy as he took what he wanted. With me freely giving it to him. I gripped his hair and raked my nails down his back. I felt myself pouring onto him, coating him in my mark. Our pants filled the room. Our kisses grew sloppy as my legs slipped off his shoulders. He pulled out and flipped me around, raising my hips in the air. Contorting my body in all the ways he wanted before filling me.

Again.

And again.

And again.

"Fucking hell, Rae. Shit, I've missed this."

"Clint. Clint. Don't stop. Please, holy hell, don't stop."

"Never. I'll never stop. Rae. I'm close. Rae!"

"Clint! Fuck!"

His hands slid down my spine. I felt him shaking against my ass cheeks. His length grew within me, pulsing and throbbing and aching for release. I gripped my bed sheets as he pinned my cheek to the mattress, wrapping his hand within my tendrils. And as I lost myself in his frantic movements, my body popped. My pelvis erupted. Electricity blinded my vision as my jaw unhinged in silent pleasure. Freezing my movements as my body clamped down around his.

"That's it, Rae. Holy fuck."

His growls raised goosebumps all over my body. The things he made me feel were outstanding. He collapsed against my body, shaking as he filled me to the brim. My pulsing pushed him out. His lips pressed sloppy kisses against the marks he left on my shoulder. I released the bed sheets from my grip, sliding my hand through his hair as he pressed his face into the crook of my neck.

I love you.

I love you, Clint.

Just say it, Rae. Say the words.

He panted for air. "You're amazing, you know that?"

I love you. "So are you, Clint."

"I just want to be like this forever."

I love you. "I don't blame you one bit."

"You mean that?"

I fucking love the hell out of you. "Every word of it."

And just as he pressed his lips to the shell of my ear, my phone rang from my jeans piled on the floor, causing me to groan as the all-too-familiar ringtone burst the moment the two of us had created.

"Fuck."

Clint paused. "Who's calling, beautiful?"

"Work."

36

CLINTON

I kissed her lips. "I promise you, I'll make it home okay."

Rae sighed. "Are you sure? Because I'm sure if I called Michael—"

"Leave Mike to his own devices. If I know boys like I know them, he's probably with Aly enjoying his time. Plus, my house isn't far from here."

"I could call them back and tell them—"

My face fell. "You'll do no such thing. They need you at work and I know you need the hours. Get ready. I'll walk home, okay?"

"I really don't feel good about this, Clint. You aren't fully recuperated. You've just been cleared to heal outside of the therapist's office. It might be too long—"

I pressed my lips against hers, sealing her words off with yet another kiss. I wrapped my arms around the girl I'd just made love to, pulling her as closely to me as I could get. Her lips smashed against mine. Our teeth clattered together. She made me feel as if I were on cloud nine, floating among the stars threatening to cover the whole of Los Angeles. I knew she was worried about me. I was, too. My stamina was still on the mend, and there was a good chance I'd have to stop for a breather or two on my walk home.

But I wasn't going to let that hold me back.

"Go. To. Work. Rae."

I punctuated the words with kisses before my hands slipped to her hips. She sighed as her forehead fell against mine. I felt her fingertips curling into my chest. My heart beat against her skin. Against her hands as they tried keeping me rooted. I knew she didn't want to go to work. They had interrupted us at a terrible time. And truth be told, I wanted to hop back into bed and hold her. I wanted to leap back into her arms, pull her against me, and fuck her into that mattress until the words poured effortlessly from both of our mouths.

I knew she needed the hours, though. Especially if she wanted to save to move out after graduation.

Rae sighed. "At least let me know when you get home safely. Okay?"

I nodded. "Of course. This'll give me time to stretch my legs. Work on my stamina. Allow me to clear my head for a bit before getting into the house."

"Is your dad still there?"

I paused. "Yeah. He's still home."

"Are you going to be okay?"

It made me sick she even had to ask. "I'll be fine, Rae. I know how to stand my ground with him."

"I don't know about this."

I cupped her cheeks. "Look. It's a twenty-minute walk. It's not even six o'clock. You'll hear from me before you get ready and leave for work in the first place. I promise."

And after a pause, she nodded. "Okay. Let's get you out of here, then."

"Atta girl."

She walked me to the front door before pulling me in for one more kiss. She fisted my shirt, wrapping it around her hand before pulling me down to her lips. I growled down the back of her throat and cloaked her in my arms. I loved it when she took control like that. When she thought she had the upper hand. I whipped her around, backing her into the wall in front of the door as my knee pressed between her thighs.

The glorious thighs I'd just relished with my lips.

Rae giggled. "We're both going to be late if you don't stop."

I grinned. "I'm not the one that initiated that kiss, beautiful."

"I guess I'll take the blame for it. But just this once."

"Just this once, indeed."

I chuckled, then captured her lips one last time. I kissed the tip of her nose, both of her cheeks, then planted one on her forehead. And after pep-talking myself in my head, I finally pulled away. I left her house, walking myself up the street and out of view before I stopped to catch my breath.

And for the first time in a long time, I admired the world around me.

I noticed the flowers lining the sidewalks as I walked by them. I noticed the cracks in the concrete where the land below it was slowly winning the war. I gazed up into the light blue sky, slowly cracking against the colors of a sunset teeming on the horizon. Things I'd never noticed while zooming around on my motorcycle. A world I had yet to experience because of the fast-paced, angry life I'd led up until this point. The breeze blew against my face, drying the beads of sweat on my brow as they formed.

It felt different than the breeze on my bike.

It felt comforting. Soothing. Not like the talons that clawed at my leather-jacketed back while speeding through town. I mean, yes. I missed my bike. But there was something about the world around me that couldn't be appreciated while on it. Like the rabbits hopping around in people's front yards. Or the laughter of young kids growing up down the off-shoot roads I passed to get to my own. The grass was green. I mean, incredibly green. A vibrant green that reminded me of those darkened neon signs in antique shops around the city.

I smiled at the life around me as I turned down the road I lived on.

I had a lot of good things going for me now. I had a great girl in my corner. I had new friends I felt I could trust. Who supported me and weren't dragging me down and encouraging me to be an absolute asshole. I had a stepmother who wanted a relationship with me. I had teachers who were helping me get through homework and missed tests so I could still graduate. Hell, even the principal of the school smiled at me every once in a while, instead of frowning my way with disapproval and frustration in his eyes.

I felt good about life, for once.

I stopped for one last breather a couple of blocks away from my house. I watched it looming in the distance, sparkling underneath the harshness of the sun. Sweat dripped down my back as I sighed. I watched the off-colored white glisten against the deep red shutters of the house. During the entirety of my childhood, I remembered that house in three distinct ways. Three different sets of colors that all popped more than the houses around it. Maybe it was the fresh coats of paint put on it every year that kept the house lively. Maybe it was the fact that it was the biggest house on the block. Or, maybe, it was the fact that we had the only house with a wrap-around porch as well as a wrought iron front gate that was barely utilized.

Either way, it stood out.

I picked up the pace. I went from standing still to walking. To speed walking. To jogging. I burst into a sprint, pumping air through my lungs and feeling them expand into my back. I felt the last pangs from my ribcage fall free, releasing the last of the pressure in my gut. I smiled at the sensation. At how free my body felt. I rushed up the driveway and leapt onto the porch, relishing the sweat that dripped off my brow. Down my nose. Drenching my neck and the collar of my T-shirt.

I felt alive, for the first time in my life.

And I wanted things to stay that way.

"Stop it, Howard! This has gone far enough!"

"Who the fuck do you think you are, yelling at me like that? Shut the hell up and listen, like you were always so good at!"

"Oh, is that why you married me? Because I kept my mouth shut and looked pretty for you?"

"The hell else are you good for? I whisk you away on all these vacations and it's not like you put out anymore!"

"You're an absolute asshole, you know that?"

Immediately, the blood drained from my face. How I could have ever convinced myself that things were getting better I had no idea. I heard my father yelling at Cecilia. I mean, just roaring at the top of his lungs. The only shocker was that she was yelling back. For the first time—well—ever . I stood on the porch, wondering if I should continue my walk. Maybe I could walk far enough to get to that coffee shop. The one where Rae got me that insanely good coffee and all those pastries.

I turned my back to the front door, readying myself to walk away. Until I heard something crash.

"Howard! Stop!"

I burst through the door, charging my sweaty ass down the hallway. I followed the sounds of my father screaming at her. Cursing at her. Calling her every single name in the godforsaken book. I grimaced at some of the shit that came out of his face. What kind of man talked to a woman that way?

A coward, that's who.

"Howard, you're hurting me. Please."

"Yeah? Well, maybe you know now how much it hurts me for you to be such a money-sucking cocktease, Cecilia."

"Howard!"

"Dad!" I yelled at him as I burst through the double doors into the kitchen. I saw him standing there, leaning over Cecilia with his hand tightly wrapped around her forearm. She leaned away from him, trying to wiggle away. And the fear in her eyes widened them as she whipped her head over to look at me.

"Clint."

I nodded. "Cecilia."

Dad glowered. "Get out."

I shook my head. "Not on your life. Let her go."

Dad slowly panned his gaze toward me, pinning me with a glare. He tightened his grip around Cecilia's wrist, causing her to squeal. She tried yanking away from him again, but he pulled her closer, almost causing her to lose her balance. I took a step closer to him, slowly reaching for the wooden spoon on the kitchen island.

And as he watched my movements, he chuckled.

"Go to your room, son."

Instead, however, I curled my hand tighter around that damn wooden spoon.

Because he sure as hell wasn't ripping another good woman from my life.

37

RAELYNN

"Welcome to Grady's Groceries. How was your shopping trip?"

"Yes, the milk aisle has changed to accommodate more items. It's over here, all the way down along the wall."

"Yes, sir. I'll make sure your coupon is acknowledged."

"We do take competitor's coupons! Because we pride ourselves on having the best prices in-store."

"I'm sorry, we stopped carrying that kind of ice cream when their ingredients were proven to be genetically modified. But I can help you find some other wonderful choices."

I put on the best face I could, even though I wasn't happy with being at work. I wanted to spend more time with Clint. I still wanted to be at home, in bed, curled up next to him. His bruises had finally faded into nothingness and I caught a glimpse of the strong, brutal boy I remembered from school. From before all this happened. His touch seemed gentler, but his movements were still powerful. Still reminiscent of the fighter I knew was still deep down within him.

I wanted to experience more of him. Especially now that he had a new lease on life.

I couldn't deny the change I'd seen in him over the past few weeks. How toned down his reputation at school had become. How much he hung around me and Michael and Allison, as opposed to going back to Roy and Marina and the rest of those dickweeds. He paid more attention in classes. Didn't crack jokes or cause a ruckus. The subdued nature that came over him during recuperation seemed to be trickling into his regular life, and I liked it. Not that I didn't like him before. But he gave off the idea that he might want to pull away from all that bullying bullshit. The poking fun at people and making people's lives a nightmare.

The thought made me smile.

"And here I thought work didn't make anyone happy."

Michael's voice ripped me from my trance. "What in the world are you doing here?"

He smiled. "Can't I come by and see my best friend while she's stuck at work?"

"How did you know I had to work tonight?"

"The distressful text you sent Allison."

I grinned. "So you were with her when I sent that text."

He shrugged. "Yeah, we've been spending some time together."

"Uh huh. And what kind of time are you spending with her?"

"Not the kind of time you and Clint are spending with one another, I'm sure."

I snickered. "Hardy har har."

"The deli still got those ham and turkey sandwiches?"

"And I know for a fact they just restocked your favorite energy drink in the vending machine outside."

"Oh. Yes. When do you take your break?"

I paused. "Give me twenty minutes, and I can probably take ten. But not more than that."

"Fair enough. I'll go ahead and get my food and annoy you until you take your break."

"Thanks."

He winked. "Anytime, Rae."

"Don't let Clint catch you winking at me. He just might slug you for it."

"I'd have a few words to say to him before he did something like that."

"Wait. Like what?"

Michael shrugged. "Like, 'Thank you for almost dying because it convinced me to kick things into gear with Allison.'"

"Maybe don't put it like that."

He chuckled. "Not exactly like that, no. But in some respects, I do owe me and Allison to what happened to him. As morbid as it sounds."

"So, there's a 'you and Allison' now?"

"I mean, not officially. But I guess being there with you that night and seeing what happened with Clint. What he did for you and what you were willing to do for him. It made me realize what I wanted, you know? I mean, with Allison. No offense."

I shrugged. "None taken. You're not my type anyway."

"I don't look very good in leather."

"I mean, you might be able to pull off leather assless chaps."

"Don't go giving Allison any ideas now."

I giggled. "You know damn good and well she'd die if you ever did that to her."

"It's one of the things I adore about her."

I had to pause Michael's story in order to check out a few customers. But they quickly dwindled down. He got his sandwich and his energy drink. And I was thankful for the soda he purchased for me. I clocked out for my ten-minute break, meandering outside to sit with Michael. We sat on a bench and watched the sun cast colors across the sky while the summer breeze slowly cooled us down.

I took a sip of my soda. "So, tell me what you adore about Allison."

Michael almost choked on his sandwich. "What?"

"That's where we left off a little bit ago. You said Allison's lack of a sexual appetite was one of the many things you adore about her."

"Not lack of a sex—Rae. Come on. You know what I meant."

I giggled. "I'm giving you a hard time. I knew what you meant."

"I mean, I just—it's Allison, you know? She's intelligent and cute. So, so cute. She's got goals and ambitions, and she likes my jokes. Her hands are as soft as they look, too."

I grinned. "Her hands, huh?"

He rolled his eyes. "Get your mind out of the gutter."

"What? I've held Allison's hands a lot over the years. I know what they feel like."

"Uh huh. I'm sure that's what you meant."

I threw my head back, laughing. "That's exactly what I meant."

"You're a terrible liar."

"Doesn't mean I can't try."

"You know I just—I keep thinking back to that night. Looking over the bridge and seeing Clint sprawled out. You know? And I just—I kept thinking about this crush I've got on Allison. Like, the fuck am I holding back for? What am I waiting for? It's not like she's going to approach me. She's certainly not that kind of girl. And what if I get pushed over a bridge tomorrow? Or the next day? Am I really going to go out like that? With Allison not knowing how much I like her? She deserves better than that shit."

I nodded. "She does."

Michael paused. "I'm thinking of asking her to prom."

I rolled my eyes. "After that entire diatribe, you're only thinking about asking her?"

"Cut me some slack. I've already asked her to the movie and she invites me over every chance she gets. Give me at least some credit."

I snickered. "All right. But only a little bit of credit."

"You think she'd go with me if I asked?"

"I swear, the two of you. You're gonna kill me, you know that?"

"What do you mean?"

I took another sip of my drink. "Do you know how long she's been asking me when you're going to ask her to prom?"

"Wait, what?"

I nodded. "Yep. I keep telling her to drop hints or just outright ask you herself. But every time I suggest that, she acts like I've slapped her across the face. I'm telling you, Michael. If you ask her, she's going to say yes. She's practically jumping out of her skin waiting for you to ask."

He snickered. "Wow. Well, that makes me feel good."

"I'm serious. You have to ask her. Our nights are going to be miserable if you don't. She'd be so happy if you asked. Hell, she'd probably say yes before you could get the damn question out."

He laughed. "Well, since we're on this same track, you think Clint will ask you to prom?"

"Yeah, I'm sure we'll go together. I mean, it's not like he has to ask. We're officially together, I suppose."

"You suppose? After everything you've been through?"

I felt myself blush. "Okay, yes. We are officially together. So, yeah. We're going to prom together."

"You still don't sound too sure of that. Is everything going okay with his recuperation?"

I shrugged. "I mean, he's always struggling with his dad. Which I'm sure is affecting his recuperation efforts. But he's okay. Far as I can tell."

"I'd like to get his dad in a room for a few minutes."

I scoffed. "Wouldn't we all."

"So, how are the two of you? You know, now that he's on the mend?"

I felt myself blush deeper. "I guess we're good."

"You guess, huh?"

"You're a dick, you know that?"

He chuckled. "Maybe a bit. Can I ask you something, though?"

"Of course. I mean, you have to spit it out soon because I only have one more minute, but—"

"Do you love him?"

The question didn't catch me as off-guard as I figured it would. In fact, it was easy to answer. I bit down onto the inside of my cheek as I turned to face Michael. And with a nod of my head, I answered his question.

"Yeah. I really think I do."

Michael grinned. "Then, you should tell him. I don't know much about Clint, but I'd like to think I know him better after these past few weeks. The lunches we've shared and helping him to class. He strikes me as the kind of guy who won't believe something is real unless you say the words. So say them."

I paused. "What if he doesn't feel the same way?"

"I can tell you, from the bottom of my heart, that's not true. Not one bit."

"But, there's a chance. Right?"

He sighed. "Rae, if that boy doesn't love you after all you two have been through and after all you've done for him, he sure as hell isn't worth any more of your efforts."

I nodded slowly. "True."

"Tell him, Rae. Tell him, like I'm going to tell Allison she's going to prom with me."

"Whoa, now. I didn't realize we were talking on that sort of a level now."

He nudged me with his shoulder. "You really are patronizing sometimes. You know that?"

I giggled. "It's why you love me."

He wrapped his arm around me, pulling me close to him. "Always and forever, girl. I'll always have your back."

"Even if I screw around with your mortal enemy and somehow make you guys friends?"

He paused. "I mean, maybe."

The two of us laughed, but his words hit home. Michael was right. If I wanted Clint to know I loved him, I had to spit it out. And there was a good chance he wouldn't do it first. Not because he didn't want to. But because he'd been through enough. He'd taken enough first steps to last someone a lifetime. It was damn time someone took the reins from him and let him rest a little bit. I didn't want to wait a second longer to tell him how I felt. Even if it blew up in my face. Even if he broke my heart. Even if I completely regretted the decision. At least I'd know. I'd know where we stood, and he'd know he was capable—and worthy—of being loved.

And I wanted to be the person to finally give that to him.

38

CLINTON

I gripped the wooden spoon, pulling it to my side. "No."

He growled at me. "No?"

I shook my head. "No. I'm not going anywhere. And I suggest you let Cecilia go."

As I stood there, staring at the fear in her eyes, I felt the entire room shift underneath my feet. My father's anger filled the space, pushing it outward and upward and downward. But, I steadied myself. I looked him straight in his eyes and held his stare. Held my ground. Held that wooden spoon in my hand, just in case that man decided to charge me.

This stopped today.

I mean, fucking hell. I was a fighter everywhere in my life except my own damn home. The fuck was that about? No more. I was done being pushed around by my father. I was done feeling weak. I'd just fought for my life, and now I felt like the time had come for me to fight for my freedom. To fight for peace. To fight for the sanity of this household and to buck up against my father.

And I was done allowing Cecilia to suffer the same angry wrath I had all my life. She deserved better. That woman had been there for me every step of the way through this shit. I wouldn't let my father hurt her. I wouldn't let him mangle her. I wouldn't let him taint her the way he'd tainted me down through the years. Because if he didn't have any issues putting his hands on her right now, that meant it had happened in the past.

Something that boiled my blood.

Dad's eye twitched. "What? You think you're a big man now?"

Cecilia tried wrenching away from him, but it didn't work. He tightened his grip further against her skin, causing her to cry out. I took a step forward, flipping the spoon in my hand. I caught it, feeling the weight of the damn thing settling against my palm. And as Dad's eyes flickered down to it, something else crossed my mind.

It wasn't simply Cecilia that deserved better.

I did, too.

"The fuck are you smiling about? Put that damn thing down and get out of here."

My father's voice ripped me from my trance and I felt my lips curling up. Further. Wider. Until my teeth gleamed at him and happiness flooded my veins. I deserved better. For the first time in my life, I felt like I deserved something more than this. Something more than Dad. Something more than the life he'd given me. Something more than the emptiness of his money. I looked at Cecilia and winked, letting her know that the two of us were getting out of this. No matter what I had to do.

Then, finally, Dad dropped her arm. "The fuck are you smiling about, son?"

I snickered. "I'm not your son."

His eyebrows rose. "Pretty sure I knocked up your mother with you. So, yeah. That makes you my son."

"Takes a lot more than sperm to make you a father, Dad."

He started walking toward me and Cecilia reached out for him. Telling him to stop. Telling him that she'd get me to go upstairs. He turned around, pushing her back toward the kitchen counter as she stumbled on her feet. And as she caught herself against the counter, she cried out. Her voice filled with panic, horror, and anger.

"He's just recovered, Howard! Stop it!"

I didn't flinch. As my father stalked toward me, I looked him straight in his eyes. I wouldn't let him control this house anymore. I wouldn't let him control my life, or my happiness, or my worth. I kept Cecilia in the corner of my eye, checking to make sure she was all right. And after she got back up onto her feet, I narrowed my eyes at my father.

"The fuck are you looking at, Clinton?"

I sighed. "I'm not afraid of you anymore, Dad. I don't know why you're so angry. I don't know why you hate me so much. But I'm done trying to figure it out. I'm done trying to figure you out. This has to stop, and it stops now. And if you don't want it to stop, I'll call people who will help me stop it. For my sake, and Cecilia's."

He put his finger in my face. "You leave my wife to me."

"Not a chance in hell."

He paused. "What did you just say?"

I stepped up to the plate, mere inches from my father's face. One on one, without a care in the world as to what he did after this. Because if he beat me to a bloody pulp, I'd take both the doctor and the lawyer up on their offers. So long as they helped Cecilia out in the process. My smile settled into a grin. A snarky grin I'd learned from him over the years. His nostrils flared with anger. His eyes bulged with revenge. I smelled the stench of alcohol on his breath and shook my head.

Pathetic. "I said, not a chance in hell, Dad."

Before I knew it, my father's hands pressed into my chest. The wooden spoon went clattering to the ground as my hands came up in defense. Cecilia screamed in the background, and the whole world fell black. Black at night. Black, like the color of my soul. Well, the color my soul had been. Rae changed a great deal of that. Cecilia changed a great deal of that. And in that moment, I wondered if Rae would be proud of me. Proud of me standing up to my father. Proud of me holding my ground. Proud of me fighting for my own happiness and safety within the walls of my father's mansion.

And I decided she would be. If she knew what was happening right now, she'd be proud. Possibly screaming at me like Cecilia currently was. But she'd be proud after the fact.

Not today, Dad. You're done with this shit today.

The only thing I processed was the smell of alcohol. The only thing I felt was my father's storm unleashing against me. He held so much anger within him. He had such fury in his fists. The only thing I saw were his angry eyes coming at me as I shoved him in his chest, listening as Cecilia screamed in the background.

"Stop it! I'm calling the police if you don't cut it out right now!"

Her voice faded away. Fell into the background as I moved and ducked my father. Whatever this storm brewed from, I wasn't going to be my father's punching bag any longer. If he wanted a fight, a fight is what he'd get. And I'd make sure to repay him for every fist that ever connected with my face. I'd repay him for every bruise he ever wrung around my neck. I'd repay him for every knee to my stomach and every elbow to my back and every time he pinned me against my fucking bedroom wall to teach me a lesson about being late for school.

Because damn it, we all deserved better.

Even my father.

"Stop! Please!"

"You're a selfish little brat, you know that?"

"Howard, no!"

Drunken fists flew around in the air and I dodged every single one of them, until a couple connected with my ribs, causing me to grunt out. But the only thing saving me was the fact that my father was completely smashed. He teetered on his feet, giving me a chance to get away from him. I slunk around him in the kitchen, moving away from him and watching as he stumbled into the kitchen counters. I gripped my stepmother by the upper arms and moved her out of harm's way, ripping open the kitchen door and pushed her into the dining room just as my father came up behind me.

And when he fisted my shirt, he ripped me away from my stepmother.

Away from the woman I'd defend tonight.

"Get back here and fight me like a damn man."

Cecilia cried out. "Howard! Stop! No!"

I scoffed. "Just getting the innocent out of the way before I teach you a lesson with your own medicine."

And as Dad slung me across the kitchen, forcing me to the ground, I heard him come for me. I felt his footsteps growing closer. I scrambled off the floor, readying myself for a fight just as his hands connected with my chest again.

Barreling me back into the garage door.

"No! Clint!"

I grunted as my back slammed into the doorknob. "Fuck."

Dad chuckled. "You want to play tough guy, not a problem. Because by the time I'm done with you, you'll know why I'm the father and you're the son."

I snarled. "In your fucking dreams, you psychotic abusive fuck."

He tossed me to the ground and I used the momentum to slide myself underneath the kitchen table. I heard Dad pulling at chairs and filling the kitchen with his growls. With his curses. With his anger. I scrambled up to my feet on the other side, then leapt onto the table itself. He looked up at me, his eyes wild and unfocused, filled with the alcohol he'd been drinking as I leapt above him, landing on the kitchen island.

Cecilia gasped. "Clint! Be careful!"

And as I hopped back down onto the floor, I scooped the wooden spoon back up, grinning at my father before he charged me once more.

"Look out!"

39

RAELYNN

I wiped down my register as I planned it all out in my head. Tonight, I'd tell Clint exactly how I felt. Tonight, I'd wrap him up in my arms, plant a kiss straight against his lips, and shout from the rooftops how much I loved him. I smiled as I thought about it. I couldn't wait to get my arms around his body again. My movements grew furious as I cleaned everything down as quickly as I could, closing up the grocery store for the second time since the incident.

My manager had been hesitant to schedule me to close after everything that took place.

"Ready to go?"

I jumped at the sound of Michael's voice. I whipped my head up, watching him as he stood at the edge of my register. Not a soul came in or left the grocery store, and I wondered how long he'd been standing there.

I furrowed my brow. "You're back?"

He snickered. "I never really left."

"You left after your break. I saw you get in your car."

"Yeah, well. I went to visit with Allison for a bit. Then I came back. Been standing here for about twenty minutes watching you clean and murmur to yourself."

I paused. "I was murmuring?"

He grinned. "Yep. And it's a good plan, what you've got going."

"Shit, you heard?"

He shrugged. "I mean, you were murmuring. And you did kind of explain to me that you were going to do it anyway. Good thing I'm here to drive you, right?"

"Then, why do I get the feeling you're not just here to drive me to Clint's?"

"What? Can't I come visit my best friend while she's working?"

I grinned. "You overprotective little thing, you. You're worried about me."

He rolled his eyes. "Look, it freaked me out, what happened to you and Clint that night. Okay? So sue me if you don't like it. But if you're closing down this grocery store again, I'd like to be here to make sure you get to wherever you need to be safely enough. You know, until Clint's back to doing that for you."

I smiled. "Thank you, Michael."

"I love you, Rae. Let me know when you're ready to go, and I'll get you over to Clint's."

I reached over the cash register and hugged his neck. Then I finished up what I needed to do. I cashed out my till and took it over to my manager's office. And I found him staring at the parking lot cameras. I cleared my throat, pulling him from his trance as he jumped in his seat. He whipped his head around with widened eyes, and my gut dropped for him.

Looked like Clint and I weren't the only ones affected by what happened.

I passed off my till and clocked out. Then Michael and I headed to his car. I felt the eyes of my manager on us the entire way. He stood at the windows of the grocery store, watching us until we got to the car and got in. I even saw him watching us in my rearview mirror as we drove off.

Making our way for Clint's house.

Michael had a smirk on his face for the entire ride. And as we listened to his bullshit classical music, I found my inner peace. I found my inner strength. I rehearsed the things I wanted to say to him as we made our way for his house. I felt myself filling with hope. Excitement. Anxiousness. But not the bad kind. The good kind.

Because I knew this meant taking another step for Clint and me.

A step I felt we'd both been ready for.

"You want to rehearse?"

I peeked over at Michael. "What?"

He snickered. "Rehearse. You know, what you're going to say to him tonight."

I shrugged. "Nah. I'm good. I usually wing it with stuff like this."

"You're going to wing it when it comes to telling Clint how you feel for the very first time>"

"I mean, I usually wing it with my English speeches and I do just fine with those."

He paused. "You didn't plan out that speech you gave last year?"

I shook my head. "Nope."

"That massive speech you gave on *1984* sort of applying today."

"Are you not hearing me right? Clean out your ears, Michael."

He chuckled. "Holy shit, you're amazing. You know that?"

I smiled. "And I hope that's one of Clint's many reactions tonight."

"If it isn't, I'll kick his ass for you."

"Michael!"

"What? Come on, Rae. I see how happy he makes you. I see how much this boy means to you. And if he doesn't love you or if he hurts you or if I even suspect he's manipulating you or leading you on in any way? He's got it coming to him. Because you're my friend, Rae. My best of friends. And we have to stick together."

I reached over, taking his hand. "I love you so much."

He smirked. "Love you, too, Rae. Now, you ready?"

"As ready as I'll ever be."

"Good. Because we're here."

I drew in a deep breath as we pulled into Clint's driveway, stopping just shy of the porch. Michael squeezed my hand for reassurance, and I leaned over to kiss his cheek softly. I wanted him to know how thankful I was for his friendship. How thankful I was for accepting Clint into our fold. And as I hugged him tightly, I pressed my lips against his ear.

"Thank you. For everything."

He nodded. "I'll hang around for a bit, just in the slightest case this goes haywire. All right?"

"You won't have to, but thank you anyway. Give it about ten minutes, then you can drive on off. I'm sure Cecilia will give me a ride home later."

"If you don't stay the night."

I scoffed and playfully swatted at Michael. Then I shoved myself out of his SUV. He wished me luck and I closed my door, grinning at him through the window.

And just as I turned around, the front door burst open.

"Clint!"

I looked on in horror as the man I loved fell to his back on the porch. I heard a door open in the distance as the world around me tunneled. All I saw was Clint lying on his back, blood dripping down his face. Flashes of him lying at the bottom of that ravine bombarded my mind. Until I heard that fucking voice.

"Get up and fight me like the man you think you are!"

His father.

I watched in slow motion as Cecilia rushed out onto the porch. She was missing a shoe. Her hair was disheveled. Her dress had been ripped off her shoulder and she looked as if she'd been crying for hours. I saw her drop to the porch beside Clint. I stood there, frozen, as Clint's father appeared in the doorway. His fists were balled up. He had blood splattered all over his face. His eye was swollen shut. His lip, split. He had the fire of Satan in his eyes.

And I watched as Cecilia helped Clint back up onto his feet.

Michael stepped up beside me. "Hey!"

I jumped at the sound of his voice. Because I had no fucking clue when he'd gotten out of the car. Time toppled over on itself. I watched Michael push away from my side, sprinting for the porch. I followed behind him, finally pulled out of my trance. The world moved in regular motion again as the smell of blood, sweat, and tears filled the space around me. Michael moved behind Clint, steadying him as he stumbled back. And while Cecilia smoothed her hands over his chest, I reached up to cup Clint's cheek, pulling his eyes to mine.

"Can you hear me? Are you okay?"

"You won't get out of this another time, son."

His father reached between all of us, ripping him away from our grasps. I lunged for him, trying to get him back as Michael held me around my waist. Cecilia screamed for him to stop. Screamed at his father for him to let Clint go. I reached out for him, kicking and trying to get out of Michael's grasp.

But if he wouldn't let me use my body, I sure as hell would use my words.

"Let him go!"

My shrieking voice filled the night as Clint's father held him tightly by the collar of his shirt.

"Let him go, you coward! I'm tired of you hurting him. Abusing him. Beating him to a pulp. You're the sorriest excuse for a father I've ever seen in my life, and mine left me when I was just a little girl!"

Michael put his lips to my ear. "Calm down. He's going to hurt you. He's drunk. I can smell it. Calm your voice, Rae."

But I didn't listen. "He's still recovering from the crash, you piece of shit. I'm going to call the police and have you thrown in prison to rot!"

The sounds of his father laughing at me fell against my ear. As Michael settled me back down onto my feet, he strengthened his grip around my waist. I reached out for Clint. I watched as his father's eyes fell onto his son. Cecilia cried in the background, slumped against the front door as that man drew his fist back. I reached my hand out, screaming with all my might. My fingertips wiggled for the back of Clint's shirt, so I could pull him out of the line of fire of his father's fight-ending punch.

Then, Clint brought his knee up, nailing his father straight in his groin and taking him to the ground.

The world fell silent as he growled out in pain. Cecilia's cries stopped. Michael's grip loosened. And my shrieking ceased. I watched as blood dripped down Clint's face. His neck. Soaking his shirt as it poured from his nose, which I knew his father had rebroken. Clint stood there in front of his father, letting his blood drip onto the top of his damn head. And once his father looked up, Clint sighed.

"You really are a piece of work, Dad."

Then, Clint struck his father with a blow of his knee that knocked the man out cold.

Everything fell silent. Everything stood still. Time itself yielded to what had just happened. Clint's father fell face-first onto the porch. Passed out in his own alcohol-laden drool. And as Michael released me from his grasp, I scurried to Clint's side, gripping his arms and slowly turning him toward me as shock and anger rolled over his features.

"Baby, can you hear me?"

I rubbed my hands up and down his arms, trying to pull him out of his trance. I heard Cecilia gasp for air, as if she'd been holding her breath. I heard her walk out onto the porch, dropping to her knees next to his father. I watched his eyes dart around. He slowly came to as he tried to get a bearing on his surroundings. He looked at me. At Michael. At his father, lying on the porch. He brought his hand up to his nose before he winced, with tears streaming down his face.

"Baby, talk to me. Can you hear me?"

He shook his head. He stumbled back away from me, holding his hand out. I tried to get to him, but he stopped me. I tried to reach out for him, but he wouldn't let me wrap him up like I had planned. He wouldn't let me pull him close, like I had planned. The words danced on the tip of my tongue. The words I knew he needed to hear.

He beat me to the punch, though. With words that shattered my heart right there on his fucking porch.

"I can't do this."

His words were such a soft whisper, I thought I'd misheard him. Until he said them again with strength.

"I can't do this, Rae."

I paused. "Do what?"

He looked away. "Us."

"What?"

"This."

"Excuse me?"

"I need you to leave."

I looked up at him, hoping this was all a dream. "You can't be serious right now. You need help. You need a—"

His head whipped around to mine. "I need you to leave. Now."

"Clint, I—"

"I. Said. Leave!"

And as the roar of his voice filled the space around me, wrapping me up in the greatest nightmare of my life, he took a step toward me. His fists were balled up at his sides. I felt someone yank me away from him, and I stumbled down the stairs. Cecilia cried as she sat by his father's unconscious body. Blood poured down Clint's face as he stared at me with lightning in his eyes. I wanted to reach out for him. I wanted to press my lips to his ear. I wanted to whisper to him how much I loved him, and reassure him I wasn't going anywhere.

I hadn't prepared for him wanting me to leave, though.

And I had no words for the true desire of his heart.

STAY WITH ME

DIAMOND IN THE ROUGH 3

1

CLINTON

My knees curled against my chest. I felt the blood caking on my face. My head spun from the aftermath of the fight with my father. How aggressive things had gotten. How proud I was of Cecilia standing up to him.

How much my heart hurt that Rae witnessed any of it.

I closed my eyes and listened to the sound of Michael's SUV pull out of the driveway. No, not pull out. Peel out. Tires squealed along the concrete and the smell of burned rubber filled the air. I placed my head against my knees as the rain came down harder than ever. Thunder boomed in the distance. Lightning flashed above my head. When had it started raining?

Could it wash away my sins?

I felt sick to my stomach. I wanted to vomit on the porch. The silence was deafening. And yet, it brought me peace. My father wasn't yelling. Cecilia wasn't crying. Things were simply… silent. The sound of the rain soothed my soul, but the booming of thunder reminded me of reality.

Reminded me of the presence of my unconscious father.

My back rested heavily against the railing as I slowly looked up. I stared at the house as water dripped from the tendrils of my hair. I wanted to go after Rae. I wanted to wrap her up in my arms and tell her I didn't mean it. But I couldn't. I knew I couldn't. Because I was bad news, and I always would be.

She had her life ahead of her.

And I had nothing in my future.

My eyes slowly gravitated to my father, lying unconscious on the porch. I didn't even know what to do with him. Did I need to call 9-1-1? Was he even still breathing? I saw his back softly moving, and I almost regretted it.

Almost regretted not having killed my father when I had the chance.

What kind of person does that make me?

I grimaced and turned my eyes away from him. Maybe if I ignored him long enough, he'd go away. Maybe if I blinked my eyes rapidly, it would somehow rewind time. Back to the last time I'd been pressed against Rae's body. Back to the last time I'd been in her arms and gazing into those gorgeous eyes.

So I blinked as quickly as I could. Faster, and faster, while I prayed it took me back in time. That, somehow, blinking in quick succession was the key to time travel.

It wasn't, though.

It only served to hold back my tears.

Rae deserves someone better.

Those four words kept rushing around in my mind. The storm grew and the wind howled. My leather jacket shrunk against me as the rain continued to batter it. Rae did deserve someone better. Someone more worthy of her time. And far less dangerous. The life I lead wasn't a life to pull someone into. The family I had wasn't a family I needed to add to.

And it killed me inside.

She went after him, though. She cares about you.

It was true. I'd seen her lunge at him. I'd seen Michael holding her back as she tried to get to me. Which only fueled my need to let her go. If she ever got hurt because of me, I'd never forgive myself. If my father ever hurt her, for any reason, I knew I'd kill him. I'd sit in prison with a smile on my face about it, too. Rae deserved much better than that. She deserved a family that would take her in. Make her feel loved. Make her feel safe. Make her feel wanted.

None of which my father could ever provide for anyone.

I still couldn't remember bits and pieces of the night, though. I couldn't remember how we ended up on the porch. Or the exact moment where I knocked my father out cold. I remember Cecilia screaming. I remember her chest heaving with tears. And the next thing I knew, we were on the porch. Before Michael and Rae pulled up. Then Rae had tried to come to my defense.

And the next thing I know, Dad was on the ground. Unconscious, in a pool of his own blood.

Or possibly mine.

Slowly, pain filled my body. An excruciating pain I didn't know what to do with. My face throbbed. My neck stiffened. My eyes fluttered closed as more tears pushed themselves to the surface. The night came back in bits and pieces. Rae, screaming from Michael's arms. Trying to pull away and get to me. Cecilia, crying on the porch as she yelled for both of us to stop. My father, chuckling in his maniacal way as his eyes briefly fell on to Rae.

My knee, connecting with his groin.

I slowly looked back over at my father. Sounds other than the rain slowly dawned on me. Cecilia's voice, rambling aimlessly as she stood in the doorway of the house.

"Yes, unconscious. Yes, he's breathing. Uh huh. From the nose. Um, it just—it all happened so fast—I know his nose is broken again. I can just tell by looking at it."

My eyes gravitated to my stepmother. To the way she looked upon me with worry and hurt. She slipped out, tiptoeing around my father's body as she came for me. She dipped down, propping a cell phone against her shoulder. She reached out and touched something on my neck. My eye twitched. Her hand cupped my cheek. And when she brushed her finger across my temple, I felt myself get sick to my stomach.

I leaned over, away from her, and began to heave. My stomach turned itself inside out as burning bile worked its way up my throat. Concussion. I had a concussion, right?

I felt my stepmother's hand softly rubbing my back as I continued to puke on the porch.

It felt like my entire body was revolting against itself. Rising up and refusing to operate anymore until I got into better circumstances. It was like my physical form had finally given up. Had finally waved the white flag of surrender. I worked my way onto my hands and knees. I shook violently as the world spun around me. Tears dripped down my face. Snot fell from my nose. And with every heave, I felt my nose rush pain around the back of my head.

"Cecilia," I whimpered.

She patted my back. "I'm right here. The paramedics are on their way. Just hold on, okay?"

I couldn't gain control of my body. I felt helpless. Pathetic. Weak, like my father had always called me. My leather coat had tightened so badly around my arms that I couldn't feel my hands any longer. And that made me cry even harder. My mother's leather coat. The one she gave me when I was a young teenager. Sent to me, for my birthday. As a present and some sort of pathetic excuse for never being in my life. For leaving me behind with a man she knew to be an abusive piece of shit.

I suddenly didn't want to wear it anymore.

I leaned up and struggled to get it off. I stumbled around as spit dripped down my chin. I felt someone tugging at my coat, trying to help pull it off me as I slowly peeled it away from my body. I coughed and sputtered. Sobs fell from my lips because I didn't have the strength to hold back my tears any longer. I felt an arm wrap around my stomach, holding me as grunts and growls came from behind me.

It wasn't until the coat finally ripped away from my arms, however, that I figured out Cecilia was holding me. Cecilia was grunting with me. Cecilia was cradling me close.

"Come here. I've got you. They'll be here soon, Clint."

I leaned heavily against her. Despite the fact that my massive body was easily twice her size, I curled into her like a newborn child, afraid of being too far away from her. I coughed as my sobs came in hiccups. The taste of puke in my mouth was fucking awful. My nose hurt unlike anything I'd ever felt and Dad still lay there. Unconscious on the fucking porch.

The thunderstorm was moving away, though.

Slowly, but surely.

The sound of sirens fell against my ears and I sighed. Cecilia positioned herself against the house and I leaned even harder against her. I didn't know what this meant for us. What this meant for our family. Would she tell the paramedics how this all happened? Would I be arrested?

Would it even matter?

I might have a better quality of life in prison.

"It's okay. Breathe for me, Clint. I need you to settle down a bit."

My chest hiccupped. "I'm sor—so—sorry, Cec—cec—"

"Sh-sh-sh-sh. They're almost here. I see the ambulance now."

The siren's sound grew to a deafening roar. And only then did my father start to stir. Footsteps landed against pavement as people made their way onto the porch. Helping my father to wake up. I heard him groaning. Grumbling. Growling out my name. I slowly opened my eyes and watched him bat people away. He even ripped a small flashlight out of one of their hands and tossed it over the railing of the porch.

"Where the fuck is my son?"

I cowered against Cecilia's body as her hand smoothed over the side of my face.

"Where the hell are you, Clinton?"

The paramedic sighed. "Sir, I need you to stay still. You could have a concussion."

My father bolted upright. "Where the fuck are you, you piece of shit?"

"Sir, can you please—"

"I'm going to rip you a new one. You don't get to knock me out on my own porch and get away with it. Cecilia!"

She snickered. "Shut up, Howard."

He snarled. "What did you say, you stupid bitch?"

"Shut up, Dad. Seriously."

He whipped his head around. "Come here, you little dipshit."

"You two. Inside, now. The paramedic will tend to you in there."

We listened to the command of the woman trying to help my father. But he was combative the entire time. His curses and slurs followed me inside, where my stepmother and I switched roles. Once I got myself on my feet, I took her in my arms and held her closely as the paramedics examined me. They flashed lights in my eyes and checked my temples. The man fiddled with my nose and it nauseated me. I felt myself heave again and Cecilia quickly stepped away, watching with wide eyes while people fussed over me.

"No concussion. But he's in mild shock."

"Pupil dilation's good."

"We need a brace for his nose!"

"He'll need surgery to fix it eventually."

I reached out for Cecilia's hand and she took it. Then, with a squeeze, she stepped back out onto the porch. She closed the door, muting my father's yelling and cursing. And as I stood there, alone, I let the tears silently fall.

In front of a paramedic that kept tossing me pitiful glances.

"This is gonna hurt. Just bear with me."

"One, two—"

I closed my eyes and let myself fall into a happy place. I saw Rae's face, smiling at me as she called out my name. I was used to traveling to happy places. That's how I'd gotten through the hurt and the pain of my childhood. I didn't even feel them snap my nose into place. I didn't feel them inject me with pain medication. I didn't feel them poking around at my bruises or putting a brace over my nose.

Because I'd lost myself in my own little world.

A world where Rae was still there. Safe from harm, and able to fall into my arms without a care in the world. I lost myself in a field of flowers as our backs fell to the petals, casting them upward as we made love underneath the summer sun. I lost myself in her laughter. In her scent. In her smile and her touch and her kiss.

And when I opened my eyes, one last tear slipped down my cheek.

No more, after this.

"Thank you, I really appreciate it. Yes, I'll make sure to file a police report. Yes, self-defense. I can promise you that. Handcuffs might be necessary to transport him. Uh huh. I'll be along in a little while. He'll be fine. Yes, thank you so much."

Cecilia's voice filled my ears and my eyes panned over to her. I saw her ushering the paramedics out. I heard the exhaustion in her voice. She closed the door and locked it, then turned to face me.

"I told them to take your father to the hospital."

I nodded slowly. "Okay."

"You really should go yourself. But they insisted you were fine."

"If something happens tonight, I'll check myself in somewhere."

She snickered. "You'll do no such thing alone."

Then she came over and took my hands within hers. "You really should call her, you know."

I nodded mindlessly. "Okay."

"I'm serious, Clint. She could really help you right now."

"I'll take that into account."

"Clint. Look at me, sweetheart."

My eyes fell to hers and I tried my best to focus.

"Call. Rae. Promise me."

I nodded slowly. "I promise to consider it."

Then I pulled away from her and walked my ass upstairs. Because I sure as hell didn't want to be part of this world anymore. I wanted to be part of my dreams.

Part of the only place where my father didn't exist.

2

RAELYNN

I sat in the passenger seat of Michael's car as we drove back to my place. I kept my eyes on the outside mirror, looking back, just in case Clint started running after us. But he didn't. He receded into the horizon as another storm unleashed, pouring forth more rain than I'd ever seen. Booming the loudest thunder imaginable. Flashing etches of lightning throughout the sky and blinding the whole of Riverbend for seconds at a time.

My heart had never hurt this badly before.

My soul shattered. It felt as if my heart were dripping blood as it slowly sank to my stomach. The butterflies in my body died, giving way to maggots that felt as if they were eating me from the inside out. It was the only way I had to explain the pain no one could see. It was the only way I knew how to explain how much Clint had just hurt me.

Maybe he didn't mean it?

It was my only hope. Maybe it was just a show he put on for his father. But that didn't make sense. His father had already been knocked unconscious. Was it possible the show was for Cecilia? Maybe she secretly didn't like me, or something like that. Or maybe, he meant it now but wouldn't mean it tomorrow.

Yeah, he'll call. Once tensions settle and he gets some rest.

"He's just got a lot on his plate right now. Give him some time."

Michael's voice pierced my thoughts, but I had nothing to say.

"You know he cares about you. I certainly know he cares about you. Just give him some space. A lot has happened in a short span of time to him."

I nodded aimlessly. "Yeah."

"He's probably just overwhelmed, and he'll call you tomorrow once he feels better."

"Maybe so."

"And besides, if we really want to be real for a second?"

I sighed. "Don't."

"We all know Clint can be sort of an ass sometimes. That's just kind of how he is."

I closed my eyes. "This was different, and you know it."

Michael didn't respond, which furthered the dread in my gut. He'd always been the voice of reason. The person that worked gracefully under pressure. Part of me was hoping he'd go against what I said. Tell me that this wasn't any different. That Clint was simply, well, being Clint. But when he didn't argue, I wanted the world to open up below me.

Taking me, and Clint's father, along for the ride.

We weaved slowly through the neighborhood as the sounds of sirens wailed in the distance. I whipped my head around, trying to figure out where they were headed. Had someone called 9-1-1? Was Clint all right? Who called? Did Michael call?

I looked over at him and he held up his hands.

"Don't look at me. My guess is his stepmother called."

Cecilia. "That makes sense."

I settled heavily into the seat as we turned down my street. I closed my eyes, feeling Michael's SUV park itself in my driveway. I didn't want to get out. I wanted to go back to Clint's place and force myself into his orbit. Force him to tolerate me until he came to his senses.

Michael's voice broke through my thoughts. And I wanted him to shut the hell up.

"Look, I know this time is different. But I want you to know I'm here for you. Me and Allison. You're not alone, even if you might feel like it right now."

I sighed. "I appreciate it."

"And if you need anything at all, we're only a phone call away. Anything. I mean that."

"Can you get Clint back for me?"

He paused. "Well, anything but that."

I snickered and opened my eyes before a groan fell from my lips. Fucking D.J.'s bullshit, rundown car was sitting in the middle of the damn driveway. Just my luck. Just what I fucking needed after this hellish night. I shook my head as I unbuckled my seatbelt. I couldn't unlock the door, though. I couldn't bring myself to open it and get out.

Michael cleared his throat. "You can always come back to my place, you know. Crash on our sofa. My parents wouldn't mind."

I nodded. "You lucked out with them, you know."

"I know. A lot of kids who are adopted end up in terrible situations. I came out lucky."

"Don't ever take that for granted."

He shook his head. "I don't. And I won't. I promise."

"Thanks for driving me home."

"The offer still stands if you don't want to be here."

"I know. I just want to be alone right now, though. I'm sure I can avoid them when I walk inside."

"Well, if you can't, I'll stay parked out here for a little bit. If you get to your window and wave me off, I'll leave. If you don't, I'll assume you're coming back out with your things."

I smiled softly. "Sounds like a plan."

I finally got my hand to move to the door handle. I shoved it open, then reached for my purse. I let myself out of his car, clutching my purse close to me. Trying to root myself in anything akin to reality. It felt like the world was spinning. Like I was floating up to the darkened heavens. None of this felt real. And yet, I knew it was real.

This torture was real.

The sirens grew, coating the neighborhood with their sounds as dogs began barking. Cats began meowing. The whole of the dirt of our side of the fence slowly woke up. People flicked on their lights. Others cursed at the animals to shut the hell up. I closed Michael's car door and made my way to the porch, fishing my keys out of my purse.

Please don't be downstairs. Please don't be downstairs. Please don't be downstairs.

I took one last peek back at Michael before shoving my key into the door. I unlocked it as silently as I could, then eased the door open. I didn't hear the television going. I didn't see any lights on. And as I slipped inside, I breathed a sigh of relief.

No one was downstairs.

I closed the door behind me and leaned against it. Heavily. I wanted to sit down and cry. But, I couldn't. Our foyer was like a fucking acoustical stereo. If there was any part of the house that required my silence, it was here. I locked the door softly, wincing as the sound of the latch echoed off the damn corners of the walls. I paused, holding my breath. Waiting for the hallway light to click on before D.J. yelled down the damn stairs at me.

But no sounds came.

I tiptoed into the kitchen. I opened the fridge and pulled out a bottle of water. It took a couple minutes of rummaging around to find a decent-enough snack. But, after finding an unopened bag of chips, I headed up stairs. I skipped the ones I knew creaked. The ones I knew might wake my mother up. And as I made my way down the hallway, I heard soft panting. Soft groaning. Soft, murmured curses coming from my mother's bedroom.

For fuck's sake.

I rushed the rest of the way to my room. I closed my door silently and locked it. I reached for my headphones and slipped them over my head, plugging the port into my phone. I turned on some music to block out the sounds. I walked over to my bedroom window and waved down at Michael. He flashed his lights before backing out of the driveway, and I stood there. Watching him leave.

With tears brewing behind my eyes again.

I had to take my headphones off in order to shed my wet clothes. I piled them onto the floor, racing the steady sounds of my fucking mother in the room next to me. I stripped myself bare, shivering as I walked over to my dresser. And as I pulled out a long shirt, the sounds grew. Morphing and growing, as if I weren't here.

Then again, they didn't know I was here.

It made me sick to my stomach to listen to. Then again, I should've been used to it. I ripped the shirt down against my body before quickly putting my headphones on again. I fell onto my bed and reached for the chips. I eased them open, careful not to disturb the disgusting party going on next door to my room. I snuggled underneath the covers and cracked open my water, chugging it back as I grabbed my remote.

I turned on my box television before immediately muting it.

I listened to music and watched the silent images of Golden Girls flash by. Mom and I didn't have cable. We each had cheap antennas on our televisions. But that was it. The nice one that D.J. purchased her was downstairs for movie nights. And the box television we'd had down there made it into my room as a 'gift.' I mean, don't get me wrong. I was grateful for it. But, knowing this television had made its way into my room because of D.J. never did sit right with me. Almost made me feel dirty every time I used the damn thing.

But I needed the distraction tonight.

I munched on chips and sipped my water. I watched the images on the television aimlessly as one song poured into another. Rock anthems. Rap songs. A few random musical numbers I'd come to enjoy. I mindlessly ate until the entire bag was gone, even though I knew damn good and well I'd hear about it tomorrow. I rolled my eyes and licked at my fingers. I tossed the empty chip bag into the small trash can beside my bed. I finished my water and threw that away, too. Then, I took a chance and eased my headphones off my head.

Only to be met with louder, more fervent sounds.

I rolled my eyes and slipped them quickly back over my ears. I wiggled down into bed, turning off the television in the process. I lay there, staring up at the ceiling and trying to figure out what the fuck to do next. I kept checking my phone. Every few minutes, I checked to see if Clint had called. Or texted. Hell, fucking emailed me or some shit like that. There was nothing, though. A text from Michael, telling me he'd gotten home safely. A text from Allison, asking me if I needed anything. Another text from Michael, asking me to respond so he knew I was still alive.

So, I shot him a quick message back.

Me: Alive and well. Uh, kind of. Avoided D.J. and Mom. About to pass out.

Then my phone fell back to my chest.

The songs fell into the background. The entire world kind of faded away, really. The ceiling darkened and the room spun around me. Almost as if the chips had made me drunk. I felt my eyes closing and my body sinking into the mattress. My head fell off to the side as my breathing evened out, but I didn't quite feel asleep.

Oh, no.

Suddenly, I saw it. The bridge. The skid marks. I heard my own voice yelling for Michael to stop the car before I leapt out, rushed to the edge and peered over it. And as I gazed into the darkness below me, I called out his name.

"Clint!"

I tried jerking myself awake, moving, opening my eyes. But it was no use. I kept calling out his name while Michael pulled me away from the edge. And the more I fought against him, the angrier he got with me. I felt licks of fire kissing the back of my neck. I tore away from his grasp. And when I whipped around, I didn't see Michael behind me.

Just a fiery being that looked like Michael.

"You're pathetic."

I shook my head. "No, I'm not."

"You want to go for him?"

"You need to help me. He's down there. His bike's right over there!"

"What bike, Raelynn? What bike do you see?"

I whipped my head over to see the bike, but it wasn't there. And neither were the skidmarks. The fire in front of me grew, engulfing Michael and swallowing the rest of him whole. I felt my body lock up. Fear coursed through my veins. And as a fiery tongue made its way for me, I leaned back.

All the way over the railing.

"It should've been you, Raelynn."

The tongue wrapped itself around my throat and hoisted me over the edge. I cried out for help. I cried out for Michael. Then I cried out for Clint. Tears slid down my cheeks. I tried wrapping my hands around the fiery tongue, trying to get a grip on it so it would let me go. So it would stop searing my skin. So it would stop torturing me.

Then the tongue dropped me.

And as the darkness swallowed me whole again, I finally jerked myself awake. Just as the sun started streaming through my window.

Signaling the beginning of a new day.

3

———

CLINTON

I barely slept that night. Between the pain in my face and the hurt in my heart, sleep stayed away. I hated it. Every fucking second of it. The worrying. The turning in bed, over and over. I'd written more in my journal that night than ever before. Page after page of angry musings, random poems with Rae at the center, and a list.

A half-done list of all my possibilities after I graduated.

The list had more numbers than suggestions. It was depressing, really. Making a list, then putting two things on it. 'Get a job' and 'move out.' Those were the two things on my list.

And I still had no idea how to actually accomplish those two things.

The sun slowly rose and I eased myself out of bed. My entire body hurt. I shuffled into the bathroom and turned on the light, shielding my eyes. My head hurt. Still. My hips hurt. Still. My knee hurt and my knuckles were bruised and even I knew my ribcage was black and blue again.

Nothing could have prepared me for the sight of myself in the mirror, though.

"Holy fuck."

The bags underneath my eyes were fierce. The soft red marks around my throat reminded me of more things that happened last night. Things I hadn't remembered until I looked at the marks on my body. The scratch marks. The bruises. The way that fucking thing on my face held my nose upright.

"I can't wear this shit to school."

I tried taking it off, but it felt like it was plastered to my nose. The bruises on my cheekbones made me angry. The light black and blue marks that peppered my ribcage made my blood boil. I turned my back to the image of myself and decided to suffer through a shower. I knew it would hurt, water battering against my abused body. But I stunk. I smelled of rain water, sweat, and hopelessness.

And if the plan was to do research today, I needed my wits about me.

I got into the shower and groaned all the way through it. Every droplet hurt. It felt like my body had gone into overdrive, like my nerve endings were exposed. I probably should've gone to the hospital. But I didn't want to be in the same facility as my father.

When the hell was he coming home anyway?

I slipped out of the shower and dried myself off, pressing the towel softly against my skin as I walked into my bedroom. Everything felt muted. It almost felt like I wasn't piloting my own body. Not really, anyway. I felt out of place. Out of time. Alert, but not really there.

Until a knock came at my door.

"Clint?"

Cecilia's voice caused me to pause. I quickly wrapped the towel around my waist before I reached for the door. I closed my eyes, drawing in a deep breath. Because I knew seeing me like this would throw her for a loop.

Then I opened the door.

She gasped. "Clint, you need a doctor."

I opened my eyes. "I'm fine."

"Your ribs. You—come with me. Come on. I'll get you somewhere."

"Cecilia."

"Your nose doesn't look much better, either. We need to schedule surgery."

"Cecilia."

"Come with me. You can skip school and—"

I snipped at her, "Cecilia."

She paused. "Yes?"

I sighed. "You shouldn't be here when my father gets home from the hospital. Whenever that is. It won't be safe for you. Not after you calling the paramedics and having him hauled off last night."

"I'm not concerned about that right now. I'm concerned about you. We need to go get you checked out. For all we know, your father's knocked something loose or busted stitches somewhere we don't know about."

"I'm fine. It's all topical."

"And how do you know that?"

I snickered. "If I were bleeding internally, I'd technically already be dead."

She stared at me and I took her in. Really, truly took her in. The color of her eyes that had slowly faded. The disheveled nature of her hair as she piled it at the crown of her head. The bags under her eyes were heavier than I'd ever seen them. And, without makeup, she looked ten years older. She had crows' feet at the corners of her eyes. Her lips were downturned, causing her entire face to sag. Her shoulders were hunched. She favored her left side.

I nodded slowly. "Didn't get much sleep, either?"

She brushed off my question. "I won't take you to the hospital your father's at, but you have to see someone."

"I'll make an appointment with the doctor I saw."

"That's the hospital Howard's at right now."

"I'll figure it out, then."

She sighed. "Why won't you let me take you?"

"Because it's not your responsibility."

I saw the hurt in her eyes. And had I not already been dead inside, it would've killed me. The truth of the matter was that all this was my mother's responsibility. But she'd abandoned me. None of this should've happened. Dad shouldn't have been an abusive fucking asshole. Nobody should have had to bear the responsibility of it.

I wouldn't let Cecilia dig her hole any deeper.

Just like I wouldn't let Rae do it, either.

"You really should take advantage of this time. Withdraw some funds. Pack up your things. Get the hell out of here and find a better life for yourself."

She stepped forward, placing a hand against my arm. "While that's sweet, it's not your job to look after me, Clinton. I appreciate it, but right now I'm worried about you. You can't go to school looking like this."

"Then I won't."

"There's nothing I can do to convince you to let me get you to a doctor?"

I shook my head. "No."

"Are you staying here for the day?"

"No."

"Where are you going, then?"

I shrugged. "Anywhere but school and here. I need to clear my head for a bit."

"Do you want me to come with you?"

"No."

"Is there anything I can do for you right now?"

You're much too good to me. "No, there isn't."

She sighed. "Well, at least keep in touch, okay?"

I nodded. "I can do that."

Reluctantly, she left my room. She walked down the hallway toward her and Dad's bedroom, but stopped in the doorway. I watched her back expand with her breath. I saw her shoulders roll back. And as she suddenly held her head high, she let out the longest sigh I'd ever heard in my life.

Before slipping through the large double doors and disappearing behind them.

You're too good for any of us, Cecelia.

I finished getting myself ready for the day and covered up the best I could. I slipped on a pair of sunglasses and went rummaging around for a coat. Anything to slide up my arms in case there were bruises I'd missed somehow. I found a light jacket shoved in the back of my closet, neatly hanging from a hanger. A bomber jacket, made out of some lightweight material, that Cecilia had gotten me for Christmas a year or two ago.

I ripped it off the hanger and slipped it on. I grabbed my notebook and pen from my bedside table and slipped my wallet into the back pocket of my jeans, cursing myself for… well, everything.

Then I made my way downstairs.

With my eyes covered and that bomber jacket covering the rest of my body, I made my way out the front door. Nothing in tow except my wallet and that fucking notebook. I had one goal in mind for the day. And that shit had nothing to do with school. By the time I was done today, I'd have that entire list filled with ideas on how to get the fuck out of here. How to start a life for myself with mediocre grades and no life skills to speak of.

There had to be a way for me to get out without using resource shelters in the area.

I walked toward school, then kept on walking. I walked past Valley High, down the mile and a half stretch until the main part of our little side of town came into view. I crossed the road, eyeing the railroad tracks off to my right. Fear seized me as images of that night bombarded my mind's eye. Including the moment where I was sure that damn river would sweep me away.

Rae saved you. And look at what you're doing to her.

"I'm saving her from me," I murmured to myself.

I trotted across the road and found my way into a coffee shop. The one next to the grocery store, actually. I walked inside and felt all eyes on me. Some random high school kid with sunglasses on, a navy blue jacket that almost didn't fit, and a nose brace on his face. But, thankfully, it was still early. Which meant the morning rush was all drive-thru. No one really came inside.

Giving me the privacy I needed.

I ordered my coffee and stood there to wait for it. I was thankful to be there. The last place I wanted to be was at school. I couldn't face Rae. I knew she'd corner me and ask me about last night. About us. About what the fuck happened. I couldn't face her right now. Because I knew if I looked her in the eyes, I wouldn't be able to lie to her.

So my only option was to avoid her at all costs.

"One large black coffee with rosewater and caramel?"

I reached out for it. "Thanks."

"Can we get you anything else?"

I paused, reliving the memory of Rae in my bed that morning. "Actually, yes. Do you have computers here for the general public to use?"

The barista nodded. "Through the doorway in the corner and immediately to the right."

"I appreciate it."

I took large gulps of the coffee as I walked through the small coffee shop. I did as I was told, and found myself in a small room with seven or eight different computers. All of them were as nice as the ones my father had at the house. It was shocking, really. This dinky little coffeehouse with such up-to-date technology.

I wasn't complaining though.

I sat down in the far corner, thankful that I was tucked away from the world. I opened my notebook and logged in using the log-in information taped across the top of the monitor. After navigating to the web browser, I picked up my pen. I scratched out the two things I'd written last night in my sleepy stupor, then typed in my first search.

What to do after high school with terrible grades.

Much to my surprise, a lot popped up. I filtered through the articles and clicked on a couple of them. I scanned through and jotted down some valuable information. The articles I really wanted to read, I emailed to myself. Good reading material if I couldn't sleep again tonight. I jotted down a few things to research. Community colleges in California with the best rates. Scholarships and shit I could get without proving good grades. Jobs I'd be eligible for as an eighteen-year old with a high school diploma.

Literally, anything that might get me out of this fucking place.

I didn't want to stay in Riverbend. And eventually, I'd want out of the state altogether. I needed to get the hell away from this shit. The hell away from my father. The hell away from my life. I needed a fresh start. With people that didn't know me and police departments that didn't profile me. My search poured me into an overall state search. States that had the best services for runaway children and had the best social programs to help people get back on their feet.

And after emailing myself over thirty links to articles to read later, I sat back and stared at the screen as I finished the coffee that reminded me of Rae. Then a thought hit me. A thought that lingered a little too long. A thought I wanted answers to, even if I didn't follow through with it. So, I typed my question into the internet search bar just to see what would pop up.

Is it legal for an eighteen-year old to steal from their parents?

A last ditch effort, just in case nothing else panned out whatsoever.

4

RAELYNN

I stood at the entrance to my neighborhood, staring up at the sidewalk. As Michael and Allison walked down to me, I held out hope that Clint might show up. That he might come meet me like we'd done those few times before the accident. Michael kept looking at me with that pity-filled stare and Allison rubbed my back. I shrugged her touch off, tired of their antics and their pity and their bullshit.

I was tired of everyone's fucking bullshit.

Michael sighed. "You know he's not coming."

Allison shushed him. "Come on, let's get to school before we're late."

"Maybe he'll show up after lunch. Once he gets some rest."

"Or maybe he went to the hospital when he got up this morning. You never know."

"Not helping, Allison."

"Sorry."

I walked aimlessly with them into the school. I peeked over my shoulder just before we walked inside, and there was no trace of him. We took up our usual spot outside of my locker, my head on a swivel for him. And while my heart refused to give up hope, my mind already had. Rationally, my mind knew he wasn't coming. Maybe not for the rest of the week. Maybe not ever again. I wouldn't blame him for that, either. Running away and never coming back.

I wanted to run away and never come back.

Allison linked her arm through mine. "Come on, it's homeroom time."

I wandered through the day aimlessly. Listlessly. I didn't pay attention in my morning classes or even take notes. I sat at the back of the classroom and worked on homework, trying to knock it out. Because I knew once I got home, I wouldn't be able to focus. I felt hollow. Empty inside. Like someone had shoveled out my soul and replaced it with helium. I was late to classes because I kept pausing in the hallway, letting my mind take over and memories rip me back into the past.

I missed Clint more than I could stand.

My heart continued to remain optimistic, though. Because apparently, torturing me wasn't enough. I stared out the window of class and counted down the minutes to lunch. That was my only remaining hope. That Clint would simply show up for school late because of a doctor or a need for sleep or another brawl with his father, and I'd see him at lunch. My eyes followed the hands of the clock. My teacher's voice stayed muted the entire time. After quickly finishing my homework for the night, I abandoned all thought processes and relegated myself to the spinning hell of my mind.

Of my heart.

Of the war raging between the two.

The bell rang and it ripped me from my trance. I gathered up my things and made a beeline for the door and raced toward the cafeteria. My legs carried me as quickly as I could run. I didn't even bother stopping by my locker to discard my morning books. I wanted to get to Clint as soon as possible. If he was here, I wanted to be the first to greet him.

But when I turned the corner, I saw the cafeteria completely empty.

"Huh?"

A voice cleared itself behind me. "Can I help you?"

I whipped around, gazing into the eyes of our football coach. He quirked an eyebrow at me. "Skipping class?"

I paused. "Uh, no. I—it's lunch time, isn't it?"

He furrowed his brow. "No. It's not. It's only ten-fifteen."

"What?"

"Are you okay? You look a little pale, Miss…?"

"Sorry. Uh, sorry. I have to get to class."

I rushed past the football coach, feeling his eyes follow me down the hallway. I'd only gotten through first period? I felt disoriented. Confused. I could've sworn I'd gone to both of my morning periods before lunch.

"Rae?"

I heard our school guidance counselor call out my name. I slowly turned around as tears rushed my eyes. She came over to me, ushering me toward the main office. And before I knew it, we were in her office. With her door closing behind me. As my books fell from my arms.

While tears streaked my cheeks.

She handed me tissues and urged me to take a seat in front of her desk. I didn't want to talk. The last thing I wanted to do was tell anyone else about what was happening. But, she didn't ask me questions. She simply typed away on her computer, her eyes glued to the screen. Giving me as much privacy as she could while I sobbed my eyes out in her fucking office.

Like a damn child.

You are a child.

I didn't feel like a child, though. I hadn't felt like one in years. The shit I'd dealt with. The bullshit my mother put us through. All this insanity with Clint and his father. Children didn't deal with this. Adults did. Adults tackled these kinds of issues.

Guess the grass isn't always greener on the other side.

I cried until I had no more tears. The guidance counselor—I couldn't recall her name—continued working until my crying subsided. I cried so hard my eyes swelled shut. I slumped into the chair until the back of my neck sat against the top crook of its cushion. I gazed up at the ceiling, wondering what Clint was doing. Wondering where he was.

Wondering if he was all right.

"Do you want to talk about it?"

I sighed, closing my eyes. "No."

"Are you sure?"

"Yeah."

"Is it something to do with Clint?"

I paused. "Why do you ask?"

"I noticed he's absent today."

"How do you know that?"

"I have more jobs than tending to the mental and emotional well-being of the student population here."

I sighed. "Gotcha."

"Would you like some advice?"

I snickered. "I haven't told you anything."

"Doesn't mean I don't have advice."

"Sure. Go ahead, then."

"Whatever's going on, address it head-on. Talk to whoever you need to in order to get things cleared up. This is your most important year. This is when you determine plans for college. Nail down your grades for scholarships. Create rapport with teachers who will give you shining recommendations for school. Whatever's happening that has you so distracted, talk to whoever you need to in order to fix it. Because when it comes to your future, you're allowed to be selfish."

It sounded like some shit out of a self-help book. And yet, it made all the sense in the world. The only problem with her advice was that I couldn't talk to them. Clint wasn't here, and if even I thought about talking to his father, I was certain he'd beat me into the ground, too. And even if I could get my mother to sit down and have a serious conversation with me about D.J., she'd brush off anything I had to say to her because 'You're a teenager and don't get it.'

But it was sound advice.

"Thanks," I murmured.

"Anytime. You're free to go to class whenever you want. But you're more than welcome to stay here. You know, until another student comes knocking on the door or something."

I slowly sat up. "How many students do you see in a day, anyway?"

She sighed. "More than I like to admit with issues I still can't believe most days."

"In a good way, or...?"

"'Or.' Yes."

Guess the grass really isn't greener on the other side.

"What time is it?"

The counselor peeked over at me. "Almost time for the lunch bell."

"I've been in here that long?"

"You have, yes."

I sighed. "Great."

"Do you lose time like this often?"

"No. Just today."

"Another reason why you should unload the stressors off your chest."

I nodded. "Yeah. I got it."

She grinned. "Just making sure."

"Actually, I'd like to ask you something."

She turned toward me. "Ask away."

"Is it possible for an eighteen-year-old to survive in this world with a high school diploma and nothing else?"

"Generally speaking? Or is this for something specific?"

"Just general. I'm curious."

She paused. "Uh huh."

"Really. I am."

"Okay. I'll bite. Yes, generally speaking, it's possible to make a good life for oneself without a college degree. But it's still hard. Most jobs will start people at the very bottom, and make them prove themselves twice over against their college-educated counterparts. And in bigger cities and states like California, that percentage drops significantly."

"So what you're saying is someone who only has a high school degree would have to get out of California before attempting to build a life for themselves." ·

She nodded. "For the greatest overall chance of success, yes."

"How can they do that without money?"

"There's the catch-22. I'll let you know once I know."

I snickered. "Well, thanks for the advice."

"My office is open to you anytime. But can you relay a message to Clint for me?"

I paused. "Sure."

"Tell him college is nothing like high school. Especially a community college. Let him know that even a two-year technical degree would set him up much better than only having a high school diploma."

I blinked. "I didn't ask that question for Clint."

"I'm sure you didn't."

She turned to face her computer just as the lunch bell rang.

And while part of me was frustrated with her for assuming my position, I couldn't hate her for it. Because she'd been right. Maybe I was frustrated because she was right. Because I'd become so easy for people to read. I gathered my things and made my way for my locker, my mind in knots as I put my books away.

And pulled out my afternoon books.

As I made my way for the cafeteria—again—I wondered how long it might take for Clint to come back to school. Or if he'd come back at all. I hoped he did. His grades were slowly doing better. I mean, not by much. He was still a hearty C average student. But the one D he had in history had come up due to his last test score. If he worked really hard at it, he might be able to get some of his classes into the 'B' range before the end of the school year. Which would greatly affect his GPA.

And any chance he had at getting into a two-year technical college out of state somewhere.

"Hey there, beautiful."

"What's for lunch?"

"You want me to go through the line for you?"

"They've got discounted sodas today."

I rolled my eyes. "You guys can stop hanging off me now."

Michael chuckled. "Not our fault you haven't spoken to us all day."

Allison nodded. "Yeah, Rae. We're worried about you."

I rolled my eyes. "You should be worried about Clint."

Allison furrowed her brow. "What makes you think we're not?"

The three of us hopped into the lunch line and I kept my eyes peeled for him. I'd never seen Clint actually eat lunch here. So I kept darting my eyes through the glassless window cutouts of the cement wall that separated the lunch line from the cafeteria dining area. I mindlessly paid for my food, grabbed a Dr. Pepper and headed for our seats in the corner. My backpack lay at my feet and my food stayed untouched as my eyes scanned the room, searching frantically for any sign of Clint.

But he was nowhere to be found.

Michael sat in front of me. "Just give him some time."

Allison patted my back. "He needs to rest. Recuperate. Process, and all that."

I shook my head. "I can't shake this feeling that something's just—"

I didn't know how to explain it.

I drew in deep, quick breaths as I cracked open my soda, chugging it back and relishing the burn of the carbonation. I tried to push my tears away, the hurt, the anguish. I didn't want people to see me break down and cry. I had cried in front of the school counselor, and that was enough. I didn't want the entire school talking about how I'd been bawling my eyes out at lunch over Clinton Fucking Clarke. Since he was nowhere in sight.

That didn't bode well for either of us. And told much more of a story than I wanted the school to know.

Especially since I had no idea what came next.

5

———

CLINTON

After sitting at that damn computer until almost eleven in the morning, I was out the door. I walked up and down the road, trying to figure out where to go or what to do next. No bike. No car. Forty bucks in my pocket. I didn't want to go home because I didn't want Cecilia questioning where I'd been or worrying even more about me. And I sure as hell didn't want to run into my father, just in case he came home from the hospital today.

I meandered until I came across a familiar sight. The park. That damned park I'd found Rae sitting in that night. I chuckled bitterly to myself. It was as if the world were conspiring against me today. Using everything it could to remind me of the girl I'd left behind. For a good reason.

Guess the world didn't care about my reasons.

I walked over to a bench in the corner, shielded by a few of the trees that still stood in the abandoned place. And as I sat down, I stared at that bench. The bench where Rae and I had our first kiss. Where I first felt her skin against mine. Where I found her, holding back tears and trying to put on a brave face while her entire world caved around her.

Like mine.

"What a fucking mess," I murmured to myself as I sat down. And the second my ass touched the bench, I felt something stiffen. I felt something preventing me from sitting down and I shot back up. I looked behind me. Had I sat on something? But I didn't see anything on the bench.

Holy shit, I have my phone with me.

I ripped my phone out of my pocket and sat back down. I opened up my email, clicking link after link as I read through the articles. Some of them were bullshit, and some of them were full of help. I pulled my notebook and pen back out, jotting down things on random pages that I wanted to remember. Names of community colleges in the state that would take high school kids with shitty grades. States in the country that would actually provide a free community college education to those who declared residency. I didn't even know that was a fucking thing, free education.

By the time I'd read through all those articles, I actually felt hope surge through my veins.

Maybe I can do this after all.

My stomach growling pulled me from my trance, so I slipped my phone back into my pocket. I gathered my things and walked back the same way I came, then slipped into the grocery store. Rae's grocery store. The one where all this bullshit started in the first place. I made my way to the deli and picked up a couple of sandwiches. Some fries. Even grabbed an energy drink from the machine. I felt people staring at me as I went through the line. The line Rae usually worked.

Only it wasn't Rae behind the register.

And I found that I didn't really like that.

You miss her.

I shook the thought away and walked my ass outside. I sat down on a bench near the front doors and tore into the food I'd bought. I wondered what Cecilia was doing. If she was worried about me. I wondered what she was thinking. If she was worried about the status of her marriage with my father. In my eyes? She needed to be more hellbent on taking care of herself. Finding a safe haven to run toward. Finding a way out of this hellhole. Because I knew my father would bring down hell on us all once he got out of that hospital.

She needed to take care of her own safety.

She's staying behind for you.

I growled to myself. The last thing I needed was yet another innocent woman going to bat for me. Rae tried it, and it almost got her hurt. And I didn't have the energy to push another good woman away. Cecilia had been a godsend. An adult who showed me what it really meant for a parent to care about a fucking child. I didn't want to push her away. The easy route would be for her to pack her shit and leave me behind. I knew how to deal with that. I knew how to write people off the moment they abandoned me. Mostly. Kind of.

Except your own mother.

Holy shit, I was a fucked-up human being.

I finished my food and tried not to give my thoughts any more energy to grow. Now I needed to concentrate on getting home. Even though cooler temperatures were falling over the city, that didn't stop the sun from beating down against our backs. Sweating me to my fucking core as I sat on the bench beside the sliding doors of the grocery store. I pulled my phone out of my pocket and checked the time. Fucking hell, it was almost three o'clock.

You'll need a ride to get home on time.

I searched for the taxi companies in the area before calling one up. I didn't want to make an Uber account and have to use it or anything. Because if I did, Dad would know I hadn't been in school. He'd see that charge to the credit card and flip his fucking nozzle. As if he didn't already do that, anyway. The last thing I needed was any more of a reason for my father to want me dead. Because I'd done enough to warrant him killing me.

I found myself dreading the moment that he got home from that hospital.

I ordered the taxi, and thirty minutes later it showed up. I rattled off my address and the man drove me home. And I just gave him the thirty bucks I still had left over from lunch. I didn't care how much the trip cost. I didn't care how much I was over-paying him by. The only thing I cared about was whether or not Dad was home. Whether or not I'd open this door and feel his wrath beating against my body.

Literally.

Until I bled to death.

I drew in a deep breath. As the taxi pulled away, I started for the front door. I opened it up and walked inside, bracing for my father's voice. But when I heard Cecilia yelp, I whipped my head up.

"What? What's wrong?"

Her hand pressed against her chest. "You scared the living daylights out of me, Clint."

I closed the door. "I didn't mean to startle you. It's just me."

I saw her book on the floor. She scrambled for it, trying to right herself on the couch again. Her cheeks were flushed, her eyes wide from the shock. My heart ached for her. How scared she was for my father to come home. But, when she lifted her eyes to meet mine again, the fear melted away. And replacing it was this cool sort of strength I'd come to learn she possessed.

A trait I envied quite a bit.

"How was your day?"

Her voice ripped me from my thoughts. "Uh, good."

"Did you make it to school?"

I nodded slowly. "Yep. I did."

"Are you sure about that?"

"Why wouldn't I be?"

"You want to try one more time?"

And when she grinned, I shook my head.

"No, I didn't make it to school."

She nodded. "I was home when the school called and told me you were absent from roll call in homeroom."

"I don't think I've ever known you to linger in this house."

"I've never had a reason to, until now."

I chuckled. "Waiting for Dad and his wrath to come wafting through the door?"

Her face stayed serious. "No. Waiting for you."

Her words clenched my heart. It became hard to breathe. I'd never had someone do that for me. Hang around all day, waiting for me. I didn't know how to process that. How to feel about it.

I drew in a deep breath. "I'm worried about you."

Cecilia nodded. "I'm worried about you, too."

"I didn't mean to scare you or anything."

"You didn't. I know you can handle yourself. I figured you went on a walk into town, or something."

"I did."

"So… how's town?"

I snickered. "It's town. How was your day at the house?"

"It was… a day at the house."

I nodded. "It's not like you to hang around here like this. Just… sitting here and biding your time."

"I suppose we're all changing, in a way."

"How so?"

"Well, for one, you stood up for yourself. In a way I've never seen you do. I mean, I expected it eventually. But I didn't expect it to be for anyone other than yourself. Not only did you stand up to your father, but you did it for my sake. You've grown a lot, Clinton."

I didn't wince when she called me by my first name. "I guess that happens as life goes on."

"You shouldn't have to worry about your father, though. About whether or not he's home. You leave him to me. I'll figure this out."

"You know I'm not going to do that."

She got up from the couch. "I know you're not. But that isn't going to stop me from reminding you that it isn't your duty as the child of this house to meddle in adult affairs like this."

"I've been meddling in adult affairs ever since my father started using his hands to parent."

I watched as Cecilia approached me. She stood in front of me, clad in a pristine royal blue dress with dainty white gold jewelry peppering her body. Her makeup looked like perfection. Her hair was completely straight and pulled back, with wisps falling into her face. She reached her hand up and cupped my cheeks, flooding my body with warmth.

A warmth I only had memories of when it came to my mother.

"You've been through a lot in your life, Clint. And while I'm not your mother, that doesn't mean I don't worry about you."

I closed my eyes. "I know."

"My only regret is that I didn't step in sooner. That I never stopped your father from—"

"It's not your fault."

"No, it's not. But, I have a responsibility in all this. I knew what was taking place, and I never did anything to stop it. Or report it. That's on me, Clint. Part of where you're standing right now is on —is—uh—"

The second she drew in a shuddering breath, I wrapped my arms around her. I pulled my stepmother closely into me and felt her arms drape around me. Her warmth brought tears to my eyes. Memories of my mother came flooding back to the forefront of my mind. Memories of my mother caring for me. Rocking with me.

Loving me and cherishing me and singing to me as she held me close.

I buried my face in Cecilia's hair, trying to cling to this feeling. To the idea that someone even remotely akin to a parent could actually give a shit about me.

I sighed. "Please don't cry."

She nodded quickly and sniffled.

"Well, um, dinner's in the oven. And you smell like you need a shower."

She pulled away from me as I chuckled softly.

"I suppose I don't smell the greatest."

She wrinkled her nose. "You really don't. Go get cleaned up, and when you're done, dinner will be ready."

I reached out and wiped a stray tear off her cheek. I saw the pain and the guilt flooding Cecilia's eyes. I'd never seen her like this. So downtrodden and… and sad. Just plain sadness. It hurt me, truly. Because through all this, I'd come to see how incredible of a woman she really was. Strong, steadfast, dedicated, and actually intelligent. Broken, like me. In a lot of ways due to her family. Like me.

I stroked her cheek. "I'm proud to call you my stepmother."

She snickered. "And I hope, one day, I earn the honor of calling you my stepson."

She quickly turned on her bare feet and padded back into the kitchen, leaving me there to hurt even more. The fact that she didn't feel she could call me her stepson hurt. Especially after everything that had happened. Everything she'd helped me through. But I knew she said that because she felt guilty. Not because I'd done anything wrong.

So I dragged myself upstairs and got myself cleaned up for dinner.

I stepped into the shower with aches and pains in places on my body I didn't know existed. When I came out of the shower, wonderful smells filled my nostrils. I smelled basil and honey. Starches and gravy. I smelled butter and blueberries and sugar in the air. It pulled me downstairs. I went down for dinner in nothing but a pair of sweatpants and an old, ragged black shirt.

And I found dinner sprawled out on the kitchen table. With two place settings.

"We're eating at the table?"

Cecilia set our drinks down. "Why not?"

I paused. "I don't know. I'm just not—used to having family dinner. I guess."

She snickered. "Well, I'm not your father. I like eating with family. So get used to it is all I can tell you."

And when she winked at me, it made me smile. Truly smile, for the first time since yesterday evening.

"I can do that," I said.

6

———

RAELYNN

I didn't want to go, but I gave my word. During my last period, Michael and Allison both pressured me to join them for dinner tonight. Sushi, apparently. I didn't feel like going out, though. I didn't feel like joining them for anything. I wanted to run myself a bath, get into the pathetic tub and cry my eyes out while indulging in a bag full of cookies. But they were my friends and I knew they were trying their best to cheer me up.

So I promised them I'd be there.

Michael wanted to pick me up, but I refused. I'd get there somehow. Some way. I pulled on an old pair of jeans and a T-shirt, then threw my hair up into a bumpy ponytail. I looked like a hazard zone. The bags underneath my eyes were more prominent than ever and my skin looked pale. Well, paler than it usually was. I sighed as I walked away from the mirror, making my way downstairs.

"Where you headed?"

I paused at the sound of D.J.'s voice.

"Sweetheart?" Mom asked.

I sighed. "Heading out to dinner with Michael and Allison."

D.J. snickered. "You aren't going to eat dinner with me and your mother? She's been cooking."

I slowly turned around. "No, I'm not. I'll be back around eight or so."

"Where are you headed for dinner? So we know where you are."

"Not your responsibility to know where I am."

Mom sighed. "Please, just answer his question."

I glared at her. "Just because you put up with his antics so our bills get paid doesn't mean I have to."

Mom gasped. "Excuse me?"

D.J. stood up from the couch. "You apologize to your mother."

I scoffed. "Yeah, no thanks. No apologies needed for the truth, no matter how hard it is to hear."

"You get over here right now so we can have a talk. Your attitude has been atrocious lately."

"Pretty big word for a drug dealer."

Mom shot up from her seat. "You take that back right now, young lady."

"Do as your mother says."

I shrugged. "Sorry that I brought up a rumor on the street."

D.J. lunged at me and I dropped my purse. I was ready for a fucking fight. I was ready to take this asshole down with nothing but my hands. Mom held him back, talking softly in his ear as my nostrils flared in anger. I silently dared him with his eyes. Dared him to come at me. To lay his hands on me.

I'd get his ass thrown in jail and we'd all be rid of this fucker.

When the two of them sat back down on the couch, D.J. snuggled my mother. Ran his hands over her thighs. I watched her kiss his neck and it made me sick to look at. I picked up my purse and stormed out of the house, making my way for my bike. And as I threw my leg over the rusted piece of shit, I made my way into town.

Straight for the sushi place.

I parked my bike, but didn't have anything to tie it off. So I simply tossed the hunk of rust down onto the sidewalk and made my way inside. The breeze of the air conditioning felt good. I stood there for a second, letting it dry off the beads of sweat working their way down my face. And when I felt partially human again, I started meandering around the restaurant.

I found Michael and Allison in a booth.

"Shit, she's here."

"Hey, Rae!"

I quirked an eyebrow as the two of them leapt away from one

another. I mean, Michael practically shoved Allison off his body. Their lips were red. Allison's neck was flushed. It didn't take a genius to figure out what they'd been doing in this back booth all by themselves.

It made me feel like the third wheel, though.

Which wasn't how I wanted to spend my dinner.

I ordered my drink as Allison made room for me on the other side of her. But I saw how they had their hands intertwined in the darkness. It made me miss Clint. It made me want him here. I wanted someone to kiss. Someone to snuggle against. Someone's hand to hold.

Specifically, his.

Michael whistled. "So what do you two want for dinner? It's on me, by the way."

I shook my head. "You don't have to do that."

Allison giggled. "That's so kind of you. Thank you."

Michael chuckled. "Hey, it's the least I can do."

Allison smiled. "You do so much more than that, you know. You're just… very kind. In general. I like that."

"Well, do you know what I like about you?"

I piped up. "What's that?"

The two of them looked at me before Allison's cheeks flushed.

"Oh, sorry. Thought you were talking to me."

I tossed them each a look before I buried myself back into the menu. I hated being that person. But I also wouldn't spend my entire dinner hour with them listening to their sickeningly, disgusting flirting back and forth. Yes, I was happy for them. But they had to respect what I was going through. Because if the tables were turned, I would've done the same damn thing.

Respected their circumstances.

The waiter came by and took our orders. Michael ordered for Allison and she giggled like the schoolgirl she was. I murmured my order before tossing the menu back to the waiter and thanking him for the extra water. I felt empty. Dead. Dark, deep within the pit of my soul. I didn't understand this kind of hurt. I'd never experienced it before. I mean, with my father, it wasn't my fault. He left well before I had any memories of him. But Clint?

Maybe I'd done something to push him away.

Maybe I'm the reason he's gone.

Michael cleared his throat. "So how's that bike holding up?"

I whipped my head up. "Huh?"

Allison smiled softly. "Your bike. That's how you got here, right?"

"Unless you took a taxi."

"You know she hates taxis, Michael."

"I mean, it's an option. You never know."

"You're so silly."

He smiled. "And you're so cute."

I rolled my eyes. "Yeah, I rode my bike. It's a hunk of rusted junk, but it gets the job done."

Allison giggled profusely. "That's what she said."

Michael snorted with laughter as I slowly panned my eyes over to her.

"What did you say?"

Allison smiled brightly. "Michael taught me those jokes. You know, using 'that's what she said' behind a phrase that could technically be construed as… dirty."

I snickered at the way she whispered 'dirty.' As if she'd be shot into the bowels of hell for saying it out loud.

"That was a good one, beautiful. Way to go."

She smiled. "Thanks, Michael."

Clint used to call me beautiful. "Well, it was a good one. Yes."

"Thanks, Rae."

Our food came and I entertained myself with eating. While Allison and Michael entertained themselves with, well, one another. They kept charging headfirst into conversations meant only for them. Which threw gasoline on the fire of my pain. When would this let up? When would it stop hurting so much? I mean, it'd only been one day. How the fuck was I supposed to keep putting one foot in front of the other and acting like things were okay if this was day one?

How did my two best friends expect me to sit here and watch them practically fondle one another when this was day one without Clint?

Every time they thought I wasn't looking, they snuck a kiss or shared bites of their food. At least, I thought so. I thought maybe they thought I couldn't see them. Because if that wasn't the case, then that meant they were blatantly making the conversation about them instead of including me.

And I didn't want to believe my two best friends were that cold-hearted.

I knew they were trying to get my mind off Clint. But, they had to know that what they were doing wasn't helping. Right? I mean, come on! They were pressing themselves against one another! I don't know when the hell their pseudo-relationship took a shift into the physical realm. But they needed to keep it behind closed doors.

Just be happy for them, Rae. They were happy for you.

Sushi was for dinner, but guilt was dessert. And instead of saying something to the two of them, I just let them roam. I didn't interject into their conversations and I turned my head every time they kissed one another. Because I knew I felt this way out of anger. And jealousy. Out of not having Clint in my life anymore.

Maybe they'll leave you, too. Now that they have one another.

Dinner wrapped up and I didn't fight Michael when he paid. I peeled away from the two of them to head outside. Because I wanted to get on my bike and go for a ride. I wanted to work off my anger. Work off my frustration. Ride around until D.J. was thrown off a bridge.

But I didn't see my bike on the sidewalk.

"Where's your bike?"

Michael's voice made me want to strangle him, for some reason.

"Uh oh. Should we call the police?"

Allison's voice grated on my ears as I stood there.

"You need a ride home?"

"Tell us what to do and we can get it done."

"Seriously, Rae. What do you need right now? Because we're here for you."

Yeah, when you aren't making out over dinner. "I just need a ride home."

Michael nodded. "I can do that."

I leaned my head against the glass of his backseat window. Allison took Michael's hand from across the console, their fingers laced together. Silent tears brewed behind my eyes. With every blink, they threatened to pour out. As if I hadn't already cried until my voice was hoarse over some asshole who didn't give a shit about me. They pulled into my driveway and I didn't bother looking to see if D.J.'s car was there. I just hopped out, happy to be out of their orbit so they could go fuck and get it over with already.

Allison rolled her window down. "If you need anything, call me. Okay?"

I nodded. "Will do."

"Promise?"

I sighed. "Yep. I promise."

"Same goes for me."

"Thanks, Michael."

Then Allison rolled up her window and the two of them took off.

I stood in the driveway, watching them fade away. Watching them ride off into their own little world. I used to do that on Clint's bike. I used to wrap my arms around him and cling to him as we rode around town. Or back to his house. Or back to my house. The horizon had been for our taking. Life had been ours to grasp. And now, I stood alone in my driveway. Watching my two best friends who were absolutely in love pave their own path into the sunset.

While I stood there.

Alone.

Like I'd always been in my life.

7

———

CLINTON

*M*idnight.

As I checked my cell phone for the time, midnight stared back at me. Midnight, on a school night, and I still wasn't asleep. I'd taken pain medication. I'd taken a sleep aid. And here I lay, staring at my fucking ceiling.

Wondering about Rae.

No matter how hard I tried, I couldn't stop thinking about her. Everything reminded me of her, and I hated it. I wanted it to be over. Every single part of this painful journey reminded me why I didn't do the fucking relationship thing. The pain in my broken heart reminded me of why I fucked and kept moving. Why I took what I wanted and gave very little back in return.

Because this was what heartbreak felt like.

I did it for her own good, though.

I rolled over onto my side. Despite the pain in my face plate, I buried myself into the pillow. I stared at the wall, giving myself yet another muted surface to look at as my mind spiraled. I wanted to call Rae and tell her about all of the things I'd researched. All the possibilities that were apparently out there for me. And if she wanted to, she could be part of that. I wanted those words to come out of my mouth. I wanted to tell her how much I missed her. How much I wanted her. How much I needed her.

How much I love her.

I sighed as I rolled onto my back again. I was a stomach sleeper. So I knew I wouldn't sleep well. Or hard. But I wanted to sleep a little bit, at least. While my father wasn't at the house still. I didn't know his condition at the hospital. Frankly, I didn't care. Hell, I didn't give a shit if the hospital kept him for weeks on end because of complications stemming from the night before. So long as it kept him out of this house.

And away from us.

Rae could be over more.

I growled at the thoughts racing through my mind. I turned over onto my other side and grabbed my phone again. 12:06. I'd killed six entire minutes doing nothing but burying myself in my own thoughts.

Why can't it be six entire hours?

I tossed my phone back onto the bedside table. I snuggled down underneath the covers and closed my eyes. Maybe if I faked being asleep, my body would eventually slip into it. I mean, everyone said *Fake it until you make it.* Maybe that shit actually worked.

So I screwed my eyes shut.

Rae's face bombarded my memories. Her laughter echoed in the caverns of my ears. And I swore I felt her lips against mine. That soft plumpness pushing against me. My eyes ripped open. I panted softly for air. I rolled over and reached for my cell phone, trying to figure out what time it was.

One-fifteen in the morning.

I tossed my cell phone onto the pillow next to my head. Then I closed my eyes. At least it worked; pretending to sleep led to sleep. Not a restful sleep, though. I didn't want to see Rae in my dreams. I didn't want to relive the beauty of her body before waking up and finding myself in an empty bed. I couldn't take it. My heart couldn't tolerate it.

Should've thought about that before leaving her.

I growled as I turned to the side. I picked up another pillow and pressed it against my ear. I blocked myself away from the world, hoping it would all fade away with time. But the further I sank into my mattress, the more my mind swirled with thoughts of her. How was school? Did she have a lot of homework? What did we talk about in history? What did she do after school today? Did she have to work? Did she get home safely?

Does she miss me?

I peeked my eye open and saw my phone sitting there. Taunting me. Mocking me. Whispering things in my ear. *Call her. Just once. It'll be okay. Once you hear her voice, you can sleep easily.*

I almost caved, too.

Instead, I turned over onto my other side. I sandwiched my aching face between two pillows and forced my eyes to close. I drew in deep breaths, helping to push away memories of her. My mind fell blank. As my medication finally took hold, I felt myself actually drifting off to sleep. I welcomed it with open arms. I welcomed the pain medication as it continued to dull the ache in my bones. And as I hovered between sleepiness and being awake, I felt myself sigh.

I need to get out of this fucking town.

My mind gave way to thoughts of my future. Darkness swallowed me whole and dragged me under. I saw the list I'd made rushing behind my eyes. Reminding me of all the choices I had at my disposal, despite my insistence that I didn't. Community colleges and jobs that paid for schooling and only required a high school diploma. Entire lives I'd plotted out that were attainable for me the second I could get away from my father.

So many pieces soared around in my head.

For instance, would my father still be legally obligated to hand over my trust fund? I knew he had one set up for me. But could he take that away? It was technically mine. The second I turned eighteen, I gained control of it. I mean, he still lorded over it. Watched my every move with it. But I still technically had access to it. Could I shift that money into another account without his consent? Could I withdraw it and stash it somewhere so he couldn't take it back if he wanted?

The last thing before I got swept under by sleep was making a mental note. I needed to look into banking laws and call a few people so they could answer some questions.

Then, she appeared again.

"Clint?"

I turned around. "Rae?"

"Hey, Clint!"

I furrowed my brow. "What are you doing here?"

She paused. "What do you mean, what am I doing here? You called me."

"No, I didn't."

"Are you sure? Because I'm pretty sure you butt-dialed me while you were moaning my name."

A grin spread across her face and I looked down. And as the world tilted over on itself, I found my legs naked. Spread. With my cock resting in my hand. Rae's face darkened and she licked her lips, causing electricity to shoot through my body.

"I uh, I don't know where—"

Rae giggled. "Looks like you could use some help."

I panted. "Are you—willing to help?"

She quirked an eyebrow. "I can't believe you even have to ask that question."

In a flash, she was on top of me. Dressed in an outfit completely different from before. Her beautiful skin, softly sunkissed with summer's grace, was draped in red lingerie. A bra with her tits spilling out. A thong that emphasized her curves. A lacy robe slipped down her arms as she straddled me, gazing into my eyes. My cock pulsed in my hand. I felt it leaking as it begged to be within her. And as her hands fell against my chest, I licked my lips.

"How's this for help?"

Her lips fell to mine and I wrapped my arms around her. Both of them. Leaving my cock to do as it wished. Her warmth drew me in. Her taste reminded me of the drug she'd become. I rolled her over, grunting as I pinned her beneath me.

Then I ripped that thong clear off her body.

"Clint!"

"You're mine, Rae."

She gasped as my lips fell to her neck.

I raked my teeth along her skin, pinning her wrists above her head as I kissed down her chest, feeling her excess fill the divots of my body. I brought her hands to my hair and had her fist the locks I'd grown out just so she could cling to me. And as I kissed my way down her body, I sucked against her skin, leaving marks that made me grin as she jumped and darted around.

"Clint. Oh, that tickl—! Oh, you—Clint, fuck."

I tossed her legs over my shoulders and settled in for a meal. Her scent filled my nostrils, letting loose the animal within its cage. I dove between her thighs. I felt her arousal coating my cheeks. I lapped until she shivered. Until she bucked ravenously against my face. I slipped my hands underneath her ass cheeks. I squeezed them, lifting her hips to my face. Feasting on the buffet of her body as her legs locked out against my back.

"Clint!"

I lapped heavily against her slit as she shook for me. I looked up, watching as her tits bounced for my viewing pleasure. Her skin flushed. Her back arched. Her sounds became choked as my tongue continued its assault. I didn't let up. I flicked her, faster. Harder. Visibly shaking her as I slowly lowered her back to the bed.

"No. No. Clint. I can't. No. I can't. Clint. Please. No."

I paused. "No?"

But she fisted my hair and pulled me back, causing me to chuckle against her pussy lips.

"More, please."

Her soft whimpers filled me with longing. The juice she offered me filled my stomach with need. My cock pulsed against the bedsheets and I started rutting, fucking their softness as I slid one finger into Rae's beautiful body. I crooked my digit and watched her jaw fall open. Her heels pressed into my back as she arched her hips closer to my mouth. Wanting everything I had for her.

So I gave it to her.

"Holy fucking hell."

Her growls encompassed me. I rocked harder against the mattress. I slid another finger inside her beautiful body, slowly working against her walls. I tickled the inside of her pussy. I felt her losing control of her body. Her toes curled and her body flushed against as broken syllables fell from her lips.

But I understood one of them. The only syllable I really wanted to hear.

"Come. Come. Come. Come."

She sprayed me and I chuckled with delight. I stuffed her full of my fingers before letting my pinky wander. Her thighs were drenched. My neck glistened with her mark. I lapped her swollen nub deeply, giving her a chance to recover as she heaved for air. Her hands fell away from my hair. She lay there, sprawled out. Ready for me to devour in any way I wished.

My pinky pressed against her puckered hole.

"Clint?"

My eyes found hers. "Yes?"

"I've never—I don't—"

I slowly rimmed her asshole with my fingertips, watching her gasp. Listening to her sigh. I felt her ass release, ushering me in as I breached her virginal hole. Goosebumps traveled along my body. Heat rose at the base of my ballsack. She quivered around my fingers, moaning for more as I sank my fingers all the way into her body.

"That's it. That's my beautiful girl."

"Oh, Clint."

"Take it, Rae. Take what you want."

"I don't know if I can come again."

"I know you can. I know you've got one more for me."

"Please, I can't. It feels too good."

"I'm not stopping until you come for me again."

She whimpered as I fucked her with my fingers. In, and out. Over and over as I watched her tremble. Her body was mine to do with what I wished. Her curves were flushed with the pleasure only I brought her. I wrapped my hand around my cock and stroked with delight. Her hips bucked against my hands as my thumb fell against her clit. I circled it softly, watching her eyes roll back. I stroked my cock to the rhythm of her hips, feeling that heady sensation finally taking over.

"Rae. I love you. I love you so fucking much."

8

———

RAELYNN

Brm! Brm! Brm! Brm! Brm! Brm!

My hand slammed against my cell phone, and I didn't know if I'd snoozed the alarm or turned it off. Either way, I rolled over, burying myself underneath the covers as I drifted back to sleep. I didn't struggle with sleep, either. All my body wanted to do was sleep. Sleep, cry, and sleep some more. I didn't want to do homework. I didn't give a shit about classes. Day two of absolute misery, and it threatened to swallow the whole of my future.

Because I didn't even give a shit about graphic design anymore.

I hadn't drawn in days. Which was unheard of. There were no doodles in the margins of my notes and textbooks. Mostly because I wasn't cracking open my textbooks or taking notes in class. There were no faint pen outlines on my arms of doodles I'd done before and after school. Because it took too much energy to pick up that pen. To trace those lines. To come up with an image I wanted to draw.

I was scared I'd end up drawing Clint's face everywhere.

Brm! Brm! Brm! Brm! Brm! Brm!

"Fucking alarm."

I slammed my hand against my phone again before a knock came at my door. I threw the covers off my head, my hair falling into my face. I blew at the tendrils, slowly working them out of my vision. And as I heaved a heavy sigh, I heard my mother's voice through the door.

"It's time to get up, honey. You have to leave in twenty minutes."

I sighed. "Great."

I threw the covers off my body and slowly eased myself out of bed. Every step I took, I groaned. Every time I lifted my arms, I grunted. I hadn't even bothered to change into pajamas last night. I still wore the clothes I'd worn to that dumbass sushi dinner. And they stank. I wrinkled my nose as I tossed them into the hamper, knowing damn good and well I'd have to do laundry after school today.

Then I shuffled to the bathroom in nothing but my underwear.

I cleaned myself up and splashed water in my face. I washed myself down with a soapy washcloth at the sink before drying myself off. I'd be late to school, but I didn't care. First time for everything, I guess. I slathered on the deodorant and threw my hair into a messy bun. I didn't have time to do anything else with it. Like wash it.

"Rae?"

I rolled my eyes. "I'm coming, Mom."

"Just making sure you're up."

I threw on some clothes and made my way downstairs, hoping beyond all hope I didn't stink. I'd have to change my bedsheets, too. But that could be left for another time. The smell of breakfast wafted up my nose. Bacon and pancakes, which only meant one thing.

"Morning, tiger."

Fucking D.J. "Morning."

Mom smiled. "You sleep well?"

I snickered. "Sure."

D.J. slid me a glass of orange juice. "Your mother asked you a question. You don't have to cock such an attitude."

I pushed the glass away. "When are you going to get it through your head that I'm not your daughter?"

"Rae."

"I'm just trying to be a help to her. And I know she needs help with you sometimes."

"D.J.!"

I scoffed. "Yeah, whatever."

D.J. stabbed at his pancakes. "I care for your mother. I'll be around for a while. We might as well both get used to it."

"Oh, really? So, do you frequently beat on and bruise up things you care about?"

Mom pulled my chair out from the table. "That's enough. Come over here."

I rolled my eyes and followed her into the living room. What the fuck she was upset about, I'd never know. Even if D.J. married my mother, he still legally wasn't my father. So he didn't have a place to tell me what to do or give me some sort of morning pep talk.

"Can you make it quick? I'm going to be late for school."

Mom narrowed her eyes. "You're already late. So suck it up and listen."

I shook my head. "No, you suck it up and listen. I don't know what happened in your life to make you think you have to stick around with a man like him. A man that beats on you and makes you feel like shit. I don't know if you really do feel like you can't provide for this family or find a job that pays the bills, but it's not my issue anymore. And neither is he. If you want to ruin your life with a man like him, go ahead. But that doesn't mean I have to accept it or bring him into some fold. For years, Mom, it's been this way. For years, you've turned to men like D.J. for comfort and solace when all they do is stab you in the back and make you cry. And instead of bettering yourself and trying to pull yourself out of whatever bullshit mindset this is, you keep ending up with these guys. You keep pursuing them. You keep going out and getting drunk, and you drag me along with it."

Her eyes widened. "You take that back."

I shook my head. "No, I won't. Because you need to hear it. You're sick, Mom. Your head isn't right. And until you get your head right, your life is always going to be like this. But just because you're willing to accept this doesn't mean I have to. I'm not listening to D.J. I'm not accepting him into my life. And I'm sure as hell not holding my tongue any longer in this house."

"I think you're done speaking to your mother that way."

D.J. came around the corner as Mom's eyes welled with tears.

"Yeah, well. Make sure not to beat on her too hard this time. Okay?"

Mom gasped. "Rae!"

I leveled my eyes at D.J. "But remember my promise. Always remember my promise."

I backtracked toward the front door and scooped up my things. My backpack, my purse, and my sanity. I tossed it all over my shoulders and ripped the front door open. Then I heard Mom's desperate voice behind me.

"Are you even coming home after school today?"

The question gave me pause. "I don't know, Mom. I'll see you when I see you."

I stepped out onto the porch and closed the door behind me. Hearing my mother cry on the other side of that door would've broken my heart had it not already been broken. I closed my eyes and drew in a deep breath. I'd already be late for school. I walked up my driveway and started for the opening of our neighborhood, wanting nothing more than to pack my shit and never come back.

Even if it meant not getting my high school diploma.

Maybe I should ask the guidance counselor about GED programs.

I walked away from my house as quickly as I could. I burst into a run before I started panting in the morning sun. I mean, come on. It was sixty-eight degrees outside. How the hell did the sun still feel hot? Just another thing to annoy me today before I got to homeroom.

"Rae!"

A horn honking caught my attention and I saw Allison hanging out of Michael's SUV. I snickered as they came screeching around a corner, blazing a trail straight for me. Michael came to a stop on the side of the curb. Allison reached back and threw open my door. I leapt in with my things and Michael whipped a U-turn, speeding off down the road toward our high school.

"Where in the world were you this morning?"

Michael cocked his head. "Thank fuck I decided to drive."

Allison gasped. "Michael. Don't use that kind of language."

He chuckled. "Sorry, beautiful."

I swallowed my groan as they leaned over and kissed one another.

"Thanks for picking me up."

Michael nodded. "Anytime."

Allison craned her head back. "What happened this morning? Why didn't you show up?"

"Yeah. We had to run back to my car before coming to find your ass."

"Michael."

I paused. "I thought you said you drove this morning."

And when they both fell silent, I decided I didn't want to know.

Allison giggled. "Anyway, how was your morning?"

Michael snickered. "I take it D.J. was around?"

I rolled my eyes. "He's always around. Only this time, I told my mother exactly what I thought of him. And her, for being with him."

"You did what?"

"What did you say to her?"

I shrugged. "What needed to be said a long time ago. That there was something wrong with her if she always gravitated to these types of men. That just because she needed him to pay the bills doesn't mean I had to accept him."

Allison's jaw hit the floor. "You said that to your mother?"

Michael's face fell. "Wow. That's pretty harsh."

I shrugged. "Had to be said either way. Not my fault she doesn't want to leave an abusive dickweed because he pays some of our bills."

Allison paused. "Does he really?"

I nodded. "Yep. Our dirty little secret."

Michael sighed. "I mean, at least you got it off your chest, right?"

Even though I made her cry, sure. "Yeah. At least there's that."

Allison sat down in her seat. "Did D.J. do anything this morning to bring that on?"

"I mean, other than trying to be my dad, not really. He was his usual asshole self. Told me he's trying to step in because, apparently, my mother needs help with me."

Michael balked. "What?"

"Yeah. That's what he told me."

Allison scoffed. "That can't be true. You've never given your mother any reason to worry. You've never really rebelled."

Michael chuckled. "Other than that one time me and her snuck out to go to a diner and got sick on milkshakes at two in the morning."

Allison paused. "You guys did what?"

I grinned. "No need to get jealous. It was three years ago."

"I'm not jealous."

Michael grinned. "That pouty bottom lip says otherwise."

I averted my gaze as he leaned in to kiss her. And the kissing evolved to giggling. Which evolved to him tickling her as we pulled into the back parking lot of the school. I gazed out the window, searching for Clint's bike. Well, not really bike. But any sort of vehicle that looked like it might have Clint in it. Part of me wanted to tell Michael to drive by his house. Maybe he just needed a ride to school.

Or maybe you know that's absolute bullshit.

I sighed and pushed my way out of Michael's SUV. He gave me a one-armed hug before Allison trotted around and wrapped her arms around my neck. I knew they were trying to cheer me up. Trying to offer me the bright side of life, or whatever. But I was slowly coming to the understanding that this was one of those things I had to ride out. There wasn't a way to make it pass any sooner. I just had to wait it out.

I glared at Michael. "If you hurt her like this, I will end you. Understood?"

Then I squeezed Allison one last time before relinquishing her to Michael.

Her new boyfriend, apparently.

I made my way to homeroom by myself. Because Michael and Allison wanted to walk hand in hand. It was the first time in my entire high school career I'd walked to homeroom alone. And it sucked. Hard. I crossed the threshold of the classroom just as the bell rang. And Allison came running in behind me just before the bell stopped ringing. She smelled like a mixture of her conditioner and Michael's aftershave as she sat down next to me.

A combination that brought tears to my eyes.

Allison took my hand. "You okay?"

I nodded, but didn't say anything.

"You're going to get through this, okay? And you're not going to do it alone."

Except, I was already alone. Mom had D.J. and didn't give a shit about my issues. Allison had Michael, and the two of them didn't give a shit as to how much PDA they graced the general public with. I was alone. Completely alone.

And I wondered if Clint felt this alone.

9

CLINTON

"Holy fuck."

I groaned as I rolled over. Something sticky and crusted slid against my skin. It made me grimace, causing me to reach for my sheets. And when I threw them off my body, memories came barreling back.

Memories of my dream.

"Are you shitting me?"

My boxers had a massive wet spot on them. My sheets were caked in cum. I snickered as I tossed my comforter off the bed, groaning at the smell. I hadn't had to deal with this shit since I was thirteen years old. And yet, some dream with Rae made me come like I'd just learned how to touch my dick for the first time.

"What a fucking mess," I whispered.

I threw my arm over my face. I didn't know what else to do. Every part of me hurt, my face included. And dream after dream last night haunted me. Every single one of them about her. Rae. That beautiful body and those soft curves and that excessive softness and those luxurious thighs. There wasn't a dream that ran through my head that hadn't been tainted by her presence. My balls felt empty. There was so much wetness on my bed.

How many times did I orgasm last night?

I sighed as I sat up. I ripped my sheets off the bed and tossed them to the side. I turned my fan on, needing to dry out the rest of my damn mattress before I inched my way out of my boxers. Feeling that crusted sensation sliding down my skin made me shiver. And not in a good way. I rushed into the bathroom and readied myself for a long, hot shower.

Hoping to wash the dreams away.

The one time I wanted to wake myself up, I couldn't. The one time I wanted to awaken myself from all those bullshit dreams, and I couldn't make it happen. I'd been practically sleepless for the past two nights. Then I pass out and my brain fucking tortures me. Just my luck, at this point. I turned on the hot water and let the steam fill the room. I stepped in, feeling the waterfall showerhead cascade hot streams down my back, carrying with it the stench of my sweat and the crusted evidence of my debauched dreams.

Tortuous dreams of a girl I couldn't have.

I scrubbed myself down. I washed my hair and winced as water beat against my face. I knew things would feel worse with my body before they got better. But I was tempted to go to a doctor. My nose fucking hurt. And it made me angry. Just what I needed to start my day. A large dose of fucking anger.

I hate my life.

I stood under the water until I felt it grow lukewarm. Then I turned it off and reached for a towel. Getting ready for the day took almost twice the amount of time. Especially since it felt like the marrow of my bones were filled with lead. I pulled on a pair of jeans and stretched out the collar of my shirt. I slid it over my face, trying not to hit my nose as I finished getting dressed. I gathered up my things and walked downstairs. I guess I didn't have a choice but to go to school today.

I didn't feel like it, though.

I picked up my bomber jacket lying on the floor. But instead of putting it on, I simply carried it into the kitchen. I figured the smell of coffee would greet me. Or breakfast. Or the sound of my stepmother's voice.

But nothing greeted me when I got into the kitchen.

"Cecilia?"

I furrowed my brow as the emptiness of my father's sprawling mansion-esque home greeted me. I didn't hear Cecilia call out for me, so I called her name again. And again. I repeated it as I walked around the house. I darted into guest bedrooms and checked the laundry room. I went back upstairs as fear gripped my heart. Hell, I even risked opening my father's bedroom doors to see if she was in there.

No one was around, though.

"Cecilia!"

My voice roared through the house. I dashed around in a frenzy, trying to locate her. It wasn't until I found the front door ajar, though, that I looked outside. And I found her. Standing there. At the end of the driveway.

With her back to me.

I narrowed my eyes and watched her unwavering body. She almost looked like a statue. One I didn't recognize. Her state of dress shocked me. Her hair was disheveled. She had her fucking robe on. Slippers on her feet with her nightgown peeking out from beyond the fluffiness of her robe. I'd never seen her step out of the house without a full face of makeup on. Designer heels. Thousands of dollars' worth of clothing and jewelry. And there she stood. Like any other stay-at-home mother.

Staring down at the ground.

"Cecilia?"

I walked toward her, leaving the front door hanging wide open. I tossed my bomber jacket onto the railing of the porch as the morning sun greeted me. The wind was brisk. Colors splashed against the sky. I kept an ear out for my father, just in case he was around. Something told me he wasn't, though.

Then, I got to Cecilia's side.

"What the—?"

She wasn't looking down. She was looking at our mailbox. Specifically, at the sign swinging below it. I blinked a few times, trying to bring the words into focus. Trying to convince myself I wasn't seeing what I knew was so plainly there.

"I don't even know when he came by."

Her voice sounded so defeated. Breathless. Exhausted. Cecilia sniffled as she raked her hand through her knotted hair. I looked over at her and saw tears dripping down her cheeks. Tears of defeat. Tears of fear. Tears of wariness. My eyes gravitated back to the sign. I reached out and touched it, trying to convince myself it was real.

Then I snickered. "Can he do this? I mean, your name's on the house too, right?"

She shook her head slowly, not saying a word. And my stomach fell to my toes. In that moment, I realized that Cecilia was more like me than I could've ever understood. A prisoner in her own home. Where nothing was hers and everything was held over her head in spite. I raked my eyes over her, watching her unwavering body. The way she stood eerily still despite the tears that flowed down her cheeks told me she was a professional at that. Crying silently. Crying so no one knew.

"Come here. It's okay. I've got you."

I wrapped my arm around her and pulled her against me. And finally, Cecilia pulled her eyes away from the 'For Sale' sign swinging underneath our mailbox. Fear filled them. Wariness wafted behind them. Confusion wrinkled her brow and when she sniffled, there were twinges of anger riding on its coattails.

"I don't know how he can do this, Clint."

Her words were nothing but a whisper. But they felt as loud as a bullhorn. All my life, I'd been telling myself that same thing. Telling myself that I didn't understand how my father got away with some of the things he did. For a while, I thought it was his money. The millions and millions he threw around only to come out on top, again and again. Never losing. Never failing. Always climbing higher. I wondered when his time would come. When he'd fly too close to the sun and fall to the earth.

And in my dreams as a child, I dreamt of that fall killing him somehow. So I'd be rid of him for good.

It killed me to see that same want in Cecilia's face.

"Do you have any idea of when he came by?"

She shook her head slowly. "I don't even know if he came into the house. I passed out hard around one. So, some time after that, I guess."

"Does Dad have any other property around here? A home or something I don't know about?"

She shrugged. "He's probably staying in some hotel or something. Or maybe he's placed a call from the hospital to someone. I don't know. It could be a million things."

"We should call the hospital today. See if he's checked out."

"I figured I would've gotten a phone call from someone."

"That's not always the case. Especially if he didn't want anyone calling you."

Her lower lip trembled. "What are we going to do?"

I thought back to the lawyer. To the doctor. The brochures and numbers they'd handed out for me. I knew they'd help me if I called them. I knew they'd talk me through this. Get me set up with resources. But I wasn't sure they'd help Cecilia. As far as I was concerned, we were a package deal at this point. Nothing happened to me without knowing there was a plan in place for Cecilia.

Because she was just as much a victim, too.

"Come on, we should get inside."

Cecilia stood her ground. "I want to rip that sign down."

I steered her toward the house. "We can't act irrationally any longer. We have to think this through."

"There's nothing to think through. Your father's about to sell this house out from underneath us and leave us homeless."

"Which means we should go inside and figure out a plan."

I guided her up onto the porch. Then I turned my head and looked down the road, toward the high school, where another day would be skipped. At least, the morning would be. My grades would slip. I might not be able to graduate. I'd be pigeon-holed into getting a GED or something and being the scum of the earth for the rest of my life. But seeing Cecilia cry was hell on earth. I couldn't leave her like this. If my teachers wanted to know what the fuck was up with me, they could call the house and I'd explain it all.

Maybe they'd let me repeat my senior year instead of expelling me for absences, if I begged them.

"That's it. Inside. One foot in front of the other."

Cecilia sniffled. "I'm sorry. Just—just give me a second to—"

I closed the door behind us. "You don't need to be sorry. You've been the strong one throughout this whole thing. You're owed a moment, at least."

"Holy Hannah, what are we going to do?"

She broke down and I wrapped my arms around her. I patted her hair down and held her close as she cried into my chest. I kept telling her it would be all right. That we'd find a way out of this. That my father couldn't possibly legally do this. Not like he thought, anyway. But I wasn't sure who I was trying to comfort, her or me.

I wasn't sure which one of us would cave and not come back from it.

Her or me.

Get on the phone with your bank.
Figure out the status of your trust fund.
Figure out how much control your father has over that money.
Start stowing things away to sell.

My mind ran away from me the louder Cecilia cried. I felt her collapse and I scooped her close to me, refusing to let her fall to the floor. She was better than that. She was stronger than this. So I held her steady as I laid out a plan of action for my day. I clenched my jaw as she cried until she practically made herself sick. I walked her down the hallway and ushered her into the bathroom downstairs only seconds before she started puking.

I stood there with my back to her, giving her privacy but not leaving her alone. And as I listened to her sounds, I resigned myself to the plan. First, I needed to call my bank. Ask them questions about my trust fund and its contingencies. If I had any access to that money, I needed to transfer it into an account my father couldn't touch. Or see. Or dip into, if he had to. And if I didn't have control of it, I needed to start stockpiling things from around this house. Selling things off, right out from under my father's nose. I mean, if he wasn't going to come home, how the hell would he know I was selling his shit?

I could put the money into an account he couldn't touch. And since my father didn't make it a habit of keeping receipts, there was no way for him to prove this stuff wasn't my stuff to sell anyway.

I didn't know. That required more research from a legal perspective.

I could call that lawyer and ask.

I felt my stepmother's hand touch down between my shoulder blades. She pushed me softly, moving me out of the way. I turned around, watching as she wiped her mouth off with a washcloth. She tossed it into the sink. "We'll figure this out," she said.

And—just like I'd questioned earlier—I had no idea who she was really talking to.

10

RAELYNN

The school day crept by slowly. As I sat in the back of my morning classes, I got caught up on my homework. I worked so quickly that I finished a week's worth of work. Which meant no homework this weekend.

Which meant a weekend of sitting around and feeling sorry for myself.

Every time I checked my phone, I had a text message from my mother. Messages I deleted without even opening. Hell, she even called me a couple of times. And I thanked my fucking stars my phone was on silent. I had half a mind to block her. However, I settled on turning off my phone instead. While I was out to lunch.

With Michael and Allison.

"This is going to be great!"

I panted. "Keep running. If we're caught, we'll get in serious trouble."

Michael unlocked his SUV. "Come on, Allison. It's time for your first-ever lunch ditch."

She hopped into the front seat. "I feel so alive!"

I shook my head as a small smile crossed my cheeks. A small one. But one that helped prove I might come out of this all right after all. I'd gotten Michael's text about skipping out on lunch today just before I turned off my phone. And I was glad I got it. He cranked up his car as Allison giggled with delight. He sped out of that parking lot and we headed straight for the sandwich shop. Their tomato bisque was calling my name. Complete with their five-cheese grilled cheese and some homemade barbecue chips to go along with it.

Then Allison opened up the can of worms again.

"You feeling better from this morning?"

Michael tossed her a look before shaking his head.

I sighed. "I'm just… tired of him. I'm tired of D.J. always being around. Always trying to act like my father when I clearly see what he does to my mother."

Michael settled into his chair. "Does he know you recognize this?"

I nodded. "Yep. I even promised him the next time my mother came home busted up, I'd be calling the police. I reminded him of that promise this morning."

Allison shook her head. "I can't imagine being in a relationship like that."

"I've been telling my mom for years that she needs help. That she needs to get her life together and stop running around with men like this. And for a while, she was doing that. Applying for jobs. Trying to find a life of her own. I don't know what happened, though."

Michael snickered. "D.J. happened. As much as it sucks, your mother's had a hard life. She just wants things to be easy. And in her mind, a bit of physical pain is probably better than the heartache that comes with being alone, working a dead end job and struggling to make ends meet."

I paused. "Okay, Dr. Phil. Let's slow down there a bit."

Allison smiled. "Have you ever thought about doing psychology?"

He shrugged. "I may or may not like my A.P. Psychology class a little more than I figured I would."

Allison took his hand. "Well, anyway, the guy's a loser. Don't worry about him. One of these days, your mom's going to look at herself in the mirror and realize what we already know."

I rolled my eyes. "That D.J.'s a piece of shit that doesn't deserve to walk the earth?"

She snickered. "Yes, and that she deserves better."

I licked my lips. "I hope it's soon, then. Because I'm not sure how much more of it I can stand."

We pulled up to the sandwich shop and hopped out. It was busy, and I grew worried that we might not make it through our lunch before we had to go. By the time we got in line, placed our orders, and got our food, we had to get back in the car. Which meant eating on the go while trying not to spill shit on Michael's leather seats.

"Just be careful. I'll drive slow."

"Did you spill something? Hurry, get it with this."

"Speed bump. Hold your food up."

I swear, no one babied their car more than Michael babied this damn vehicle of his.

"Is there a long way around we can take? I won't be able to finish this with the regular route. And I'm starving."

Michael smiled at Allison. "Anything for you. I'll drive us through some neighborhoods."

And of course, the neighborhood with the easiest streets to drive was Clint's.

I gazed out the window as I sipped my soup. Instead of eating it with a spoon, I'd stuck a straw in it. My eyes lingered out the window while Michael and Allison talked with one another. And every once in a while, their laughter pierced the foggy haze of my mind. I was happy for them. I really was. But sometimes, I wanted to slap them both. Could they just put that shit on hold for one second? I mean, once we got back to school, it was game on.

Did I really have to be in the car for it, though?

I heard the smacking of their lips as they kissed. I caught a glimpse of Allison feeding a bite of food to Michael. I stared hard out the window, trying my best not to get angry or shut down. Trying my best not to seem like a bitch.

It wasn't easy, though. And it gave me a new respect for how they both felt when I first started dating Clint.

The closer we got to his house, the more silent they became. Until not a sound was made in Michael's car. I finished up my soup and tossed it into the paper bag. I reached for my grilled cheese and unwrapped it, holding my drink still with my thighs. But the second Allison gasped, I whipped my head up. And when Michael cursed to himself, my eyes darted around.

Then I spotted it.

The sign hanging off their mailbox.

"'For Sale'?" I breathed.

What the fuck?

Allison drew in a short breath. "You think that's why he ended things?"

Michael shushed her. "Leave it alone."

"I mean, it's right there. Plain as day. Might give Rae some closure."

"That's not yours to determine."

I shook my head. "He would've told me about something like this."

Michael paused. "I mean, are you sure? Maybe he just didn't get around to telling you about it? Or didn't know how you'd react? Or something?"

"Drop me off."

Allison whipped around in her seat. "Say what now?"

"Drop me off. Now."

Michael shook his head. "Can't do that, Rae. We're going to be late for school if I have to wait for you."

"I didn't ask you to wait. I asked you to stop your fucking car."

Allison reached for me. "Just get through the school day. We can come back after classes are done."

I leveled my eyes with her. "Let me out of this goddamn car, or I'm pouring my soda out on the leather seats."

Michael shook his head. "Fucking hell, Rae."

He came to a stop at the curb and I abandoned my food. I wasn't hungry anymore, anyway. I chugged the rest of my drink before I slipped out of the car, slamming the door behind me. Windows whirred down. I slid my purse over my shoulder. Allison handed me my backpack through the window as Michael stared at me with fire blazing in his eyes.

"Don't you fail school because of him. You've worked too hard for all this."

I scoffed. "Like it's any better watching the two of you neck and make eyes at each other."

Allison furrowed her brow. "Hey. What did we do?"

I shook my head. "Nothing. Get to school. I'll see you guys tomorrow."

Michael groaned. "Rae, you can't just—"

"Michael. Get back to school and leave me be."

Allison sighed. "Good luck, Rae. Really."

"Thanks."

Michael was getting on my fucking nerves, and I needed him to leave. His hands slammed against the steering wheel before he pulled away, leaving Allison watching me with worry on her face. Her head fell out of the window and she craned her neck back, waving as they faded away. I watched them leave before turning back to face Clint's house.

Please be home. Please be home. Please be home.

The chant seemed familiar as I drew in a deep breath. With my things slung over my shoulder, I resigned myself to missing my last few classes. The only thing that gave my solace was keeping up with my homework. I wasn't sure how I'd fare come midterms. But I'd deal with that once it came around. Right now, I had bigger things to deal with. I needed answers. I deserved answers.

And I wasn't leaving until I got them.

I started up the driveway, making my way to the porch. I stared at the front door and couldn't help but pause. Listening out for his father. With every step I took up to the front door, I remembered that encounter. Only two or three days ago, but it felt like an eternity. It took my breath away. I stood on the porch, unable to move. I saw the front door, but my arm didn't move. I saw the doorbell, but my finger didn't extend.

The whirlwind of life hit me all at once, pushing tears to my eyes.

I held my breath as the still-life images bombarded my mind. The first time Clint ever picked on me. How I'd yelled at him and he'd grinned at me. The cascade of effects that came after it all. How he'd call me out in the cafeteria. Make fun of my clothes. Of my house. Of my mother. How he called me names and laughed at me with his buddies.

He's come such a long way.

I saw that night. Where he found me in the park. How angry I'd been that, of all people, he was the one that found me. I remembered how I vibrated with anger at the idea of him sitting next to me. Interjecting himself into my life like I wanted him there for some reason.

Then our first kiss.

That thing sent shivers through my body.

I closed my eyes and relived the first time we had sex. How magical it felt. How his hands felt against my skin. How waking up with him made me feel like a princess. Only, I couldn't stay. I thought about how he ravaged my thoughts. Occupied my mind after that moment. After understanding that he was like me. A boy lost in a world his parental figure had torn to shreds. Used and abused. And angry with the world.

He understands me.

I relived that night. Those boys. The chase. That crash. The ravine. It made me sick to my stomach to think about. And yet I couldn't stop it. It was as if the reel had been started up in a booth somewhere, designed to torture me. I blinked back tears and tried to move. But fear and anguish paralyzed me.

I feel helpless.

I saw Clint in the hospital. Hooked up to tubes. Filled with stitches and bruises. I wavered on my feet as I reminisced on his release. All those times we tried to do his homework, only for him to seduce me with his body. With his words. With his compliments and his eyes. How I wanted to be wrapped up in him again. How I wanted to be his again. How I wanted to tell him how much I loved him.

Does he love me, though?

Had someone asked me that question four days ago, my answer would be 'yes.' But now? I wasn't sure. The reel spiraled me into silence. It held my voice captive. It choked off my tears and my ability to breathe. And it wasn't until I fell forward that I snapped out of it, gasping for air as I snapped out of my trance and slammed my hands against his front door.

Just in time for the front door to rip itself open.

11

CLINTON

"Howard, it's me. You really need to call me back. I've got a lot of questions to ask you that I deserve answers to."

"Howard, it's Cecilia. I don't know if you've blocked me or if you're dodging me, but where in the world do you expect Clint and me to go? Are you leaving me? What is your son going to do about school?"

"Howard, damn it. You pick up this phone right now or I'm hiring a lawyer. I'm serious. This is ridiculous. You started that fight!"

"Howard, it's me."

"Howard."

"Howard, pick up this damn phone!"

I sighed as I listened to Cecilia shriek her head off into the phone. She hung up and threw her cell phone across the room, damn near shattering it against the wall. I walked over to her and rubbed her back. She put her head in her hands and started sobbing, she was so angry. Or confused. Or scared.

Possibly, all three of them.

I knew she wanted answers to her questions. But I also knew my father would never give them to her. He didn't operate that way. Once he set his mind on a mission, he saw it all the way through. She shouldn't have threatened a lawyer, either. Because now, he'd go through with it and cut her off.

Like he'd apparently done to me.

While Cecilia had been blowing up his phone, I'd gotten on the phone with the bank. I mean, it took me a little while to figure out who the fuck managed my trust fund. A call to my regular bank led me to three other phone lines before they told me they had no idea. So I had to go poking around in my father's study. I pulled out drawers and sifted through files. I came across all sorts of random documents with monetary numbers on them that made my head spin. And finally, I came across a couple of names that looked promising.

So I called them both.

The first one told me they didn't manage funds like that. The second one told me I wasn't privy to the information. Which meant I was on the right track. I pulled out all the fucking paperwork for that place. And while my father was shit at a lot of things, keeping a paper trail wasn't one of them. He had records dating back to when he opened the damn account in the first place. I was able to trace that account from its inception all the way up to a few months ago.

When I had turned eighteen.

Cecilia sniffled. "What did the bank say?"

I sighed. "Not much."

"What do you mean?"

I shrugged. "According to the paperwork, that account became mine the second I turned eighteen. But the man I spoke to said that until I was twenty-two, I couldn't have unfettered access to it."

She turned around. "Has it always been that way?"

"Not from what I can tell. I went into Dad's study and read through the agreement."

"He's not going to like that."

"He's currently smoking us out of our own home by controlling the only thing he's got control over. I don't give a shit what he likes."

She paused. "Do you still have access to the money?"

"The man on the phone said I did. But I can't transfer any more than five thousand at a time without Dad's permission. So I initiated a transfer of $4,999.00 into my own bank account to see if I can actually get it to go through. And if I can, that opens up some doors."

She shook her head. "How in the world did it all come to this?"

"The second Dad realized he couldn't use his money and influence to yank our chains any longer."

"Can I admit something to you?"

"Sure."

"I'm scared, Clinton."

I nodded. "I know you are. But we'll find a way out of this, okay? Come the end of the day, I should see a pending deposit in my account. And if that money's there in the morning, I'm calling that guy from the bank back and initiating transfers until Dad stops it."

"Is this what's going to happen now? Scrounging around for scraps?"

"With Dad, preparing for the worst is what you have to do. Let's hope there's a better outcome, but make a plan in case there isn't. Okay?"

She sighed. "Yeah. All right."

I knew my father would shut that money down. The second he caught wind of that transfer, he'd try to cancel it. I'd be lucky if I saw that money in my account in the morning. Cecilia went and retrieved her phone, poking away at the screen. And as she held it to her ear, I heaved a heavy sigh.

Before running down a plan in my mind.

I need to call that lawyer.

I didn't know how much I was really privy to in this house. What could I sell without my father getting me into trouble over it? Could he claim I was stealing from him? Extorting him, somehow? Those were questions for a lawyer. But I didn't know if I'd open another can of worms trying to ask those kinds of questions.

My eyes darted around the house. Everything expensive came into view all in one get-go. But if Dad was going to sell the house, then downsizing was reasonable. Right? I sell off his things, keep the money, and claim downsizing efforts in the process. I didn't know. It didn't make a lot of sense. I clocked the suede couches and the paintings on the walls. The sculptures standing on columns around the room. The projector television. All the fine china we had in a cupboard in the dining room. Legitimate silverware for days. Like it was plastic wear to us.

Even selling the small things would net me well over a hundred thousand dollars.

Could I get away with it, though?

A slam against the front door ripped me from my trance. Cecilia came rushing back into the room with her eyes wide as saucers. I held my arm out and stopped her in her tracks. I peeked down at her and mouthed 'stay put' before making my way for the door. I slowly approached it and peeked out the frosted windows to try and see who was out there.

But when I opened the door, the last person I expected to be there stood in front of me.

"Can you talk? Because we need to talk."

Rae's voice filled my ears and it wasn't a dream. It wasn't a fantasy. I ran my eyes down her body, clocking her crooked form. Her tired eyes. The bags underneath them that accentuated how pale her skin looked. Had she lost weight? Her cheeks looked a little sunken in. That could be from exhaustion, though.

Why is she so tired?

I looked back at my stepmother and she nodded, urging me to go outside and sit on the porch. I turned my eyes back to Rae and stared at her, our eyes connecting for the first time in days. My heart skipped a beat. My stomach exploded with butterflies. Hell, I felt my knees fucking go weak.

This isn't good.

"Are you all right?" I asked.

She glared up at me. "Outside, please."

"Rae, I can't—"

"The least you owe me is that."

I sighed as I stepped out onto the porch. Mostly because I knew she was right. Out of all this insanity and all she'd done for me, the least I owed her was an explanation. But would she accept it? Would she accept my words and leave with a lighter heart? I wasn't sure if she would.

I wasn't sure if *I* would.

I closed the door behind me and ushered her over to the rocking chairs. Her disheveled hair got tossed around in the wind as it whipped around the house. A smell crept underneath my nose, forcing it to curl up. And as I sat down next to Rae, the smell grew.

What is that smell, anyway?

"You look good, considering."

I focused on her. "You—you do, too."

She snickered. "You're a terrible liar. But thanks anyway."

"I'm not lying."

And when she shot me a look, I kept my mouth shut.

"Moving, Clint? Really?"

I shrugged. "I'm just as surprised as you were."

She paused. "Wait, you didn't know?"

"Not even Cecilia knew. We woke up this morning and the sign was out there. She's freaking out so badly that I didn't have the heart to leave her for school today."

"Have you heard from your father at all since…?"

I shook my head slowly. "No. We're not really sure he's the one who even came by to do it. She's been calling around all morning, trying to figure out where the hell he is."

"Has she tried the hospital?"

"I think she's doing that now."

"So, for all you know—"

"Dad's contacted a realtor to take over the sale of the house."

I leaned back into the rocking chair and closed my eyes. The wind felt nice. The harshness of the sun seemed to have finally abated. If the wind blew just right, I could smell the sea, its saltiness wafting in from a coastline I hadn't visited in months.

But, other times…

Is it Rae that smells like that?

"How are you doing?" I asked.

She scoffed. "Some question for you to ask."

"I'm serious."

I opened my eyes and looked over at her.

"How are you doing, Rae?"

She shrugged. "As good as I can be."

"Are you sure?"

"No, I'm not sure. All right?"

The harshness of her words wasn't like her. And I wondered who else had taken the brunt of her anger when it should've been me.

"Sorry. Sorry, Clint."

I shook my head. "No need to be sorry."

"So what are you guys going to do? I'm sure your father can't just sell the house like that."

I shrugged. "Honestly? It won't shock me if he tries anyway. I think this is payback."

"Payback for a fight he started?"

"How did you know he started it?"

"Your father is *always* the one to start shit."

I snickered. "True."

"Would he really do that to you guys? Just sell the house and leave you homeless or something?"

I shrugged. "I mean, I don't know. Dad's well… not a good guy. And neither one of us have heard from him since the other night. Since the paramedics took him to the hospital. Cecilia hasn't been to visit him. No one's called us to update his condition. I think he's on a warpath now. And it's a matter of riding it out."

"How do you ride something like this out, though?"

"I don't know. But I guess we'll figure it out."

"Do you have a plan for if he does sell the house?"

I sighed. "You mean 'when'? Because I'm betting money on the fact that he'll go through with it."

She rolled her eyes. "Whatever word you want to use, Clint. Just answer my question."

"Sorry. Uh, I'm trying to come up with some plans. Poking around at my trust fund. Trying to get money deposited into my account. Things like that."

"What about selling some of the stuff in the house?"

"I don't know what the legal ramifications would be from something like that. But it's crossed my mind."

"Well, you might not be able to sell stuff he's purchased and can prove he purchased. But you and Cecilia can sell things he's given to you or gifted to you. Because in the eyes of the law, those things are technically your possessions."

I paused. "How do you know that?"

She shrugged. "You're not the only one who's contemplated running away more than once."

"Rae, I'm so sor—"

She held up her hand. "Selling things like silverware and paintings might not be a good idea. But the furniture in your room? Your clothes? Jewelry or wallets or watches? Or any of Cecilia's clothes? You can sell those things and be just fine. Just in case you need that information."

I nodded slowly. "I appreciate it."

"Also, your father's a fucking jerk-off."

Like father like son, I guess. "Yep. He really is."

"Are you coming back to school?"

"I honestly don't know. Right now, I can't leave Cecilia. Not alone with my father, anyway. And something tells me he's waiting for that moment."

"Waiting for you to leave your stepmother here alone."

"Yeah. I mean, I don't know. It sounds paranoid. But it just doesn't feel right."

She drew in a deep breath. "Then you do what's best for your family and I'll talk to your teachers."

"Rae, you don't have t—"

She held up her hand again. "Will you shut up and just let people help? You don't have to be fucking me in order for me to want to help."

Her statement tore my heart out. "Thank you, Rae."

"No problem."

But the more we talked, the icier her voice became. Her face etched itself into stone and her statements grew colder. Which told me we had many, many problems.

Despite her choice of words.

12

RAELYNN

Even though he answered my questions, I saw his walls up. His face seemed guarded and his eyes looked dead. He answered me, sure. But he wasn't opening up to me. I had to pry his answers to my questions out of him. He wasn't freely talking about anything. My questions were carrying this conversation. And I knew that if I stopped them, he'd stop talking.

Which pissed me off.

I heard my voice growing icier and felt myself becoming distant. I didn't want my anger to become the focus of this conversation. But I couldn't help it. I was hurt. Angry with his father. Angry with Clint for pushing me away and frustrated with my mother and the bullshit she kept pulling with D.J. I'd lost the only person in my life who understood me. The only person who seemed to get what I was going through. Talking with Michael and Allison didn't feel the same anymore because they came from great families. Parents that were still married. Two-income households with parents that worked jobs that made them happy. They didn't understand what I was going through. Clint did, though.

And it pissed me off that he'd taken that away from me.

He kept pushing me away. Pushing my advice away. Trying to get me to stop helping him under the guise that I didn't have to. I wanted to smack him across his face. Despite how much of a terrible person that made me. I wanted to grab his shoulders and shake him until he got it. Until he understood that breaking up with me was the worst possible thing he could've done during something like this.

I didn't have the energy, though.

I cleared my throat. "I'm serious. I'll talk to your teacher. I'll make sure you can still keep up."

He nodded mindlessly. "Thanks."

"And as far as your possessions go, I'm sure there are things you'd love to get rid of. Use that to your advantage."

"I will."

"Call the lawyer you spoke to as well. I'm sure he'd have some great advice on how to proceed next. Or even if what your father's doing is legal."

"I'm sure."

I sighed. "And if he doesn't, I'm sure he can point you in the right direction."

He blinked. "Yeah."

"Clint?"

"Hmm?"

"Are you going to even look at me?"

He slowly panned his gaze over to mine, and I found his nose wrinkled. Like something up above us stunk. There was this look of disgust on his face that made my heart sink. He didn't even want me there. He didn't want me near him. Talking to him. Interacting with him. It was as if our relationship had reverted back to its normal ground. Square one, with him being an absolute asshat and me getting stuck in his crosshairs.

Still, I pressed on.

"What your father's doing is wrong. What he's doing to you and your stepmom is downright despicable. Fight him. Fight him on it. And I'll be here if you need anything."

His eyes met mine. "Thanks, Rae. really. I'll take your advice into account. But Cecilia and I got this. We can handle it."

His words burned. I felt the crack of the imaginary slap across my cheek. He stood from his chair and my eyes followed him, watching as he rolled his shoulders back. I saw the last of his walls drop down. Like iron bars trapping him into his own little corner. His arms extended above his head and I hated myself for how my eyes lingered. The skin of his lower back came into view. Those cute little dimples that sat just above his buttbone greeted me.

Called to my fingertips. I closed my eyes and shook the thoughts away. Clint wasn't mine anymore. I had no right to see him that way.

But I deserved an answer to the question running around in my head.

"Clint, do you really want things between us t—"

"Clinton? I need you. It's imperative."

Cecilia's voice interjected into my question and Clint whipped around. I stood up, facing his stepmother as she covered herself up. She held her silken robe closed, her hair a disheveled mess. She looked terrible, for lack of a better word. Like she hadn't gotten a lick of sleep in weeks.

Clint strode to her. "What's wrong?"

But her eyes fell to me. "I need to borrow him for a second. I'm sorry."

I shook my head. "No, no. It's fine. You seem flustered. I hope everything's okay."

The two of them looked at one another before Clint nodded for her to go back inside. I hated being on the outside like this. I hated no longer being a part of their lives. I mean, I'd always felt like an outsider. But I never thought I'd feel that way with Clint again. Truth be told, it hurt worse than anything else. Being privy to Clint's life and bonding with Cecilia only to see them completely shut me out felt like hell on earth. Like I'd ascended into Dante's Inferno and was living it for myself.

I snickered. "Yeah. I'll just—I'll head out."

Clint reached for me. "It's nothing personal. We're just—"

I waved my hand in the air. "If you need me, you know where to find me."

I scooped up my things and hopped over the railing of his porch. I fell to the ground and skinned my knees, but I didn't give a shit. I heard Clint rushing for me, but I held out my hand. Two could play his game. If he wanted to shut me out, then I'd shut him out.

No holds barred.

I glared at him before I walked across his lawn. With dirty knees and a hole where my heart used to be, I made my way down the road, slowly creeping toward the school. I knew something had flustered Cecilia. I knew something serious had gone down. But the way they treated me was unacceptable. Like I hadn't saved Clint's life, helped him keep his grades afloat in the hospital, and helped him transition back into school. Like none of that shit had occurred. At all.

Like it had all been erased from time.

You're being selfish, Rae.

"I know I'm being selfish," I murmured.

They're about to lose their house.

"Yeah, well. When do I get to be an important part of the equation?"

You are important.

"To who? Not Clint. Not my mother. Not Michael and Allison."

They're your best friends.

"Yeah, but I'm not their number one anymore. I'm no one's number one."

I felt like I'd blown a gasket in my brain, arguing with myself. But who else was I going to talk to? Michael and Allison were sucking face every chance they got. I couldn't have ten uninterrupted minutes with Clint. Cecilia wasn't someone I could talk to. And my mother had lost her damn mind with D.J. coming into our home and trying to run it as he saw fit. I had no one. Nothing. No one to turn to. No one who understood me. No one who loved me enough to put me first for once.

I just want to be important to one person. Just one. Anyone.

Fucking hell, I'd take the stray cat in the neighborhood at this point.

I walked aimlessly until I found myself staring at the front doors of the school. I walked inside and looked at the clock before heaving a heavy sigh. I felt like that's all I did now. Sighed, cried, and turned in homework. I'd missed lunch. History only had about thirty more minutes left. If I walked in now, the teacher would berate me for sure. But if we'd had a pop quiz or something in class, she'd still let me take it.

So I headed into history class.

I walked inside and saw Allison turn around. Her eyes widened as I came into view, closing the door behind me. Our teacher leveled me with a stare. Students snickered at me from all angles. And as I made my way to my seat, the teacher asked me.

"Not the time to start slipping, Miss Cleaver."

I nodded. "It won't happen again."

"It better not."

There had been no pop quiz. But I had just enough time in class to read through the next chapter. Doing homework while not paying attention to the lecture. That had become my signature move here recently. The bell tolled for classes to switch, but the teacher asked me to stay behind.

I couldn't stay long, though. Otherwise, I'd be late for my last class of the day.

"And where were you, Miss Cleaver?"

I packed up my things. "I had to go see someone."

"Is this someone your boyfriend?"

I winced. "Not technically anymore, no."

"Then why did you have to go see this someone?"

I stood. "Because he's going through a hard time and I wanted to know if I needed to keep bringing him homework or not."

"It's not your responsibility to keep up Mr. Clarke's grades."

"It is when his father is abusive and preventing him from coming to school."

My teacher paused. "What did you say?"

I shook my head. "Clint's going through a very tough time. And I'm sorry I was late for your class. But he's going through a lot right now, and if he doesn't have to fail his classes I'm not going to let him fail."

"Did you say 'abusive'?"

Shit. "If you want to know, visit him. But I won't be late for your class again. Even though it means possibly not helping out someone in need."

Then I turned on my heel and left my teacher in the room.

I sprinted for my last class. I only had three minutes to make it damn near to the other side of the school. The bell rang as I ran up the ramp, signaling that I was late. Fucking hell, late for another class. And because of a teacher chewing me out for shit I didn't deserve to be chewed out for! My grades wouldn't suffer. They never suffered. I was a straight-A student. Had been since middle school.

I leapt into the classroom just before the teacher closed the door.

"Nice save, Miss Cleaver. Stay after class with me, please."

I sighed. "Good thing I'm not a bus rider."

The class gasped and I froze.

"What was that, Raelynn?"

I closed my eyes. "I said, 'Okay. I'll stay behind.'"

"That's what I thought you said."

I swallowed a growl working its way up the back of my throat. It was like a damn catch-22. Late for one class, bitched out by a teacher. Only to be made late for another class so I could get bitched out by another teacher. As I dropped myself into my seat at the back of the class, my eyes found Allison. Michael. The two of them were staring at me as if I'd grown a third head. I nodded at them before pulling out my things, preparing myself to get homework done while my teacher rattled on about bullshit I didn't care about.

Because I'd gotten a small glimpse at Clint's world.

Teachers that didn't care. That didn't own up to when they made their students late for class. Teachers that didn't give a damn about someone's well-being. Or aptitude. Or test scores. This small debacle made me empathize with him more. Because while I'd only gone through it with a couple classes, he'd been going through it for years.

And as I started in on my homework, my mind fell back to Cecilia.

Her, and the emergency that had ripped Clint away from me in the middle of the most important question I needed to ask him.

13

CLINTON

I wanted to rush to her when she hopped over the railing. I saw the second she fell over a bit too far that she wouldn't plant herself on her feet. I moved for her, my arms outstretched. All pretenses gone out the window. I wanted to scoop her into my arms and apologize. Take it all back. Tell her I was sorry for my life turning out this way. But when she threw me a look that could've killed me where I stood, I stopped in my tracks.

And I watched as she made her way across the lawn.

The anger in her eyes haunted me. It made me worried that I had officially lost her. That I'd never be able to reconcile things once I could dig Cecilia and myself out of this hole. However much I might've dreamed about it, I feared the worst. That this was it. That this was the last time I'd ever see Rae, and I was watching her walk away from me.

For good.

I wanted to go after her. No matter how much I wanted to, though, I couldn't. There were so many things going on. I couldn't leave Cecilia like this. Too many things were at stake. Including this fuckery going on with my father. We needed answers, and we needed them quickly. So I kept my eyes on Rae until the horizon swallowed her whole.

Then I went inside.

"Cecilia?" I called out her name as I closed the door behind me.

"In the kitchen."

Her voice was so soft. Breathless. Worried. I made my way into the kitchen and saw her sitting there with a crystal glass of whiskey. She twirled it around in her fingertips. The sadness in her eyes was unbearable. I placed my hand on her shoulder and squeezed, knowing damn good and well that whatever she had found out wasn't good. I walked to the fridge and got me a soda. I wanted a glass of whiskey, too. But I figured Cecilia wouldn't allow it.

I sighed as I sat down in front of her, watching her glassy eyes find mine.

"What happened?" I asked.

Her eyes fell to her glass. "What time is it, again?"

I shrugged. "Sometime past lunch."

"Good." She put her whiskey glass to her lips.

She chugged. And chugged. She swallowed until the amber liquid was gone. And when she got up to get a second glass, I knew it wasn't good. Whatever she had to speak with me about would be life-altering. That much I knew for sure. How badly, I didn't know.

But I braced for the worst.

Cecilia eased herself back down and leaned heavily into the chair. I brought my soda to my lips, mindlessly sipping as I gave her the space she needed to collect her thoughts. Part of me wanted to yell at her to spit it out. The rest of me knew how much she was struggling, though. The look in her eye. The sadness in her features. The way her eyes teared up and dried out. Like her body didn't know whether to be sad or angry.

Or both.

"Did Dad call you back?"

She nodded slowly.

"Did he answer any of your questions?"

And again, she nodded.

"Whenever you're ready to talk, Rae's gone."

She drew in a short breath. "You should really call that girl and apologize."

I nodded. "One thing at a time."

Cecilia reached for my hand. "Your father's already—"

I took hers, wrapping my fingers around her hand. "He's already what?"

Though I knew what was coming.

"Your father's already found a buyer for the house, Clinton."

I drew in a deep breath. Anything to keep my head from popping off. I had to keep my cool. I couldn't let loose on her. I couldn't become Dad in this moment. I squeezed her hand before I sat back. Her touch fell away and I replaced it with the cold soda in my hand. I brought it to my lips and chugged, wishing it were alcohol. Wishing it were something to wash away the pain and hatred and disdain I had circulating through my system. The carbonation burned. I let it burn, too. I didn't stop until the damn drink was gone. And even then, I wanted something stronger.

Something harsher.

Something more potent than a fucking Dr. Pepper.

"What else did Dad say?"

She sighed. "A lot. He blames you for what happened. Though I kept telling him it was his fault. That he started it after having one too many drinks. That you were only trying to defend me."

I shrugged. "Dad doesn't like chivalry unless it suits him."

She snickered. "So I'm figuring out."

"I'd really like to see the version of my father you've seen all these years."

"You know, I'm not so sure it was ever different. Just… masked. By presents, and clothes, and jewelry."

I nodded slowly. "You think?"

She sniffled. "Guess it's easy to get me to shut up with money."

"Don't say that about yourself."

"No, no. I'm serious. I mean, I grew up with nothing. I grew up with no voice. No things that were my own. No dreams or hopes of having a life I could live of my own volition. When I met your father, he promised me the world. Trips around the globe and nights spent in penthouses and fashion beyond my wildest imagination. I was so taken by all the things he could provide that I never saw the similarities between him and my father."

"You still can't blame yourself."

"I'm an adult, Clint. I can blame myself all I want. I can't control how I was raised. But I can control how I act as a result of it now. You'd do best to keep that in mind."

I nodded slowly. "I will."

"I guess I saw all the freedom of traveling with him and the freedom to eat whatever I wanted, and mistook it for actual freedom. An actual life. When really, I was still underneath someone's thumb. Unable to move or speak or think unless it was demanded of me a certain way."

"Sounds like Dad."

She wiped at her eyes, though her voice never cracked. "Anyway, this isn't about me."

"It's about us. You can talk about whatever you want to."

"I don't know how the fuck your father sold this house so quickly, but he did. We've got six to eight weeks until they close, then…"

I felt anger surging through me. "It's only been, like, two days. How the hell did he orchestrate all of this from the hospital?"

"He wasn't in the hospital when he called me."

"That makes more sense."

"Yeah. He's in a hotel on the other side of town somewhere. Said he got out that next morning and he's been there ever since."

I snickered. "Fucking bastard."

Everything was changing too quickly. Six to eight weeks? Where the hell did that man expect us to go? What did he expect us to do? I tried to figure out where I could start listing some of our things. We needed money, and quickly. I closed my eyes and tried figuring out all the jewelry I'd seen Cecilia in over the years. How much of it did she have in the house? She'd have to give up her luxury, but we could make this work. Even if we only sold—

"He wants me to go with him, Clint."

My eyes slowly opened. "What?"

Her eyes lined with tears. "He says he wants me to come with him."

"Go with him where?"

She shrugged. "I don't know. He said I'm his wife. And wherever we end up, I need to be there."

"Need to be? Or that he wants you there?"

"Do you really have to ask that question?"

"So he wants you to uproot, but you don't even know where you're going? Did he ask you to pack? Or anything like that?"

She shook her head. "No. Just to get ready. Which I assume means packing. Maybe."

I narrowed my eyes. "What aren't you telling me?"

"Clinton, it's not that simple."

"What's not that simple? Come on. Dad said something and I deserve to know what it is."

"I know. I know. Just… please. Just give me a second."

Don't explode like him. "He wants me to be some sort of rental tenant in this house, doesn't he?"

"No."

"He wants me to go live with Roy? Or Rae?"

"No, that's not it. He's just—"

"He's just what? Tell me, Cecilia. What am I supposed to do here? He's sold the house. You're going with him. Am I supposed to come, too?"

And when her eyes teared up, I fell back into my chair.

"You've gotta be fucking kidding me."

She sniffled. "I'm sorry. I tried reasoning with him. I'm still going to try and reason with him. Just give me some time, okay? He's still very angry."

"He doesn't want me coming with you guys?"

I slammed out of my chair. My fists balled up at my sides. I felt myself spiraling out of control as Cecilia yelped in shock. The kitchen table came off its fucking feet. It fell to the ground, raking across the marble of the kitchen floor. I felt my mind exploding. I felt my heart combusting. It felt like the pain and anger in my body was ripping me apart, limb for limb.

I had no words to describe the hurt coursing through my system.

"He said you're eighteen and you can figure it out. But I'm going to talk to him. You're his son. You're *my* son, Clint. And I'm going to do whatever it takes to talk some sense into him. To get him to back out of selling this house. Even if he puts it in my name. Even if he washes his hands of it that way. I'm not going to let him do this to you, Clint."

I heard her voice, but it seemed so far away. I felt her hand on my arm, but it barely rooted me to reality. Hot tears streamed down my cheeks. She eased me back into the kitchen chair. I sniffled as I stared at the wall, my chest jumping in anger. In hatred.

In defeat.

"He wants you to go with him, but not me."

Cecilia crouched down beside me. "Clint, look at me."

"Just say it. Just—just so I can hear it."

"Look. At. Me."

I slowly turned my eyes down to hers. She cupped her hands around my knee, steadying herself as her own tears flooded her face. I wiped mine away on my shirt, wishing and willing this life to be over. Hoping and praying I'd wake up from this fucking nightmare I'd been plunged into.

"I'm going to talk some sense into him. I've got weeks to do it. And I'm going to research legal avenues. See what I can do about fighting this. It isn't over. Okay? Can you hear me, Clint?"

I chewed on the inside of my cheek. "I just want to hear you say it."

"Say what?"

"Say, 'Your father wants me to come with him, but not you.'"

"I'm not saying that."

"Cecilia, just say it."

"I'm fighting this, Clint. Please, give me time. Give this entire scenario some time."

I gritted my teeth together. "Just. Say. It."

She sighed. "Why? What good is it going to do?"

It's going to help me let go of my hope. "Just trust me. Please. I'm begging you. If you give me nothing else, give me this."

And with a defeated sigh, she nodded.

"Your father wants me to come with him wherever he buys his next house, but not you."

Finally, after years of being bound to this hellhole, I felt the chains burst free. Any hope of ever finding the decency within my father popped off, leaving scars behind as the animal in me stood up. The animal he'd been starving and torturing and beating for years. The wounded animal he was more than willing to abandon out of sheer pride. Out of sheer anger. Out of sheer... abusiveness.

I was finally free of the dream of him. Of the dream I'd had ever since I was a little child. Of the dreams where my father loved me. Cared for me. Enjoyed my presence. Free of the expectation that I somehow had to make him happy. Make him proud. Do whatever he wanted simply because he commanded it. Weight after weight rolled off my shoulders. It felt easier to breathe. And as my tears dried up, I stood, helping Cecilia off her feet.

"Thank you for that."

She drew in a shuddering breath. "It hurts to say."

I nodded. "It does. But maybe it'll give you some perspective on what to do next, and show you that you always have a choice."

Then I pulled her into my arms and the two of us cried together, releasing emotions we'd been holding in for ages and finally freeing ourselves from the prisons my father had kept us in.

I only hoped she made the right decision for herself.

Because she was important, too.

14

RAELYNN

"**F**ucking teachers."

"Giving me a hard time."

"Once. I was late once!"

"They're judging me because of Clint."

"They shouldn't even be teachers!"

"Prejudiced fucks."

I kept my head down as I walked home from school. I murmured to myself, pissed off that all my afternoon teachers kept me behind to give me a lecture. I'd been late to their classes once. How the fuck did that warrant pulling me aside and berating me? What the hell did they expect from me? Yes, if a teacher pulls me aside, I'm going to be late for my next class. That isn't my fucking fault!

That didn't even touch what I found with Michael and Allison, though.

Michael sent me a text, telling me they were waiting out back in the parking lot. The only damn bright spot to my entire day. But, when I walked out of the back school doors, I didn't see Michael's big-ass SUV. It wasn't until I squinted that I saw it at the back corner of the parking lot, parked underneath some damn trees. I should've known not to go near the damn thing. But I was naïve. I figured they wanted to get out of the sun while waiting for me.

Didn't take a fucking rocket scientist to explain why the windows were fogged up.

Gross.

I didn't even bother them. I simply turned around and headed for the road. The last thing I wanted to do was get in a car that smelled like pheromones and sexually-frustrated teenagers. This day had been a nightmare. Straight from the asshole of hell. And all I wanted was to get upstairs, get to my room, and close myself up for the weekend.

I didn't even want to bother with school tomorrow.

I deserve a long weekend.

I didn't know which to be angry about more: the fact that my teachers didn't give a shit that I was a straight A-student, or the fact that my best friends didn't give a shit about really waiting for me. I mean, why fog up the windows and perch yourselves for a make-out session if you know someone's going to be joining you soon? That's downright selfish! I would've never pulled that shit with Clint.

Are you sure about that?

I rolled my eyes and muted the voices in my head. I rushed across the road and tore into my neighborhood, because I wanted to get into the house as quickly as I could. I didn't know what to do with all this anger. All this hurt. All this betrayal I felt. I mean, rationally? I understood it was stupid. I knew my emotions were raging out of control and that I needed to pull them back a bit.

But I just couldn't.

I looked up just in time to see D.J. getting into his car. Fucking really? He was here? Just my luck. I moved quickly. I practically jogged into the driveway as he turned his engine over. It wasn't until he started backing out, however, that I realized he was leaving.

Finally, someone's having mercy on me.

"Hey, kiddo."

Spoke too soon. "Hey, D.J."

He rolled down his window the rest of the way. "How was your day today?"

I flashed him a bitter smile. "Getting worse by the second."

He snickered. "What did I ever do to you to make you hate me so much?"

I shrugged as I passed his car window. "I don't know, Deej.

Breathed air? Opened your mouth? Set your sights on my mother? Sent her home with bruises? Pick one. They're all valid."

"Spoiled brat."

"Ignorant prick."

I looked back at him as I made my way to the porch. I glared at him as he sped out of the driveway, his tires peeling off into the distance. The smell of burnt rubber filled the air, and I grimaced as I made my way inside. I drew in a deep breath of fresh air. Well, fresh air tainted with something terrible my mother had obviously cooked. I closed the door behind me as tires squealed in the distance. Probably D.J. taking a tight turn out of the neighborhood. Because he thought he was cool.

Asshat.

I leaned against the door and sighed, closing my eyes. I dropped my purse. My backpack. I felt my knees weakening as I closed my eyes. I wanted this day to be over. Hell, I wanted this year to be over. I wanted to be graduated so I could get the fuck out of here and the fuck away from Clint. And everything that reminded me of him.

"Rae? You all right?"

Mom's voice hit my ears and I drew in a shuddering breath. The last thing I needed to do was break down. I was tired of it. Tired of feeling weak. Tired of feeling alone. Tired of feeling disposable. Like I was second-best.

But, when I opened my eyes, I saw Mom standing at the end of the hallway.

"Rae, what's wrong?"

I swallowed hard. "Do I smell cookies or something?"

She nodded slowly. "I tried making your favorite. But I think there's something wrong with the stove."

"Burning the cookies?"

"Which is saying something, since we both know I'm a slow baker."

"And a terrible cook."

She snickered. "I'll let you get away with that this time."

I nodded. "Sounds good."

She paused. "Do you want to talk about it?"

I shrugged, but I couldn't say anything. I felt the knot forming, my knees buckling. My entire world was crumbling around me as the loneliness in the pit of my black soul ignited. The light blinded me behind my eyes. It hurt to feel the heat of that searing anguish. My hand came up to my chest and I gripped my shirt. Tugged at the collar because it was now too close to my throat.

"Oh, Raelynn. I've got you. Come here."

I held my hand out. "No. No, no. No hugs. Please. I just—"

"Stop it. You have to let it out. You know better than that."

The second I felt my mother's arms around me, I collapsed. I threw my arms around her neck and my knees finally buckled. She gasped as she sank us to the floor, her arms holding me tight. And as I tucked my face into the crook of her neck, I sobbed. I cried like I did when I was a child. When I first skinned my knee, or when I first jammed my neck. When Allison first hurt my feelings, or when I got my first failing test in middle school.

"What's wrong? Talk to me, sweetheart. What's happening?"

My lower lip quivered. "I-I-I, Clint—he's mov—mov—school just—"

She kissed the top of my head. "Deep breaths, Rae. Even breaths. You're close to a panic attack."

"My chest. It hurts."

"I know."

"I can't—"

"Just do as I'm asking. Breathe in through your nose, out through your mouth. And focus on keeping the rhythm even."

I did as she asked. My chest kept jumping, but I kept at it. She murmured softly in my ear. She cradled me as if I were still a child. She rocked me side to side, groaning and grunting underneath my weight. She didn't let me go, though. She didn't push me away. She simply let me cry into her neck until my breathing finally stabilized.

Then the words poured from my lips like water from a backed-up fountain.

15

CLINTON

California state assistance for teenagers.
Jobs that require only a high school degree.
Cheap motorcycles for sale.
Places for homeless students to sleep in Riverbend
Can I sell my dad's stuff if he's selling the only place I live in?

I slammed my finger against the 'enter' key and watched the search engine whirl away. I picked up my third cup of coffee and chugged it back, groaning at the taste of rosewater. Fucking hell, I loved this coffee place. I'd miss it when I left. And I was damn lucky they didn't charge me for the usage of their computers.

Because my neck had grown stiff researching shit on my cell phone.

I typed in everything I could think of. Any search that might give me some sort of reprieve from the insanity coming down around me. Weeks. I had only weeks to figure out what my next moves were. Otherwise, I'd be homeless. I'd have to sleep on the streets. Possibly drop out of school. Make my way in this world scrubbing dishes for less than minimum wage in some food truck while I sweated my ass off.

"Come on, there has to be something."

I clicked around and sent myself articles. I highlighted things I jotted down in the notebook I carried around with me now. More and more, my notebook filled with ways to live. Ways to eat. Places that might take me in versus poems and short stories and novel ideas that came to me at the drop of a hat. My notebook had gone from creative to proactive. Artistic to sadistic. I felt like it mocked me some times, laughing at me. Like my father probably was right now.

Satanic.

The devil. My father was Lucifer himself. How he could do this to his own flesh and blood, I'd never know. How my mother could leave me with a man like this, I'd never understand. I didn't want to understand. I never wanted to be as cold-hearted and as desolate as the two of them were.

I just wanted to find a safe place to be myself.

After hitting dead ends and growing tired of frivolous searches, I broke down and called that lawyer. I found his card I had taped to the inside of my notebook, figuring I'd have to make an appointment with him. I reached his secretary and gave my name. The reason for me calling. And just when I thought she'd rattle off his schedule to me, she told me to wait.

"Clinton Clarke?"

I paused. "Uh, yes?"

"I was wondering if I'd ever hear from you again. How are you?"

I was so shocked, I couldn't even remember the man's name. "I'm good. I mean, well, I have a question. But, otherwise, I'm good."

"Are you wanting me to answer that question for you?"

I sighed. "No, no. I just—I want to pick your brain a second."

"About what?"

"I have a hypothetical for you."

"Question for a friend. That kind of thing?"

"You could say that."

"Got it. Shoot."

"Let's say there's a house up for sale. Just went on the market. And there's already a buyer."

"Nice. That happens sometimes."

I snickered. "Yeah. Anyway, the issue is that there are two people still living in the house. A high schooler of legal age and a woman."

He paused. "Uh huh."

"Yeah. And it's assumed the woman is going to move when the

house sells. But it's not assumed the high schooler is going to move."

"Okay?"

"What rights does that high schooler have? Can he—I mean—can this high schooler somehow stop the sale?"

"Does this high schooler want to?"

I snickered. "I mean, the high schooler won't have anywhere to go."

"So, this kid not going with the move isn't a decision he's made."

I paused. "No. It isn't."

He clicked his tongue. "Clinton?"

"Yes, sir?"

"You want to drop the veil of pretense for a second and talk seriously?"

"That depends. Are you going to interject your services and make things worse?"

"Not unless you hire me. Otherwise, this is simply a phone consultation where I tell you the kind of rights you have and how I can help you."

I sighed. "All right. Shoot."

"Your father's sold your house, but has he explicitly said to you that he doesn't want you going with him?"

I cleared my throat. "He said that to my stepmother. Not me. I can't get him on the phone."

"Is there any way for you to get a copy of the sale contract of the house?"

"I have no idea."

"Okay. You need to try and do that first. I can place a few phone calls if you—"

I shook my head. "No. I don't want to make things worse."

He sighed. "I can leave your name out of it."

"Please, just—do I have a right to sell some of the things in the house to get some money for myself? Because I can't leave town right now. I need to graduate first."

"Kid, I know. That's what I'm trying to tell you. If you can get that sale contract on your hands to make sure your father hasn't sold the furniture and the possessions inside the house, then you can sell those off yourself."

I paused. "I can?"

"Yep."

"Even, like, the silverware and the furniture?"

"All of it."

"Seriously?"

"Yep. Dead serious. Even if he takes you to court and tries to prove that you 'stole his stuff' by selling it out from underneath him, the second you prove that he did it to you with the house, a judge is going to throw it out of court. It'll be seen as neglect, and that won't shine a good light on him."

I sighed. "I don't have proof of that, though."

"You said he said it to your stepmother, right?"

I nodded. "He did, yes."

"If you can get him to say it to you, too, or get it written down electronically somewhere, you're good. You can't record him without notifying him of the fact that you're recording. But what he says in emails or text messages…"

"I read you loud and clear."

"But even so, there are things in that house you're privy to that aren't specifically your belongings. Not sculptures and priceless art he might've gotten at an auction or anything. But neutral items the entire family uses, like couches, chairs, china. You have a right to that."

I sighed. "Thank you so much."

"And before we hang up, I just want to put this out there. If you need me—for anything—it'll be pro bono work."

"You don't have to do—"

"Pro. Bono. Do you hear me?"

I swallowed hard. "I do. Thank you."

"Keep my number handy. Know you're not alone in this fight."

"I will. Thank you, sir."

"Call me in a few days and let me know how you're doing. All right?"

I snickered. "Why?"

He paused. "Because I care. And I get the feeling that idea is foreign to you. So let me start teaching you that."

It wasn't foreign when Rae was around. "Okay. Sounds good."

I hung up the phone with him and leaned back into the chair. I pressed the heels of my hands into my eyes and sighed with relief. Okay. That was a better outcome than I had hoped for. Now, how the fuck was I going to get my hands on a copy of that sale contract?

Time to start searching the internet again.

The more I searched, the more insane this scenario became. A few weeks ago, I'd been hanging out with Roy, biding my time until graduation, and dreaming about plans to get out of this place. And now, I'd loved. I'd lost. I'd almost died. Only for my father to come to the decision he was going to throw me out on my ass. Force me to survive alone, no matter what.

Wait. The bank account.

I picked my phone back up and punched in my information on my banking app. And when I saw that the $4,999.00 transfer had actually gone through, my jaw hit the floor. I pushed away from the coffeehouse computer as I sifted through the numbers I'd recently dialed. I called the guy back I'd spoken with at the beginning of the week, hoping to initiate another transfer.

But things didn't go as planned.

"Your account's been locked down, Mr. Clarke."

I sighed. "Figures. I take it my father did that?"

"I'm not allowed to discuss the specifics of—"

"A few days ago you could. I'm still a beneficiary on that account, right?"

He paused. "Actually, sir, no. You're not."

I blinked. "What?"

"Your name has been removed from the account."

"You're being serious right now, aren't you?"

I guess I shouldn't have been surprised. But it didn't lessen the sting.

"I'm sorry, Mr. Clarke. But if I can be of service to you at all—"

"You're good. Thanks."

And I hung up the phone before the tears crested the folds of my eyes.

I tried to focus on the good. If I could just get my hands on a sale contract, I might stand a chance at reaping a great deal of money before this six to eight week period was up. And until then, I still had things I could sell. I threw away my empty coffee cup and started out of the coffeehouse. I flagged down a taxi and got in, then rattled off my home address.

I needed to go home and start preparing things to sell off.

It didn't shock me when I found Cecilia at the kitchen table. She'd practically taken up permanent residency there. I had come downstairs this morning and seen her sitting there, staring into her mug of coffee. And when I left to skip school and come back to the coffeehouse, she'd still been sitting there. Now, as I walked back inside around three in the afternoon, I found her still sitting there. Still in her robe. Still with that same damn mug of coffee.

Had she even moved?

"Cecilia?"

The two of us hadn't spoken since yesterday. Since she told me the offer my father had made her. And that the invitation wasn't open to me. I walked into the kitchen and sat down in front of her, waiting for her to lift her eyes to mine. Waiting for her to acknowledge me.

But she didn't.

"Cecilia?"

She sighed, but didn't say anything.

"Cecilia, we can do this."

She licked her lips. But again, stayed silent.

"I know you think this is hopeless. I know you don't think you have a choice. But you do. You have a choice in all this. You have a choice to stay with me and not go with him."

She closed her eyes. Drew in a deep breath. And still, she fucking stayed silent.

"I'm serious. I know you don't believe me, but I'm dead serious. You deserve better than him. Better than this. You won't be safe with my father."

"But I'll be safe with you."

I sighed. "I talked to that lawyer. Remember him? We've got some avenues we can take to get money."

She shook her head. "You and I both know how unpredictable your father is."

"And angry. Which is why you shouldn't be with him. Don't live alone in a house with him. You know it won't be better. Don't you? Can't you see how happy we've been as a familial unit every time he's been gone?"

She shook her head. "If we try something, he'll find a way to snuff it out."

I reached out for her hand. "Which is why we have to fight."

Her eyes fell to my palm. I wiggled my fingers, beckoning for her to take my grasp. She slowly moved her hand over mine and I closed my fingers, holding her trembling hand within my own. Tears slipped out from her eyes. It made me sick to see her crying so much. After everything this woman had done for me—after stepping up for me the way she had—it killed me to watch her go through this. To watch my fucking sperm donor yank her around like this.

"You have a choice, Cecilia. You just need to see that for yourself."

And instead of answering, she fell silent, refusing to answer as the tears continued to silently fall.

16

———

RAELYNN

The weekend came and went. As empty as my heart and as angry as my soul. Neither Michael nor Allison called me once the entire time. Probably because they were spending every waking moment doing everything but having sex. D.J. kept waltzing in and out of the house like he fucking owned the place. Which meant I had to listen to him and Mom fight all weekend. More of the same. More of him accusing her of shit she wasn't doing. More of Mom crying. More of him storming out. More of her getting drunk and bringing some random guy home from a bar before D.J. showed up with flowers and make-up sex.

The cycle made me sick.

I hated being at home. I hated being in this town. I wanted to graduate, leave it all behind, and get the fuck out of Dodge. The plan had been to move with Allison. Get a place together near her college campus. But I wasn't sure I wanted to do that anymore. How could a best friend forget about her heartbroken friend all weekend? And for a guy? If Allison's heart had been broken and I was still with Clint, I'd bat Clint off in a fucking heartbeat to go be with her.

Guess I didn't mean as much to Allison as I figured I did.

Monday morning couldn't come fast enough. But even then, it still sucked. I walked to school by myself, went to class by myself. I got out of one toxic environment and plunged headfirst into another. I didn't see Michael or Allison until I got to homeroom. Allison's face was flushed with a red I was all too familiar with. She smiled with a dopey smile I'd once had on my face.

She was in love.

And making out in the back stairwells of the school.

I didn't feel like facing Michael and her at lunch. It was too painful and I was too angry. Sure, maybe my anger wasn't warranted. But that didn't stop me from feeling angry. From feeling like they needed to tuck shit in a bit. So I took my lunch to the library. I bypassed the table I usually occupied and headed for the middle of the room. A table surrounded by rows and rows of books.

People had to navigate a labyrinth in order to come find me.

And that was how I wanted it.

I sighed as I tried studying. I opened my books and munched on some snacks I managed to steal from my pantry at home. But I wasn't hungry. I was tired. I needed caffeine. I needed a pick-me-up. I needed coffee, otherwise I wouldn't make it through the back half of my day. I looked up from my books, spotting a clock down one of the rows of books, hanging cock-eyed on the wall at the end. I squinted my eyes to take in the time. Only halfway through lunch before my studying period started.

I hadn't taken my study period lately.

But today I needed it to get some damn coffee.

I packed up my things and snuck out of school. I made my way out the back doors and sprinted for the main road. I had over an hour before history class started. So I took my time. I walked into town and crossed the road, heading straight for the coffee shop by my work. It still gave me the creeps to walk around in that parking lot. I stayed as far away from that dumbass tree as possible. I ripped open the door of the coffeehouse and sniffed deeply, drawing in its wonderful scent.

Then I got in line.

I pulled out my phone while I waited and scrolled through the pictures I had saved. The only thing that gave me any sort of distraction this past weekend was looking at prom dresses. I mean, I wasn't going. Not now, anyway. I wouldn't have a date. My two best friends would be tonguing each other down all night. Not something I wanted to endure for some 'high school memories.'

Still, looking for dresses and saving pictures pulled me out of my nightmarish life for a little while.

Gave me something else to focus on.

"No. No. Too short. Why did I like this one again? Nuh-uh. Too expensive. Don't make it in my size, I don't think."

I deleted dresses I didn't like. Ones that were too sparkly after sleeping on them for a couple of nights. I eliminated them, one by one. Until I was left with dresses that were more simplistic. Elegant. Full-length dresses with soft, silken material. And definitely no fucking sparkles. Something green. Or blue. Possibly navy. Though not black.

A tapping on my shoulder ripped me from my trance.

"Can I help… you…?"

I turned around and gazed into Clint's eyes. I looked up at him, my brow furrowing in confusion. His eyes fell to my phone and I quickly closed out the pictures. Then I slipped my phone into my purse.

"He—hey, there. Hi. Hi, Clint."

He grinned. "Hi, Rae."

I cleared my throat. "How are you doing?"

He nodded. "Been better. Yourself?"

"I'm getting along."

"Study session time, I take it?"

"Huh?"

He nodded toward the door. "At school. Study session time?"

I snickered. "Oh. Yes. It is. I need a pick-me-up."

"Don't blame you. Sleep's hard to come by nowadays."

"Yeah. I suppose so."

The cashier sighed. "Can I get you anything?"

I whipped around and saw there was no one else standing in front of me. Just an impatient woman behind the cash register softly glaring at me. I scurried up to the front and placed my order. An iced caramel macchiato. With an extra shot.

Then Clint leaned over. "And I'll have a large rosewater and caramel coffee. Put it on the same ticket."

I looked over at him. "You don't have to do that."

But he didn't answer me.

Instead, he simply handed the girl his card, paying for my drink without so much as a glance down at me. I didn't know whether to be thankful or frustrated, irritated or flattered. Clint ushered me over to the side where we waited for our drinks. And I watched as the girl behind the cash register followed Clint with her eyes.

Making me very jealous.

"So, how's school?"

His voice pulled me from my jealous trance. "You'd know if you were there."

He shrugged. "Finding a place to live is a bit more important right now."

"So your father's really selling the house?"

"Got a buyer and everything. I'll be out on my ass in a few weeks, if I can't come up with something. Oh, those are our coffees."

I reached for mine. "Thanks."

Clint took a sip of his. "Anyway, it is what it is."

"Will you please let me help?"

"There's nothing you can do to help. It's just a shit scenario."

"All I'm asking you to do is let me back in. We don't have to date. We don't have to see one another. Just let me help you. When have I proven to you that I can't help?"

"This isn't your issue to deal with anymore, Rae."

I sighed. "Then why passive-aggressively bring it up like that?"

He paused. "What?"

"If it wasn't my issue and you didn't want me worried about it, then you wouldn't have brought it up at all. But you did. Which tells me you at least want to talk about it. So I'm here. You've already bought me coffee. Why don't we sit, or take a walk, and at least talk about it?"

His eyes danced between mine. "Are you taking a psychology class or something?"

"Michael is."

"Ah."

"That's beside the point, though. Are you going to let me back in long enough to help you? Or are you going to silently suffer and then proclaim the world's against you?"

He grinned. "Did you just call me out?"

"Yes. I fully and completely did. But only because I want to help."

"Rae, it's just—"

My glare shut him up. "You don't get to make choices for me, Clinton. If you push me away one more time, it's because you want to. Not because you're protecting me. Because the only thing you've caused me is heartache and sleepless nights. Don't you dare fool yourself on that."

And with a heavy sigh, I watched sorrow rush behind his eyes.

"Want to take a walk with me?"

I nodded. "I'm more than happy to. Come on. You lead the way."

17

CLINTON

I opened the door for Rae. "I don't really know where to start."

She walked out the door. "Well, you can start from the beginning."

"You already know the beginning. Kind of."

"Then, start from what happened after the last time I came to your house."

"You mean where you almost killed yourself jumping over the porch railing?"

She shrugged. "I would've done anything to get away from you in that moment."

Her words struck me hard. "I'm sorry."

She waved her hand in the air. "It's in the past. Talk to me, Clint. What's going on? What did Cecilia want to talk to you so badly about?"

I sighed. "Ah. That."

"That doesn't sound good."

"I mean, it's not. But it also doesn't shock me. Cecilia finally got in touch with Dad. He confirmed that he was selling the house. That he already had a buyer for it. And that I wasn't welcome to come with them to their next destination."

She stopped in her tracks. "What?"

I nodded slowly. "Yep."

"Wait, can he actually do that? Just… abandon you like that?"

"I'm eighteen. I'm a legal adult. He doesn't have to take me anywhere."

"That can't be right. Clint, that just can't be right."

I sighed. "Well, it's the reason why I haven't been at school. I've been here every morning, giving the illusion I'm at school in case Dad randomly stops by the house."

"But Cecilia knows you aren't in school right now?"

I nodded. "She does. We aren't talking about it. But she does."

"Why are you coming here?"

I started walking again. "I'm using their computers to do some research. Figure out my options. Find my next moves."

Rae walked alongside me. "Have you come up with anything substantial?"

"I mean, not really. Some working theories. There are states where, if I live there and declare residency, community college is free. But that's assuming I can get out of school with the grades I need. Which we both know won't happen."

"You never know, Clint. If you get back to school and let me help you, we can easily ace your classes. That'll bring your GPA up."

"Yeah, but even if I did that, I'm not sure more school is my route. I hate school. I can't stand it. I'll need money, and quickly."

She nodded. "So what kind of jobs can you get? There isn't much out there for someone without a high school diploma. Which means you'll still have to come back to school and graduate."

I paused. "How did you know that?"

And when she blushed, my heart went out to her.

"Who did you ask?"

She shook her head. "It was nothing. Just a passing question."

"Rae, what happened?"

"Just a rough conversation with the guidance counselor. That's all."

I reached out for her, stopping her in her tracks. "What did you say to the counselor?"

"Nothing that implicated anything was going on. It was just a passing question. Nothing more. Okay?"

"Are you sure?"

She scoffed. "Do I look like I'm lying to you?"

I searched her eyes. The last thing I needed was for someone at the school to be breathing down me and my father's necks. Things were bad enough. I didn't need them to get any worse.

"Why were you in the counselor's office?"

Rae shrugged. "Does it matter?"

"It matters to me."

"Well, maybe that'll be our next conversation."

I sighed. "You want me to talk, but you won't talk?"

"The focus isn't on me right now. We can put the focus on me after we're done with this conversation. Okay?"

"You promise?"

She gazed into my eyes. "With all my heart."

The look in her eye tugged at my gut. At my soul, really. How she still had care for me in her eyes, I'd never know. Rae was a mystery. Unlike any person I'd ever met in my life. And I had no idea how the fuck she still cared about me. I wanted to take her in my arms. I wanted to kiss those lips of hers. I wanted to taste her coffee on the tip of her tongue and erase any fear or pain or doubt from her mind.

I still care about you, too. Can you see it?

"Clint?"

I blinked. "Yeah. Sorry."

"It's okay. It's fine. Just—traffic's picking up. So we better cross the road now."

Without thinking, I took her hand. We jogged across the intersection, and the heat of her skin against mine sent tingles up and down my spine. But once we touched down on the side of the road, I dropped her hand. I couldn't stand to hold it. I didn't have a right to hold it.

Even though I wanted to thread our fingers together and lead her onward.

"What else is going on?"

Rae's voice forced me to speak. "I mean, that's really it. I got in contact with a lawyer. You know, that one I went to talk to after my accident?"

"What did he have to say?"

I shrugged. "He gave me some good advice. Apparently, many of the things in that house are mine, though I didn't purchase them. He said something about 'common use,' or something like that. You know, the couches and fine china. Since we all used it in the house, it all belongs to us. Just like he can't force me to replace it if I break it, he can't sue me if I sell it."

"So you're thinking about getting money that way."

"Not thinking about it. Doing it. I put some things up for sale last night. Took pictures with my phone. That's the reason I was at the coffee shop today. I was meeting various people with things that already sold."

She looked over at me. "So you've got some money in your pocket now."

"More than 'some money.' Let's just say I'm itching to get back to the house so I can stash it away somewhere. It's making me nervous to carry it around."

She smiled. "I mean, I hate that you're having to go to those kinds of lengths. But I'm glad it's working out for you."

"It sucks, but it'll give me what I need to take my next steps."

"How much are you hoping to get?"

"If I can sell everything I want to? Three hundred thousand."

"Holy shit! Are you serious?"

I chuckled. "I don't expect to sell all of it, though. That's a lot of money in a small amount of time. I'd be fine with even a third of that."

"Do you mind me asking how much you have right now?"

"Including what's in my bank account? About twenty grand."

Her jaw dropped open. "Wow. Then, yes. We need to get you to a bank or something."

"Not a bank."

"Why not? Don't you have a bank account?"

"I do, but my father can access it at any time."

She paused. "Wait, your father still has access to your bank account?"

I nodded. "He does. I'm working on that, though. I placed a call today to a completely separate bank. I wanted to open up an account and I've already got an electronic transfer in the works. Come tomorrow morning, the account I have right now should have all my funds transferred into this new account my father can't touch. Then I'll put this money in my account."

"Once you know your father can't access it."

"Exactly."

She puffed out her cheeks. "It makes me sick you even have to go to these lengths."

"My father's a control freak. Any amount of control I can rip away from him puts me in a much better position."

"Is it bad that I kind of want to wring his neck?"

I chuckled. "You and me both."

I worried that being seen with me would be bad for Rae. But she didn't seem to give a shit at all. We got to talking so much that we weren't paying attention to where we were walking. It wasn't until the smell of her neighborhood caught my nose and I realized I'd walked her to her doorstep that I understood why I had aimlessly walked here with her.

Because for days, all I'd wanted was to come over and lie down with her.

"I probably should've walked you back to school, huh?"

She snickered. "I'm kind of over school right now."

I furrowed my brow. "Why?"

She shrugged. "I don't know. Just not resonating with me right now."

"Rae, you can't let your—"

"I know, I know. Clint, my grades aren't slipping. I'm not behind on work. In the whole of my high school career, I've had four absences. I'm good. I promise."

I sighed. "Okay, then."

"I just don't want to be bad for you. And I feel like the more I'm around you, the worse for you I become."

She opened her front door. "I mean, if you want to get technical, none of this shit started happening until you broke up with me. So, I guess I have an argument for how *not* being with you is bad for me."

"Do you always have an argument for everything?"

"When people try to dictate what's best for me instead of letting me do that? Yes. Come on in."

I stood my ground. "I'm not sure if that's smart."

Rae snickered. "Stop denying yourself what you want and get the hell inside. No one's home."

"Which is the issue. I'm bad news, Rae. And the more wrapped up in me you get, the more of my life you get with it."

"And how is that bad? When did I ever give you the impression I didn't want to be wrapped up in it? You do get that, right? You do understand that you don't get to decide what's bad and what's good for me. Right?"

"I just want to keep you—"

Her face turned red. "Damn it, Clint. Cut the shit for a second! I want to *be* with you. Really be with you. How the hell is that a bad thing? You aren't your father. I know you *think* you are, but you aren't. You aren't a culmination of the bad things that have happened to you. You're just you. Why can't you see that? Why are you punishing me because *you* can't see that?"

I stood there, dumbfounded as she reached for my hand. She took it and threaded our fingers together. An action I hadn't had the balls to do myself. She softly tugged me inside. And after she closed it, she held my hand tightly, physically refusing to let go as I looked down into her gorgeous eyes.

Eyes I had missed.

"You're all I want, Clint. And whatever life comes with you, I'll weather it. Because that's what people do when they care about each other. And I care about you. I always will."

My eyes danced between hers. I felt so shell-shocked by her words that I couldn't move. She rose to her tiptoes and pressed her lips softly against mine. I froze. I didn't pucker my lips or flinch as her hand slid up my arms. I tried to stand my ground for as long as possible. I tried to resist her warmth and her loving demeanor and her perfect words.

Until I couldn't any longer.

"Just let me have you. That's all I'm asking," she whispered.

Settling my hands against her hips, I backed her against the door as my tongue invaded her mouth.

18

RAELYNN

My God, how I missed him. His kiss. His touch. His forceful nature. And when his hands fell to my hips, I opened my mouth for him. I felt his tongue slide across the roof of my mouth and I could have cried.

He ripped my shirt off and kissed down my neck. I managed to slip off his jacket and wondered where his leather one had gotten off to. Clothes came off in a flurry as his lips slid down to my chest. Kissing and sucking. His teeth sank into my skin and marked me as my hands slid through his hair.

It had grown so long, and I loved it.

I slid my hands down his back. He buried his face into my cleavage. His warmth encompassed me as his hands slid up and down the backs of my legs. I panted with need for him. I had to have him. And as he picked me up, he slung me over his shoulder, my eyes level with his lower back as he carried me into the living room.

But not before cracking his hand against my ass.

"Clint!"

He growled as he tossed me to the couch. I watched him with wild eyes as he slid out of the rest of his clothes. Those rippling muscles came into view before he ravaged my body, pulling off the rest of my clothes. I was bare, naked underneath him as his lips crashed back to mine. The heady feeling I got from his body settling against mine turned my brain to mush. I raked my fingernails across his skin. He kissed down my stomach before shifting me how he wanted me. And with my back melting into the couch cushions, he knelt between my legs.

Before diving into my body.

I moaned. "Clint, yes."

His tongue parted me and my back arched. My hands twisted into his hair as he stroked me to a constant high. He kept me on the edge. Teasing me. Filling me with his fingers. Stroking those wondrous parts of me I had ached for him to touch. My legs wrapped around his head. My heels dug into his shoulders. He drank from my fountain as I poured forth for him, ravenously bucking against his face. Feeling his stubble against my lower lips. Feeling his hands meander up my curves until he massaged my breasts.

"Clint. Clint. Clint. Clint."

His name fell from my lips like a desperate prayer. And as my body locked out, I spiraled into a darkened abyss. I felt like I was floating and sinking at the same time. Light burst behind my eyes before being swallowed up by the darkness. My toes curled as he buried his tongue between my lower lips and my nails raked along his scalp. He held me to him. Drank every ounce of arousal I offered him.

And when I collapsed, heaving for air, he kissed my inner thighs.

A trail of wetness followed his lips as he kissed up my body. My arms fell to the side, unable to move. I shivered with anticipation, puckering my lip as I waited for him to press against me once more, pick me up and mold me however he wanted, so long as it made him happy.

But he didn't kiss me with the fury he did before.

His lips softly captured mine and I tasted myself on him. He wrapped his arms around me and effortlessly picked me up. He swung me around, settling himself on the couch as I straddled him. I sank against him, resting my naked body against his muscles. My curves dripped into the divots of his strength. I gasped for air against the crook of his neck. His hands massaged my back. My thighs, my hips, until I was strong enough to lift my head.

"Please tell me this isn't a dream," I whispered.

His forehead propped up mine and my eyes fell open. I found

him staring at me with a smile on his face. A genuine smile. One that reached his eyes. And my heart felt fuller than it had in days. I felt as if my broken heart were mending with every massage of his palms. With every stroke of his fingertips. With every kiss of his lips.

Then his cock pulsed underneath me.

"No. It's not a dream," he murmured.

His hands fisted my hips and he lifted me up. Like a rag doll, there for his pleasure, he slowly sank me down his girth. Inch by inch, until he filled me in all the ways I remembered. My head fell back. My eyes fluttered closed. His arm wrapped around my lower back, holding me to him as I adjusted. I felt him pulsing, his heat already filling me. My hands pressed against his chest, sinking him deeper into the cushions of the couch.

And as our eyes connected, his hands slowly pushed back.

"Let me guide you, Rae."

I captured his lips. "I'm all yours."

Our eyes held one another as he steadily moved my hips, showing me how to please him. How to stroke him in all the ways he wished. My arms wrapped around his neck and I clung to him as I slowly found my rhythm. His arms cloaked my back, holding me to him as I rolled and bounced, pulling groans and grunts from the back of his throat.

"Rae. Shit."

"That's it, Clint. Like that."

"Don't stop. I can't—you're—don't stop."

"I won't. I won't. I won't ever stop. Never."

Faster and faster, until our breaths became one. I breathed the air he afforded me as his hands explored my body. I bounced in his lap, feeling my arousal dripping against his skin and marking him, the way he'd marked me with his teeth. His hands slid around to my ass cheeks and gripped them tightly, rolling me deeper against mine. And as his face fell to my bosom, I felt him sucking deep, dark marks against my skin.

Until the two of us sought our end with one another.

"Clint, yes!"

"Fucking hell, Rae. You're perfection."

He pounded into me and my body jumped for him. His growls overpowered my whimpers as I spiraled out of control again. I collapsed against him, feeling him hold me as he thrusted quicker.

Faster. Harder. He worked me through my orgasm. Jumping my bones and making my muscles twitch as I felt him mark my warm walls.

And as my head fell into the crook of his neck, he collapsed against the couch. Holding me. Splaying his hands across my skin.

As the evidence of our lust dripped from between my legs.

19

———

CLINTON

I stroked my fingers through her hair as her weight rested against me. Home. I felt as if I were home again. And I didn't know if I'd ever feel this way about anything again. A place. Or a person. Or a city. Or a state. I felt more confused than ever about my future. And yet, none of it mattered.

Not when Rae was in my arms.

"We should clean up."

I grinned as she slowly lifted her head.

"You think, huh?"

She smiled. "I know. I'm leaking."

I chuckled. "I thought you liked that feeling."

"No one likes that feeling."

I paused. "True. I don't like leaking, either."

She snickered. "So, shower?"

"Together?"

"Is there any other kind?"

I felt a renewed sense of strength rush through my muscles and I quickly picked her up.

"Clint!"

"Up the stairs, I presume?"

She kicked her legs. "We need our clothes, you idiot."

I dipped down. "I've got them. I can get them."

"Put me down. You're going to drop—Clint!"

I chuckled as I bent down, picking our clothes off the floor. I slowly made my way to the stairs with her tossed over my shoulder, her legs kicking and her hands gripping tightly to my hips. I walked up the stairs and found my way into the bathroom upstairs. And after kicking the door closed behind me, I dropped our clothes before settling her onto the bathroom counter.

"I didn't drop you."

She frowned deeply. "Don't you ever do that again."

I kissed the tip of her nose. "No promises."

"Clint!"

I captured her lips and felt her giggle against me.

"I missed you, Rae."

She sighed. "I missed you too, Clint."

"I'm sorry."

She nuzzled my nose. "I'm sorry, too."

"You have nothing to be sorry for."

"Just take the apology, crazy."

I snickered. "Not when it isn't warranted. I put us in this situation. Let me own up to that."

She cupped my cheeks. "Fine. You can make it up to me by washing me down in the shower."

"Doesn't sound like much of a punishment."

"It is when you realize I'm not letting you have sex with me in that shower."

"Oh, really. Is that a challenge?"

Fifteen minutes later, I had Rae pinned to that fucking shower wall. I rolled against her, feeling her cling to me as her muffled moans fell against my shoulder. I loved being encased by her. I loved the feeling of her pussy squeezing me dry. And as bubbles popped against my skin, I made love to her in that shower.

And I hope she felt it as much as I meant it.

We washed one another down, and it took all I had not to indulge in her a third time. We dried off and put our clothes back on, then made our way downstairs. The heat of the shower followed us. I couldn't take my eyes off Rae's glistening hair, damp from the shower and begging to be fisted. Begging to be wrapped around my wrist and tugged on as I took her from behind.

Focus, Clint. Don't fuck this up.

"So, you hungry?"

Rae's voice called to me from the kitchen, helping me focus.

"Starving, actually."

She giggled. "I figured. So how does a pizza and movie kind of night sound? I mean, you're here and we might as well make the most of the moment.."

"On a Monday night? Won't your mom be back soon? And you can technically make it to your last class of the day, if we leave now."

She shrugged. "I already finished up the homework and read ahead. Plus, there's a note here in the kitchen from Mom. She'll be out for most of the night tonight."

I paused. "When did your mother come home?"

"I'm not sure. I guess it's a good thing we were quiet in the shower."

I furrowed my brow. "I wasn't quiet in the shower."

And her laughter filled the hallway that separated us. Drawing me down the corridor until I found her in the kitchen.

"What do you like on your pizza?"

I shrugged. "Anything you want is fine with me, so long as it doesn't have peppers on it."

"So, pepperoni, mushrooms, and tomato all right?"

"Sounds fine to me."

"If you want, you can go pick the movie while I get this ordered."

I grinned. "Just make sure you tell the delivery guy you're paying with cash."

Rae turned to me. "Why?"

I quirked an eyebrow. "Already forgetting our prior conversation? I've got money on me. I'll take care of it."

"You don't have to do that, Clint."

"I want to. Tell him you'll be paying with cash. And get whatever else you want."

She smiled so sweetly at me and it tugged at my heart strings. I didn't think this day could get any better. But I also didn't want to jinx it. I left the kitchen as she started placing our order, making my way into the living room. With the scent of us still lingering in the air, I blushed. Actually, truly blushed. Because holy fuck, her mother must've known something was up from the smell of this room.

Hopefully not, though.

I turned on their television and flipped through the few channels they had. Until finally, I settled on a movie just starting. It looked like a sappy romance movie. One of those kinds of movies where women cried at the end. But I didn't give a shit. So long as I got to stay with Rae, I was happy.

"Pizza's ordered. What'd you find?"

I tossed the remote control to her. "Just this romance movie, I think."

"Oh, no. Not that one. I'd rather watch the news."

I snickered. "Then, by all means, find something else."

She flipped through the channels for a while before rushing up the stairs. I heard her thundering around and my brow furrowed deeply. Until she came jumping down the stairs with DVDs in her arms. She sprawled them out on the floor for me to take in, then yanked me down to the floor with her.

"Here, take your pick."

I glanced at the titles. "These are all action movies."

Rae paused. "And?"

"You don't want to watch something more…?"

She snickered. "Girly? What? Girls can't like action movies, too?"

Fucking hell, I love you. "The Expendables, then. Definitely."

"Ugh, I love these movies. I hope they make a third one. Really."

"We can watch both of them tonight, if you want."

"Yes!"

The way she hissed with delight pulled a smile across my face. One that made my cheeks ache. I went and sat on the other couch in the room, the love sofa, so I could cuddle Rae close to me. She started up the movie and flopped down, pouring her legs over my lap. And as our hands found one another's, our fingers laced together.

It felt good, being back together with her.

"Thank you," I said.

"For what?"

"For fighting with me through all this."

She giggled. "You aren't getting rid of me that easily."

"Most days, I feel like you're the only reliable thing I have in my life. And I'm scared of fucking that up."

"Well, try not breaking up with me this time around. That might help."

I chuckled. "Yeah. I'll try that tactic this time."

I felt her staring at me and I turned my head.

"What?"

She smiled softly. "Say more sweet things."

My thumb stroked her skin softly. "You're amazing."

"Again."

"You're the best thing that's ever happened to me."

"Again."

"There isn't a night that's gone by that you haven't been in my dreams."

Her eyes welled with tears. "One more time, please."

I brought her hand to my lips to kiss. "I feel bad for people who don't have something like this."

And when she smiled, it filled my heart with sunlight.

"Me, too, Clint. I feel bad for them, too."

The ringing of her doorbell severed our moment. But it brought along a completely different moment. A set of moments forever seared into my memory. One where we gorged ourselves on pizza and rooted on the good guys in the movie. One where we watched back-to-back movies with full stomachs and barely-opened eyes. One where Rae tugged me upstairs, insisting that I stay the night with her in her bed.

Making memories I knew I'd never forget as I stripped her body down, kissed every valley she had to offer, and made love to her until we both passed out from exhaustion.

20

———

RAELYNN

My eyes fell open and, for once, my chest didn't hurt. My eyes weren't sore. My legs weren't trembling with exhaustion. I felt something warm draped over my waist and I sighed with relief, seeing Clint's hand splayed over my bare stomach. I reached for my cell phone slowly, not wanting to disturb him and the soft breaths that fell against the shell of my ear. And as I gazed at the time, I quickly navigated my phone to turn my alarm off.

Before it started blaring and woke him up.

"Mm-mm. Come here."

I giggled as he pulled me close.

"We have to get up soon, handsome."

"Mm-mm. No."

He buried his face into my hair and I smiled broadly. I slowly turned around, abandoning my cell phone for one last glance of his sleepy face. He peeked out of one eye before screwing it shut tight. I kissed his forehead. Then the tip of his nose. And finally, both of his cheeks.

"It's Tuesday morning. We can't skip school."

He groaned playfully. "I've been skipping school for days."

"Which is why you need to get up with me and come to school."

"I don't have a change of clothes."

"Are the ones you have dirty?"

"If I say 'yes,' will that get me out of school?"

I snickered. "You're insane, you know that?"

"And you're too comfy for your own good."

He buried his face into my breasts and held me close. I laughed softly as I stroked my fingertips through his hair. As I stared up at the ceiling, I felt life falling back into place again, my anger dissipating, my frustrations melting away. He kissed my skin mindlessly, allowing his leg to slip between mine. He trapped me underneath his body, pinning me to the mattress.

"I know what you're doing, Clint."

He slid on top of me. "No moving."

I wrapped my arms around him. "Clint."

"Just five more minutes of this."

"We don't have long as it is. School starts in an hour."

"It won't take me but about twenty minutes to get ready."

I scoffed playfully. "And what about me?"

He kissed my neck. "What about you?"

"What if it takes me longer than twenty minutes to get ready?"

He rose his head up. "Does it?"

"I mean, no. But that's not the point."

He snickered. "You're amazing to wake up to."

He kissed me, and I didn't even mind his morning breath. The sun shone through my window and my heart felt fuller than it had in, well, what seemed like forever. I wrapped my arms around him and let him slide between my legs. My hips ached in all the right ways and my body felt as if it had been run over by an eighteen-wheeler.

And yet I let him slide into me.

I gasped. "We have to be quiet."

He kissed my nose. "I know."

"Clint, I don't know if—oh."

And when he captured my lips, he swallowed my sounds.

Slowly, deftly, he rolled against me, pulling us both out of our hazy stupors. He swallowed my moans and I held on to his groans. My hands slid down his back as his skin prickled underneath my touch. I'd never get used to waking up to him like this. It would always be a treat. Feeling him fill me would always be a surprise encounter I hoped would never end.

He moved so easily my bed didn't even rock. He ground his tightly-wound curls against my body, shivering me to ecstatic heights. I kissed him, sucking on his lower lip. I relished how he felt first thing in the morning. I wanted to always experience this. Him. Inside me. Slowly waking us both up.

Whatever I had to do in my future to get that, I would.

Because Clint was my future.

We climbed up the precipice before throwing ourselves over the edge. And as he collapsed against me, I felt him filling me. Time and time again. His body quivered as I clung to him. I locked my legs around him, refusing to let him move. He growled against the crook of my neck, kissing and nibbling my collarbone. And once our bodies stopped shaking, I sighed with relief.

"We really do have to go to school, Clint."

He groaned. "You really know how to ruin a moment."

I giggled, kissing the side of his face. "Come on. Up, up, up."

"I don't want to go to school."

"You sound like a toddler. Get up and let's go."

"You're so mean, stupidhead."

His pouting voice made me laugh out loud.

"Come on, now. Don't make me scold you like a child."

He harrumphed like a toddler and I fell apart in laughter.

"Quit being the lazy son of a bitch you've turned into and get your ass to school."

He scoffed. "Wow, Mom. So harsh."

I smiled. "I know. But sometimes, you test me."

He cupped my cheeks and captured my lips. He rolled me on top of him and it took all I had to wiggle away from his grasp. I knew if he kept distracting me, touching me, and sliding between my legs, I'd stay there. All day. Enjoying him and feeling him as our bodies writhed together.

And we really needed to get to school.

I stood up. "Come on. School will help us get our minds off things."

He grinned. "You take my mind off things."

"It's not working, Clint. I'm not coming back to bed."

"Oh, really? Not if I… do this?"

He wrapped his arms around my waist and I clapped my hand against my mouth. I cried out into my palm as he picked me up and tossed me back onto the bed. I turned over and tried to scramble off the bed before he fell on top of me. But I didn't move fast enough and his body pinned me to the mattress.

Giggles fell from my lips. "I'm in the wet spot. I'm in the wet spot."

Clint kissed the back of my neck. "Should've thought about that before telling me no."

"Clint! We're going to be late."

"And if you keep yelling my name, you're going to wake up Mother Dear."

He tickled my sides and I pressed my face into my mattress. I wiggled around, trying to buck him off as laughter made my voice hoarse. I felt myself sweating. Growing red in the face. And if we didn't get a move on it, we'd both be late.

"Clint! Mercy! Uncle! I give!"

He chuckled. "Ready to give up and spend all day gazing into one another's eyes in bed?"

I sighed. "We really have to go to school. We have to get you graduated. Your future depends on it, if you want a decent one."

Reality crashed back down around us and Clint wiggled off my body. He helped me to my feet and I turned around, readying myself to apologize. But he pressed his finger against my lips, silencing any plea I might have had. And as his hand slid through my knotted hair, his eyes danced between mine.

"I know you're right. I also want you to know how much I cherish these moments we have together."

I smiled. "Well, because of your antics, I now need a quick shower."

He grinned. "So do I."

"Care to take one together?"

"Do we have time for a distraction?"

"No, we don't. Because you spent it tickling me."

"Damn."

I swatted his chest playfully. "Consider it a lesson learned, then. Come on. We have to be quiet. Mom's still snoring, but she won't be for long."

Clint paused. "Wait, you can hear her snoring?"

My face fell and I walked over to the door. I felt him watch me, his eyes on my naked hips as they swayed. I cracked the door open and let the bombastic sound fill the room. I mean, my mother was sawing some fucking logs in her sleep. Pulling the damn curtains in from downstairs. I grinned as I watched Clint's eyes widen. But we didn't have any time to waste. I nodded my head down the hallway, motioning for him to follow me. And quickly, we crept down the hallway, making it into the bathroom with nothing but the sound of Mom's snores following us.

Then we hopped into a hot-ass shower.

Clint's hands wandered, but he didn't try to distract me. He washed me down like he had last night, taking great care with my inner thighs. I narrowed my eyes at him. I silently scolded him as he slipped to his knees. He kissed random parts of my body, causing my skin to flush as my eyes slowly closed.

Teasing me. Relentlessly.

A few minutes before we needed to start getting dressed.

"Clint."

He chuckled. "Just giving you a taste of what you could have had."

I moaned. "Please, we have to go—"

"I know. I know. We do. I know."

He punctuated his sentences with kisses, though. Against my hips. Inside my thighs. Against my lips.

My lower lips, at least.

I gripped his hair and pulled him up from his knees. I crashed our lips together, seeking some sort of a release. I needed it. I couldn't go to school like this. But I'd have to. I got out of the shower without washing Clint down. I wouldn't be able to touch him without forcing him back between my legs. He chuckled as he washed himself down, and I stewed in my frustration as I dried myself off.

It was good frustration, though.

Frustration I couldn't wait to relieve after the day was done.

Clint hopped out of the shower and I handed him a towel. He dried himself off and we crept back down the hallway, greeted with the sounds of my mother's awful snoring. How any man slept beside her with that nonsense was beyond me. And together, we quickly got dressed. I slipped my phone into my back pocket, threw my hair up into a ponytail, slipped my backpack over my shoulders and led Clint down the hallway, trying to maneuver around the creaky steps. I didn't want to risk waking my mother up. I didn't want to deal with any of her bullshit on such a perfect morning. After such a perfect evening.

With the boy I adored.

"Come on. We can still find Allison and Michael. If they're waiting for me."

He paused. "What do you mean 'if'?"

I sighed. "It's a long story."

His fingers threaded through mine. "Care to fill me in on the punchline?"

"They're together now and can't keep their hands off one another."

"Ah, the honeymoon stage. I like that stage."

I snickered. "I know you do."

"I mean, good for them. They seem like a cute couple. I take it they've kind of… set you off to the side, though?"

I shrugged. "I mean, I get it. Just kind of came at a shit time. Them making out all the damn time while I'm nursing a broken heart."

He kissed the back of my hand. "Well, no more of those."

"Promise?"

He kissed my cheek. "I promise with all I am."

I smiled. "Good."

"Is that Clint!?"

Allison's squeal made me smile.

"Guess they're waiting this morning," I said.

Michael waved at us. "Hey! Clint! Good to see you, man."

Clint squeezed my hand. "You think he's serious?"

I nodded. "I think Michael's loosened up a *lot* since he and Allison started officially dating."

Allison came running at me and I wrapped my arms around her in a massive hug. Part of me was still hurt, but the bulk of me was simply happy to have my friend back. I saw Michael walk up and give Clint a pat on the back. One of those dude hugs I saw around school. Allison released me and wrapped her arms around Clint's waist. And I saw a look of jealousy flash behind Michael's eyes. It was cute, really. How protective he'd become of her.

Clint made sure to do nothing but pat Allison's back, though.

"Good to see you, Mike. Aly. How you guys been?"

Allison pulled away. "Oh, my gosh. We have so much to catch you up on."

Clint grinned. "Like how you two are an item?"

Allison smacked her lips. "You told him already?"

My eyebrows rose. "Was I not supposed to?"

Michael grinned. "She wanted to tell him. Well, she wants to tell everybody. I'm assuming that also included Clint."

Allison nodded. "If he ever got his butt back to school. Really, it's good to see you."

Clint smiled. "It's good to see you two as well. And I'm happy for you guys. Congrats."

Michael clapped his back again. "Thanks, man."

Silence fell around us before Clint sighed.

"So I take it you guys know?"

I looked up at him. "They don't know everything."

Michael cleared his throat. "You know where you're moving to?"

Clint snickered. "Who said my father wants me moving with him?"

Allison sighed. "Oh, Clint. Really?"

He nodded slowly. "Really."

Michael's face fell. "Well, we've got an extra room at my place. My parents can fix you up. You can stay there until graduation. You know, finish out the school year and everything."

Clint shook his head. "I don't wanna put you and your family out."

Allison furrowed her brow. "Who said you are? I mean, you have to graduate. With us, you know?"

I linked my arm within his and looked up at him.

"Think about it, at least? Michael's parents are really nice. You'd like them."

Clint looked down at me. "You sure about that? My own father doesn't even like me."

Michael put his hand on Clint's shoulder. "I'm sure. You take my word for it. All you do is let me know, and I'll have it fixed up for you. Okay? If you need a place to stay, I've got you."

Clint sighed. "Why, though?"

Allison shrugged. "Because that's what friends do."

Michael nodded. "Yep. It's what friends do for one another. Though, if you break Rae's heart again, we're going to have to have a talk."

Allison's face fell. "No hurting my best friend again. Got it?"

Clint grinned. "I read you loud and clear."

Michael smiled. "Good. Now, let's get the hell out of Dodge before we're all late for class."

21

CLINTON

Aly linked her arm with Mike. "So I can help you get caught up in the classes we have. I mean, other than history. Out of all the subjects, I'm terrible at history. And Rae's great with dates."

Mike nodded. "Yep. I'll shoot my dad a text during class changes to see about you staying in the guest bedroom. I'll just let him know your parents are moving and you need a place to crash to get to and from school."

"Oh, oh! I can get you notes as well in your classes. I'm sure I know someone that can photocopy things for me. I'll get you copies so you don't have to worry about it."

"And you can ride with me to and from school. Since I'm assuming you haven't replaced your bike or anything."

"Are you going to replace your bike? I don't know if I could, after what you've been through."

"You're going to need some money, too. I mean, unless you've already got that worked out."

I paused. "Actually, I do. But that puts me in a bind."

Aly furrowed her brow. "Why?"

Rae gasped. "Oh, shit."

I rubbed her back. "It's okay. It's fine. Let's just get to school and we can figure it out."

Mike started walking. "What puts you in a bind? What's going on?"

I sighed. "I need to check something first. Hold on."

Him mentioning money reminded me of that damn bank account. As we continued walking toward school, I pulled out my phone, checked my email notifications and smiled. I went and checked my current bank account and laughed when I saw an account balance of zero. I threw my fists into the air and Rae started clapping. Then, she leapt at me and wrapped me up in a massive hug.

Leaving Aly and Mike in confusion.

"Yes! Yes! This is a great step in the right direction."

I snickered. "If only I had time to get to the bank."

Rae shook her head. "No, no. No focusing on the negative for now. Promise me."

I grinned. "I promise."

Mike paused the walk. "Someone want to fill us in now?"

Aly nodded. "Yeah. I want to celebrate with you guys, too."

I sighed. "So, this whole thing with selling the house? It's kind of a backlash from my father. You know, from what happened. I take it you told Aly?"

Mike nodded. "I told her some of it, yeah."

"Yeah. He's doing it out of spite. Because he's not in control anymore and that pisses him off. He's told my stepmother she's moving with him, but I'm not welcome. So I've been scrambling for money."

Aly held up her hand. "Wait a second. He actually told you that you can't go with him?"

Rae scoffed. "Yeah. It's been a massive thing. He's an absolute asshole."

Mike murmured. "You can say that again."

I held my hand up. "Anyway, long story short? I'm selling things off I have a right to in order to pick up some money. The good news is that I sold off a lot yesterday. But I haven't been able to get to a bank yet."

Mike narrowed his eyes. "So you have that money on you right now?"

Rae nodded. "He does, yeah."

Aly shook her head. "Do you have a bank account you can put it in?"

I smiled. "That's why Rae and I are celebrating. I opened up my own bank account that my father can't touch and transferred everything from my old account to my new one."

Mike patted my back. "Dude, that's awesome. But keep that money stowed away in your locker. You know, in case something happens at school today. And after classes I'll get you to a bank so you can deposit it."

"That means more to me than you realize. Thanks, Mike."

He squeezed my shoulder. "Anything I can do to help, you just let me know."

I felt loved again, like I had friends again. I didn't know what the fuck I did to deserve these people in my life. But I was determined not to fuck it up again. We all rushed into school and the girls darted off to go to homeroom. And Mike? Well, he did exactly as he said he would. He escorted me to my locker and stood guard while I stashed the wads of cash I had on my person. I placed it under a stack of books and shoved it all the way back. I piled some shit in front of it before grabbing my books. Then I slammed my locker closed and booked it to homeroom, getting there just before the late bell rang.

And as I dropped into my seat, I felt all eyes on me.

Even though people kept giving me funny looks, it felt good for things to be returning to normal. Well, not really normal. But a sort-of-kind-of normal. School felt familiar. Mike and Aly felt familiar. Rae felt very familiar. And I needed familiar in my life right now. I needed something I could count on. Depend on. Lean on.

Even if that 'something' was school.

The one thing on this planet I hated more than my own father.

My phone kept vibrating in class, so I turned it on silent. But the vibrations were good. People were snatching up these things I was selling left and right. If I could get Mike to drop me off at my house, I had the potential to make another seven grand before tonight was over. That had me smiling all throughout the morning. I had a pep in my step and slowly, things felt less and less overwhelming. I had money in a bank account my father couldn't touch. I had a little over fifteen grand in checks and cash in my locker, waiting to be deposited. And if I could get my hands on one last decent sale, I'd be set for a while.

At least, until I got back on my feet again after graduation.

I liked this kind of normal. The kind where Mike waved at me in the hallways and Rae rushed up to kiss me between classes. Roy and Marina weren't aimlessly laughing at stupid jokes and trying to rile me up over dumb, useless shit. This reality was much better. I had friends that gave a shit. I had my girl back. I had money coming in to help me once my father abandoned me for good.

And this time, I wouldn't fuck it up.

Or let someone else fuck it up, either.

I'm all in, Rae. One hundred percent.

The bell for lunch rang and I rushed to the cafeteria. I found Mike already sitting down with his food tray while Aly unpacked their lunchbox. I waved at them before hopping in the food line, finding myself standing behind Rae. I tapped her on the shoulder and she turned around. And very quickly, I captured her lips.

"Mmm, hello there."

I grinned. "Hey, beautiful."

"Ahem."

The lunch lady cleared her throat and she blushed. Which pulled a smile across my cheeks. We walked through the line and got our lunch. I even had the cashier charge Rae's lunch to my account. Despite her protests, I did it anyway, winking at her as we picked up our trays. We walked over to were Mike and Aly were already cuddled up, smiling as they gazed into each other's eyes.

As I sat my tray down, I leaned over to whisper in Rae's ear. "Is that what we look like?"

She shrugged. "I don't know. But if it is, I don't mind it one bit."

I smiled. "Neither do I."

I kissed the top of her head before we sat down with them. Mike and Aly paid us no mind. Which didn't bother me one bit. They deserved some time with one another, just like Rae deserved some time with me. So as I picked at my pathetic hamburger, I turned my attention to the beautiful girl sitting next to me.

"So are you free tonight?"

Rae sighed dramatically. "No, I have to work."

I quirked an eyebrow. "You sound overly thrilled at the idea."

"Really? Should I try that sigh again?"

And before I could stop her, she sighed and leaned against me. She placed the back of her hand against her forehead, causing me to chuckle. Wrapping my arm around her, I kissed the top of her head again. I breathed in the smell of her conditioner, letting it pull me back to the memories of last night. This morning. Memories of having her whenever I wanted her and making love to her every waking moment she'd let me.

I held her close as she rested her head against my shoulder.

"I wish I was free, though. I'm having to close again tonight."

I nodded softly. "Well, that's all right. I'll come visit you."

"Yeah?"

"Yeah. I'll get a taxi or something. We can go get a milkshake afterward at the diner up the road from where you work."

"Mmm, that sounds like heaven."

I smiled. "Only if you're there, though."

I closed my eyes and let myself slip into another world. Another place. Another time. Where nothing existed except Rae and me, trying to make a way for ourselves in the world. I wanted her by my side. Always. Now more than ever, I understood how much I needed her. She was my rock. My shelter. My safe place to fall. The one person I felt I could be weak with and not be judged for it.

I needed her in my life for as long as she'd stick around.

Mike sighed. "So how are classes going for you two?"

I snickered. "As good as they can for now. I'm completely lost in them, though. It'll take me some time to catch back up."

Rae kissed my chest. "Don't worry. We'll help."

Aly smiled brightly. "Yep! Study sessions at my place in the basement. We have all the good snacks, too."

Mike nodded. "They really do. I'm jealous. My parents are health freaks. You'll have to watch out for that."

I shrugged. "I can go and buy myself some ice cream and chips whenever I need them. That's not an issue. And with this stuff I'm selling off, I can help with—"

"Oh! That reminds me! I sent the text off to my dad and he said he wanted to talk with Mom before they made a decision. But he also said it shouldn't be an issue. I should know by the end of the day today. We can talk about it while I take you to the bank."

I nodded. "It's appreciated more than you realize. Seriously."

Aly leaned against Mike. "It's really not a problem. We just wish you would've talked to us sooner."

Rae nudged me. "Yeah, Clint. You should've talked to us sooner."

"Yeah, Clint. You should've talked to us sooner."

The mocking voice made me swivel around, although I already

knew who it was. I'd never forget the voice of Marina. That piercing, tinny, Valley girl voice. There she was, chomping on that banana like she was sucking down Roy's dick. I eyed her closely before I looked over at Roy, watching him practically hover over the four of us.

"Enjoying lunch, losers?"

I shrugged. "Of course. Are you?"

Marina snickered. "We always enjoy lunch until you assholes show up."

Aly rolled her eyes. "Nice one, Marina."

Mike nodded. "Yep. Very creative. A-plus for effort."

Marina glared at them. "At least I'm not a pathetic loser that goes around helping charity cases just to feel better about myself."

Rae cleared her throat. "I'm sorry. Do you mean 'charity cases' as in us? Or 'charity cases' as in you? Because I'm pretty sure the two of you can't be helped."

Marina jumped at Rae and she stood out of her chair. Like lightning. I'd never seen her move so quickly, and I shot up from my own seat to step in front of her. To shield her from the nonsense of the crew I used to run these halls with. I stared Roy down, refusing to look over at Marina. Because I didn't believe in intimidating a girl, no matter how much I figured she deserved it.

"What? The two of you are back together now? Rumor had it you dumped her for another piece of ass."

Marina grinned. "Yeah. People are talking about how you're fucking your stepmom now. That how you roll over there in the Clarke household? Fucking family members."

Rae growled. "I'll claw your damn eyes out."

Marina stepped forward. "You want to try that statement again?"

I moved with her and felt her shove me in the chest. I slowly looked over at Roy, but all he did was fold his arms over his chest.

"What? You got your girl fighting your fights now?"

He smiled wickedly. "She can handle her own. Question is, can you?"

I nodded slowly. "I don't swing at girls. I'm better than that. Rae won't hesitate, though. And I wonder who's going to win in a battle of women? The one who knows how to fight, or the one who tips over in her own heels?"

Roy shoved Marina out of the way in order to stand toe to toe with me.

"You think you can come into this cafeteria and stand up to me? Huh? After fucking around with pathetic assholes like these three? You think you can still rule this school and get away with bullshit like that? With abandoning the only friends you could count on?"

I grinned. "You really thought you were my friend?"

He shoved my chest. "You deserve everything your father fucking hands you."

My eye twitched. "And I've had about enough of your shit, Roy."

22

RAELYNN

I rubbed Clint's chest. "Hey, hey. It's not worth it. They're not worth it."

I saw his nostrils flaring, and I knew he was only half paying attention to me. I had to calm him down. The teachers weren't in the cafeteria yet, but they would be soon. And the last thing Clint needed was to get expelled just as he'd gotten back into the groove of things here. We needed to get him graduated, and this wasn't the way to do it.

"Clint. Listen to me."

Roy snickered. "Yeah, Clint. Listen to her."

I eyed him hotly. "You shut the hell up before I punch you myself."

Marina jumped in front of him. "You lay one hand on my man and I'll—"

Allison's voice came from behind me. "Or you'll what, you snide little bitch?"

My jaw fell open and I whipped my head around. Michael laughed as he rubbed her back, and Clint started chuckling. I smiled and winked at her, then turned my attention back to the two goons in front of us. And I noticed something.

None of the other guys from the table across the cafeteria had joined them. They all just sat and watched. With smirks on their faces before rolling their eyes and turning their backs.

Seemed as if Roy and Marina were losing their position with those assholes as well. So I decided to use that to my advantage.

"You know, I figured more of your friends would be here to back you up."

Roy grinned. "I know what you're trying to do. And trust me, they're backing us up."

I shrugged. "Then where are they?"

Michael piped up, "You know, other than sitting over there and not paying one bit of attention to what you're doing over here."

When Marina and Roy looked over, I saw their faces falter. Their confident, cocky smiles slowly begin to fade. I looked up at Clint, ready to relish the victory. Because we might actually get out of this without some sort of a fight.

But the look on his face hadn't changed. His nostrils still flared with anger, his shoulders rolled back. He was still on guard. Still watching, waiting for something to break out. I hated seeing him so riled up like this. I rubbed his arm and moved it to his chest. I patted his heartbeat softly, trying to talk him down from his heady high.

It didn't work.

Roy snickered. "Anyway, now that the distraction's over—"

Marina smiled wickedly. "Want to settle this? Woman to woman?"

I rolled my eyes. "When you show me a woman, sure."

"What did you say?"

She lunged at me and Clint stepped in front of me again. She started beating her fists against his chest, but he didn't move. Roy stood behind his girl like a fucking coward, letting her wail on my man. But, even though Clint's fists were gripped tight, he didn't swing one punch.

He simply let her get it out of her system before she backed away.

"Yeah. And that'll be your girl's face if she ever talks to me that way again."

Clint shook his head. "You won't touch Rae."

Roy narrowed his eyes. "You threatening my girl?"

I snickered. "No. He's not. He's simply telling you Marina won't touch me without consequences."

Roy licked his lips. "And what kind of consequences are those?"

Clint sighed. "The kind of consequences that get you both

expelled and thrown in jail for all the underage drinking parties you throw."

Marina hissed. "You mean the parties you helped us throw? The parties you got drunk at? The parties where you hooked up with random bitches and boasted about it later? Yeah? Those parties, you damn drunk?"

Michael came to my side. "Doesn't matter what he did in his past, so long as he's moved past it."

Allison came up to Clint's other side. "Yeah. We don't care about that stuff. We only care about what he does now."

I nodded. "Which is why you two aren't worth it. Clint, they aren't worth it. Let's just sit back down, okay?"

I looked up at him, hoping he had relaxed. But he hadn't.

"I'm good. I'll sit down once they leave."

I tried to tug him into the seat, but he shrugged off my touch. He looked down at me and winked, but it didn't provide me with any solace. I didn't like where this was going. I just wanted everyone to go back to their respective places so we could eat and get the hell back to class.

Roy snickered. "You got something to say, asshole, then say it."

Clint nodded. "Fine. I will. I'm tired of you and Marina pushing me around. Pushing us around. I'm tired of you thinking you're a big shot when the only reason you got into your position is because I took pity on you. Befriended you when I didn't have anyone else. It's time someone taught you a lesson. It's time you were reminded of who's better with their fists."

"Oh, you want a fight. Is that it?"

I placed my hand on his chest. "Clint, don't do this."

He shook his head. "I don't want a fight. But, sometimes, that's the only way people listen. Getting the ever-loving shit beat out of them. If that's what it takes for you to get the picture, then I'm all for it."

Marina stood behind Roy. "Get him, baby. Break that fucking jaw of his."

Roy put up his fists. "Fine, then. Come on. Hit me."

Clint shrugged. "You first."

Roy didn't hesitate. He swung at Clint and he shoved me out of the way. Michael caught me and pulled me away from the scene as I watched it unfold. Allison ducked and Michael rushed for her, clamoring over the lunch table to get to her. He picked her up and climbed back across the table as Clint caught Roy's fist mid-swing and twisted his arm. He backed Roy against the wall. Marina cried out and whipped around, looking for some sort of support for Roy.

But everyone at their table kept their backs turned.

"Someone help him! Where the fuck are you guys!?"

Her cries echoed across the cafeteria and I saw students turning our way. With each punch Roy threw, Clint caught them. Not once did that asshole land a punch. Clint brought his knee up into Roy's gut and took him to his knees. The stupid boy heaved for air as Marina fell down beside him. Clint hovered over them, a dark look on his face. Not once had he swung a punch, though. All he did was warn. And promise.

Then he made good on that promise.

Roy pushed Marina away again and lunged at Clint. He shoved Clint down, back first, onto the table. Into the food we had just purchased. I reached for Clint, wanting to pull him away. But Michael held me back.

"He's got this. He knows what he's doing. Let the teachers see him defending himself."

My eyes widened as Roy's fist came up in the air. I cried out Clint's name, watching as he caught it. He rolled Roy over and straddled him, pinning the boy's hands to the table. Then, Marina came up behind him and gripped his shirt.

And my vision dripped red.

"Oh, no you don't."

I tore away from Michael's grip and rushed toward Marina. I wrapped my arms around her and picked her up, moving her away from Clint. I set her down on her feet and glared at her, and she cocked her hand back to slap me. But out of nowhere came Allison, who jammed her heel down into Marina's toe. Marina bent over and grabbed her foot.

I grinned. "Good one."

Allison frowned. "We have to get out of here. The teachers are coming."

By the time I got back to the table, I saw Roy's elbow come up into Clint's jaw. He stumbled back into the wall and Roy pushed himself off the table, heading straight for Clint. His fist connected with Clint's jaw. Clint wrapped his hand around Roy's throat, and just as Clint pushed him away, teachers came around the corner.

"Clarke! Emerson! Principal's office, now!"

Teachers pushed us out of the way and wrapped their arms around the boys. Roy kept clamoring for Clint, cursing and yelling as Clint backed away. He didn't fight the teachers or try to pull out of their grasp. Roy, on the other hand, bucked and kicked and cursed like a toddler not wanting to go into time out.

It was pathetic to watch.

Even though Clint had come out on top, it also looked as if he'd started the fight. I knew damn good and well those teachers hadn't seen Roy attack him. And I wasn't sure how all of this would go down. I saw them haul Clint down the hallway toward the principal's office. He peered over his shoulder at me and winked again. Like he somehow had everything under control. I went to walk after him, but both Michael and Allison grabbed me, wrapping their hands around my wrists and pulling me back as teachers hauled a kicking and screaming Roy out of the cafeteria.

With Marina in tears, following behind them.

"I have to go after him."

Michael sighed. "Let the teachers sort it out."

Allison stroked my arm. "Yeah. You know the principal will get to the bottom of it. He knows Clint's trying to turn over a new leaf."

I pulled out of their grips. "You know they'll throw Clint under the bus in a heartbeat."

Michael nodded. "Yes. But there are plenty of people here who will say Roy started that fight. Not Clint."

Allison smiled softly. "Yeah, it'll be okay. Plus, there's us who can attest to that, too."

I sighed as I turned back to the entrance of the cafeteria.

"I don't know, guys."

They rubbed my back, but I felt more overwhelmed than ever. I couldn't fucking catch a break. Every time I made a step forward in my life, two steps were taken away from me. For all I knew, this would lead to Clint's suspension. Or expulsion. And we'd all be back at square one. Me, with my broken heart. Clint, dealing with shit at home by himself. And us, graduating without our newfound friend.

I hate this so much. "Why does he have to be like that all the time?"

Michael patted my shoulder. "What do you mean?"

I shrugged. "I just—why did he have to egg Roy on like that? Why did he have to instigate things?"

Allison took my hand. "I have to say, I'm with Clint on this one."

I furrowed my brow. "What?"

Michael squeezed my shoulder. "Me, too."

I paused. "Wait, what?"

Allison giggled. "You see a fight. You see Clint slipping back into his old ways. But if there was ever a fight to engage in, that was the one."

I shook my head. "I don't get it."

Michael snickered. "Of course you don't. He was standing up for you, Rae. That asshole had it coming. And Marina, too. I'm sure it felt good for Clint to blow off a little steam and to be the bigger person in the process."

I rolled my eyes. "Fighting doesn't make anyone the bigger person. It makes them a bigger target."

Allison came into my vision. "Even when he's standing up for his girl?"

Michael rubbed my back. "Even when he's big enough to defend himself and not start the fight in the process?"

I shrugged. "I don't know. I don't know anymore. All I know if that if this fight leads to him getting suspended—or worse—we're right back to where we started."

Allison paused. "How do you figure?"

I cracked my neck. "I mean, think about it. He'll be back home dealing with this shit by himself. Caught up in his father's whirlwind instead of here, where he should be, trying to graduate. He can't make a life for himself without a degree. And once we graduate, who in the world is going to help him do that? Because I don't know about you, but I don't see anyone else jumping up to defend him or help him. Do you?"

And when they both fell silent, I knew I had them.

"That's why I'm scared right now, guys. Because if we graduate without Clint, he doesn't stand a chance."

23

CLINTON

I picked at my fingers and fidgeted in the principal's office. I kept stealing glances at Roy, who sat there with a holier-than-thou grin on his face. I still heard Marina crying outside. Like she'd somehow been wrapped up in all this. The little bitch. I wanted to stick my head out into the hallway and tell her to shut the hell up. The principal was calling all of our parents. First, Marina's. Then Roy's.

And when he hung up the phone, I slowly lifted my eyes.

"Please, sir. I didn't start this fight. There's no reason to call my father."

Roy snickered. "You start every fight you're in, Clarke."

The principal held up his hand. "Who started the fight and who didn't isn't my concern right now. Mr. Clarke, you're clearly not in any condition to be in school right now. By the looks of your nose and the accident we all know you've been in, you should be home. Resting."

Roy rolled his eyes. "Can I go now?"

The principal glared at him. "You can sit right there until your mother gets here. I just called her. Then you can explain to her how a boy who's just been in a life-threatening accident suddenly has a bruise on his jaw and across his face."

He stood from his chair. "I didn't do that to Clint's nose! It was probably his fucking father or some—"

The principal slowly stood. "Sit down and stop that language in my office. Now."

Roy flopped back down into the chair and I sighed. If that man called my father, he was sealing my fate. I'd never recover. I'd never recuperate. Because my father would beat me until I was dead. I drew in a deep breath and closed my eyes, trying to settle my heartrate. I thought of some way to try and get myself out of this. Anything that didn't force me to own up to what was happening in my own home.

Because if my father got arrested because of me? And he paid his way out?

He'd chase me to the ends of the earth if it meant retribution.

"Sir, please."

The principal held up his hand. "I'm sorry, Mr. Clarke. But you know the rules. No matter who throws the first punch, all parties are to be picked up so they can cool down. We can start fresh tomorrow. I'll make sure your teachers get your homework to you somehow."

I shook my head. "Sir, you don't understand. If you call my father—"

He blinked. "What happens if I call your father?"

I felt Roy grinning at me. Marina's crying stopped as footsteps came into the front office. I swallowed hard, watching as the principal leveled his eyes with mine. All I had to do was say it. Tell him these bruises were from my father. Tell him what he was doing. How my father was about to abandon me and never return.

But I was also eighteen. The hell was some principal going to do?

I sighed. "Can't you just trust me on this?"

The principal picked up his phone. "You know we don't compromise rules. It sets a dangerous precedent."

I wanted to strangle Roy when I heard him chuckling at my side.

His mother came and collected him as I sat there. No explanation of how I got my bruises. No having to grovel to his mother. She cooed at him and checked him over. Made sure he was all right before tossing me a disgusted look. I ignored it, though. I had larger worries on my plate.

Like the words coming out of the principal's mouth.

"I'm sorry, Mr. Clarke. But I'm going to need you to come pick up your son. Yes, sir. Immediately. A fight with another student. Though, one I'm not sure he—no, I'm not sure he start—Mr. Clarke, your son didn't start this fight. But he does have to be picked up from school. Yes. Uh huh. He'll be in my office."

It wouldn't matter, though. Not to my father. The only thing that mattered was the word 'fight.' The fact that I was probably interrupting his day. I pulled out my cell phone and quickly started texting Rae. Spitting out everything I could before my father stormed through those doors.

"Mr. Clarke, you need to put your phone—"

I whipped my eyes up. "I've got things I need to take care of. Things that are beyond the scope of your reasoning and what I want to tell you. Now, you can either let me send a message to Rae so she can take care of it, or you can throw me out. But I'm not putting up my phone until I send this message. Are we clear?"

The principal sighed. "Tuck in that attitude."

"Let me send one message to make my life just a little easier, and it'll be put away."

My eyes fell back to my phone and my fingers flew across the screen. I didn't bother editing it. Because any second now, my father would walk into this office with steam pouring from his ears and I'd be dead.

Or, at least wish I were.

Me: Rae, I need something from you. The money, it's in Mike's locker. Make sure it stays safe until I can get to it. Dad's about to pick me up. It looks bad. I won't be here after school. Don't come check on me until you hear from me. I don't want you hurt. I'm sorry you have to deal with me all the time.

And just as the principal's door whipped open, I slid my phone back into my pocket.

I slowly turned around and saw my father's angry eyes. I swallowed hard as I stood up. I took one last look at the principal and I could've sworn I saw regret in his eyes. But it didn't matter now. The smoke blowing from my father's ears had nothing on the daggers flying from his glare. He watched me as I walked out the door, then left the principal's office without a second thought. The heat of his body worried me. The fact that he hadn't laid a hand on me yet only put me on edge. What would he do to me once we got home? Were we even going home?

I slipped into his car and neither of us spoke a word as he drove us back to the house.

He didn't say anything as we got out of the car and walked inside. Or even as he slammed the door behind him. Which gave my mind more than enough time to theorize what might happen next. I felt my body already crumbling. I didn't know if I'd be okay after this. I jumped when the door slammed shut. But dread filled my gut when I heard him flip the lock.

"You are a mystery to me, Clinton."

The growl of his voice kicked my body into overdrive. I whipped around, but not soon enough. His hand came down against my neck and he slammed me into the wall, pressing my cheek against the pristine white walls. I pressed my hands into the plaster, struggling to breathe as his fingertips closed down against my pulse points. Tears welled in my eyes, but I refused to give him the satisfaction of seeing me cry.

Although I felt the little boy within me screaming out for help.

"Did you really think I'd punish you for some stupid little fight? Hmm?"

He ripped me away from the wall and tossed me against the banister of the stairwell.

"Did you really think I'd let you get away with what you've done to me? To our lives? After that stunt you pulled last week?"

He fisted my shirt and pulled me up to his face, and my body fell limp. I didn't have the strength to fight him any longer. I didn't have the ability to push him away. I hurt in so many places. My muscles ached for death. My mind went blank and I found myself traveling to my happy place as my father's voice melted away into nothingness, growing further and further away the deeper I sank.

Like the river waters that almost swallowed me whole.

"Well, rest assured, Clinton, I don't give a flying fuck what you do at school. This is going to be for putting ideas into my wife's head. For trying to take her from me, you pointless little bastard. She's mine, and you will do nothing more with her. Do you understand?"

As he tossed me to the floor, I closed my eyes. And the last thing I remembered was his foot jammed into my lower back. I let the tears fall as my happy place swept me away. Back into the arms of Rae. I saw her face smiling at me, felt her lips pressing against my cheeks. Her soft fingertips brushed my tears away, making me smile. Making me feel better about things.

Making me feel loved.

"Come. Follow me."

Her voice filled my ears. Drowning out my father's rage. I felt my body being tossed around, but I didn't register the pain. Only the intensity. Only the pressure. Like my body had been filled with morphine and was numb from head to toe. Rae took my hands and pulled me into a beautiful wildflower meadow. Fraught with colors that warmed my soul. Yellows and pinks and blues. Purples and reds and so much green. A sparkling lake with fish jumping out caught my eye. And as the wooded landscape backdropped all around the meadow, a cabin magically appeared.

A cabin, in the middle of a meadow, situated on a crystal clear lake. A massive three-story behemoth, with a wrap-around porch. It was gorgeous. It called to me as Rae pulled me closer. She pulled me past the lake. Past the fish that called to my fingertips. To my hungry stomach. She pulled me up the porch steps and inside, showing me its glorious majesty.

And it left me stunned.

"Welcome home, handsome."

Rae kissed my cheek, and I knew this had to be heaven. She threaded her fingers within mine and guided me through the cabin. The massive kitchen with marble countertops. The roaring fireplace with microfiber furniture, ready for me to flop against. She walked me up the stairs, showing me the bedrooms. The bathrooms. The hallways and the library.

Until finally she stopped at what looked like an office.

"What is this place, Rae?"

She giggled. "You've been gone too long, sweetheart. I take it the book tour went well?"

I paused. "Book tour?"

"Yeah. For your latest novel. Are you feeling all right?"

I blinked. "Yes. No. I'm fine. Sorry. I guess I have been away too long."

"You got any ideas for your next book? Or are you taking some time off to hunt?"

"To hunt."

"Yeah. And fish! Though, if you ask me, we don't have

anywhere else to put any more meat. The deep freezer in the basement's already full."

I stared at Rae, dumbfounded. I had no idea what the fuck she was talking about. And yet, I wanted to. It all sounded magical. Like utter perfection. Her, in this house that was clearly ours. With a lake to fish in and woods to hunt in and food to feed ourselves with and money from books I wrote to keep us afloat. I smiled as I wrapped her up in my arms. I walked her into the wall as her giggles filled the space around us. My lips pressed against hers and I drank her in. The sweet concoction of her tongue as it slid across the roof of my mouth.

"Mmm, I guess things did go well on this latest book tour."

I nodded softly. "And oh, how I missed you."

We sank to the floor of my office space and I kissed her body, peeling her clothes back and sucking marks against her skin that I wanted to see for the rest of my life. She scratched her nails along my back as I pounded into her, diving deeper into the life I wanted. The life I needed. The life that ripped me away from my current reality. The image shook from time to time, and I tried to keep it still. I lost myself in her curves and buried myself between her legs. I took her from room to room, marking the house with her scent as she fell weak against me.

And I found myself hoping to never wake up from this amazing dream.

Even if it killed me to stay there.

24

RAELYNN

Clint's text made me fucking sick. I couldn't concentrate for the rest of the time I was in classes. Allison and I went around to his teachers after school, explaining to them that he had a family emergency he was dealing with. That he needed his homework. Tests. Any reading assignments he might have missed. Pop quizzes he needed to take. The teachers seemed less inclined to work with him after today's little spat, and I wanted to slap them all. How dare they judge him when they didn't know shit about him?

Still, they gave us what we needed.

Michael jogged up to us. "All right. I've got the money out of his locker. I don't feel comfortable keeping it there. Should I take it and stash it at my place?"

I nodded. "If you could, please. I don't know when he's going to be able to get it, but I want it somewhere safe that isn't here until he can get back to it."

Allison swallowed hard. "Should we call the cops or something?"

I paused. "I honestly don't know."

Michael shook his head. "Have you heard from him at all since that text?"

I closed my eyes. "No, I haven't. And I have to work tonight. So I can't drop by."

Allison put her hand on my shoulder. "Michael and I can just do a drive-by, if that makes you feel better."

Michael piped up. "And if you want to give me his number, I can call him. You know, keep at it until he picks up."

I drew in a deep breath. "I'm really hoping he makes good on his word. He said he'd come by after I was done working and we'd get a milkshake or something tonight. If he doesn't come by, I might need a ride home."

Michael hugged me. "Consider it done. Just call, okay?"

I opened my eyes. "Please tell me everything's going to be all right."

Allison rubbed my back. "One way or another, we're all getting out of this. I promise."

After coming up with a plan, I headed back to my house. Michael had his money, Allison had his homework, and I had the task of trying to get Clint on the phone. But it wasn't any use. Every time I called him, his phone went to voicemail. Every text I sent went unanswered. I stood in front of the small mirror on the wall of my room, trying not to cry. I wanted to put on a bit of makeup for work, make myself look more presentable, in case Clint did come around.

But I kept crying it off.

"For fuck's sake, come on."

I hissed at myself as I wiped at the mascara running down my face.

"Lip gloss. Lip gloss and some powder so my face isn't so red."

It would have to do, because I had to be at work within the hour.

Just as I swiped on a layer of lip gloss, I heard something crash downstairs. Mom started screaming and I heard D.J.'s voice rising above the commotion, which sent me running. I ripped my door open and made my way to the top of the steps. I heard them yelling at one another as more things crashed against the wall. I heard tears in Mom's eyes. I heard blood in D.J.'s voice. And as I turned the corner, heading for the kitchen, I saw a plate crash against the wall.

"D.J.! Stop!"

"Stop? Stop? You want me to stop when I hear my girl's been fucking other men around town?"

Mom sniffled. "D.J., please. Calm down so we can talk."

He roared. "I'm not calming down when I've just learned my girl is nothing but a fucking whore!"

I ducked as a glass went flying. Shards of the damn thing scattered all over the place as I shielded my head. Anger rushed through my veins. I wanted this man dead by the end of the night tonight. I saw my mother crouched down in a corner, her face in her hands while she sobbed. And D.J.? Well, he just kept destroying our stuff and yelling bloody murder. As if that might help things.

"How many men, huh? How many men did you let inside you?"

Mom sobbed. "I don't know. Please, it was just when we were broken up. I'd never cheat on you, D.J."

He snatched her arm. "Like hell you wouldn't. You already did! We never broke up. We just had fights. And we always made up."

"Let me go!"

"I'm not doing a damn thing you ask of me. You can't even keep your fucking pants on, you bitch."

"Stop!"

I came around the corner and picked up a glass filled with water. I chucked it at D.J.'s head and hit him square in the jaw with it. He released my mother and glared, lunging at me. But Mom threw herself at him and tackled him to the floor.

"You won't lay a finger on my daughter. Do you hear me?"

D.J. snickered. "And that's the issue. Like mother, like daughter. You're an ungrateful bitch, just like she is."

Mom screamed out as she raked her nails across D.J.'s face. I rushed over to her and pried her off his body, praying for all of this to stop. I couldn't take it any longer. The chaos. The confusion. The insanity. It would drain my next paycheck just to replace all this shit in the house he'd already broken.

Because God knows Mom couldn't afford it without D.J. funneling money into her purse.

"She's just as fucked up as you are, Lucy."

Mom shrieked. "Don't you talk about my daughter that way!"

I shook my head. "Mom. Stop. It isn't worth it."

D.J. grinned. "Yeah, Lucy. It's not worth it."

I pushed my mother behind me and leveled my eyes with the bullshit excuse of a man on the floor. He stood up and dusted himself off, but I saw his arm and the side of his face bleeding, where the little shards of glass he had splintered all over the ground had come to wreak havoc on his body. I snarled at him and picked up a knife off the kitchen table. He chuckled at me as his eyes fell to the dull instrument in my hand. Then he quirked an eyebrow.

"I have to admit, your mother wouldn't have the guts."

My eye twitched. "Get out, or I will."

Mom hissed. "Raelynn."

I held my hand up to her. "Get the hell out of this house and don't you ever come back."

D.J. grinned. "I take it you're not calling the police, then?"

I shook my head. "I never said that. I only said to get out. I'm more than willing to give you a headstart."

Mom panicked. "She's not calling. D.J., I promise she's not calling."

I rolled my eyes. Mom sounded pathetic, but I wasn't afraid of this loser. I hated him. Every ounce of him. And I didn't care if I had to carve his fucking eyes out with a spoon.

I'd do it just to get him out of our home.

D.J. chuckled. "Think your mom still loves me."

I nodded. "Maybe so. But she won't be getting back with you. Not this time. You've got five minutes before I call the police. Whether you're here, or there, it doesn't matter."

He narrowed his eyes. "You don't have the balls, kid."

I dropped the knife, reaching for my phone. "Want to bet?"

I felt my mother's hand around my wrist and I had to resist the urge to smack her. To push her down. Because she had endured enough of that in her life. Instead, I wrenched away from her grasp. Stepped away from her and held my finger against the red button on the front of my phone. D.J.'s eyes darted from my finger to my eyes. Again and again. Almost as if he were testing me.

Then I pressed it.

"No! Rae!"

D.J. backed up. "Fuck you both. I'm out."

"No, D.J. Come back. We can talk this out, please!"

"9-1-1, what's your emergency?"

I held the phone to my ear as Mom collapsed on the ground. She sobbed against the glass, not caring that it gouged her knees. Her shins. The palms of her hands. I stared at a carcass of my mother. Unlike the woman I used to know.

Or maybe the mother I thought I had never existed. And I simply grew up.

"Hello? Is anyone there?"

I sighed. "Yes. Hi. I'm not really sure if it's an emergency, but there's been some domestic issues at my house and I think my mother needs medical help."

"Sounds like an emergency to me. What's going on?"

"Her ex boyfriend stormed in and broke a lot of our things. Mom's bleeding from some glass shards. I also think she might need some mental help."

Mom slowly looked back at me, and the daggers she shot from her eyes were forever etched into my memory.

"Is the assailant still there?"

I shook my head. "No."

"Do you have a name for him?"

"D.J. I don't know his last name."

Mom snarled. "You hang up that phone now."

I licked my lips. "No, Mom. You need help."

"What was that?"

I cleared my throat. "Sorry. Are you ready for my address? I won't be here, I have to go to work and I can't be late. But I'll make sure someone keeps my mother here until you arrive."

I rattled off my address to the 9-1-1 operator. Then I hung up the phone. Mom picked herself up off the floor, but every time she dusted herself off, she created more cuts. My feet crunched over the glass as I wrapped her arm around my shoulders and guided her to the couch, easing her down. She refused to look at me as hot tears burned their way down her cheeks.

Then I spoke my own truth.

A truth I'd wanted to proclaim the last time she pulled this.

"Mom, I need you to stay here."

She snickered. "No, thanks."

I sighed. "I know you hate me now, but once you get the help you need—"

"I'm not fucking crazy, Raelynn."

"No, you're just depressed, anxious, and addicted to any man who will give you attention because you never healed from Dad leaving."

And when she didn't say anything, I brushed her hair back.

"You're going to stay here and wait for the paramedics to get here. They're going to offer you help and you're going to take it. Okay?"

She leaned into the couch, away from my touch. "And if I don't?"

I stood upright. "Then I'm moving in with Allison and never coming home."

She snickered. "So you'd leave. Just like your father."

"If anything, I'm the only one who's stayed and fought for you. Fought with you. But I can't fight against you any longer. I'm tired. I'm eighteen years old. I'm at a point where I'm about to go live my own life. And you expect me to dig you out of your messes and pay your bills and watch you tramp around with men coming in and out of this house at all hours of the night. What kind of life is that for me?"

She refused to meet my stare. "I can change, you know."

"I know you can. With help, Mom. So you'll take their help once they get here. Or I move out. Your choice."

"You're more like your father every day, you know."

I shrugged. "And if that means fighting for my own life when you won't even fight for yours, then so be it."

I left my mother to her choice and walked back upstairs. I gathered my things, shoving them into my purse. I packed a change of clothes and my phone charger. A few toiletries. I packed down my purse in case I got the opportunity to stay somewhere else. Then I grabbed my backpack for good measure. I reached for the bike Allison had loaned me and walked it up the driveway, listening to sirens roar in the distance. And as I walked up the street, I turned to look back. To take one last look at my house before I went to work.

Committing it to memory, in case I never saw it again.

I felt numb. As I peddled out of the neighborhood, I felt the rest of my body grow numb. An ambulance and two police cars raced by me. I didn't even stop to watch them as they made their way into the neighborhood. I didn't even debate on whether or not to skip work and stay with Mom. Because I knew my time was better spent earning money to get me the hell away from this place. I peddled faster. I broke a sweat getting to work. I let my worries about Clint and my mother and D.J. and my future fall to the wayside as I cycled into the parking lot.

I chained up Allison's bike and walked into the grocery store, leaving my proverbial baggage outside as I went to put my backpack and purse underneath my register.

25

CLINTON

I hissed as I moved the ice packs. Three of them, to be exact. Sliding around my body as bruises kicked up, grew hot, then subsided into nothing but a dull ache. As I lay on my bed and stared at the ceiling, I laughed bitterly to myself. It was a wonder no bones had been broken. That, miraculously, I wasn't bleeding all over the place.

Because judging by the state of things downstairs, Dad had really tossed me around.

Pictures crashed to the ground and dents were impacted into the walls. The banister was crooked now, cracked in three separate places. Now, I didn't know much about moving. But I figured the new tenants of this place wouldn't be happy with the destruction. Which meant that my beating had bought me a little more time in this place.

Unless Dad dropped the price of the house for them substantially.

That was the furthest thing from my mind, though. The only thing I focused on was the ceiling while Cecilia and Dad yelled at one another downstairs. Hearing her angry voice waft through the floor was definitely a treat. One I thought I'd never hear again. But I supposed she had gotten her footing. Found the courage to stand up to my father after waking me up in my bed.

How I got here, however, I still didn't know.

All I knew was that when I opened my eyes, I saw her. Cecilia. The image of Rae faded away and was replaced by the face of a woman that had been more my mother than my own had ever been. And even though concern was etched across her face, anger flooded her eyes.

Anger she now unleashed against my father.

"You've gone too far, Howard. You should be jailed for this!"

"And you'd go back to living on the street. What are you going to do, huh? Have sex with men for money? You're not even good at it, Cece!"

"And you're even more abusive than my father, you pretentious asshole!"

They argued for a little while longer. Then the front door slammed. The only reason I knew that Cecilia had stayed behind was because I heard her still screaming downstairs. Still yelling at nothing as my father peeled out of the driveway. I tossed the ice packs off to the side. I needed a shower. Something to flood rejuvenation back through my pulsing muscles.

Anything to get my mind off the shitstorm of my life.

I eased myself out of bed and stripped out of my clothes, leaving them in a pile on the floor as my phone continued lighting up in my back pocket. I saw it flashing on the floor. Notification after notification. People wanting me to meet them as soon as possible to pick up the things I was selling. I cast it off to the side, though, as I turned on the water as hot as I could stand it and eased myself underneath the waterfall stream.

"That's it."

I groaned as I settled down onto the floor. With my legs outstretched and the water pouring over me, I opened myself up to a stream that hurt before it cleansed. And as I sat there, my mind swirled with so many things.

All the things I had to get done.

I had to get those people their items. Collect my money. Damn it, I still needed to get to the bank. What did Rae do with that money? I had to call her and figure out where it was so I could pick it up. I didn't want anyone feeling responsible for that kind of money for very long. It came with a heavy burden and a constant paranoia I didn't want anyone else experiencing. I had to figure out what kind of deal I could strike with Mike's parents. Because I didn't want to freeload off them. And with the damage done to the downstairs, I wondered how much free time that bought me to sell off more things.

"Shit."

The hot water made me feel clean again. But the dirt settled back in the second I turned off the water. I heaved myself off the floor and out of the shower, settling back into a life my father had carved out for me. The dumbass bathroom he'd renovated two years ago for my birthday. Before he left for a month to be anywhere else other than here, celebrating it with me. A bedroom he'd decked out with expensive items, gifts to apologize for every bruise I'd grown up with. This bedroom had become a museum to the pain he'd caused me, the pain I lived with every day. And as I stared at my mahogany bed frame and matching dresser, it made me sick to think about.

"I'm selling it all."

I wrenched my phone off the floor and started snapping pictures. Then I started responding to those who had already claimed items online. I made appointments for tonight, telling them I'd knock fifteen percent off the price if they met me between eight and ten o'clock on the corner of my street. I watched them respond with fervor, taking me up on my offer and thanking me for this reason or that.

I didn't care about the reasons. I only cared about the money.

I slipped into a clean pair of sweatpants and a T-shirt. The hot water loosened my body up a bit, though I was still very bruised. I slipped my cell phone into my pocket and put my sandals on. I needed to start gathering things in my duffle bag for later. However, a knock came at my door. A small, soft, subtle knock.

"Come in."

The door eased open. "How are you feeling?"

I snickered. "Uh, good considering?"

"I suppose that was a stupid question."

I sighed. "It's not stupid. We're just in a hard situation. How are you doing?"

And when she let out a shuddering breath, I looked over at her.

"I've decided to leave him, Clint."

I rushed over to her and wrapped her up in my arms. I held her close, rocking her softly side to side. She sniffled against my chest and patted my back. I closed my eyes and silently thanked my fucking stars she'd come to her senses. I knew this was a turning point for us. A moment in time we'd never forget. I knew she was trembling with fear. But I also knew how strong she was. How far she'd come in life. What she had survived.

"We're going to make it. I swear to you, Cecilia."

She sighed. "After what just happened…"

She shook her head as she pulled away from me.

"I can't forgive him. I'll never forgive him, Clinton. I mean, look at you. Just—just look at you."

I nodded slowly. "I know. Trust me, I've lived with it my whole life."

"I'm so sorry I didn't intervene sooner."

"No, no, no. Don't you start doing that. Don't you start blaming yourself for things we can't change. You've done a hell of a lot for me. More than any other adult in my entire life. I won't let you feel guilty for anything else."

She sniffled. "I love you. I hope you know that."

I grinned. "I know. I love you too, Cecilia. Now, come on. I'll help you pack. Because you damn well know we aren't keeping this house."

"I wouldn't want to stay in it anyway."

"Honestly? I feel the same way at this point."

We walked out of my room and down the hallway, heading for the double doors. I'd only ever been in my father's room once. One time, in my entire life. She threw the doors open and it was even bigger than I remembered. A sprawling room, easily three times the size of my bedroom. Cecilia walked through it as if it didn't faze her. As if the grandeur of it all didn't shock her in the slightest. She walked over to a door in the corner and opened it up, flicking a light on that seemed to cascade down sprawling corridors.

I walked over to her and peeked inside as my jaw dropped to the floor.

"This is my closet. It's a lot to pack up, but I figure I'll have to sell some of it anyway."

I scoffed. "All of this is yours?"

She nodded. "Your father's closet is on the other side. The other door in the corner. The petty part of me wants to burn his clothes in a bonfire tonight. But I know better than that."

My cheeks puffed out with my sigh. This would be a long night, packing all this shit up. But she was right. If she wanted to leave my father for good, he'd cut her off. Completely. Which meant she'd have to sell a lot of this stuff just to keep herself afloat.

I cleared my throat. "All right. Where are your suitcases?"

Cecilia walked inside. "I definitely don't have enough to pack up all this stuff right now."

"Do you want to sort it first, then?"

She paused. "I suppose I could make a pile of clothes I'm willing to sell now. What's that site you're using?"

"Facebook?"

She giggled. "Oh."

"Yeah. Their marketplace is fantastic. I'm targeting just this area to get things sold quickly. But if you broadened your selling area even twice that, you'd sell this stuff like lightning."

"How do you price it?"

I shrugged. "I just look up the listing price for things like this in the store, take ten percent off the top for wear and tear. Then drop it another hundred bucks. It's worked for me every time."

"That's actually not a bad price."

"We can sort, then take pictures of everything. If you get even a few items up tonight, by morning you'll have an inbox flooded with people waiting to buy your stuff."

"Is that what you've been doing?"

I paused. "It is."

She grinned. "I noticed some things missing."

"Is it that obvious?"

She shook her head. "No. It's obvious because I've been around here for more than a week at a time. It wouldn't have been had I been dipping in and out like your father."

I breathed a sigh of relief. "Okay. Good."

"Are you using a separate account? Or, just your regular Facebook?"

"Oh, no. I'm not that dumb. I created a separate account. Which is why you only post a few items at a time this first time around. If you post too many, the site flags you as a bot and shuts your account down."

"How many did you post the first time?"

"Five. I got those items sold first. And now, I've got eight more people I'm meeting tonight to sell things."

Her eyes bulged. "Eight more people? Really?"

"Yep. So come on. Let's get sorting and start taking some pictures."

"Will you help me make an account? You know, on this site?"

I threaded my arm around her shoulders. "I'll even help you post the pictures and come up with neat ways to sell the items."

"Thanks, Clinton."

"Of course."

I kissed the side of her head, then we got to work. In the midst of sorting her dresses and shoes, accessories and bags, I took breaks to pack up things of my own. Silverware I'd sold and a set of fine china I'd found in the attic. Dusty from being up there for years. Never touched. Never seen. Never used. I found a shit-ton of things in that attic to sell, actually. Old Armani suits. Genuine leather Gucci shoes. All sorts of things that hadn't seen the light of day in at least a decade.

I packed it all away in my duffle bag, preparing it to be sold.

There were moments where I saw Cecilia tearing up over items. Things she tossed into the 'sell' pile I knew she didn't want to get rid of. And my heart ached for her. But I kept reassuring her this was the right decision. That she was taking the right strides to try and get away from my father. I rubbed her back and listened to her stories. Romantic tales of my father that were almost too much to believe. The man she'd once known was foreign to me. It was as if she were speaking about another person entirely. But, I still listened. I still cried with her. I still held her and helped her through the pain.

Of course, until it was time for me to make my way to the corner.

So I could make some money of my own.

26

RAELYNN

I kept an eye on the door as I checked people out. And every time there was a lull in customers, I started cleaning down my area. I went through my usual duties as work, watching as the cashiers I worked silently with slowly phased out for the night. Until no one was left except myself and the night manager. I closed in an hour, and Clint still hadn't shown up. Which worried me. Not that I hadn't been concerned since that fucking text in the middle of the school day.

But, now I had more of a reason to be concerned.

Me: It's okay if you can't come to the grocery store. I understand. Just let me know you're all right. Please.

I sent the text off to Clint in the middle of customers. My manager gave me a look and I slid my phone into my back pocket and continued on with my duties, hoping I'd feel my phone vibrate against my ass cheek. I didn't, though. Which made me even more worried.

What did his father do to him?

I feared the worst. Clint was back in the hospital. Unable to communicate. Maybe he had packed up his stuff and run away. Or, maybe his father had finally beaten him to death.

Tears rushed my eyes and I had to take a bathroom break.

I turned off the light on my register and raced to the back of the grocery store. I slammed through the door of the women's restroom with my hands trembling. I splashed cold water on my face, trying to calm myself down. I wiped off the little bit of makeup I'd managed to paint on my face before leaving, and my mind bounced from Mom to Clint. Mom to Clint. Mom to Clint.

Why couldn't my life just settle the fuck down?

I pulled out my phone and crafted a message to my mother. One I hoped she responded to. I asked her if she was still at home or at the hospital. Though I wasn't sure of the hospital's policy on phones for their patients. I sent it off before checking on Clint again. He hadn't seen my message yet, and I felt bile creeping up the back of my throat.

Please be okay. Please be okay. Please be okay.

I drew in a deep breath before heading back out to my register. And after checking out seven more people, it was time to close down. I wiped down my register, as well as the remaining ones that looked terrible. I swept, making sure to get up and down the aisles where people waited. Then I cashed out my till and took it to the manager, who proceeded to count it and tally it up before we left.

He stood and watched me as I hopped on my bike.

"You get home safe, okay?"

I heard the tremor of his voice and I sighed.

"I will. I promise. Okay?" I asked.

I took off into the night, peddling back home. What I needed to do was call Michael and ask him to give me a ride home. But what I did was exactly the opposite. I pumped as quickly as my legs would let me go. I felt my backpack and my purse weighing me down as I made my way back toward the school. I didn't head home, however. I headed straight for Clint's house.

I needed to know if he was all right.

I pulled into the driveway and came to a screeching stop. My eyes danced over the lights that lit up the windows of the house. Nothing looked out of place. Or broken. I didn't hear screaming or crying. No one burst out on the porch with bodies flying in every other direction.

So far, so good.

I placed my bike down on its side in front of the porch steps and shifted my bags onto my shoulders as I walked up the steps. I knocked softly on the door, but no one answered. No footsteps. No voices. Nothing.

And with each knock, the silence grew.

"Clint?" I called out.

I reached for the doorknob and found the door unlocked. With what felt like a brick of lead in my gut. I slowly opened the door and listened for yelling. Or screaming. Or crying. I didn't hear any of that, though. I heard nothing, which was worse. Was anyone even home?

Because if no one was home, why were all the lights on?

"Clint? Cecilia? Anyone here?"

"Rae?"

Hearing Clint's voice rushed relief through my body. I heard thundering footsteps upstairs as I dropped my things to the floor. I closed the door—and locked it—behind me. And as Clint came rushing down the steps, I found him in one piece.

Bruised, but in one piece.

"Clint," I breathed.

He wrapped me up in a massive hug and picked me up.

"I'm sorry. I'm so sorry I couldn't make it. It's been a whirlwind of a night."

I buried my face in his neck. "I'm just glad you're okay."

He kissed the side of my head. "I'm sorry I worried you."

"What happened with your father?"

He set me down on my feet and cupped my cheeks. The smile on his face lit up my insides. He crashed his lips against mine, weakening my knees. And as he caught me in his arms, he smiled against my lips.

"Come upstairs. I'm helping Cecilia pack her things."

I paused. "What?"

He snickered. "Cecilia's leaving my father. Finally. Come on. Upstairs, with me."

"What do you mean, 'leaving him'?"

"I mean, she's leaving him. Filing for divorce. Not going with him to this new house."

He tugged me up the steps behind him like a kid at Christmas time.

"I mean, that's great. But I don't get why that's good news for you," I said.

He laughed. "It's not, but it's great news for her and I'm happy for her. I'm proud of her, Rae!"

I still didn't understand. But, I rejoiced with them all the same. He pulled me into the massive master bedroom and I gawked at its beauty and size. I looked up toward the vaulted ceilings and slowly turned around. It was beautiful. This one room was half the size of my fucking house alone.

"It's good to see you, Rae."

Cecilia's voice hit my ears and my eyes whipped over to her. She smiled at me and held out her arms, prompting me to hug her. I rushed over to her and held her close. The room felt different. Her aura felt different. Even her smile looked different.

I giggled. "Divorce looks good on you."

She barked with laughter. "I'm not divorced yet. But I'm getting there."

Clint piped up. "We've still got a lot to pack up. You in?"

I nodded. "I'm in for helping, yeah."

Cecilia drew in a short breath. "Oh, by the way. If you see anything in the 'discard' pile you or your mother might like, feel free to take it. It's all going to a donation place anyway."

I smiled. "I appreciate that. Thanks."

Clint took my hand. "Here, I'll show you what we're up to right now."

Clint led me into a closet that was easily the size of my bedroom. Probably bigger, to be honest. There were drawers pulled open showcasing sizzling diamonds. Ruby red gems. Bright gold and rose gold jewelry. An entire wall of sunglasses. Purses tossed onto the floor. It looked like a bomb had gone off in this place. And in its wake, designer clothes for people to rummage around in.

Cecilia definitely had great taste in fashion.

"This is the packing pile. And believe it or not, it's only half the size it was. Everything else is kind of scattered around, but they are the 'discard' piles. We're going to sort all the discarded stuff by accessory and clothing type before boxing it up."

I blinked. "Wow. there's a lot of stuff here."

Clint chuckled. "Yeah. And we've been at it for three hours."

Cecilia called out. "Except for that break you took!"

I furrowed my brow. "What break?"

He grinned. "I sold more stuff tonight."

I threw my arms around him and rejoiced with him. Even though things felt more disconnected than ever, I knew they would fall into place the way they needed to. I felt it in my bones. The chaos was slowly coming to a close, this chapter of all of our lives coming to an end.

Finally.

After struggling for weeks.

I jumped into the sorting and packing. Cecilia handed off some used luggage she didn't want anymore, and I snickered when she handed it to me. Louis Vuitton luggage. A beautiful brown with creamy tan logos emblazoned onto it. Clint ended up tossing all sorts of things into the luggage. Random purses he thought I might like. Sunglasses that looked absolutely ridiculous on me. Jewelry Cecilia didn't want to lug with her that he thought my mom might enjoy.

There had to be at least two hundred thousand dollars' worth of stuff in one of these suitcases.

"No, no, no. I can't take any more. This is too much."

Clint smiled. "Oh, come on. This dress still has the tags on it. And you don't think this would look great on you?"

I snickered. "I'm flattered you think it might fit."

Cecilia rubbed my back. "I think it would fit you. The material stretches. It's supposed to mold to your body. You're, what? A size twelve?"

I paused. "How did you pinpoint that?"

She winked. "It's a gift. Hold on."

I watched her walk into the back of the closet as Clint folded that dress up. He shoved it into one of the suitcases before zipping it up, and I heard him struggling with it. The damn thing was almost bursting at the seams. And I didn't know what to do with— well—any of this. The jewelry they wanted to give me. The designer sunglasses. The outfits.

I'd never worn stuff like this before.

Nor my mother.

"Here we are. Take a look at this."

Cecilia came around the corner with the most beautiful dress in her hands. A hunter green dress, with silken fabric that sparkled in the lights of the closet. She held it up, and my eyes followed it. A full-length dress with off-the-shoulder straps and a built-in bra laid into the corset top.

"It's—it's beautiful."

Cecilia smiled. "A ten-twelve. Which I think will fit you just fine."

She handed it to me, and the first thing that flashed through my mind was 'prom.'

It was the perfect prom dress.

Before I knew it, I had matching shoes in my hands. Dainty white gold jewelry that matched. Even a clutch purse that went with that dress, and that dress alone. Clint took it all out of my hands and packed it away. They continued filling those bags with things they thought I might like until there was no room left in the luggage. Tears rushed my eyes. I didn't know what to say, or think, or do.

"Thank—thank you. I don't—I wouldn't—how do you even wash stuff like this?"

Cecilia smiled. "I'm sure Clint can talk you through that."

I paused. "Clint?"

He chuckled. "I'm not completely inept in the ways of cleaning expensive clothes. I am my father's son, after all."

My face fell. "But you're nothing like him."

Cecilia shook her head. "No, he's not. He's much better than his father could ever be."

He slipped his arm around my lower back and I realized we hadn't gotten much packing done at all. They'd taken their time to fill up luggage for me, and not one ounce of time had been devoted to packing her things. I felt guilty. But they didn't. Which made me feel a bit better, but only a bit.

"Well, I'm going to go have myself a glass of wine downstairs. I have some things I want to pack up down there anyway. We can give the clothes a rest."

Cecilia's voice caught my ear and pulled me out of my trance.

"Do you need any help?" I asked.

She waved her hand in the air. "I'll be fine. Clint's been packing with me for the past three hours. And I know you came over to see him."

"But I'd like to help. If you'll let me."

Clint chuckled. "And we will. After she's had her glass of wine."

Cecilia nodded. "Exactly. I need a break. And if you're still here after my break, you can help. How's that sound?"

I grinned. "Sounds good. I'd like to repay you somehow for... all of this."

Cecilia snickered. "Nonsense. You're more than welcome to it."

27

CLINTON

I watched as Cecilia winked at me, then left us in the closet by ourselves. I felt how overwhelmed Rae had become. I felt her tensing next to me, and I wanted to help her relax. I guided her to my bedroom and closed the door behind me, locking it for good measure. In case Dad decided to storm the house again. Rae stood in the middle of my room, her eyes locked onto a spot on the ceiling.

Then she let out a heavy sigh. "I can't take all of that stuff."

I walked over, taking her hands in mine. "You can, and you will."

She shook her head. "It's too much. It's too nice. I don't know what to do with it."

"You dry clean it. Any stain, just take it to a dry cleaners."

"I don't have the money for that."

I shrugged. "Sell the jewelry. Then you will."

"That jewelry is beautiful, though."

"Then, sell some of the purses and sunglasses to afford the jewelry cleaning and dry cleaning."

She snickered. "So this is how the rich live."

I licked my lips. "Trust me, it's not as nice as some people think."

Her fingertips reached out and fondled a bruise against my jawline. Her eyes flickered over to worry, and I didn't want her to feel worse. I wanted her to feel better. I wrapped my hand around her wrist and brought her fingers to my lips, kissing the tips of them. All of them. Watching as she softly relaxed.

"It's okay, Rae. I'm okay."

She sighed. "I could've sworn your father had—"

I nodded slowly. "I mean, it wasn't pretty. He was angry. He lashed out. He did what he usually does. But it didn't come out as bad as I figured it would."

Tears rimmed her eyes. "I hate him so much."

"Come here. It's okay. I promise, I'm all right."

I wrapped her up in my arms and felt her cling to my clothing. She shook against me, and it made me silently spit fire at my father. Once he was finally out of my life, things would be so much better. For me. For Rae. For us, and my future.

Our future, if we had one together.

I walked her slowly into my bathroom and closed the door behind us. We both needed to unwind, and I needed to wash the stench of sweat off my body. Packing up Cecilia's shit was a big job. Because she had a lot of stuff. She certainly had access to my father's money over the years. But, she wasn't as materialistic as I'd taken her to be.

Especially after watching her easy generosity with Rae tonight.

I reached into the shower and turned on the hot water. I tempered it with some cold, then stripped myself of my clothes. Rae's eyes roamed over my body, clocking the bruises as tears continued to slip from her eyes. And as I helped her out of her own clothes, I ran my hands along her curves, stealing her warmth and her softness. Prepping a soft landing into the one person I called home.

"Come here, beautiful."

I pulled her into me for a voracious kiss. One that stiffened my cock almost instantly. I accepted the effect she had on me. The electricity she pushed through my veins. I pulled her into the walk-in shower and turned the hot waterfall into a wet mist. The entire stone shower turned into a wet sauna, coating us in a sheen of sweat and water vapor as our teeth clattered together.

"Oh, Clint."

I growled. "I'll never get tired of hearing you say that."

I pressed her against the wall and kissed down her neck. She opened herself up for me, and I took my fill of her. I marked her breasts. Sucked on her nipples. Tugged them to painful peaks with my teeth as her hands threaded into my hair. She pushed me further down her body. Aching for me to be between her legs. And as I fell to my knees, I slipped one of her legs over my shoulder before slipping the other.

"Clint, no, no, no. You're going to—drop—fuck!"

"Mmm, what was that?"

I gave her all my strength. All my devotion. I gave her all of me as I hoisted her off the ground. My hands pressed into the stone wall to steady me as her nails raked along my scalp. I opened my mouth and devoured her. My tongue slid up and down her slit, readying her for my assault as her heels dug into my back. Her body hovered above the shower floor.

"Shit, Clint."

"Mmm, that's it."

"Don't let me fall."

"I'll never let you fall, Rae. Not on my watch."

My tongue found her swollen nub and I flicked against it. Over and over, feeling her tremble against my face. I had her right where I wanted her. And I never wanted her to leave. I drank every droplet she had for me as she poured into my mouth. Opening herself. Relaxing herself. Offering herself up as my dinner.

A dinner I'd never forget.

"Clint! Yes!"

"Be as loud as you want, beautiful."

"Oh, fuuuuck. Please, don't stop."

I lapped harder against her. Deeper into her body. My fingers curled into the stone wall as my cock leaked from its tip. I felt her trembling and shivering against me. I felt her hands wrapping themselves around the tendrils of my hair that had grown far too long. She bucked against me, ravenously chasing her release on the tip of my tongue.

But when she unraveled, I didn't stop.

"Clint! Clint! No, no, no, n—yes. Oh, right there, yeah."

I chuckled as I continued my assault, following her every command. A little to the right. Back to the left. Down. Down. No, no, no, up. I smiled against her. Every chuckle I filled her pussy with made her jump. She hissed with delight and moaned my name. Until her words became choppy and her gasps became groans. I felt her unraveling again, losing control. Her arousal dripped down my neck as I coaxed her over the edge again, feeling her grow weaker against my assault.

Which still didn't stop, even as my body shook with exhaustion.

"Clint, I can't. I can't. You have to—oh, fuck, what are you doing to me?"

Her moans fell from her lips with ease. I felt her juices dripping down my chest. My cock leaked thick threads of precum as it pooled on the shower floor. Sweat dripped down my brow. Mist flooded my back. I rocked my face against her, digging deeper and keeping a steady rhythm as she slowly began bucking against me again.

"Oh, yeah, Clint. Yeah, yeah, yeah, yeah, yeah."

Her pleasure choked off her sounds. I heard her gasping as her body spun out of control. It was the most beautiful sound I'd ever heard in my life. And I never wanted a day to go by where I didn't hear it. I slowly slid her to the floor, my muscles trembling with exhaustion. I lay her down on her back, kissing softly up her stomach. Her breasts. Her neck. All the way up to her lips. And as our mouths met, I felt her legs spread apart.

"Fill me, Clint."

She didn't have to ask me twice.

I slid deep inside her as the mist of the sauna-shower cloaked us from the rest of the world. I threaded our fingers together, pinning her wrists above her head. Her pussy swallowed me whole. Her walls clamped down tightly around me. I felt her shivering. Quaking, for my viewing pleasure. And with every thrust I afforded her, I watched her breasts jump and her eyes roll back. I watched her jaw unhinge in silent pleasure as she entrusted me with her most vulnerable form.

A gift I'd never take for granted.

My growls met her moans. Her glance met my stare. I kept my eyes on her, unable to pull away as her face contorted with pleasure. She was a shaking mess. Dripping with sweat, flushed with ecstasy, and dripping with cum. And yet, she'd never looked more beautiful. Writhing beneath me. Helpless to my pleasurable assault.

I love you. I love you. I love you, Rae.

I pounded into her. I dug my knees into the stone and bit back the pain. I gnashed my teeth together as she lifted her hips, offering them to me as a sacrifice. Her walls squeezed me as her legs locked around my calves. Her fingernails dug into the tops of my hands as her pussy pulled me deeper, trapping me within the confines of its warmth. I dropped my lips against hers and hovered over her as my cock pulsed once. Twice. Three times, inside her body.

And then I burst.

Bringing her along with me.

Her moans filled the back of my throat as my grunts filled hers. I rutted against her, like a wild fucking animal, my threads of arousal filling her to the brim. Her pussy pulsed so hard it pushed me out. And with it came our intermingled juices, shooting against my pelvis. I grinned against her lips and chuckled as our teeth clattered together. What a mess we were. The two of us.

A perfect mess made for one another.

I love you, Rae. With everything I have.

I hoped she felt it, too. Because one of these days, I'd have the balls to say it. One of these days, I'd have the guts to tell her myself.

One of these days, if she kept me around long enough, I'd have the courage to look her square in her eyes and tell her.

But for now, I settled with holding her close, pulling her against me as we lay there, our bodies intertwined at the bottom of my shower. I kissed her shoulder and she jumped, giggling as I nuzzled her and threaded our fingers together as she slipped her shaking leg between mine.

I settled for feeling her press against me, wanting to get as close to me as she could.

In the hopes that one day soon, I'd tell her how I truly felt.

And hear those words from her in return.

28

RAELYNN

*Raelynn*One Week Later

I smiled as I tried on my prom dress for the fourth time that week. I still couldn't believe all the stuff Cecilia had simply handed away. I ran my hands down the silken fabric, watching as it molded to my touch. To my body. To the curves I apparently had. I even held the clutch in my hands to get an idea of what I might look like at prom.

If Clint ever asked me to go.

I felt much better than I did last week. And not just because Clint and I were back together. I mean, yeah. That played into some of it. We were spending a lot more time together, especially since we were working on catching him back up with classes. Getting his overdue homework turned in. Things like that. But work was also going well. I'd gotten a small raise. Only twenty cents more than I was making, but every little bit helped.

And selling off some of the jewelry Cecilia had passed to me helped cushion my bank account.

After Mom got back from her stint in the hospital, I gave her some of the clothes. Not all of them, but some. A couple of the sunglasses and a few of the purses. Some tops and pants and dresses that definitely didn't fit me. She ogled and swooned over them. She even put on a little fashion show for me as she twirled around in them. I hadn't seen my mother smile like that in years. And it warmed my heart to see her that happy.

Without D.J.

"Rae!"

I opened my bedroom door. "Yeah, Mom?"

"I'm off to my therapy session. I should be back in a couple of hours. I was thinking of picking up lunch for us."

"Don't worry about it. I'm graduation dress shopping with Allison today. I'll see you for dinner!"

"Sounds good."

"Love you! Have a good time at therapy!"

I heard Mom snickering as she walked out the door. That was another new thing, too. Because of our income status, she qualified for free therapy lessons through the hospital that had treated her. So, twice a week, she was scheduled to go in and talk with someone to help her sift through these issues she clearly still struggled with. I was so proud of her for finally pulling away from all the abusive nonsense and getting her happiness back and starting down a path to find her way in life.

Though another decision would be coming soon. Because eventually, she'd have to get a job.

That's when the real test would come.

Don't think about that now. Focus on the present.

I smiled as I slipped out of the dress. It still needed to be hemmed, since Cecilia was a good four inches taller than me. But I had the money to get that done now. Most of the money from selling off that jewelry was stashed in a savings account. But I'd kept a little bit of the money in my own checking account. You know, to have it there in case Mom and I needed something.

Or if I really did need to move in with Allison until graduation.

I got dressed into some jeans and a T-shirt. Then I peeked at the back of my closet. That luggage was still piled up, still half-full of things I knew I'd never use. I did grab a pair of the sunglasses, though. The one pair I did like. They were black, swirled with brown. And the frames were large. They almost covered my face. They were muted, not like the sparkling ones that twinkled at me every time I opened the small suitcase.

These I'd keep for myself.

I gathered my things then headed out the door. Allison had convinced her parents to let her borrow the van for today. So off we went. She pulled into my driveway just as I locked the door behind me. I was excited to go dress shopping with her. I rushed to the van and hopped in, with her exclaiming over my sunglasses.

"Oh, my gosh. Where in the world did you get those?"

I pulled a sparkling pair out of my purse. "Want a pair?"

She gasped. "Rae. Do you have any idea what kind of sunglasses these are?"

I shrugged. "No clue. But I know they're expensive. So treat them with care."

"Wait, are you giving these to me? Where on earth did you get them?"

"Oh, do I have some shit to fill you in on."

"Okay, okay. Hold on. Let me get us out to the main road first."

She slipped on the sunglasses and giggled like a little girl. I clapped my hands as I laughed, watching the way she enjoyed them. I had a pair set aside for Michael, too. Sunglasses that could easily pass for a men's pair. All black. A beautiful matte black. With sharp edges and a red streak going down either side of the arms.

I couldn't wait to give them to him Monday at school.

Allison pulled out of the driveway and headed toward the opening of the neighborhood. She drove like an old woman, though. Five under the speed limit, no matter what. I grinned as we made our way onto the main road, getting ourselves into traffic that made Allison white-knuckle the damn steering wheel.

I held off on my storytelling until we got to the mall. But the second she eased into a parking space and turned off the van, I whipped my head around to hers.

"So, last week after I got off work, I went to go check on Clint. You know, his first day back?"

Allison turned to face me. "Yeah? I mean, I take it he was fine. He's been back at school all week."

I nodded. "Yep. He was just fine. Apparently, Cecilia's leaving his father."

She gasped. "Nuh-uh."

"Yeah. She's really leaving him. They were packing up all her stuff when I went by. Her closet is massive, Allison. I mean, easily the size of my bedroom. If not bigger. She was packing away all the things she wanted to take and donating what she didn't want to keep."

"Let me guess. She let you pilfer through the donation pile."

"More than that, she and Clint loaded me down with stuff. You wouldn't believe the kinds of things I've got in my closet right now. Stuffed inside brown and tan Louis Vuitton luggage."

"What!?"

I laughed. "I know, right? It was insane. I've actually sold some of the jewelry she gave me just to put some money in my savings. You know, for after graduation. I gave a few pieces to Mom. I kept a few for myself—including my prom dress."

"Wait, wait, wait, you have your prom dress and I haven't seen it yet? What gives?"

"You can come inside after you drop me off and I'll put it on for you. Cecilia gave me matching heels and a clutch and everything."

"So, you got these sunglasses from her?"

I nodded. "Yep. I've got a pair for Michael, too."

"What will you do with the rest of the clothes?"

I shrugged. "I don't know. I mean, I've already got the things I want to keep folded away at the bottom of my dresser drawers. I guess you can come take a look at what you might want. But I figured I'd hang onto the things and sell them if I needed the money."

"Oh, that hurts my heart. I bet they're gorgeous clothes."

"Well, then come upstairs after we're done shopping and you can take a look. There's purses and dresses and shirts and pants and jewelry still up for grabs."

She threw her arms around me. "Your life is so insane."

I giggled. "Yeah. I know."

She released me from the hug. "So, what about the house? Is it actually being sold?"

I sighed. Because this was the one bad thing that happened this past week.

"It's actually sold, yeah. They have to be out in a little over two weeks. And according to Clint, neither of them have heard a word from his father since he came to pick Clint up from school that day."

She snickered. "What a butthead."

I giggled. "Yes. He's definitely one of those."

"Oh! Michael said Clint stopped by to pick up his money. Did he ever get it deposited?"

I nodded. "Yep. And he's still selling things off. I think he'll have a nice little nest egg going for himself."

"Has he given Michael's parents' place any thought? I mean, he'll need a place to go."

"If he has, he hasn't mentioned anything to me. And honestly, I'm trying not to press so much. I know he's overwhelmed, and we just got him caught back up with school. The last thing I want is for him to stop coming again because he feels like he's drowning and has to cut something out."

"That makes sense."

"So, ready to get this shopping done?"

She giggled. "You're just ready for the food that comes after."

I unbuckled my seatbelt. "You know I hate shopping."

"Which is terrible, because you look good in so many things. I'd kill for the curves you have. I'm nothing but a stick."

I rolled my eyes. "I know. Such a burden being thin and beautiful."

The two of us linked arms, then headed into the mall. We walked through store after store, with Allison turning her nose up at most everything she came across. I mean, I had planned for an entire afternoon of shopping. But, usually, shopping required trying things on.

And after walking through four stores, she hadn't tried on a damn thing.

"Are you okay?"

Allison sighed. "I think I should be searching for prom dresses instead of graduation dresses."

"You still haven't found yours yet?"

She shook her head. "No, and I'm still not sure if I'm even going. I mean, Michael's hinted at it. I think he kind of asked me, but I'm not sure."

"What do you mean, he kind of asked you?"

"Well, we were having this talk about it on Wednesday. And he started talking about his suit and all the colors he wanted to wear. And then he looked at me and asked me what color my dress was. I told him I didn't know because I hadn't gotten one yet, and that was that. He didn't formally ask or anything. Just... assumed? I think?"

I nodded. "It sounds like he assumes you guys are going together."

"I want him to ask, though. That's the fun part of prom."

"Well, maybe start dropping some hints. You know, like you did back before you two were dating."

She rolled her eyes. "Are guys always this clueless? Why do I have to do all the legwork?"

I snickered. "Trust me, you will *always* have to do all the legwork."

"Great."

"If you want to look for prom dresses instead, I'm all for it. Means I don't have to try on shit."

She snickered. "Yeah, you'd like that part, too. Oh! Wait! Has Clint asked you to prom?"

I shook my head. "No. Not yet."

"You think he will?"

"I really hope so. I mean, I've got that dress his stepmom gave me. I'd like a chance to wear it for him."

"For him? Wow, who are you and what have you done with my best friend?"

I laughed. "Oh, shut up."

"You've got it bad for him."

"And this is news to you?"

She giggled. "Nope. Just cute, is all. Love looks good on you."

"I never said I was—"

"Yeah, yeah, yeah. You're in love, whether you want to admit it or not. And it looks good on you. Take the compliment and come on. I see a dress I want to try."

And before I could fight her any more on the matter, she tugged me into a store. Headed straight for a pale yellow and purple gown that screamed Allison's name.

A gown I knew would look fabulous on her, even though it still hung on a rack.

29

CLINTON

The strip of tape made a bombastic sound as I pulled it across the cardboard boxes. I'd done everything I could. Sold everything I could without throwing red flags up to my father. And now the time had come. Cecilia and I had two weeks to get our asses out of this place before the new owners were due to move in. And I still had yet to figure out where the hell I was headed. I hadn't even talked with my stepmom about it. Were we sticking together? Was she leaving to do her own thing? Did I need to take Michael up on the offer from his parents?

Stay focused. Just keep packing.

As I dug through my room, I set aside a few more things I didn't mind selling. A genuine leather belt I hadn't touched once. Shined leather shoes that still smelled new. An entire tuxedo tailored to me I never planned on wearing again.

Well, after prom.

Shit, I have to ask Rae to prom.

My phone rang in my back pocket and I tossed my tuxedo onto the bed, which had been stripped of its sheets. If I really was being forced out of this house, I'd take with me anything and everything that could even possibly be mine. Towels. The decorative bathroom set. The sheets on my bed. Hell, I was still in the process of trying to arrange a storage facility so I could take my bedroom set, too.

The mattress. The bedside tables. All of it. I'd gotten so much money from selling off the small things in this house that I had no need to sell that shit. Which meant I could start my new life off with some furniture of my own.

Though, part of me wanted to torch every bit of it and start from scratch. Erase the painful memories that came with the pieces of this bedroom set.

I pulled my phone out and saw an unknown number calling, so I ignored it. I got back to taping up boxes I already had packed. Then that number called back again. No voice message. No text. Nothing. It was our area code, though.

Just pick it up, Clint.

"Hello?"

The woman cleared her throat. "Is this Mr. Clinton Clarke?"

I paused. "Who's asking?"

"My name is Rena Nichols. I'm a lawyer in the area."

I furrowed my brow. "What can I do for you, Miss Nichols?"

"I'd like to speak with you, in person, about the charges against the three kids that ran you off the road last month. Do you have some time to come in?"

"On a Saturday?"

"Yes, sir."

"You don't have to call me that."

"What do you prefer to be called?"

"Clint is just fine."

She paused. "All right, Mr. Clint. Yes, as soon as you can get in here, I'd like to speak with you. Preferably with an adult present."

I snickered. "I'm eighteen. I can come by myself."

"I know. But it might behoove you to have an adult here. To help you absorb what I have to say."

"Has something happened? How did you get my number?"

A knock came at my door. "Clinton? Everything okay?"

I turned around and looked at Cecilia. I pressed the phone to my shoulder as I tried gathering my thoughts. She walked over to me, her eyes filled with concern. And just as she went to reach for my phone, I drew in a sharp breath.

"There's a lawyer on the phone for me. Says she's got information on the charges against the boys that ran me off that bridge."

Cecilia nodded. "You want me to speak with her?"

"She's saying I should come into her office today with a legal guardian or something. Says it's not required, but I should anyway."

"Let me get my things. Get her address and we can head out now."

"Are you sure?"

She backtracked out of my room. "Positive, Clinton."

I put the phone back to my ear. "You still there?"

"I'm ready to give my address whenever you are."

I searched around for my notebook and pen before scribbling down the address she rattled off. I didn't know what this was about, but it sounded urgent. And not good. I hung up the phone and turned around, finding Cecilia standing in the doorway with her purse slung over her shoulder and her hair piled high on top of her head. We made our way out of the house.

"Did she say what this was about at all?"

I shook my head, closing the front door behind me. "All she says was it was important. I don't even know how she got my information."

She nodded slowly. "All right. Well, let's go figure out what this is all about. Then, we can get back to packing."

"You think she might be able to help with this house thing? You know, prevent the sale from happening?'

She sighed. "It's already happened. There's nothing we can do about that. And honestly? I'm not sure I'd even want to stay here, given the chance. Would you?"

I shrugged. "Where else am I going to go?"

She nodded slowly. "We'll figure that out. Together. Okay? I promise. But, right now, let's focus on what's in front of us. Which is the lawyer."

"Mr. Clint, it's nice to meet you."

I shook the lawyer's hand before reaching for Cecilia.

"This is my stepmother, Cecilia Clarke."

Miss Nichols shook her hand. "Thank you for coming in on such short notice. Please, make yourselves comfortable."

It was clear from the size of her office that she was a prominent lawyer. A successful one. The bookshelves were lined from floor to ceiling with all sorts of law textbooks and reference materials. Binders were open on her desk. There were filing cabinets tucked into every corner of the room. Miss Nichols walked with poise and grace, dressed to impress but not dominate.

She ushered for us to sit down in front of her desk.

"To answer your questions, I received your case file from a colleague of mine. A colleague that might have promised some pro bono work?"

I nodded slowly. "So, why are we in your office instead of his?"

She sighed. "My colleague's schedule has become filled. But he didn't want your specific situation falling through the cracks. He'd been keeping tabs on the police investigation, but once a major case fell into his lap, he wanted to make sure yours got passed on to someone he knew would take care of it."

Cecilia cleared her throat. "Which he feels is you."

Miss Nichols nodded. "Yes. And I have to admit, your case has caught my eye. It's an easy open-and-shut case. The police charged them for the speeding and reckless driving. I'm curious as to why you haven't pressed formal charges yet."

The women looked at me and I sighed.

"Just—a lot has happened lately. A lot is going on that needs my attention."

The lawyer nodded. "Something more important than putting bars around the boys that almost killed you."

Cecilia butted in. "You said pro bono, right?"

Nichols nodded. "Correct."

"And you think this is an open and shut case?"

"Once we go to court, I can prove within the day what these boys are guilty of and have them slapped in handcuffs."

I sighed. "Look, we're in the process of moving. And—"

The lawyer held up her hand. "My colleague gave me quite an interesting hypothetical over the phone."

Her eyes met mine as Cecilia looked over at me.

"Okay. Great," I murmured.

Nichols sat against her desk. "I'll answer any questions you want. I'll help in any way I can. But these kids can't walk. They need to be taught a lesson. And as far as this house situation goes, I'm more than willing to help you navigate it."

I snickered. "The house has been sold. It's a non-issue at this point."

"Then I can help the two of you get back on your feet. Get you established in the area. And if you don't want to stay here, I can reach out to colleagues I have up and down the West Coast. Have them help you get settled where you need to be without that man's influence ruining everything."

Cecilia drew in a shuddering breath. "You can do that?"

Nichols nodded. "I'm more than willing to, yes. The position you two have been put in sounds almost impossible. You're going to need someone on your side."

I felt so overwhelmed. And yet, so relieved. Cecilia started firing off all sorts of questions. How this woman could help. What court might feel like. Whether or not we'd have to get up and testify. How long the process took. I sat there, thankful that I'd brought her along. Because had she not been there beside me, I wasn't sure I would've come up with half the questions she had asked.

Cecilia took my hand. "How are you feeling about all this?"

I drew in a deep breath. "It's a lot to process."

Nichols stood up. "I want you to take your time and think about it. The police will push forward with charges, one way or another. But they can't charge the boys with attempted murder without you filing those formal charges. Which I'm more than willing to do."

I nodded slowly. "And, you're willing to help with the rest of this stuff, too?"

Her eyes met mine. "Anything you need. Pro bono."

I looked over at Cecilia before I stood up. I walked over to the lawyer and stared straight into her eyes. I search for any lie. Any manipulation. Any fault in the programming of what she was saying. And when I found none, I offered her my hand.

"You have a deal," I said.

Nichols took my hand. "Wonderful. The first thing I'm going to do is file the formal charges on your behalf. I'll need a written account of what happened that night for my own records. I know you've already written one for the police, but I'll need one, too."

Cecilia shot up beside me. "I'll get him back sometime this week. And thank you for answering all my questions."

She shook my stepmother's hand, too. "Anytime. I'm going to

give you my information so you can contact me any way you wish. Phone. Email. Stopping by. You're welcome anytime."

"I'm confident my stepson's in good hands with you. Just make sure those reckless kids can't ever get behind the wheel of a car again and hurt anyone else."

Nichols nodded. "Don't worry. My firm and I will take care of it. Cases like this are easy ones."

After exchanging information, we left the law office. And I felt another massive weight roll of my back. It became easier to breathe. My legs didn't feel as sore. It was as if some of the chains had fallen away, allowing me a few inches closer to the exit of this terrible dungeon I'd been stuck in for years.

Cecilia wrapping her arm around my waist pulled me from my trance. "So, I know this is terribly irresponsible of me to ask. But, how do you feel about me picking us up a six pack of cold beers for the night? There are some things I want to talk to you about. Things we have yet to discuss."

I snickered. "Beer? I thought you were a wine person."

She shrugged. "I have my surprises every now and again. Do you have a beer you prefer?"

"I'm honestly not really a beer person."

"I shouldn't be shocked that you know that."

I chuckled. "How do you feel about a wine and whiskey night?"

She unlocked her car. "Sounds like the only thing I need to pick up is food, then."

"Oh, what about that Indian place across town? Their curry and naan is fabulous."

"The little place with the bright pink roof?"

I slipped into the car. "Yep! That's the one."

She dipped in beside me. "Indian food with some wine and whiskey sounds fabulous. What do you usually order, other than the curry?"

"Their curry, extra jasmine rise, and garlic naan. You?"

"I love their chicken tikka masala. Extra spicy. With two orders of rosemary naan and their mango milkshake."

"They have mango milkshakes?"

"Oh! You haven't lived until you've had one of those. I'm going to get you one."

And as she cranked up the car, a smile crossed my face. I was in completely uncharted territory with her right now. But I loved it all the same. My stepmom was a lot cooler than I'd given her credit for. She was a completely different person from what I had assumed her to be.

I enjoyed spending this time getting to know her. Having her open up to me. Feeling as if I could rely on her.

I just hoped this conversation she wanted to have tonight ended with us sticking together instead of splitting apart.

30

RAELYNN

"I can't wait for Michael to see you in that dress."

Allison pulled into my driveway. "If he ever asks me to prom. And I still didn't find a graduation dress for myself. Mom's going to kill me."

"Oh, boo. You needed a prom dress anyway. And that thing looks perfect on you."

"You think?"

I smiled. "The dark purple with the pale yellow under the tulle? You're going to look like the next Disney princess."

She smiled. "I'd like to find some yellow shoes. You know, to keep the continuation of the colors going."

"But do purple jewelry, if anything. Small items. You definitely want people focused on that dress."

She giggled. "Look at you, getting into fashion and all that."

I rolled my eyes. "Don't get used to it. Clint's stepmom can only rub off so much."

I reached over and gave Allison a tight hug. Then I gathered my things. I'd ended up finding myself a nice casual dress for graduation. I mean, I had the money in my account. It was already marked down on sale anyway. Why not? It fit me nice. It didn't have to be altered. And I already had a pair of flats that would go well with it. It wasn't a color I wore regularly. The pale blue and white swirls were definitely brighter than my entire wardrobe put together. But the cotton dress would breathe, according to Allison. And it was sleeveless. Came just above my knee. So, it would be light enough for the California summer heat.

"Are you seeing Clint at all tomorrow?"

I opened my door. "I'm not sure. But, if I don't, want me to give you a call?"

Allison paused. "Actually…?"

I waved my hand in the air. "Tell Michael I said hey. And have fun. I'll see you Monday."

"Love you."

"Love you, too."

I slipped out of the van and made my way for the front door. I went on inside, knowing it would be unlocked. Allison and I had stayed out far longer than I had anticipated. It was nearing dinner time, and I smelled something simmering on the stove. I closed the front door behind me and made my way for the stairs, ready to hang up my dress.

Until Mom's voice piped up.

"Where have you been all day?"

I furrowed my brow. "Dress shopping with Allison, remember?"

She paused. "Dress shopping?"

"Yeah. I shouted it down to you this morning before you left for therapy. How did that go, by the way?"

"Prom dress shopping, or graduation dress shopping?"

"Graduation dress shopping. I already have a prom dress."

She coughed. "Wait, you do?"

I nodded. "Mm-hmm. Cecilia gave it to me."

"Who's Cecilia?"

"Clint's stepmom?"

"Since when have you been over at Clint's? I thought you two were broken up?"

I shrugged. "Not anymore. We worked things out."

I went to go up the steps, but Mom stood up.

"Wait, wait, wait, wait. Hold on."

I held back a sigh. "I have an exam to study for, Mom."

She walked over to the stairs. "Can I… see you in your prom dress?"

"Maybe later. I really have some studying to do."

"And you didn't want to go dress shopping with me?"

I paused. "No."

I looked over at my mother and saw her eyes swell with hurt.

"I wanted to go shopping with you for that dress. Graduation's been a long time coming. I thought you wanted to go with me?"

I licked my lips. "Mom, I just—don't know how to have quality time with you anymore."

"What do you mean?"

I shrugged. "Just, with everything that's happened."

"You mean with D.J.?"

"I mean, in general. But, yes. That includes D.J. I couldn't spend time with you without being around him. And it's been so long since we've hung out that I don't even know how to do that anymore with you."

She placed her hand over mine. "Honey, why didn't you tell me you felt this way?"

I snickered. "Because I was too busy telling you to leave someone who kept smacking you around."

"Will you at least take out your dress so I can see it?"

"You don't just want to see it on me later?"

She eyed me carefully. "Why haven't you asked me about my therapy appointment yet?"

"Okay. How did it go?"

"No, no. That's passed. Why aren't you curious about it?"

"Mom, you're reading too much into things. It's fine. Things are okay."

"Things aren't okay. If there's anything I learned at therapy today, it's that things haven't been okay for a while and I simply haven't seen it."

"Well, keep up with your therapy sessions and maybe we can start to pick through some of it."

She paused. "Is that it?"

I rolled my eyes. "Is what it?"

"Do you feel like I'm not going to stick with my therapy sessions?"

"Mom, I don't have time for this. I have a test I really need to study—"

"In a minute. Right now, we need to talk."

"No, we don't. You're blowing something you've always known completely out of proportion. And now, you're getting in the way of my studies because *you* want to do something. It's selfish."

Her eyes welled with tears. "I'm sorry I can't seem to do right by you."

I swallowed my rising anger. "I just need some time. You need to heal, and so do I."

"Things are over between me and D.J. For good. I swear to you. We've had our last fight, Rae. I mean that."

I nodded. "Then time will tell. Okay?"

She squeezed my hand. "I'm getting better. I already feel better. My therapist and I talked about a lot today. Started unpacking some of the things I never let go of regarding your father leaving."

"I'm glad. I'm really glad to hear that."

"I feel like a new person, almost."

I smiled weakly. "Yes. So, let's just keep taking it week by week. Okay?"

She squeezed my hand harder. "You don't believe me."

"Mom, it's only been a week. And if you really want me to be honest? I've seen you go longer spans of time before accepting D.J. back. No doubt he'll come up to this door someday with money and flowers and promises of a future together, and that will be your real test. Surviving without him. Making something of yourself instead of being so scared of the world out there."

She sniffled. "When did you grow up on me?"

"I did it while you were arguing in your room with D.J. and out at the bars on the weekends with mysterious men."

I knew that comment smacked her across the face. She physi-cally stumbled away from me. Tears streamed down her cheeks and it killed me to hurt her. But at the same time, I had a right to express how she'd made me feel. How much she had abandoned me over the years. How very unlike my own mother she had become the further she slipped into this mania of hers. I shifted my bag into my other hand, giving her the silence she needed to dry her tears. I felt my heart breaking. But, at the same time, she needed to hear it.

Maybe if she finally heard the truth, she'd stick with this new path she had carved out for herself.

"You really believe that little of me?"

I snickered. "Mom, I don't want to fight tonight."

She scoffed. "I'm not fighting. I'm asking a question I want an honest answer to."

"I don't think you're little. I think you're lost."

"I'm not lost, Rae. I was hurt. And I never recovered from that."

"And you lost who you were in the process. Don't you lie to me."

She looked at me pointedly. "I'm not lying. And don't you dare take that tone with me. No matter how you view me, I'm still your mother."

"And no matter what you choose to do with your life, I'm still the daughter you've neglected in the process."

"How have I neglected you, huh? Tell me. You've got a roof over your head. Food in your belly. Clothes in your drawers. Tell me how you've been neglected."

I shook my head. "I need to go study."

"Oh, no you don't. You wanted this fight, we're going to have it."

I spun around. "I didn't want any fight, okay?"

Mom stood in front of me as I slowly backed up the steps.

"I didn't want to fight with you! I just didn't want to lie to you! But, that's what I get when I tell you the truth because you don't like it. You don't like your truth. Which is why you need therapy. And I'm proud of you. I really am. But you broke my trust a long time ago when you continuously let an abusive man into this home where I live without asking me how I felt about it once. You broke my trust the second you started relying on that man for money and then preaching to me about how I had to stand on my own two feet and rely on myself. You broke my trust the second you tried to mold me into the kind of girl I am today while denying yourself that same strength because the world out there is too scary and too hard and too judgmental. Well, you know what, Mom? It's going to take more than a week for that trust to come back. So take it or leave it. Because that's all I've got for you."

"You don't believe a word coming out of my mouth, do you?"

I turned my back. "I'll believe it when I see it."

I started up the steps, leaving my crying mother to wallow in her own self-pity. On the one hand, I felt like an utter bitch. And on the other hand, I felt relieved. Now that the truth was out there and she knew exactly how I felt, I didn't feel like a stranger in my own home. Yes, it was a harsh truth. But, speaking my truth helped me to breathe a little easier.

Even at the expense of my mother's tears.

Hearing her cry downstairs broke my heart. But I didn't let it deter me. I closed my bedroom door behind me and hung my new dress up in my closet. I tossed my purse onto my bed, went into my closet and pulled out my backpack. And as I started pulling my books out, exhaustion washed over me.

I had no more pity to give out to anyone.

I tossed my books onto my bed. But staring at them made me tired. The test wasn't until Wednesday. I could study in the morning. I turned my eyes back toward my closet. They fell to the luggage at the bottom. And one by one, I pulled them out and dumped everything onto the bed.

I picked out the few things I figured Allison might enjoy. I set aside the sunglasses for Michael. Then I picked out one specific piece of jewelry I wanted to give Mom for her birthday. It had her name written all over it. Big. Beautiful. Loud. Just like her. I sighed as I set it off to the side. Her birthday was next month. I would wrap it up and give it to her. Something nice she could be proud of. A piece of real jewelry, instead of that fake shit D.J. always bought her. I wanted her to have something to remind her of what she deserved. To remind her of the beauty this world had to offer if she simply strived for it.

And after picking out a few more things for myself, I started taking pictures.

I wanted to post everything else online for sale. Because it made me nervous to have all this expensive stuff at the bottom of my closet. I had to look up the pieces of clothing in order to estimate how much to sell it for. And the prices boggled my mind. A few of the less expensive things I set off to the side. I slipped the items into the smallest luggage case I had as a back-up reserve of money. The big things, though, I posted immediately. The more expensive the item, the more nervous it made me.

The more I heard my mother cry, the more I wondered if she could stick with this. I kept posting pictures and getting hits on them. People who were interested. Who were asking for verification of the jewels and diamonds. I worked to answer their questions as more pictures uploaded. Because in the end, I needed a fall-back plan. If Mom fell through with all this—if Mom took him back—I needed enough money for an exit plan. Enough money to run my own life and completely disconnect myself with her. Because I meant what I said.

If he came back, I was gone.

And I needed to be ready for the worst.

31

CLINTON

I sipped my whiskey as I leaned back in the chair. It softly rocked, and the fall breeze kicked up. I swear, I smelled the fucking ocean in it. I closed my eyes and relished my full stomach. Lunch had been fantastic, which left us with more than enough to heat up for dinner. And after two rounds of Indian and whiskey, I was feeling limber. Light. Carefree. Relaxed.

Especially with Cecilia.

Things were just comfortable with her. I enjoyed having her in my life. Having her support on things. I never had evenings like this with my father. We either ate in separate rooms or I ordered take-out simply because he wasn't home. Never had we shared a meal like this. Not even during the damn holidays.

I wonder what holidays would be like with her.

"So, how are you feeling about today?"

I sighed. "You know, I feel good about it."

Cecilia nodded. "That lawyer was generous with her offer."

"She was, yeah."

"It's nice to know good people really do exist."

I snickered. "Maybe she'll help you with your divorce."

"I've actually already called her about that. She can't, but she's referring me to another one of her colleagues that has a really good win rate."

I nodded. "Good for you. Seriously. I'm proud of you."

She smiled softly. "But there's still the matter of you."

"What about me?"

"You'll need to stick around here and finish out high school."

"I'll figure a way around that. I've got a friend at school whose parents have already offered to let me use their spare bedroom."

"Oh?"

I nodded slowly. "I still don't know if I'm going to take them up on their offer. I mean, I'd have to find a storage unit. Store all my things. Only take what's necessary. Then, there's still the plan of what to do after high school. It would make more sense for me to keep selling things, or finding a part-time job now, so I can get a place of my own."

"What kind of job would you get?"

I snickered. "Hell if I know. Maybe a cashier somewhere. A sandwich maker or a barista."

"Mmm, I don't think I can see you in an apron and a hair cap."

"It would definitely be a sight."

I sipped my whiskey as night time slowly fell upon us. The beauty of the sunset faded, leaving us with cars rushing by in the distance. The glow of the city rose above our heads, muting a lot of the stars. The ones that did twinkle seemed to almost be laughing. They flashed and blinked. Flickered, as if they were waving down at me.

But suddenly, I heard a chair scraping across the cement.

I looked in front of me and saw my stepmom pulling up her chair. She sat with me, knee to knee, before digging out her cell phone. She set her wine glass down on the ground, and I couldn't help but notice the glow on her face. She looked radiant. Happier than I'd ever seen her before.

Everything about this night was refreshing.

"So I've been taking your advice over this past week with selling some things off."

I paused. "Oh?"

She nodded. "Mm-hmm. I mean, I'm entitled to half of what your father owns, but—"

"Wait, wait, wait, wait. You guys don't have a prenup?"

She shook her head. "Nope. We don't."

I blinked. "Are you serious?"

"Yep. Dead serious."

"That doesn't sound like my father at all."

She snickered. "Like I said, the man I've come to see now and the man he used to be when we first got married are two incredibly different people. He didn't want me signing a prenup. That's how much he believed in us at the time. I don't know if he was that generous or I was that stupid. But, given your history with your father…"

"You're not stupid, Cecilia."

"Well, I definitely wasn't this strong of a woman when I first met Howard. I was his puppy. I spoke only when he spoke to me and I was more than happy to accept his expensive handouts in exchange for loyalty. It was masked as love. But I don't think we ever really loved each other."

"What do you think happened then?"

She shrugged. "He provided me with a life I never had. Opulence. Expensive things. Wealth. All those concepts that were bad in my childhood he gave freely, and without me even asking. To me? It was romantic. And I fell head over heels for it. But not him."

I nodded slowly. "Why are you telling me all this?"

"I don't know. I guess because you have a right to know. Or maybe I don't want you thinking badly about me. Or maybe I just need to talk about it."

"I could never think badly of you. Not after all you've done for me."

She smiled. "Well, you've done me a great deal of good. You helped me find my voice. Find my strength with your father. And when that happened, I saw the angry side of him. The side that wanted to control me. If I stayed his little toy, he was fine. We were happy. The presents and traveling kept coming. But, in the end, I had to stay that way in order for him to love me. And that isn't love at all."

"No, it's not."

She drew in a sharp breath. "At any rate, I must've been so silent and airheaded in the beginning that he didn't think I'd ever change. Or leave him. So, yeah. I'm entitled to half of what he has. I'm sure he'll rake me over the coals to make sure I don't get it. But all of the things he's gifted me with are mine. That's what Miss Nichols told me over the phone today, anyway."

"So your car?"

"I can sell it."

"I take it you've already sold the clothes you were going to donate?"

She nodded. "And the ones that didn't sell got taken to the donation place. I want to wait until I get moved out of here to sell the car. But that's easily sixty grand in my pocket. I still have a ton of jewelry I can sell off. Shoes I know I'll never wear, even though I've kept them for now. And there are some things I insisted we have in this house that your father can't stand."

"Like…?"

"Some of the artwork on the walls. The decorative vases. There's artwork in the attic that should be on display that isn't. Even three or so of those paintings sold at auction would set me up in this city for almost a year. And that's if I wanted to keep living as opulently as I am right now."

My jaw dropped open. "Dad's got shit like that in the attic? All I found was the china stored up there."

She giggled. "That attic is expansive. That's my next project, actually. I won't take anything off the walls. But, in exchange for that, things that have collected dust in the attic for years are mine to sell. That's how I'm going to frame my argument. The lawyer advised me to cut up my credit cards, too. Take dated pictures of them. It's all about covering my ass now in court. Proving that I'm not taking him for all the money in the world."

"And cutting up your cards to his bank accounts would start to prove that."

She nodded. "Exactly."

I sighed. "It's insane we even have to go to these lengths."

Her hand settled on my knee. "It is. But I want you to see something."

She pulled out her phone and started scrolling through it. I furrowed my brow as I watched her. When she handed it to me, I looked at the pictures. Beautiful pictures of what looked like a condo. Or an apartment of some sort.

"Is this what you wanted to talk about tonight?"

Cecilia nodded. "Yes. This is a two-bedroom condo for lease not far from here. Just on the other side of the high school. It's in a nice area. Has some nice amenities. And they have yearly leases that aren't going to break the bank."

"Twelve hundred a month? That's pretty reasonable."

"I thought so myself. It's two-bedroom, two-bathroom, with a shared kitchen and living space. Open concept. Around fifteen hundred square feet. And, it's got a pool with a deck as well as a gym and a yoga room."

I grinned. "And you'll love that yoga room."

I kept scrolling through the pictures and was amazed at the quality of the place. The building itself was only six or seven years old. The pool looked outstanding. There were tennis courts. A playground for kids. A pool, as well as an indoor hot tub. I couldn't believe a place like this in California only went for twelve hundred a month. I kept looking for the catch. I kept waiting for the other shoe to drop.

"Why is this apartment so cheap?"

Cecilia smiled. "I'm glad you asked. Apparently, we aren't the only two people your father has pissed off. I got to chatting with the front desk manager as I was calling around to places the other day, and it turns out your father's gotten into a pretty decent spat with the man who runs it."

I sighed. "Of course."

"I didn't ask for details. All I said was that I was looking for a place to stay. He asked if Howard was coming with me. I said 'no'. And I guess he read between the lines. The apartment dropped seven hundred bucks on the spot, making it affordable for me."

I handed her phone back. "Well, I'm really happy you've found a place. It really is nice. It suits you."

She took her phone. "The bathrooms are ensuite, too. So, ultimate privacy."

"That's nice."

"And they're big. About the same size. So, no one's sacrificing room size because one of them is a 'master' or anything like that."

"Sounds like you'll really enjoy the place."

She smiled. "I do. I'm going to look at it Monday. I have a scheduled tour at four-thirty in the afternoon."

"You deserve this, Cecilia. You really do. Just make sure this front desk manager isn't giving you this kind of a deal because he's into you. I'd hate for you to get caught up in that kind of scenario."

"I promise, he's not. He and his husband have been proudly married for six years."

I barked with laughter. "All right. Good. Well, then make sure you check the appliances. Make sure they all work so you aren't liable for damage you didn't incur."

"Well, you could check them out for me. If you're worried about that kind of thing."

I shrugged. "I don't mind going with you after school."

"You're really not getting this, are you?"

I paused. "Getting what?"

She settled her hand on my knee. "I don't want you to just come look at this place with me, Clinton. I want you to move in with me."

"Wait, what?"

"I want you to come with me."

"You do?"

"Yes. This is what I wanted to talk to you about. You might have to help me with some things. Depending on how selling off this stuff goes, I might need help with food and stuff. But, yes. I want you to move into the second bedroom. I want you to have a place to go that at least remotely feels like home."

I blinked. "Are you being serious right now?"

"We're family, Clint. Maybe not blood related. But we're family. And we're going to need one another. Yes, I'm completely serious. I want you to come with me. If you want to, that is."

And as I sat there, completely dumbfounded, tears burned behind my eyes.

32

RAELYNN

"Welcome to Grady's Groceries. If I can help you, please let me know."

"Welcome to Grady's Groceries!"

"Raisins are on aisle four."

"No ma'am, we don't sell peppermint ice cream this early in the year. That hits the shelves two weeks before Thanksgiving."

"We do have some Halloween decorations! All the way back in the corner, near the bathrooms."

Even though Sunday afternoons were the busiest, I was glad they called me in. I needed out of the house. Mom had been moping since I came home yesterday. And every time I looked over at her, she started crying again. It was exhausting, and I was running out of sympathy. I couldn't handle her stuff anymore. And it shouldn't be my responsibility. I needed to focus on school and keeping my grades up.

"Ma'am?"

I turned at the sound of the voice. "Yes?"

"Where do you keep paper products?"

"I'm so sorry, we only have reusable products here. But if you're still looking for plates and silverware, that's on aisle nine."

"Is it more expensive?"

I nodded. "It is, yes. But, you'll only have to buy it once. Unless you back your car over it."

She giggled. "Well, I don't plan on doing that. Though I can't say much for the grandkids."

"Well, you could make them eat off paper towels. We have earth-friendly ones on the same aisle. Toward the back of the store. That side of it."

"Thank you for your help, dear."

"Any time. I'm here to help as much as I can."

I kept myself busy as the hours ticked by. The sun started to set and my dinner break was coming up. It wasn't a long break. Thirty minutes, as opposed to the ten-minute breaks I was usually afforded after school. Still, I thought about working through it. Keeping myself busy and keeping my mind preoccupied with other things. But the automatic door opening pulled me from my thoughts.

"Welcome to Grady's Groceries! My name's Rae. And if you need anything—"

"Just ask?"

"Clint?"

I looked up and saw him walking toward me, a smile on his face and pep in his step. I furrowed my brow as he came over to my register, then leaned over to kiss me. Captured my lips right in front of everyone without a care in the world.

It made me blush.

"Wow, what's gotten into you?"

He smiled. "Any chance you've got a break coming up soon?"

"If you give me fifteen minutes, I'm about to hit my dinner break."

"Perfect. Fancying some coffee?"

"'Fancying'? Who are you and what have you done with my boyfriend?"

He chuckled. "I'll hang around outside while you finish up."

I kept stealing glances at him out the window as he stood there. Whistling. With his hands in the pockets of his jeans. Every time he peeked over his shoulder, he winked at me. Like he didn't have a care in the world. It made me smile, and puzzled me at the same time. What the hell had put him in such a good mood?

"Rae!"

"Yeah?"

"Time for your dinner break. Wrap it up and shut it down. You've got thirty minutes."

I rang up my last customer and turned off my light. I made my way outside and threaded my arm through Clint's, watching as he smiled down at me. A playful wink, a nod of his head, and away we went. Toward the coffee shop next door that he had practically claimed as his second home.

"Dare I ask what's got you in such a good mood?"

He chuckled. "Let's get some coffee first. You hungry?"

I sighed. "Starving."

"What can I get for you two this afternoon?" the cashier asked.

Clint nodded. "Yes. I'd like two large caramel coffees made with rosewater, two of your ham and cheese sandwiches, two cinnamon rolls, two apples, and two packages of chips."

The girl behind the counter smiled. "What kind of chips?"

I looked up at Clint. "Doritos for me."

He nodded. "And salt and vinegar kettle chips for me."

The cashier rang it all up. "Will that be all for this evening?"

Clint slid his wallet out. "Yes, it is. We'll be sitting here, too. Thank you."

We paid and got our stuff, then he escorted me over to a table in the corner. Near the window. Where the sun shone and lit up the table in front of us. He divvied out the food, pampering me in ways I'd never experienced with him. He opened up my chips and handed them to me. Passed me my sandwich, but unwrapped half of it first. I narrowed my eyes at him as he hummed to himself. I'd never seen Clint this happy in all the time I'd known him.

"Okay. Spit it out."

Clint's eyes met mine. "What?"

I snickered. "What do you mean, 'what?' Spit it out. What's happened? What do I not know?"

He grinned. "Cecilia's moving out."

I blinked. "That's it?"

"That's it."

"You're happy Cecilia's moving out."

"I am, yes. She's found a great place on the other side of the high school. About ten minutes down the road. The front desk manager gave her a great price on the place."

"And that's why you're whistling."

"What's wrong with whistling?"

"Other than the fact that I didn't know you could do it? Nothing. I just figured—"

"I mean, she's asked me to move with her, but you know. Semantics."

I paused. "She's what?"

He started laughing as my hands flew to my mouth. I shot out of my chair and threw myself at him, wrapping him up in the biggest hug imaginable. I kissed his face. His neck. His shoulder. Tears rushed my eyes and I swallowed them down.

"She really asked you to go with her?"

He nodded against the crook of my neck. "She really did."

"Oh, Clint. I'm so fucking happy for you."

I felt him sniffle and it broke my heart. I slid into his lap as he wrapped his arms around me. I stroked my hand through his hair, which seemed to be growing longer by the second. I was so overwhelmed with happiness. With relief. I almost couldn't contain myself as I blinked back batches of tears.

I kissed his ear. "I'm so happy for you."

"She really asked me to go with her, Rae. Like, legitimately."

I rested against him as he held me close and shook underneath me. I was so thankful for Cecilia. Thankful that the two of them had grown so close over these past few weeks. Clint needed a fucking adult in his life that gave a shit about him. Who genuinely wanted him around. I knew how worthless he felt on a day-to-day basis. How pointless and unloved he felt by the adults around him. His father. The teachers at school. The principal, for crying out loud. He deserved Cecilia's love, and so much more.

"When do you guys move?"

He lifted his head. "I don't know. We're going to look at the place tomorrow after school. I guess we'll sign the lease there if we like it well enough."

"And you say it's not far from here?"

"Nope. I'll still be able to finish out my senior year here. Though I'll have to ride the bus or something."

I snickered. "That's crazy talk. I'm sure Allison and Michael and I can start picking you up or something. I'll talk to them about it."

"I don't want you guys to go out of your—"

I cupped my hand over his mouth. "We're your friends. We love you. Hush."

He furrowed his brow. "You… you love me?"

I nodded. "We all do."

And as his eyes searched mine, I felt my heart stop in my chest.

"Well, I love you guys, too."

I grinned. "All of us?"

He captured my lips in his before he slid me to my feet. His hands held my hips as our lips sat languidly together. A soft, genuine kiss. One that preached our truth even though we still couldn't say it.

Though, I hoped one day I'd build up the courage to tell him how much I loved him.

He patted the back of my thigh, then I went to sit back down. He kept grinning at me as I ate my sandwich, sipped my coffee and crunched on my chips. His feet slid against mine underneath the table where we sat. And I felt like one of those girls in the movies Mom always watched.

I finally understood how they felt.

"So, how's your weekend been?"

I sighed. "Pretty good, considering."

"Considering…?"

I shrugged. "I mean, things with Mom have been… interesting."

"Interesting, how?"

"Well, she's started therapy."

He paused. "Wait, she did?"

I nodded. "There's been a lot that's happened that I haven't told you about."

"Why not? Why haven't you told me?"

"I mean, things have been pretty chaotic in your world."

He put his food down. "That doesn't mean I can't be there for you."

I shrugged. "It's nothing bad. Just all happened at once, that's all."

He took my hand in his. "What happened, Rae? Talk to me."

I drew in a deep breath and told him everything. The fight with D.J. Him shattering things against the walls. Me telling him to get out. How hard my mom was crying. I told him about me finally calling the police on him and Mom's cuts as she fell to the floor trying to go after him. And the more I talked, the more Clint squeezed my hand.

With rage flying behind his eyes.

"I'm so sorry I wasn't there, Rae."

I shook my head. "It's fine. I mean, it really is okay. That happened the day your father came to pick you up from school."

"The same day?"

"Yeah. Like I said, it was a lot. And I just didn't want to talk about it, I guess? We were dealing with your stuff and—"

He looked me square in my eyes. "I want you to hear me. Are you listening?"

"I am, yeah."

"There is never going to be a point in time where my shit overshadows your shit. All right? The next time something like this happens, you speak up. Let me be there for you. I think I've proven to you how much of a big boy I am. Let me be a support to you like you've been to me."

I blushed. "Okay. I'm sorry."

"You don't need to apologize, Rae. But you don't need to protect me, either. That's my job."

"Hey, now. I can protect you just as much as you protect me."

He grinned. "I suppose you can. If you open up enough to let me protect you."

"I know, I know."

"So she went to the hospital?"

I nodded. "She did. She got help. With our income issues, she qualifies for free therapy through the hospital that treated her. And she had her first appointment with them yesterday morning."

"How often will she go?"

"Starting next week, twice a week. Wednesday and Saturday mornings. She said everything went really well and that they already started unpacking some things. But time will tell."

"You don't think she'll stick with it?"

I sighed. "I've seen my mother go without D.J. for almost a month before he comes swooping back in. Wanting her back. Coming with flowers and make-up sex and money to smooth things over. I'll believe her when I see her actively turn him down."

"I don't blame you on that."

"She's upset with me for that, though."

"What do you mean?"

I threaded our fingers together. "We kind of got into a fight last night. She was upset that I went dress shopping with Allison and not her. And it kind of spiraled into this same conversation. She was upset that I didn't believe she had changed, and I told her that she had broken my trust so much after promising to not go back—only to go back again and again—that I'd believe it when I saw it."

"Ouch."

"Yeah. It felt good to get off my chest, but Mom hasn't been okay since. And the worst is, I don't even fully feel bad."

"Because you're numb to it."

"I guess."

He grinned. "What kind of dress shopping did you do?"

Time to drop the hints. "Graduation dress shopping. Though Allison ended up picking up her prom dress instead."

"Has Mike asked her yet?"

"Not according to Allison."

"Let me guess. He's doing the whole 'assuming they're going together' thing?"

I paused. "How did you know?"

"I've been talking to him about it. I've told him that formally asking her is what girls like. Assuming things is only going to upset her in the short term."

I narrowed my eyes playfully. "What else have you and Michael been talking about?"

He winked. "Does it matter?"

"Yes, it matters. I didn't even know the two of you talked outside of school."

"I guess we've been getting along, yeah."

"So are you wanting to go to prom?"

He smiled. "Are you asking me to go with you?"

"No. Just wondering if that's your scene."

"And if it is?"

Just ask me already. "I don't know. Just wondering."

"Uh huh. Just wondering? That's all?"

"Yeah. Why?"

He shrugged. "No reason."

"Now, you're just being frustrating."

He chuckled. "And even when you're frustrated, you're gorgeous."

33

CLINTON

R ae still had three hours to go on her shift before she was done for the day. And I decided to stick around. I stayed at the coffee shop and did some writing in my notebook. I checked my bank account. Started on a budget. I wanted to have what finances I did have in line for my trip with Cecilia after school tomorrow. I wanted her to know exactly what I could contribute and what I wanted to take care of once we moved.

Because I'd certainly move with her.

That much I knew. Well, almost. I stopped banking on things a while ago. Nothing in my life was guaranteed, so that's how I saw everything now. Including this apartment, even though my stepmom wanted me to come with her. I would, too. If the offer still presented itself tomorrow.

But, if my life had taught me anything, it was the fact that twenty-four hours changed a hell of a lot.

Still, having a budget was good. So, for the first time in my life, I started jotting one down. I kept track of everything and rounded to the nearest dollar. I placed some calls. Like to the phone company my father used for our phone plan. Truth be told, now that he no longer had access to my bank account—and I no longer had my trust fund—the only thing connecting the two of us was the phone. I had no more bike. So no more insurance. Once I figured out how to separate myself and get my own phone bill, that was that.

No more strings to Daddy Dearest.

The phone call was long. Much longer than I had anticipated. And I was painfully honest with them. No use beating around the bush. I was moving out. Away from my father, and I wanted a new phone plan. One that didn't have my phone under his name. There wasn't much I could do other than open another phone plan under my name and have him eventually disconnect my line. Which I didn't have an issue with at all. They rattled off their available phone plans and I circled the two in my budget. Then I thanked them for their time.

Seven o'clock came around quicker than I had anticipated. I packed my things up and waved at the girl behind the cash register, thanking them for letting me take up a space. Then I stood in front of the main window of Grady's Groceries. I smiled as Rae came around the corner, purse in hand and fresh off of work. She rushed outside and laughed, throwing her arms around me.

It felt so good to hold her close.

"What are you still doing here?"

I snickered. "Can't a guy wait for his girl to get off?"

She grinned. "Cheeky, cheeky."

I quirked an eyebrow. "I see what's on your mind, beautiful."

"Are you going to whisk me home and help me decompress?"

"While that's a tempting offer, I'm craving ice cream. Care to go get some with me?"

"Trying to make up for the lost milkshake date?"

"Depends. Want to split some fries with me, too?"

She smiled, and it gave me all the answer I needed. She slipped her hand into mine and we walked toward the main road as I tried flagging us a cab. It took a few waves. But eventually, someone pulled over. I opened the door for her and told the driver where I wanted to go. And six minutes later, he pulled into the parking lot of the very busy diner.

"Is that line out the door?" Rae asked.

I groaned. "Well, fuck."

"Care to get a cone instead? We could walk home while eating them."

"Are you up for walking home after working this afternoon?"

She shrugged. "If we go slow, sure."

I grinned. "Slow and steady is my specialty."

She shoved me playfully and I laughed as I paid the driver. We hopped out and pushed our way inside, then placed our to-go order for ice cream cones. Rae ordered a banana-mocha swirled cone dipped in hardened caramel coating. And that damn thing sounded so good I ordered myself one, too. I paid for the ice cream and we pushed our way back out of the diner, heading in the direction of school.

Keeping a languid pace as we cracked into the hardened caramel shell.

"Mmm, my God, this damn thing is always so good."

I moaned. "I've never had the hardened shell before."

Rae gasped. "Oh, you wound me, Clint. That hurt. Physically hurt."

"I think you'll have to introduce me to more of your favorite treats around this area."

"You mean now that you're staying?"

I paused. "Was there ever a fear that I wouldn't?"

She shrugged. "I don't know. I guess there was always a fear that you'd use this opportunity to leave. And no one could have blamed you for it. Not even me."

I slipped my free arm around her shoulders. "I'm sorry I made you feel that way."

"It's okay. I'm just glad you've made the decision to hang around."

"I've got too many options on my plate not to."

She snuggled into me. "So, any idea what you might do after you graduate?"

I snickered. "No fucking clue. I mean, there are plenty of avenues. So I'm finding. But they all require a great deal of money. Money I might not have at my disposal if I move in with my stepmom."

"Why's that?"

"I mean, I'll be helping her with bills and such. Neither of us will have a ton of money. At least, until she gets through the official divorce with my father. Which you know he'll drag out in an attempt to get her to shut things down instead of raking him clean."

"I hope she drags his ass through the mud."

"Me, too. He fucking deserves it. But if my father's coming at us this hard, I can only imagine what she'll go through during the divorce."

"You think you might stick around and help her with that?"

I shrugged. "I honestly have no clue. I'm still just trying to not fail my classes. That'll be the key to getting a decent enough job to support me while I'm on my own."

"Did you ever think you'd say those words?"

"Actually, no. I didn't, to be honest."

She giggled. "They sound good. I know you can do this. We all know you can. And you won't fail your classes. Because you have me and Allison and Michael to help you get to graduation."

"I still don't know how I ended up with friends like them."

She scoffed. "Me, you asshole. I was your 'in' with them."

The two of us laughed as we rushed across the road. Cars honked at us as our laughter grew, and we continued running until we got into the shade. We stood there, panting and eating our ice cream cones as the autumn breeze kicked up. We began to shiver as we stood to catch our breath.

"Still a damn good cone," she said.

I smiled. "You're right about that one. But you haven't answered your own question."

"What?"

"What are your plans after graduation, smarty pants?"

She started walking again. "Well, it was to move with Allison into an apartment near her college campus. But I'm not so sure about that anymore. I mean, she and Michael are becoming a thing. And I'd hate to be a constant third wheel because I'm living with her. Plus, I'd really like to do something with my doodling and love for graphic design. And I can't afford a four-year institution."

"What about two-year? Or whatever?"

"That's an option, if I go part-time. But none of the community colleges around where Allison's headed have those programs. Which means I'd be on my own."

I held her close. "You're not alone, so long as you have me."

The two of us talked and laughed as we made our way to her house. I wanted to walk her home. I wanted to make sure she got there safely. Especially since the sun had fully set. I was still paranoid from that night. I wouldn't head toward my house until I knew she was safe within hers. But, as we slowly approached her home, we heard voices.

Her mother's voice, and a man's.

"Who is that?" I asked.

"Shh," she said harshly.

Rae tugged me into a neighboring yard before we crept closer. We stayed in the shadows, hanging out as Rae's mother stood on the porch. I narrowed my eyes. The man looked familiar, but I couldn't place him or his voice. But, my question was answered by the next thing that flew from Rae's mother's mouth.

"D.J., you're not coming inside. I've already told you no."

He snickered. "Come on, baby. It was just a stupid fight. We have them all the time."

D.J.? This was the fucker Rae always complained about?

Rae's mom sighed. "I know we do. But we've had our last fight. This isn't happening anymore. It can't. I can't do it anymore with you, D.J."

"You're being unreasonable. Why don't I take you out? You love that wine at that little Italian place—"

"I'm not going anywhere with you, either."

He took a step toward her. "You're not done with me. I'm not done with you, either. I'm not giving up on this. On us."

"Well, good thing you aren't the only one who can make decisions around here."

He paused. "Did your daughter get under your skin? You know she doesn't like me. But she won't be around for much longer. She's off to college soon. Or wherever. Then it'll just be us, baby. Like we always wanted."

"Like you always wanted. It's not my fault you were a jerk to my daughter. You had your chance. And now, I want you to leave."

He took another step toward her. "You'll never be done with me, Lucy. We still love one another. There's still love here between us."

I went to step out of the shadows and confront this asshole. Because he was already pissing me off. But Rae slipped her arm in front of me, stopping me in my tracks.

"Hold on. I want to see how she handles this."

So I held my ground. Even though I wanted to jam my fist into that fucker's face.

"You know, Deej, I never thought I would be, either. You've been a big part of my life for a long time. And at one point in time,

I thought maybe you were the one. That we just had some kinks to work out and struggles to work through."

He sighed. "See? I knew you still loved me. Just let me come in. We can talk rationally about this."

She shook her head. "No, Deej. You're not welcome any longer. It takes more than love to make something like this work. And we don't have it."

He pointed his finger. "You don't get to tell me that. You're not the only one who dictates what happens here."

"And neither are you. But this is my home. Not yours. And I don't want you here."

"I'm coming in."

She lifted her chin. "If you push past me, I'm calling the police. I won't repeat this cycle with you anymore. It's amazing to me that you haven't already replaced me with some young, dumb, perky little thing. I don't know why you keep coming back, either. Why I keep letting you treat me like shit. But I need to grow up. And so do you. I need to be the mother my daughter deserves, and you need help. Just like I do."

"I'm not fucking crazy like you and that spoiled bitch are. Where the hell are you gonna be without my money, huh? How are you gonna eat? Pay your bills? Remember what I do around here, Luciana. Remember it before I walk away. Because if I walk away, I'm not coming back."

She sighed. "Good. Now, get the hell off my lawn before I call the cops. And don't you dare step foot on my property again."

I felt Rae sigh with relief. I looked over at her and saw happiness fill her eyes. They sparkled in the darkness. The pride that washed over her made my heart soar. We watched D.J. walk away and get in his car. And as he peeled out of the driveway, I heard Rae's mom sniffle before heading back inside.

"Go see your mom. She needs you. And I'll see you soon, okay?"

I gave Rae a kiss on the cheek before I watched her head for the front door to go take care of the mother she deserved.

34

RAELYNN

My eyes opened and I stared at the ceiling with a smile already falling across my face. Monday morning never felt this good, and my heart soared with joy. Last night with my mother was fantastic. I held her while she cried. I told her how proud I was of her. And after venting to me about how stupid she'd been for so many years, we sat down and took stock of her life. We cuddled up on the couch together and came up with a budget. We looked up the exact totals of all our bills and searched around for all sorts of services in the area. Mom was eligible for a great deal of help, from food stamps to free resume services to help her nail down jobs. We created a vague outline of what needed to happen. What bills were due when. How much money we needed a month in order to keep our heads afloat.

Then we figured out where we could cut back.

To an outsider, it sounded boring as fuck. But, to me, it was the proof I needed to know Mom really was turning over a new leaf. We looked up jobs online she was already eligible for and jotted them down. Most part-time work. But part-time was better than no time at all. With the last of the money D.J. had offered Mom, we figured we had three more months of smooth sailing until we hit an issue. Because even though my paycheck from the grocery store could cover most things, it couldn't cover everything.

By the time we were done, we had a very confusing outline of what needed to happen. Ways we could cut back our bills. Things we could get rid of completely to save money. I promised her I'd research cheap meals for two and she promised me she'd put in two job applications every day from now until she snagged one.

And as I slipped out of bed, I felt the dawning of a new day upon us.

My feet planted into the ground and my body didn't feel so heavy. Getting dressed didn't feel like such a burden. I didn't bust a sweat taking a shower because I had to move around to get myself clean. I even took the steps downstairs two by two, jumping at the end before scooping up my backpack. I felt great. I felt alive. For the first time since Clint and I came together as one, I didn't feel burdened. Or stressed. The hopelessness that had plagued me no longer reared its head.

What a damn good feeling for a Monday morning.

Things were finally back on track. I made sure I had all my books in my bag, then double-checked my purse. I had my wallet, my keys, my phone. I had some snacks and some chewing gum. I even had some lip gloss in here, in case I wanted to spruce up a bit.

All I needed was something to snack on for breakfast.

"Rae?"

Mom's voice pulled me into the kitchen.

"Rae, you got a second?"

I plucked an apple from the fruit bowl. "Not much more than that. Gotta get to Clint and everyone."

"About that."

I paused. "Everything okay?"

Mom's face looked worried. That is, until a grin slowly slid across her face. I sighed as I bit into the apple, ready to chuck it at her for worrying me like that.

"Come on. Spit it out. What are you hiding, Mom?"

She sipped her coffee. "I called your school this morning."

"Oh? Why?"

"To tell them you aren't coming in today."

I paused. "Wait, why?"

She grinned. "Because we're going shopping for accessories to go with your graduation dress."

"We are?"

"Mm-hmm. I take it you probably didn't get any while you were out?"

"I mean, I have a pair of shoes that probably match."

"You know good and well 'probably' isn't good enough for an accomplishment like this. And plus, you have your ears pierced. I hardly see you wearing earrings. Is the dress low-cut?"

"No, but it's strapless."

"I'll need to see the colors of it so we can pick something out accordingly. But if it's strapless, a nice bracelet will accent things well."

"But… our budget?"

She sighed. "I can buy my daughter some accessories to go with her graduation dress."

I narrowed my eyes playfully. "You found some money in your purse, didn't you?"

"Yes. And I want to spoil my daughter with it."

I shook my head, but deep down I was screaming with delight. I hadn't spent a day with my mom in years. And I couldn't wait to go out with her. Plus, I had a bit of my own money to spend. My paycheck from the grocery store had a nice bump in it because of my raise. So, I silently decided to treat Mom to lunch while we were out.

But first, I had to tell the gang I wasn't coming.

Me: Hey, Clint. I won't be at school today. Mom and I are spending some time together. I'm sorry for missing school, but Allison can help you with things today for classes. Text me if you need anything.

I sent the message off and didn't have to wait long to get a response.

Clint: You two have a blast. Have fun, and I'll let you know how things go at the apartment after school.

I slipped my phone back into my purse and dropped my backpack to the floor. Mom came over and hugged me, holding me for the longest time. I sighed. I relished her touch. Her embrace. Her companionship. I closed my eyes and sank my cheek against her shoulder, feeling embraced by a mother I'd lost some time ago.

"I'm so sorry, Rae."

I shook my head. "Stop. It's in the past. We can only go forward, okay?"

Mom snickered. "I don't know when you grew up on me."

"And that's okay. Just keep getting better. For me, and for yourself."

She set her coffee down and swayed side to side, rocking me like she used to when I was a child. I felt myself falling back into those memories. Into the first memory I had of gazing up into my mother's face. I'd been sick with the flu. Coughing and unable to sleep. Hurting in places I didn't understand. And she had been there, with her own version of the flu. Making me sip water, giving me popsicles, and singing my favorite lullaby.

"Hush little Raelynn, don't say a word. Momma's gonna buy you a mockingbird."

My eyes welled with tears as she started singing it to me. Right there, in my ear, as we swayed in the kitchen. I didn't even try holding back my tears. I simply let them fall, dragging with them the pain and anguish I'd dealt with for all of my teenage years. I shook against my mom. I felt her wrap me up tight. My knees clicked together and my toes curled as I tried keeping up my strength.

With Mom singing in my ear.

"I've missed you so much, Mom."

She sighed. "I love you so much, Rae."

"Can we just—stay like this for a bit?"

"For however long you want, princess."

I don't know how much time we spent in that kitchen. But after a while, Mom started moving. Walking me down the hallway as I kept clinging to her. She walked us into the living room. We sat down on the couch we had occupied for hours last night. I crawled into her lap. Eighteen years old, five-foot-six, and one hundred and fifty-two pounds. All of me curled against her. And her arms somehow still wrapped around me. Her hands locked, her lips fell against my forehead, and she kissed me. Repeatedly. As the tears continued falling.

"Hush little Raelynn, don't you hurt. Momma's gonna promise to keep her word. And if this Momma does relapse, you have permission to kick her ass."

I sputtered with laughter as I sniffed back more tears. My head fell against her shoulder as she looked down at me. Still the giant of a woman I'd always known, despite the fact that we were the same height. My tears dried up as she smiled at me. I slowly raised my head as I slipped off to the side. With her arm around my back and my legs tossed into her lap, she settled into the couch. Smiling at me with a happiness I hadn't seen in her face since… well?

Since, ever.

"Independence looks good on you, Mom."

She snickered. "Let's just hope it stays that way. I'm getting old, you know."

"Oh, boo. You're hardly in your forties."

"That's almost mid-life crisis age."

"Don't tell me you're going to go out and get yourself a hot rod."

She giggled. "Don't be silly. Women go out and bring home a pool boy. Not a hot rod."

I threw my head back with laughter as my back fell to the couch.

"You're absolutely insane, you know that?"

Her hand wrapped around mine. "You had to get it from somewhere."

I smiled up at the ceiling. "So, any chance I can talk you into having lunch with me while we shop?"

"I take it you got paid?"

"And got a raise at work."

She gasped. "Rae! That's fantastic. When did that happen?"

"Not too long ago. I'm only, like, five days into my raise. But that five days gives me enough extra money for us to get lunch somewhere. Like that sub place you love so much."

"Oh, they have the best roast beef sandwich."

"I don't know how you eat that stuff. It stinks."

"Now you know how I feel when I watch you drink pickle juice."

I hummed. "Mmm, pickles. I need to pick some up the next time I'm working."

"You can keep your pickles and I'll keep my roast beef. How's that sound?"

"Fine by me. Just don't burp in my face. I'm not liable for my actions if you do."

She began tickling me and I started squealing my head off.

"Mom! No!"

"I don't burp. Take it back."

"Mom! I hate being tickled! Mommy!"

She giggled profusely. "Take it back."

"You don't burp! You don't burp! Uncle! Uncle!"

She stopped tickling me and I gasped for air, rolling off the couch. I hated being tickled. It was the worst sensation. But, as I slowly stood to my feet, a grin crossed my face.

"You fart like an old man, though."

She shot up. "You've got double tickles for that."

And as I took off up the stairs, I laughed my ass off, hearing her hot on my heels as I darted into my room.

35

CLINTON

A horn honking caught my ear as I walked out of the front of the school. Cecilia sat there in her bright red car, shining like the sun as she waved me down. She smiled brilliantly, and I couldn't recall ever seeing that kind of smile on her face. I jogged over and dropped down into the car, discarding my backpack between my legs.

"You look nice. What's the occasion?"

She rolled up my window. "Because today, if we play our cards right, we'll have a new home."

I chuckled. "I take it you're excited."

"I'm more than excited. I'm ready to get this party started."

The second I had my seatbelt buckled, she took off, zooming out of the cul-de-sac in front of the school and careening down the road. She had the music blasting with classic rock as she bobbed her head to the beat. Driving barefoot, of all things, as we raced down the road. I rolled my window down and let my arm rest out in the sun. I couldn't stop stealing looks over at her. How happy she looked. How carefree her hair was tossed on top of her head. It looked as if her own bonds had fallen away. Her face was barely covered in makeup. Her ears displayed simple stud earrings instead of the expensive, glistening diamonds I was used to seeing on her.

Simple suited her.

We drove in silence, but by no means was it empty. We jammed out to music and she played air guitar behind the wheel of the car at stoplights. I laughed at her as she yelled the words to her favorite songs. I'd never seen this side of her. Hell, I would have never guessed it existed. If she was nervous, the only thing that gave it away was how hard she gripped her steering wheel.

Her knuckles were practically white with tension.

We drove for maybe four miles before she turned on her blinker. Got into the left-hand lane. I looked over and saw the sprawling complex scattered with trees and greenery. It looked so different from the other places in Riverbend. The apartment buildings were brightly colored on the outside with stone work peppered in that felt pleasing to the eye. It looked like each apartment had its own private balcony. Beautiful white-washed wrought iron. This place screamed 'Cecilia'. It was definitely the kind of place I'd find someone like her in.

I hoped, for her sake, we qualified for something like this.

We pulled up to the parking lot in front of the lobby and got out. She slipped her heels on and stood up, smoothing her hands over her dress. She looked over at me and smiled. I held my hand out, ushering her toward the front door. And as we walked inside, a man dressed in a pale pink button-front shirt stood up, holding his arms out for her.

"Cecilia. You look amazing."

She hugged him softly. "Matthew, it's really nice to meet you in person. Finally."

I waved. "Hey there."

The man grinned. "And you must be Clinton. Cecilia called me and told me you were coming with her today. Nice to meet you."

He held his hand out to me and I shook it.

"Yeah, I wanted to come along with her and check out the place for myself."

He quirked an eyebrow. "Oh? Cecilia made it sound like you were moving with her."

I grinned. "If that's the best course of action for everyone, yes. But I'd like to see the apartment before either of us make a decision on anything."

He nodded. "Of course. I've got the golf cart cranked up and ready to go, if you guys would like a tour of the complex?"

Cecilia nodded. "We'd love one, thank you."

We followed Matthew out back and hopped onto the cart. Me

in the back and Cecilia up front with him. We drove around the massive grounds, racing by the tennis courts, the beautiful blue pool that housed a deck, a small cobblestone pathway to the enclosed hot tub, as well as grills for the people living in the complex to use. It really was a nice place, tucked back away among lush trees and rich, green grass.

It felt more and more like home as we continued pressing onward.

"So, are we seeing a model room? Or the actual apartment you're wanting to rent to us?" I asked.

Matthew pulled into a parking space. "Oh, no. This is the actual apartment. And it's a good one, too. First floor, back right corner. Only one side of the apartment gets the harshness of the sun, so your energy bills won't skyrocket during the summer."

I nodded. "And all the appliances come with it?"

Cecilia snickered. "Why don't we get inside and see?"

Matthew smiled. "He's okay. It's good that he's asking questions. It means he cares about where you end up. Remember that."

I liked this guy.

We walked down the small hallway before he pulled out some keys. And the second the door to the apartment opened, Cecilia drew in a soft breath of air. Even I stood there, shocked. In all the best ways.

"Holy shit, this looks better than the pictures."

Matthew chuckled. "I told my boss those pictures we threw up there online were shitty. Excuse my language."

Cecilia slowly walked in. "The hardwood floors are beautiful."

I furrowed my brow. "Are those granite countertops in the kitchen?"

"And look! A built-in breakfast nook!"

I shook my head as Matthew ushered us in. He closed the door behind us and gave us the grand tour, with my jaw dropping to the floor. There was so much room in this fucking place. I mean, for an apartment? Hell, yeah. I went into the kitchen and checked all the appliances, which I found had been recently updated. I walked over to the balcony, shaded by the trees and the balcony above it. The white-washed wrought iron made the little nook cozy, and it overlooked a long stretch of grass that led softly down a hill.

Where I heard people splashing in the pool.

Rae and I could spend the summer by the pool after graduation.

I imagined her in a cute little bikini. Me, slathering tanning oil on her back. Driving me wild all summer while I wrote in my note-book and she rested between my legs. I hadn't even seen the bedrooms, and already this place felt like home.

Michael and Allison could even join us.

"Clint? Honey?"

I whipped around at the sound of my stepmom's voice.

"Yeah? Sorry. Just thinking."

Matthew grinned. "About that nice pool you saw?"

I snickered. "It was nice."

"We have the biggest apartment complex pool in Riverbend. And the hot tub comfortably seats fifteen people."

Cecilia's eyes widened. "Fifteen? That's a small pool in and of itself."

"We pride ourselves in providing the best for our apartment dwellers."

I sighed. "So, what's the catch?"

They both fell silent and all eyes were on me.

"There is no catch," Matthew said.

I snickered. "There's always a catch."

Cecilia cleared her throat. "We already talked about this."

I nodded. "I know. But you guys will be losing a profit on our lease at twelve hundred for a place like this. I want to know there isn't some catch. Something you expect us to do in exchange for paying such a low cost of rent here."

Matthew walked over to me and placed his hands on my shoul-ders. I didn't like him being so close. But it was better than my father being that close. I stood my ground, keeping my eyes connected with his. I wasn't backing down on this. I wouldn't let my stepmother get swindled by anyone else. Not again.

Not as long as she protected me.

"I'm not going to assume to know everything about your story. But let's say I get the gist."

I furrowed my brow. "Okay?"

Matthew licked his lips. "I watched my mother, for many years, get treated as less than by my stepfather. I watched her get taken advantage of for years. And she didn't live long enough for me to see her become the strong woman I knew she was, deep down."

I sighed. "Dude, I'm sorry."

"I got a soft spot for your stepmother's story. For what I think she's gone through. And I'd like to think I'm pretty good at reading between the lines."

"I'm sure you probably are."

His hands fell from my shoulders. "There are some catches. But they're small. You'll provide your own bulbs. Batteries for the three smoke detectors. If any major plumbing issues pop up that our maintenance men can't resolve, you're responsible for the bill. But that's it. If you blow a bulb, the maintenance men will use your bulbs and replace them. Same with the batteries. It'll all be written out in your lease agreement. Along with the twelve hundred for rent."

"And that's it?"

He nodded. "That's it. Those three things. That will keep our cost down substantially on this apartment and give us the ability to offer this at a price that suits you and your stepmother's current situation."

"And your management knows about this?"

"They're the first people I convinced of it."

My eyes darted over his shoulder to Cecilia, who was standing anxiously waiting for my response. I didn't mean to make her so nervous. I just wanted to make sure she'd be okay here.

That we'd both be okay here.

I shrugged. "Well, can we apply today, then?"

My stepmom stepped forward. "Yes. I'm prepared to apply today, if we can."

Matthew smiled. "I'll do you one better. The place is yours if you can pay the deposit today. Equivalent to first month's rent."

I nodded. "Done."

Cecilia smiled brightly. "Will you accept a direct transfer? Or Paypal? Or anything like that?"

Matthew chuckled. "We can do Paypal. Let's get back to the office and get it set up. We'll get you confirmed before you leave here today."

The air smelled fresher as we rushed back to the front office. Cecilia transferred the money and I practically forced her to let me cover half of it. Going in together, so she knew I was coming with her. Moving in with her. Staying with her. We sat there in Matthew's office as everything percolated. As Paypal loaded and emails were sent off and confirmations sat there, pending.

Then, things started dinging on the screen.

My electronic transfer dumped into Cecilia's bank account. The apartment complex got our deposit. Our confirmation number popped up on screen and Cecilia laughed with joy. I wrapped my arm around her, pulled her close and kissed the top of her head. This was fantastic. Finally, things seemed to be looking up for the two of us.

"All right. So, when do you two want to move in?"

Matthew's question brought a still to the room as Cecilia sat up.

"Is it possible for us to move in soon?"

He shrugged. "That depends. How soon?"

I butted in. "Two weeks from yesterday sound okay?"

"So, not this coming Sunday, but the Sunday after?"

Cecilia nodded. "Yes. Do you guys do move-ins on Sunday?"

Matthew typed around on his keyboard before a smile crossed his face.

"We do now. Just put myself on the schedule to be here in two Sundays to welcome you guys to the property. Once you get here, I'll hand over the keys and we'll sign the lease agreement then."

Cecilia clapped her hands. "This is fantastic! Thank you so much, Matthew. Really."

I nodded. "But the apartment is ours even though the lease isn't signed?"

He nodded. "Yes, sir. That money secured your spot. It's yours, as of two Sundays from now."

And the sigh of relief that left my mouth relaxed me from head to toe.

36

RAELYNN

"Sweetie, can you pass me the—"

I tossed her the seasoning. "Catch!"

"Girl! Wai—shit!"

I giggled. "You owe me another cookie."

Mom glared at me. "You're doing this intentionally now."

"What? What did you think would happen when you promised cookies for whoever cleaned up their cursing first?"

"Look, all I'm saying is that it's not becoming for either of us to walk around dropping 'fuck' and 'damn it' all throughout the day."

I grinned. "Do those words count toward the deal?"

She slowly looked over at me. "No. They don't."

I snickered. "Fine. I'll let you off the hook this time."

As I stood at the stove, saucing up the enchiladas, I giggled to myself. Things with Mom were going wonderfully. After shopping yesterday, though, Mom came to the conclusion that both of us cursed too much. Between getting poked with earrings, dropping jewelry on the floor, and looking at the prices of some accessories, she thought we needed to tone down our language a bit. So, we made a bet: whoever could go the next week and curse the least got to have their choice of cookies with ice cream next weekend. Complete with their own movie night that the other had to suffer through.

And since I had no intent on changing how I spoke, my goal

was to make Mom curse more than me. You know, by pissing her off and shit.

"What other meals did you find that were under three bucks a pop to make?"

I scooped the enchiladas out. "All sorts of things. Buffalo chicken wings with mashed potatoes. Vegetable stir fry. Burgers and sweet potato fries. The list goes on really. It's all about cooking it in-house. I've found a cheap recipe for just about everything I know you like, with the exception of steak. Steak just isn't cheap."

Mom shrugged. "Eh, steak can be one of those things we go out and treat ourselves to."

"I'm fine with that. Because while it might look easy to cook, it's also easy to fuck up. And I don't think either of us want to sink twelve bucks a pop into steaks only to make them like hockey pucks."

I felt Mom grinning at me and I rolled my eyes. I tossed the rice into the enchilada pan and started cooking it up a bit. Letting it soak up all those juices. We had some in the back of the fridge that had been sitting there for a couple of days. It needed to be eaten, otherwise it would spoil. And if there was one thing Mom had ingrained into me, it was the fact that food had to be eaten. Never spoiled. Never thrown away. And never, ever wasted.

"Pretty sure that makes us even now."

I snickered. "Not even close. I heard you upstairs trying to wrangle your clothes off."

"Wait, what?"

I tossed her a smile. "What? You think I wouldn't hear? I don't know what the hell you were wearing up there, but I'm pretty sure I've got the whole night to let my tongue fly before we're even again."

"You were spying on me? You little—!"

I held up my finger. "Uh, uh, uh. Do you want your cookies next weekend, or mine?"

"Your cookies suck. Who likes oatmeal raisin?"

"I suppose the same people who don't like cinnamon pecan cookies. You weirdo."

The two of us started giggling at the stove. Mom swatted me playfully with a rag before she took the black beans off the stove. She started setting the table, with the rice almost ready in this beautiful enchilada flavoring. The sauce created this rich red color that went perfectly with the black of the beans and the red and white of the enchilada. With the salad Mom quickly whipped up, we had all sorts of colors on that table. Complete with some orange soda we found at the back of the pantry.

Though we said a small prayer over it. Because we had no idea how long it had been back in that pantry.

Mom cracked the soda open. "Bless this soda, Lord, for I know not where it comes from."

I snickered. "So dramatic. The worst it can do is burn holes in our throats."

Mom started pouring the drinks just as a knock came at the door. I furrowed my brow and she looked at me, but I saw her tense. Which put me on alert. I knew we weren't completely out of the woods with D.J. yet. We knew there was a possibility he'd be back.

"Want me to get the door, Mom?"

Then a soothing voice fell down the hallway.

"Rae! It's me!"

I gasped. "Clint."

I rushed to the door and ripped it open. I smiled as I lunged myself into his arms. He held me tightly as he spun me around. And I peppered his cheek with kisses.

"What are you doing here?" I murmured.

"Your mom wanted to surprise you tonight with me coming over for dinner."

I paused. "Since when do you and my mom talk?"

"Since he came over late the other night to check on us."

Mom's voice caused my brow to furrow. "What?"

Clint settled me to my feet. "I was worried about you two after D.J. left. I tried going home, but Cecilia knew there was something on my mind. So we did a little drive-by just in case he came back or something."

"You—you did?"

Mom rubbed my back. "Yep. He did. Came up and knocked on the door and everything."

Clint grinned. "Your mom invited me to dinner tonight with you two after my worries settled a bit."

"Which I think is really cute, how he wanted to check in on us," she whispered.

I cupped his cheek. "You're amazing, you know that?"

Mom reached for his hand. "Plus, I want to get to know him more. I hope you like enchiladas, Clint. Because it's a family recipe, and it's what's for dinner."

"Sounds fantastic, Miss Cleaver."

"Nonsense. Call me Lucy."

Clint's eyes widened. "Oh! I brought these."

I watched him reach for the chair on the porch and him pick up two gorgeous bouquets of flowers. One of them, green and white with dusted gold, he handed to Mom. And the other one, filled with beautiful fall colors, reds and yellows and oranges, he handed to me. I slowly looked up at him before burying my nose in the flowers. Oh, they smelled heavenly. Mom reached out with her arm and hugged Clint's neck, patting him softly on the back.

They murmured to one another, but I didn't catch what they said.

I did see Mom smiling, though. Which was a very good sign.

"We should get these in some water," I said.

Mom released Clint. "Definitely. Come on. I've got some old vases somewhere in the cabinets."

Clint stepped inside. "It smells incredible in here."

I closed the front door. "Mom knows how to throw down in the kitchen."

She laughed. "I'm teaching Rae how to, though."

Clint laughed as my jaw dropped open.

"Hey!"

Mom put her hand up. "I'm not saying you can't cook. You've got your dishes you're good at. But none of them are those traditional recipes that come from your heritage."

I scoffed. "I think I did just fine with the enchiladas."

"Yes, you did. After I walked you through the first batch. That's how you learn, sweetheart."

Clint snickered. "First batch? Sign me up. I'm starving, and it all sounds delicious."

I put my hand on his arm. "Just know we aren't liable for the damage the orange soda does to your throat."

He paused. "Wait, what?"

Mom and I laughed our way into the kitchen before getting the flowers in some water. Then we all sat down to eat. For the first time in as long as I could remember, it felt like a family again in this house. Mom telling stories to Clint. Him returning the favor with his foot pressed against mine underneath the table. Mom and Clint got along wonderfully. And as the two of them talked, I couldn't stop staring at him.

He had come back to check in on us.

My heart fluttered in my chest at the idea of it.

Mom took a sip of her drink. "So do you have any plans for after school and all that?"

Clint and I paused, staring at her as her eyes danced between us.

"What?" she asked.

Clint narrowed his eyes. "How are you feeling?"

She shrugged. "I feel fine. Why?"

I licked my lips. "So, the soda's okay to drink?"

She scoffed. "You two are made for one another. Eat your damn food and hush."

I grinned. "One more point in my favor."

Clint furrowed his brow. "One point?"

"Let's get back to the question at hand. I want to know what Clint's plans for after high school are."

I looked over at him, trying to let him know that he didn't have to answer. But he looked confident. Much more confident than I would have been at that question had I been in his shoes.

"Well, Miss Lucy, I know college isn't for me. Not that I don't like a good education, but I'm terrible at it. I don't do well in classes with formal testing and things like that. I'm more of a hands-on kinda guy. I think I'd be better suited to start from the bottom somewhere, get certificates as I go along, and work my way up. Learn at the lower level and apply those types of things at upper levels."

Mom nodded. "That sounds like a plan. Are you staying around here? Or moving away?"

"For now, I'm staying around here. But there are plenty of job offers I can apply for. And I'll have a small support system in the area with my stepmom and everything like that."

"Are things going okay at your house, Clint?"

He sighed. "They're going. I don't know how much Rae's told you and all that, but Dad's selling the house and she doesn't want to go with him. We're getting an apartment together on the other side of the high school so I can finish out my senior year."

"That's wonderful news."

He smiled. "Thanks. It took a lot of weight off our shoulders, finding that place. I'm really just playing it by ear right now. But I'm in a good place with money. Dad hasn't been around to say anything else about it. Thanks to Rae and Allison, things are looking up for my grades."

Mom reached over and patted his hand. "Well, if you ever need somewhere to go, we don't have much here. But you're welcome to it."

I nodded as my eyes found Clint.

"Yeah. You're always welcome here. Okay?"

He smiled gratefully. "I really appreciate it. Thank you."

"You seem like a great boy, Clint. I'm glad my daughter found someone like you. It was very sweet of you to check in on us the other night."

He shook his head. "It's not a problem. I was worried, so I figured I'd stop by. That's it."

"Well, thank you for it."

I nodded quickly. "Yes, thank you for doing that. Even though I didn't know shit about it."

We all laughed softly before we went back to eating. Mom and Clint went back and forth with questions, warming my heart as to how well the two of them got along. I felt full of sunshine. Full of hope. Full of happiness instead of despair. We scarfed down dinner and he helped us clean up, washing dishes for me to dry while Mom put away the leftovers. We each poured ourselves some more orange soda before popping some popcorn. Then we settled ourselves in the living room for a movie.

Thankfully, I got Mom to put on a comedy instead another one of her romantic comedies. Which meant Clint and I wouldn't be bored out of our minds.

Mom stood up. "Oh, I forgot napkins. Does anyone want a napkin?"

I nodded. "Yes, please."

Clint murmured with his mouth full. "Mm-hmm. Please."

I snickered as Mom made her way out of the living room. I heard Clint swallow hard before he chugged back his soda. Then he gripped my chin.

"I've been waiting all night to do this."

He guided my lips to his and his tongue fell against the roof of my mouth. I shivered against him, moaning softly as his lips pressed against mine. I opened myself for him. I tasted him for the first time that night and I felt heat pooling in my gut. I lifted my hand to cup his cheek, stroking the stubble on his jawline. Blood rushed through my ears, drowning out the sound of the movie as the entire world faded away.

That is, until Mom cleared her throat.

"Shit," I hissed.

She tossed the napkins at me. "Save that for a time when I'm not here, got it?"

I giggled. "Got it, Mom."

"My apologies, Miss Lucy."

She pointed at Clint. "Protection, young man. Use it."

My eyes widened. "Mom."

"I don't care that she's on birth control. Use it."

My jaw dropped open. "Mom!"

Clint laughed. "Noted, Miss Lucy."

"Good."

And as Mom fell back down beside me on the couch, I wanted to curl up and die from embarrassment.

37

CLINTON

*Clinton*Two Weeks Later

I sighed as I stood in the empty, grand foyer of the house I grew up in. I'd call it a 'childhood home,' except that it held nothing positive. No memories of Thanksgiving dinners where families laughed around a table. No family breakfasts where we all talked about our upcoming day. No sitting around a television watching the news. No movie nights.

Just destruction. And darkness. And death.

"I won't miss you one bit," I murmured.

I looked over my shoulder, out through the open front door. There Cecilia sat in her new SUV. Even after trading in her cherry red luxury vehicle this past week, she was able to purchase a new car with money still going back into her pocket. An affordable, family SUV. With regular fabric seats, a basic Bluetooth interface, an extended overall warranty, and twenty grand more in her bank account. No payments. No hassle. No fuss.

And sadly enough, all of our things fit into the damn car.

"Take your time, Clint!"

Cecilia's voice ripped me from my trance and I waved at her. I turned my gaze back into the house and slowly started walking around. Down the hallway leading into the kitchen. Back around into the living room. I walked upstairs, making sure we hadn't left anything behind. No jewelry. No chargers. No random pairs of socks. Nothing like that.

And when I got to my bedroom, I sighed.

Everything looked so empty. What Cecilia and I didn't sell off, Dad had sold off himself. He didn't even seem to notice the lack of silverware. Or china. Or items in the attic. He emptied the house for the new owners, who were due to move in tomorrow morning. Empty.

That was the definition of this house.

I walked back downstairs and slid an envelope out of my pocket. I set it on the one piece of furniture that had stayed behind. A curio in the corner of the foyer Dad hadn't sold yet. I remember that curio distinctly. I remember the day Mom bought it. Right out of a thrift shop that angered Dad to no end.

We buy new, sweetheart. We don't have to rummage through people's garbage.

Does it have termites?

It looks diseased. Take it back.

I'll buy you a better one for your birthday. Just get it out of my house.

That curio symbolized everything. It was the one fight my mother won over my father. The one fight where my father actually gave in. Granted, he left us alone for three weeks after telling Mom she wasn't welcome on his latest business trip to China. But that didn't matter. To her, that curio symbolized her strength. Her ability to put her foot down.

It gave her enough strength to walk away from the marriage.

It gave her enough strength to leave me behind.

Place the note and get out of here.

I sighed as I walked over to the piece of furniture. I pulled the tape out of my pocket and taped the bright blue envelope to the front glass. I knew the color would stand out. When Dad came by, I knew he'd see it. Whether he read the note addressed to him or not, I didn't know. And honestly? I didn't care. Getting it down on paper helped. Handing it over to him helped even more. I did my part. I said what I had to say in that note.

And now, it was time to move on.

I sighed before I turned my back. The note was the last piece. It wasn't much either. Just a paragraph or two on what he could expect of me from this point on. I told him I no longer wanted him in my life. Nor did I want to be part of his. I told him I'd find my own way. That I wouldn't ever ask him for anything again. That I wouldn't reach out, either. And I didn't expect him to. I wanted him to know that we could go our separate ways and be done with all this shit. All this abuse. All this insanity.

Writing that note helped bring me peace.

And I hope it served to keep my father far away from me.

I walked out of the house and closed the front door behind me. I jiggled the knob, making sure it was locked. Then I headed for the SUV. Cecilia rolled up her window as I walked around to the passenger's side. Ready to drive off into our new future. I climbed into the car and buckled my seatbelt. And as Cecilia reached over for my hand, I shook my head.

"I'm fine. I promise."

She squeezed it. "You want to go get some food before we head to the apartment?"

I shook my head. "No. I'm ready for this. We can unload everything, get the furniture arranged, and order something in."

"Mmm, I haven't done that in ages. How do you feel about Thai?"

I grinned. "Sounds like a plan."

My stepmom drove away from the house, and with every piece of distance I felt the last of the weight lift off my shoulders. Peace overcame me so intensely it pushed tears to my eyes. I didn't try to mask them, either. As Cecilia held my hand, I let them fall down my cheek. I let the memories assault my mind. I let myself feel the pain I'd been experiencing my entire life.

And she sat there, silently. Driving us to our new home.

Without an ounce of judgment in her form.

I wanted this. As much as it hurt, I wanted this more than anything in my life. I wanted a new chapter in my world. I wanted to start the part of my life where I made things right. Where I made good choices. Where I surrounded myself with good people instead of toxic people. I wanted kindness in my life. People like Rae and Allison and Michael. And Cecilia. I wanted to surround myself with people who were healing, too. Healing from abuse and hurt they couldn't always control, like Luciana.

"You okay, Clinton?"

I sniffled. "I am."

"Are you sure?"

I nodded slowly. "I'm ready, Ma."

She paused. "What did you call me?"

I smiled as I looked over at her.

"Is that okay? If I call you that?"

She smiled brightly. "You can call me whatever you want, son."

"Thanks… Ma."

"Is there anything else you want to do before we get there? Any place you want to stop?"

I shook my head slowly as we came to a stoplight. Right by the school. Only five minutes away from our new home.

"I just want to get the hell away from that house."

And with a snicker, she nodded.

"Then, allow me to speed as quickly as I can to the apartment."

I smiled. "Sounds good to me."

38

—————

RAELYNN

Michael pulled to a stop. "I think this is it."

I looked at the apartment building number. "Yep. 1824."

"You going to take pictures for me?"

I snickered. "I'm sure you and Allison will get the tour soon enough."

"So that's a yes?"

I giggled. "You know that's a yes."

"Good. Because you know Allison's going to be bugging me over dinner as to whether or not you've sent them."

I reached over and gave Michael a big hug as I laughed.

"Thanks for bringing me over."

He kissed my cheek. "Anytime. You know I don't mind giving you rides."

I pulled back. "Have you talked to Clint about the new school riding schedule?"

"I haven't yet. I plan on it tonight, though. You know, after the two of you are done doing your thing."

"There's no 'thing' happening tonight. His stepmom's home."

Michael gave me a knowing look. "Uh huh. Whatever. Have fun, Rae."

I rolled my eyes. "Screw you."

"That's Allison's job one of these days."

"I'm telling her you said that."

We laughed as I unbuckled my seatbelt. I slid out of his car and waved him off, watching him drive out of the neighborhood. He and Allison had a dinner date. *The* dinner date, really. The one where he picked her up at her house and officially met her parents.

I'd already told Allison to text me and let me know how it went.

With Michael's car out of sight, I turned around and looked up at the massive apartment building before walking onto the first floor. I came to the apartment number and knocked softly on the door. I checked my text message, making sure I had the right place.

And when Clint opened the door, I smiled broadly.

"Come here, beautiful."

He picked me up and swung me around. I giggled as he carried me into the apartment. He closed the door behind me and set me back down on my feet. Then he proceeded to give me the grand tour.

"This is my bedroom. It's back down the hallway. Cecilia's is right off the main room."

I nodded. "So her bathroom is the one guests use?"

He paused. "She said that, too. Why the fuck is that such a big deal?"

Cecilia called out from her room. "Because boys have nasty bathrooms, and guests aren't using nasty bathrooms!"

I snickered. "She's got a very big point."

Clint rolled his eyes. "I'm not nasty."

I giggled as he continued leading me around the apartment. He showed me his bedroom and bathroom, which were much larger than I expected them to be. Cecilia showed me her room and bathroom. And I was shocked at the amount of furniture they had. The decorations that had already gone up. It looked like they'd been slowly moving in all week. The place looked phenomenal.

"Want to see the balcony?"

I smiled. "Hell, yeah."

Clint's hand fell to the small of my back and he ushered me out a door. The white-washed wrought iron was gorgeous, and it overlooked a stretch of land shrouded in green grass and trees. The leaves were turning colors, casting yellows and oranges and reds against the sky. I smiled brightly as Clint closed the porch door, giving us some privacy out there all by ourselves.

"Come here. Sit with me."

I squealed as he pulled me into his lap. We sat down in an over-sized chair on the small private balcony, and I leaned against him. My legs curled up as he held me. My forehead fell against his temple. I hadn't seen Clint smile like this in a long time. And the smile stayed prevalent on his face. He looked more relaxed, more at ease. I kissed the shell of his ear softly and he turned his head, nuzzling his nose against my own.

"What was that for, beautiful?"

I snickered softly. "You seem happy."

He held me tight. "I am happy."

"No, I mean… happy. Really, truly happy."

He nodded slowly. "I'm relieved, more than anything."

"Have you guys been moving in all week?"

He shrugged. "More or less. We still have a storage unit filled with things. But we pooled our money and bought new pieces of furniture. A new couch. A new television and a place to set it. Things like that."

"It really looks nice."

"Thanks for coming over."

The porch door opened and Cecilia stuck her head outside.

"Sorry to interrupt. But I'm about to order some Thai. Rae, are you hungry?"

I paused. "Thai food?"

She nodded. "Mm-hmm. Is that okay?"

"I don't know. I've never had Thai food."

Clint gasped. "You what?"

Cecilia shook her head. "That won't do. I know exactly what to start you with."

"How the hell are we dating? How did this happen?"

I laughed as Cecilia went back inside and closed the door.

"How have you never had Thai food?" he asked.

I shrugged. "Mom's not a fan of it, so we don't eat it."

He sighed. "I have to rethink my life choices now."

"No more sex for you, then, I guess."

"Hey, now. I didn't go that far."

I grinned. "It's cute that you think I could actually resist you."

"Oh, really now?"

His lips captured mine, silencing my laughter. I moaned as I sank against him. I felt my phone vibrating, but I ignored it. I could get back to Allison and Michael at a later time. I sat up as I straddled Clint's lap, letting my arms languidly drape around his neck. The kiss was slow. Deep. My head fell off to the side as his hands journeyed around my back. I rolled against him, wanting him more than ever before.

If only this balcony were more private for us.

"Mm, Rae. Rae."

I kept kissing his lips. "Mm-hmm?"

"Rae, Rae. Listen."

I paused. "Yeah?"

Clint cupped my cheek. "Some other things have happened this week."

"Oh? Like what?"

His hands settled on my hips. "Things are moving forward with the court date."

My eyebrows rose. "Wait, what court date?"

"The one against the boys. You know, that pro bono lawyer?"

My jaw dropped open. "The woman who called you? You took her up on her offer?"

He nodded. "I did. And she's confident we have it in the bag."

"Are you serious?"

He chuckled. "Very."

"Holy shit. Clint."

I threw my arms around him as tears rushed to my eyes. I clung to him, feeling him wrap his arms around me. He stood up and carried me with him, opening the balcony door and walking us back inside. I curled against him, tucking my face into the crook of his neck as I heard Cecilia still on the phone ordering food.

I drew in shuddering breaths as I tried keeping my tears at bay.

"I'm so happy you decided to go with it," I whispered.

Clint kissed my cheek. "I know you are. And I knew it needed to happen. I guess with everything going on with the house and my dad, I didn't want more on my plate. But she's made this process pretty painless."

"I'm so proud of you."

A door closed behind us and I lifted my head. I watched Clint's bed come into view before he walked me over. He settled me down on the edge, then patted my back. Trying to get me to let go.

"I've got one more thing I want to show you."

I sniffled. "What is it?"

He stood up. "Something Cecilia helped me pick out."

I watched him walk over to his closet. He slid the doors open and plucked something out from the back. He turned around and my hands flew to my mouth, taking in the beauty of the pristine black suit. Crisp. Clean cut. Tailored specifically to him. The button-front shirt had a glossy texture to it, juxtaposing the matte black jacket. The black collar was velveteen. But it was the dark green bowtie that caught my eye.

The color reminded me a lot of that dress Cecilia gifted me.

"Clint, it's—it's beautiful."

He nodded. "It is. But it's nothing unless you're on my arm."

I blinked. "What?"

"Rae, will you go to prom with me?"

And as I rushed off the bed, I lunged at him. I wrapped my arms around him as tears welled in my eyes. I hugged him tightly, peppering his cheek with kisses. He chuckled as he wrapped his arms around me, the suit dragging along the hardwood floors of their new apartment.

"I've been waiting forever for you to ask."

He snickered. "Then say yes."

I nodded quickly. "Yes, Clint. Holy fucking—hell yes. Hell yeah, I'll go to prom with you."

39

CLINTON

I smiled into her shoulder as I wrapped her up tight. I tossed my suit over into the corner, wanting to hold all of her in my arms. I breathed in the scent of the luxurious body spray she started wearing a few weeks back. I loved its smell. Like cotton on a cool fall day. I kissed her neck, hearing soft moans fall from her lips. And as I journeyed up her neck, I felt her head fall to the side.

"No. I want to taste you, Rae."

I fisted her hair and brought her lips back to mine. I needed her. I wanted her. And now, I had her. Fully, without my attention being divided. No father to worry about. No being scared of going home. No fretting over the situation Cecilia was in. I was free. Free of worry, and doubt, and chains my father locked me in. I was free to graduate. Free to live my life. Free to come home and never wonder about having to brace for impact.

Which meant I could devote myself to the girl I loved.

My hands slid down her back. I felt her slipping my shirt over my torso. Our clothes came off in a flurry, our hands sliding against one another's skin. I puckered for her. Goosebumps flooded my skin. My cock jumped at the sight of her. At the sight of her naked body standing in front of me.

I licked my lips as my eyes traveled down her toned curves.

I slowly walked over to the door. With my girth at full attention, it wept at the need to be inside her. I locked my bedroom door.

And the sound of the lock flipping snapped something inside Rae. She rushed me, pushing me against the door. My back fell against it, and I tried my best to muffle the sounds. Her fingernails slid down my skin and rumbled over my abs as she fell to her knees. My eyes bulged as she wrapped her hand around my girth. Stroking it. Spreading my leaking arousal up and down its shaft.

"Rae, you don—holy fuck."

And the moan she let out around my dick made my body shiver.

I groaned as my hand found her hair, twirling up in her tendrils, commanding her every move. Her tongue slid down the underside of my cock, licking me and stroking me as her cheeks hollowed out. My toes curled into the hardwood floors. I felt my thighs already quaking as she swallowed down my cock. I heard her gag and felt the tightness around me. And as my eyes rolled back, I started moving my hips.

"Yes. Rae. Shit, just like that."

The whispered words filled the space around us. She bobbed her head quicker. Faster. Hollowed out her cheeks harder. The suction was too much. Feeling the back of her throat made my head spin. I felt my balls curl up and my eyes jumped open. I didn't want it to end like this. I wasn't ready for it to end yet.

"Oh, no you don't."

I growled as I tugged at her hair and pulled her up from the floor. She fell into me, my lips capturing hers. And the taste of my cum on her tongue unleashed the animal. I dipped down and gripped her ass cheeks, hoisting her against me. I walked her over to the bed and tossed her onto the mattress, watching her tits bounce for me.

She panted. "Clint. I need you."

And she didn't have to say anything else.

I gripped her ankles and pulled her to the edge of the bed. I tossed them over my shoulders as I stood there, my cock falling against her pussy lips. She unfurled for me. Her clit throbbed for my viewing pleasure. I grinned as I stroked my girth, feeling it pulsate in my hands. Her hands fisted my comforter. I stroked myself up and down her glistening slit.

Then I pressed into her, giving her no time to catch her breath.

"Cli—!"

I folded her in half and fell down against her. With my hands on either side of her head, I snapped my hips against hers. I felt her hands sliding along my back, her nails marking me as growls came out of the back of her throat. Our bodies became one as she rolled against me and I pinned her beneath me. I swallowed her sounds, the cries for more and the chants of my name. I pounded against her. Quicker. Faster. Harder. And it was only by the grace of whatever god existed that the bed didn't rake across the floor.

"Rae," I grunted.

I felt her closing around me and her body trembling beneath me. Her legs locked out. Her thighs quaked. And her hands cupped my cheeks. She kissed me over and over, gasping for air and whimpering as I sucked on her lower lip. I felt my balls pulling up as her juices dripped down my thighs. And as I sank myself deep into her, I ground my pelvis against her swollen clit.

"Clint. Clint. I'm coming. I'm so close. Yes. Right there. Like that. Oh! I love you. Clint. I love you. I love you. I love you. I love you."

I grunted at her words. I gnashed my teeth together and forced my eyes open. I saw her staring back at me, with pleasure and desperation in her stare. She arched her back. I watched her eyes close. And as my cock finally spilled into her, I choked out her name.

"Rae—lynn."

I collapsed against her, sliding her legs softly off my shoulders. As she quivered beneath me, my cock still sheathed within her, my face fell to her shoulder. I nuzzled her pulse point, feeling her heart beating wildly against mine. I kissed her skin. Her jaw. Her cheek. All the way over to her lips as my trembling arms held me up.

"I love you too, Rae."

And as her hands brushed away tears I didn't know I had been crying, I opened my eyes. I stared into hers. Into the loving eyes of the girl I'd come to love. The girl I had loved for weeks now.

"I love you with everything I am," I whispered.

EPILOGUE

Raelynn
Four Months Later

Allison cupped her hand over her mouth. "Oh, my gosh."

I smiled. "How do I look?"

"Rae! Are you insane right now?"

I laughed as she rushed over. She wrapped her arms around my neck and hugged me tight. The tulle of her purple and pale yellow gown rushed against my legs as she jumped up and down, taking me with her. Jumping in heels while I stood there in flats, trying to make sure she didn't knock me down.

"You. Look. Amazing. Oh, my gosh, Rae. Mom! Lucy! You guys! Get up here!"

Allison's voice rang my ears as she finally released me. I stuck my finger in my ear and wiggled it around. But not too soon after that, the clicking of cameras filled the space around me. Flashes went off and I shielded my eyes. Allison got beside me and tried to pose me as best as she could. With my hand on my hip. With our arms around one another. One with us smiling, and one with us being serious. As if we were models.

"Allison, you're killing me here."

She sighed. "Just one more. Okay? One with our parents."

I snickered as I went and stood beside my mother. She couldn't stop stealing glances. Shaking her head. Letting her eyes well with tears. I mean, I knew prom would be a big deal. But, all this crying? The squealing?

It was a bit much.

"You look amazing, sweetheart."

I grinned. "Thanks, Mom."

"I won't make a big deal out of it. I've only taken a few. And I'll only take one of us together."

"I know you'll steal some from Allison's parents later."

She snickered. "You're damn right, I will."

The two of us started laughing and I ignored the sounds of the cameras. Mom held her arms out for me and I hugged her tightly. I tried my best not to cry, too. Because Allison insisted I wear makeup for the night. She'd worked on my face for almost an hour, trying to get everything right. The last thing I needed to be doing was ruining it with tears.

"I love you so much," Mom whispered.

"I love you too, Mom."

Allison called out. "Hey! Rae!"

I released Mom. "What?"

"Did someone order a limo?"

I paused. "No, why?"

"Because a limo just pulled into the driveway."

All of us looked at one another before Mom and I started rushing down the steps. Allison and her parents weren't too far behind us. And just as we got to the front door, the doorbell rang. Allison squealed her head off. I heard Michael laughing behind the door. But when Clint's chuckle followed behind, I felt myself blush.

"You ready for this, honey?"

I looked over at Mom. "I'm very ready."

Allison's father opened the door and there the boys stood. Michael, in a white tuxedo suit with a black collar and a black pair of pants. His button-front shirt was purple. The same color purple as Allison's dress. And his boutonniere was pale yellow. Just like the corsage he had for her in his hand.

"You look—"

Michael was stunned speechless. I smiled as Allison wrapped her arms around him. Her parents snapped pictures as Michael slipped the corsage onto her wrist and the two of them posed for pictures. I stood off to the side with Mom, taking in how happy and wonderful my two best friends looked.

Then I felt someone appear at my side.

"She doesn't hold a candle to you, Rae."

I slowly looked up and saw Clint standing beside me. In his all-black suit, except for this bowtie. The dark green bow tie that matched my dress perfectly. I smiled up at him and he turned to me, his eyes locked with mine. He had a boutonniere on his collar, too. Dark green, with little sprigs of silver that were dotted with the smallest of pearls.

"This is for you," he said.

I looked down at the corsage, and all eyes turned to me. Pictures were snapped. Mom wiped at her eyes. I smiled brightly at the matching corsage as Clint popped the plastic container open. He took my hand softly and slid the band over my wrist. And as my eyes rose to meet his again, he winked.

"The limo is courtesy of Cecilia, if you're wondering."

I snickered. "Why doesn't that shock me at all?"

He shrugged. "She wants us to have a good time. And she's going to want some pictures."

We looked around at the adults and they nodded. Letting us know he'd get them, in due time.

"Wait, how did Cecilia afford the limo?" I asked.

Michael snickered. "Not going to lie, I'm wondering the same thing."

Clint shrugged. "Her lawyer has informed her that, until the divorce is final, my dad can't completely cut her off. Especially after proving that he sold the house right from underneath us."

My jaw dropped open. "Wait, so…?"

He grinned. "Let's just say Dad's mailed her a new credit card to appease her in the hopes she won't bleed him dry before they can get papers signed."

All of us had a good laugh before Clint offered me his arm. Allison's parents and my mother continued taking pictures as we walked outside, all the way to the limo. The leather seats called to us. They were soft. Like butter. And out of the corner of my eye, I saw something chilling on ice.

"What's that?" I asked.

Michael picked it up. "The finest sparkling grape juice. Chilled to perfection."

Allison and I giggled as Michael screwed the top off.

Clint grabbed crystal champagne flutes and we each had a glass. The driver had music blaring, preparing us for a wonderful night out. I cuddled against Clint as we drank through the juice. We sang to the songs and waved our glasses in the air. Toasting, over and over, a night to remember.

A night that signaled putting all this bullshit behind us.

The limo drove us to the hotel. To the ballroom the high school had rented out and decorated. I slipped my arm into Clint's, then Allison took my hand. And together, the four of us journeyed into the hotel. We followed the red carpet all the way to the ballroom. All the way into the entrance. And as the beat pulsed and lights flashed, a smile crossed my face.

This was going to be awesome.

"Care to dance?"

Clint's lips pressed softly against the shell of my ear to be heard. And a shiver worked down my spine. I peeked over at him and nodded, then pulled Allison over to me. I wrapped her up in a one-armed hug, kissed her cheek softly, and told her how beautiful she looked. Then, I told her I'd see her out on the dance floor.

Just before Clint started tugging me toward it.

He twirled me around. The bass of the beat wound down. And as his arm slipped around my lower back, the music slowed down. The song became sensuous. He pulled me close, holding my hand up with his, swaying us softly to the beat.

"I didn't know you could dance, handsome."

He grinned. "I'm full of surprises at times."

I paused. "Michael taught you, didn't he?"

"First—and last—time I ever dance with a dude."

My head fell back in laughter as he dropped my hand. He slid his arms around my lower back, holding me close to him. I slipped my hands up his chest. My arms draped around his neck. My head came back up and our eyes connected as the music filled the small spaces between us. Nothing else existed. Just me, him, and the song. Our song.

A song I started softly singing as my eyes danced between his.

"I know you haven't made your mind up yet. But I would never do you wrong."

Clint smiled as his cheeks tinted with a blush.

"I knew it from the moment that we met. No doubt in my mind where you belonged."

He pulled me close and took over the lyrics.

"I could make you happy; make your dreams come true. Nothing that I wouldn't do."

Tears rushed my eyes as I changed the lyrics.

"Drop down into a ravine for you."

And as his nose nuzzled against mine, we sang the last of the song together.

"To make you feel my love."

DON'T FOLLOW ME

DIAMOND IN THE ROUGH 4

1

—————

RAELYNN

I breathed in the salted air as I rollerbladed down the boardwalk. Despite our small patch of town being attached to one of the biggest cities in the nation, it still felt like this quaint little place. We had our own stretch of beach. Our own boardwalk. No world-renowned restaurants that drew a crowd or nationwide festivals for people to purchase tickets to. The warmth of the sun on my skin felt wonderful as I swerved around people. Couples eating ice cream cones and people walking their dogs. Children aching to get to the sandy shorelines and college kids coming out of the beach stores with bags full of cheaply-made merchandise.

This place would always be home to me.

"Rae!"

Allison's voice rose above the crowd and I skated across the boardwalk. The wooden planks rumbled underneath me as I headed for the opening of the small shop. She held out her arms for me and I skated right into them, spinning around as the summer sun beat down against my back.

Holy shit, we were officially graduated.

"You're really getting the hang of those things," Allison said.

"I'm just glad Mom bought them for me. No offense, but your bike seat practically rides up my crack."

"Why do you think I never rode it myself?"

I hugged her tighter. "I hate you so much."

"Me too, Rae."

The two of us laughed as I took her hand. I skated alongside her as she jogged, and we found the last table with an umbrella to shield us from the scalding rays. I'd never known the California sun to be this hot. I usually never ventured out much in the sun during the summer. I stayed in my bedroom, went to work, and occasionally crashed at Allison's.

But Clint had gotten me out more during these hot summer days.

"The boys here yet?" I asked.

Allison and I sat down before she sighed.

"I haven't seen Michael yet, no."

I nodded. "And I'm assuming Clint's coming with him?"

"Do you ever know the two of them to go anywhere without each other anymore?"

I paused. "Actually, now that you mention it?"

She giggled. "I mean, it's sweet, but... do you ever wonder what in the world they're doing all the time?"

I furrowed my brow. "Have you been tanning?"

"You like it? I've been out on the beach a lot with Michael."

"It looks really nice on you."

"I mean, it's not like you don't have one."

I rolled my eyes. "I have a nice farmer's tan going on. I'm not sunbathing in my itty bitty bikinis like you are."

She gasped. "I don't wear itty bitty bikinis!"

"Says the girl who wears string bikinis."

"They aren't thong bikinis, no. And mine are strapless so I don't get those lines on my shoulders."

"Face it, Allison. You're dangling your body in front of poor Michael and you love it."

She grinned. "Maybe just a tad."

I laughed. "So do we want to order our ice cream? Or wait for the boys?"

"You know they're going to pitch a fit if we don't let them pay."

"What is that, anyway? We've got our own money."

She snickered. "I think it makes them feel important."

"Figured Clint might feel that way when I'm riding his dick."

"Rae!"

I laughed. "Oh, come on. You don't say so now, but give it a few more weeks with Michael. When we're all off at college soon. You'll finally give it up and then you'll be insatiable."

"Nope. No, thank you. Waiting until marriage."

"Uh huh."

"Well, it's true."

I grinned. "Good luck with that."

And after a brief pause, Allison spoke.

"Can you believe we're going to all be in college in a month?"

I shook my head. "It doesn't feel real."

"My parents are already helping me pack my things. And I haven't even found an apartment to live in yet."

"So they aren't making you stay in the dorms on campus like they were?"

She shook her head. "No. I finally convinced them to let me have my own place after swearing to them Michael wasn't moving in."

I barked with laughter. "You're kidding."

"Not one bit. They thought I wanted my own place so he could move in."

"You'd kill him."

"You know how I need my space. And he'd never give it to me to study and all that stuff if we were under one roof."

I grinned. "Though, you having your own place might come with some other perks."

Her face fell. "Stop it."

I held my hands up. "I'm just saying!"

"I'm not sleeping with Michael anytime soon."

"But maybe sometime in the future."

She paused. "Did he put you up to this? Did he tell you to try and wear down my walls?"

I snickered. "You know damn good and well Michael wouldn't ever have the guts. I know he respects your boundaries. And you do, too."

"Then why are you riding me so hard about this?"

I shrugged. "Because I think you're stuck in a mindset that's going to hold you back in college. I mean, if you can't take control of your sex life as a girl, who's to say you'll take control of your education?"

"What makes you think that not having sex until marriage is

something I've been relegated to? Why can't that also be a personal decision I make because my sex life is mine?"

"Good point. Is it a decision you've made?"

She nodded. "Yes, it is."

"Okay, then. Subject dropped."

"Thank you."

I sighed. "Mom's having a hard time with it."

Allison took my hand. "Still crying and stuff like that?"

"I think she's just having a hard time letting go. And instead of being productive, like your parents are, she's wallowing in her own self pity at night when she thinks I can't hear her."

"Not going to lie, sometimes it feels like they can't wait for me to get out of the house."

I snickered. "Because you've been dreaming about the day you leave for college ever since we started high school. I'm sure they're happy for you. Proud of you. Same with Michael, especially since he's going with you to college. The two of you are practically prodigies in your fields. I mean, a full ride, Allison? Come on now."

"I didn't think they'd give it to me, you know."

"Oh, I knew from the get-go they would. They'd be stupid not to. Especially with how hard you busted your ass in high school."

"Still, I wouldn't go as far as to say 'prodigies.'"

I giggled. "You're both going to Stanford, idiot."

She smiled. "That statement kind of seems like an oxymoron."

When Allison approached me the day after prom and told me she was applying to Stanford, I couldn't believe it. After getting into what I thought was her dream school, she decided to take a chance for once in her life. She applied, sent in the separate application for their architecture department, and they sent her information on their scholarship programs. With her GPA and her extra curriculars, she was eligible for a slew of their financial aid packages. And after two weeks of trying to convince her to go for the gold, she applied for one of them.

She applied for one of three full-ride tickets they gave out to incoming freshman students.

"Do you regret changing colleges?" I asked.

Allison shook her head. "Not one bit. I never even set my sights on Stanford or anything like that because I figured I wouldn't make it. I mean, usually you have to be related to someone to get into that school. Or from a historical lineage. Or make a massive donation. I didn't think I'd get in there on grades alone."

"Are you excited?"

"I kind of feel excited and I kind of feel as if I could puke."

I giggled. "So, normal. Got it."

"I still can't believe Michael applied, though."

I furrowed my brow. "Is that a bad thing?"

"No! No, no, no. I just--well, he had his ticket secured to the University of California. I didn't think he'd switch over to something so…"

"Prestigious?"

"I mean, yeah. Expensive. Hard. You name it."

I shrugged. "Michael's intelligent. And he's head over heels for you. Of course he'd switch. He's in love with you."

She smiled. "I still can't believe those words come out of his mouth sometimes."

"And at least you won't be stuck where I'm going."

"Oh, come on, Rae. Cal State is an excellent school. Don't be such a downer."

"Says the girl with a full ride to Stanford."

Her face fell. "I'm serious, Rae. I'm proud of you. I honestly didn't think you'd do the college thing, you know. Community college, maybe. But four years?"

I shrugged. "I didn't think I'd do it either. But if I want to do graphic design and things of that nature, all the research I did tells me I need a bachelor's degree. So why not just start out in the four-year program?"

"And why not be an hour away from your mother?"

"I mean, she's not going for that as much as I thought she would."

"Meeting halfway wouldn't be terrible for either of us to have dinner or something."

"Yeah, if two and a half hours of driving isn't considered 'terrible.' And if we don't hit traffic."

Her smile faltered. "Well, at least you can tell your mom you'll still see her every other weekend. Or once a month. And you're close enough to get back quick in case of emergencies."

I paused. "Are you trying to make her flood this town with her own tears?"

She roared with laughter. "It'll work out, Rae. Come on."

I sighed. "Yeah, yeah, yeah. I know. I know."

Allison released my hand and I leaned back in the wooden booth. As I gazed out over the water to the left of us, I felt uncertainty bloom in my stomach. It made me feel sick. My appetite for ice cream was gone. The more I talked about school, the more fearful I was of it. The more I heard my mother cry, the more I felt as if I was making a wrong decision.

I sighed. "How am I going to get through with you and Michael six hours away?"

Allison smiled weakly. "We can make things work. We can do this, okay? Weekends together. Parties at Stanford you can come to. When we all come home for holidays and stuff. We'll see one another more than you think."

But, is that enough? "Yeah. Sure."

"Rae."

I waved my hand in the air. "It's fine. Really."

"It's not fine. Something's on your mind."

"I'm just worried. It's nothing. I'll sleep it off."

"Talk to me, Rae."

I groaned. "It's just all easier said than done, you know? I mean, sure, the beginning of the semester might be easy enough. But, what happens once classes ramp up? What happens when you get bogged down with reading? And schoolwork? I mean, think about all the times I've come over and interrupted you doing homework, Allison."

She looked at me, but she didn't speak.

"Think about all the times I've had to track you and Michael down in order to spend time with you."

"Rae, it's not--"

I shook my head. "I'm not trying to be a downer. But I am trying to be a realist. This is a massive change. And everyone's acting like things will be hunky dory."

"I mean, do you want me to tell you that we'll never see one another and eventually drift apart? Is that going to make you feel any better?"

I snickered. "I don't know. Is that what's going to happen?"

I searched Allison's eyes for a signal. Or a sign. Anything to tell me my paranoia wasn't grounded in anything real. But all she did was shrug. A shrug. My best friend of years and years, and she didn't even know if we'd be able to preserve our friendship. I slumped back into my chair and stared back out over the ocean. I didn't know where the boys were, and I didn't care. I was losing my best friend. My life. Leaving it all behind for a school I wasn't even sure I wanted to attend. The last semester of our senior year changed so much. Allison and Michael grew even closer. Clint and I spent every waking moment together. He was talking about his future plans with starlight growing in his eyes. He practically bubbled over the brim with excitement!

And then there was me. Dreading every second. Counting down the days until doomsday. Still not sure about the decisions I'd made with my life. Every plan I laid out before myself had been obliterated when Allison got into Stanford. No apartment-sharing for us. Because fuck-only-knew I'd never make it into a school like that with my mediocre grades. And there weren't any community colleges around Stanford that had a graphics design associate's.

So there went the shared apartment.

Now I had all this money saved up and nothing to do with it. If I got a place of my own, I'd eat through it in three months before I'd be broke. I was two weeks away from my last day on a job I'd had for years. I was three weeks away from packing up my things and moving into a dorm room that would house another stranger under its roof with me. Instead of Allison, in our apartment, like we had always planned.

Life had already changed quickly around us. And I knew it wouldn't stop.

Which meant there wasn't a damn thing any of us could do to stop it.

2

CLINTON

"This fucking traffic. Come on!"

Michael honked the horn in his SUV as we sat in standstill traffic. The girls had been at the boardwalk by themselves for damn near forty minutes, and we couldn't get there to save our lives. Despite the windows being rolled down and the classic rock station turned up, I shifted in my seat. My eyes darted around. My pulse ticked up.

I wanted this to be a stress-free day for Rae.

And it was turning into anything but that.

"What the hell is all this traffic about?" Michael asked.

I shrugged. "Who the fuck knows?"

"I mean, wouldn't they have cleared it by now if it was an accident? Do you see any orange cones for construction?"

"We'll get there when we get there. Not much we can do unless we want to pull over and walk."

He snickered. "Had we done that before, we'd already be there by now."

"Well, in a few weeks you guys won't be here to experience any of it."

Mike put his car in park. Never a good sign when sitting in traffic. But, I knew exactly what I had said to trigger his response. I felt him turn to me, but I refused to meet his stare. Because I wasn't ready for the question about to fly out of his face.

"Clint?"

I rolled my eyes. "No, Mike."

"Clint. Look at me."

"No, thanks."

"You going to man up and have this conversation? Or am I going to have to pull it out of you?"

I snickered. "I'd like to see you try."

And when I rolled my eyes over to his, he grinned.

"Gotcha."

My face fell. "You're a fucking child."

He shrugged. "Yeah, well. I'm a manchild who's worried about my best friend."

I'd never get used to him calling me that.

"You know, that title is usually designated for--"

He waved his hand in the air. "Yeah, I know. You always remind me. Best friends are reserved for those who have known each other the longest. But not this time. I consider you a very good friend. A best friend. Because you're awesome, and I like you, and you fit in with our group, and you make Rae happy, and I don't mind shooting the shit with you."

I grinned. "Thanks."

"So time to shoot the shit since we're stuck in traffic."

My grin fell. "No, thanks."

"Dude, come on. It's painfully obvious you haven't made a decision yet. Why not?"

"Why the fuck is it so hot in your car right now? Fucking hell."

"The air conditioning in my car gave out yesterday. Got an appointment for tomorrow to get it fixed."

"Couldn't have told me that before we decided to get trapped in your black box of sweltering heat?"

He chuckled. "Nice try at a diversion. But it's not working."

I scoffed. "Yeah, just like your A.C. Fuck!"

I stuck my head out the window. And to my shock, it was cooler outside with the sun burning the top of my head than it was inside his car. His leather seats made my skin stick to the fabric. I breathed in deeply as sweat dripped down my face. And since my head was out the window, I tried to see what the fuck the hold-up was.

Then my phone vibrated in my board shorts' pocket.

"That Rae?" Mike asked.

I sat down. "Probably."

"What does she want?"

I pulled my phone out and looked at the text.

Rae: You guys close? Pretty sure I pissed Allison off with more college talk.

I sighed as my fingers flew over the screen.

Me: At least you've made a decision. Mike's about to wind up and knock it out of the park with how bullshit it is that I haven't made a decision yet.

I sent the message off and promptly got one back.

Rae: I mean, it would be nice for you to make one. You know, so I know how to declare my housing. Which I have to submit by the end of next week. Just letting you know.

I rolled my eyes and put my phone away. But I felt Mike's eyes on me. I jammed myself against the door, hanging my arm out as Aerosmith came on over the radio. I reached over and turned it up, trying to drown out his eyes with music. I bobbed my head and murmured the words. Thanking my fucking stars that traffic was slowly starting to move. For two whole blocks.

Until it stopped again.

"Fucking hell!" I exclaimed.

Mike snickered. "Maybe if you talk about your game plan for August, the traffic will pick up as a reward for your service."

I sighed. "You're not going to stop riding me about this, are you?"

"Not at all."

I rolled my eyes. "Fine. What do you want to know?"

"Have you figured out what you're going to do?"

"You'll have to be a bit more specific with that request."

"Okay. Did you apply to college? Or are you still sticking with the whole 'no college' deal?"

I sighed. "No. I didn't apply to college. School isn't for me. Not even some pointless two-year school."

"Good. Off to a nice start. So, are you staying with Cecilia? Or moving closer to Rae?"

"I'm… not sure on that yet."

"Which is fine. You got choices to talk through?"

I snickered. "Sure. I've got choices. I've always got choices. I can choose to stay with Cecilia in the apartment. Or I can move out and live in some downtown studio apartment close to Rae's school and hopefully convince her to move in with me. You know, if she doesn't already get a place of her own."

"Has she been talking about that?"

"She's been talking about everything. Mostly, how her former plans have gone to shit and what she's supposed to do now. She hates the idea of a dorm room. But apartments by herself are too expensive. She's all but said she wants to live with me."

"But…?"

I shrugged. "But I don't know."

"Why don't you know?"

"I just don't know, Mike. All right?"

My eyes fell out the window and I sighed. Finding a job around here hadn't been nearly as easy as I'd figured it would be. Even with setting aside as much as I could to help Cecilia pay for bills and shit, I was running through money fast. Between treating Rae to some things and my father making this damn divorce as hard as possible, I was tearing through money.

And as of yesterday, I'd run out of things to sell.

"Taking Rae out of the picture for a second. What do you want?" Mike asked.

I sighed. "My own life."

"Okay. Good start. What does your own life include?"

"A job I don't hate. A studio apartment over a bakery or some shit in downtown L.A. I fucking love downtown L.A."

"Well, that's close to Rae's school. Maybe the two of you could swing a place together."

"Yeah, well. She's making it seem like she can't swing something like that until she's got more money in the bank. Which is so weird to me, because I thought she was selling shit off, too."

"What do you mean?"

"You know, that stuff my stepmom gave her? Back when Cecilia and I first moved? Rae told me she was giving some of it away, keeping a few things for herself, and then selling off the rest to really cushion this transition and do what she wanted. Now, she's talking about not having money at all. And every time I ask her about it, she doesn't fucking say anything. I feel like she's lying to me. Or hiding something."

"Is that why you haven't made a decision yet?"

I shrugged. "The fuck am I supposed to do? I lived with a man who forced me to walk on eggshells my entire life. And now I'm doing it with my own fucking girlfriend. I won't go back to living like that, man."

"Have you told her any of this?"

I snickered. "You want to try telling me how to tell Rae that she's lying to me and I don't appreciate it because she's making me miserable?"

"If it were the other way around, I'd tell her to speak with you immediately. So…"

"Yeah, yeah. I hear you."

My eyes drifted out the window as traffic picked up again.

"Can I be real with you for a second, Clint?"

"Please. I'd appreciate it."

"Downtown L.A. is expensive as hell. You're going to need a decent sum of money just to make it through a year."

I nodded. "I know. I've already run the budget. For six months, by myself, in a studio apartment where I'd like, with bills and groceries and shit, I'd need just shy of forty grand. And that's without a car, just walking everywhere."

"Exactly. Which means, splitting that down the middle, that's still forty grand for each of you during the year."

"So what are you saying?"

I looked over at Mike and watched him shrug.

"I'm saying that being together means compromising. You can have an ideal life, sure. Then, you have to come together with your partner and figure out a compromise that works for both of you. Both with money and with school."

I paused. "And you think I don't know that?"

He scoffed. "Says the guy who hasn't told Rae he's miserable yet."

"I'm not miserable."

"That was the word you used."

"Well, I didn't fucking mean miserable."

"Might want to choose your words better when you talk with her, then."

"Dude, this is why I didn't want to have this conversation. Get off my nutsack."

"You get off it first."

I sighed as I leaned heavily into the seat. Sweat dripped down my back and I merely accepted my fate. I'd boil to death in this car before we got to the fucking boardwalk. Since when did things get so complicated? Since when did money drain this quickly? Holy fuck, I'd need a serious job if I wanted to keep living my life around this area. Especially around Cal State. Where Rae had decided to attend college for four. Fucking. Years.

Shit.

"What kind of jobs have you been looking for?"

I shook my head. "No."

Mike paused. "No, what?"

"No, I'm not talking anymore with you."

"Oh, come on. We've moved on from Rae."

"And I'm done talking."

"Just answer the damn question. What kind of jobs?"

"All kinds of jobs, Mike! Mechanic, part time cashier, a fucking sub sandwich maker. Gas station attendant. Construction. Internships. Fucking internships, dude! And no one gives me anything. No callbacks, other than people telling me *We've found our candidate, thank you for fucking applying.*"

"Do they say 'fucking' or…?"

I growled. "I'm going to slit your throat."

He chuckled. "Hopefully you don't list that as a skill."

I reached over and tried to fist his shirt, but he caught my wrist. He tossed my hand back into my lap before shooting me a look. Traffic slowly rolled down the block. Inching us closer to the boardwalk before we came to yet another standstill.

Then Mike put his car in park again.

"You can be pissed all you want, Clint. But we both know the only reason you're this angry is because Rae doesn't have her shit together, so you can't. And you won't get your shit together until you talk to her. Until you have a firm foundation with her again. Or at least a firm enough foundation to tell her whether or not you actually want to follow her to college or strike out on your own again."

I shrugged. "I mean, her college is only an hour away. And that's with traffic."

"Yeah, well. Look at this traffic. We were fifteen minutes away from the boardwalk. And we've been sitting in this damn car for forty-five."

Point taken. "I mean, if we really wanted to--"

"Dude, quit being a pussy."

"I'm not being a pussy."

"Yes, you are. You don't want to piss Rae off so close to all of us splitting, so you're hoping that if you ignore it the issue is going to go away. But you know that isn't how it works."

I sighed. "Yeah. I know."

"So boss up and bring up the conversation. You don't have to do it today. But you need to do it soon. Rae needs a firm plan of action on your end in order to work through what she's going to do on her end."

"And what if I need the same from her?"

"That's why you sit down and fucking talk about it, dude."

He sat back down in his seat as the song on the radio changed over again. As some Van Halen ballad filled the SUV, I let my eyes fall closed. While most of me was thankful I didn't have to put up with school anymore, part of me was disappointed. Even if, by some miracle, I wanted to go to school, I didn't have the option. Decisions I made in high school ruined my odds for that sort of thing. And Rae hadn't been happy with me when I decided not to apply.

In fact, it sparked a fight between us we still hadn't recovered from.

And that damn fight was four months ago.

My best bet at this point was to find a job with room for growth. With room for me to pull a decent-enough salary that helped support a lifestyle in this expensive-ass state. Otherwise, I'd fall behind. I'd forever be destined to scrape by with nothing but scraps underneath the table for hard labor twelve hours a day. Which was a life I didn't want for myself. I wanted to prosper. I wanted to be proud of myself. I wanted to be able to provide Rae with what she needed instead of her constantly worrying about things and checking her bank account and hiding things from me like she'd been these past few weeks.

I felt like I was on the verge of losing her. Losing Rae. Losing the love of my life.

And I had to find a lifestyle that made sure that didn't happen.

3

———

RAELYNN

I looked beyond Allison's shoulder after much too long of a silence. And when I saw Clint emerge from the throng of people pushing their way to the beach, I sat up.

"Oh, thank fuck."

Allison turned around. "What? What is it?"

Michael waved and Clint started jogging for us. I smiled as I stood up, steadying myself on my rollerblades. He picked me up and swung me around, peppering my cheeks with kisses. I smiled as Michael and Allison embraced, watching him dip her back for a deep, passionate kiss.

Then Clint did the same to me, making me giggle as his tongue slipped across the roof of my mouth.

It felt so good, having him there. In my arms. Wrapped up in me after so many tense nights together. Things hadn't gone according to any plan after prom. And it was the little things keeping us all hinged right now. We all knew it, though none of us wanted to talk about it. It was disappointing when Clint announced that, after all the hard work we all put in, he wasn't going to apply for college. Even with a 2.9 GPA, I knew he stood a chance. Especially with his senior grades showing how he finally applied himself, and how it paid off.

But, no matter what I said, I couldn't convince him to apply for school.

Much less for the school I got accepted to.

"Mmm, I don't know about you, gorgeous. But I'm ready for ice cream."

I giggled. "Why are you so sweaty?"

Allison snickered. "I take it you haven't gotten your air fixed yet?"

Michael scoffed. "Fine. Fine. Blame the terrible traffic on me. It wouldn't have been that bad in my car had we not been stuck in it for an hour."

I furrowed my brow. "What in the world made traffic stop like that? You guys were just at Michael's right?"

Clint kissed my forehead. "Doesn't matter. We're here now. What would you like to have?"

Allison and I placed our orders, then the guys headed inside. I sat down, making enough room for Clint as I scooted over. I kept my eyes on him as they walked inside. As they ventured up to the counter. As they ordered our milkshakes. I didn't want an ice cream cone that would melt all over my hand before I could get the damn thing eaten. I had watched Clint struggle with one too many of them over the course of this summer.

And yet, he didn't seem to learn.

Because he came out with the biggest ice cream cone for himself I'd ever seen.

"A double fudge brownie milkshake for you," he said as he handed me my drink.

"And a massive waffle cone for you, I see."

Allison reached for her milkshake. "Thank you, baby. I really appreciate it."

Michael kissed her cheek. "Of course. Anything for you."

And after watching Michael kiss Allison on the cheek, Clint kissed me on the cheek. Like he was getting his cues from him.

Like he didn't know what the hell to do otherwise.

Michael sat down. "So, what have you girls been getting up to?"

Clint sat down, too. "Yeah. Any good conversations we should know about?"

Allison giggled. "You guys never gossip about your conversations. Why should we gossip about ours?"

Clint smiled broadly. "You owe me twenty bucks, man."

Michael rolled his eyes. "Really, Allison? You had to take that approach?"

I furrowed my brow. "Wait, what just happened?"

Allison paused. "Did you idiots bet on me again?"

Michael pulled out his wallet. "I mean, really. I would've figured I knew my girlfriend better by this point."

Clint snickered. "Your loss is my gain. Pay up."

I narrowed my eyes. "You guys have never bet on me before."

Michael snickered. "Because you're completely unpredictable."

I cocked my head. "Thanks?"

Allison murmured, "Yeah, well. I don't like this at all."

Clint took the money from Michael. "Plus, I like you unpredictable. Keeps me on my toes, gorgeous."

But, again, he didn't kiss me until Michael kissed Allison.

I mean, I loved the fact that Michael and Clint had grown close. I liked the fact that they hung out and had their own inside jokes and were there for one another. Michael had been a good influence on him. Definitely. Plus, Clint's anger kept itself in check the more time he spent around Michael. Clint hadn't flown off the handle once since the two of them became connected at the hip.

But, still. Something didn't feel right.

"So who's looking forward to the road trip?"

Michael's voice ripped me from my trance and I took a sip of my milkshake. Leaving room for Allison to butt in.

"Well, I'm looking forward to it. Two hotel rooms for the weekend? We can celebrate and have a great time while Rae's doing orientation."

Clint slipped his arm around me. "Ready to get the lay of the land, gorgeous?"

I nodded, but I didn't stop drinking my milkshake. Which made Michael chuckle.

"Chug that any quicker and you're going to get brain freeze."

Allison giggled. "Leave her alone. We've been sitting here sweating our butts off for almost an hour waiting on you guys."

Michael kissed her temple. "I'm sorry we were so late. Had I known traffic was going to be that bad, I would've just walked it."

Then Clint kissed my temple. And the action was so stunted and empty that Allison furrowed her brow.

"You okay, Clint?"

He nodded. "Yeah. Why wouldn't I be?"

I shrugged. "I don't know. You just seem… off?"

Michael grinned. "Off like a camera? Or off like a horse?"

"Wait, huh?"

Clint and Michael burst out in laughter as I sat there, staring blankly at Allison. Another inside joke. They seemed to have a lot of those.

Allison snickered. "What--what does off have to do with a--?"

Michael held his hand up. "Had to be there. Holy shi--hoo! Had to be there."

Clint snorted. "Your father's a fucking mess, you know that?"

For some reason, I felt more alone than when Clint and Michael weren't here.

Allison rolled her eyes. "Anyway... Rae, you ready for orientation?"

Michael cleared his throat. "Yeah. You waiting until orientation to figure out whether or not to stay on campus?"

I shrugged. "I figured I'll end up staying on campus. For at least the first semester, to get my bearings."

Clint stopped laughing. "Wait, what?"

I looked over at him. "What?"

He furrowed his brow. "You're staying on campus? Since when?"

I shrugged. "Since you won't make a decision on where you want to live. I have to turn in the paperwork. Might as well do it at orientation since it's around the due date. The last thing I want is to be left without a room because I didn't make the decision on time."

He stared at me blankly before Michael interjected.

"Any good frat parties going on at this thing, you think?"

Allison smacked him playfully. "Michael. Stop it."

"What? I mean, Rae can go there. Meet her new peers. Fraternize with new people. Get her party on a bit."

"We're not there to party. We're there to support her."

I kept staring at Clint. "And maybe party a little bit."

Michael reached over, slapping Clint on the shoulder. "I mean, if he can keep his nose out of his notebook long enough. Am I right?"

It wasn't until Clint looked away that I settled back into my seat. But I felt his arm move from around me. I sipped on my milkshake as I gazed out over the ocean, and I felt someone's leg press against mine. I looked underneath the table and saw Allison's shoe.

I looked up at her and found her casting me some sort of a pity glance.

Well, I didn't want her pity.

I just wanted this limbo of hell to be over.

"Just because I'm writing doesn't mean I can't go party with you guys. It's a hobby. That's all," Clint said.

Allison smiled. "Writing about anything good?"

Michael took a bite of his ice cream. "Yeah. What is it you write?"

Clint shrugged. "All sorts of things. Poems. Ideas for short stories. Character outlines. A dream I may have had. Shit like that."

I sighed. "It's not shit."

Clint snapped back. "Well, it's not good."

"You're your harshest critic. I think you should do something with it."

"Yeah, like I should've gone to college?"

I bit down on the inside of my cheek. "You could've gotten in, with all the hard work you did."

Clint fired back. "Yeah. I know. But that doesn't mean school was ever my dream. You know I hate school. Why are you so pissed about this?"

"I'm not pissed, okay? Just confused."

"Yeah, well. So am I."

I paused. "About what?"

Clint murmured, "Nothing."

I heard a 'thwap' underneath the table, and then Michael and Clint started glaring at one another. Clint's eyes fell to his notebook, which he practically carried everywhere now. He slid it off the table before his ice cream started dripping down his hand.

"Fuck," he hissed.

I snickered. "Yeah. That's why I keep telling you to get anything other than a cone."

"Well, maybe I want a fucking cone anyway."

I shook my head and kept sucking on my straw. Why he always had to make things difficult sometimes, I'd never know. They continued talking around me, but I paid them no mind. I wasn't looking forward to this orientation at all. Not one bit. Because I'd have to share a room with Clint. And right now, things weren't good between us.

In fact, they hadn't been for a little while now.

I fell into my own mind and thought about his words. I mean, did he not want to live together? Did he not want to be closer to me? It wasn't like he didn't have the money. He'd been selling shit left and right and banking thousands upon thousands of dollars. Why couldn't he afford to come with me? Why was he hesitant?

Why did it take me bringing up staying on campus to piss him off enough to talk about it?

At this point, I was inclined to stay on campus. The last thing I wanted to deal with was constantly fighting with Clint when I wasn't in class. But I sure as hell didn't want to room with a stranger. I don't know. It was all so confusing. Everything seemed so clear-cut at prom. So good. So… perfect.

How did things get so bad this quickly?

I wondered about Mom. How she had really taken this to heart. I'd tried to find the closest school to home, but I knew it still took me farther away than she wished. I mean--I don't know. It wasn't as if I felt like I could really leave her anyway. And I knew why she wanted me to stay. Well, kind of.

Fuck, why is everything so damn difficult?

"Rae?"

"Rae, you there?"

"Gorgeous? Can you hear us?"

I slowly panned my gaze back to my friends. "Huh?"

Michael snickered. "You going to suck the life out of that milkshake?"

I looked down and saw I had drained it. And not only had I drained it, but my empty suction had pulled in the sides of my plastic cup. And holy fuck, my head hurt. I grimaced as I set it back down on the table. Michael chuckled as Allison reached out for my hand. Clint wrapped his arm around me, pulling me close, kissing my temple and trying to warm the skin around my face that had chilled so suddenly.

Holy fuck, I didn't think that brain freeze would ever end.

"You okay?"

Clint's murmur almost brought tears to my eyes. Because, no. I wasn't okay. I hadn't been okay for months. I hadn't been okay since he'd announced that he wasn't applying to college. I hadn't been okay since he told me he wasn't sure where he wanted to live after graduation. I hadn't been okay since he told me he was struggling to get a job and somehow didn't have the money to move with me. Like, where the fuck had all his money gone? He had way more than me to sell off. Why the hell didn't he have any money?

Probably for the same reason you don't have much, either.

I sighed as the brain freeze finally released me. I leaned against Clint, closing my eyes and soaking him in. Sometimes his embrace felt empty. But it didn't right now. I soaked it up and committed it to memory for all those times his embrace and his arms and his kisses *did* feel empty. I mean, relationships went through down points, right? This wouldn't last forever, right?

This wouldn't do us in.

Right?

"You okay, gorgeous?"

I sighed as Clint kissed the top of my head.

"I mean, I'd be better if I knew how we were getting into these parties."

Michael clapped his hands. "That's the spirit!"

Allison groaned. "You three are relentless."

I snickered. "Oh, come on. You know you enjoy parties, too. Remember the one after graduation?"

She laughed. "The one where you got so drunk that we had to haul you home in the back seat with a bag in front of your face?"

I pointed my finger at her. "Hey, now. Mixing liquors isn't a good thing. I wasn't drunk."

Clint paused. "She's actually got a point there. Mixing liquors like that is the devil."

Michael threw his head back. "THE DEVIL!"

And when they burst out laughing again, I rolled my eyes.

"You guys have too many inside jokes," Allison said.

Michael smiled. "Now you know how Clint and I feel whenever we're around you two."

My jaw dropped open. "Hey. Hey, now. We don't have nearly that many inside jokes."

Clint nodded. "She's right, you know. We have more because we're more awesome."

The guys high-fived as Allison giggled.

"Oh, and don't you guys worry about those parties," Clint said with pride in his voice. "With someone as devilishly handsome as me in your posse, you're bound to get in."

4

———

CLINTON

After indulging in an ice cream cone that dripped down the length of my arm, I washed up. Giving Rae some space, and giving me the ability to splash some water in my face. Maybe it was the heat. Or the pressure of looming decisions, but she'd been a lot snappier lately. And it wasn't just at me. Mike asked me more than once if she was all right. And sometimes, I saw Ally's face contort in pain whenever something flew out of Rae's mouth directed right at her. I knew something deeper was going on with my girl. I knew something was bothering Rae.

I just didn't know what.

Or how to begin to fix it.

I made my way back out to the booth and slid in beside Rae. I got the feeling she didn't want to be held, so I simply sat there, watching her as she watched the ocean. In any other world, this should've felt like a utopia. A perfect world, where nothing else mattered except the two of us.

But it didn't feel like that at all.

And what was worse was that these times were quickly coming to a close. In a few weeks, we'd all be tossed to the corners of California's map. Without any way to get back and see one another easily. Mike and Ally were on their way to Stanford, of all places. Which didn't shock me one fucking bit. They were both smart. More intelligent than I could've ever been. I mean, all I was doing was working on some sort of stupid book. An idea that flourished in my head just before we all graduated.

The shit thing was, I didn't even feel comfortable telling Rae about it.

Mike knew about it. But that was it. I didn't want to tell Ally, because I knew she'd mention it to Rae. Which would then kick up yet another fight about why I didn't tell Rae first. And how the hell was I supposed to phrase that answer? *Hey, I didn't tell you about something happy going on with me because you've been miserable and I don't know why?*

Yeah. That'd get me a speeding ticket as I zoomed through Relationship City and crash-landed in Single Town.

"You guys want to take a walk along the pier?"

Mike's voice pulled us both from our trances and I nodded.

"Sure," I said.

But Rae had a different answer.

"Nah, you guys go ahead. I'm going to sit here a little while longer."

I furrowed my brow. "You don't want to go?"

She shrugged. "My legs hurt from rollerblading. I just want to rest."

"I'll carry you, if you'd like."

"Clint, it's fine."

"Piggy-back style?"

"Clint, I said I don't want to go."

"Bridal style? I know you like that one."

"Clint."

I sighed. "Rae, please. Come take a walk on the pier with me. Let's watch the sunset together."

After a long pause, she finally nodded her head. I helped her out of the booth before she jumped onto my back, and away we went. I carried her effortlessly as Ally and Mike walked in front of us. Hand in hand, unable to get enough of each other. Their arms bumped together and they kept whispering to each other. Giggling. Laughing and playing around. I missed things like that with me and Rae. I missed having those moments with her.

All I got from her nowadays were heavy sighs and rolls of her eyes.

We all walked to the pier and I set Rae down. She rollerbladed softly at my side as I kept up with my long strides. With our hands cupped, but no fingers threaded together, I felt us drifting apart. The more we walked, the further away our bodies became. Until her hand fell away from mine.

And she skated up further by herself.

Mike and Ally kept peeking back at me. Shooting me glances and looks I wanted to slap right off their fucking faces. It made me angry, seeing those glances. And I hadn't experienced that kind of anger in months. Not since the turn of the year, when things really settled down with Cecilia and myself.

Despite the bullshit Dad kept throwing our way.

We all got to the end of the pier and I gazed out over the water. I didn't bother going after Rae. If she wanted to come stand beside me, she would. I kept stealing glances over at Mike. Over at Ally. At the way they intertwined with one another. At the way Ally let Mike hold her close. I ached to have that with Rae again. I couldn't even remember the last time we'd made love.

"Hey there."

Rae's voice ripped me from my trance. She slipped her arm around mine and relief flooded my veins. As the sun slowly set, we stood there. Leaning against the pier. Taking in the sun's murky reflection in the ocean water.

Then, Ally spoke. "Things will never be the same again."

My stomach dropped as Rae sighed.

"You're right. It won't."

Mike piped up. "That doesn't mean we can't get together, though. This isn't an end."

Rae snickered. "Yeah. Just a massive change that never goes according to plan."

I slowly looked over at her. "What was your plan?"

She shrugged. "Does it matter now?"

I furrowed my brow. "It's always mattered to me, Rae."

Her eyes turned up toward mine and I saw tears in them. Pain. My girl was hurting, and it killed me inside. I wrapped my arm around her and pulled her close to me. And as her cheek fell against my chest, she sniffled. The sound was enough to cripple me. I felt like my body had been broken all over again. I kissed the top of her head, over and over. Trying to physically kiss the pain out of her body.

A body I hadn't felt against mine in weeks.

"The distance won't keep any of us apart. Not in spirit, anyway," I murmured.

Mike nodded. "He's right. We're going to have our phones. Which means video conferences. Weekends with one another."

Ally giggled. "And don't forget holidays. We're still exchanging New Year's presents like we always do."

I nodded. "Yeah. I've only gotten to do that once with you guys. I'm not missing out on another chance to do it."

Rae snickered. "I guess so."

Ally shrugged. "Well, I don't guess. I know."

Rae whispered, "At least one of us does."

I held her as close as she'd let me as her tears fell against my shirt. She cried softly as the sun set, and it felt as if the weight of the world had settled back onto my shoulders. I kept looking over at Mike's and Ally's worried faces. We were all worried for Rae. She'd shut all of us out, in some way, shape, or form. None of us knew what to do about it, either.

Especially after all we'd been through this past year.

The sun set and darkness blanketed us, forcing us to turn around. Rae skated in front of me, making a quick exit away from my embrace. I slipped my hands into my pockets. I heaved a heavy sigh. I walked behind Mike and Ally, trying not to stare as they kissed underneath the moonlight.

"You girls want a ride home?" he asked.

Ally smiled up at him. "I don't know about Rae. But I'd love one."

By the time we got to Mike's car, Rae was standing there. She had her rollerblades in hand and she looked eager to get into the stifling car. Mike unlocked the doors and we all piled in. We rode home silently, and not once did Rae let me take her hand. She didn't look at me, or talk to me, or lean in to kiss me.

The only thing that gave me hope was her climbing out behind me once we got back to my apartment.

"Rae, you staying here?" Ally asked.

She nodded. "Yeah. Just want to spend some time with Clint for a little while."

Mike leaned over. "Need me to come get you in a couple hours?"

She shook her head. "I'll catch a ride or hail a cab."

Mike looked at me before he nodded his head. Ally rolled up

her window, and they slowly pulled away. I looked down at the woman I loved. The girl who was growing into such an angry, closed-off, uncertain woman. She bit her lower lip and shuffled on her feet. Clearly waiting for me to make a move.

So I did.

"How are your feet?"

She shrugged. "Kind of sore."

"Want to go inside and soak them?"

She sighed. "I'd actually really like that."

"Sure. Yeah. Of course."

I escorted her to the apartment and let her inside. I called out for Cecilia as I shut the door, but no sound was heard. My stomach dropped for a split second. Had the door been unlocked before I walked in?

"A date?" Rae asked.

I whipped my head over to her and found her holding up a note.

"It says here that your stepmom's… on a date?"

I grinned. "Oh, damn. She must've accepted."

Rae's eyebrows rose. "She's already dating?"

I walked over, taking the note from her. "I mean, I knew this one guy was into her. Kept coming around with flowers and shit. But I didn't think she'd actually do dinner with him."

"Has the divorce been finalized?"

I nodded. "Yep. She got the official paperwork in the mail… two weeks ago?"

"Why didn't you tell me?"

I paused. "I, uh… guess it slipped my mind."

"Really, Clint? Something you and Cecilia have been battling against for months just slipped your mind?"

And when she scoffed, I felt like I'd taken three steps back.

She walked out of the kitchen and made her way to my bedroom. I didn't even get the damn note settled down onto the counter before I heard my bath running. Rae kept murmuring to herself. I stood back to try and hear what she was saying. I couldn't make it out, though. The damn water was running too loudly for me to hear.

"Clint, is it okay if I just take a bath?"

I stepped into the bathroom. "Of course. You can make yourself at home. You know that."

"Do I, though?"

She shot me a look I couldn't read. Which was pathetic, because she'd been giving me that look a lot. I watched her peel her clothes off, my hands aching to rush over her toned curves. I hadn't held her naked body against mine in weeks. I felt my cock jumping to life as her clothes fell to the floor. I wanted her. I needed her. I'd do anything to get between those legs just for a few minutes.

Which is all it would take at this point.

Rae eased herself into the bath as steam slowly filled the room. The bubbles mounted around her body, shielding it from me as she sank into the tub. I went and closed the toilet before sitting down. She leaned her head back and closed her eyes as her arms fell into the water. She sighed with relief. Much like she used to do whenever she was in my arms at night.

Then silence wrapped around us.

"The divorce was finalized a couple of weeks ago. But Dad really gave us the runaround on it."

Rae's brow furrowed. "Oh?"

I nodded. "Yeah. He came by more than a few times and kicked off arguments with Cecilia."

Her eyes popped open. "Wait a second, you never told me that."

I shrugged. "I didn't want to worry you. I took care of it. Though once I had to call the police to have him escorted off the property."

"See, this is what I don't get about you. Why are you leaving me out of the loop all of a sudden?"

"I'm not leaving you out of the loop. I'm trying to fill you in now."

"Yeah, two weeks later. How many times have we had alone time in the past two weeks?"

I paused. "Once, Rae. And that was only for a few minutes before your mother interjected and you invited her to join us for our pizza and a movie night."

She swallowed hard. "Oh."

"Yeah. So… anyway. The divorce is over. But things didn't quite go our way."

"How so?"

I sighed. "Dad fought in court that if Mom wanted her half of his money, then she should also assume half of his debt."

She sat up. "What?"

I nodded. "Yeah. His lawyer argued that if she wanted to get her hands on his money, then it was only fair to 'split up the red as well as the black' between them."

"Don't tell me the judge went for it."

"Yeah. He did."

"You know damn good and well your father paid off that fucking judge."

I shrugged. "Maybe so. But when the divorce was finalized, more than half of the money she got from my father was eaten up in past-due debt. Credit cards she racked up that he stopped paying on. Shit like that."

"Wait, the card he had to legally let her use until the divorce finalized, he stopped paying on?"

I nodded slowly. "He manipulated this every step of the way. By the time Cecilia was done paying off the debt she inherited from the divorce, she had enough money to do one of two things. Set it aside for an eventual retirement if she wanted to ever have any solace in her later years. Or live frugally without a job until she could figure something out."

"What did she pick, Clint?"

"I told her it was financially responsible for her to set that money aside. Let it grow, like a retirement fund. Maybe in a decade, if she invests wisely, it'll grow to a point where she only has to work part-time. Because that's the only kind of work she can find right now with absolutely no work history."

"And until then?"

"I've... been helping her as much as I can."

Realization washed over Rae's face. And for the first time in months, she softened toward me.

"Why the fuck didn't you just tell me this was going on?"

I shrugged. "Things between us have been rough lately. I didn't know if you were going through something at home, and I didn't want to pile on."

"Why didn't you just ask then, Clint? You never ask if I'm okay."

"I ask how you're doing all the time."

"It's not the same."

I sighed with frustration. "Then tell me how you want me to ask if you're okay. Because I ask, every day, how you're doing. And every damn day, I get the same damn answer. Just tell me what you want, Rae. And you'll have it."

"Why do I have to tell you everything? You've been with me for how long now, Clint?"

"You know, I never took you for the kind of girl to play these kinds of games. I'm not a mind-reader, and I never will be."

I reached over and turned off the water before it overflowed the tub.

"I'm not playing games, Clint. But, there's a difference between you saying *Hey, what's up?* and *Rae, you don't look so good. You okay?*"

"I asked you if you were okay over ice cream!"

"And I wasn't ready to talk about it over ice cream. Not with Allison and Michael there, anyway!"

"Well, are you ready to talk about it now? Because I'm tired of this bullshit."

"What bullshit?"

"This. The walking on eggshells, and the uncertainty. And your mood swings. And the lack of intimacy between us. And the lack of communication. You don't even act like you want to be around me anymore, Rae. Do you know how that makes me feel?"

She teared up. "I'm sorry. I didn't mean to--"

"I know you didn't mean to. My father never meant to beat the shit out of me, but he did."

She sat up straight. "Don't you fucking dare compare me to your father!"

"Then stop making me feel like my father did and talk to me. I love you, Rae. Now cut the bullshit and tell me what's wrong. Because I know something is."

5

RAELYNN

I slumped back down into the bubbles. I didn't know how to answer that question. My heartrate ticked up and my eyes wouldn't focus. My hands shook underneath the water and it became hard to breathe. I closed my eyes and it felt as if the world were tilting around me. Over and over, trying to make me sick. And still, all my body wanted to do was sink underneath the water and fall asleep. Just give in to the silent fight raging within me.

I'd felt like this for weeks.

A black pit opened up in my gut, swallowing whatever fear I had. Leaving me with… nothing. An emptiness inside I didn't know how to explain. How was I supposed to look at the boy I loved and tell him I didn't feel anything? Tell him I didn't know anything? Tell him all I wanted to do was fall asleep and never wake up?

I couldn't put my finger on it.

All I knew was that the mere idea of school made me tremble with nerves.

I didn't want to go to this orientation. I didn't want my friends coming with me. I just wanted to stay home and bury myself in my own misery. But every time I thought about staying with my mother, more of that emptiness popped up. Sleep had eluded me for days. It grew hard to think straight. And spitting out the fact that I was living in a dorm room for the first semester of college made me want to puke.

College.

Whose fucking idea was that, anyway?

"Rae?"

"Can you hear me?"

"Rae, talk to me. You've got me worried."

Clint's voice finally pulled me from my trance and I drew in a sharp breath.

"Yeah, yeah. I can hear you."

"You're trembling, Rae. The fuck's going on?"

I snickered. "You're yelling at me. That's what's going on."

He paused. "I'm sorry. I'm just frustrated."

"Yeah, well, me too."

"Tell me what to do."

"I don't know what to do, Clint!"

My voice rose with such fervor that it echoed off the corners of the walls. Clint flinched away from me and I slid my head underneath the water. Underneath the bubbles. Relief. The water provided relief. It muffled the sounds of the world around me and muted the screaming inside my head. I felt as if I were floating. As if I weighed nothing. As if I were nothing, and that was all right. Because even in my nothingness, I was still exactly where I needed to be.

When my lungs started burning, I came up for air. And when I wiped the soapy water from my eyes, Clint was gone. No longer did he sit on the toilet, begging me to talk. Instead, I heard him stripping his clothes down in his bedroom. Going to bed, most likely. I needed to get out of the tub and get home anyway. I needed to sort through all this shit before I talked to him about it. I knew he was feeling out of place, anyway. Being the only one of the four of us not attending college of any sort. Floating around from place to place. Not really knowing where he belonged.

I understand that feeling all too well.

"Up."

I whipped my eyes up and saw Clint's naked body for the first time in weeks.

"Wh--what?"

He motioned with his hand. "Up. Scoot up."

"Clint, I don't--"

"Up, Rae. Now."

Curling my knees toward my chest, I moved myself forward. Clint stepped into the hot bath behind me, hissing softly as he eased himself down. Steam still rose from the water. The bubbles sloshed over the edge. His hands fell to my shoulders, making me jump as he guided me against him. My naked back was seated against his strong chest. A feeling I hadn't indulged in weeks.

It brought tears to my eyes as his arms slid around my waist.

"Just try for me, please," he murmured.

I sniffled. "I don't know if I can."

"Just try. That's all I'm asking. Even if it's jumbled."

So, with a deep breath in, I tried for him.

"I'm worried that when things change, it won't be as good. Or maybe I won't fit in. Or maybe college is a mistake."

He kissed the top of my head. "Keep going. You're doing great."

I sighed. "Home has been terrible. And yet, it's all I know."

"Why is home still terrible?"

"Mom stopped looking for a job months ago. She just… floats around during the day. Asking me for money. Telling me to take care of this and that. Telling me how proud she is of me for taking care of our family."

He paused. "Wait, you're paying your mother's bills?"

I shrugged. "What else am I going to do? She stopped looking for a job and bills had to get paid somehow. I've drained almost all the money I got selling stuff. I-I-I mean, D.J. tried coming back again and I was so fucking happy with her for turning him away. But all she did was turn to me."

"Rae, why didn't you--?"

I groaned. "Because I didn't want to burden you, Clint. You've got your own shit going on. I know how hard your father made this divorce. I didn't want to bog you down."

"You're not bogging me down. I want to help you. I want to be here for you like you're here for me."

"And I get that. I do. It's just--"

He held me tighter. "It's just what, Rae?"

I sniffled. "I don't know. It's just… so much. All at once. I thought I could trust Mom with my finances and shit. I told her about my college plans. Getting my own place. Maybe with you. And she was happy about it, until she wasn't. She started asking for money here and there. Money for milk. Groceries. Picking up the tab if we went out to lunch. Then it just kind of grew."

"And you didn't feel as if you could say no."

I shrugged. "She's my mom, Clint. She was there for me after Dad left. And yeah, she's not perfect. But at least she tries. You know?"

"You don't owe her for that."

"Yes, I do."

"No, you don't, Rae. She's supposed to give that to you because you're her child. You owe her nothing."

"Yeah, well. I don't have anything else to sell off to recuperate the money. So, I'm back to scraping pennies off the ground and working as much as I can at the grocery store while hiding how much I'm working so Mom doesn't keep asking for more fucking money."

"Is that why you want to live in the dorms for the first semester?"

I paused for a long time before I spoke.

"If I can find a job on campus to work, not having rent or anything will put more money in my pocket for a place, yeah."

He kissed the back of my head. "You don't want to stay on campus, do you?"

I shook my head. "No."

"Why didn't you just tell me that, then?"

"Because living off campus is my idea and you shouldn't be financially responsible for my idea."

"That's bullshit. Do you even hear how much bullshit that--?"

I sighed with frustration. "I don't care if it's bullshit, okay? I just--do you know how envious I am of Michael and Allison right now? I mean, full fucking rides? Allison's parents paying for her place off campus? Michael, going to school right along with her? I mean, fucking hell. Their parents are setting them up to succeed while my mother's so sad because her goddamn meal ticket's leaving!"

"You don't really think your mother feels that way, right?"

"How the hell else would she feel, Clint? Tell me. How the fuck is she gonna get money if I'm not the one putting it in her hands? Because I'm sorry, but the woman is never going to get a job if she doesn't have to."

"Then maybe you leaving will force her to."

I snickered. "Or she'll find some other man to slap her around before paying her bills. And that'll be my fault."

"Rae, your mother's inability to live her life in a productive way isn't your fault. Your home is toxic, just like mine was. You need to leave, and college is your way out."

Out, and away from you. "Yeah, whatever."

He scoffed. "You sound like me last summer."

I felt him nuzzling against the back of my head and it made my body ignite with life.

"You have to put your foot down with your mother," he murmured.

I rolled my eyes. "Easier said than done."

"You're not responsible for her, Rae. I need you to hear me when I say that."

"Yeah, I hear you. But it's not that simple. So long as I'm living with her, I'm going to be held responsible until she starts blaming me for bills going unpaid because I'm being selfish with my money. I'm responsible there, just like you're responsible here."

"That's different."

"How the hell is that any different?"

I turned around to look at him, but he didn't have any answer for me.

"Things will change, Rae. All relationships do over time. But change isn't always a bad thing. I mean, look at me. I've changed."

Yeah, I figured you didn't have an answer. "You have, yeah."

"And has it been a good change? Huh?"

He cupped my cheek and a soft smile crossed my face.

"It has been a good change, Clint. I'm so proud of you."

"I mean, I used to pick on you relentlessly."

I rolled my eyes. "Don't remind me."

He grinned. "Calling you names. Sticking my fingers in your food. Calling you out in the middle of the cafeteria."

"You're about to make a quip about se--?"

"And now, I can't get you out from underneath me. Who'da thunk it, huh?"

My head fell forward as laughter rolled from my lips. Genuine, unadulterated belly laughter.

"You're so insane, Clint."

He gripped my chin, lifting my eyes. "And you're a marvel, Rae. You've changed my life for the better. I went from your bully to your partner. I get to hold you in my arms. Be your confidant. I've got friends in Allison and Michael now because of you."

His lips pressed softly against mine and I sank against his naked body.

"Everything will work out, Rae. I promise. And I'll be next to you the entire time."

Oh, thank fuck. "Promise?"

And as his hands meandered along my naked skin, more water sloshed over the edge.

"Promise promise, Rae."

6

CLINTON

Holy fuck, it'd been a long time since she kissed me that way. With her tongue softly falling into my mouth as my lips parted. My hands slid along her back, running warm water along her skin as bubbles popped around us. She moaned, and oh, how I growled. I missed her moans. I missed her body. I missed everything about her. I gripped her hips, pulling her into my lap, and she straddled me as more water trickled over the edge.

Making her giggle against my lips.

"We're going to make a mess, Clint."

I fisted her hair. "God, I fucking hope so."

I kissed her so furiously our teeth clattered together. Her arms draped around me, grinding against my quickly-rising cock. Weeks. It had been weeks since I'd filled her. Fucked her. Made love to her. And as her bars finally came back down, I felt her letting me in again. Baring her heart and soul for me again. Even if she couldn't make sense of it. Her hands ran down my chest and I felt my skin puckering at her touch. She sucked on my lower lip, causing my cock to jump as it fell between her pussy folds.

Where she stroked it softly.

"Such a tease," I grunted.

She sighed. "It's been so long."

"I've missed you. I've missed you so fucking much."

"I'm sorry, Clint. I'm just so scared."

I shook my head and cupped her cheeks. She sure as hell had nothing to apologize for. I brought her back in for a kiss before my arms cloaked her back. I held her to me, feeling her heart fluttering against my chest as my legs contracted with joy. I smiled against her lips and she giggled. I helped her to her feet before guiding her out of the tub as we slid across the bathroom floor.

Before crashing into the wall.

"Rae!"

She threw her head back in laughter as she fell against me.

"Rae. Are you okay? Look at me."

Her eyes met mine and she smiled. Her eyes sparkled, and damn it, it had been months since I'd seen that. I slid my thumb over her cheek. She turned her head and kissed the pad of my finger. I traced my thumb over her lower lip, watching it softly pull down before flipping back into place.

"I love you," I murmured.

Her lips journeyed to mine. "I love you too, Clint."

I wrapped her up in my arms and carried her the rest of the way. Our lips fell together once more as my eyes screwed shut. I walked us out of the bathroom, keeping my balance as her legs wrapped around me. And as my cock wept for joy to have her naked against me again, we toppled to my mattress.

Not giving a fuck whether or not my blankets got wet.

I kissed down her neck and felt her pulse fluttering against my lips. I nibbled against her shoulder, losing myself in her as my pulse quickened. I knew things were about to change. For better, and for worse. My friends were going off to college--my girlfriend, too--and I'd be stuck back here, still trying to find odd jobs and hoping I could keep finding shit to sell to make ends meet. But the taste of Rae's skin pushed that all away. As I kissed down her body, venturing straight to that delectable pussy of hers, I let all those insecurities fade away. All those fears.

So I could devour her the way I always did.

"Oh, Clint."

I growled. "Oh, Rae."

"Shit, shit, shit. Like that. Ooooh, Clint."

She whimpered as our fingers threaded together. I tugged on her arms, bowing her back as her hips fell closer to my face. I lapped my tongue up her slit. I flicked her clit before sucking it between my lips. Her tits bounced for me as she rolled. Her juices dripped down my neck the more I licked. I drank down every last drop of her, wanting nothing more than to feel her come against my face.

"Cl--int."

And when she choked out my name, I got what I wanted.

Her body vibrated as her pussy pulsed against my lips. I dug my tongue against her clit, feeling it pulse with every throb of her walls. She rutted against my skin. My stubble. My mouth. Taking what she wanted before she collapsed.

The second I stood, she quickly slid off the bed.

"Rae, what are--fuck!"

"Mmm."

She swallowed me down as my hands fell to the mattress. My eyes widened and the animal inside me rattled within its cage. Her throat closed around me, taunting my balls. Teasing my body. Building me close to my end. Electricity washed through my veins. My eyes rolled back as she hollowed out her cheeks. I forced myself to stand. I slipped my fingers through her wet hair. And as I hung on, I pumped her lips up and down my cock.

"That's it. Suck it down, gorgeous."

She giggled around my girth and my eyes rolled back. I teetered, causing her to wrap her arms around my hips. She fisted my ass cheeks, curling her nails into my skin. And when my eyes popped open, I fucked her face. Ravenously hard, feeling her gagging around me. My breathing came in short pants. I felt sweat mingling with the water as it trickled down my back.

But, just before I popped, I pulled her off me.

"On the bed. Now."

She scrambled to her feet and threw herself onto my bed, beckoning for me with her legs already spread. I fell into her arms and her soft body welcomed me home. I wasted no time sliding inside her, feeling her walls cradling me as her nails raked down my back.

"Clint. Oh, Clint. I'm sorry. I'm sorry. I'm sorry."

I kissed her neck. "It's okay. I've got you. I'll always be here."

"Clint."

Her whimpers were both desperate and wanton. I snapped my hips against hers, holding myself up with my hands. I gazed into her eyes, watching them roll back in pleasure. Her tits jumped for me while her skin flushed, painting the most beautiful picture I'd ever seen. Her lips puckered and I kissed them. Her hands cupped my cheeks and I held my position. I swiveled my hips, stoking that fire in my gut as her walls clung to me. Pulling me deeper. Massaging me harder.

Until I started pounding into her body.

"That's it. That's it. Clint, you always know. You always know. You always know."

"Mine. You're mine, Rae. Forever. Always. You're stuck."

"Yes. Yes. I wanna be. I wanna be. Clint, please. I'm gonna come. I'm gonna come."

Her pussy clamped down around me and my knees went weak. I fell against her body, feeling her pull me down as she moaned out into the room. Her pussy pulled me deeper. Her arms held me tighter. And as I buried my face into the crook of her neck, grunts poured from my lips.

As her end triggered my own.

"Oh, fuck Rae. I've missed this."

She shivered beneath me as my legs jumped. My cock spilled inside her with her juices flooding my balls. I felt spent. Emotionally. Physically. Spiritually. All I wanted was for Rae to stay, to sleep next to me tonight so I could wake up with her in my arms.

But, when she sniffled, I quickly rose up.

"Rae?"

She giggled breathlessly. "I'm so sorry. I don't know why I'm crying."

I smiled softly as I brushed her tears away.

"It's okay. It really is."

She snickered. "I just feel so stupid."

I shook my head. "You're not stupid. You're scared. Confused. A bit hurt. All at once. It's natural, and if there's anyone that understands, it's me."

She paused. "Clint?"

"Yeah, gorgeous?"

"Could I stay with you tonight?"

My heart swelled with joy. "I'd love nothing more."

We wiggled ourselves up toward the pillows before I tucked us in. Pulling up the covers, I laid them across her, feeling her wiggle back against me. Her ass pressed against my pelvis. Her back, seated against my chest. I smiled as a feeling of comfort and reassurance fell over me. Like it always did whenever I got to hold Rae in my arms.

She was my home. And I never wanted that to change.

It won't change, if I have anything to do about it.

I kissed Rae's shoulder as her breathing evened out. Her chest rose and fell. And soon her breaths became soft snores. I smiled while she slept, nestled against me. Underneath the covers of my bed. But I still had a mess to clean up. So, reluctantly, I slipped away from her.

"I'll be back soon," I whispered.

I walked back into my bathroom and unplugged the tub. I let it drain as I pulled out towels, tossing them onto the wet floor. I mopped it up as much as I could before I turned on the fan. I gathered everything wet--including our clothes--and walked it out to the dryer. I tossed everything in with a nice dryer sheet before getting it all started. Then I turned on my bedroom fan to try and help dry up what was still damp in the bathroom.

And as I curled up next to Rae for the night, I smiled.

Thankful to have her in my arms for the night again.

7

RAELYNN

As I scanned groceries through my kiosk, the beep forced me to register my future. I only had one more week left of working here before I was done. For good. I had decided to take the last couple weeks of summer vacation to pack and enjoy the road trip with my friends and Clint. Even if it meant staring down the barrel of some decisions I knew would make life with my mother a living nightmare. While I wanted to spend quality time with her--and I would--inevitably, I knew what topic would come up.

The topic of money.

It was my mother's favorite thing to discuss.

"I can pay you back once one of these applications go through."

Yeah. The applications she put in months ago.

"I'm doing some odd jobs for people around the neighborhood. So I can carry the light bill if you get the water bill."

Yeah, except she paid it late and I had to foot the late fee because she couldn't afford it.

"Why don't we go out to lunch? There's a great Mexican place across town, and I know how much you love Mexican."

"No, you love Mexican, Mom. I enjoy Italian."

"What was that, sweetie?"

I whipped my eyes up and saw an elderly woman standing in front of me. I smiled at her and took the money from her hand, then charged her out. I counted her change out in her hand before bidding her a good evening. Then I silently chastised myself.

I had to stay out of my mind so I could get through this damn shift.

Rationally, I knew I was being an idiot about this. School really wasn't all that far away. And all I had to do was keep telling Mom that. I needed to help her put in some applications. Or simply leave. Like Clint told me to do. I guess our situations were a bit different. Mom was expecting me to contribute and Cecilia didn't have that same expectation of him. I just--

I wanted so badly for Mom to change.

I wanted her to be the mom I knew she could be. The mom I knew she wanted to be. I mean, yeah. I was proud of her for keeping up with her therapy appointments. But things had stopped changing. It was almost like she reverted. Or morphed into a similarly toxic version of someone different.

I don't know. I was confusing myself at this point.

Just focus on work. Then on packing. Then on the road trip.

"I can do that," I whispered.

"So! Ready for the next big step?"

Pauline jumped up to my register and it snapped me out of my trance.

"What?" I asked.

She giggled. "The next step, silly. College? You know, the big leagues?"

I felt homesick just thinking about. "Yeah. Sure."

"Oh, come on. It won't be that bad. What are you going to be studying?"

I sighed. "Pauline, I'm really not--"

"Please, please, please, please, please?"

Why was she hired again? "English."

"Oh, nice. Whatcha wanna do with it?"

"I want to teach elementary school kids."

"Shouldn't you be getting an education degree, then?"

"Those classes don't come into play until junior year. Still have to declare a major other than 'education' until then."

"Gotta have a specialty. Got it. Nice."

I nodded. "Yeah. Nice."

"So are you excited?"

I sighed. "Not really."

"Why not? I've heard college is great. Lots of parties. Lots of boys. Lots of friends to make and food to eat. Sounds like paradise, if you ask me."

Not when you're losing friends over it. "I'm sure it does."

"Have you always wanted to teach kids?"

"No."

"Have you always wanted to do English?"

"No."

"So, what made you make that decision with your degree?"

I sighed. "I don't know. It just seemed right."

Pauline nodded. "Nice."

In truth, I didn't know if I was making the right decisions. But I did enjoy English. It was the only subject in school I didn't hate. And kids were fantastic. So why not combine them? Seemed logical enough. I didn't have any other passions. I mean, other than the graphic design. But I didn't figure out until I enrolled in this fucking college that they only had a graphic design minor. Not major.

My fucking luck.

I don't know, I felt pressured into going to college. With all this confusion, I heavily leaned toward taking a year off there for a bit. Staying behind. Hanging out with Clint. Continuing to work at the grocery store and helping Mom with the house. But the scholarships I ended up snagging paid for my first year of college if I enrolled this year. I couldn't postpone them, or defer them. I had to use them or lose them.

Talk about extra pressure when trying to figure out my life.

I mean, I hadn't even turned nineteen yet! What was the rush? Why did I have to have everything figured out by the time I was eighteen? That didn't make any sense. In some respects, I still wasn't seen as an adult. Sure, legally I could sign my name on shit. But that was it. I still couldn't rent a car, or a hotel room, or drink. Was I really adult enough to be making decisions that would affect the rest of my life?

How fucked up was that?

But Clint had a good point. Everything was a chance. A risk. And I could either take it or not. This degree felt the safest, along with my graphic design minor. So, why not? And despite Mom not wanting me to leave her, ever, she was excited about me wanting to pursue something with my 'doodles,' as she called them.

It was selfish of me to ask for more than that.

"All right, spit it out," Pauline said.

I blinked. "Spit what out?"

"What's bothering you so badly. You're zoning out in your shifts. You're not paying attention to the customers. I know a distracted person when I see them. My father's always distracted."

I nodded slowly. "I'm sorry."

"No, no, no! Not a bad thing. Just an observation. There's something on your mind. Why don't you talk about it?"

I shrugged. "Don't want to."

"I think it might help if you do, though."

I sighed. "Pauline, I really--"

"Come on. You know you can trust me. I'm your co-worker. I see you during your shifts. We talk on our breaks. I've got your back, girl."

Fine, whatever. "I just don't know why I have to have it all figured out now is all."

"Oh?"

"Yeah. I mean--I'm only eighteen, right?"

"Right."

"So what's the issue with taking a year off? Why do I have to be pressured to take scholarship money now or lose it forever? Am I not worth their money in a year? What's up with that?"

"You make a good point."

"And, fucking hell, I'm leaving the only place I've ever known. I'm leaving my friends behind. My mom. My boyfriend. And I don't even know if he wants to come with me! Or meet up with me eventually! For all I know, I go off to college and that's that."

She whistled lowly. "Sounds like you need to talk with him."

"Yeah, well. He's got his own shit going on. And don't get me started about leaving this job. I don't even have a job on that end yet. What if I don't find one? It's not like my mother has money to give me. If anything, I'm giving *her* money!"

"Mooching mothers. That's some shit right there."

"Yeah. It is. And to top it all off? I don't even know if I'm going to want to teach once I get out of school. I might graduate with this expensive degree and then want to do something completely different. Something with graphic design and art. I'll really be shit out of luck, then."

"Why don't you do graphic whatever instead?"

"The college I'm going to only has a minor in it."

She nodded. "Well, fuck."

"Yeah. Fuck."

I sighed, but with relief. It felt good dumping this on to someone instead of letting it swim around in my head. But why was it easier to talk to my annoying twenty-two-year-old coworker than it was my friends? Or Clint?

"You want my advice?" she asked.

I shrugged. "Try your best."

"I think you still have plenty of time to change your mind. I mean, even if you decide at the beginning to pursue English with education or whatever, your first two semesters are going to be used to get requirements out of the way. Math. Science. Shit like that. And if you figure out that school isn't for you at all, you can drop out and get most of your money back if you don't complete the semester."

I blinked. "Don't I pay for the whole year upfront, though?"

She shook her head. "Nope. They bill you by semester."

Huh.

"Look, I've been where you are. I went to school to become a vet tech. I mean, my entire life I dreamt of working with animals. Night after night. I thought it was my life's calling, you know. And then I got into school and realized I couldn't handle sick animals. Too emotionally taxing. And gross."

I snickered. "So what did you do?"

She shrugged. "I'm in the middle of a career shift. I took this job a couple months ago to help out with money and bills. And I'm back home with my parents while I take a condensed program to become a dental hygienist."

"And that's what you want to do?"

"More than anything. It's a nice balance of not dealing with sick people, not dealing with sick animals, and pulling a nice paycheck."

I nodded. "Congratulations."

"The point I'm trying to make is that figuring out what's important to you takes time. And even if you do feel locked into college, it can always change. Keep focusing on getting good grades. Apply for those scholarships. And when you stumble across what you want to do with your life, you'll know. Deep down."

I smiled. "Thanks. I appreciate that."

She patted my hand. "I like helping people. And I like working with kids, too. Like you. That's my specialty going into my dental hygienist program. But there are stepping stones I still have to follow. I'm only twenty-two, though. And you're only eighteen. Find your stepping stones, Rae, and take them one day at a time."

I felt a weight lift off my shoulders. "This means a lot. Thank you."

"And don't be so damn hard on yourself. Switching directions isn't a big deal. It's your life. Live it how you see fit. Okay? Promise me."

I nodded. "Okay. I promise."

"Good. Now, take care of these customers coming down the aisles. They're headed straight for you."

I rang up the customers with a smile on my face. But not a forced smile. Not like my smiles had been. It felt a little more effortless this time around. And I kept stealing glances at Pauline. As annoying as she was at times, I found her words comforting. I'm glad she took the time to prod at me until I talked. Because I needed to hear what she had to say.

And hopefully, as time passed, I could become as brave as her.

Ready to take on the world, no matter what anyone else thought of my path.

8

———

CLINTON

I was thankful Cecilia let me borrow her car for the night. Because I really wanted to pick Rae up from work before this dinner with her mother tonight. I wasn't sure I wanted to go after everything Rae told me about her, though. I wasn't sure I'd be able to keep my mouth shut. What she was doing was wrong. Bleeding money from Rae was wrong. And I wanted to put my two cents in on the matter.

But I'd promised Rae I wouldn't say anything.

I pulled into a parking space at the front of the line and sat. I turned up the music, bobbing my head as I watched Rae through the window. She stood there, wiping down her register. And I saw someone new walking up to her. The girl looked like she worked there. But I didn't recognize her. And when Rae looked over at her, she smiled. Genuinely. With that light in her eyes.

It was good to see that light coming back.

I listened to music and mouthed the words as I waited for her to come out. And when she came out through the automatic doors, I beeped my horn and flashed my lights, rolled my window down and waved at her, finally catching her attention. But when she looked up at me, her smile didn't light up.

Not like it did with her friend inside.

Huh.

"Ready for dinner?" I asked.

She walked around and got in the car, sighing.

"As ready as I'll ever be."

I took her hand. "Are you sure you don't want me to—"

She shook her head quickly. "No. Don't say a word. It's not your place."

"Since when is it not my place to defend you against people taking advantage of you?"

"Since that person is my mother who likes you."

I shrugged. "I don't care if she likes me. All I care about is how she treats you."

"Well, I care if she likes you. So don't screw that up tonight, okay?"

I paused. "I'm sorry. I didn't mean to press a button."

"Can you just drive, please?"

I pulled out of the parking lot and we rode back to her house. Silence fell between us, and I hated it. After the night we'd spent together this past weekend, I figured things might change. That her attitude toward me would change. That her opinion of the things I did might change. But after we woke up the next morning, it felt as if nothing ever happened, like we hadn't made passionate love before falling asleep beside one another. She couldn't wait to get home. She didn't even stick around for a cup of coffee before she rushed out the front door.

Like I was nothing but a little booty call that got too out of hand.

I hated all of this.

"I'm sorry," she said.

I drew in a silent breath. "It's okay."

"No, it's not okay. Nothing about me is okay right now."

"We'll get through it. Like we always do."

"We've been trying to get through it for a while, now."

I came to a stop at a light. "Can I be blunt?"

She nodded. "Sure."

"Is this you trying to break up with me?"

She whipped her eyes to mine. "No. Hell, no! Why would you think that?"

"Just seemed like the perfect wind-up before the swing, that's all."

She took my hand. "I'm not breaking up with you, Clint. I just-

-know I'm not okay right now. And I don't know how to get okay again."

I brought her hand to my lips for a kiss. "Just stop shutting me out. You're doing it all the time. Like I told you, even if your thoughts are jumbled, I want to hear them. I want to help you work through them. Like you did for me."

"I'm not good at this, am I?"

I chuckled. "You're really not. But that doesn't mean you can't get better."

"Sorry."

"Don't be. You're used to being everyone's rock. And sometimes, a rock that has been standing on its own for too long forgets how to lean against another structure. Because it's too dug down into its ways."

She paused. "Where in the world did you pull that from?"

The book I'm writing. "Just came up with it."

She giggled. "You should write it down somewhere. Use it in one of your stories."

Just tell her about the book, Clint. "Maybe I will."

As we pulled into her driveway, guilt flooded my stomach. Here I was, telling her to be open with me when I couldn't even tell her about my latest venture. Writing my own book, for once. A dream gone wild one night that spurred on the daydreaming I did of an entire world beyond our eyes. Fantasy. Epic fantasy, with sword fights and magical powers and dragons galore. I'd never been so eager to write in all my life. Every night, I recorded conversations I wanted to happen between my characters. Every morning, I took my ass to the coffee shop and used their computers to type up my character's next moves.

"Ready to go in?" Rae asked.

I nodded. "Ready when you are."

I'd tell her in due time.

When she wasn't struggling so much.

The two of us walked inside and the smells of enchiladas wafted underneath my nose. I heard Luciana humming in the kitchen as I closed the door behind me. My hand slid to Rae's lower back. I guided her into the kitchen. Though, it didn't shock me that I felt some resistance on her end.

"Perfect timing! Sit, sit. I'm almost done with the rice. Can I get you a drink, Clint? Water? Soda? Juice? Milk?"

I chuckled at Luciana. "Water's fine. Thank you."

Her mother smiled. "And you, honey?"

Rae paused. "Uh… soda?"

Her mother giggled. "You sure about that?"

Rae murmured. "I'm not sure about anything."

The words caught me off-guard as her mother continued to whirl around the kitchen.

I rubbed her back after we sat down at the table. Rae kept her eyes forward, even as her mother set her soda down in front of her. She looked almost dazed. Like she wanted to be anywhere but here. I was worried about her. Especially after that comment.

She wasn't sure about anything?

Did she also mean us?

"So! How was work tonight, honey?"

Rae nodded. "It was good. Five more shifts, and all."

Her mother sat down. "How do you feel about that?"

Rae shrugged. "It is what it is. Time to move on, I guess."

Her mother paused. "You could always take some time off, you know. Postpone school. Stick around here with your old mom for a bit."

I butted in. "She's already put in her two weeks."

Rae cast me a glance. "I'm just taking it a day at a time."

Her mother sighed. "Well, know my doors are always open for you. Okay, honey?"

So long as you can get your hands on her wallet.

We all dished up our food, but the table was pretty silent. Very tense. Definitely not the kind of family dinner anyone wanted to have. Rae's mother kept peeking over at me and winking. And whenever Rae looked up, her mother patted her shoulder. Rubbed her back. Tried to comfort her daughter.

"You sure there's nothing you want to talk about?" Luciana asked.

Rae sighed. "Well, I did have this conversation with my co-worker today."

I paused. "That new one I saw you with?"

She slowly looked over at me. "Yeah. Pauline."

Her mother butted in. "What did you two talk about?"

Rae cleared her throat. "Just about college. Decisions. You know, how she thought she wanted to be one thing, but is now making a life change. Or career change. Or something like that."

I nodded. "What did she want to be?"

Rae snickered. "A vet tech. Until she realized she couldn't handle sick pets."

I chuckled. "Wait, really?"

She nodded. "Yeah, really. So, now she's living back with her parents and finishing up a dental hygienist degree. Says it's the happiest she's ever been."

Her mother scoffed. "And she's working at the grocery store to make ends meet? Doesn't sound like much of a life."

Rae licked her lips. "It's admirable when someone wants to work for something better, Mom."

Her mother shrugged. "I don't know. Seems kitschy to me."

I blinked. "Working toward a life that makes someone strong and independent is kitschy?"

Rae tossed me another look. "I found the conversation very uplifting, actually. Really reassuring. You know, just in case I'm making the wrong decision."

Her mother put her hand over Rae's forearm. "Which is why I'm telling you to take a year off. Come on, Rae. What's a year going to do? If anything, it'll only reaffirm what you're doing now and you can go off to college with confidence."

I sighed. "Or, she can follow the path she's leading now and make herself stronger through facing her fears."

Rae pursed her lips. "I'm not scared. I'm just wary. There's a difference."

Her mother sighed. "It's okay to be scared if you are. All the more reason to take the year. You've got a home here. You've got a job at the grocery store. You've got Clint here."

I butted in. "Don't bring me into this as a reason for her to stay behind."

Rae closed her eyes. "Will you two stop it?"

I leaned back into my chair as her mother drew in a deep breath. Then Rae's cheeks puffed out with her own heavy sigh.

"It was just a nice conversation. Nothing more. Nothing less. Sorry I brought it up."

Her mother smiled softly. "And thank you for sharing it with us. All I want you to know is that you have options. My door will always be open to you. On the one hand, I hate that this girl wasted so much time and money figuring out what she wanted to do. But, on the other hand, it's her journey. And I can respect that."

"Thanks, Mom."

Her mother nodded. "Just know that the worst that could happen is that a year off changes your mind. Which isn't a bad thing. And best case scenario? You go back to school next fall with the reassurance you need."

"I know, Mom."

"And if you stay on this path? There are a lot of very lucky children right now being born who will have you as their teacher. As their guiding light."

"I appreciate that, Mom."

Luciana was so hard to pin down. On the one hand, she had pride in her voice when it came to talking about Rae. And on the other? She was trying too hard to get her to stay behind. Rae was so much bigger than this place. So much better. And the idea of her mother having one more year of influence on the girl I loved made me sick. I didn't want her turning out like her mother. Just like I didn't want to turn out like my damn father. She deserved better than that. She deserved a better life than this. Better than the dilapidated house and the men coming and going from her mother's bedroom and her mother begging for money like a fucking child.

But I saw the way Rae's shoulders slumped. Something was up, and I knew it wasn't just about the money. Or the decisions. Or going off to college. Something else was in the works here, and that worried me.

What hadn't she told me yet?

Had she told that co-worker of hers?

"Well, let's all dig in. This food's going to get cold if we don't eat it."

Luciana started eating, but Rae only poked around at her food. Pushing it around to make it look as if she'd eaten it. Her mother didn't pay her any mind, but I did. I saw the sadness on Rae's face. The confusion behind her eyes. The way she hunched. The way she kept her eyes down. The way her smile slowly sank as she tried to keep it plastered on her face.

Her façade was breaking.

And that broke my heart.

She never needed a façade before. Why does she need one now?

I had so many questions I wanted to ask her. So many things I needed to know. Did she feel she could confide in this Pauline girl more than me? Her own boyfriend? Did I need to take a step out of the picture until she got through her first semester of college? Hell, her first year? Was there something I wasn't doing that she needed from me? Did she need some space?

I'd give her anything at this point if it made her smile. If it made her eyes light up like I saw with her co-worker earlier.

Fucking hell, I missed gazing into that smile.

Especially when I was the cause of it.

9

***

RAELYNN

"Thanks for dinner, Mom."

I nodded. "And thanks for the to-go for Cecilia."

Luciana waved at us. "Tell her I said she can stop by anytime she likes! I'd like to catch up with her."

Clint snickered. "I'll let her know. Promise."

"Bye, Mom!"

I tugged him out the front door and breathed a sigh of relief when the door slammed shut. We made our way for Cecilia's car, thankful we had that instead of having to walk around. Thunder rumbled in the distance and I felt the temperature dropping. Pretty soon, the world would open up above our heads and dump water on us all night.

And I didn't want to be home for it.

"Want to go for a ride?" Clint asked.

I smiled. "I'd love to."

He opened my car door for me. "Where to?"

I shrugged. "Honestly? Anywhere that isn't here."

I climbed up into the car and he closed my door. Lightning flashed across the sky and I saw my mother's silhouette at the window. She watched as Clint and I pulled away. I felt her eyes following us up the road, watching us until we disappeared from sight.

Fucking hell, I was glad to be away from that woman again.

"Are you hungry for dessert?"

I shook my head. "Not really."

"What about some coffee?"

I shrugged. "Probably not the best idea when it's nine at night."

"So, we park and talk? Maybe with some snacks?"

I snickered. "You didn't eat enough at dinner, did you?"

He sighed. "Can you blame me for wanting to get out of there?"

I giggled as he pulled out onto the main road. We drove through a fast food place and he got himself a soda along with two large french fries. I shook my head at him when he offered me one. He set it in my lap anyway.

"I know you didn't eat dinner. The fries are there for when you stop being stubborn."

I snickered. "Gee. Thanks. My hero."

He held his french fries between his legs so he could eat and drive. And when he pulled into the parking lot of the abandoned park, I smiled. Brightly. I looked over at the bench where Clint found me that night. Found me wallowing in my own self pity before I came to understand why he was the way he was. I plucked a french fry from its container and nibbled on it. One, and then another. I picked up Clint's large soda and took a sip, feeling him grinning at me.

"What?" I asked.

He shook his head. "Nothing. You just look beautiful tonight."

I blushed at his words. "So much has changed, you know."

He nodded slowly. "Yeah. I know."

"Who would've predicted the change in our lives after you found me on that park bench over there?"

"Oh, is that the bench? I couldn't remember."

I shoved him playfully and he laughed.

"Come on. Quit being a dick."

He winked at me. "Maybe I do remember."

I snickered. "A complete accident changing our lives. I'd never experienced anything like it, up until that point."

"Back when you were still nerdy Rae Cleaver."

"Yeah, and back when I thought you were still a jerk."

He smirked. "Hey, you were the stuck-up know-it-all. I'm not the only guilty one in this party."

I shrugged. "Not my fault I know everything."

He laughed, and the effortlessness of my own laughter took me by surprise. Clint leaned toward me, his salted lips pressing against mine. And I loved it. I cupped his cheek, keeping him there as our lips lingered, our tongues softly exploring. I wanted it to stay this way forever. This carefree. This exciting. This easy.

I didn't want things to ever change.

His forehead fell against mine and I panted softly. Catching my breath, my eyes opened. And I found him staring at me. He gripped my chin softly, causing me to gasp. His gaze kept hold of mine as he tilted my head up further, exposing my face to him. Exposing my breaking façade as he stared straight into my soul.

I still didn't know how he did that.

"Rae."

His voice was steady. Even. My breath hitched in my throat. I'd miss that. I'd miss hearing him say my name like that. Surely, I wouldn't hear it as much once I went off to college. I wouldn't feel his touch enough or kiss him enough or sleep next to him enough. It killed me, not getting a place with him. It killed me, him not coming to college with me. I didn't want to leave him behind in this town. In this small slice of hell we somehow made our home in. He deserved so much better. So much more than this life.

And it angered me that he wouldn't reach for it.

"Yeah?" I asked breathlessly.

His eyes danced between mine as his tongue darted out to lick his lips.

"Something's bothering you. What is it?"

I bit down onto my bottom lip to keep from kissing him. Because if he pushed me away from that kiss, I wouldn't be able to bear it. I looked away, trying to shake his grip. But he held my chin harder, keeping my face pointed toward his.

"Clint--"

"Stop fighting me and look at me, Raelynn."

I snickered. "Don't use my full name like that."

"I'll do whatever it takes to get your attention."

"Even doing something I don't like, *Clinton*?"

His eye twitched. "Why are you intentionally trying to hurt me?"

I furrowed my brow. "What?"

"You have to know how much this is hurting me. You're pushing me away and it's killing me inside. Why are you doing it?"

"I--you--what are--?"

"I know you, Rae. Sometimes better than you know yourself. And I know you're actively aware of how much you're pushing against me. How much space you're putting between us. You're smarter than that. Even if you refuse to see it, you know it's there. Staring us in the face. The gap that keeps widening because you won't talk."

Dread filled my gut. "I'm sorry."

"I don't want you to be sorry. I want you to change it. Sorry only covers up so much. And I'm begging you, damn it. Let me in. Talk to me. I mean, how the hell can I be there for you if you won't let me in?"

His hand moved to my cheek. He cupped it, and I nuzzled against his palm, feeling his calluses and the warmth of his skin. My eyes closed and I sighed with relief, stealing the bit of comfort he provided me. My heart broke. It shattered into a million pieces on the floor. I knew he was right. I knew I was pushing him away. And yet, I had no idea how to stop it.

Other than to talk, of course.

"Have I made a mistake with school?"

It came out as nothing but a whisper. But I knew he heard it. His hand tensed and he raised my head up, forcing my eyes back open. And when I found his stare, I felt rooted to my seat.

"Do *you* think you've made a mistake, Rae?"

I shook my head. "I-I-I--I don't know. I mean, you saw the mixed signals Mom sent me. How proud she sounds when she talks about me going to college, then how hard she pushes me to stay home."

"And we both know why that is."

"Yeah. I know. But--I mean, I love English. Don't get me wrong. It's the only subject I don't suck balls at. And kids are great. I could be around them for the rest of my life. But…"

He smoothed his thumb over my cheek. "But?"

I sighed. "I don't know if Mom actually wants this for me. And I mean, if she doesn't, what if she fights me all the way through school? Or moves closer and wants me to live with her? She'd pull that shit, you know. Selling the house just to move closer to campus to keep me on her leash. And that would be torture, you know? But I don't know if I could tell her no. And this degree? English, teaching kids? I don't know if it's what I want to do. I've always loved graphic design. So did I choose that just because they only have a graphic design major? And if I did, is it worth taking at least a semester off to find a school where I can get a full degree in it? And then, there's the fucking scholarships. One year paid in full to help me with grades that will enable me to apply for more scholarships. Because fuck only knows Mom doesn't have the money to put me through school. And what if I give that up to wait a year and it's not there? Then I'm stuck with no way to pay for school. At least right now, I have a year to think shit through while I'm getting requirements out of the way. But what if I get into the graphic design classes and don't even like *those*? What the hell am I going to do then? I don't have anything else I enjoy. I don't have anything else I'm good at. Why the fuck do I have to have my life figured out by the time I'm eighteen? Why can't I at least be able to drink first!?"

The more I spoke, the quicker the words came. And by the time I was done, I panted for air. Clint's eyes widened as his hand slid down my neck, cupping my shoulder before leaning back against his car window.

"Wow. Okay."

I collapsed against my seat. "I know."

I hid my face in my hands and tried to hold back my tears.

"I know, I know. I'm an idiot. I'm an indecisive, anxious idiot. Talk about first world problems, right?"

"Hey, hey, hey. Come on, now. You're far from an idiot."

"I feel like an idiot."

He pulled my hands away from my face. "If anything, you're lucky."

I blinked. "Lucky?"

"Yeah. Lucky. I mean, think about it. Nothing's set in stone yet. You have the luxury of a bit more time and the chance to make a different choice. You go, get some classes out of the way that transfer anywhere you need them to, and you get time away from your mother to really think this through about what you want for *your* life."

I paused. "I--I guess, yeah."

He chuckled, shaking his head. "You know, for a smart girl, you're really dense sometimes."

I shoved him playfully. "Dick."

He held up his hands in innocence. "All right, all right. Maybe that was a bit mean. But look. Okay. Let's see how you can figure out if this is what you want. I'm sure there's a way."

"I'm not so sure there is."

"I mean, what about this road trip coming up? With your orientation, or whatever? Maybe you can talk to someone about sitting in on some English classes. Upper level ones. The ones you'd tackle once you got into your senior year. And maybe an education class. To get a feel for both of those worlds."

"I'm not sure if they'd let me do that."

"It doesn't hurt to ask. And you're going to a school that's fairly close. Maybe one of the teachers at the high school can put in a good word for you or something. I'm sure someone is networked in there. Cal State is a pretty big campus with a lot of faculty."

I sighed. "But what if I can't do that? What then?"

He shrugged. "In the meantime, do some digging to see what else might be out there for you. I can help, if you want. I'm kind of a pro at that now anyway."

"Really? You'd help me with something like that?"

"Did you think I wouldn't?"

I guess my pause was long enough. Because Clint leaned forward with a determined look on his face. He cupped my cheek, forcing me to pay attention to him as his face fell stern. I'd never seen him like this. So guiding. So reassuring. So firm in what he was talking about.

The look suited him.

"Rae, whatever you need me to do, I'm here for you. I know that whatever you choose, you're going to be brilliant in. All you have to do is figure out what that is. Figure out where your heart lies. Where your passion lies. And yes, that takes time. But you have time to figure it out. Your future hasn't been decided yet. You have avenues. Many avenues. But you can't find them until you start seeking them out. Sitting here and worrying about it isn't going to make it any different. It's only going to make it worse."

I nodded. "You're right."

"In this particular instance, I know I'm right. What you need now is action. Movement forward. You've been stewing in an endless purgatory, waiting for some impending date. So put some motion in these long days. Make daily goals of what you'll find out, what you'll accomplish, and what answer to what question you seek. Even if it's only one question. It's going to help. I mean, it helped me, at least."

I sighed. "You're amazing, you know that?"

He nodded. "I do. I also know we've knocked our french fries onto the floorboard of the car. They're kind of useless now."

I giggled. "You're insane."

"And you're okay. At least, you're going to be."

"You think so?"

He kissed the tip of my nose. "I know so, Rae."

I threw my arms around him and buried my face into his neck. He scooped me up, pulling me into his lap as I curled my knees up to my chest. He rocked me softly, kissing my forehead and murmuring how we'd all make it out okay in the long-run. That, at the end of the day, we both had each other. And with that, we could get through anything.

I could only hope he was right.

10

CLINTON

C ecilia knocked on my door. "Clint? Michael's here."

I zipped my suitcase up. "Thanks, Ma."

She opened my door. "Sorry to barge in, just wanted to make sure you didn't want to take anything that's in the dryer. It just stopped."

"Actually, yeah. I think my coat's in there."

"You think you'll need it during this hot summer?"

I shrugged. "Better to be safe than sorry."

I knew she was worried about me. But she didn't have to be. It was just a weekend trip to Rae's orientation at Cal State while the rest of us palled around until she got out. Sure, there might be a party we got ourselves busy with. But nothing serious. Nothing that would get us into any trouble.

"It'll be fine, Ma. I promise."

She sighed as I hugged her.

"I know it will, Clint. I just--I'm worried. You know how it is."

I kissed the top of her head. "I do."

Things hadn't necessarily gotten better once the divorce was finalized. Cecilia was worried since my father knew where she lived. She thought he might pop by one day unannounced, like he did about two months into the divorce proceedings. It freaked her out then, and put her on edge every time she was home alone. Hell, even when she was with me, she had a tendency to jump at the sounds coming from outside. Or above our heads. Or the creaking of the walls as the apartment expanded and contracted from temperature drops.

"Why don't you invite your friend to come over?"

Cecilia patted my back. "I'll be okay. Just worried about you."

I grinned. "I know you don't want to talk about it, so I will. I'm going to be gone for a few days. This would be a perfect time to invite him over and show him around. You know, since I haven't officially met him or anything."

"Clint."

I chuckled. "Seriously, Ma. If he's a good man, he'll come stay with you. Or at least check up on you. There's nothing wrong with leaning on someone. Especially during times like these. Okay?"

She sighed. "How did you get so smart?"

I kissed her forehead. "You can blame Rae for that."

I slipped beside her and went to pull my jacket out of the dryer. Mike stood in the living room, grinning from ear to ear as I passed him by. He slapped me on the back as I went to go get my suitcase. Then, I hugged Ma one last time.

"Call me if you need anything, Clint. Okay?"

I nodded. "I will. I promise."

"And you've got enough money?"

"Yes, I do."

"Promise?"

I sighed. "Goodbye, Ma."

"Love you, Clint!"

"Love you, too!"

And when I got the apartment door closed behind me, Mike chuckled.

"Awww, how cute."

I grinned. "Yeah, well. Better than getting tossed around."

His face fell. "Dude, I totally didn't mean it like that."

I snickered. "You're gonna have to learn to take those jokes. That's how I process things, you know."

"Really, though. You two doing okay?"

We walked to his car. "You know what? I think we are. I mean, it's not easy. But we're good at budgets and pinching pennies. Ma's teaching me things about saving money here and there I didn't know about."

"What your father did to her is bullshit, you know."

I shrugged. "From an unbiased perspective, it makes sense."

"Still fucked up."

"Never said it wasn't."

I piled my things into his trunk, then climbed into the backseat. I knew Ally would want to sit with him. And I sure as hell wanted to cuddle with Rae as we drove into the city. He pulled away from the apartment complex and made his way out, readying us to go get the girls.

And as I gazed out the window, Mike cleared his throat.

"So, how are things with you and Rae?"

I nodded. "Good, actually. Really good lately. I think we're a bit apprehensive about how much things will change in the fall, but we'll work it out."

"Trust me, Ally's worried about the same thing."

"She is?"

Mike nodded. "Yep. We've talked about it a few times, but I can tell it worries her. How far away she and Rae will be. Whether or not classes will get in the way of us. Things like that."

"And plus, we've all been through a lot of hell together. A lot tougher things than starting college, right?"

He snickered. "You're damn right we have. You and Rae, especially."

"Side note, you should really step on it. The girls are gonna ride our asses about being late."

"I'm not the one who had to kiss my momma on the lips."

I rolled my eyes. "Pick at me all you want, but I couldn't imagine my life without Ma in it."

"Does she like you calling her that?"

I smiled. "Yeah. She does."

"Good. That's really good."

"So how are you and Allison?"

He snickered. "You want me to talk? Or get to the girls on time?"

"You can't do both?"

He chuckled. "Takes concentration to time when I can zoom through the yellow lights and when I can't."

"Ah, if we're a few minutes late, I'm sure they won't mind. And if they ride us? We'll stop for snacks. Snacks always hush Rae's mouth."

"You want me to tell her that? Or do you want to offer up that little tidbit to her when they're complaining in the car later?"

I chuckled. "Answer the damn question, Mike."

He smiled. "I mean, we're good. Planning things together. Trying to get everything figured out. Packing up our things and trying to keep our families at bay."

"Still writing up flow charts of how you two will spend your free time once you're both Ivy League bigshots?"

He rolled his eyes. "I hate you for bringing that back up."

My jaw dropped open. "Holy shit, is she still doing that?"

"Yep. Especially now that I changed my schedule around a bit. It's driving me fucking crazy, dude."

I laughed. "Well, just show her she doesn't need to meticulously plan all this stuff out."

"Is that even possible with someone like Allison?"

"Look, nothing is impossible with a girl you like."

"Love."

I paused. "Come again?"

He snickered. "I love her, Clint."

I blinked. "Holy shit, have you told her that?"

He shook his head. "Not yet. But I want to. You think it's too soon?"

I clamored up beside him. "Hell, no, man! Congratulations! When did this happen?"

He shrugged. "I don't know. I just looked at her the other day while she was talking about her schedule and when we might encounter one another on our walks to classes, and it just hit me. I love her. I said it in my head and it made me smile. I love Allison, man."

I clapped his shoulder. "Sounds like you should do something special with her this weekend while Rae and I are in orientation."

"Wait, this is your orientation, too? Did you decide to go to college?"

I snickered. "Hell, no. You know me. But I did tell Rae I'd walk with her around campus and attend a couple of the formal gatherings of incoming freshman with her. She's really nervous."

"Is she finally talking to you about things?"

"She's getting better. It's not perfect, but nothing is ever perfect."

"Tell that to Allison."

I chuckled. "But, back to my original--well--thing. Plan something nice for her while we're out. Let her know with your words that you want the same things she does when you start school. Let her know you want to keep her as a priority going forward. Even with school changing. All she needs is a bit of reassurance. Because if she's still on this trip or something, you probably aren't communicating the way she needs you to."

He sighed. "Fuck, girls are complicated."

I shrugged. "Not really. They want reassurance, romance, and good snacks. Oh, and they want to know they don't have to be strong all the time."

"Uh huh."

"No, I'm serious. Half of the shit between me and Rae cleared up when I looked her in her face and told her I was here for her. That she didn't have to be strong for me anymore. I mean, we started our relationship with her being strong for me. I had to let her know it was okay--and time--to switch gears."

I watched him ponder my words as we turned down the main road through town toward Ally's house.

"When the fuck did you get so wise?"

I threw my head back, laughing. "You sound like Ma now."

"Maybe she's got a point. You definitely don't sound like the Clint Clarke you used to sound like."

I shrugged. "Shit changes. But not always for the worst. The girls need to know that. Because I think this college things is freaking them both out way more than it should. Also, you're a dick."

"What? What did I do?"

"I've always been wise. Just never had anyone to share my wisdom with."

Mike looked down at the clock. "Shit."

"What?"

He sighed. "I told the girls we'd be there to pick them up with enough time to swing through somewhere and get lunch."

"So… what?"

"Look at the time."

My eyes fell to his very fancy dashboard and I snickered. "Whoops."

Mike took a sharp right. "Yeah, they're not going to be happy."

"Wait, where are we--?"

"The coffee shop. Coffee will smooth this over."

I snickered as we pulled into the parking lot. He had a point, and I knew exactly what to get Rae. I remembered it from so long ago. Back last year, when she scared me so badly after coming back from picking up coffee and pastries. We walked inside and rattled off our orders. Then I picked out some treats for Rae. Mike and I piled everything into his car before slipping into a sandwich shop on the corner, grabbing all of us small meals just in case.

"Think this'll be enough?" Mike asked.

I snickered. "I fucking hope so. We have enough food to feed a small army. I'm sure they'll find something they like in all this."

"Think it'll make up for being an hour late?"

I shrugged. "Guess we'll find out."

I sipped my coffee as Mike drove us toward Ally's house. I mean, the college was only an hour away, at the most. Check-in for the hotel wasn't until three anyway. There was no reason for us to leave at noon in the first place. I leaned back in the seat, watching as the world passed us by. We were lucky that Mike's father had an 'in' with the hotel we were staying at. Because otherwise, we wouldn't have been able to check in without an adult present.

Thank fuck for connections.

"This weekend is going to be awesome, dude."

Mike sounded absolutely jovial as he wiggled around in his seat.

"I'm going to have Allison all to myself. I mean, assuming we're going to be switching up rooms. We're still doing that, right?"

I shrugged. "If the girls want to, yeah."

"Yes. I think I can convince Allison. I haven't slept with her yet. I mean, not sexually. But not like that, either. I think it would be great, waking up to her like that. Making her coffee. Snuggling her close. Maybe turning on a movie before we get out of bed for the day."

I smiled. "Oh, yeah. You got it bad for her."

"Can you blame me? She drives me nuts, but she's still perfect as ever."

"I know how you feel," I murmured.

I was looking forward to spending the time with Rae. But the smallest part of me was concerned she wouldn't go along with the plan. Usually, I was concerned Ally wouldn't go along with it. So conservative. Not wanting to cross any lines that possibly meant temptation. But, with how rocky things had been with me and Rae,

I wondered if she'd use this time to be with Ally instead of me. I mean, Mike was awesome. He'd become a very quick best friend. But I didn't want to share a hotel room with him.

Not if my girl was in the room beside us.

"I think Allison will be happy with the arrangements. I mean, I brought it up to her the other day and she didn't completely shoot it down. She's worried about it, sure. But I reassured her that my hands wouldn't go anywhere she didn't want them. And that seemed to alleviate her worries a bit. I think she might actually go for it, Clint. You know, sharing a room with me."

I paused. "These rooms have two beds, right?"

He nodded. "Yep. Two queen-size beds each. And a balcony. It's a great hotel."

My eyebrows rose. "Wow. That does sound like a nice room."

"Dad said for us to charge whatever we wanted in terms of room service, too. I think, mostly, to settle his mind that we're ordering food and not out getting our asses in trouble. You know what I mean?"

"We might go out a couple of times, though."

Mike grinned at me in the rearview mirror. "Doesn't mean we can't order something before we leave."

I shook my head. "You remind me of the old me."

"Hey. It's possible to have fun without destroying property and being a dick."

"Hey! I--didn't destroy property. Kind of."

Mike laughed. "At least you own up to the other part."

I chuckled as we pulled into the driveway of Allison's parents' house. A very nice house. One like what I hoped to own one day. A modest home compared to the ones that surrounded it, and yet it was perfect. Not too big, not too small. A white picket fence and a smooth concrete driveway. A glistening white house with one of the few lawns in the neighborhood that boasted green grass instead of fake turf.

I just hoped the girls weren't too upset that we were running behind.

11

———

RAELYNN

Allison sighed. "I knew the guys would be late. I swear, Michael can't ever stay on schedule."

I rolled my eyes. "Quit giving those guys such a hard time. We can't check in until later this afternoon anyway."

"I know. But, what's going to happen when he has to stick to a rigid schedule in college? Stanford isn't going to settle for a boy always late to his classes."

"Was he late to classes in high school?"

"No, but he was also locked down into the building for seven hours. He had nothing else to do *but* go to class."

Point taken. "I just think you're riding him a little too hard, Allison. That's all. I mean, Michael is smart. He's quick on his feet. Just because he runs late to outside functions doesn't mean he's going to treat college the same way."

"I don't know. I mean, I know my schedules and outlining things is making him upset. But what else can I do? I want to help him succeed. And it's like he won't let me."

I snickered. "The two of you are going to be fine. Just try not controlling every aspect of his world for once. It's okay to live. There's a life outside of school."

"Yeah, once we get out of school."

I shook my head as she gazed out the window. Allison was wound much too tight for any of this. Hopefully, this weekend would do her some good. Hopefully, we could convince her to go to a party and just breathe. She really needed to. Because if her panties wound themselves any tighter, her ass crack would slit right up her damn back. I was tired of watching her talk herself in circles. I was tired of seeing how exhausted Michael was with her fucking graphs and schedules and string-to-string play-by-plays outlining the next four years.

The girl had to take a breath.

My phone rang and I closed my eyes. It rang and it rang, and I wanted to ignore it. I knew who it was. She'd called me three times already to rattle off in my ear. I didn't want to talk to my mother anymore. Because while I knew she had my best interests in mind, there was always that reminder of her own selfish motives.

"You going to answer that?" Allison asked.

I sighed. "I guess I should."

"She'll just keep calling until you do."

"I know. I know."

"Maybe you should tell her how you're feeling. She might understand."

"Yeah, no. Maybe when I'm settled at school the cyclone of crazy can miss me because I'm an hour away."

She giggled. "You don't give your mother enough credit."

I pulled my phone out. "And you give her too much."

I swiped my finger across the cracked screen of my phone before I held it to my ear.

"Hey, Mom."

"You forgot your cell phone charger! I found it in your room."

I paused. "What--? Are you--? No, Mom. I have two. One of them I keep in my purse. Why--why are you in my bedroom?"

"Because something stinks in your room, so I'm cleaning it."

"Mom. Don't go in my room. I'm serious."

"I can't let the smell just linger."

"Mom!"

"Do you want me to run you over an extra pair of underwear? I mean, you've got some laying out on your bed. Did you mean to pack them?"

I groaned. "Mom. Just spray some Febreeze and I'll fish out the scent when I get back. I'm sure it's nothing."

She sighed. "I can't live with that smell while you're gone. And we're out of Febreeze."

I paused. "I bought a three pack of it a week ago. They should be under the sink."

"Oh, it'll be fine. Let me just--what's this?"

"Mom!"

Allison squealed. "The boys are pulling up."

"Mom, I have to go. Please, just get out of my room."

"What's this box? That's what stinks so badly."

"The damn box doesn't stink, Mom! Put it down!" I roared.

Everyone froze. Allison stared at me with wide eyes and Mom fell silent. I didn't want her touching that box. Holy fuck, I'd make Michael take me back to the house just so I could take the box with me. In fact, that was a great idea.

I sighed. "I need that box with me, actually. It's got some information I need in it."

Mom cleared her throat. "I can, uh, fish it out for you if--"

"Mom, I love you. And I get this is hard for you. And I'm sorry I yelled at you. But you have to start coming to terms with this. I'm going off to college in a couple of weeks and you have to find a way to be okay with that. You can't snoop around in my room. You have to trust me on this, okay? Just... just be proud of me? Okay?"

She sighed. "I'm so very proud of you. You have no idea."

No, I don't. "Just take the box with you downstairs. I'll come by and get it."

"What's in it?"

I bit down onto the inside of my cheek. "Just stuff I need. I meant to pack it. Then I can figure out why it stinks and you won't have to deal with the smell anymore. How's that sound?"

She sighed. "Okay. I'll take it downstairs with me."

"Thank you."

"Oh, do you have your list of questions you wanted to ask during your orientation?"

I paused. "That's what's in the box."

I fucking hope she bought my lie and didn't try to open the damn thing.

"Ah, well. Come get it, then. Anything else you need from your room?"

I shook my head. "I'll take one last look at it before I leave. I promise. Okay? And I'll give you a big hug."

"I'd like that very much."

I hung up the phone and sighed. I stood up from the bed as

Allison eyed me carefully, then reached for my bag. I slipped my phone into my pocket as we silently walked downstairs. I heard Michael and Clint talking to Allison's parents, promising they'd take good care of us.

Normally, I'd interject with a quip of some sort.

But I was too focused on getting back to the house.

Michael gave Allison a big hug, but I slipped by Clint. I wanted to get out of there. I needed to, really. I tossed my stuff into the back of the car, then hopped in. I waited impatiently for the three of them to make their way back to me. Everyone climbed in silently as Allison waved at her parents. Clint climbed over me, seating himself next to the window before he took my hand.

"Everything okay?" he asked.

"Michael, can we go back to my house for a minute? I left something."

I tossed Clint a knowing look and he sighed. I snickered to myself and Michael drove to my place, and I quickly hopped out of the car. I motioned for Clint to stay behind. I didn't want anyone to witness this. Because if something broke out between my mother and me, I didn't want anyone bearing witness to it.

I was tired of everyone seeing the destitution of my life.

"Hey there, sweetheart."

Mom rushed me the second I walked in the door and hugged me tight.

"Hey, Mom."

She kissed my cheek. "The box is on the kitchen table. And I packed a couple of sodas for you and everyone else for the road."

"Thanks."

I walked into the kitchen and sighed with relief. There was the box. With the lock on the front of it. It didn't look tampered with. Or as if it had been broken. So I scooped it up before reaching for the shoulder-strapped cooler. I nodded at Mom with a taut smile on my lips, then quickly made my way upstairs.

I should've done this a long time ago anyway.

I locked my bedroom door behind me and started whirling around my room. I picked up one of the larger bags I'd kept from Cecilia's stash and started stuffing it with all sorts of things. The box. The underwear. I pulled out my dresser drawer of panties and dug all the way to the bottom. Until my hand fell against the white envelope. I shoved that into the purse. I picked up my piggy bank

and put that in there, too. I reached above my closet with a yard-
stick I kept in the closet and scraped along its shelf top until two
tied-off socks fell in my face. I stuffed those in the purse, too, before
gazing around the room.

And when my eyes fell to my bed, I sighed.

The measures I'd gone to in order to keep my money out of the
hands of my mother had become exponential. It almost made me
want to cry. Almost, anyway. I walked over and pulled up the lower
corner of my fitted sheet. I jammed my hand into the small slit I'd
made in the mattress. Just big enough for my fingers to fit through.
I grabbed the wads of cash, shoving them into the purse. One,
after another, after another. Until all six of them were safely at my
side.

If Mom was going to start sifting through my room, then I had
to make sure she wouldn't find anything I intended to keep.

I put the expensive sunglasses I'd kept on top of my head. I
packed away the few pieces of jewelry I'd convinced myself to
keep. The two silken scarves I was saving for a rainy day. I folded
up really tight the couple outfits I had yet to sell. Then I shoved the
pair of heels I wore to prom down at the very bottom of that
massive purse before zipping it up.

Thank fuck, the bag was huge.

"Wow, looks like you forgot a lot."

I snickered, coming down the stairs. "Yeah, well. I'm glad you
convinced me to come back."

Mom grinned. "Sometimes I do know best."

Yeah, maybe. "All right. I'm heading out. I'll see--"

"Uh uh uh. You forgetting something?"

She held her arms out for me and I internally cringed. I walked
over to her and hugged her, feeling her kiss my cheek. Over and
over. As if she weren't ever going to see me again. I hugged her
neck one last time before pulling away, and tried my best to give
her a reassuring smile.

"Oh, you got those questions?"

I nodded. "They're in the box."

"Let me know how it goes!"

"Will do, Mom!"

Then I was back out the door with my purse bursting at the
seams with money.

I climbed into the SUV and music hit my ears. Classic rock. A station Clint had gotten Michael hooked on. They were all singing at the top of their lungs as I closed my door. I wasn't in a singing mood, though. I clutched my purse tightly against my chest as I gazed out the window. Clint's hand settled onto my knee as I saw my mother peeking her head through the curtains, watching us pull away. And as we got further away from the house, I felt myself growing less and less stressed.

Maybe college wouldn't be terrible after all.

Especially if it came with this kind of peace.

"This is going to be awesome," Allison said.

Michael nodded. "Are you two okay with me and Allison rooming together?"

I paused. "What?"

Clint squeezed my knee. "Mike and Ally are wanting to bunk together. But don't worry. The bedrooms have two beds each."

Allison furrowed her brow. "Why would she be worried about something like that?"

I cleared my throat. "That sounds good. I could use some time with Clint anyway."

He looked at me. "You could?"

I smiled softly at him. "Yeah, I really could."

When he smiled back at me, a weight lifted off my shoulders. I slipped my hand on top of his as everyone started talking around me. Michael said something that made Clint laugh. Allison said something that made Michael roll his eyes. The music blared as we headed for the highway, pulling further away from my house. The only place I had called home for the past eighteen years. I had orientation tomorrow morning on campus. Then a tour of campus just after lunch. But, after that? The rest of the time was ours to do with what we wanted.

And as I let my eyes linger over Clint, I knew exactly what I wanted to do.

12

CLINTON

I gawked at how massive the campus was as we passed it. While Rae clung to my hand and her purse full of money, I stared out the window, listening to Mike and Ally chatter on about their own plans. We made our way to the hotel as the sprawling campus faded into the background, and I felt myself filling with nerves. Why did I feel so anxious all of a sudden? Why were my hands sweating? Why did I feel so overwhelmed?

It wasn't my fucking orientation we were going to.

As we pulled into the parking lot for the hotel, we got out. And the sheer number of guys walking around that passed me by made me bristle. Young boys in groups, staring at me and glancing over at Rae. Whistling softly at Ally and making Mike take her into his arms. I walked to Rae's side and guided her into the hotel. Away from the prying eyes as dread filled my gut.

I didn't like how many guys were around campus.

"Hi there! You guys all checking in?"

The peppy front desk attendant chirped her voice across the lobby as we made our way for her.

"Uh, yes. The reservation's under my father's name. Dale Vance."

The woman started typing. "I need your I.D. as well as a valid credit card."

Mike pulled out everything he needed for the woman. But she

looked displeased. She kept checking his I.D. and looking up at him, and I watched her eyebrows rise. I looked down at Rae. I saw her shuffling on her feet. She tucked herself against me, and I felt her trembling softly.

I kissed the top of her head to try and calm her down.

"I'm sorry, but you need an adult here to help you check in."

Mike nodded. "There should be a note underneath the reservation explaining everything."

The woman shook her head. "Doesn't matter if there is. The law states--"

"Michael Vance! I was wondering when you'd be here to check in."

A very bubbly older woman came out of the back room and walked out to us. She hugged Mike softly, and the three of us looked around at one another.

"Mrs. Autumn. It's really good to see you again," he said.

She ruffled his hair. "When did you get taller than me? What is happening right now? Are you actually college age?"

He chuckled. "College bound for Stanford."

She gasped. "Your mother's alma mater. Oh, I know she's so proud of you right now."

I furrowed my brow. "I didn't know your mom went to Stanford."

Mike shrugged. "She doesn't talk about it much because she didn't have the best time. Her dad kind of forced her into the family tradition."

Ally paused. "You don't feel that way, do you?"

Mike smiled at her. "No, baby. Not at all."

The woman grinned. "Baby, huh?"

Introductions were made and I shook the woman's hand. And slowly, I saw the girl behind the counter sinking into shame. I felt bad for her, honestly. Being run over by the likes of her manager and the son of some rich guy. But Mrs. Autumn got us checked in and assigned to the rooms we'd be in for the weekend. We went and gathered our things from the car before heading up.

Where Mike and Ally quickly disappeared.

"Well, I guess this is our room," Rae said.

I snickered as the door slammed, closing us off from our two friends.

"Yeah, I guess it is."

"You want to do the honors? Or should I?"

I kissed her head again. "It's your weekend. You can go in when you're ready."

With a heavy sigh, she slipped her key into the hotel room door. And when the air conditioning slapped us in the face, the two of us sighed with relief. I helped Rae get her things into the room, and as she flopped onto the bed I walked over to the window. I pulled back the curtains and looked down the five stories all the way to the ground. More boys walked by. Laughing and punching one another in the arm. Having the time of their lives during orientation weekend.

Boys that had their life together.

Unlike me.

I've just got my notebook and bullshit side jobs.

"So, do you wanna talk about it?"

I turned away from the window as my question lingered in the air. Rae sat up and looked my way, then heaved a heavy sigh. A sigh I heard much too often nowadays.

A sigh I didn't know how to fix.

"I don't know. It's just--"

I walked over to her. "What happened with your mom?"

She scooted over, giving me room to sit. "She called me at Allison's and started rattling off all sorts of nonsense. How she was in my room supposedly cleaning or whatever and wondered if I left my charger cable for my phone behind."

"Why was she in your room in the first place?"

"I don't know, but she flat-out lied to me about it. She said there was 'a smell coming from a box under my bed.'"

"She didn't."

"I've had that box with me this entire time. Have you smelled anything?"

I sighed. "Oh, Rae."

She shook her head. "I've let up lately on the money I'm giving Mom and she's actively snooping around for it. I know she suspects something. That's why I gathered all of it up and shoved everything I figured she might find into that purse."

I nodded slowly. "I figured that's what it was."

"What the hell am I going to do? She's literally going through my room trying to find shit. What the hell is wrong with her?"

"Rae, your mother is sick. Maybe not physically. But, mentally? Possibly. Is she still going to therapy?"

"With as easy as it was for her to bold-faced lie to me about some stupid shit? I don't even know anymore."

"Is she telling you she is?"

She nodded. "Yeah."

I wrapped my arm around her. "I don't want to seem as if I'm walking all over what you want. But I really do feel that one of the reasons you need to give at least this first semester a chance is to get away from your mother. Figure out how to live your life without her influence and her presence."

"I know."

"And who knows what's going through her mind right now?"

She snickered. "I've got an idea as to a few things."

I kissed her temple. "I know you do. But we're away for the weekend, so one of the first things we can do is find a branch of your bank to put all that money in."

"Well…"

I paused. "What? What is it?"

She sighed. "I know what you're going to say, so don't do it. Okay?"

I nodded. "Okay…? What's going on?"

She cleared her throat. "I thought I could trust my mother, so I kind of gave her a card to my bank account."

"You did what?"

"I know! I know. I know it was stupid. But she was on such a good path with getting rid of D.J. for good and going to therapy and putting in job applications. I figured it would be easier for her to just get what we needed if she had a card to the account instead of me always having to, you know, *give* her money."

"You didn't."

She stood up. "I know it was stupid. But that's why I started storing money not in my bank account. I know she's run it a few times already and it's probably been declined. I've only been putting in there exactly what is necessary, then storing the rest away elsewhere."

I sighed. "Fucking hell, your mother."

"Yeah. Tell me about it."

I paused. "Okay. Well, we go to a branch of your bank and we open up another account. One that doesn't have any cards attached to it. Or put it in your savings account. There's a way for us to store this money without your mother getting access to it that doesn't require you to haul it around in a purse all weekend. That's just as dangerous."

"I know," she whispered.

I took her in my arms. "It's going to be okay, Rae. I promise you."

She leaned against me. "I don't know some days."

"You know, I might have something that'll cheer you up."

She sniffled. "Really?"

I nodded. "Mm-hmm. Can I get over to my bag for a second?"

"Does that mean I have to let you go?"

Her words warmed my soul. "Not at all."

I dipped down and gripped her ass cheeks. I hoisted her against me as she giggled into my neck. With her arms and legs tightly wound around my body, I carried her over to my bed. I sat her down on my lap as I reached out for my suitcase, clumsily unzipping it.

Before reaching out and pulling out a bottle of champagne.

"Clint!"

"Sh sh sh sh sh," I said, chuckling.

She lowered her voice. "Where the hell did you get that?"

I grinned. "A 'congratulations' from Cecilia. She bought it for us."

"Your stepmom is a fucking saint."

"Yeah, Ma is pretty awesome. I told her I wanted to celebrate with something special. And she came back with this for us. She scolded me, of course, did the whole one-finger pointing thing and told me to drink responsibly."

Rae laughed. "I bet that was a sight."

I smiled. "It really was. I wish I would've gotten it on video for you."

"So want me to go unwrap some of the plastic cups over by the coffee machine?"

"And I'll do the honors of popping open the bottle."

As Rae scrambled off my lap, I stood. With a smile on my face and the cork pointed in the other direction, I effortlessly popped the top. The love of my life came over and I filled up our clear plastic cups. Then I ushered her over to the balcony.

Where we had a view of the hotel pool and hot tubs as yet more boys walked by.

"To your future," I said.

I raised my glass and Rae followed my motions.

"Wherever it takes you and whatever you decide to do with it, I'll always be here."

She smiled. "Promise?"

I slipped my free hand along her waist. "Promise, promise."

"Then I'm going to toast to our future. Cal State or not, it's the two of us against the world."

And when she clicked her cup against mine, I felt more at peace than I had in months.

Rae turned to look out over the part of L.A. we could see, so I stood behind her. With my arm around her stomach, we silently sipped our drinks. I drew in the fresh air. I listened as guys and girls from all directions laughed and cracked jokes. I knew there would be mounds of parties thrown here. Probably in this hotel alone, but definitely around the campus. I wasn't sure if Rae would be up to any of them. But if she wasn't, I didn't mind spending our evenings in with room service and her body cuddled against mine.

After all, I missed having her like this anyway.

It felt nice to get away with her.

Imagine what you'd feel like if you moved with her.

I shook away the thought. I rested my chin on top of Rae's head and finished my drink. She handed me her cup and I went inside to refill them, already feeling the champagne loosening me up. I kicked the air up another notch and filled our glasses again before I turned around. I figured I'd go back out onto the balcony to find Rae. But instead, she stood in front of me.

While slowly easing the balcony door closed.

"I think opening a new account for that money is a good idea. Maybe putting some of it in an investment or whatever?"

I nodded. "Okay. I'm sure we can work that out tomorrow after your orientation."

She sauntered toward me. "Then, maybe we could come back here and have some lunch. Maybe order in, since Michael and Allison will probably want to do dinner out tonight."

I swallowed hard. "Sure. Whatever you want."

Her hands slid up my torso. "Whatever I want?"

I nodded. "Oh, hell yeah."

She grinned. "Good."

She plucked her drink from my hand and slammed it back. I mean, she fucking chugged it. I tipped mine up and did the same, feeling my cock already aching for her. With her flushed cheeks and lust filling her eyes, she pushed me down onto the bed. She crawled on top of me, her eyes connected with mine. And as she straddled my fucking stomach, her shirt came over her head.

Revealing her luxurious curves as I licked my lips.

I watched in awe as she unfastened her bra. It slid down her shoulders as her shirt fell to the floor. Her lovely tits came spilling out, her nipples already puckered. Already begging for my lips. And as a smirk settled across my face, I rose up.

Until Rae pushed me back down.

"Uh, uh, uh. Stay there," she said.

My eyebrows rose as she slowly slid off my body. I watched her as much as I could from my position although she stepped out of my view a couple of times. She took off her clothes, casting them to the side. And when she came back into view, she bent and ripped my pants off, literally pulling them down my legs before pulling my cock out through the slit of my boxers.

Rock hard, and ready for her.

"Rae," I grunted.

"You stay just the way you are, handsome."

I lay there on my back, watching as she straddled me. Her pussy hovered above my lips as her hand fisted my hair. I smelled her. I salivated for her. Those enticing pussy lips glistened for me and I wrapped my arms around her legs, wanting nothing more than for her to drop down.

Then she did exactly as I wanted.

13

RAELYNN

I groaned. "Oh, yeah. Just like that."

I sat myself against his face and my head fell back. With his large hands gripping my hips, I rocked against his lips. I felt him give his face as an offering, reeling as I sat my pussy lips against his face. Electricity washed over me as I rocked. His tongue parted my folds as my chest flushed with heat. I ran my fingers through his hair, gripping him as he held me close. Feasting on me. Swallowing me down. Pushing me to heights I hadn't known in so long.

I'd never neglect this part of our relationship again.

"Clint. Don't stop."

He answered me with a growl before he continued teasing me with his tongue.

I lifted my head and looked down at him. His eyes peered back at me with hunger and need. My thighs quaked. My toes curled. And my gut ached for me to fall over the edge. I panted for air as I felt myself climbing. As I rolled quicker against his face, my breathing became broken. My eyes rolled back as he held me close. His tongue pressed deeply against my clit. And as I fell over the edge, I collapsed.

Falling against the mattress.

I whimpered as my body twitched. I felt Clint manipulating me before he spread my legs wide. He tossed them over his shoulders, his cock falling between my swollen folds. And when he slid against my walls, my jaw unhinged.

"Ooooh, *fuck.*"

He snapped his hips against mine. He folded me in half. He rested his body against the back of my thighs as my eyes rolled back. I felt him filling me, and it was all too much. Being able to let go with him--knowing no one could walk in on us--felt surreal.

I didn't want it to end.

"That's it, Rae. Take it. Let it wash over you."

"Clint. Yes. Harder. I need you--hard--yes! Clint! Shit!"

My back arched and I fell over the edge. Much quicker than I wanted, but we had all weekend. His face fell to my breasts as he stilled inside me. Pulsating, but not exploding. Growling, but not releasing. Swiveling his hips, but refusing to let himself burst.

Which meant our time wasn't over.

"Clint," I whispered.

My legs slid lazily from his shoulders. He rolled us over until my body rested against his. I heaved against the crook of his neck, feeling my heartrate skyrocketing as his girth stayed inside my body. Resting there, as if it had found its home.

Just like my cheek found its home against Clint's heartbeat.

"You're breathtaking," he whispered.

I snickered. "Take me any way you wish."

He growled just before the phone rang. Which caused me to giggle as he fumbled with it. The ringing sound filled our room and I forced myself to get up. I smirked down at him as he held the phone to his ear. Planting my knees into the mattress, I shifted myself as he held back his groans. He shot me a look before he drew in a quick breath. But the second he opened his mouth, I slid up his girth.

"Hey th--hmph--hey. Yes? Hello? Oh, hey, Mike."

I bit down onto my lower lip as I squeezed my walls around him. His eyes widened as he pointed to the phone.

Like I gave a damn who he was on the phone with.

"Yeah, dinner at six? Uh… Rae?"

I giggled as I bounced against his body, causing his jaw to unhinge silently.

"Yep. That's good. Six, in the hall--hallway."

I clapped my hand over my mouth as I pressed myself up before sliding all the way back down again. Making him more frustrated than ever. And yet, I knew he liked it. The thrill of it. Michael in his ear, me teasing him on his cock.

"Can we do steak, Michael? I'd really like a nice slab of beef tonight," I called out.

I rolled my hips, causing Clint to groan out before he drew in a quick breath.

"Yeah, yeah, yeah. I'll tell her. See you guys at six. Bye."

And just as quickly as he'd hung up the phone, my hands fell against his chest.

"They know now, you know," he murmured.

I grinned. "Like you care."

"You're going to pay for that, Rae."

"I'd like to see you tr--ah!"

I giggled as he quickly flipped me over, reaching for my clit as he kept himself sheathed within me. His fingers moved quickly, working me as my legs pulled taut. I gasped for air, whimpering with broken moans as I choked on my own ability to speak. He knew just what buttons to press. He knew exactly how sensitive I was. He played me like a damn fiddle, and I adored that about him.

Until his fingers stopped.

"Wh-wh-wh-wh--what? Why? I don't--"

"Payback really is a bitch, beautiful."

He captured my lips before pounding into my body. Over and over, swiveling his hips against my swollen nub. I gasped for more. I needed more of him. But every time I got close, he stopped. Every time I reached that peak, he pulled back. It was sheer torture, not falling over that cliff with him. I felt his length swelling. Pulsing. Practically screaming out its own needs. And yet Clint wouldn't indulge them.

Neither of us.

"Please. I can't anymore."

Clint nuzzled me. "Oh, is the little tease tired of being teased?"

I sighed. "Come on. It wasn't this bad."

"Well, it's not my fault you look so beautiful when you're flustered."

He bit against my neck and I arched. His hands moved all over my body, tracing my outlines with his palms. He pounded into me, then rested. He languidly moved, then rested. He rutted against me, short, quick strokes as his pelvis lapped at my clit.

Then fucking rested.

Beads of sweat dripped down the nape of my neck. My entire body flushed from head to toe. I couldn't move. Couldn't breathe. Couldn't think straight. My limbs went limp against the mattress. Immobile against the force of his body. Every inch of me was covered in his kisses by the time he was done. And yet, neither of us were done.

Because he wouldn't fucking let me come.

"Clint," I said hoarsely.

He captured my lips, making my heart flutter.

"You ready, my love?" he murmured.

All I mustered was a nod before he chuckled.

"Good. Because I am, too."

"Oh, thank fuck," I breathed.

He laughed as he pulled out of me and my eyes widened. I didn't want him to leave. I reached for him, but he was nowhere to be found. I was too weak to lean up and search for him. Too weak to open my eyes and find him. But, when I felt warmth settle against my ears, I smiled.

"Taking a page out of my book?" I asked.

"And if I was, gorgeous?"

I slowly opened my eyes and moaned with hunger. His cock, dangling for me, glistening for my viewing pleasure. He hovered over me, nuzzling my hip bones. I jumped at the feel of his cool nose against my skin. I slid my hands softly up his thighs, trying to find a place to hang on to before I guided him to my lips.

I should've known he had things under control.

"Open wide."

He slipped down my throat as his face fell between my legs. And the pleasure that skyrocketed through my system threatened to burn through my gut. Every single part of my body felt as if it were on fire, roaring with a desperate need only Clint could fill. I felt myself overcome with helplessness. And yet I felt freer than I had in my entire life. As I bucked ravenously underneath him, the whole of my throat opened up. I felt all of my muscles release, slipping down the warm embankment of a river and floating off into the sunset. I let the moment consume me and my mind fall blank. All there was were our bodies, desperately searching for something only we could give one another.

Nothing else mattered.

And I never wanted this to change.

He growled between my legs and my eyes sprang open. He spread me further as his girth pulsed against my cheeks. All I did was offer myself, because I sure as hell didn't have the energy to move. I slid my nails up and down his thighs, shivering as I tried to regulate my breathing. Sensations I'd never experienced before engulfed me, sweeping me underneath his torrential current.

And as my hips rose from the bed, I felt myself finally pop.

"Clint! Clint! Yes! Keep going!"

My muffled cries caused him to growl. I watched his balls pull up before his hips stilled. He shoved himself down my throat as my hands gripped his ass cheeks, digging into the strength of his muscles as his tongue did its own work. I snapped my hips against his face, rocking as hard as I could. Another orgasm rolled over me, forcing my eyes closed as I felt his girth finally pumping.

Releasing into me and marking the whole of my body.

I shivered against him. His tongue dug in harder, and I came again. Three times, back to back, locking up my body and causing me to go weak. Clint pulled himself from my mouth and I felt trails of spit and arousal mark everywhere the tip of his dick touched. I gazed up at the ceiling, watching it ebb and flow like waves of the ocean. Spinning around and around. Threatening to cast me off into another dimension as my body catapulted through the clouds.

Before I came crashing back down to earth.

"Holy shit," I breathed.

I coughed as Clint rolled off my body. He pulled himself upright long enough to turn around. I rolled over, catching his eyes and seeing how flushed his face had become. The dew glistening against his lips. The beads of sweat framing his face. He was a mess. And I knew I looked like one, too.

He reached out and wiped off my cheek with his thumb.

"You're so beautiful," he murmured.

I smiled. "I love you."

He cupped my cheek. "I love you too, Rae. Never, ever forget that."

And when he kissed me, I felt our souls intertwine.

I nestled into his body, feeling him shaking. Just like I was. He pulled me close with his strong arms, then dragged the covers over us. The feeling of those cool sheets against my skin made goose-bumps tingle along the edges of my body. Out of nowhere, I heard the television turn on and the flipping of channels caught my attention. I looked up and saw the reflection of the screen in Clint's eyes. I smiled as I kept watching. A reflection of a reflection. Finally the sitcom Clint landed on was exchanged for my face as he looked down at me.

"Dinner's at six. We're going to a steakhouse," he said.

I kissed his cheek softly. "Want to take a nap until then?"

He snuggled down into bed with me before reaching for his phone. He put it to his face as my leg slid between his. I snuggled close. My naked body pressed against his. I heard his phone beeping before he set it down. Then his lips fell to the top of my head.

"Alarm set. We'll have an hour to get ready. And until then, we can do whatever it is we want."

I nuzzled against him. "What time is it?"

"Not quite four."

"Mmm, okay. Time for a bit of a rest."

And as he held me in his arms, with my eyes fluttering closed, I wondered why he didn't want this all the time.

Why he didn't want to move in with me and have me all the time.

14

CLINTON

My eyes fell open as the sun barely peeked through the black-out curtains of the hotel. As I shifted against the comforter, I felt my cock hissing with need. It shot electricity through my groin, aching my pelvic muscles. And even after last night--even after fucking Rae into oblivion before we both passed out--my body wanted more.

"Morning, handsome."

Her greeting came with a soft giggle, which did nothing for my raging hard-on. I tossed my arm over my eyes as I tried to pull myself out of my entranced slumber. I wanted to roll over and go back to sleep. I wanted to sink myself into Rae from behind and fuck her slowly. Gently. Until we both passed back out with me still sheathed inside. I wanted that more than anything. Her naked body pressed back against mine. Like she'd been all night.

But when I rose up on my elbows, I found her at the foot of the bed. Fully clothed.

Putting on makeup.

"What are you doing?" I asked groggily.

She giggled. "Trying something new."

"Why?"

She shrugged. "I don't know. It's college orientation day. Might as well make a good impression.

"You can do that by just being yourself."

"You sound like you need coffee."

I sat my back against the headboard. "Is there coffee?"

She pointed and I followed her arm. I wanted to kiss it. Massage it. Tug on it until she fell back against my body. I slipped my hand underneath the comforter and rearranged myself, trying to find some sort of relief. My bones needed her. The marrow of them pulsed with fire. It almost hurt to pull away from her. To slide out from underneath the covers and make my way to the coffee pot.

"I also took the liberty of ordering some things for breakfast. You know, pastries. There's some bacon, I think. Oh, and cereal."

I nodded. "Cereal."

Rae giggled again. "I had some myself."

I walked over toward the silver rolling tray and stumbled around trying to make my coffee. I spilled milk trying to get shit into the bowl, which required me to chug a mug of hot liquid before I could even eat. I turned around as milk dripped down my chin. I watched as Rae painted makeup on her face. I mean, I'd seen her wear it from time to time. Especially for prom. My God, she'd looked incredible at prom.

I didn't want her looking that incredible for the guys on campus.

"What are you staring at?"

Her voice pulled me from my trance and I took another bite of cereal.

"You."

She blushed, and the color impeded on the foundation she'd slathered all over her face.

"Since when did you start wearing heavy makeup?"

She sighed. "Are you really going to give me a hard time about this?"

I shook my head. "No. Just making sure you aren't doing this because you feel like you have to. This is just orientation."

"It's not just orientation, Clint. This is where I meet the incoming class. Even some of my professors. There's a tour of the campus, and I want to make sure that anyone I come into contact with gets a good first impression."

I grinned. "Then you may want to go easy on the lipstick. You look like you're back at prom."

"Thanks."

The flat tone of her voice made me sigh. I had to pull myself out of my own headspace and put myself in hers. She was nervous. I got that. I just had to make sure my worries about her didn't trump her own worries. Because hers were the most important. I had to keep her grounded and settled during these meetings and tours. I had to make sure she digested information and didn't get too overwhelmed. Or lost by herself on campus.

"I think you look great," I said.

And when she smiled softly, I felt my heart skip a beat.

"Thanks. But you're right. I think lipstick is a bit too much. So just lip gloss."

I nodded. "Good idea."

"You know, I don't know how late this thing will go today. So, if you ever want to dip out at some point in time, feel free. Okay?"

I shook my head. "No need. I want to be there with you through this."

"Are you sure? Because I might end up doing some last minute things. You know, if there's another tour or if there's an option to meet the English teachers. Things like that."

I paused. "Do you not want me to go?"

"No, no, no! It's not that at all."

"You said that pretty quickly."

She closed her lip gloss and sighed before turning to face me. "It's just…"

I set my bowl of cereal down and went to sit beside her. I took her hand within mine, stroking my thumb along her skin. Her eyes wouldn't meet mine, and I knew why. Even before I asked the question, I knew the answer.

"You want to do this alone, don't you?"

She sighed. "Is that bad?"

I shook my head. "It's not bad. I get it."

"It's just that having you on campus with me even though you won't actually be on campus or around campus might, I don't know…"

I brought her hand to my lips to kiss. "It's okay, Rae. I promise, I get it."

"But, that leaves you being the third wheel with Michael and Allison all day. And I don't want that to--"

"Hey. Hey, hey, hey. This is your experience. And I want you to have this experience the way you want to. You've got your phone on you, right?"

She nodded. "Right."

"Great. So, if you realize you want me there with you, all you have to do is call. I'm sure Mike will drive me over. Or I'll catch a cab. Something like that. Okay?"

She sighed. "I feel so bad."

I cupped her cheeks. "Stop it. You've got enough pressure on yourself right now. You don't need this perceived one, either."

She sighed. "When did you get so wise?"

I snickered. "Popular question, apparently."

She furrowed her brow in confusion, but I only kissed the tip of her nose. I stood up and walked back over to my cereal, intent on finishing it. I wolfed it down before pouring myself another mug of coffee. I watched Rae gather her things, double- and triple-checking her purse.

"How much time do you have before you go?" I asked.

She sighed. "Uh, fifteen, twenty minutes?"

I wiggled my eyebrows. "How about a quickie for good luck?"

She laughed. "I just did my hair and makeup. It's not happening."

"Oh, come on, gorgeous. You know how fast I am in the mornings."

She shook her head, giggling. "Not a chance. But if you play your cards right tonight, you won't have to make it quick."

"Mm, is that a promise?"

She smiled up at me and I chugged back the rest of my second mug of coffee. I walked over to her, threading my arms around her waist. Touching her ignited a fire in my gut. Gazing into her eyes seized my heart within the palm of her hands. Every time I held her, she held me back. And the idea that there would come a time when an hour would sit in between her holding me held my gut hostage with terror.

"I promise, but you'll have to wait until later. You know, after we find a fun party to go to and all."

I grinned. "I'm holding you to it, then."

She giggled. "Good. Because you know you're my favorite way to unwind."

"Oh, really now?"

"Mm-hmm. Really."

"Well, I'll keep that in mind while I'm watching Mike and Ally suck face all day."

"What in the world do you think they did for all that time before dinner yesterday?"

I snickered. "Do you really want me to recount it for you?"

She paused. "Wait a second, am I missing something? Did you and Michael talk? What happened?"

I threw my head back in laughter. "I don't know any details for sure. But I'm sure it involved a lot of cuddling, heavy petting, and Mike begging to get between her legs before Ally came to her senses and wrapped herself up in a petticoat."

"You're so mean."

I chuckled. "Do you have another idea of how that went down yesterday?"

"Actually, no. I don't."

I kissed the top of her head, trying to respect the boundaries of her makeup. I didn't like that, though. It wasn't Rae, and I didn't like the fact that she felt she had to doll herself up to make a good impression. Especially without me next to her on campus while those horny-ass college boys roamed around. Even in her nice black pants and button-front shirt, she looked outstanding. Her clothes didn't have to cling to her like some girls in order to show-case the beauty of her body.

And I wouldn't be there to protect it.

"Call me if you need anything, okay?" I asked.

She nodded. "I promise I will."

"And you're sure you don't want someone with you? Even if it's Ally?"

"I promise. I need to do this on my own. Mom is still concerned as to why I need an entourage with me on this thing. I know she'll use it against me if she thinks someone came with me to orientation. I need to show her I can do this alone so the next week and a half with her isn't atrocious."

I grinned. "All right. Well, get out of here before you're late. I told you. No quickies, no matter what you try to pull."

She laughed, and the sound filled me with joyous pride.

"You're insane, you know that?" she asked.

I kissed her nose softly. "Insane for you."

"I'll keep in touch."

"I'll keep my phone on me."

And as she pulled away from my grasp, it took all I had to not put my foot down and tell her I was coming with her.

Especially since I wanted to be at her side for purely selfish reasons.

15

RAELYNN

Butterflies took flight in my stomach as I took a cab to the bank. The first thing I wanted to do before this damn orientation was get this money in a separate account. A place where neither myself nor my mother could touch it. The bank line was long, and I feared I might miss opening orientation. But I needed this money to be safe.

And this was the only way I'd get away from my mother without her asking questions in order to get it done.

"Welcome to P&R Banking. How may I help you today?"

I sighed. "Yes. Hi. I already have a checking and a savings account with you guys. I'd like to maybe open a third account? Or open an investment account?"

"Well, I can certainly help you with choosing the right one out of the ones you have open. But if you want to open an investment account, you'll have to go take a seat."

She pointed and I looked over at the overflowing chairs in the corner. There was no way in hell I'd open up something like that without being late to orientation.

"Okay, well, can I make a cash deposit into my savings account, then?" I asked.

The woman smiled. "Of course! Just fill out this deposit slip and hand it over with your money. I'll get your account looked up and get you squared away."

I filled it out quickly, then started pulling wads of cash out of my purse. I felt all eyes on me as I kept taking them out. Counting them in front of the woman before jotting numbers down. I didn't know exactly how much I had. All I knew was that I had to get it off my person.

Can I open a security box for the diamonds and other shit?

"Here, let me help," the woman said.

I started handing her money I hadn't unraveled. And after ten minutes of people cursing behind me, we had a final tally. Seven thousand dollars. I had seven thousand dollars stashed in my bedroom. And at least that in diamonds and jewelry at the bottom of the purse. I smiled warily at the woman and she gave me the side-eye. Like I was someone to be warned against.

"Do you guys have safety deposit boxes here?" I asked.

"We don't," she said flatly.

So much for good first impressions.

After the money got deposited and I had my receipt in my hand, I made my way quickly out the door. I used the little bit of cash I kept on hand in a small wad at the bottom to pay the driver, then rushed across campus. I had to find the sports stadium. I felt myself sweating down the nape of my neck and my forehead. Ruining my fucking makeup as I sprinted as quickly as I could.

"Come on, where are you?" I groaned to myself.

Finally, after what seemed like hours of running around, I saw a bunch of kids filing into a massive building. As I dabbed at the sweat on my forehead with a tissue, the butterflies of nerves turned into butterflies of excitement. Older kids at the doors greeted me. One even handed me a water bottle before giving me another tissue. I thanked her and giggled, to which she giggled right back. Then I was handed a program.

And a small map of the university.

Everything felt and looked fantastic. The dean got up and made a speech as I took a seat next to a few girls. They looked at me before one of them patted me on my knee, asking me my name. Passing notes to me back and forth on our programs. Already, I'd found some girls to tag along with. Something that definitely wouldn't have happened had Clint been with me.

"Where are you from?"

"What's your major?"

"That shirt is so cute, where did you get it?"

"Converses! I've never been brave enough, my feet are so wide."

"Do you have any of that lip gloss with you? It's gorgeous."

I didn't even pay attention to the ceremony. Or the speech. I was too excited about finding some girls to pal around with. After we were dismissed, the girls dragged me over to a tour of the dorms. Which were bigger than I imagined.

"If we requested one another, we could be roomies!"

"I'd much rather room with someone I've met than leave it to chance."

"Do you like classic rock? I listen to it while I'm trying to sleep."

I smiled. "I love classic rock. My boyfriend does, too."

One of the girls slipped her arm around mine and I walked with them around campus. The dorms we saw had private bathrooms connecting two rooms apiece. And there were four of us, which made us very excited. There was chatter about not sharing bathrooms with strangers and we all jotted down our names and numbers, hoping it wasn't too late to get in our roommate requests. With every tour we took, I saw myself on this campus. Walking around with my books. Studying in the library. Rooming with these three girls I'd hooked up with.

This is perfect.

"All right, who's ready to try the cafeteria?"

"I hope they have salads and soups. Otherwise, I'll have to do the most expensive plan."

"If the cafeteria food isn't bad, it'll be worth the money you'll save."

"Yeah, these meal plans are ridiculous."

"But you get more flexibility with off-campus plans!"

"Rae, what do you think?"

I looked between the three girls and shrugged.

"Why not have the best of both worlds?" I asked.

"Oh, I like that idea."

"Do they have a plan like that?"

"Oh! It's the middle tier plan!"

"Rae, you're a genius."

I smiled as the four of us walked into the cafeteria. The tour broke up and we all got in our respective lines, and I couldn't believe the selections of food. There was a hot bar and a salad bar.

Soups and sandwiches and wraps. There was a stir fry station and an all-breakfast bar. Which I quickly went toward.

"Oh, just like me. I love breakfast."

I looked over at the girl and I couldn't conjure her name.

"Don't worry about it. Rae, right? I'm Meredith," she said.

I snickered. "Sorry. Today's been a bit of a whirlwind."

"Right? I mean, it's been insane. But I'm glad I found you guys. I was terrified I'd do this orientation alone."

I heard Kristen call out. At least, I thought her name was Kristen.

"Over here, guys! We got a view with this table!"

Meredith lowered her voice. "Kirstie, right?"

I snickered. "I thought it was Kristen."

The two of us picked up our trays and made our way to the table. We all sat down, and I gazed out through the window I sat against. It looked like the whole of the campus could be seen from here. There were lush trees and brick walkways. People walking below us and professors strutting across campus. I saw two or three different tours walk underneath us before someone cleared their throat.

And when I looked back at the girls, I found them staring at me.

"So, did you say something about your boyfriend liking classic rock?"

I paused. "Kayla, right?"

She smiled. "Yep! Kayla and Kristie."

Kristie. That's it. "Do you two know one another?"

Kristie smiled. "We went to the same high school. Not really friends, until we figured out we were coming to the same college."

Kayla nodded. "And now we're best buds!"

Meredith giggled. "Well, I'm Meredith. And this is Rae. We don't know each other, but she's cool."

Kayla nodded. "Totally. But, I want to know more about this boyfriend."

Kristie smiled. "Is he hot? High school sweetheart? Coming with you to college?"

Meredith snickered. "Who brings a boyfriend to college with all these hunky men walking around campus?"

I paused. "Wait, is that not a thing?"

Meredith looked over at me. "Is what not a thing?"

I sighed. "Not bringing a boyfriend to college. Because he's definitely here with me right now. He's waiting for me to get back from orientation."

Kayla held up her hand. "Wait, wait, wait, wait, wait. Your boyfriend is here with you, but not on campus with you?"

Kristie grinned. "Sounds like trouble in paradise."

Meredith took a sip of her water. "Why bring him anyway? I mean, if he's not going to be with you here, what's the point?"

I furrowed my brow. "I'm not following."

Kristie interjected. "What she means is, college changes people. Friends grow apart and people fade away. They find their own group of friends to fall into. Like the jocks and the geeks and the sorority girls. I mean, it's why I broke up with my boyfriend last week."

Kayla gasped. "Wait, you did? With Jared?"

Kristie nodded. "Uh huh. I mean, he's going to college on the other side of the country. What's the point? Besides, did you see those guys in front of us at orientation? I've already got my eye on the redhead."

I looked over at Meredith and she shrugged.

"I mean, there are a lot of college guys around here. It's a completely different ball game with dating and stuff," she said.

Kayla smiled. "Don't you want to know what it's like to be with a man instead of some high school boy?"

Kristie grinned. "I sure as heck do."

Kayla giggled. "And this way, you can date as many guys as you want! You don't have to be tied down. In college, no one expects you to be. You could have four or five guys taking you out on nice dates and fawning over you and wanting to make out. It's a girl's dream out here, and having some high school boyfriend back home kind of ruins that. Don't you think?"

I didn't like how they were talking. Nor did I like the way any of this sounded. I expected it to grate against my ears. I expected myself to kick back and defend myself. But I found myself listening instead. Leaning in as they chattered on about stories they'd heard from friends. Romantic dates and never settling down. Trysts with professors and forbidden loves that made classes all the more exciting. I found myself hooked, listening to their stories. Meredith and I leaned in as Kristie and Kayla chattered on.

Kristie sighed. "And I mean, how in the world can I know what kind of guy I want in my life if I haven't even declared my major yet? I don't know what I want to do for the rest of my life, or where I want to go. Much less who I want to be at my side for it. No, no. Coming into college single is the best decision I've made."

And holy fuck, did she ever have a point.

16

CLINTON

Ally swallowed her food down. "Don't worry, Rae will be fine. She's always been independent like this. It actually shocked me when she was okay with the idea for all of us to come along with her."

Mike nudged her. "No one said anything about Rae not being okay."

She shrugged. "It's written all over his face, Michael. I mean, look at him."

I sighed. "I'm literally in front of you right now."

Sitting at breakfast with Mike and Ally was awkward enough. But having them watch me watch the clock? That was just embarrassing. The minutes ticked by like quicksand, slowly swallowing me whole. Never going fast enough. Was Rae having a good time on campus? Was she okay? Did she feel overwhelmed?

Ally was right.

I was worried about her.

"Well, I don't know what you've got planned for the day. But Ally and I figured we'd make it a hot tub and pool day. You in?"

I looked over at Mike, sighing. "Actually, there's something I want to do before Rae gets back from campus."

Ally cocked her head. "Oh? What's that? Do you need any help?"

Mike nodded. "Yeah. I mean, we don't mind keeping you company so you aren't alone today."

I snickered. "Thanks. I appreciate it, but it's not necessary. I don't need company. It'll be quick, then I'll join you guys at the pool. Okay?"

Mike smiled. "Good. Ally and I plan to be there around eleven."

I nodded. "I'll meet up with you once I'm done."

I slammed back my last mug of coffee before I pushed out of the chair. I could've wasted all day just sitting and talking with them. But I had my mind made up. I walked over to the elevators until Mike and Ally turned their heads. Then I darted off toward the business center. I'd been working all morning on a rudimentary resume on my phone. It wasn't much, but it was something. I sat down at one of the computers and logged into my email. I had to get the damn thing edited and professional-looking before I could print it out. Turns out, there were some decent jobs in the area I qualified for.

So why not put in some applications?

After printing a few of them out, I paid for them at the front desk. I didn't want something like this being charged to Mike's credit card. The last thing I wanted was anyone knowing what I was doing. Not because I was ashamed or shit like that. But because I didn't want anyone getting excited. Or getting their hopes up. I didn't want them to be cheering me on and making plans only for me to disappoint them.

That petrified me.

I flagged down a cab and quickly got in. I had to pull up the names of the places hiring before I could rattle off the address. Thank fuck, I had enough sense to jam my wallet with some money. And then, away we went. I turned around and watched the hotel fall into the horizon. We made stops along the way, allowing me to get out and rush in to hand over my application. I knew I wasn't overly qualified for the positions. But sometimes that played in people's favor. Sometimes, being overqualified was just as bad.

If I could sell myself as 'room for improvement' and 'willing to be molded,' I stood a chance.

"Hello. My name is Clinton Clarke. I wanted to drop off my resume for the job position open in your establishment."

"Hi there! Clinton Clarke. I saw you had a part-time job opening and I was hoping I could apply. I have my resume right here."

"Hello, Clinton Clarke. It's good to meet you. Here's my resume. I know I don't have much experience, but I'm a quick learner and willing to be molded for the position."

"Hello."

"My name is Clinton Clarke."

"Thank you so much for your time."

I put my best foot forward. I was as cordial and open as I could be. And while a couple of the jobs practically tossed my resume in the trash before I got out the door, a few sounded promising. Two of the places where I applied sat down with me immediately. Asked me a few questions. Whether or not I was going to be working around a college schedule. And one of the managers lit up when I told him I wouldn't have a schedule to work around. That I'd fit wherever they put me.

It wasn't the most glamorous job. But it was one of the full-time positions.

After dropping off twelve different applications, I promised most of them I'd follow up in a week if I didn't hear anything. I got pretty good at snuffing out who to follow up with, too. Those who smiled at me, or offered me paperwork to fill out, gave me cues that they were interested. And those that simply nodded their heads before stowing my resume away got tossed out in my mind. If they called, great. If not, no skin off my back.

And when I looked at the clock, I smiled.

"Oh, hell yeah," I murmured.

I'd spent three hours out, which meant it was almost noon. The morning had flown by, and that made me smile. Only three more hours to go and Rae would be done for the day. I was looking forward to asking her how her day had gone. I wanted to know everything. I told the driver to take me back to the hotel before I paid him for his time. And after I tipped him, I rushed back upstairs.

Where my eyes landed on my journal.

Suddenly, thoughts sprang to my mind. New places to take my book. New plot holes I needed to fill. I snatched it off the bedside table and flipped it open. All the way to the very back of the pages.

It was getting full. I'd need a new one before the weekend was out. My hand flew across the page, scribbling in my chicken scratch. I used as many truncations as I could. Anything to make the writing go faster before the images faded away. A smile grew across my face as the stories unfolded. Stories I'd eventually type up and string together.

Possibly hand over to an editor one day.

Wow, what a dream.

For now, everything was a simple stream of consciousness. Not much punctuation. Definitely no formatting. Thoughts in the margins of the pages. Some of it highlighted. Others crossed out. One of these days, I needed to start putting my words into a real document. A legible one. Instead of scratching down in this thing and letting the ink slowly fade away.

Once I get a job, I can save up for a laptop.

I smiled at the thought. As I finished writing and closed my journal, I thought about all the things I could do with my musings. With my thoughts. With my writings. With my poems. I had all sorts of things in my journal. And while the back third of it was being taken up by a fantastical story of betrayal and brotherhood, it wasn't the only thing I had in here. I had poems dating all the way back to my middle school days. Short stories of love and lust. Pride and humor. Darkness and blood. I wrote whatever came to mind. Whatever inspired me. And over the years, I had collected a great deal of journals.

Twenty-two of them, to be exact.

My writing had fallen off in high school. Mostly because it wasn't 'cool.' I snickered at the thought. How I could've been such an idiot was beyond me. But ever since I could write, I'd been writing. Jotting my thoughts down. Turning those thoughts into stories to tell. Lessons to teach others one day with my words. I sighed as I looked up. I set my journal down and walked over to the window. I slipped the curtains open before sliding the door to the side, then I stepped out onto the balcony.

Gazing out over the expanse of L.A. that I could see.

All this time, I'd been waiting for things to feel right. Waiting for things to fall into place. Waiting for pieces to snap into their rightful positions. Maybe the timing would never be perfect. Maybe there wasn't such a thing as pieces falling into place. Maybe it was all our own doing. Putting things in a prioritized line and feeling good about it.

Seize the chance, Clint. Like you just did with those resumes.

And as the thought crossed my mind, a grin slid across my cheeks.

17

RAELYNN

"Hey! Allison!"

I waved her down as Michael popped up from his lounge chair. I slipped through the fence with my bathing suit on and my T-shirt hanging just past the middle of my thighs. Allison slid off her chair and came running for me. She slipped around in the water before crashing into me, holding her wide-brimmed hat to her head. I caught her and laughed as we stumbled together before ultimately crashing back into another chair.

And as Michael walked over, he pulled up chairs for all of us.

"Tell me everything," Allison demanded. "All of it. How was orientation? How was campus? Did you meet any of your teachers?"

Michael chuckled. "Settle down, Suzie Q, with your tirade of questions. Let the girl breathe."

Allison sat down next to Michael and the two of them threaded their hands together.

"Are you breathing now?" she asked.

I snickered. "Has anyone seen Clint? I went upstairs to find him, but he wasn't there."

Michael shrugged. "He said he had something to do before you got back from your orientation. But we haven't seen him yet."

Allison nodded. "He said he was going to join us around eleven or so."

"Rae! Hey!"

I turned around at the sound of his voice. I got up from my chair and rushed for him. I jumped into his arms, smiling and laughing as his bare torso caught me. His legs were clad in a pair of board shorts, just aching to get wet.

He kissed my cheek and my heart exploded with happiness.

"Oh, I'm so glad to see you, Clint."

He murmured. "I thought your day wasn't done until three."

I shrugged. "The tours were pretty pointless. So, after lunch, I decided to walk around campus before coming back."

He squeezed me tight. "Well, I'm glad you're here."

"Me, too."

I committed how I felt to memory. The feel of his touch. The warmth of his skin. I tried erasing all those things the girls had said at lunch as he peppered my cheek with kisses. He set me down on my feet and I looked up into his eyes. Into the loving, tender, gracious eyes of the boy I loved. Clinton Clarke. The boy I'd once hated, but who was now in my corner. The boy who had my back, no matter what.

Those girls are wrong. I could never give him up.

"So how did orientation go? Was it as boring as you figured it would be?"

His question ripped me from my trance, and I found myself not wanting to talk about it. Instead, I took his hand and slowly walked us toward the pool. I slipped my shirt off, watching as his eyes danced down my body. I grinned as I took another step toward the edge. I held my arms out, ready to do a back dive off the side.

Before Michael crashed into me, sending me hurtling with him into the pool.

"Gotcha!"

I shrieked. "Michael!"

We fell into the water and I heard splashing all around me. I clamored for the surface, emerging with a massive smile on my face. Allison's laughter followed her into the pool. I felt a pair of arms around me before Clint popped up. He smiled brightly with his face dripping wet, and I wrapped myself around him. My legs around his waist. My arms around his neck. Getting as close to him as I could before our foreheads fell together.

"You're not avoiding my question, are you?" he asked.

I heard the worry in his voice. "I'm not. It was just--I mean, orientation. We toured one of the dorms. Ate food in the cafeteria."

He chuckled. "Was it terrible?"

"Actually, it wasn't half bad."

"What about the dorms. As small as you figured?"

I shrugged. "Maybe not as small. I'm just glad there's no communal hallway bathroom."

"Wait, that's a thing?"

I nodded slowly. "The dorm we toured had a bathroom that connected two rooms at a time. That's it."

"Well, thank fuck for that."

I giggled and captured his lips with a kiss. But guilt still crawled around in my stomach. I wanted to be able to forget about it. I wanted to erase that damn lunch from my memory. Even as I kissed him, though, the conversation was still there. In the back of my head. Like a damn virus trying to infect me.

Just keep kissing him until it goes away.

I slipped my tongue into his mouth as he held me close. We bobbed along in the water, not a care in the world given to who might see us. I moaned down the back of his throat and clung to him as he danced on his tiptoes in the water. And as our teeth clattered together, I felt him chuckling.

He slowly eased away.

"Mmm, I think someone missed me."

I giggled. "Maybe a bit."

He kissed my forehead. "Let me come with you next time, then?"

"Maybe. Oh! Wait."

Clint paused. "What?"

I grinned. "I heard about a frat party worth checking out tonight."

Michael swam over. "Sorry, did I hear someone say something about a party?"

Allison held on to his back. "Will there be drinking?"

I rolled my eyes. "It's college. Everyone drinks."

She frowned. "Even though they aren't allowed to?"

Clint laughed. "You're too cute, Ally. You know that?"

I giggled. "Come on. It'll be fun. A college party, welcoming the freshman to campus. It should be worth a stop-off, at least.

Maybe after dinner? If it sucks, we can go get ice cream or something somewhere."

Michael smiled. "Or come back and night swim."

Clint pointed at him. "That code for skinny dipping? I'm all about skinny dipping."

Allison grimaced. "Count me out."

I nodded. "Me, too. You boys can have a sausage fest while you're naked in the pool while Allison and I watch movies on television."

"No, no, I meant out of the party."

We all groaned at Allison's words.

"Come on, live a little. Have some fun," I said.

Clint nodded. "It's really not going to be that bad. If someone offers you a drink, just say 'no' and they'll leave you alone."

Allison shook her head. "That's not what I see on television. People keep asking until they wear you down."

Michael laughed. "Sweetheart, no one is going to press their good alcohol onto someone who won't enjoy it. Trust me."

Clint sighed. "Ain't that the fucking truth."

I snorted. "Fine. If you don't want to come, Allison, you can stay behind while we go have a good time."

Michael nodded. "Yep. I'll go with Clint and Rae."

"Hey, I don't want you to go alone, though. What if there are girls there?"

Clint grinned. "There will be. Might want to come and make sure your territory stays marked."

Allison rolled her eyes. "Fine. Whatever. Okay. But I'm not drinking or doing any of the drugs."

I snickered. "None of *the* drugs. Got it."

Michael wiggled his eyebrows. "Anyone up for some pregaming before the party tonight?"

I paused. "What are we pregaming with?"

Clint nodded. "Yeah, we can't drink at the bar here."

Allison giggled. "Michael snuck some alcohol in his suitcase."

My jaw dropped open. "You've been holding out on us!"

Clint gasped. "Mike. I'm hurt. We're supposed to be besties, bro."

He barked with laughter. "All right. Dinner in, then the pregaming shot happens at eight. Sound good?"

I paused. "Better make it nine. I've heard these parties don't really get going until then."

Michael nodded. "All right. Dinner in our rooms, pregame shot at nine, then we head out to this elusive party Rae heard about on her new campus."

We swam around in the pool before Clint eventually tugged me out. He stopped asking me about orientation--thank God--but I saw that look in his eye. He couldn't keep his hands off me in the pool. He couldn't get away from Michael and Allison quickly enough. I barely snatched up my things as he pulled me toward the back entrance of the hotel. Ready to get into our room.

"I've been waiting for you to come home all day," he murmured.

The second our hotel door closed behind us, his lips were against mine. His hands ripped my bathing suit off me as I fiddled with his trunks. His raging cock called to me. I felt my thighs warming. Oh, yes. Those girls at lunch were completely wrong.

No college man would ever make me feel the way Clint did.

"You looked smoking hot in that bathing suit."

He wrapped his lips around my nipples before shoving me to the bed.

"Fucking hell, I couldn't stop thinking about you, gorgeous."

I watched him stroke his cock as his wet bathing suit slipped to the floor.

"And now? You're mine until nine," he growled.

18

CLINTON

When my lips fell against her wet skin, the animal inside me popped. I needed to claim her. Mark her. Take her as mine as quickly as possible. I bit into the meat of her breast. I felt Rae arch against me as moans left her lips. Her legs curled up, exposing that wet pussy for me as her curves dripped with water from the pool.

I quickly tossed her thighs over my shoulders.

"Clint. Clint, I--I-I-I--"

I panted between the valley of her breasts as my cock rubbed against her pussy folds.

I slicked myself with her, shuddering at how wet she was for me. Her legs clamped around my cheeks as I raised up, fisting my cock at its base. I watched as I pressed my tip against her entrance. Her body opened for me as her back arched. Her pussy swallowed me down. Inch by inch. Disappearing into her body as my balls pulled up.

I grunted as our hips fell together.

"Rae. So fucking perfect."

"I love you. Take me, Clint. Please."

I gripped her hips and pulled her closer to the edge of the bed. Then I folded her in half. With my hands pressed into the mattress, I snapped my hips against hers, rendering her helpless as she got pinned underneath me. Her jaw unhinged. Her body vibrated. I felt her walls already clamping down around me as I pounded into her. The bed slammed against the wall. Over and over again, with my thrusts. I didn't care who heard, either. I didn't care if Mike and Ally heard. If they were giggling, or making fun of us. I needed Rae. I needed her presence. Her warmth. Her body. I needed to be reminded of our connection. Of the reason I put in those damn resumes in the first place.

Because she, alone, was the only reason I'd ever pull away from my duties at home.

"I love you. I love you. Fucking hell, I love you, gorgeous."

"Yes, Clint. Harder. Oh, fuck me harder. Yes, that's it. Fuck!"

The sounds of wet skin slapping wet skin filled the room. I felt myself growing against her walls. Her nails raked down my arms, leaving behind red marks I'd wear with pride tonight. I captured her lips and folded her knees all the way to her fucking chest, feeling her tits bounce against me. I swiveled my hips and dug myself into her clit. And as our teeth clattered together, I felt her unraveling. I swallowed her moans as she fell off the edge.

Quivering around me and tempting my own fate.

"Yes. Yes. Yes. Yes."

I growled as I swallowed her desperate sounds.

"Oh, Clint. Yeah, baby."

I rutted against her. Like a fucking beast. My hands found hers and I threaded our fingers together before pinning them above her head. I raked my curls against her clit. I felt her squeezing my cock. And as her pulsing pulled me over the edge, I felt myself filling her. Pump after pump. Thread after thread.

Until I fell against her, absolutely spent.

"I love you, Clint."

The whispered words warmed my heart as I kissed the crook of her neck.

"I love you too, Rae. More than anything in this world."

I stayed there, sheathed inside her body. I kissed down to her nipples, lapping at them softly as she trembled from the aftershocks of her orgasm. I expected my dick to dwindle, to shrivel up and fall right from between her legs. But it didn't. I stayed hard as I pressed against her walls, her legs sliding from my body. Our eyes connected. Our souls intertwined. And as I slowly slid myself out, she gasped.

"Clint."

I eased myself back in. Watching and reveling in how her eyes fluttered closed.

We had hours to burn before this pregame shot of ours. Before our night kicked off and the party consumed us.

And I knew just how to pass the time.

19

RAELYNN

I sighed. "Maybe this wasn't the best idea."

Clint chuckled. "I think that's the shots finally talking."

Michael snickered. "Told you not to do three on an empty stomach."

Allison giggled. "Hey. We know they had a good time. Gotta release those muscles somehow."

I gawked. "Allison!"

She roared with laughter. "What? Michael and I are in the next room. We had to crank up the television to drown you two out."

Clint rubbed my back. "Should've eaten something before those shots, gorgeous."

I rolled my eyes. "And whose fault is that?"

I sighed as I gazed up at the house. Freshman and other college members of all sorts and ages and races hung off the porch. Poured from the front door. In and out. Like a constant rotating shuffle of craziness. Music blared onto the porch. Bodies swayed to the beat. Red cups were hanging in the air, connected to bodies with hazy, alcohol-dimmed eyes.

"I don't know about this," I murmured.

Allison slipped her arm around mine. "Oh, come on. It's all part of the experience, remember? And if we hate it, we can always leave. That's what you told me."

I nodded slowly. "Just didn't think I'd be the one to bail."

Clint kissed my temple. "And I'll be here with you the entire time. You'll be fine. I promise."

Michael stood in front of me. "Yeah. You've got us this time around."

They were my best friends. Clint was my comfort. My soft place to fall. So why didn't I feel reassured by their words?

Why wasn't I reassured by his kiss?

I drew in a deep breath and tightened my grip on Allison's arm. I looked over at her and she gave me that innocent smile I'd come to love over the years. We were complete opposites who just happened to fit each other perfectly. Two lost pre-teens navigating the sea of middle school while trying our hardest not to get picked on. Me, with my ratty clothes and mangled hair and angry eyes. Her, with her perfectly-matched outfits and straight hair and soft smile. Two girls who never had a chance of meeting one another outside in the real world.

Somehow sitting next to one another in homeroom back in sixth grade.

"I love you, Allison," I said.

She giggled. "That's the alcohol talking."

"No, I mean it. You're my bestest friend in the whole world. I love you."

"Bestest? What kind of word is that?"

I grinned. "The only word that fits right now. That's what kind of word it is."

"No more alcohol for you."

I laughed. "Maybe just one more drink. Or two."

Michael took Allison's other hand. "You guys ready to go in?"

Clint placed his hand on the small of my back. "Ready when you are."

And I found myself bristling at his touch.

We all walked inside where the music was thumping so loudly I couldn't hear myself think. People rushed around. Couples were making out in corners with their clothes half off. There was a strobe light somewhere, making it harder to see. And as someone passed by me, they shoved a drink into my hand. Michael's, too. Clint's hand had one, and even Allison ended up with one before the darkened blur passed us by.

"No, thank you," she said.

Allison set her drink on a table and abandoned it. I sniffed mine. There were hints of fruit punch and pineapple. A tantalizing combination. I sipped the drink as Allison snuggled tightly against me. It hit my tongue and my eyes widened. There was cinnamon in this, too. A heady combination that had me chugging the entire drink back.

"Okay, let's slow down a bit," Clint said.

He took the cup from me, but my lips followed it. I cast a glance up at him before Michael took Allison from my side. The two of them started dancing, with his hands sitting low on Allison's hips. My eyebrows rose as a grin crossed my face. But then I felt someone's hands on my shoulders.

"Wanna dance?"

I heard Clint's voice in my ear and I looked up at him. He smiled down at me, but for some reason I wasn't comforted by his presence. We moved with the beat for a little bit. He caught me as people shoved me around. Someone else came by and shoved a drink into my hand. And already, I smelled that fruit punch and cinnamon.

Before Clint tried taking my drink away.

"What are you doing?" I asked.

I looked up at him as I turned around.

"I'm taking your drink from you. You've had enough."

I snickered. "Since when do you make that decision for me?"

He paused. "I've just never known you to drink."

"Well, why don't you get a drink and join me? It's my college orientation. Let's celebrate! Woo hoo!"

"Woo hoo!"

The entire room stopped to cheer with me and I burst into laughter. How cool was that? I swiveled my hips and tipped back the drink, swallowing it all down without once removing my mouth. We all got sucked into the party. Into the dancing and the laughter and the conglomerate cheers. Someone started tugging on my arm and I found myself by the counter with Allison while we snacked on chips. My best friend leaned against me as we watched the boys get roped into a game of beer pong.

"Hey! This is Rae. She's my best friend. She starts here in September."

Someone jutted their hand out and shook mine as I tried to focus.

"Hey there. I'm Matt."

"Hey! I'm Jessica."

"Rae? That's such a pretty name. I'm Ralph."

"Nice to meet you! I'm going to be a freshman, too. Well a transfer freshman, but still. I'm Rebecca!"

"DeShawn."

"The name's Curtis. Rae's a very pretty name."

Allison introduced me to anyone and everyone that walked by. I was beginning to think she'd had too many drinks, too.

"Rae! Hi!"

I perked up at the familiar voice. "Meredith! Hey there!"

The girl from lunch walked up to us and I leaned over to Allison.

"I met her at orientation. She's cool," I whispered.

Meredith walked up. "Here you go. Drink for you, and a drink for--"

Allison held out her hand. "No, no. It's okay. I don't drink."

"Oh! Well, I'll get you a water, then. You know, once I make my own trip back."

Meredith winked before she stumbled a bit. Which made me smile.

"A bit too much there?"

She snickered. "Never. Not at parties like this. Oh, my gosh. I'm so glad you made it out. Have you seen Kristie? She's here with Kayla."

"Who?" Allison asked.

I peeked over at her. "Two other girls I had lunch with."

Allison smiled. "Hey! See? You're making friends already. Where are they? I'd love to meet them."

"Kristie! Kayla! Over here!"

Meredith's voice boomed across the kitchen and the two blondes bounded out from the corner. We all hugged and I introduced Allison to the group. And before I knew it, we were diving into conversations about the party and the guys and how good the drinks were. Allison was like a unicorn, the only person at the party not drinking. And while the girls were pretty drunk, it helped me to forget about lunch. About what we all talked about.

Until I found Clint staring at me from the beer pong table.

20

CLINTON

"Yeah! Another one!"

I clapped my hand against Mike's as the guys on the other end of the table had to chug. Again. While I enjoyed a rousing night of getting drunk, it didn't appeal to me right now. It was clear I'd have to keep my eye on Rae. Which I did. From my perch at the game. Allison kept pulling people over to introduce to Rae. Boys and girls alike. And while I didn't like the way some of the guys lingered around them, they eventually dissipated.

Eventually the dynamic duo were surrounded by three drunk, stumbling idiots.

I nudged Mike. "Any idea who they are?"

"Yeah! Got one! Wait, what?"

I nodded. "Over there with Rae and Ally. Who are they?"

Michael shrugged. "Who cares? They're having a good time and--yeah!--so are we. You gonna pay attention or what?"

"Chug! Chug! Chug!" the guys at the other side of the table chanted as their drunken horse of a buddy slammed back yet another beer. He stumbled into the table, almost knocking it over as Mike and I caught it. How in the world had I considered this fun? Everyone was acting like a bunch of children. I sighed as I helped get the table set back up. Readying myself for a rematch.

But, when I looked over at the little girl's huddle, I noticed they were gone.

"Hey. Hey, Mike."

"What?"

"Where did the girls go?"

I looked over at him and saw him rubber-necking around the room.

"I don't know. Did you see where they went?"

I shook my head. "Nope. I'm gonna go find them."

I left the beer pong table and went on the hunt. Rae didn't need to be walking around here with Ally without someone at their side. She'd had way too much to drink already, and Allison didn't know how to navigate parties like this. Mike followed hot on my heels as we pushed our way through the crowded house. The smell of pot slowly began wafting through the air.

We need to get out of here.

The last thing Rae needed was to be caught at a party where there was both underaged drinking and marijuana. Yes, I get it. This was California. But she'd ruin her chances at this school if she was caught in a place like this. Especially by the police.

No. I had to look out for my girl.

"Let's try the back porch," Mike said.

I nodded. "Good plan. They aren't out here anywhere."

We walked around the house and found a wooden gate hanging open. I heard the splashing of water and an in-ground pool quickly came into view. Girls giggled and boys stood around them, ogling their bodies clad in bikinis. Red cups had been discarded in corners. I saw two wallets and a damn cell phone just sitting in the grass. I shook my head. How the hell had I done this with my life? And in high school, no less.

Mike slapped my chest. "There they are."

I lifted my eyes and heat shot up my spine. What the fuck was Rae doing with a group of guys? I saw Ally standing next to her, clinging tightly to her arm as Rae laughed. Her head fell back and I saw those boys eyeing her. One of them was standing much too close. I saw those three other girls gathered around them. All of them, huddled around the edge of the pool.

"Cannonball!"

Some asshole ran off the diving board and curled up his legs. He splashed everyone standing at the edge of the pool and it made Rae roar with laughter. Her face lit up as she looked over at Ally, who was laughing her ass off, too.

It's nothing, Clint. Just your girl having a good time with her best friend.

But I felt a stir of jealousy erupt in my gut.

Even though I tried stuffing it down, it sat there. Churning. Blending. Igniting a fire in my chest. That was the old Clint. Not the new Clint. I wouldn't smother Rae tonight. She was enjoying herself, and after all the shit she had to put up with, she deserved a chance to unwind. A chance to let loose. A chance to be free.

But, at the expense of her getting arrested?

"Wait a second. Is that--?"

I looked over and saw Mike narrowing his eyes.

"What is it?" I asked.

He snickered. "Allison's holding a red cup."

My head whipped back over. "What now?"

One of the guys moved out of the way and I saw it. Ally, with one arm wrapped around Rae's, and her free hand holding a fucking red Solo cup. My jaw dropped open. I watched Mike lunge, headed straight for the two of them. I saw his nostrils flaring. I reached for his arm and held him back. I stood in front of him, holding my hands against his chest.

"What the fuck is she doing? She's never had a damn drink in her life!"

I leveled my eyes with his. "It could just be water, dude. You don't know what's in that cup."

"Clint, have you seen one drop of water around this shithole?"

I sighed. "Okay, but we go up there calmly. We aren't here to police them. Just keep them safe."

"Yeah, and my girl--who hasn't ever had alcohol--is drinking some fucking cinnamon concoction from hell. Get out of my way."

"Mike!"

He shoved me out of the way and stormed up to the girls with me right behind him. The guys in the group turned around with grins on their faces as their gazes ran up and down our bodies. My stare found Rae and her smile dropped. Ally looked at Mike and her jaw fell open. He walked up to her and peered into her cup as I went to stand beside Rae. And when a look of shock dripped over Mike's eyes, I sighed.

Ally shook her head. "It's just a bit of wine. It really isn't anything. I tried a sip of Mom's once."

Mike took her glass. "How many have you had?"

Ally balked. "What? That's my first one. I'm not some lush."

Rae slipped in between them. "What the hell's wrong? She's just having a drink."

Mike snickered. "Yeah. And you've had one too many. Come on. We're going to the hotel."

Ally shook her head. "I want to stay, though. We made some new friends. See?"

I looked over at the girls, who seemed to be grinning. They had these 'I told you so' faces on and their arms were crossed over their chests.

What the hell had they been talking about over here?

"Clint, do something."

Rae motioned over toward Mike, but all I did was shrug.

"He's right. I think things are getting a little out of hand here."

Rae scoffed. "Are you serious right now?"

Ally sighed. "Come on. Just a little more time."

Mike shook his head. "We're going back to the hotel. Now."

I nodded. "I think that's a good idea."

Rae glowered. "Oh, sure you do. You get to party, but I don't. You get to get it out of your system, but I don't. Because then who would take care of you? Right?"

I blinked. "We need to get you some water and some food."

Then, some asshole I didn't recognize stepped in on behalf of our girlfriends.

"Come on, guys. Your girls are having a good time. I'm Lance. This is Chris and DeShawn. The two blondes are Kristie and Kayla. Meredith's the one with the bow in her hair. Why don't you guys stay and have a drink? I promise, we don't bite."

I felt Mike seething with anger. I peeked over at him and saw his nostrils flaring. And when I saw he wasn't going to give in, I nodded, not giving him a chance to respond.

"Sounds like a plan," I said.

Rae sighed with relief, but Ally kept glancing over at her boyfriend. Mike stood tight at her side, claiming what was his in front of the guys. I knew all too well about that game. And he'd figure out at some point that it was a game that never worked. Eventually, Ally would feel smothered. And she'd either talk with him about it or leave.

Then again, I felt myself hovering around Rae, too.

"Clint, back off a bit, would you? I can barely breathe."

"Honey, seriously. Your elbow's in my ribcage."

"Clint, just--there. Like that."

Every time I tried to touch her, she shrugged me off. Every time I tried to offer her something, she waved her hand in the air. Like she was trying to shoo away a needless fly. I didn't like this. Not one bit. The alcohol seemed to change Rae, and not for the better. I understood that road all too well. I didn't want her to make the same mistakes I did.

And yet, as she dragged Ally off for another drink, I saw her making those mistakes.

I was helpless to stop her from ruining herself tonight.

"Come on, man. Is this really their scene?"

Mike's voice pulled me from my trance and I sighed.

"I mean, Ally's having a new experience. Rae's getting the lay of the land when it comes to college. What can we really do?"

He snickered. "The hell are you talking about? You always know what to do. Rae's never been like this around you. How do you fix it?"

I shrugged. "Like you said, she's never been like this around me. I don't know how to fix it. I'm not really sure there's anything to fix."

"You're right. There isn't."

I looked over at where the tinny sound came from and I saw one of the blondes walking up to us.

"Kayla?"

She shook her head. "Kristie. You really should lay off the two of them."

Mike jumped in. "Or what?"

I glared at him. "Dude, take a breath."

Kristie snickered. "You know, this kind of behavior is the exact reason why good girls like them dump their boyfriends before coming to college."

I paused. "Excuse me?"

She smiled. "You heard me. Coming to this party. Getting angry that they're drinking. Getting jealous of other guys watching them. That kind of behavior gets you dumped, gentlemen."

Mike shook his head. "My girlfriend and I are going to the same college. She'd never do that to me."

The girl giggled. "Do you even hear how stupid you sound right now?"

I stepped in. "You can tuck in that language with my boy here."

She ran her gaze down my body. "Then listen closely. If you try to check your girls all the time on their actions, they're going to start hiding things from you. It's only natural. They'll do what they want, but they won't include you. College is to let them fly freely. To help people experience things. You want to be there for that? Then enjoy it with them. But if you don't…" She looked between us and giggled. And with those words, she turned around and left.

"If we don't, what?" Mike asked.

I sighed. "If we don't, they'll dump our asses. That's what she means."

"Follow me," I whispered.

Allison craned her neck back. "Where are we going? Should we tell the guys?"

I rolled my eyes. "Do you really want to check in with Michael every step of every day that you take? Because that's what he's making you do right now. And I know you're uncomfortable."

"I--I mean--I've just never seen Michael like that before."

I snickered. "Well, it's called 'jealousy.' And he'll get over it. Or he won't, and he'll turn into an insecure little dick."

"You think he'd really do that?"

"I think he's doing it now. What do you think?"

I stopped in the middle of the living room dance floor and stared down my best friend. The boys were trying to ruin this night for us, but I wasn't having any of it. Allison was finally having her first drink! Just some wine, but I was proud of her. Finally, she felt comfortable enough to have new experiences. Make new friends. Branch out and try things and step out of her comfort zone a little bit. I was beyond proud of her. I mean, it wasn't like she was chugging back bottles without any regard for herself.

Just a damn glass of wine.

"I think we should go back and find them," she said.

I grabbed her arm. "Oh, no you don't. You're staying with me."

Allison sighed. "But what if he's upset? Or not doing well?"

I smiled. "Then he's got his buddy. Clint. We're here to have fun. I want to celebrate my best friend's first drink."

She blushed. "I've had some of my mother's wine before."

"But this isn't your mother's wine. This is your wine. Come on. Let's go out onto the porch. I need some room to breathe, don't you?"

I tugged her through the gyrating bodies of the living room before we stumbled out onto the porch. The smell of weed hung heavily in the air and it turned my head. There was smoke pouring around the corner. Allison started coughing softly as I moved away from her.

"Where are you going, Rae?"

I furrowed my brow. "Just to check things out. You wanna come, or are you staying?"

I looked back, watching as she shook her head. "No, thank you. I'm staying behind."

"Suit yourself!"

I found my way around the corner and saw Kayla sitting with Meredith. They smiled up at me before Meredith patted the seat on the porch swing next to her. A couple of guys I didn't recognize leaned against the porch railing. One of them had a joint in his hand, and he inhaled deeply. Holding his breath. Staring straight at me before puffing the smoke back out.

And slapping me in the face with it.

"Want some?" he asked.

Meredith grinned. "It's the good kind. Just one puff will relax you."

Kayla giggled. "And by the sounds of it, you do need to relax a little bit. Did you shake off your entourage?"

I shook my head. "What?"

Meredith lowered her voice. "The boy that keeps ruining your evening? Did you shake him?"

Kayla snorted. "See why girls dump their boyfriends before college? They all do that. They all get possessive and weird and clingy. Happened to me. Happened to Mere. It'll happen to you."

The guy handed me the joint. "Try it. Take it in slowly, hold, then let it out."

I looked down at what looked like a large turd. I wrinkled my nose at it, the smell already getting to me. But I wanted to fit in. I wanted to make friends. I wanted to fucking relax. I looked around, making sure Clint wasn't anywhere to be seen. Then I saw down next to 'Mere.'

She patted my back. "There you go. The first hit's gonna be rough. Just work through it. Force your lungs to take it all in."

I nodded as the guy handed me the rolled-up joint. I sighed as I held it to my lips, tentatively sucking on it. The smoke filled my lungs and I already felt my body working against it. My throat jumped as I opened my lungs, forcing the smoke to go in.

"That's it."

"Hold it."

"One, two, three."

"Now, let it out and do it again. Quickly. Come on, come on."

I let out the smoke and quickly took another puff. Only this time, it went down a little smoother. I sucked a bit more down for good measure, then held my breath as I handed it off to Meredith. She smiled at me before taking a puff, and I felt the world slowly tilting around me. I felt lighter than air. Relaxed, and full of happiness.

And as I let out the smoke, the guys in front of me clapped.

"Ten seconds. Good one."

"You want in on another round?"

I nodded. "Oh, hell yeah."

I sank back into the porch swing with Meredith. She threw her leg over my lap as my head fell back. The joint came back around to me and I lifted my head long enough to take a long drag of it. My lungs filled with the smoke and I battled to keep it down. I let myself fall away from my own mind. I didn't think about anything. Not my mother. Not orientation. Not Allison, or Michael, or Clint. Not home, or my money issues. Nothing, except the fact that it felt like my body was floating around in the air.

"Oh, this feels so nice," I moaned.

Meredith groaned. "Here comes trouble."

My head snapped up. "What?"

"Rae? Are you serious?"

My eyes slowly panned over to the corner and I saw Clint emerge. He walked around, his gaze landing directly on me. Smoke from the joint caught his gaze and he snickered. He shook his head, like he was some sort of disappointed parent.

Then he came to stand in front of me.

"What has gotten into you tonight, gorgeous?"

I quirked an eyebrow. "What do you mean?"

Meredith giggled. "Yeah. What do you mean?"

He glared at her before his eyes came back to mine.

"This isn't like you. Getting drunk. Getting high. Are you crazy? What if you get caught?"

I shrugged. "It's part of the college experience. Everyone does it."

He blinked. "Seriously?"

I snickered. "Don't look at me like that."

"Like what?"

"Like you know better than I do. Really, Clint?"

His face softened. "That's not what I was--"

"Yes, it is!"

I leapt off the porch swing and everyone turned their attention to us.

"I don't need you protecting me, Clint. I can look after myself. I did before you came into my life, and I will after you're gone. That's what this is all about. Me standing on my own two feet and carving out a life I want for myself. Not the life you want for me. This is about me taking care of me. Not about me being dragged around like a damn child by my fucking boyfriend."

His eyebrows rose. "Dragged?"

I snickered. "Yeah, Clint. Dragged. Look around you."

I gestured at the party as I slowly circled around.

"Look at it. All of it. I've been so fucking afraid to leave high school behind. But look at all this. Do you think these people brought their high school with them? Their friends and their boyfriends? No, they didn't. They came alone, like I didn't have the balls to."

"What are you saying, Rae?"

"All right, I think it's time to go home. What do you say?" Michael asked.

I felt his hand come down against my arm, but I ripped away from him.

"You might be Allison's boyfriend, but you're not mine. You won't touch me that way."

Michael narrowed his eyes. "Yeah, but you're my best friend, Rae. And you're drunk. High, too. It's time to get out of here."

Allison peeked around the corner. "I'm ready to go whenever you guys are."

I pointed at her. "Did they put you up to this? Did Michael threaten you or something?"

Michael scoffed. "Threaten her? Do you even hear yourself?"

Clint sighed. "This is what happens. Alcohol and weed create paranoia."

I stepped back. "I'm not paranoid!"

Meredith piped up. "She's just trying to have a good time and you guys are trying to control her."

One of the guys spoke up. "Yeah. Not cool, dudes."

Clint snickered. "Yeah, dude. Well, see your way out of this conversation. Come on, Rae. We're going back to the hotel."

I crossed my arms. "And if I don't?"

Clint sighed. "Pouting doesn't look good on you when your eyes are bloodshot. Now, come on. You need food and a shower."

I licked my lips. "Maybe what I need is another boyfriend."

Michael held out his hand. "Whoa, whoa, whoa. Let's take it easy with all this shit."

Allison came up to my side. "You're going to regret this in the morning. Just come with us. You can sleep with me tonight."

Michael paused. "Wait a second, what?"

Clint sighed. "Fucking grand."

I narrowed my eyes at him. "Yeah, sorry I don't feel like bouncing on your cock tonight, you jealous asshole."

He snickered. "Oh, I'm the asshole? You're the one preaching about new boyfriends and not giving a shit how any of this makes me feel. But I'm the asshole?"

I glared at him. "Yeah, that's right! You're the asshole!"

I pulled away from Allison and stumbled over something. Whether it was my own two feet or Allison's shoelace, I didn't know. All I knew was that my drink went flying into the air, all over Clint. And his arms fell open to catch me. My cheek pressed against his chest as I struggled to stand up. And feeling him against my body made me shiver.

But not in a good way.

"Rae, you okay? Can you stand?"

I shoved him away. "Leave me the hell alone."

I pushed my way through the crowd as blood rushed through my ears. I stumbled against the porch, trying to prop myself up.

"Rae! Wait up!"

I rolled my eyes at Allison's voice and kept going. I pushed my way through the crowd as guys held out their arms to catch me. I couldn't stand up. I couldn't keep myself fucking upright. I felt someone guide me to a couch in the living room as music thudded against my ears. Asses swayed in my vision. Guys looked at me and winked before sticking their tongue down someone else's throat.

"Rae, there you are."

I sighed as Allison dropped down beside me. I felt her rubbing my back, but I shrugged her off. I didn't want her concern or words of encouragement. What I wanted was to relax. To forget about everyone and cast all hell to the clouds, for once in my fucking life. I leaned into the couch cushions and closed my eyes. I let the beat of the music whisk me away. And as Allison batted away people who tried to offer me drinks, I felt the world tilting around me.

Must be the weed.

Clint got to do this with his life. If anything, he should understand. He got to party to relieve stress. He got to drink. I'd seen him more than once come into school with bloodshot eyesand the smell of pot on his leather coat.

I wonder what happened to his leather coat.

"Rae? You need anything?"

I sighed. "I need you to shut up."

Allison murmured, "Sorry."

My head fell off to the side. Smoke started filling the room. Someone 'woo hoo''d off in the distance and I shoved my fist into the air.

"Woo hoo!" I exclaimed.

But Allison didn't join me in the exclamation.

I rolled my head over to her and opened my eyes. And when I saw her, I sighed. She had her arms crossed over her chest. Her leg crossed over her knee. She stared down at the floor, her lips moving as she talked to herself.

"Allison, don't let Michael ruin this night for you."

She shook her head. "And what makes you think he's the one ruining it?"

Her eyes met mine.

I scoffed. "I'm not the one ruining it. You were having a good time with a drink and everything before they found us in the backyard."

She sighed. "Did you have to be so mean to Clint?"

"He wasn't getting the picture. He never gets the picture."

"Do you ever talk to him about the picture?"

"I talk to him plenty enough, thanks."

Allison sighed. "What's really going on, Rae?"

I shrugged. "You mean other than my mother stealing my money, wanting to keep me home as a permanent paycheck, and Clint not wanting to move anywhere near me? Nothing."

She blinked. "Wait, what's this about your mother?"

I shook my head. "Nothing."

"It doesn't sound like nothing."

"It is nothing, okay? You know how my mother is. You give an inch, she keeps taking miles until you piss her off for good."

"Does Clint know you want him to move with you?"

I closed my eyes. "If he really loved me, would I even have to ask?"

And when Allison didn't answer, I knew I had mine.

22

CLINTON

Mike put his hand on my shoulder. "She's just drunk, man. You guys are solid."

I barely heard his voice. I barely registered his touch. My mind reeled as I watched Rae storm off, her tense body falling away from me. She peered over her shoulder, casting me a look that could've buried an army six feet under if she had commanded it.

I sighed. "I should've seen this coming."

Mike slipped his hand off my shoulder. "See what coming? The fact that she was going to get drunk and high at a party and lose her mind? Come on, you know the kind of pressure she's been under."

I nodded. "Yeah, I do. And she's been pulling away. Nothing's been the same ever since I told her I wasn't applying to college. I know she resents me for that."

"Dude, she doesn't resent--"

"You mean after all those times she helped me with homework? All those tests she helped me study for? All the work she put in to helping me bring my grades up? And you don't think she resents me for not going to college when she helped with all that?"

Mike snickered. "She helped you graduate. That's all she wanted. It's not her fault her mother started breathing down her neck around the same time."

I shrugged. "Maybe so, but can you see why my mind is doing what it's doing?"

"Sorry. Excuse me. I'm going to go get her," Ally said.

I shook my head. "It won't work."

She snickered. "Then don't have faith. But I'm still going after her."

I watched Ally push between the two of us as she went after Rae. Raelynn Cleaver. The girl who saved me more times than I could count. The girl who pulled me up from the mire of my life and helped me to fly. The girl I had fallen madly in love with.

This shit was never about what school program she wanted to enroll in.

This was about me. It had always been about me. At least, it seemed that way. Had I become too controlling of her actions? Did I not give her the space she needed? Did she feel smothered? Or manipulated?

Have I turned into my father?

"Don't think that," Mike said.

I scoffed. "You don't even know what I'm--"

"You're wondering if you turned into the asshole that raised you. And I can tell you, that's not anywhere near true."

I rolled my eyes. "Seems to me like it is."

"Clint, Rae isn't acting this way because of what you're doing to her. She's acting this way because she doesn't understand how to mitigate her stress levels properly. I love her, but she's always felt as if the world sits on her shoulders. Like she has to save it all in order for her to mean something."

"That's because she's always had to be the strong one."

He shrugged. "Maybe so. But at some point in time, that type of mindset is going to become destructive. It's going to wear her down. She has to learn at some point that she doesn't owe the world anything. That she can't save everyone. That it's okay for things to not go as planned. Even if she has to learn it the hard way."

"I don't want her learning the hard way. The hard way hurts."

"And yet, if that's what she chooses to do, you can't do a damn thing about it."

I shook my head. "I hate that you're right."

He chuckled. "Me, too."

"Do you really think she's afraid of bringing me with her, though? You think she'd have a better college experience if--"

"Don't even say it, Clint. You know that girl is head over heels for you."

I shrugged. "Doesn't mean I'm good for her. At least, not right now in her life."

"Is that how you really feel about it? Or are you trying to justify how she feels and convince yourself her way is the right way? Because I have to tell you, you do a lot of that with her."

I blinked. "What?"

Mike grinned. "You do a hell of a lot of bending over backwards for her and always seeing her point of view on things. The first time I ever saw you stand up to her and speak your piece was when you fought her about applying to college. Maybe this is what she needs. Someone bucking up to her and showing her that she doesn't always have the answers. Maybe that's how she learns this lesson."

"I just wanna love her, man."

"Then love her. But don't feel like loving her means always leaning to her side."

I snickered. "When the hell did you get so wise?"

He gasped playfully. "Clinton. I'm hurt. I've always been wise. I just haven't had anyone to be wise with."

I rolled my eyes and he clapped me on the back. I stood there waiting for Ally to bring back Rae. The throng of people went back to their party after witnessing the drama.

But they didn't reappear.

And it made me sick to my stomach.

"Well, it's pretty clear she doesn't want me at this party," I said.

Mike sighed. "Dude, you can't think about--"

"And if she didn't want me here, then she should have come alone. Left me at the hotel. Or back home, for all I care."

"Wait a second, I thought we ended this shit on a good note. What's happening? Talk to me."

I shrugged off Mike's hand. "You're right, but I'm also right. It's been very clear to me all night that she hasn't wanted me here with her. At her side. Hanging out with her and making memories. She didn't want me on campus with her. She didn't want me to help her with her mother before we came here. If she didn't want me around on this damn trip, she shouldn't have brought me."

"Co--come on, Clint! Please, don't be a drama queen."

I shook my head and made my way off the porch. If Rae needed space, then I needed space. I stormed around the house and made my way into the backyard. I headed straight for the makeshift bar, reached behind it and picked up two beer bottles. I cracked both of them open, then turned around and held one out.

Knowing damn good and well Mike would be there to take it.

"You sure about this?" he asked.

I clinked my bottle against his. "To not chasing the girls down."

He sighed. "Yeah, yeah. Whatever."

I chugged the beer back and my love for it came rushing to the forefront of my memory. I groaned with every gulp. I sighed with relief at the burn working its way down my throat. I tossed the empty bottle in the trash can before reaching for another one, cracking it open on the edge of the bar.

And as I threw the second one back with ease, a crowd gathered around me.

"Chug! Chug! Chug! Chug! Yeah!"

The crowd cheered as I tossed the second one into the bin. I reached for another and broke that one open with my fucking teeth. I held the bottle up and spit the cap out, watching in my peripheral as Mike stepped away. The crowd shut him out, pushing him all the way to the back as he stumbled around with the beer in his hand.

And as I watched him make his way into the house, I gulped down my third consecutive beer.

"Chug that beer! Chug that beer! Chug that beer! Yeah!"

I had people step up to compete, throwing up before getting their second beer down. People offered me shots and I chased them back with beers and cocktails. I filled my stomach with more alcohol than I'd had in months. It tasted amazing. I felt myself relaxing. And as the crowd of college students slowly grew around me, I found myself in a drinking contest with three other muscley men.

"My money's on the bald one."

"Nope, the one in the blue shirt."

"My money's on the guy still drinking. Get him, freshy!"

I chuckled at the nickname as all care and accountability for my life fell to the wayside. I felt the old Clint emerging. But I welcomed it. I didn't stuff him down or try to get him to go away. I brought him out to play as I made new friends. Girls in scanty outfits offered me snacks to soak up the alcohol, winking at me. And all I did was nod. None of them held a candle to Rae. Not in body, not in spirit, and not in soul. I wanted to drink until Rae's memory fell away from my mind. Until her words were drowned out by the beer and tequila washing through my system.

I wanted to drink until I didn't remember this night at all.

Because if she could, then so could I.

"Yeah!" the kids cheered.

"I'm Leslie."

"I'm Carlie."

"I'm Ashley."

I snickered. "You three plan those names, or what?"

They giggled. "Or what."

When I finally looked over at their unanimous answer, I found myself staring at triplets. Fucking triplets. Brown-haired, doe-eyed beauties with massive tits and beautiful hips. One of them wore nothing but a bikini. Another one wore a long shirt and knee high socks with her boots. The last one was clad in glasses with her hair pulled back. Definitely nailing the librarian sort of look.

"Want a drink, ladies?" I asked.

The one in the bikini stepped up. "Actually, I want to challenge you!"

The crowd roared and all the guys shoved their way to the front. My eyebrows rose as she giggled, but her giggle wasn't quite like Rae's. It was harsher, with a snort at the end. Not light and airy and carefree, like Rae's. Still, I ushered her up to the front and gave her the benefit of the doubt. I knew girls that could drink. No use in denying her a shot to drink me under the table.

Which I knew would never happen.

She smiled before taking her first shot. Then another. She chugged back a beer before wiping her spindly little lips. Then she handed me a beer and picked one up for herself before nodding her head. Silently counting down from five.

And when she hit one…

"Go!" she exclaimed.

The bottle hit my lips and I tilted my head back. And as I drowned my sorrows in cheap-ass college-town beer, Rae's words spun through my head. I didn't want anyone else but her. I didn't want another girl in my life. But she'd obviously been thinking about life after me.

That was painfully clear from her words.

I mean, she'd said it. Just like that. She'd taken care of herself and protected herself before me, and she'd do it after I was gone. Those were her words. She saw a life after me, and I didn't see a life after her. I saw a future with her. But nothing else. I didn't see my life without Rae in it. Without her love, and her support, and her beauty, and her intelligence, and her help, and her body.

I hadn't once considered the idea of being with anyone but her.

But she had apparently considered it.

You didn't give her enough romance.

I slammed the beer bottle down and found the girl staring at me.

"Took you long enough, handsome."

You didn't give her enough space when she needed it.

She handed me a shot and I threw it back.

"Looks like he enjoys his tequila!"

Maybe your cock isn't good enough anymore.

She placed a snack in my hand and I threw it back.

"Ready for round two?"

Maybe she just doesn't love you anymore because you're a pathetic loser with no future and no college degree and no aspirations like she has.

I hiccupped as I reached for another drink. Any drink. Whatever drink someone had for me.

"Five, four, three, two, one!"

Just drink until you don't care anymore. It'll happen. It always did before.

And as I tipped the disgusting wine cooler up to my lips, the voice in my head finally got drowned out. I stumbled backward, my hand catching me against the bar as I opened my throat. I let it slide down, mingling with the chips and the cheese and the crackers. Trying to find anything else to focus on.

Like the churning force inside my stomach reach to protest my actions.

23

———

RAELYNN

I didn't like the realization. I didn't like the idea of Clint not loving me. Of him never having loved me. I pushed myself off the couch and tore through the crowd, stumbling against people that cursed me out.

"Fucking hell, bitch. Get out of the way."

"That's my man. Go get your own."

"The fuck!?"

"Rae!"

I sighed. "Leave me alone, Allison."

I heard her hot on my heels and all I wanted was for her to leave me alone. I wanted to go back to the hotel. I wanted to go home. And I didn't even know where home was! It sure as hell wasn't with my mother. She couldn't care less about me and what I wanted. All she gave a shit about was money. What I could give her. What bills I could pay so she could be a lazy bitch. I had no home. Not with Clint. Not with Allison and Michael while they sucked each other's faces off.

I have to get out of here.

"Rae!"

"Leave me alone!" I shrieked.

I pushed through the kitchen and it felt as if the walls were closing in around me. Everyone multiplied and it felt like I couldn't move. Couldn't breathe. Couldn't take a step without knocking into someone. My chest rose and fell quicker than normal. My heart leapt into my throat. My palms started sweating and my back started aching and my muscles locked up.

"Rae? Where are you?"

Allison's voice sounded so far away.

I need quiet.

I felt my body careening to the side as someone shoved into me. I felt pairs of hands on me as the room knocked me around like a damn pinball in a machine. I couldn't get my bearings. Everyone had turned into blurs. I couldn't focus. Couldn't breathe. Couldn't see straight.

Space. I need space.

My back fell against the wall and a door burst open beside me. I yelped, watching as a guy came out of the bathroom. The most horrendous smell followed behind him. The smell of shit and puke. But the safe haven of the bathroom called to me. And I sucked it up enough to slip inside and lock myself in.

"Rae!"

Allison pounded on the door as I drew in quick breaths through my mouth.

"Rae! Open up, please!"

She pounded again as I looked around the small bathroom.

It wasn't any bigger than a half bath. Just enough room for a sink and a toilet. It smelled like death in here. But I was alone. I closed the toilet and sat down before reaching for the air freshener. I sprayed it around me. All over the floor. All over my clothes. All around in the air. Trying to mask that god-awful smell as Allison kept shaking the fucking door on its hinges.

"Will you stop it!?" I screamed.

The knocking ceased and I sighed with relief.

"Please let me in, Rae. Let someone in."

The pleading of her voice made me sigh.

"Just leave me alone. I just want to be alone."

"I know that's not true, Rae. I know you think that's what you want, but I know it's not what you actually want."

I scoffed. "And what do I actually want, genius?"

"Someone you don't always have to take care of."

I sniffled. "Please, go away."

"I'm not going anywhere. Not until you let me in."

"Then you'll stand out there all night."

"Can you get her out of there? I have to take a piss."

Allison hissed behind the door. "Go upstairs, asshole. I'm talking right now."

My eyebrows shot up. "Did you just say 'asshole'?"

"Well, if you weren't acting like one I wouldn't have already made the connection."

I snickered. "Thanks."

"What in the world is going on right now? Do you not want to be with Clint anymore?"

"I'm not talking about this through the door."

"It's either that, or you let me in. There's no other option. So take the help."

I laughed bitterly. "You think this is helping?"

"Well, getting high and drunk isn't helping. So let's try another route."

I sat there, staring at myself in the mirror. My skin had grown pale. My eyes had become sunken in. The bags underneath them were beginning to become a problem as the world tilted around me. I closed my eyes. I drew in deep breaths. I didn't know what I wanted. But I knew I didn't want this.

"Don't shut me out now. Please," Allison begged.

I sighed as I reached over. I unlocked the door and heard her quickly slip in. Her flats slid along the floor as she closed the door. But I didn't hear her lock it.

"You're going to have to--"

"Here we are. All right," Michael said.

I rolled my eyes. "Of course he's with you."

He closed the door, then locked it. "Yeah, because that's what good partners do. They look after those they love."

I snickered. "Glad you're an expert in love now."

Allison pulled me up onto my feet. "You want to tell us what's going on now?"

"And why aren't you with Clint, Michael?"

He shrugged. "He stormed off. Seems you two have that in common."

I rolled my eyes. "Of course he did. Because it always has to be about him."

Allison shook her head. "No it doesn't. You feel like that because you met him during a time when he needed help. And a lot of it. Now you need some but, for some reason, you're not letting him help."

Michael sighed. "You're not letting any of us help."

My face fell. "Because I don't need it."

Allison waved her hand in the air. "Yeah, yeah, yeah. Whatever. Look, I don't care what you've got going on right now. I love you, but I don't care. The only thing I care about is whether or not you're happy. And you haven't been happy for a while. So you can either talk to us, or you can keep it all inside until you explode and alienate everyone around you. Those are your two choices."

I rolled my eyes. "Like you're an expert."

Michael groaned. "Come on. I'm going to go find Clint. We just need to get them out of here so they can sleep this shit off."

I paused. "Wait, he's not with you?"

Michael shook his head. "I told you less than a minute ago that he stormed off. You don't remember that?"

I shook my head slowly. "No, I don't."

Allison sighed. "All right. Time to go back to the hotel. Michael, go find Clint. We can flag down a cab, or call an Uber, or something like that once we get out of this stupid house."

I panicked. "Where's Clint? I need to see Clint."

Michael snickered. "Yeah, well. Don't kick him in the balls before storming off next time. A dude's got feelings, too."

My gut churned with guilt. He was right. I'd completely obliterated Clint before I stormed off. Wait a second, I was in a bathroom? How the hell did I--? People were standing too close to me. The walls were caving in again. They undulated and pulsed, like the blood rushing through my veins.

"Five minutes."

"Rae, you okay?"

"Go get Clint. I've got her."

"She's going to puke."

I nodded. "Yep. Yep, I am."

The guilt turned my stomach. And the alcohol took over. I whipped around and opened the toilet back up with just enough time to erupt. I fell to my knees, shaking as tears streaked my cheeks. I felt someone gathering my hair back before blowing cool air against my sweating skin.

"Worst. Night. Ever," Michael murmured.

Allison sighed. "Just go get Clint. Go. I'm serious. Get the hell out of here."

Michael paused. "Did you just curse?"

I heaved. "Go, damn it!"

Feet scurried across the floor before someone groaned outside. The bathroom door closed and I heard someone flip the lock. It kept coming. And coming. And it hurt like hell. Now I realized why the bathroom smelled the way it had when I first came in. Because with every heave, my asshole opened up, letting out gas that could knock over a damn horse brigade.

"I'm sor--fuck."

Allison sighed. "Just save it for the morning."

"Please, I--oh."

"Seriously. Stop talking. You're going to aspirate if you keep it up."

It felt like my stomach was tying itself in knots. And the entire time, tears dripped into the toilet. Every once in a while, Allison flushed. She picked up the air freshener and sprayed it right on my ass crack hanging out of my jeans. My shirt kept riding up. Why was my shirt riding up? And every time I pulled it down, my jeans fell lower.

"Oh, fuck."

A knock came at the door and I heaved again. I heard Michael's voice, but it sounded far away. I felt my body slipping into nothingness, into a dark expanse that I wanted to swallow me whole and never spit me back out. I'd never felt so miserable. So lost. So afraid before. Was this what a panic attack felt like?

Because I felt more panicked than I ever had in my life.

Allison's voice sounded in my ear. "All right. How we doing down here?"

I heaved. "Oh, shit."

"That good? Great. Well, Michael's got Clint. They're headed out front. Maybe we should try and wash you off long enough to get you out there."

Another knock came at the door and I vomited again.

"Just kidding. Ten more minutes, and then we're going to meet them out there at the Uber. All right?"

She rubbed my back and I started crying.

"Rae?"

Between the heaves, I sobbed. I pressed my cheek against the rim of the toilet and let it all hang out. With my ass crack halfway out of my jeans and my tits shoved up against the warm porcelain, I heard Allison murmur something about a disaster. I didn't care, though. I felt more inclined to cry myself the river that almost swallowed Clint whole all those months ago than pick myself up.

I was tired of picking myself up.

"Why did he leave?" I asked.

Allison paused. "What was that, honey?"

"Why did Clint leave? Why didn't he just stay?"

"From the sounds of it, he's pretty--"

I sniffled. "Why didn't he let me help him with things? Why couldn't I have stayed with him and Cecilia?"

She sighed. "Are you talking about last year?"

I drew in shuddering breaths. "I just wanted him to take me back so I could help, Allison."

"I know. And he did take you back. You're together, honey."

"Not really. Not since them. He's staying for her. For his step-mother. He doesn't wanna come with me because she's family and I'm not family and I'll never see him again because he'll find someone closer and he won't be able to come see me because he doesn't have a bike and he doesn't want to move in with me because he hasn't brought it up because he doesn't love me, Allison."

She snickered. "Oh, boy."

I sniffled. "And all I wanted was for him to love me and for him to like me and for him to always be with me and then he left when things got hard. So how do I know he's not going to leave when college gets hard? When I get stressed and frustrated and hard to be around?"

"I mean, he's doing a good job of sticking around right now."

"Yeah, until I leave to go to college and he's free to do whatever because I'm not around to do anything with and he finds someone else. Maybe he's using college as a way to distance us. Maybe if I stay with Mom, he'll stay with me."

She dropped next to me. "No, Rae. You have to get away from your mother. Even Clint knows that."

"Then why won't he come with me like Michael's going with you?"

She rubbed my back. "Is that what this is about?"

I heaved. "I thought he'd want to come to college with me and move in with me and we could live our lives together and never look back but he's staying for Cecilia so maybe I should stay with Mom until he's ready to move away and make a life for himself."

"Honey, you have got things so backwards it's sickening."

Snot dripped from my nose. "Yeah, I know I'm sick."

And as I went back to dry-heaving into the toilet, I continued to cry. I cried and I cried. The bathroom filled with fumes from my ass, and still I cried. I cried until my voice was hoarse. Until my eyes were so swollen I couldn't see out of them.

Then I felt Allison pull me away from the toilet.

"All right. Come on. Time to go home."

I sighed. "I don't have a home."

And there it was. The five words I'd been scared to utter for months. Clint was my home. And without him coming to college with me, I didn't have a home.

I had *nothing* without him.

24

———

CLINTON

"I don't understand why she can't just talk to me. I mean, am I hard to talk to? Do I seem hard to talk to?"

The girl in the bikini sat beside me, twirling a strand of her hair around her finger.

"I don't think you're hard to talk to at all… what did you say your name was?"

I hiccupped. "Clint. Clarke Cli--no. Clint Clarke."

She giggled. "I'm Ashley."

I nodded. "That's right. The triplet."

Her hand settled against my thigh. "Uh huh."

"You know, I miss her. I miss what we used to be. All the good times and the laughs and the random pastry runs to our coffee house. I mean, we have our own coffee house. And now we have nothing. She's just… we're nothing, you know? At least, it feels that way."

"That's not really fair to you."

"It's not fair to her, either. I just want her to be happy, and she's not. And I don't know what to do. She tells me she needs space, then she's knocking on my door at three in the morning. She tells me she needs time away, and then she's hopping on my dick."

"Oh, lucky girl."

I snickered. "She changed me. I mean, for the better. Like, she's awesome. You'd like Rae."

"Mmm, I bet I would. Does she like girls?"

"Eh, I don't know. She's got Allison as a friend, but I don't see her hanging out with so many--"

I hiccupped and it felt like the alcohol was talking back at me. I managed to not puke at the bar, but I knew I needed to get away from that drinking contest. I stumbled up the porch and flopped back down into the porch swing. Just swinging back and forth. Trying to figure out how the hell things got so far out of control.

And this awesome girl was willing to talk to me about it.

"Tell me more about you," she said.

I snickered. "Me? Well, I'm not the same guy I was before Rae, you know? My father was a dick. I mean, just as absolute asshole. Left me with my stepmom and it's the best thing he ever did for me."

"What's your favorite color?"

I grinned. "The color of Rae's cheeks when she blushes."

She giggled. "What's your favorite vacation spot?"

"Anything with Rae in it. Maybe a nice field somewhere. With a cabin, and a lake. Me working on my book."

I felt my head falling forward before it snapped back up.

"Oh, so you're an author? I bet you make tons of money."

I barked with laughter. "I wish. Maybe one day. Then I can get that cabin in the field with the lake and a great big bedroom to--"

The girl in the bikini--what was her name again?--snuggled tightly against me.

"--to what, handsome?"

I sighed. "To make love to the woman I love. Forever and ever. Until she smiles and all her worries fade away. That's all I want. For my woman to be happy. With me. While we're both succeeding. But what if she doesn't want that?"

She leaned her head on my shoulder. "Oh, you are just so hurt and wounded, you know that? Sitting here, looking all pathetic."

"Yeah, maybe that's it. Maybe I've become too soft for her. Maybe I need to man up. Buck up. Take the reins back for a little while. Maybe that's the issue. She feels like the man in this relationship and not the woman."

She snickered. "You really are something, you know that? I think I know just how to heal you, too."

My eyes widened as her hand fell against my cock. I jumped as she got up, crawling into my lap.

"Whoa, whoa, whoa, whoa. I've got a girl--"

She giggled. "Yeah, don't worry. They all do, until they don't."

Her lips leaned into mine and I dodged her. Though my movements were slow. She ground her ass into my pelvis and I practically tried pushing her off me. Why the hell were my movements not coordinated enough?

"Like it a bit rough, huh?"

She reached for my wrists and pinned the down.

"What the--? Get off me. Hey!"

"Mmm, you really are strong, huh?"

"What the fuck is going on!?"

The guy's voice boomed over my head and the girl shrieked. Fucking hell, what in Satan's hell was her name? She quickly stood from my lap and I rolled off the porch swing, crawling on all fours to try and get away. The world tilted around me again. I felt something grip the back of my shirt before hoisting me up. I stumbled to get on my feet as the guy turned me around, then pinned me to the porch column.

"What the fuck are you doing with my girlfriend?"

I held my hands up. "We were just talking and she came on to me."

His nostrils flared. "Bullshit."

"I-I-I--I'm serious. I'm here with my girlfriend, too. Not the best night. But we're getting through it."

"Yeah, by fucking around with my girl."

He tossed me to the porch and people started gathering around. I didn't want to cause any more of a scene at this damn party. Not with Rae walking about high as a kite somewhere. I got up and tried to get off the porch, but no one let me move. They crowded around us, blocking my only two exits. And while I could have jumped off the porch, every time I looked over the edge it felt like I was looking into the darkness.

I felt like I was on that damn bridge again, with that car chasing me.

I swallowed hard. My forehead started sweating. The more I looked over the edge, the more my hands shook. Flashes of that night came barreling back. The sound of the horn. The screeching of the tires. I felt myself teetering. My heart sank to my toes. I blinked a few times to try and clear the hazy fog from my vision. Only to feel something dripping down my cheek.

"Are you fucking crying!?"

"Maybe you should man up."

"Fight! Fight! Fight! Fight!"

I felt his fist crack against my face and the world faded away. Red dripped down through my vision, and the only person I saw was my father. His sneering face. His gangly arms. I heard his laughter echoing inside my head.

You'll never be good enough.

Get it the fuck together.

What have I told you about this?

You'll never be a man. Not without me.

"I'm more of a man than you'll ever be," I glowered.

The guy paused. "What?"

I roared as I charged him. I knocked him clear off his feet. With one punch to the side of his head, he fell to the porch. And I straddled him. Right fist. Left fist. Right forearm. Left elbow. I laid into him as he blocked my fists from hitting his face. Girls shrieked around me. People tried pulling me off him. I whipped around, batting their hands away before wailing into his stomach.

Knocking the wind clear out of him.

"Get off him! You're going to kill him! Baby!"

The girl in the bikini dove into the picture and I stopped. I felt others dragging me off this guy as I heard my name. It was off in the distance, but unmistakable. And as I felt myself sobering up, the clamoring of Mike's footsteps fell against the porch.

"What the fuck!?" he exclaimed.

He helped me to my feet as the guy I'd knocked to the ground got up. With the help of his girl, of course. He growled at me before he lunged again, and Mike stepped in the middle.

"Move," the guy commanded.

He shook his head. "Back off. I'm serious. This guy behind me? I've seen him take on his own fucking father. You don't stand a chance."

The girl behind him snickered. "No wonder your girl wants to leave you. Maniacal asshole."

Mike slowly peeked over his shoulder at me. "Say what now?"

I teetered on my feet. "I wasn't trying to fuck your girl."

The man growled. "I saw her in your lap."

I snickered. "Yeah, because she crawled there. She likes

wounded guys. Men she can fix with her pussy. Maybe make yourself look a little more wounded and she'll actually stick around."

The guy lunged at me, but Mike stood his ground. He gripped the fabric of the jerk's shirt as I turned and walked off. I brought my palm to my face, but I knew I wasn't bleeding. Hell, I wouldn't even have a bruise with how pussy-whipped that guy's punch had been. I pushed through the whispers of the strangers on the porch and leapt off, forcing myself to stay upright. And as the cool summer breeze kicked up, I felt myself sobering up a little more.

"Hey! Will you wait the hell up?"

I whipped around at the sound of Mike's voice, only to lose my balance. I felt myself plummeting and was helpless to stop it. It was as if my body refused to work any longer. Mike rushed over and caught me just before I hit the ground. Like some bomb-ass dude scooping up a little girl.

Fucking hell, I felt like a lost little girl.

"All right. You're coming with me. The girls should be ready soon. Time to go home."

My words slurred together. "I have no home."

Mike dragged me over to the curb, and I leaned against him as he pulled out his phone.

25

RAELYNN

"**F**ucking hell," Allison breathed.

Dread filled my gut. "What in the world has you cursing now?"

I clenched my stomach as she led me out of the house. The jostling alone was enough to make my body want to turn itself inside out. But as we made our way off the porch, my mind quickly wafted back to how sick I felt. Why the hell had I drunk so much? And what the fuck had convinced me to mix pot into it all?

What did I say to Clint?

I can't remember anything.

"Come on, Rae. To the curb. That's it. You got it."

I groaned. "Why did you curse again?"

"Just focus on you right now, yeah? Let me do the rest."

Allison helped me stand upright before shoving something up to my lips. The cold water poured down my chin a bit before I opened my mouth. It sloshed to the back of my throat and I gagged. Which caused me to retch onto the pavement. I heard Clint's voice off in the distance, but I didn't hear what he was saying.

Allison sighed. "Get it together, Rae. You need water."

"Then stop trying to fucking choke me with it."

I spat onto the ground before she helped me raise up. And when the water bottle touched my lips again, I started drinking.

She kept pouring quickly and making me cough. Which made me angrier. But every time I tried to pull away from her, I felt myself falling.

"Would you stop fighting and just accept it? My God, Rae."

Her words stopped me in my tracks. My throat opened up as the cold water poured down into my stomach. With each drop, I felt better. And I wondered if I was the cause of my own issues. What if I stopped fighting in other areas of my life? Stopped fighting my mother and stopped fighting my fears and stopped fighting against Clint?

Would things get better?

Am I the reason for all this?

"All right. With me. The Uber's here," she said.

My head fell against her shoulder. "I'm sorry."

She sighed. "You don't owe me anything. Clint, though? You owe him big time."

I never should have gone this far. I never should've come to this party. I mean, I'd never been a partier! I didn't know my limits. I didn't drink excessively. I hadn't ever tried drugs of any sort. What the hell was I thinking? I wasn't. That was the issue. I hadn't been thinking, and now the entire night was ruined.

You're an idiot, Rae.

Allison's sighs grew heavier as I leaned harder against her. And then, I felt someone wrap their arm around my shoulder. My body heaved from one side to the other, with the water sloshing around in my stomach. I burped. The taste made me shiver as I leaned against someone strong. Someone tall.

"Clint?"

Michael chuckled. "Nope. He's on the pavement. It's me."

I whispered, "Michael."

"Hey there, beautiful. Come on. Let's get you two back to the hotel."

I felt my body being dragged over to the curb. And when I sat down, I looked over at Clint. My eyes widened when I saw the red marks on his face and neck, bloodshot eyes and disheveled hair.

"What the fuck happened to you?" I asked.

Clint slowly looked over at me as Michael spoke up.

"We need to get out of here before that giant ape decides he wants another go at Clint."

Allison groaned. "I thought you said the Uber would be here in ten minutes?"

"I'm sorry, baby. The app shows the car is here. But I don't see it. Let me go search around for it. Maybe it's up a block or something."

My eyes fluttered around Clint's face. He kept swaying. Teetering. Like he couldn't even keep himself upright. Allison and Michael kept talking around us, but I wasn't paying them any attention.

"Where you in a fight?" I whispered.

He slowly looked over at me, and the pain behind his eyes stabbed me in the gut. Tears rushed my eyes and freely poured down my cheeks as he looked away. His shoulders hunched. He looked absolutely defeated. And as I sat there, wondering how the hell this night had careened so far out of control, I tried with all my might to conjure what I had said to him.

But I came up with nothing.

"There it is!"

"Over here!"

"Hey, hey, hey. Slow down! It's us!"

Allison and Michael started yelling before a car pulled up in front of me. My head fell back as someone helped me up. I didn't know who. A car door opened and I felt my body falling against a seat. Allison kept cursing to herself as my head fell onto someone's shoulder. I wasn't registering anything. I couldn't even remember what color the damn car was. Why did my throat hurt so badly? Why was my chest sore?

"Fuck," I groaned.

Michael rattled off the address to the hotel before another door closed. I heard the locks flip, and I nestled into the person next to me. My eyes wouldn't open. My body couldn't prop itself up a second longer. I felt myself falling in and out of sleep. Trying to find relief as the car's swaying lulled me into a peaceful slumber.

I woke up to my shoulder being shaken. My head jerked up as my arm slid around someone's shoulders. Allison groaned as she pulled me out of the car, and my feet stumbled underneath me.

"You're going to have to help just a bit here, Rae."

I snickered. "I'm trying. But I can't."

"Yeah, well. Story of your life, I guess."

I scoffed. "We can tuck in the attitude a bit."

"You first."

"Why the hell is everyone so mad at me right now?"

Michael butted in. "Because had it not been for you and your asinine tricks, Clint wouldn't have started drinking to forget shit."

"Oh, so you're mad at me, too, now?"

"Yeah, I am. Because a night that was supposed to be fun for all of us was ruined because you decided, out of the blue, that you wanted to be alone. Which is fine, if you had fucking come alone, Rae. Now, let's get you in the room."

I rolled my eyes. "What the hell ever, asshole."

Allison sighed. "Save it for the morning when you're sober."

The hotel door crashed open and the next thing I knew, I was being piled into a bed. My eyes fell open and the ceiling circled around. Twisting and turning as my stomach started rolling again. I clenched my eyes shut. I pressed the heels of my hands into my eyes. I tried to shake this terrible feeling in the pit of my gut. And as Clint's groans hit my ears, I felt the mattress jump with the force of his fall.

"All right, can you two hear me?"

Michael's voice filled my ear and I nodded along with Clint's grunt.

"Good. We're not changing rooms. I'm going to sleep with Allison, and the two of you are going to fix this on your own. Rae, had you not been an absolute bitch, none of this would've happened. I don't know what the hell's wrong with you lately, but figure it out."

I snickered. "The tough guy act doesn't sound good on you."

Allison interjected. "I don't care what you think. All I care about is you two fixing things. Whether you stay together or break up before college starts, you need to figure it out. You're making everyone miserable, and that's not okay."

I furrowed my brow. "Break up with Clint? What?"

Clint sighed. "Don't act like it's news."

What the hell did I say at that party? "No, seriously. I can't remem-
-"

Michael chuckled. "Yeah, yeah. In the morning, I'm sure you'll remember. But until then? We're going to bed. No more parties this weekend. Fix your shit. Come on, Allison."

And as the hotel door closed behind them, I licked my chapped lips.

"Clint?"

I felt the mattress undulate before something thudded against the floor.

"Clint? Are you okay?"

He groaned, but didn't say anything. I managed to open one eye without feeling as if I might puke. I watched him stumble over to the balcony doors. He slid them open and walked out, flopping himself into a chair. I hiccupped as I sat up, propping myself up on my elbows, watching him gaze out over the darkened horizon.

"Clint?"

Instead of answering me, though, he ignored me. Cold shoulder and all. I closed my eyes and flopped back down onto the mattress, trying to wrack my brain as to what I had said. I couldn't remember anything, though. I remembered the shots we took. Arriving at the house. I remembered feeling a bit smothered by Clint's presence. But that was it.

"Is that why you're mad? Because I felt smothered?" I asked.

I didn't get an answer, though. Just the wind softly blowing through the open sliding door.

"Clint, are you hungry?"

"Do you want some water?"

"I think I can get up to get some water. Do you want me to order you anything?"

"A snack from the vending machine?"

"I think one of the restaurants is open right now."

"Want me to move to the other queen bed?"

Every question I asked went unanswered. And I hated that. I reached over and picked up the hotel phone, haphazardly dialing the kitchen. I needed food. I needed sustenance. I needed the growling of my stomach to go away. I also needed some Tylenol.

Could they deliver Tylenol?

"Room number, please," the man said.

"Uh, yeah. Room… uh… well, the name's Rae Cleaver. The reservation is under--"

"I'll look it up later. What's your order?"

"Do you guys have Tylenol?"

He paused. "Tylenol."

"I mean, I want food. But I also need Tylenol. And I don't have any."

"It'll be charged to your room from the pharmacy down here at the snack bar."

"Perfect. That's fine."

"And the rest of your order?"

I licked my lips. "Uh… water. Coffee. Um, some french fries and a double bacon cheeseburger."

"Anything else?"

I scratched the top of my head. "Do you have any pasta? With alfredo sauce?"

"Got a spicy chicken pasta with broccoli."

"Perfect. That."

"Dessert?"

"Mmm, something with chocolate."

"Fair enough. Anything else?"

I paused. "Ketchup, garlic breadsticks--or something like that--and… a bowl of fruit."

"Great. I'll look up the name and have it delivered within the hour."

I sighed with relief. "Thank you so much."

"Uh huh."

The man hung up and I fumbled the phone, dropping it to the floor. I figured I could deal with it later. I rolled back over onto the bed and closed my eyes, feeling myself quickly drift off to sleep again.

Before a knocking at the door jerked me awake.

I looked over at the balcony and Clint still sat there. His head bobbing. His leg jiggling. Almost as if he were listening to music. Another knock came at the door. A bit harder this time. And I forced myself off the bed.

"Guess I'll get it," I murmured.

Then again, I did order it for us.

I opened the hotel room door and expected the man from the phone on the other side. The smell of the food made my mouth water and I couldn't wait to get Tylenol in my system. But when the door opened, I found Allison standing there, clutching the rolling silver tray of food.

"Mind if I come in? They delivered it to our room. And I'm pretty sure Michael stole some of your breadsticks."

I shrugged. "It's fine. Come on in."

I went back and sat on the edge of the bed. I took Clint's tray of food and sat it beside me, in case he wanted to come eat. Then I poured myself a glass of water. I chugged it before taking a bite of my pasta, moaning over its taste. The creaminess of the sauce. The spice of the chicken. The crispy broccoli. Oh, it was damn near perfection. I almost forgot to take my Tylenol until Allison held it out for me. And as I tossed it back, I guzzled down another glass of water.

"Clint, I've got a burger in here for you."

But he still didn't budge.

"He talking to you at all?"

I sighed at Allison's question. "No. He's been out there ever since we got back."

Allison tried. "We've got Tylenol and water for you. Want some?"

Like magic, Clint got out of his chair. His eyes avoided mine as my best friend poured him a drink. She handed him the Tylenol and he tossed it back, then chased it with a few sips of water. And when he set the glass down, his eyes met mine.

Those pain-stricken, angry, empty eyes.

I remember those eyes.

He picked up his tray of food and took it back out to the balcony. He slumped into his chair and started mindlessly eating. My eyes darted around the tray before I found the ketchup. And I went to go give it to him.

Until Allison took it from me.

"I better do that, you think?"

Holy fuck, I think I ruined things for good.

26

CLINTON

I felt like fucking garbage. No, worse than garbage. I felt like the garbage's garbage. The shit that shit threw out. My face kept swelling and I felt a bruise forming despite the fact that the guy at the party couldn't fight worth shit. Or maybe the alcohol had dulled my senses. I didn't know. My pride was wounded. And for some reason, my damn ribcage hurt. When the hell did I hurt my ribs? I pulled my shirt up and sighed. There were bruises there, too.

Apparently, there was shit I didn't even remember.

I did remember Rae's words, though. How much they stung. How determined she was to spit them out. Thinking about them made my heart crack that much more. I forced myself to think about something else. The fries. Oh, these extra crispy fries were the fucking bomb. I inhaled them as the Tylenol kicked in. Along with the hydration of my water. I wanted to get up and get a second glass, but I didn't want to be anywhere near Rae. I didn't want to talk to her. Or look at her. Or even smell her.

I just wanted to get away from her.

Mike had been a good sport for hauling me into the room. Tossing me on the bed. I wished he hadn't tossed me near Rae. No matter, though. I owed him big time for helping me away from that party. I picked up my burger and felt the juices of the meat dripping down my face. I took massive bites, swallowing it after barely chewing. My stomach yearned for the nourishment. Yearned for the carbs and the grease to help me sober up. Holy fuck, I'd had way too much to drink.

Never again.

"Clint? Do you want more water?"

"I've got some brownies and chocolate cake here. You want dessert?"

"I'm not going to eat all of my breadsticks. Here, I'll bring you some."

Rae brought me another glass of water, a mug of coffee, and a bunch of other shit I didn't want. I refused to look at her as she set everything down. She stood there, waiting for me to acknowledge her. But I didn't have the energy. I was still licking my wounds. Still dwelling on her words. Still trying to figure out how much she meant and how much she didn't.

I knew if I talked to her, she'd tell me she meant none of it.

But I knew that wasn't the case.

All I wanted to do was fill my stomach and pass out in bed. Without talking to Rae. I didn't want to sleep with her. Or beside her. Or even in the same room as her. I found myself wishing I had never come on this trip. That I had told her she needed to do this by herself. Maybe then, all of this could've been avoided.

Or maybe, it would have prompted her to break up with me sooner.

I wasn't sure which one was better. Or worse.

I cracked my neck and set my dirty plates on the concrete floor of the patio. Then, I continued staring off into space. Not really focusing on one particular thing. Rae kept trying to strike up conversations with her stupid questions. I let her voice fade into the background, jiggling my leg with anxiety that filled my veins. I bobbed my head to a song that was playing on loop in the back of my mind. Some electronic song from the party those idiots kept playing over and over again.

The song sucked.

But it blocked out Rae's voice.

I hated the way she was talking to me. The way she kept trying to interject herself. Like nothing was fucking wrong. Or like everything was wrong. Why couldn't she just leave me alone? That's what she wanted, right? Her space. To be left alone. To leave me and never look back.

I couldn't shake my anger off. And until I was able to swallow it down, I knew it was best for me to keep my distance.

I mean, hell, she probably didn't remember it anyway! And I wasn't in the mood to recount her drunken words. I wasn't ready to rehash it. To experience that pain all over again so quickly. I wasn't a damn masochist. I didn't want to do that shit. And for once, I prioritized what I wanted over what I figured Rae wanted.

Can I even be mad if she doesn't remember?

Yes. Yes, I fucking could. Because it still hurt. Because it still happened. Murderers that didn't remember the murder were still tried and found guilty for it. So even if she didn't remember breaking my heart, that didn't mean she hadn't. I licked my lips. I didn't know why I tasted blood, and I didn't get up to figure out why. Because going to the bathroom meant crossing through the hotel room.

Which meant passing by Rae.

I blinked back tears. What she'd said at the party kept rushing through my head. Torturing me, as if I deserved it. And maybe I did. Maybe I had been a shitty boyfriend that gave her too much space or not enough space or wanted sex too much or not enough. Maybe I had broken her heart or pushed her away or pulled her back too much or not apologized for something. Fucking hell, I didn't know. And I'd never know, because she didn't want to speak with me. Or talk about it. All she wanted to do was act as if this shit didn't exist.

And that didn't fly with me anymore.

I couldn't shake the feeling that things were over between us. That it was only a matter of time before we parted ways. I wouldn't blame her, though. This was miserable for both of us. I should've seen it coming. The way she'd been pulling away. The distance between us lately. How upset I knew she had been when I told her I wasn't applying to college. She probably expected me to repay her for helping me this year. Repay her by going to college and making something of my life. But I didn't operate that way.

If you wanted to help someone, you shouldn't expect anything in return. Otherwise, it wasn't really help.

It was debt.

And even still, I knew Rae was a good person. She deserved a good man at her side. A good person of a man. Not like she'd stay with a no-good, dead-end asshole like me for too long. I was lucky to have had her for this long. I knew it was only a matter of time before she realized she could do better. And with the way those men were flirting with her behind that damn frat house, she'd probably realized it tonight.

Hence, her words.

I burped and the world tilted for a second. I finished my glass of water and chased it with the lukewarm mug of coffee. I needed enough energy running through my veins to get a shower. To wash the stench of that damn house off me. I drew in a deep breath before hoisting myself out of the chair. I stumbled against the railing before a soft gasp trickled against my ears.

And as I turned around, I saw everyone staring at me.

Ally, Mike, and Rae.

"Yeah?" I asked.

Mike licked his lips. "We've been talking."

I nodded. "I'm sure."

Ally cleared her throat. "And we think it might be best for everyone involved if you stay in the room with Mike tonight."

Rae balked. "Wait, what?"

Mike held up his hand to her. "You can get your things and come take a shower. Our room has a really nice tub, too. You can soak, if you want."

Rae snickered. "I thought you said we were staying in our own rooms? So you could be with Allison?"

I nodded. "Thanks, man. I appreciate it."

Ally tried to perk up. "I mean, we can have a girl's night this way. I'm not tired. We could order another round of desserts and watch a movie. How's that sound?"

Rae frowned. "I don't want to eat sweets and watch a movie. I want to talk with Clint."

I snickered. "Yeah, well. You already did that tonight. Why don't we save some talking for tomorrow?"

We all fell silent and Rae's eyes filled with tears. I didn't want to feel bad for her. She didn't deserve it. I did anyway.

"But--"

Mike cut Rae off. "Really, Rae. We all need to cool our jets for the night. You said you wanted space, so here it is."

Rae sighed. "I don't remember saying that."

I scoffed. "Doesn't mean you didn't."

Her eyes rose to mine and I walked inside. I couldn't have her staring at me like that all night. I'd cave. Eventually. And I didn't want to do that. For once, I needed to be away from her. I needed to not be in the same room as her. I quickly grabbed some clothes and got my toiletry bag from the bathroom.

"Ready when you are, Mike."

I watched him kiss Ally's forehead before he nodded at Rae. I saw the way Ally looked at Mike. The way their eyes connected with love. It was the way I looked at Rae. Every single time I set eyes on her. But she hadn't looked at me like that in a while. Rae's eyes fell against me, and I turned away. I couldn't look at her. It hurt too damn much. The last thing I needed was a reminder of what we didn't currently have because I couldn't take much more tonight. And as we left the bedroom, I heard Rae sniffling and Ally trying to cheer her up.

"It's okay, we can all talk tomorrow."

"Maybe over breakfast in the bedroom?"

"Or we could go out."

"What movie do you want to wat--"

The hotel door closing behind me cut off their voices. And while I figured it would bring me relief, it didn't. I felt more tense than ever. I followed Mike to the adjacent door, where he unlocked it and ushered me in.

Holy fuck, their room was much bigger than ours.

"I see you were holding out on us."

Mike snickered. "Hey, this is Allison and my first time alone like this. Away from parents. I wanted to spoil her a bit."

I nodded. "Yeah, I remember that stage."

He sighed. "After some sleep, we can all talk with a clear head. I know Rae feels like shit. But she should feel like shit for a little bit before we fix it. Maybe she just has to learn the hard way."

"Maybe so."

"Bathroom's over there. Use it however long you want. But don't expect some movie night with treats. My ass is grass, and I need sleep."

I chuckled. "Thanks. Don't worry, I'm passing out after a hot shower, too."

"Good. Hope you don't snore."

"Rae's never said I do. So..."

"So, fall asleep first. Got it."

I shook my head as a smile crossed my face. Leave it to Mike to cheer me up with some stupid-ass joke. I walked over and patted his shoulder before making my way to the bathroom. I heard the shower calling my name. I paused, gazing around the bathroom. The damn thing was three times the size of ours next door. I closed the door and shed my clothes, then walked beyond the swinging glass door.

I could've lain down on the damn floor and gone to sleep, it was so big.

I fiddled with the knobs until that hot water battered against my muscles. It stung at first. Then I adjusted. I felt the stench of the night rushing down my body and swirling down the drain as I soaked myself. My hair dripped into my face. I closed my eyes and let it run over me. I opened my mouth and filled it with the hot water, then gurgled. Multiple times.

Washing the beer from my teeth.

I washed everything twice. My hair. My body. My feet. My hands. The achiness of my bruises went away, and my back fell against the wall. I slid down to the bottom, extending my legs. Resting. Relaxing. Trying to center myself.

I hadn't felt this off-kilter since my last fight with my father.

Fucking hell, Rae.

I didn't know what this meant for us. Or if there was an 'us' any longer. All I knew was that I needed to relax enough to sleep. I needed to stay away from the parties and the weed. Just in case any of those jobs called me back for an interview.

Shit, the interviews.

Should I still interview around town?

I slid down the wall until my back fell against the floor. I gazed up at the ceiling as steam enveloped me. I didn't know what to do any longer. I mean, I had passed out my resume because I wanted to surprise Rae with it. Getting a job around here so I could move with her. So I could be with her. So I could be next to her and cheer her on instead of having to commute an hour just to see one another.

But if we broke up, what was the point?

What was the point of any of it?

27

RAELYNN

"Okay, that's it. There you go. Get it out, Rae."

I coughed and choked as I thrust my head into the toilet.

"Maybe, next time, opt for some soup. Might come up easier."

I groaned. "Shut up, Alli--oh."

She rubbed my back and held my hair up as my entire life came up into the hotel room toilet. Two o'clock. My stomach woke me up at two o'clock and I almost didn't make it to the bathroom. My entire body hurt. In between my heaving spells, Allison helped me get out of my clothes. I was in nothing but my bra now. Completely bare, except for my tits being held up.

"There we go. Think you got enough time to get this off?"

I felt her unfasten the bra and it slid down my arms. I coughed into the toilet. I spat. I tried desperately to get that taste out of my mouth. And as I sat back onto the floor, Allison finished getting my bra off my body.

Leaving me stark naked on the cold floor.

"I'm going to get you a shower going. You can sit down in it and finish getting sick there."

I sighed. "I'd rather die."

She snickered. "Don't talk such nonsense. Once we get you showered and cleaned up, you'll be fine."

"I fucked everything up."

I curled my knees up to my chest and wrapped my arms around myself. I placed my head against my knees, wondering how the hell I'd fix this. I heard the shower turn on and the heat of the water called to me. I felt my stomach already gearing up for round three. Or was it four?

Allison helped me up.

"All right. In you go so I can clean up the bathroom."

Tears rushed down my cheeks as I stepped inside.

"Holy shit, that's hot."

"Yep. And it'll wash you clean. It'll relax your body so you can get this stuff out of your system."

I hissed. "Why did I insist we go to that party?"

She snickered. "Because you're an idiot. That's why."

She closed the curtain and I sat down on the floor. I heard her cleaning up. Flushing the toilet. Spraying perfume around. I leaned against the wall and let my tears fall. And on the other side of the wall, there was nothing. I hadn't heard a sound from the guys in a while. I mean, sure. I'd been asleep. But they had been making noise over there before I passed out.

Now there was nothing.

I sighed. "Do you think he'll come back?"

Allison paused. "I'm not sure, actually. You really hurt him tonight."

I tried not to cry anymore. "What did I say?"

"You really don't remember?"

"Only bits and pieces of the night."

"But not the fight?"

"No. Not really."

"Convenient."

I furrowed my brow. "What?"

She cleared her throat. "We can talk about this tomorrow. We're all really tired, and I honestly don't feel like recounting the night right now."

"Must've been bad if you don't want to talk about it."

"Yeah, Rae. It was. And honestly, I'd like to know where in the world it came from."

I shook my head. I opened my mouth and gargled some hot water just to get the taste of vomit off my tongue. How in the world could I explain my doubts to Allison? This fear that had been implanted within me? Would Clint understand if I tried explaining it to him? Probably not. I mean, he was very supportive. All the time. Hell, he'd offered to help me in any way possible with figuring out what I wanted to do with the rest of my life!

It didn't get better than that.

So why did I still have doubts?

"You awake, Rae?"

I nodded. "Yeah. Unfortunately."

Allison sat next to the shower. "Don't talk like that."

"Well, it's how I feel."

"Still?"

"If you don't want to know, don't ask."

She sighed. "You've been angry at the world for a long time now."

"I'm always angry at the world."

"Not in a brooding way, Rae. In a lashing-out kind of way. It's been like this for weeks. Since before we graduated."

I shrugged. "I don't know what to tell you."

"Want to know my theory?"

"Sure. Why not?"

"I think you're upset that Clint doesn't want to go to college."

I snickered. "He can do whatever he wants with his life. Just like me."

Allison laughed bitterly. "If you don't want to have this talk now, you sure as hell won't be able to have it tomorrow. So either get honest with yourself and own up to things, or shut up and deal."

My eyebrows rose. "I've never heard you curse so much."

"I've never been this upset with anyone before."

"I'm sorry, Allison."

"Me, too. For you and for Clint. So let's try to sort at least a little bit of this out before tomorrow comes."

"I love you."

She stuck her hand in the shower. "I love you, too. So talk to me. Be honest with yourself for once."

I gazed at the shadow beyond the shower curtain. The shadow of my wise, intelligent, beautiful best friend. I cleared my throat and gargled some water again. Trying to give myself some time to gather my thoughts.

"Clint's been so good to me, you know. He deserves better than all this."

Allison nodded. "Yes. He does."

"And you're right. I'm a bit upset with him that he won't go to college."

"You know he doesn't owe you that for helping him, right?"

I paused. "Who the hell said anything about him owing me?"

"That's why you're upset, right?"

"Hell, no. I'm upset because it wasn't even a decision for Michael to follow you to school. But Clint doesn't--"

She squeezed my hand. "You think Clint doesn't want to be with you as badly as you want to be with him."

I shrugged. "Wouldn't he want to come to college with me if he did?"

"Not necessarily. We all know school isn't Clint's thing. He talked all the time about sticking around home. At least for a little bit. It wasn't like it came as a surprise."

"I guess I was hoping he'd change his mind and come with me."

"Can't he come with you and still not do school?"

I sighed. "I don't know. He doesn't make it seem like that. He says he's got responsibilities to his stepmom. Helping her stay afloat after the divorce and all."

"And you want him to choose you over her."

"No. Not at all."

"That's the only decision you're giving him right now, from the sounds of it."

"I just--" I groaned as I tried centering myself. "I just… wish things were different for him. For me. For us. It looks easy with you and Michael. Free rides. Aspirations. Dreams. Parents to pay for things."

Allison snickered. "You think it's easy for us? I've got parents that want all the doors in the house open when he's around. I've got a father that still comes with us on dates."

"Wait, what?"

She giggled. "Yeah, Rae. I envy the alone time you get with Clint. All the time, it seems."

"I didn't know any of this."

"It's not easy for us. It just looks easy because you're seeing what you don't have instead of seeing what you do. Michael and I?

We're just excited to get away from our parents. I'm shocked my parents agreed to me having an off-campus apartment with Michael coming to my same school. I can't wait to have him over. Have some space to ourselves to just exist."

"I just wish Clint wanted to follow me. That's all."

She squeezed my hand again. "Then tell him that."

I shook my head. 'I can't tell him that."

"Why not? Rae, you've helped him through so much--"

"Yes, to get to where he is now. Away from his father. And now, I'm supposed to be the one to tell him to leave the only shred of a parent he's ever had to come with me? Really?"

She paused. "I guess I never looked at it that way."

"Yeah, well, it's the only way I've been looking at it. He has to want that for himself. Because otherwise, he'll resent me for it. Me, always at school. Him, sitting around some studio apartment waiting for me. If he doesn't want that for himself, he'll eventually accuse me of isolating him or some shit. I know that happens. I've seen that happen."

"Have you told him any of this?"

I licked my lips. "No."

"Rae, I need you to listen to me. We all make mistakes. Lord knows Clint has made his fair share of them. But you two need to talk through this. You need to tell him how you're feeling, because I know he'll hear you out."

"And if he doesn't?"

"Clint might be scared and hurt, but he's not stupid."

"I know he's not stupid."

"And he's not fragile. Or weak. He can take this. He can take anything. But if you keep babying him, nothing is going to get fixed."

I sighed. "I know."

"I mean, I hate to say it, but there was probably some truth to what you said at the party."

I snickered. "Are you going to remind me what I said now?"

"There was one particular thing you said. Something I can't shake. And it makes me feel like maybe you're scared."

My gut seized. "What did I say?"

"You said something to the effect of, 'I protected myself before you, and I'll protect myself after you're gone.'"

"I fucking what?"

I ripped my hand away from Allison and threw open the shower curtain.

"I fucking said what!?"

She shushed me. "Hush. Everyone is sleeping."

My eyes watered. "I said that to him?"

She nodded slowly. "You're afraid of college right now, aren't you?"

I shivered in the shower as tears escaped down my cheeks again.

"I'm petrified, Allison. I'm scared that when we all leave, that's it. No more friendship. No more late nights. No more phone calls. No more surprises. No more friends, or loving boyfriend, or memories, or gift exchanges on New Year's. I'm scared that when we leave for college, it's all going to go away. Like it never existed. And I'll be alone, with no one to support me, no one who believes in me, and a mother that would do anything to get me back home with her."

Allison cupped my cheek. "I'm scared too, Rae. This is big. Moving away and doing our own thing is massive. College changes things, and you need to start dealing with that. The only constant we have in our lives is--"

"Don't give me that shit."

"Well, you need to hear that shit. Because if you don't digest it, you'll feel like this forever and keep ruining everything good around you because of your anger. Got it?"

I nodded. "Yeah. Got it."

"What I do know is this. I love Michael. With everything I have. And all he and I can do is make the best decisions we know how to right now. In this moment. Because it's all we have."

I slowly looked over at her. "You love Michael?"

She smiled brightly. "More than anything. I cherish him. He's perfect for me. And yeah, we're scared. We don't know what's ahead. Our routine is about to change, and we're about to be six hours away from home, and we're about to be taking classes that are going to bury us alive. We know that. So we cling to one another because we do have that constant, and that comforts us."

"Well, I don't have Clint."

"You do now."

"I won't when I go off to college."

"Girl, I hate to break it to you, but if you really can't see what I'm telling you? You're flunking out of your first semester."

I giggled. "Thanks for that."

She shrugged. "It's true. You're trying so hard to see the negative, and I don't have a clue as to why. But you need to fix that. College will be ruined for you if you don't, with or without Clint."

"I don't want to be without him."

"You can't control every variable though, either. Trying to is only going to end in failure. Which is what you're anticipating anyway. Don't be that person. Don't do that self-fulfilling prophecy thing. I can tell you one thing."

"What?"

"This thing you're doing right now? This cyclical arguing with yourself while you talk yourself out of something that could be good for you? It's the exact reason why your mother does what she does."

I paused. "I'm not following."

"You think your mother sits there with nothing to do all day and plots how she's going to take your money? That's certainly not the case. She's scared, Rae. I'm sure she probably sits there, talking herself in circles. Telling herself why a job won't work out or why it's not worth putting in applications just for her to get her hopes up and everything blow up in her face. I bet in your mother's eyes, she's somehow saving herself from a lifetime of hurt. While, in the process, creating the hurt herself."

I blinked. "Holy fuck."

"Yeah."

"Ho-lee. Shit."

"Yeah, Rae."

I drew in shallow breaths. "How do I stop it?"

Allison shook her head. "I don't know. I'm not you."

"I have to stop it, Allison. I can't turn into her."

"Well, now that you understand and recognize it, you can do what you need to in order to fix it. And you can start by talking with Clint tomorrow. Now, finish up in here and let's get to bed. I need sleep."

She closed the curtain and started cleaning up the water on the floor. Then she left me alone to dry off. My mind kept reeling with our conversation. One I knew I'd never forget. How did I let go of all this? How did I move forward? There was so much unknown.

And none of it felt right. Not my major. Not this college. Not this hotel room. Not leaving. Not staying.

Clint feels right, though.

And I hurt him tonight.

Badly.

28

___

CLINTON

The first thing I felt was my head. It felt as if someone had it in a vice. Cranking it tighter and tighter, trying to get my brain to slide out of my damn nose. Fucking hell, my head hurt. I couldn't open my eyes because even the darkness shook around me.

The second thing I felt, though, was my heart.

Except it wasn't my heart. It was the black pit in the middle of my chest where my heart needed to be. It brought back memories of last night. Snippets of Rae's angry face. Her harsh words. That girl, climbing into my lap.

Did I do something with that girl?

My jaw started aching. Followed quickly by my ribs. Holy hell, it felt like I had been run over by a truck. Some eighteen-wheeler, barreling down the highway at high speed. Flashes slammed against the shaking darkness behind my eyelids. Some angry dude. My fist against his face. His knees in my ribs.

No. You didn't do anything. You just beat the shit out of some guy.

"You up?"

Mike's voice rang in my ears. I groaned as I shifted onto my side. My body felt as if it were made of lead. Like the marrow of my bones was filled with the stuff. With every sharp breath of air I drew through my nose, more of my night came back.

The hot shower. Sleeping in Mike's hotel room.

Rae constantly bombarding me with questions.

"Fuck," I grunted.

The burp that came up my throat was rancid. It made me grimace and forced me out of bed. It felt like I was going to be sick. The floor underneath me tilted, trying to knock me off balance. I heaved myself out of bed and fell against the wall before the sound of scrambling was heard. All the sounds around me meshed into one as my arm lifted itself into the middle of the air.

Before coming down around something.

"Come on. Toilet. Now."

I groaned. "Shut up. Your voice sucks first thing in the morning."

Mike snickered. "Pretty sure that's the hangov--fuck. There you go."

My stomach ejected its contents as I fell to my knees against the hard floor. I groaned in pain before tears rushed the back of my eyes. I couldn't remember the last time I got so drunk it made me sick. Holy hell, puking was a terrible sensation. It felt like my body was being ripped apart. Limb from limb. My ribs felt as if they were trying to break through my skin. The pain behind my eyes mounted, as if it were trying to squeeze my eyes from their sockets.

What the fuck was coming out of my nose?

It's my brain. I'm melting. I'm dying.

"Your nose is bleeding, dude. Hold on."

Water ran and the toilet flushed. My heaves became dry as I sat back on my haunches. Something cold landed underneath my nose and I flinched. Someone's hand clapped against the back of my head.

"Holy fuck, that hurt."

Mike sighed. "Don't move away. You're really bleeding good, man."

I sighed as I sat there, with the stench of vomit filling the air. Why the hell had I gone to that party last night? Hell, why the fuck did I come on this trip? I should've known Rae better than that. I should've known she would have wanted to do this alone. I mean, we'd been together almost a year. One year come next month. How the hell did I not know her better than this?

Maybe that's why we're not working out.

"All right. It's finally slowing up. How's your head feeling?"

I laughed bitterly. "That a serious question?"

Mike snickered. "I'm trying to figure out if you need breakfast, or another four hours of sleep."

"Fuck, no food. Definitely no food."

"Coffee? Water? Excedrin?"

I sighed. "All three?"

"Done, done, and double done. Except, maybe not something that thins the blood. Your nose is uh… well, yeah. Let's just say if it starts up again, I'm taking you to a doctor."

"Got it."

I opened my eyes for the first time that morning and the world didn't tilt. The pain in my stomach slowly subsided, but it only made room for the pain in my chest. My hand flew to my pec. I gripped it as the emptiness washed over me. How the hell could something so miniscule feel so death-defying? I wanted to cry. I wanted to scream. I wanted to storm into Rae's room and demand the answers she hadn't given me yet.

And yet, the rest of me wanted to lie back in bed and fall asleep for a few weeks.

"Okay, well. You've got two choices. You can hang out here while I take a shower, or I can get you back to bed before I take a shower. What's it gonna be?"

I cleared my throat. "The last thing I need this morning is to see your dick."

Mike chuckled. "Don't worry. I'm not gracing you with something so beautiful until I know you can remember it. All right. Up we go."

My arm fell back around his shoulder and he heaved me off the floor. The world tilted for a second, but it quickly righted itself. Good. Much better than the first time I tried getting up. Mike helped me into my bed and I lay back down before I heard him ordering room service.

Breakfast for him, and all of the liquids and Tylenol for me.

I listened to the water of his shower as I stared at the ceiling. The foggy haze of sleep and my hangover started to lift. Leaving me with nothing but my thoughts. My theories on what the hell really happened last night. My hand fell back against my chest. It was hard to breathe. Hard to think straight. I turned over onto my side and gazed out the massive window with the sun pouring through the balcony windows.

Sun.

I needed the sunlight on my face.

I pulled myself out of bed and dragged my ass over to the door. It took an embarrassing amount of time to figure out how to unlock the damn thing before I slid it open. I walked out and flopped into a chair, relishing the heat against my skin. The sun against my face.

I relaxed back into the chair as the sounds of cars zoomed down below.

"You should talk to Rae, you know."

Mike's voice came from behind me and I sighed.

"I'm good, thanks."

"You know she's going to feel bad. She already felt bad last night."

I shrugged. "She should've thought about that beforehand."

"Come on, Clint. I'd like to think I know you a little better than this."

I cleared my throat. "What happened last night wasn't completely her fault. I played a part in it, too. Even if I didn't realize it at the time."

"Still. You two need to talk."

I shrugged. "What do you expect me to do, then? Haul my hungover ass next door and try not to puke while I drag out of her whether or not she wants to stay together?"

"You know damn good and well that girl is head over heels for you."

"And yet, that wasn't how things came out last night."

"She was drunk. And a bit high."

I snickered. "Yeah. I've been both before. Separately and together. I know getting high relaxes someone and getting drunk makes them more suggestible to things their subconscious is wanting to explore. If anything, shit like that makes you more prone to being honest. Not lying."

"Do you really believe that?"

I nodded slowly. "I've lived it too many times in my own life to think any differently."

"Still, that doesn't--"

"If you were in my position, what would you do?"

He stepped up beside me. "I'd talk to Allison and figure ou--"

"If you found out your girlfriend was worried about still being with you when she went off to Stanford, what would you really do,

Mike? I mean, if you found out that Allison had doubts in her mind about you. If you knew…"

I licked my lips as my next words stained my tongue.

"If you knew that if you ended things--right here, right now--and she'd be better off for it, would you? Would you end it for her sake? If you really loved her?"

Mike snickered. "Bullshit."

"Is it really, though?"

"You know damn good and well that girl isn't better off without you. If anything, you've improved her quality of life. If anything, you've shown her what love is in a world that has chewed her up and spit her out time and time again."

"It's not bullshit and you know it. I mean, the distance between us? The lack of passion? Of dates? Of sex? Of intimacy? The times where she's shut me out? Shut you out? Refused to talk to Allison, all of a sudden? I know you've heard the stories. I know you've experienced it. Do you really mean to tell me--?"

"Clint, she's been pushing all of us away. It's not just you."

"Then what the fuck am I supposed to do, Mike? Follow her here? Work a dead-end job because I need to pay rent and never get my foot in the door anywhere to make a difference while she studies her ass off, makes new friends, and builds a new life? A life she deserves?"

"What the fuck is so wrong with that?"

I growled. "I don't--"

The dark hole in my chest clenched together as I chewed on my words.

"I don't think I fit in her future anymore, Mike."

His hand came down onto my shoulder. "I don't know what I'd do in your position, man. But I do know that if something was wrong with Allison--no matter how big--I'd start by talking with her. That's for sure."

I shook my head. "Do you want me to recount the amount of times I've tried talking with Rae this summer? About anything serious, other than the shit her mother's pulling on her right now?"

"Well, the difference now is that she's actually said something that needs to be addressed. She's showing her cards, even if it took pot and booze to show them. Now you have something that needs to be discussed. Not just a hint. Not just a feeling. Not just a theory. Something concrete."

"What if she shrugs it off and tells me it was just her being intoxicated?"

Mike sighed. "Then you need to cut your losses."

"And you believe that."

"Yeah. I do. Look, I love Rae. She's my best friend. But if she's really not willing to address what happened last night, at all, then you need to cut your losses for you. You've been miserable this whole summer. A summer where we all should be happy and looking toward the future. Instead, you've been stuck up Rae's ass trying to make her smile without her giving you any feedback. At all."

I grimaced. "Yeah. I know."

He squeezed my shoulder. "Go over and talk to her. Open up the conversation. Even go so far as to tell her that she owes you one after last night. Then, depending on how she reacts, you know where to go from there."

I pinched the bridge of my nose. "Is that breakfast shit here yet?"

"Yep. Came just as I got out of the shower."

"Why the hell did I not hear the door?"

He chuckled bitterly. "Probably because you've got some shit on your mind. Come on. Coffee, water, and Tylenol. Lots of it. Let's get you feeling better before you head over there."

I sighed. "Yeah. Sure. Sounds like a plan."

I stood from the chair and it became easier to move. Just that small conversation with Mike had lifted some of the weight off my shoulders. Now that I had a direction to head in that someone agreed with me on, I felt a little more confident going into this conversation. Rae and I had to talk. That much was for sure. But I wasn't sure if she was willing to.

I wasn't sure what I'd do if she didn't.

"This coffee smells fantastic," I murmured.

Mike popped open a pill bottle. "We're going straight to four. Don't pass Go, don't do shit with your life until you take these."

I held out my hand. "Thanks, man. I really appreciate this."

"Of course. You'd be doing the same thing for me if the roles were reversed, and I know it."

I nodded. "Yeah. I would."

He shook the pills out into my hand. "No matter what happens, know you're not alone in this. Okay? Even if things go south with you and Rae, you've still got me and Allison. It doesn't work any other way. All right?"

"Thanks. I appreciate it."

"And no shutting us out. It's bad enough Rae's freezing us out after all the years we've known her. We don't need you doing that to us, too."

I poured myself a glass of water. "I won't. You have my word."

"Good. Now, you sure you don't want any of this bacon? It's double-fried and extra crispy."

I shook my head. "Maybe after this Tylenol kicks in."

"Then I'll save you a couple of slices just in case."

29

RAELYNN

I groaned. "I hate my life."

Allison giggled. "Yeah, well. We all have those points, I suppose."

I sniffed the air. "Is that coffee I smell?"

"Yep. And eggs. And pancakes. And greasy bacon. I had the kitchen make it extra crispy."

I peeked out from under the blankets. "Can I have some?"

"Depends. Am I going to be cleaning up regurgitated food after you do?"

"I don't… think so?"

She giggled. "Doesn't sound very confident."

"I mean, the room isn't spinning. That's a plus."

"Yes, that is a plus. I also got you some more Tylenol. And some water. And some orange juice."

I sat up slowly. "You're the best."

"Don't speak too soon. There's still a lot to talk about from last night."

I winced at her words. I watched her pour me a mug of coffee before dousing it in creamer and sugar. And when she walked it over to me, she had this look in her eye. I mean, I couldn't blame her. I deserved every look that came my way. Every curse word. Every terrible thing. Every fate that could befall me after something like this.

Allison made me a plate of food. "Hopefully this will help the rest of your headache and nausea."

I sipped my coffee. "Never again am I doing this."

"Good. Because being drunk, high, and a bitch doesn't look good on you."

My eyes widened. "Damn, Allison. Back at it with the cursing again."

She sighed. "I'm sorry, but the situation calls for it. You were an absolute maniac last night. You hurt a lot of people in the process. Clint more than anyone."

I nodded. "I know. I know. I don't--"

"Mmm, no. I don't think you do know."

She handed me the plate of food and I took it. But I felt my appetite quickly dissipating. Allison was in rare form this weekend, and every time she cursed, it took me by surprise. I set the plate on my lap and picked at it with my fingers. I held up the extra crispy bacon before putting it back down. I slid the plate onto the bedside table and reached for my coffee, desperate for the caffeine.

"You need to try and eat."

I nodded slowly. "And I will. Once I have the energy to move my jaw."

Allison sat on her bed. "You're moving it now."

I tossed her a look. "You know what I mean."

"Actually, I don't. Are you not hungry?"

"I'm fine."

"Are you not hungry because you feel guilty?"

"Allison. I get it. Okay?"

She took a bite of her bacon. "I don't think you do get it, though. Do you remember anything else from last night?"

I paused. "I thought you told me all of it?"

She giggled bitterly. "I told you what I thought caused Clint's drunken tirade once you stormed off. But that wasn't the only thing you said."

"Clint got drunk last night?"

"Uh, yeah. And apparently, he did it in spectacular fashion. Hence, the fight."

I blinked. "The fight?"

She scoffed. "Are you serious right now? Yes, the fight. The bruises. You were with him for a while last night before we switched rooms. How much time have you lost?"

My eyes danced around the room. "Why is everything so fuzzy?"

"Because that's what getting high and drunk instead of talking about your feelings does."

I licked my lips. "What else did I say last night?"

She shrugged. "That you felt smothered. That you wanted space."

"I know. You've told me that part. But why do I get the feeling there's more you won't tell me?"

"Because I feel Clint has some right to jog your memory of it."

"Seriously? You're playing that card right now?"

"You don't have any cards to play, Rae. You've spent all of them. Every single one of us got caught in your tirade of insanity last night. And not one of us got out unscathed. So yes. I'm playing that card right now."

I blinked. "What did I say to you?"

"It isn't what you said. It's what you did. I care about Clint. He's become a good friend of mine. And what you did last night to him was completely and utterly wrong."

"I'm begging you, Allison. Tell me what I said."

She sighed. "You aren't going to like it."

"I already don't like it, so that won't budge."

"After I tell you this, you have to be strong enough to talk with him today. You know he's going to want to talk. There's no falling apart like you did last night."

"I get it. I won't fall apart."

She drew in a deep breath. "You told him that you felt as if he was dragging you around like a child. You told him you were afraid to leave high school behind, but that going to the party and seeing everyone so confident helped you to see that you needed to come alone. To do this all alone."

"I said that?"

"I'm paraphrasing. Clint accused you of being paranoid because of the booze and drug mixture, and I'm pretty sure he was right. That made you angrier, though. Clint said you needed to go back to the hotel to get a food and some shower, and you told him 'maybe what I need is another boyfriend.'"

A chill ran through my veins. "Please tell me that was paraphrasing, too."

"Actually, no. 'Maybe what I need is another boyfriend' was a direct quote from you last night."

"Are you fucking kidding me?"

"No. I'm really not. After that, I'm pretty sure you called him an asshole before storming off."

"I called *him* the asshole."

"At least you're sober enough to see the irony."

I sat there, stunned. "Why the hell did I say that?" I shook my head at myself as tears rushed my eyes. "My God, he's never going to forgive me."

Allison sipped her orange juice. "Sure he will."

"He really won't. If he's got any sense about him, he won't."

"But he loves you. So he will."

I stared blankly at her. "Fine. Say he does. But he won't ever forget I said those words. And I can't take them back."

She licked her lips as we sat in silence. I watched Allison nibble on her food. Sip her orange juice. Generally look at every part of the room except for me.

"Allison?"

Her eyes came back to mine. "Yeah?"

My voice lowered to a whisper. "I think I'm making a mistake."

"With Clint?"

I shook my head. "With school."

My gaze fell to the floor as Allison got off the bed. She came over and sat beside me, her hand rubbing softly against my back. I let the tears fall. There was no use in expending the energy to hold them back. But saying it out loud? Admitting it to someone?

It felt good.

"How do you figure?" she asked.

I shook my head. "None of this is me. Last night wasn't me. This campus isn't me. The closer we get to the school year starting, the worse I feel. I don't know if I picked Cal State because I really wanted to come here, or if I wanted to get away from my mother."

"It did shock me when you told me you didn't want to pursue graphic design."

"Right? But, when I was talking to Mom about the community college not too far up the road from the house, she started talking about getting a part-time job to help with things and I could go to school part-time and stay at the grocery store. She talked about our girls' nights and me staying at home and commuting and how we could pool our money together and get a reliable car and it fucking freaked me out, Allison. Like, big time."

"And rightfully so."

"I don't think I chose to come here because it's what I want. I think I chose to apply and come here because I wanted to get away from Mom. And now that I'm here?"

"It doesn't feel like where you're supposed to be."

My lower lip quivered. "I've ruined everything."

She shook her head. "No, you haven't."

"Do you feel this way at all? As you and Michael get closer to going off to school?"

She paused, then shook her head again. "No, Rae. Not even a little bit."

I sighed. "So none of this is normal."

"No, it's not. For as long as I can remember, you've been dead set on making something of your artistry. Graphic design. Drawing. Something like that. I wanted to jump down your throat when you said something about doing English. It's not at all like you. You know who that sounds like, though?"

I blinked. "Who?"

"Clint would've been good at an English degree. Especially with how much he loves to write in that journal of his."

"You think I did the English degree to please Clint?"

"No. I think you chose English because the second biggest thing you love in your life is him. And you wanted something to remember him by once you went off to college. I bet you anything that, in the back of your mind, you chose English when you were asked to declare a possible major on all that paperwork because thinking about Clint made you happy. And English made you think about him."

"I mean, I can't fail at English, either. I've always been good at it. The reading. The papers."

She nodded. "That, too. Rae, I don't think I could commit to the workload I'm going to get at Stanford if I wasn't absolutely positive that I was supposed to be there. I'm all in, and that's what college takes. Same with Michael. So, if this isn't where you want to be, you need to take some time and cool your jets."

"But with Mom--"

She cupped my cheek. "Whatever you choose to do, she'll understand. And there are plenty of ways to fix what's going on with you and your mother. Starting with putting your foot down on some things."

I sniffled. "But why do I have to keep doing that with my own fucking mother?"

She giggled softly. "Because it's your mother, Rae. None of this should shock you, or scare you. But I think with the idea of coming to a college you hate, it's making you freak out about everything else because you've never encountered this kind of fear before."

"I did once."

She nodded. "With Clint's accident."

My lip trembled. "I remember how helpless I felt. How terrified I had become. How out of control everything was around me. I feel like that again. And I don't know what to do."

"Do what you did last time."

I paused. "What?"

"You're an idiot, Rae. Cling to Clint. No matter what. You battled his father for it. You battled the doctors for it. You battled school for it. But, in your moment of fear, you clung to Clint. Do that now."

"I'm sure he doesn't even want me looking in his direction, much less clinging to him."

"I think you'll find that Clint is a lot more graceful and accepting than you give him credit for. You're being way too hard on yourself. What you need to do with him is start by apologizing. Then you need to tell him exactly what you've told me. Start to finish."

I paused. "But what if he thinks--?"

Allison smiled. "Say it. You need to."

I licked my lips. "What if he--he thinks I'm--"

"It's going to sound just as insane when you say it. But releasing it into the wild is going to help you process it. Come on."

A tear streaked my cheek. "What if he thinks I'm weak and leaves?"

She giggled. "You're the girl who saved his life, Rae. If anything, he's scrambling to try and figure out how to repay you. How to help you in your own time of crisis."

"Fucking hell, that does sound insane."

"It really does."

I turned away from Allison and picked a piece of bacon off my plate. I crunched on it mindlessly as I sifted through all sorts of things. I wasn't convinced Clint would simply forgive me. And I knew damn good and well he'd never forget. I still wasn't convinced I hadn't irreparably damaged things. But could I really back out of college last minute like this? And even if I did, it was probably too late to enroll into the community college where I had planned on going. Plus, that meant fighting with my mother. If I wanted to put my foot down with my own money, that meant a fight. And I wasn't sure if I had the energy to fight with her anymore like that.

Then, there was fixing things with Clint. Which was a monumental task in and of itself. Especially after everything I had already pulled.

If there was anything left to fix.

"You think the boys are up?"

Allison nodded. "I heard them talking out on the balcony earlier this morning."

I paused. "Do you know what they were saying?"

She shook her head. "I figured they deserved the privacy. But Clint was talking to him. So, I suppose that's a good sign."

"Does Michael hate me?"

"He's upset with you. Disappointed, probably. I think he's a bit shocked as well because none of us have ever seen you like that. But hate you? Nah."

"I hate myself. I wouldn't blame him."

"Well, good thing we aren't you, then."

I snickered. "Yeah. That's the best case scenario for you guys."

"Stop being so self-deprecating, Rae. This isn't about you anymore. You've dragged us up here and into your tangled web of un-talked-about issues. It's time to put on some big girl panties and deal with it. Whatever might come of it in the process."

And for once, I had a direction I needed to walk in.

"When might be a good time to talk with Clint?"

But before Allison could answer me, I heard the door next to us slam open.

Then Michael called out for Clint.

30

CLINTON

"Clint! Come on, man."

I stormed down the hallway as I made my way for the elevator.

"Michael, what's going on?"

Allison's voice wafted behind me as I jammed the heel of my hand into the elevator button.

"Clint? Where are you going?"

I stiffened at the sound of Rae's voice. I heard the elevator whirring up the shaft as I slowly turned around. And when my eyes fell onto her, I chastised myself for how I felt. My heart stopped in my chest. My body ignited with life again. Even though she looked terrible, my body still wanted to move toward her. Rae's skin had gotten pale. Her lips were chapped and her eyes looked sunken in. Bloodshot. Like she had cried herself to sleep or something like that. But I needed out of the hotel for a little while.

I had a lot to think about.

The elevator opened behind me and I stepped in. Rae took a couple of steps toward me, but I shook my head.

The doors closed.

I leaned against the wall and sighed. I had a lot to think about, and I couldn't do it with Mike pestering me about when I was going to talk with Rae. I mean, I wanted to think I knew that girl better than anyone, despite how long Ally and Mike had known her. I knew she was stressed about school. I knew she was stressed about the transition. And I knew shit with her mother was throwing her for a loop.

But there was something else I couldn't put my finger on.

Something she wasn't telling me.

I knew that thing I couldn't place was the source of her anger from last night. And even though her words kept echoing off the corners of my mind, I was able to think rationally. I drew in deep breaths as the elevator carried me downstairs. My biggest fear, in all of this, had been losing her. I didn't want to put words to the idea because I was terrified of speaking into existence such a damning thing. But after last night, I wasn't afraid to admit it.

My biggest fear was losing Rae in all of this.

I mean, I couldn't see my life without her. Some of my darkest days had been lived with her in them. I didn't know where I'd be had it not been for her this past year. And I wanted to repay her. I wanted to find a way to help her through this dark time in her life. Through the shit with her mother. Through this shit with school.

Through this shit with us.

The elevator doors opened and I strode through the hotel. I pushed my way out the doors and started for the sidewalk. Thinking about going back to a time without Rae made me sick. Sicker than I had been last night. I shook my head at the thought. No, I wouldn't go back to a time like that. Rae wasn't leaving me. Not like this. I'd go back to my old ways in a heartbeat if she did. Last night was proof of that. Even with just her being mad at me-- not wanting me around at the party—I'd slipped down a rabbit hole that almost got me beat up and tossed into a ditch.

I'd be that angry guy nobody could save.

And that wasn't an option.

You don't deserve Rae.

You have some serious decisions to make.

You know she meant those words last night.

You know she's not telling you something.

"I love her," I murmured.

As I passed by people on the sidewalk, my mind spun. The voice in my head fought me every step of the way. But uttering out loud how much I loved her seemed to help. I felt people looking at me as if I were a crazy person. I didn't give a shit. Above all else, I wanted to make sure Rae made the right choices for her life. Not for me, or for her mother, or because she wanted out of town. Or away from her mother and that bullshit.

She needs help.

She needs guidance.

She needs someone to be her rock right now.

"I'm going to help her," I murmured.

I mean, it wasn't as if I wasn't guilty of doing much worse. I had actually ended things between me and Rae because I thought it was good for her. Because I thought getting her away from me would help her live a life she deserved. I actually broke the fuck up with her when things were at their worst. So spouting off a few words? Shit, that was nothing compared to what that girl had been through with me.

Compared to what I had done to her.

Time for you to be there for her like she was with you.

I looked to get my bearings so I could turn around. Get my ass back to the hotel. Sit down with Rae poolside or take her out for lunch and figure out where the fuck we went from here. We. As a unit. But when I saw the Cal State campus in front of me, I laughed bitterly.

Of course I'd end up here.

How the hell was it that my fucking feet had led me here? To the place I felt was stealing my girl from me? I shook my head as I picked up my foot, then stepped off the sidewalk. The grass gave way underneath my feet. I kept putting one foot in front of the other until I passed by the college's welcome sign. I gazed around at all the buildings. Some of them were tall, some of them only one story. I looked at all the guys and girls walking around campus. Chatting and laughing in their groups. They all looked as if they belonged together. As if their future purpose in life came from the veins of this very campus.

I wondered if Rae had felt the same way at orientation.

I slipped my hands into my pockets and walked around. I drew in the humid summer air and picked up snippets of conversations around me. Girls talking about their semester schedules. Boys talking about the next party. Upperclassmen talking about their graduation dates. A few professors, talking about their class schedules and trying to work out lunch times.

Then I came to a grand set of cement stairs.

My eyes wafted up the stairs before the sign on the front of the building came into view. Library. I was standing in front of the college campus library. Could I go in? Was it open to the public?

No harm in trying.

I rolled my shoulders back and walked up the steps. I got behind a group of disheveled students who already had stacks of books in their hands. I walked behind them into the library, then scanned the room. Aisles and aisles of books came into view, stretching from the floor to the ceiling. I walked over toward the library desk and looked up, craning my neck to get a view of the place. The middle of the building was open all the way to the top with rotunda levels that had thick, wooden banisters with chairs and desks bucked up to them.

"Can I help you with something?"

I whipped around at the sound of the elderly woman's voice.

"Uh, yes. Do you have computers here for students to use?" I asked.

She smiled. "Depends. Are you a student?"

"Are you going to kick me out if I'm not yet?"

"Ah, a prospective student. You're more than welcome to use our facilities to get a feel for them. You can't use any of the computers on the upper levels. Those are reserved for students who are already enrolled. But over there in the corner is a small computer lab with some you can use without a student I.D. card."

I nodded. "I appreciate it. Thank you."

"And if there's anything I can help you with, please let me know. My name's Rhonda."

I smiled. "Thank you, Mrs. Rhonda. I'll keep that in mind."

I made my way into the computer lab and picked one of the monitors in the corner so I wouldn't be disturbed. I knew Rae enjoyed English. But I also know she adored graphic design. But, to make matters worse, she had no idea what she wanted to do with the rest of her life.

So how could I help her make the most of the next year while she figured things out?

"Graphic design CSU."

I murmured the words to myself as I typed them into the search engine.

"English major graphic design minor CSU."

I kept talking softly to myself as my fingers typed at lightning speed.

"Graphic design major CSU."

I frowned at the lack of a major in that department before opening a couple of tabs.

And as I continued my internet search for some answers to take back to the hotel, the voice at the back of my head haunted me.

She's just going to break up with you.

No use in all this.

You're an idiot, Clint. Cut your losses.

She's going to hurt you.

But she couldn't hurt me any more than I had hurt her that day. The day she came to my house and I ended things with her just to protect her. It couldn't possibly be any worse than that. And after fighting to get me back, she deserved nothing less than the same treatment.

So I'd fight to win her back.

No matter what it cost me in the process.

31

RAELYNN

"Clint, it's me. Please pick up, okay? I'm worried about you."

"Clint, you don't even have to call. Just text. That's it."

"Clint, do we need to come looking for you?"

I went to dial his number again, but Michael took the phone from me.

"Hey! Give me that back."

He tucked my phone in his pocket. "No can do, Rae. You've called him enough."

I scoffed. "Yeah, and he hasn't picked up. He's been gone for over two hours. Where is he?"

Allison sighed. "Just give him some space. He probably left because he needed space."

I pointed with my hand to Michael. "He can't even tell us why Clint left! For all we know, he's headed home and got into a car accident. Or is being chased down. Or is in a great deal of trouble. We have to know where he is, okay? All he has to do is call me back."

I reached for Michael's pocket, but he stepped away from me.

"While I get that's a legitimate concern with you, he's fine."

I snickered. "Sorry if I don't take your damn advice."

Michael sighed. "He's already messaged me, Rae."

I paused. "Say what now?"

He rolled his eyes. "Clint messaged me a few minutes ago. He's fine. He's just taking a walk."

Allison butted in. "Show us."

I threw my hands in the air. "Thank you! Someone who doesn't make me feel crazy for being worried."

Michael pulled out his phone. "I don't think you're being crazy. I just think you're going overboard. Here. Look."

He held up his phone and I saw Clint's name. Clint's number. And the text message from Clint. Sure enough, he had messaged Michael to let him know he was all right. But he hadn't returned any of my texts or phone calls.

Which broke my heart a little more.

"Happy?" he asked.

I held out my hand. "I want my phone back, please."

Michael shook his head. "No."

I wiggled my fingers. "Give me my phone."

Allison sighed. "Just give her the phone and stop making things worse."

Michael rolled his eyes, but listened. He slapped my phone back into the palm of my hand and it took all the energy I had to slip it into my pocket. I wanted to keep calling Clint until he picked up. Just to hear his voice. Even if he was angry with me for calling a bajillion times, at least I'd hear his damn voice.

At least he messaged someone.

"Did he seem angry when he left?" I asked.

Michael shrugged. "No. Not at all. He just got up, announced he was leaving, and left."

Allison rubbed my back. "That's all that happened?"

He nodded. "I swear, that's all that happened. He didn't even take his damn notebook. It's still in the room."

I swallowed hard. "But he takes that thing everywhere."

He sighed. "Which is why you can bet your ass he's coming back. He has to come back at least for that."

But not for me.

I sighed. "You think he'll want to talk once he gets back?"

Michael shrugged. "I don't think you're really in a position to dictate that."

Allison interjected. "Michael, she's been raked through the mud enough. Back off."

He snickered. "I mean, I'm just saying. The man needs his space. I get that. He has enough on his mind right now, and that was before the party shit last night."

I furrowed my brow. "What else does he have on his mind?"

Michael rolled his eyes. "If you really don't know that, then you're more removed than I thought you were."

Allison scoffed. "Michael!"

He threw his hands up. "Well, it's true!"

I shook my head. "Even if he does need time to think, he's thinking the wrong things. I have to get him on the phone. Clint is the only rock I have and--"

Allison smacked her lips. "Rude. You have us."

I rolled my eyes. "I know, I know. It's not like that. That's not what I mean. I just--Clint is different, you know? I mean, I'm your rock, but Michael is also your rock. And his rock is a different kind of rock."

I looked over at Allison and watched her shrug.

"You have a point," she said.

I sighed. "I mean, Clint is…"

The room fell silent as I wracked my brain for the right word. I wasn't even sure there was a word to describe what Clint was to me. My brain felt muddled. My body felt as if it were trapped in a vat full of Jello. Suspended in mid-conversation, with no way out.

"Forever?" Michael asked.

His voice pulled me from my trance and I found him arching his eyebrows. Allison watched me carefully, waiting for me to confirm or deny. I let the word tumble around in my head. 'Forever.'

Then a soft smile slid across my face.

"Yeah. I think so. Clint is forever. And I have to tell him that."

Allison grinned. "He'll come around. He has to, okay? We're his ride home."

That made Michael laugh. But I didn't find it funny at all.

"He technically has the money to catch a cab," I said flatly.

Michael shrugged. "Like I said, he left his notebook behind."

I rolled my eyes. "I don't really know how I feel about being second place to a notebook."

Allison giggled. "Then, don't get high and drunk again before turning into a raging--"

Michael interjected. "And I was supposed to lay off."

I glared at her. "Yeah, Allison. Lay off."

She held up her hands. "Sorry, sorry. But, he's not the only one you hurt last night. He's just your main focus right now. Remember that."

I nodded slowly. "I'm sorry. I know. And I swear, I'm going to make it up to you guys."

Michael chuckled. "Steak dinner, anyone? I'm ready for some surf and turf."

Allison sighed. "If you're hungry, order some food. But we aren't leaving until Clint shows back up."

I smiled. "Finally, someone with some sense."

Michael ordered us all food to be delivered to the hotel room. But it was hard for me to concentrate on eating. I kept staring at the door, waiting for Clint to knock on it. I kept pressing my hand against my phone, waiting for it to vibrate. I wanted to hear his voice so badly. I wanted to get down on my knees and apologize. But, if space was what he needed, then it's the least he deserved.

Just come back to me, Clint. I can take it from there.

"You should eat."

Allison's voice pierced my thoughts and I sighed.

"Not hungry."

Michael threw a fry at me. "Eat."

I snickered. "Throwing food at me isn't going t--"

Allison tossed broccoli at me. "Eat."

"Now, come on. If I'm not eating a french fry, what makes you think I'm eating--?"

Michael threw another fry at me and I smiled. I tossed the fry back at him before picking up a piece of rice. I flicked it at Allison and she wrinkled her nose before tossing another small piece of broccoli in my direction.

Then, I armed myself with mashed potatoes.

"Whoa, whoa, whoa, whoa! That kind of ammunition isn't approved for this hotel room," Michael said.

I giggled. "Then, stop throwing food at me."

Allison smiled. "How about this? You eat half of your meal, then we go to the pool."

I paused. "I don't know if I feel like lounging by the pool right now."

Michael took a bite of his food. "Why not?"

I shrugged. "I mean, what if Clint comes back up to the room?"

Allison reached for the pen on the bedside table. "We'll leave him a note."

Michael held up his finger. "In both rooms."

I shook my head. "I don't know. I'm just not really up to--"

Michael picked up some cauliflower and threw it at my nose. It bounced off the tip before falling into the gravy for my mashed potatoes. Allison and I both giggled.

"It's either the pool, or I cover you in food. Your choice," Michael said.

I grinned. "I mean, my answer might be different if you were--"

"You can stop that statement right now," Allison said quickly.

I threw my head back with laughter as Michael started picking up the food on the floor.

"Fine, fine. I'll go to the pool. Under one condition."

Allison nodded. "Name it."

"I get to play on my phone without Michael ripping it away from me."

He stood up from the floor. "Stop bombarding Clint's phone with shit and I don't care what you do with it."

I smiled. "All right, deal."

We all got ready and headed down to the pool. But I didn't feel much like getting in. I was too anxious, and my eyes kept watching the gate. I lounged around on one of the pool chairs in the shade, trying to block out Allison and Michael's obnoxious flirting. He tossed her around in the water before swimming to her. He'd capture her lips before she wiggled away. At one point in time, he trapped her at the corner of the pool. His hands were on either side of her, their gazes connected. I looked down at my phone, trying to distract myself. I pulled up the texts I'd sent to Clint and forced myself not to send him another one.

I wanted to so badly, though.

My two best friends giggled and laughed like there was no tomorrow. And as I watched them, a longing tug in my gut surfaced. I wanted Clint to be with me. Next to me. Pulling me into the pool or resting his hand against my thigh. Anything, just to show me he was here. I mean, I didn't deserve it. I didn't deserve his presence right now. But it didn't stop me from wanting it.

It didn't stop me from wanting to apologize and make things up to him.

I looked down at my phone and scrolled through my contacts. I came across Clint's number and hovered my finger over it. I peeked up at Michael and Allison, watching as they sucked face. I mean, that boy had his tongue all the way down her throat. And she looked to be enjoying herself.

Way to go, Allison.

I licked my lips and looked back down at my phone. It would be nothing to press his number and listen to see if he picked up. But I'd made my friends a promise. I told them that I wouldn't call him. I mean, what kind of friend would I be if I couldn't keep a single promise like that? Especially after last night.

But this was Clint.

And the anxiety forced me over the edge.

I pressed his number and forced the guilt away. I'd deal with their anger later. I closed my eyes and listened to the phone ringing through the receiver as Allison giggled in the background. A massive splash happened, muting the sounds of my phone. And as panic filled my veins, I held the phone to my ear.

"Clint, you there?"

The sounds of the water died down and I heard his phone still ringing. Still unanswered. It would shoot me to voicemail any second. I put the phone back down in my lap as tears rushed my eyes. I heard the smacking of my best friend's lips as they made out, essentially in front of me. I pulled up my text messages to Clint again, standing up as my fingers flew across the screen.

"Rae, what are you doing?" Michael asked.

But I wasn't paying attention.

Me: I'm sorry. For everything. If you still want to talk, I'll be in the room. I really hope you're okay. Please be okay, Clint.

Allison cleared her throat. "Rae?"

I picked up my things. "I'm going back up to the room to wait for Clint. I can't do this any--"

The sound of Clint's text messages dinged in the distance. The familiar trilling sound pulled my eyes upright as I gazed over at the fence. And standing there, with his stare heavily on me, was Clint.

Watching from the sidelines.

"Clint," I whispered.

My knees went weak as he opened the pool gate. He walked

toward me, his stare never wavering from mine. I felt tears of relief well up behind my eyes. My hands trembled as my phone threatened to fall to the concrete. I felt Michael and Allison watching us as Clint approached and stood in front of me. He gazed down upon me, blocking the sunlight from my face.

And the bruises against his skin forced tears down my cheeks.

32

CLINTON

W orry.

The first word that came to mind as Rae's gaze danced over my face was worry. She analyzed my bruises. I saw her hand come up before she hesitated. Tears streaked her cheeks as I stood there, hovering over her. Watching her from my perch.

"I'm so sorry," she whispered.

I'd spent the better part of the afternoon away from the hotel. Trying to get a grip on things. Trying to find the information she needed. The information she didn't know how to find herself. I understood what that felt like. I understood that kind of struggle. But it all faded away as I studied the worry in her eyes.

"I'm so sorry. Clint, my God. I--What can I do to--?"

My voice softened. "Rae."

"I was such an idiot. I don't know why I said those things. I was freaking out about school and completely drunk and I've never done any drugs bef--"

I took her hand and brought it to my cheek. She drew in a shuddering breath as her fingertips brushed against my bruises. With my hand wrapped around her wrist, I trailed her touch along my skin, wincing with every mark that hurt a little more than the last. I slid her hand down my neck. The warmth of her touch filled me with healing power. I felt myself growing stronger. Becoming happier. Finding the strength to move forward.

To press on.

"I know, and it's all right."

Rae shook her head. "No, it's not. None of this is right. Clint, I just--"

I brought her fingertips to my lips. I kissed them softly, one by one, as tears dripped down the expanse of her neck. It seemed as if the entire world around us stopped. Muted itself, so we could focus on one another. Her lower lip quivered. I wanted to capture it with my own. My gaze danced between her beautiful eyes.

Eyes filled with such sadness and guilt.

"I'm so glad you're okay," she whispered.

I nodded. "I'll always be okay as long as I have you."

She drew in a slow breath. "So we're still together?"

I snickered. "Did you break up with me and I not realize it?"

She shook her head quickly. "No. No, no, no, no. Not even a little bit."

I shrugged. "Then, we're still together, as far as I'm concerned."

"Can we go somewhere and talk, please?"

"You mean you don't want to keep standing here with everyone watching us?"

She giggled through her tears. "You are insane, you know that?"

"And you're finally smiling. Hello there, Rae."

She sniffled. "Hi, Clint."

I pressed her hand back against my cheek before releasing her. I slid my knuckles against her skin, wiping the tears away. I felt them sliding against my own skin. I brushed them away, wanting nothing more than to capture her lips with my own.

But I didn't feel it was the right time yet.

"I needed some time to think things through."

Rae nodded. "I know. I'm sorry I couldn't leave you alone."

I snickered. "You don't ever have to apologize for that. I would've been more concerned had you not contacted me at all."

"Hear that, Michael?"

Water splashed Rae and she squealed. The sound made me smile from ear to ear.

"I did take some time to think, though. And… I understand where you're coming from."

Rae's eyes whipped back to mine. "What?"

My hand fell to my side. "If you need a fresh start here at Cal State, then that's what you need. It's what you should do."

"Clint, wait--"

"This is your future, Rae. This is your life. And you deserve to paint it how you see fit."

"Clint, no, no, no, jus--"

"It's okay. Look, you don't need to constantly try to accommodate me into your plans. I can figure out my own way."

"Clint, list--"

I sighed. "Really, Rae. I promise. I'll be okay. This is your life. And if the timing isn't right for us, then maybe it will be in the future. You know, when your college years are behind you."

"Wait, what?"

I nodded. "We've got all the time in the world. And if our time doesn't ever come back around? Then it doesn't."

She searched my eyes as I waited with baited breath for her to say something. Anything to give me relief, or confirm my notions, or tell me to fuck off. I had researched this speech all the way back. I walked from the library back to the hotel in the glaring sun just to give myself time to get this right. For once.

"I promise you, it's going to be okay," I whispered.

Rae's eyes dried up. Her tears evaporated in the sun. She didn't move, though. She seemed rooted to her place. I didn't know if she was shocked, or relieved, or angry, or hurt. She didn't give me anything to go on, and I started worrying.

So I proceeded forward.

I slipped my hand into my pocket and pulled out a sheet of paper. I unraveled it, scanning the notes I'd made in the library. I grinned at the recent memory. How hard I'd tried tracking down a simple piece of paper and a pen before the librarian told me I could type up a Word document and print it out. At no cost to me. I felt like an idiot. Then again, I'd never been partial to typing things up. I preferred writing them down. It helped me to remember things.

But that meant Rae wouldn't have to sift through my chicken scratch to read my notes.

"Look, I don't know why I ended up at campus today. But that's where my feet took me. So I took advantage of it."

I handed her the piece of paper and she took it.

"What's this?"

I grinned. "Notes I took for you."

She looked back up at me. "What kind of notes?"

I snickered. "The kind that might help you going forward with your degree."

"I'm not following."

I chuckled softly. "Once I got to campus, I found my way into the library. I started looking things up. Trying to figure out how I could help you. How I could help, maybe, sift through some of this confusion you're feeling. Or experiencing deep down. I looked up all sorts of things. There's some description on the graphic design classes they have here. Concentrations in their English department."

Her eyes fell to the piece of paper as I continued rambling.

"I even looked up some things you could do between now and next semester. You know, if you decided to postpone for a semester to try and work things out."

She cleared her throat. "I can do that?"

I nodded. "Yep. C.S.U. has a policy that allows all enrolled students to postpone their schooling for a semester before they either have to drop or declare a transfer to a different school. I listed some jobs around here that would work well with your grocery store experience. A few places hiring part time. I also looked up some rental places you could take a look at. You know, so you can root yourself here and not have to go back home to deal with your mother if you don't want to."

She swallowed hard. "You looked all this up for me?"

I nodded. "Yeah. I mean, it's what I did when my father threw my life for a loop last year. I spent as much time as I could looking up all sorts of avenues for my life. I figured you could use the same information. Plus, there's lot of other things you can do that I can't. Like, working in a call center. Or online English tutoring services. There are some freelancing websites you should check out. It's really cool."

"Clint," she whispered.

"Oh! And no overhead cost. Just the website taking a small percentage of the money you're paid for jobs. All you'd need is a place to live and an internet connection."

"Clint, I--"

"I mean, if you really made something of it, you could travel. I know you like traveling. Anywhere with an internet connection would work. I read a few stories online where people did this full time. They didn't even go to school. Just did this freelancing work, and then did what they wanted on the side. You could do this, and then sell your drawings for--"

"Clint."

I blinked. "Yeah?"

Rae sighed. "This is--this is generous."

I shrugged. "It's what you need. Options. I needed options, at least. And I figured they might help. I mean, you've got everything from what you can accomplish here at C.S.U. all the way to working and traveling at the same time. If you travel to the right places, too, you could make that look really good on an application form for some hoity-toity job along down the line."

She giggled. "Hoity toity?"

I grinned. "Or something like that."

"Clint… this is--"

I pressed my finger against her lips. "Your choice to make. Not mine."

"Will you just listen for a second?"

"In my defense, you've done a lot of talking lately. Let me finish. Please?"

She nodded slowly. "You're right. Okay."

I sighed. "I'm not going to push you in any direction. You take the time you need to think about this. Pour over those notes. Think about what really would make you happy. I mean, just you. Not me, or Mike, or Ally, or your mom. Just you. If you fell asleep tomorrow and woke up with any of those options in play, which one would you want it to be? Once you know that, you know what your next step is."

"You're too good to me, Clint."

"At one point in time, Rae, you were too good to me. I left you over less, because I thought I was protecting you from something. You helped me get through high school. I graduated because of you. I know it upsets you that I'm not going to college, but--"

She shook her head. "It doesn't upset me."

"Well, however it makes you feel, I know you're not very happy with it. Which is okay. You guys put in a lot of work to help me graduate. And I won't let you down because of that."

"Clint, you don't owe us any--"

"Will you just listen, Rae?"

She licked her lips. "You're talking from a good place, but you're missing some information you really need to know."

"Can I finish anyway?"

"Yeah. Of course."

I cupped her cheek. "You're the best thing that's ever happened to me. You saved my life. You saved me from myself. In a lot of ways, Cecilia and I got away from my father because of you. Because you kept pushing. Because you kept coming back. Because you kept talking, even when I wanted you to stop."

She smirked. "It's what I do best."

I chuckled. "I know, trust me."

"Hey, now. Them's fightin' words."

I stroked her cheek with my thumb. "I need you to know that whatever you decide you want with your life--or need with your life--I support you. Not because I feel I have to, but because I want to. I love you, Rae. And watching you flounder like this kills me. If anyone deserves a clear path to happiness, it's you. I hope the information on that page helps."

She nuzzled against my skin. "I'm sure it will, Clint."

I brought her in for a hug. "Come here, beautiful."

She sighed against me as her arms slipped around my waist. I buried my nose in her hair, sniffing deeply. Committing her scent to memory. I felt a weight lifting itself off my shoulders. I felt lighter on my feet as I stood there, swaying us side to side. I didn't care that I was sweating down my back. I didn't care that my feet hurt. All I cared about was soaking in this time with Rae before she made a decision.

Then she pulled away.

"I might not know what I want for my future, but I know what I want right now."

I nodded. "Name it."

She took my hand. "I want you to come up to the room with me."

And as she tugged me toward the gate, I saw heat ignite behind her eyes.

A heat I had missed seeing in her stare.

33

RAELYNN

I closed the hotel room door behind me and locked it. I turned around, facing Clint as he gazed out the balcony window. I watched him slowly turn around, lumbering around on his feet. He kicked his shoes off as his gaze met mine, and I felt my heart skip a beat.

He was putting on a damn good show of being fine with all this. But I saw the pain in his eyes. The limp in his step. His body hurt. His heart ached. And I hated being the one responsible for it.

I felt no better than his father.

"Clint, I don't want us to be over."

He sighed. "Me neither. But--"

I nodded. "But… you're right. I do have to look at everything from all angles."

"Yes. You really do. You deserve that. You know, for yourself."

"I need you to understand--"

"Rae, that isn't necess--"

"You had your chance to talk, and now it's mine."

He snickered. "This how we're going to be talking to one another from now on."

I grinned. "If that's what it takes for you to hear me out."

He nodded. "All right. Hit me with it."

"What you've given me is more generous than anything I figured you'd come back with. I thought maybe you'd pick up the phone and tell me it was over. Or come back and get your things before going home."

"I'm not going to lie, I debated it."

"I'm sure you did. And you had every right to. I want you to know that I'm thankful you chose to stay."

"Actually, I'm not sure if I'm staying still."

I blinked. "What?"

He sighed. "It's obvious you don't want me here."

"That's not true."

"It is. Even if you don't want to admit it, it's--"

"It's not true!"

"Rae, take a breath. I'm not accusing you of anything, nor am I upset."

I drew in a deep breath. "I'm still upset. And despite what Michael and Allison have to say, I have a right to be upset."

He nodded. "Yes, you do. Wait, what have they told you?"

I shook my head. "Let's just say they've really let me know how much of a shithead I should still feel like."

"What did they say to you?"

He took a step toward me as my back fell against the door.

"Don't be mad at them. Please. There's been enough anger."

He approached me. "I'm not upset with them. But if they hurt you--"

"They didn't hurt me. Just told me some hard truths I needed to hear."

His body heat pulsed against me. "Like what?"

I swallowed hard. "Like... stuff. And, uh, things."

"You might have to be a bit more specific about that."

"Then you're going to need to back up."

"Do you want me to?"

My gaze slid up his body. As my palms pressed into the door, I felt my heart come alive. That black pit in my chest quickly filled with something akin to fire and my spine sizzled with a need for him. A need for this boy standing in front of me.

No, not boy.

Man.

"Rae?"

I swallowed hard. "Yeah?"

"What do you want?"

"You," I whispered.

I stood on my tiptoes and captured his lips. Even if he pulled away from me, I wanted to taste him one last time. Commit it all to memory so I could conjure it no matter where life led me. I didn't know where we stood. I didn't know what would become of us. But I did know one thing.

I'd never stop loving this man in front of me.

He didn't pull away, so I took that as a good sign. My tongue softly fell against his lips as my hand cupped his cheek. It slid through his hair, feeling those soft tendrils for the first time in what seemed like years. Though I knew that wasn't really the case. I cupped the back of his head, holding his lips to mine.

And when a growl worked its way up his throat, my body sizzled for more.

His hands fell against the door. His body pressed against my own. His heat robbed me of my breath and I felt my knees trembling. I wanted his affection. I needed his touch. My mind spun out of control as his lips finally parted for me. I moaned down the back of his throat. He let me explore his mouth, not fighting me in the slightest. His touch set my skin on fire, and for the first time since getting to this fucking hotel I felt at peace.

With life.

With love.

With work.

With school.

With the future.

With… everything.

"Clint," I moaned.

His arms cloaked my back. He picked me up and pulled me away from the door. He tossed me onto the bed, his eyes watching me as I bounced. I reached out for him and he collapsed into my arms. His lips pressed against mine and the world tilted on its axis. I opened myself up for him. Gave myself over to him as he stripped me of my clothes and they fell to the floor in piles.

And I didn't stop tugging at his clothes until his skin met mine.

"Clint."

"Fuck, Rae."

"Don't stop. Do whatever you want."

"Dangerous words, gorgeous."

I looked into his eyes. "Whatever. You want."

He growled before his lips captured mine once more. He raked his teeth over my lower lip as he frogged his knees out, spreading my legs wide. I felt him. All of him. His hands pinned my wrists down as his lips slid down my neck. I arched for him. I felt my breasts puckering at the heat of his breath. He lapped at my nipples, sending me spiraling as he pinned me beneath him.

Preventing me from moving.

"So beautiful."

I gasped. "Oh."

"So smart."

"Clint, please."

"So mine."

He growled those last two words before he moved between my legs. He flopped onto his stomach, bouncing my body against the mattress. With his face between my thighs and his hands still around my wrists, he pulled my arms down. Arching my back and pulling my hips closer to his mouth.

Before his tongue pierced me.

"Clint!"

He lapped me up. And with every stroke of his tongue, I saw the heavens part. Fire burned through my body as I shook for him. He controlled every aspect of my movements, from my thighs jumping to my back arching. He manipulated me into a position I'd never been in before. The pain increased with the pleasure as lines began to blur. I didn't know whether to tell him to stop or keep going. I didn't know whether to tap out or double down. He folded my body. Pinned my arms. Arched my back further by tugging on my wrists. His tongue pulled floods of arousal from me, dripping down my skin and coating his cheeks. His stubble made my eyes roll back. My toes curled into his skin, though I couldn't have told anyone what part of his body my feet touched.

"Clint," I choked out.

"There it is, gorgeous."

He pressed his tongue deep between my folds and I soared over the edge. He lapped me deeply, slurping me down and drinking what I had to offer him. I trembled for his viewing pleasure. I felt my walls quivering with a need for him. My breasts jumped and my world spiraled into a dark expanse of nothingness.

And as my back dropped to the bed, he rushed up my body.

His lips crashed against mine before he slid deep inside me. Our bodies moved as one, his hips snapping against mine. My vision grew blurry with tears of happiness. He pinned me down and took me in all the ways I remembered. How I had missed him. This closeness. This passion. It seemed few and far between for us nowadays.

I wanted it to last forever.

"Rae. Fucking hell, Rae. Shit. You feel so--so good."

I moaned. "I love it when you growl. Do it again."

He did as I asked and goosebumps slid along my skin. He pulled out and flipped me over before pinning my face against the mattress. With his hand wrapped up tightly in my hair and his cock seated between my thighs, he pressed into me, taking me from behind as his pelvis slapped against my ass cheeks. I groaned into the sheets, taking what he had for me as his dick thickened against my walls. His balls smacked my clit, sending my eyes rolling back as my toes curled so deeply my calves cramped.

"Clint. Clint. Clint. Yeah, don't stop. Please. Please. Please. More. More. More."

"So close. That's it. I'm coming. Rae. I'm co--co--min--"

He exploded inside me and my heart seized in my chest. I held my breath, unable to speak as his pulsing cock pushed me over the edge. The world around me sizzled. Colors burst and died against the darkness behind my eyelids. My entire body shivered as our intermingled arousal dripped against my skin. Down my folds. Along my thighs. Coating me in the memory we created.

"Clint," I choked out.

He collapsed against me, his cock still sheathed inside my body. He panted against the pillow just above my head as he weighed me down against the mattress. I moaned. I shivered. I panted for air as my heart restarted itself. Fluttering wildly before settling down, as if I had come back to life.

As if Clint's body had pulled me back from certain death.

Neither of us spoke. I didn't dare disturb the moment. As Clint lay there, like my own personal weighted blanket, I thought about that list. All the research. All the suggestions. Completely and totally devoid of any personal bias on his part. How was he capable of it? I sure as hell wasn't. I'd never been capable of such selflessness. I always wondered what I'd get out of it. Or what I'd get at the end of a particular project. Or class. Or goal.

Clint continued to amaze me with every day that passed.

"I love you," I whispered.

But, if he heard me, he did a damn good job of acting as if he hadn't.

And my mind quickly spiraled back into the darkness he'd pulled me from.

Does he even love me anymore?

34

CLINTON

I heard the words, but I didn't know if I believed her. My heart fluttered, but I felt my gut cringing. I mean, what was I supposed to say? I loved Rae. I really did. But I didn't feel loved. Was I supposed to tell her everything would be all right? That we were fine? That we'd be okay?

Was I supposed to lie to the girl I loved?

I didn't want to say anything that would start another fight. So I kept my mouth closed. I let my eyes fall shut as I held her, feeling her even breaths rise and fall against my own. I held her close, tightening my grip around her body. And as we drifted in and out of sleep, I let my mind wander.

I let sleep take hold.

Every time Rae moved, I moved with her. Every time I shifted, she shifted along with me. It felt good, having her there. But the rift was still present. We needed to talk. Even in a dead sleep, I knew that much. Every time my eyes peeked open, I was reminded of the reality waiting for me. Every time I snuggled tight against her body, I was reminded of the conversation headed my way.

But I needed rest if we were going to tackle it tonight.

"Clint?"

Her soft voice against the shell of my ear made me groan.

"Mm?"

"Clint, you gotta wake up. Allison wants to go out to dinner."

I rolled over. "Five more minutes."

Rae giggled. "We can get more rest tonight. But right now, we have to get ready."

Her giggle made me grin as she helped me upright. My eyes slowly fell open and I was disappointed at the sight of her clothed body. I wrapped my arms around her and pulled her down on top of me. She laughed with delight as my hands slid up and down her legs. Gripping her ass cheeks. Massaging her hips.

"Clint, come on. I just got dressed."

I kissed her neck. "I can get you undressed, no problem."

She snickered. "Trust me, I know. Now, come on. I'm hungry."

"Worked up an appetite, huh?"

"Come on, you horndog."

I smiled groggily as she slid off my body. I got up and forced myself to get dressed even though I wanted to fall back into bed with her. I put on some clean clothes and splashed water in my face. I followed Rae out the door before the four of us headed for the lobby.

However, I kept seeing Michael shoot Rae glances.

Almost glares, really.

"You good?" I asked.

I nudged his shoulder and he nodded.

"Yeah, I'm good."

I narrowed my eyes. "You sure?"

He unlocked his car. "Just hungry."

I knew my friend better than that, though.

Ally must've already told Mike where she wanted to go, because we headed out without discussion of where to go eat. Rae leaned against me and I slipped my arm around her, kissing her mindlessly on top of the head. And every once in a while, I caught Mike peering back at us through the rearview mirror.

Maybe I can diffuse the tension.

"So, did you two get some good sleep like Rae and I did?"

Ally snickered. "Yeah. Rest. Is that what you call it?"

Mike pursed his lips. "More like covering something up."

Rae sat up from my shoulder. "What was that?"

Mike shook his head. "Nothing."

Ally turned around, smiling. "We're headed to one of those hibachi places. I hope that's okay?"

I nodded. "I love those damn places. Sign me up. Extra rice, please!"

Rae sighed. "Mmm, my stomach's already growling."

Mike licked his lips. "Bet it is."

I furrowed my brow. "You good, man?"

Rae nodded. "Yeah, you seem a little tense."

Mike came to a stop at the stoplight and I saw Ally wrap her hand around his.

"Michael, take some breaths," she said.

Rae paused. "What's wrong?"

I caught Mike's gaze in the rearview mirror before he shook his head.

"I don't know how you did it, Clint."

I blinked. "Did what?"

Mike scoffed. "Forgave her the way you did. I mean, the whole damn hotel probably heard you two. Did you guys not talk at all?"

Rae sighed. "We're getting there."

Mike turned around. "Getting there? You completely laid into Clint for unresolved bullshit you can't deal with, and you're only getting there?"

I felt my anger mounting. "Dude, lay off. She feels bad enough."

"And she should! That party was fucked up, and you're not the only one she hurt."

I shrugged. "Yeah, well. There's nothing we can do about it now except roll with the punches and keep moving forward."

Ally jumped in. "Like I told you, Michael."

"Yeah, whatever," he murmured.

Horns honked behind us and he sped away from the stoplight. He turned around and slouched in his seat as Rae pulled away from me. We traveled silently to the restaurant. Ally got us checked in with reservations she'd apparently made. We sat around that damn hibachi grill with strangers on the other side, staring at us as if we were prized possessions in a museum.

Then Rae spoke up.

"Just spit it out, Michael, and get it over with."

He grimaced. "It's best if I don't say anything."

Rae locked her eyes with the profile of his face. "Spill it, or stop acting like someone pissed in your cereal. You don't get it both ways and I'd kind of actually like to enjoy this dinner with you guys. So talk about it or tuck it in."

Ally cleared her throat. "Maybe not in front of others?"

Mike didn't listen. "Fine. You want me to talk? I'll talk. Something you're apparently unwilling to do."

He leaned forward before Ally caught his shoulders, trying to hold him back. I shifted myself in front of Rae, hoping he'd take the hint so we could do this when we weren't in a crowd of strangers. But Rae put her hands on my shoulders, squeezing them and moving me out of the way. No amount of talking from Ally's point of view got Mike to back down and Rae sure as hell stepped up to the plate.

"Guys, can we not--?"

Mike pointed his finger at Rae. "You acted like a spoiled brat at that party. Not once did you hold yourself with any sense of decorum or decency. You couldn't even handle your emotions at one part. One, Rae. Because the second there was temptation, you threw yourself straight into the line of fire."

"Your point, Michael?"

He snickered. "I don't think you're ready for college. I don't think you have the willpower or the want to do it after seeing you like that. And I think that's what's making you miserable."

"What?"

"I don't think you're upset with Clint at all for not wanting to go to college. I think you're upset with him because he had the balls to choose the road you wish you could travel."

I glared at him. "Mike, cut it out."

He shook his head. "No, no I won't. Because someone has to tell Rae the cold, hard truth. You went off on Clint, a man that loves you. A man that has followed you around blindly and would do anything for you. But watching you go off on him like that? Go off on me? He didn't deserve that, and neither did I. Allison didn't deserve to clean up your mess. You dragged all of us through the mud that night. And I think it's all because you don't actually want to be here."

Rae gritted her teeth. "I know what I did to you guys that night. I know this is all my fault."

"Do you? Do you really, Rae? This was supposed to be a fun end of the summer road trip for the four of us before everything changes. Because that's all you've been talking about. How it's going to change. How we're going to change. So we had this. And then you go and pull this shit and then get angry because we're angry? Come on."

I leveled out my voice. "Mike, cut it out."

Ally shook her head. "Just let him say it, please."

I looked over at Rae and saw tears cresting her eyes as Mike continued.

"It's easy to make plans and talk a big talk, but when it comes down to it, Rae, life gets busy and shit happens. This was supposed to be good for all of us. And now, you've made it all about you. You and your wishy-washy decision-making skills and your drama and your crap. I'm over it."

I stood up from my chair. "Enough, Michael."

He glared up at me. "You should be more pissed than I am."

I cocked my head. "Leave it alone. Now."

I heard Ally softly apologizing to the people on the other side of the hibachi table. But it was too late. They had already gathered their things and gotten up. Everyone working in that damn place stared us down as if we were maniacs ruining their evening. I wasn't backing down, though. Mike had gone much too far. Especially with the way Rae was sniffling. I made sure he heard my tone. Saw my fists balled up at my sides. Because I didn't have any issues coming to blows with him again.

He was lucky I wasn't already wailing on him because he made Rae cry.

"Just sit."

Rae's whispered words came along with a tug at my arm. And I did as she asked. Mike shook his head as he flopped back into his chair, looking as desolate as I'd ever seen him. Ally rubbed his leg with her hand. Tried comforting him as much as she could. But even she looked a bit empty inside.

This entire weekend had drained all of us.

"Good evening, you guys! Oh, did the other party leave?"

The waitress's cheery voice grated against my ears.

"I'm not really sure what happened to them," Ally said.

"Oh, well. No matter. What can I get you guys to drink?" the waitress asked.

We all placed our drink orders, then fell silent again. Our salads came and I saw all of us stabbing our food a little harder than usual. Other than talking with the chef at our hibachi grill, we didn't utter a word. Not to one another, and certainly not among ourselves. The food tasted bland. My appetite quickly faded away as my plate was stacked higher with food. Even drenching it in ginger sauce didn't do much for my appetite.

I ended up packing up most of it into a to-go box.

"I'm not paying for her meal," Mike murmured.

Ally sighed. "Well, it's a good thing I'm paying, then."

Rae piped up. "It's okay. I can pay for--"

I held my hand out, silencing her words. "Thank you, Ally. I really appreciate you being the bigger person you are."

Then I cast a heavy glance at Mike as he stood from his chair.

He picked up his food and his to-go drink. I saw him shake his head at Ally before he stepped away from the table. My eyes followed him, watching as he slinked out the door, shoving his way between people to try and get away that much faster. Rae sighed heavily and I wrapped my arm around her. Ally kept whispering how sorry she was for the way he acted.

But she didn't have to be sorry on his behalf.

That was his damn job.

35

RAELYNN

The night was a blur. Clint and I didn't talk. We fell asleep in opposite beds with our leftovers from the hibachi restaurant sitting out on the counter. I ate the unrefrigerated food for breakfast. I didn't bother waking Clint up as I packed my things. I was ready to get home. Ready to get up to my room. Ready to cry myself to sleep for the next week or so before I had to be back at this campus.

Alone.

With no friends in sight.

The morning turned into a blur as well. Clint and I didn't say anything to one another. Allison didn't come over to check on me. And while I didn't expect Michael to say anything to me, it still hurt that he didn't. We all silently piled into Michael's car just before eleven. Just in time for the hotel-wide checkout. I leaned heavily into the leather seats. I gazed out the window. Allison sat beside me in the back seat while Clint sat up front with Michael.

There was so much distance between all of us I almost couldn't see straight.

"So, does anyone want to listen to some music?"

Allison's words pierced the silent car ride as we got onto the highway.

"No? Not even Barbie Girl?"

I shook my head, but didn't say anything.

"Did anyone eat their leftovers for breakfast? Mine were fantastic. Hibachi is always good the day after."

I knew what she was trying to do. She was trying to lighten the mood. Preserve what was left of our weekend. But her efforts were fruitless. No one wanted to talk and no one wanted to engage with anyone else. Michael kept his lips pursed like the sour-puss he was. Clint's body tensed and stayed that way, and I just felt sad.

Sadder than I'd ever felt in my entire life.

Allison finally fell silent with a soft sigh. The world passed by the tinted windows as I gazed out toward the world. The outskirts of Los Angeles rolled by. A city that gave birth to me. A city that tried to bury me. A city that, oddly enough, felt like home more than anyplace else.

Well, except Clint's arms.

Why didn't he want to sit next to me?

This was all my fault. Michael was right last night. I ruined this trip for everyone who had been looking forward to it. I *had* been talking about things changing all summer. We *had* planned this trip together. To try and ease our souls. To try and give us some hope. To try and give us one last memory to take to college with us.

And it was a terrible memory.

What was worse was that I felt like I had ruined my friendships. My relationships with those I loved most. The three most important people to me in my life. In one fell swoop, I had alienated all of them. Clint, the man I loved; Allison, my best friend; and Michael, the first man I ever trusted after my father left.

You're a fuck-up, Rae.

I couldn't stop turning Michael's words over in my head. Those things he'd said to me over dinner last night. Jealous of Clint? Was that even possible? I mean, I had never considered any other path other than college. Sure, a four-year institution hadn't been in the plan. But college had always been there. Some sort of higher education after high school had always been there. How the fuck could I be jealous of Clint for not going?

Going had been my dream.

Are you sure about that?

I shoved the thoughts off to the side. I focused my eyes out the window as the air conditioning pummeled against my face. I kept myself as silent as I could and pressed myself as close to the window as I could get. Away from the tension in the car. Away from the fact that I wanted to scream.

Away from the fact that I wanted to keep crying until I drowned myself in my own tears.

You're pathetic, Rae.

Despite the fact that Clint's apartment was the first place we hit, Michael didn't stop there. I pulled my head upright from the window and gazed out the windshield. Watching as Clint slowly looked over at Michael.

"You missed my--"

"I know," Michael said plainly.

I looked over at Allison and she sighed.

He's taking me home first.

It shouldn't have shocked me. In some ways, it didn't. It just... hurt. Then again, I deserved it after what I pulled. Michael picked up the pace. Raced down streets doing fifteen over before turning into the opening of my neighborhood. He couldn't get there fast enough, and it made my stomach sink.

"Home sweet home," Michael said flatly.

I opened my door. "Thanks for the ride."

He didn't answer as I climbed out.

I quickly gathered my things from his trunk and turned around. I said goodbye to Allison with a soft hug as Michael threw the car into reverse, backing down the driveway before we even let go.

"Michael!" she exclaimed.

I dropped my things in the driveway. I watched Allison struggle to get the door closed. I saw Clint wave at me through the windshield before he looked over at the wild man driving. The tinted windows quickly covered their faces the further back they pulled away from me. And as Michael sped down the road, his tires skidded on the pavement.

"Rae?"

Mom's voice pulled me out of my trance and I felt myself tense up. I closed my eyes and picked up my things, then headed for the porch. The worry on her face made me sick to my stomach. Fucking hell, would I really have to talk about this with her? I didn't want to. The only person I wanted to speak with was Clint.

Then Michael.

But certainly not my mother.

"Come on. Here. Let me help."

I pulled myself away. "I've got it, Mom."

She pulled my suitcase from my hand. "No, you don't. And that's okay sometimes."

I snickered before I dropped my things near the staircase. I walked into the kitchen and headed straight for the fridge. I pulled out a soda and cracked it open, then found my space at the table in the corner.

I dropped down and guzzled it until the pain of the carbonation took over the pain I felt in my chest.

"So the weekend went that well, huh?"

I set my soda can down as Mom sat beside me.

"I really don't want to talk about it."

Mom shrugged. "Well, too bad."

I rolled my eyes. "Great."

"Hey, I know you. I raised you. And I know that the more bothered and stressed you become, the more you lock up. The more you shut people out. Which does no one any good."

I shrugged. "Doesn't matter anymore."

She placed her hand over mine. "It matters to me."

I stared into my mother's eyes and tried to come up with a reason to move away from this conversation. Because I knew if I started, I wouldn't stop until it was all out on the table. Including the shit I had to deal with when it came to her.

"You really don't want this, Mom."

She squeezed my hand. "I'm a bigger girl than you give me credit for."

All right. Your funeral. "I don't know if C.S.U. is for me, Mom."

She nodded. "That's fine. We can find you another school, if that's what you want."

"I went to a college party and got so plastered I told Clint I needed a new boyfriend."

She blinked. "You got drunk?"

"And high. I lost complete control, Mom. I'm not ready to be on my own. Not like that."

"What else happened this weekend?"

Tears crested my eyes. "Everything, Mom. I said so many disgusting things to Clint. I ruined my friendship with Michael. He won't even talk to me. He's so angry for what I did at that party. The mess I made of things and the hurtful things I said to Clint."

"Oh, honey. Come here."

Mom scooted her chair closer and wrapped her arms around me.

"I don't know what's wrong. I'm petrified of going off to school. I want school. But I don't know if I want English. And I don't know if I want school right now. I don't know if I'll like teaching kids or if I'm playing it safe or if me going off to college will ruin me and Clint or if I'm not going to be friends with Allison and Michael anymore and I probably won't now anyway because they hate me and want nothing to do with me and Clint didn't sit beside me in the car so I think he hates me, too--"

"There, there. It's okay. Sh, sh sh sh sh sh."

I drew in a shaking breath. "And you're always asking me for money. And I don't have money to give you. I have my own plans to have my own place and you stopped looking for a job and I don't get why you did that and I've had to hide money from you just to keep it for myself and I'm so tired of you complaining about me contributing to a house I don't want to call home in an area of the city that I want to leave in a part of the state I don't even know I want to continue living in!"

I felt my mother's arms go slack and I pulled back.

"What?" she asked.

I wiped at my eyes. "I know you stopped looking for a job because I had money to contribute. I became your financial enabler and I didn't speak up until it was too late."

Mom blinked. "You're upset with me about money?"

I sighed. "Not just money, Mom. Everything. It's like you're scared you're going to fail at a job or something, so you don't even try. You psyche yourself out before anything ever happens and you fall back on what's easiest because you're content with the life you have. Even if it does make you miserable most of the time."

"I'm not miserable, Raelynn."

I rolled my eyes. "And now you're upset with me, too."

"Yeah, rightfully so. Just because I ask you to contribute to some of the bills you help rack up around here doesn't mean I want to drain you of all your money."

"So, the fact that I pay for all these lunch outings we randomly have now and order the pizza all the time for our movie nights and do all the grocery shopping and pay over half of the bills doesn't strike you as odd. Especially when I only worked a part-time job at a grocery store?"

"I mean, you had the money from all those--"

She stopped herself in her tracks and I nodded slowly. I stared at her with tired eyes, waiting for her to look at me. Waiting for her to respond to me. Waiting for her to say something--anything--acknowledging that I was right about this.

That my assessment of the situation wasn't completely off.

"Mom?"

She licked her lips. "Everything will be okay. It always is."

"Mom, please look at me."

She took my hand, but refused to look. "I didn't know you were feeling like this, sweetheart."

"I honestly thought it would go away, Mom. After I went off to college and confirmed for myself that I needed to be there instead of here. That maybe, me going away would help you to find your footing somehow."

She snickered. "You've been planning on going to college to get away from me, haven't you?"

And as the question fell from her lips, my world came to a grinding halt.

Had I planned on going to college to get away from her?

36

CLINTON

"**H**ere you go."

Cecilia placed a mug of coffee in my palm before closing the balcony door behind her. She sat beside me in the reclining lawn chairs I'd purchased for this little concrete slice of paradise. I knew she felt relieved. Especially after coming in the way I did last night. I practically took the door down trying to get inside. And after she saw the bruises on my face and my ribs, she promptly got me to a doctor this morning.

She wanted me to go to the E.R. last night with her. But I'd refused.

"Have you heard from her yet?"

I shook my head. "No."

My stepmother nodded. "Don't worry. She'll reach out when she's ready."

I shrugged. "Not so sure about that."

"I'm just glad you have a clean bill of health. Because those bruises sure aren't getting any better."

"They don't hurt."

"I'm sure they do. They just don't hurt more than your heart right now."

I snickered. "Ever the wise one."

She giggled. "I come with my own perks."

I sipped my coffee. "Is there anything I could've done differently?"

She patted my leg. "From what you've told me about how the weekend went? No, there isn't."

"Somehow, I don't believe that."

"I know you don't. You're a fixer. That's what you do. And you're very good at it. But this is something you can't fix. And you struggle with that."

"I wish I could fix it, Ma."

"I know you do. And so do I. Knowing Rae is hurting like that reminds me of the kind of person I was when I first met your father. Lost. Scared. Afraid of being alone and willing to grab on to anything just to feel as if I meant something to someone."

"She means something to me."

She shook her head. "Doesn't work that way. If Rae doesn't feel as if she belongs anywhere or that anyone is happy with her, she's going to feel alone. Whether or not you feel she should feel that way."

I groaned. "So fucking complicated."

"It really isn't. Not when everything is stripped away. If you take away the emotions and the events of the weekend and boil it all down, what you're left with is an eighteen-year-old girl who was forced to grow up too soon who doesn't have any more answers when she's used to having them."

I thought on her words. "You're right, actually."

"I know I am. Because I was her once."

"I made her this list, you know."

Ma turned to face me. "What list?"

I sighed. "The day after the party. I left the hotel and found myself on campus. I used one of the library computers to list out all sorts of avenues Rae had that she probably hadn't thought about. I gave it to her hoping that, maybe, her knowing her options might help her out a bit."

She smiled softly. "You're a good man, Clint."

"I just want her to not feel like this."

"Because you love her."

I nodded slowly. "Yeah. Because I love her."

"What were some of the suggestions?"

I grinned. "One of them was to travel."

"Travel?"

"Yeah. You know, work from one of those freelance sights with her art or whatever and use the money to travel around. People do that nowadays as a full-time job all the time. I really think she could do it."

"And you think that would make her happy?"

"I don't know. But at least it would give her some time to figure out what might make her happy instead of being so damn miserable all the time."

I looked over at Ma and found her smiling fondly.

"What?" I asked.

She sipped her coffee. "My rebellion against my parents was traveling after high school. Well, I mean, I was homeschooled. We all were. And then I was expected to settle down. Have kids. Live that very traditional, religious lifestyle. My middle finger to them was traveling on what little I could scrounge up after I turned eighteen."

"How did that go?"

"Oh, it was fantastic. I had a couple of friends in the area where I lived that wanted to do the same thing. We'd always sneak out and get together and daydream about life beyond our yards. Beyond the fields and the trees and the chickens that woke us up well before sunrise. We even went so far as to reach out and get passports without our parents' knowledge. Then, once we had those in hand, we packed up our things and left."

"That's… that's insane, Ma."

She giggled. "We pooled our money together and could barely afford one-way tickets to London."

My eyebrows rose. "The three of you went to London?"

She nodded. "Oh, yeah. I think the ticket lady took pity on us, too. Which is why we could afford them. Either way, we got the tickets, got to London, and started hopping from country to country. Working odd jobs just to afford the train tickets and food. We lived out of hostels and experienced the world and all it had to offer."

"I'm surprised you guys were safe."

"Ah, I think we were lucky in that regard. If something felt off to us, we just kept going. There was no pressure to do anything or live up to any standard, so we didn't hold ourselves to one. Just three girls trolloping through Europe trying to soak up as much as possible. We did that for a little over three months before it got old."

"Did you have fun, at least?"

She sighed. "It's one of the fondest memories I have in my life."

"That's amazing, Ma."

"I learned so much about life and food and culture and music. I learned more than I ever would have in a classroom. That much is for certain. I picked up on languages and learned traditions. I became a connoisseur of wine and fashion."

"Sounds like you."

She smiled. "All this to say, if Rae wants to travel, she should jump on it now."

"Well, maybe she will."

"And you should go with her."

My eyes narrowed. "What?"

"I'm serious, Clint. There's no time like now. And as you get older, it gets harder to do things like that. You get trapped into things like leases and mortgages and car payments and kids."

I snickered. "No offense, right?"

She winked. "Never."

I shook my head. "I mean, it sounds nice. But I don't think she'd want me to."

"How do you know that?"

"Because I'm holding her back."

Ma rolled her eyes. "Oh, please. Don't be so dramatic. That's her job."

I chuckled. "What?"

"Clint, the two of you do nothing but build each other up. I mean, look at what you did for her this weekend. Despite how much she chewed into you because she was loaded with all sorts of nonsense at that party, you still managed to help her. And when you broke up with her? Completely pushed her away? What did she do?"

I grinned. "She kept making sure I was okay."

"And kept up with your homework. And your tests. And encouraging you. It's what you two do for one another. That's what couples *should* do for one another."

I shrugged. "I don't know, Ma."

"And look at it this way. Even after you were punched in the gut by some random guy at this same party, you were still prioritizing her in your efforts. If that's not true love, then true love doesn't really exist."

"Maybe. But I still wouldn't be able to come up with that kind of money. Traveling takes a lot nowadays. And I screwed up big time. I don't have any qualifications. The money I set aside from selling those--"

Ma took my hand and squeezed it tight. She urged me to look at her as she tugged at my arm. I leaned back in my chair, completely forgetting about my lukewarm mug of coffee. And as she stared directly into my eyes, she snickered.

"First of all, you owe me nothing."

I groaned. "You need help here."

She shook her head. "Not as much help as you think I do."

"What do you mean?"

She smiled. "I got a raise over the weekend."

"What?"

"Yeah. A raise. From my part-time work. I mean, it's not a lot. But it's enough to take the phone bill off your shoulders every month. And after doing away with cable and going directly to streaming services, I'm trimming down the budget. With a couple more moves, I'll be able to completely take the bills off your shoulders."

I blinked. "But, what about your--?"

"I'm a grown woman, Clint. I know how to make a budget and stick to it. I know how to set money aside and find ways not to touch it if that money can't be touched."

"I never said--"

"And as far as having no qualifications goes? That isn't even kind of true. Sure, you might not have a stamp of approval from teachers and such. But you have talent you can capitalize on. You're a writer, sweetheart. And do you know what the most wonderful thing in the world for a writer is?"

I paused. "What?"

"Travel, Clint. The best thing you could do for your writing is to travel."

37

RAELYNN

I sat in my bed, scrolling through all sorts of things on the internet. And all the while, I thought about Clint. I wanted to call him. I wanted to text him. I wanted to see how he was doing. But I also suspected he didn't want to hear from me. Not right now, at least. So I dove into the list he gave me. That typed-up piece of paper that held so many options for me.

And the one I kept gravitating back to made me curious.

I searched through airfare and hotel deals online. I looked up how much it would be to rent a car in some places and jotted down a budget on the back of that sheet of paper. The only option on his list that gave me any sort of peace was traveling. Working, and traveling, and living off just what I needed. Things were still expensive, though. I'd have to dip into the money I'd saved up in order to get to a few places. But I did find a lot of ways to cut costs.

Like booking rooms that were cancelled at the last minute. And using coupons for Air B&Bs. And taking trains all around Europe instead of being hellbent on flying.

Walking around instead of always taking cabs.

The suggestion to travel had worked its way underneath my skin. It took over my dreams last night as I tossed and turned. I couldn't shake it either. I figured once I drew up a schematic of the costs of something like this, I'd be swayed away from it. Back to the original plan of going to college. Getting a degree. Living my life by the book.

But the more I researched, the more I found myself trying to make it work.

I mean, no teachers? No homework? No stressing out about midterms or deadlines or schedules? It sounded like a damn dream. Learning on my own time by submerging myself into an atmosphere I'd never get in a classroom. And it wasn't as if the traveling and the working and the learning would cost me that much more than college. The thought made me excited. Not anxious, like school always had.

But what about Clint?

Adding another person to the traveling picture automatically increased all the prices. Airfare. Food. Cab rides. Even train tickets. I wouldn't be able to foot the bill on my own. Not by a long shot. And I knew Clint felt compelled to stay behind and help take care of Cecilia. I couldn't blame him for that, either. Not after she took him in as her own.

The thought of leaving him behind to travel made me sick to my stomach, though.

I made a list of all the places I wanted to visit. London and Galway. Belize and Rio De Janeiro. Costa Rica and the fields of Scotland and those tulip gardens I always saw online. They were located in the Netherlands, I found out. So I added that to my list. There were so many places I wanted to see. So much I wanted to learn. So many places where I could apply the skills I already had to scrape up some extra cash to do extra things. Like indulge in the country's finer foods and go on train tours around Italy's wineries and sip all their fantastic blends.

Clint would enjoy something like that.

I sighed as I flipped over to airplane flights. I started typing in some of these locations, seeing how much it would take for me to fly out of LAX. Most of the prices were what I expected. Especially for one-way international flights. But I did come across one particular airline running a deal on their international flights.

Specifically, to Rome.

"I wonder how long that's lasting," I murmured.

I started reading the fine print. And with every word I devoured, my soul soared with delight. Holy shit. They were running this special for all sorts of international flights. Ones to the

Polynesian Islands. Others to Australia. And the Rome flight? It was less than half the cost it usually was for business class. My stomach burst to life with butterflies. The deal lasted for the next week. That meant that if I played my cards right, I could be in Europe in four days.

"Four days," I whispered.

I smiled at the thought. My soul felt at peace and my heart felt fuller than it had in, well, ever. Tears of happiness rushed my eyes. And as the feeling overwhelmed me, I slid out of bed, stood to my feet and shook my arms out, trying to expel the excess energy that had crept up in my body. Rome. In four days.

This is what going to college should feel like.

I hadn't understood this excitement Michael and Allison had for their future until now. I paced my room and continued scrolling through my phone. I bookmarked the purchase page for those flights and started looking up hotel deals. Bungalows in the area. Comparing prices and drawing up a mental budget in my head.

"Yes!" I exclaimed.

Air B&B had a fantastic deal on a studio apartment with a great view. I favorited it and flipped back over to the freelance website. One of the many Clint had jotted down for me. If I could get my English tutoring thing up and running, even if I worked the bare minimum required for the site, that would cover my train tickets all around Europe. A few cab fares, too. That meant my travel costs would drop substantially and give me more wiggle room with my initial budget.

"Oh, my gosh," I whispered.

I rushed out of my room and ran down the stairs. I tucked my phone into my bra and scrambled to get my purse. I pulled it over my shoulder as I ran around downstairs, making sure I had everything I needed.

"Honey? You okay?" Mom asked.

"I'll be back later, love you!" I exclaimed.

Then I ripped the front door open.

"Be safe, honey! Text me when you get--!"

"I'll call later, Mom. Bye!"

"Where are you going!?"

I didn't bother answering her question.

I ran up the street, making my way for the exit of the neighborhood. With a renewed sense of vigor flooding my veins, my legs pumped as fast as they could go. My lungs filled with fresh air as I turned the corner and rushed across the street. I didn't know how long it would take me to run to Clint's. I didn't know when I'd get there. I had to talk to him, though. Face to face.

And I needed to do something with this excess energy I'd never experienced before.

Unless I was around him, of course.

38

CLINTON

"Hey, Ma!"

"Yeah, Clint?"

"You sure it's okay that I use your car for the afternoon?"

"Yep! I'm just going to be around here cleaning. And I have another dinner date tonight, so feel free to stay out if you want."

I grinned. "He picking you up?"

She popped her head into my room. "He is. Why?"

I peeked over at her. "You not wanting me to meet him yet?"

"It's not like I'm keeping you a secret. But we aren't at that point where I want to start introducing him to family and all that nonsense."

"Well, make sure he treats you right. Because if he doesn't--"

"Yeah, yeah. I know the rundown."

I smiled. "Good."

I didn't know much about this man Ma was dating. Well, other than the fact that they'd been doing dinner a lot lately. She seemed happy enough with him. Which was all that mattered. But the idea of her dating someone she didn't want me to meet did rub me the wrong way. I knew it wasn't an insult or anything. Just her taking things slowly. I just didn't want her misjudging someone and ending up with another man like my father.

Gotta give her more credit than that.

I was envious of her, really. For being able to have the strength to move on like she was. I would've never been able to do that. Hell, I was still having a hard time doing that. And I never proclaimed to love my father. There were moments where I wanted to do nothing else except call him. Talk to him. Get some sage advice he'd been holding back his entire life. There was nothing more I wanted than someone guiding me through this life. Showing me the path I needed to carve for myself.

Ma already gave you that advice.

I sighed. I knew I wasn't being fair to her. I don't know, I guess I was just coping with the idea of never having the kind of father I wanted. The kind of father I needed. And that would take time. Either way, I was looking forward to heading over to Mike's. I needed some guy time after the shit from this weekend. I was glad he'd called. Though, I'd kind of hoped Rae would have called me by now.

Just give her space. It's what she needs right now to make her decision.

"Clint?"

"Yeah, Ma?"

"Rae's here for you."

My eyes widened and I leapt toward my bedroom door. I stared down the small hallway and saw her standing there, sweat dripping down her brow. Ma handed her a glass of ice water before ushering her in. I couldn't believe my eyes.

Rae was here.

"Why are you so sweaty?" I asked.

She chugged the ice water back before setting the glass down on our small kitchen table. She was panting. Still sweating. And as Ma went to refill her glass, she walked toward me, her eyes never leaving mine.

"I ran here," she said breathlessly.

My eyebrows rose. "You what?"

"Here, have another glass," Ma said.

Rae took it and chugged it back, groaning as it went down. I peeked over at Ma and she shrugged her shoulders, then nodded her head to my bedroom. Yes, Rae and I needed to talk. Something she had been encouraging me to do. I'd be late for Mike's. But what the hell.

I could send him a text and things would be fine.

"Can we talk?" Rae asked.

"Sure. You want a shower first?" I asked.

She shook her head. "No, no. I'm good. But we really need to talk."

I nodded. "Yeah, we do."

I ushered her into my room and took one last look at Ma. At the flick of her wrist, I closed the door behind me. I turned around and saw Rae pacing the room and wringing her hands together. Despite the fact that she had sweated a ring around her T-shirt and her hair was matted to her face, she kept moving. Refusing to rest.

"Rae, you need t--"

"I need to travel," she blurted out.

I blinked. "You… made a decision."

She sighed. "Honestly, it's a decision I should've thought about sooner. Something that should have occurred to me. Then, maybe, I wouldn't have made such a terrible mess of everything. You know, me acting like a total psycho and losing my mind."

"Do you want to sit?"

"Actually, no. I don't. I'm so full of energy that I just…"

I cocked my head. "You look happy."

She smiled brightly. "I am happy. Clint, I was scared. Fucking petrified of committing to something I didn't want. I mean, college has always been the plan. Get out, get away, get my own place. But the underlying reason was the issue. I didn't want college for me. I wanted it to get away from Mom. To get out of here. To leave this shit behind and never look back."

"I mean, it makes sense."

"In a lot of respects, Michael was right. At the restaurant, you know?"

"How do you figure?"

She ran a trembling hand through her hair. "I am jealous of you."

I blinked. "Wait, what?"

She sighed. "I'm jealous. You don't know much about your future, but you knew college wasn't for you. And you were brave enough to make that decision. I wasn't. I caved to my fears. To this idea that things would magically work out if I kept not thinking about it. And yes, I know how stupid that sounds. But I'm jealous of your bravery. Of at least partially knowing what you kind of want."

"I don't have it together as much as you think I do."

She took my hands. "That's the thing, Clint. You do. You knew school wasn't for you. You know your writing is. You have a place here, with Cecilia. I don't have any of that."

"You have a place here with me."

She blinked. "Do I really?"

I furrowed my brow. "Of course you do. Last time I checked, we were together. Still in love. Going through a rough time, sure. But still together."

She smiled. "You have no idea how relieved I am to hear that."

"Rae, what's going on?"

She kissed my hands. "I'm sorry. I'm so fucking sorry. The guilt is eating me alive that I let things come to this. I don't think there are words I can string together to tell you just how sorry I am. Because you're the person that has been there with me through everything. And you didn't deserve what happened this weekend."

When her eyes came back up to mine, I felt a weight lift off my shoulders. I pulled away from her hands and cupped her cheeks, my eyes dancing between hers. She looked different. Seemed different. She held herself a bit differently, and I knew a great deal had changed.

She looked lighter on her feet.

Just like I felt.

"It's okay, Rae. I forgave you the morning after."

She shook her head. "You shouldn't have. You can be angry. It's okay to be angry. And you can yell at me. Say anything you want to say. You can--"

I dropped my lips to hers, silencing her words with a kiss. Her hands fell around my wrists as a smile crossed my face. I kissed her lips again. And again. I captured her lower lip softly between my teeth. I felt her take a step toward me. Her hands slid up my arms before sliding down my chest. I cloaked her body with my wing-span, feeling her mold to me as our foreheads fell together.

"Shut up, Rae. I love you. And I just want you to be happy."

She snickered. "Then kiss me again, you big lug."

I crashed my lips against hers and my tongue fell into her mouth. She battled me for control as I backed her toward my bed. All thoughts of heading to Mike's completely fell away from my mind. I felt my phone vibrating in my pocket, but I didn't bother to answer it. My hands splayed along Rae's back. I held her close to me as we tumbled to bed. And as I stripped her of her damp clothes, the smell of her womanhood filled my nostrils.

"Oh, Rae."

I growled as I kissed down her neck. The salted taste of her skin had my cock pulsing for more of her. I wrapped my lips around her pert nipples. I felt her rolling against me as she pressed herself further up my bed. With my face between her breasts, I shed my pants. I stepped out of my shoes and leaned up just enough to rip my shirt over my head.

And when Rae's eyes fell upon my body, she licked her lips.

"Come here, handsome."

I knelt against the mattress. I crawled to her, stalking her. Like the prey meant for my lunch. My lips fell to her calf and she sighed, lying down against my pillow. Her legs spread for me. I watched her body unfurl for me, her lower lips glistening with want. I kissed up the inside of her thigh. The heat of her smell battered against my face as I slid her legs over my shoulders. I massaged her with my hands. I felt her muscles jumping as I nibbled at the dollop of excess on her inner thigh.

Then, I let my tongue slide all the way up her slit.

"Clint, yes."

I grinned. "Ma's still here. Might wanna keep it down."

She picked up a pillow and pressed it over her face. An action that made me chuckle. I lapped up her slit again, feeling her shiver as she groaned against the soft surface. I wrapped my arms around her thighs, pulling her as close as I could get her. I felt her heat encompassing my lips as I played her like the fiddle she had become. Her body was an instrument I had mastered. I knew exactly how to make her buck. How to make her moan. How to make her shiver and ache with need. My tongue traced the familiar track, tasting her before I swallowed her down. And as my finger slid into her pulsing entrance, her back arched.

"Clint!"

I'd never get tired of hearing her call out my name.

39

RAELYNN

I pressed the pillow against my face as he buried himself between my legs. He bent them forward, pressing my knees against my chest with his forearm. His fingers filled me, pumping as I reached my peak of ecstasy. Fire ignited behind my eyes and all thoughts of traveling fell away from my mind. All I thought about was him. How me made my heart soar. How he made my soul complete. And as my toes curled deeper with every stroke of his tongue, I wailed into the pillow.

"Clint, that's it. Right there. Right there. Right the--"

My body locked out and my legs fell hard against the mattress. I felt the pillow being ripped away from my face before his lips fell against mine once more. I kissed him deeply. I licked myself off his skin. And as he eased his aching dick inside my body, it solidified what I was thinking.

I couldn't travel without him.

I wouldn't.

My nails slid down his back. I felt every single muscle on his body rolling and jumping for my pleasure. We moved as one, our eyes never parting. I felt his heart beating against my chest, matching the rhythm of my own. I breathed the air he afforded me. I couldn't stop smiling up at him. With my legs locked around his waist, I fell deeper into the boy I loved.

Oh, no, no.

The man I loved.

"You're perfect, Rae."

I gasped. "Clint, please."

"I'll never leave you behind. Never."

"Clint, yeah."

"You're mine. Always. Until you tell me to leave."

"Never. Don't leave me. I'm sorry. I'm sorry. I--"

He growled. "Stop it. Tell me what I long to hear."

His hips snapped against mine before he ground his pelvis into my aching clit.

"I love you, Clint."

He grunted. "Again."

"I love you so much."

"Louder."

"I love you! Oh, fu--"

His mouth swallowed my sounds while his tongue explored me. I wrapped my arms around his neck and pulled him down against my body. I couldn't get enough of him. I needed him closer. I needed him filling every part of me. The way he kissed me. The way he fucked me. The way he made love to me. I needed it in my life.

I needed *him* in my life.

He rolled us over and I straddled his hips. I ground deeply against him, with my hands against his chest. I smiled down at him as my hair curtained us off. He rose up, capturing my lips as his arms cloaked my back once more. He bucked against me, filling me as his cock grew against my walls. And as I rocked my body against his, our movements became one.

We became one with each other.

"Rae."

"Clint."

"So close. So close."

"Come with me. Please."

"Rae, fuck."

My head fell back as he groaned out into the room. His hands held me steady, my body attached to his. I felt him filling me with his mark. Thread after thread, triggering my own release. My eyes rolled back. Stars burst with delight against the darkness. I gripped his forearm tightly, feeling him shaking underneath me. His arms brought me back. My forehead fell to his shoulder. I whimpered and shook, my orgasm never-ending as his cock continued to fill me.

While my heart surged to life for him.

"Oh, Rae."

I sighed. "Clint."

He kissed the shell of my ear. "I love you so fucking much."

Tears rushed my eyes. "I love you, too."

We fell to his bed and curled up against one another. I gazed into his eyes, watching as he smiled brightly at me. He tucked a strand of hair behind my ear. I reached up and wiped away a few beads of sweat. He cupped the back of my neck and kissed me again, allowing his heat to linger.

Then Clint sighed.

"We should go see Mike, you know."

I furrowed my brow. "Now?"

He nodded. "Now. We all need to talk and fix things before next week comes."

I shook my head. "I don't think he wants to see me right now."

"Maybe not. But he won't come around unless you keep coming around. We can remind him that there's still a bit of summer left. We can still end things on the right note."

"Mmm, I don't know if that's going to work."

"We can pick up his favorite drink along the way. Snack, too."

I wrinkled my nose. "That terrible bubble tea shit?"

He nodded. "And Doritos. The man's got weird taste in food combinations, but it'll soften him to our arrival."

I narrowed my eyes playfully. "You made plans with him, didn't you?"

"My phone's been vibrating off the hook since you came into the apartment."

I giggled. "Thank you for giving me your time."

"You'll always have it, if you want it."

"I want all of you."

"Then you have all of me, Rae."

His words filled me with happiness. More than I thought my heart could handle. But he didn't back down from his plan. We were going to see Michael, whether I wanted to or not. He rolled out of bed and I groaned. I was able to take a quick shower before I had to pull my nasty pants back up my clean legs. Clint loaned me another shirt. But that didn't do much for the damp bra sitting against my skin.

"I need to take a cab next time," I murmured.

Clint snickered. "Or just call. I would've come and picked you up."

"Noted."

We slipped out of his bedroom and Cecilia was sitting out on the porch. No doubt, giving us our privacy. She peeked her head around the corner and I caught her stare. And I could've sworn I saw her wink. Clint led me outside and we went to find her car. He opened my door and offered me his hand like the true gentleman he was. My hand sat against his knee the entire time we drove around. Trying to track down that stupid bubble tea place.

"Do you remember where it is?" Clint asked.

I shrugged. "I can't ever remember where that damn thing is located."

"All right. Chips first while I try to look it up on my phone."

"I'll buzz into the grocery store really quickly. I need to pick up my last proof of pay anyway."

"Sounds like a plan."

He pulled into the grocery store parking lot and I looked over toward the corner. Where that tree stood. I slipped out of the car and watched the shadows, remembering all that had happened. The night Clint saved me. The night he risked his life to make sure I was all right. Before we barely even knew one another, he had been protecting me. Risking himself to make sure I was okay. I sighed as I closed the door. I forced myself to go inside, even though the memories of that night bombarded me.

No. It was determined.

I had to convince Clint to travel with me.

I picked up a large bag of Doritos for Michael and walked back out to the car. And I found Clint staring at that tree, too. With glossy eyes and a tranced look on his face, I gave him the time he needed to process. To remember. To pull himself out of it.

Then he sighed. "Ready to go?"

I nodded. "Did you find that drink place?"

"Yep. Just up the road a bit."

"Do you think they have sodas for those of us that aren't weird and like chewing on our drinks?"

He chuckled. "I can definitely check it out. You got the chips, so I get the drinks."

"Fair enough."

I saw Clint texting on his phone as he stood in line. But I didn't pay it any mind. Probably telling Michael we were on our way. The both of us. You know, so he could prepare the firing squad for my arrival. The closer we grew to his house, the more nervous I became. He had never been this upset with me. And not hearing from Allison at all made it worse.

Until I found the two of them sitting on Michael's parents' porch.

"What's going on?" I asked.

Clint parked the car. "I figured both of them should be here so we can all talk."

I slowly looked over at him. "And when were you going to tell me this?"

He shrugged. "I just did."

I snickered and shook my head. Then I walked the hall of shame. I offered my peace offering to Michael before Clint passed off the drink. And I watched as he ran his eyes up and down my body. Clint pulled a couple of chairs over for us and I peeked over at Allison. She had her hand on Michael's knee, softly massaging. Trying to keep him calm as her eyes avoided my gaze.

Fuck. I really hoped I could fix this.

"I'm sorry," I said.

Michael opened the chips. "That's a start."

Clint motioned for me to sit down and I gladly took the invitation.

"I know you guys are mad at me. And you have every right to be. Michael, you were right at the restaurant."

He paused. "What?"

I snickered. "You were right. You and Allison, about different things. I was jealous of Clint. I am jealous of Clint, really. He had the guts to admit that he didn't want to go to college, despite what others might've thought. I was jealous that he had at least an inkling of an idea of what he might do after high school. Even if that idea was what he wouldn't do."

Allison furrowed her brow. "But you've always wanted to go to college."

I shook my head. "No, I've always wanted to get out of here. And I figured school was a good enough excuse. I could save up, get a place of my own. With you."

I nodded toward Allison before drawing in a deep breath.

"Get our own place near wherever you went to college so we could keep rooming together. And then, you and Michael happened. Me and Clint happened. Plans got turned over on their head and it didn't become an issue of where I'd go to college, but how I would afford getting away from here on my own. I didn't see the issue like that, but that's what it really was."

Michael sipped his drink. "Why couldn't you just talk about it?"

I shrugged. "I didn't know it was an issue. Or, at least I didn't know the core of the issue. I was treating the topical issues that kept falling apart, but not the underlying issue. Because Allison's right; college was always the plan. And I thought that deviating away from that plan meant that I had somehow failed my teachers. And myself. And you guys. And my father, somehow."

Clint slid his hand over my knee. "You could never be a disappointment."

Allison nodded. "He's right. You've been difficult. But you've never disappointed us."

I looked over at Michael and he leaned back in his chair.

"So I take it you're not going to Cal State then?"

I shook my head. "No, I'm not. I've already contacted the enrollment office and told them I wouldn't be enrolling in this semester."

Michael nodded. "So you're going next semester?"

I looked over at Clint and smiled. "I don't know yet."

Allison's eyebrows rose. "And you're okay with that?"

Clint nodded. "Are you okay with that?"

My eyes panned back to Michael. "Yeah, I'm okay with that. I have an idea of what I want to do. But it's still a rough plan. What I know is that college isn't the way for me to get out of this place. I don't know what the right way is, but I do know what the wrong way is. Just like Clint knew what the wrong way was for him."

Clint squeezed my knee. "We'll figure it out."

I nodded. "Like we always do."

And as we all stared down Michael, I watched a grin crawl across his face.

"Anyone interested in hitting the beach tomorrow? It's supposed to be a very sunny day."

I leapt out of my chair and hugged him as Allison started laughing.

"Yes, yes, and even more yes," I said.

It felt good to have my family back.

EPILOGUE

Raelynn
Three Months Later

As I gazed out the window of the café, I watched the tourists walk by. The massive plaza that sprawled out before my eyes housed one of the most incredible fountains I'd ever seen. My cappuccino was the best I'd ever tasted.

Then again, most of the food in Rome tasted better than anything I'd ever had before.

I smiled at the children that walked by. They waved at me through the window and I waved back. Mothers smiled at me. Husbands that walked by nodded their heads. Locals stood out on the street, flooding the corners of the city with their music.

It tickled my funny-bone whenever they rolled their eyes at the tourists passing them by.

People pulled out their cameras and took pictures of everything. People posed for all sorts of group pictures as I peeked down at my laptop. My student still hadn't logged in yet. She had ten more minutes to sign on before the freelance website charged her for the session anyway. I liked that tutoring policy. Twenty-four hours to cancel. But if a student missed a session without cancelling, the tutor still got the full amount for the missed session.

I'd made half my traveling money that way.

I drew in a deep breath as the café brewed more espresso. I basked in the afternoon sunshine two thousand miles from home. I closed my eyes, taking it all in. And as I leaned back into my chair, I heard my laptop ding.

Signaling that my tutoring session had ended.

"Guess we have the rest of our day to ourselves."

I smiled as I opened my eyes. I looked over and saw Clint close my laptop. He sat down across the rounded table from me and smiled, holding his own cappuccino in his palms. Then a plate sat down in front of me from one of the baristas behind the counter.

Holding, just for me, a buttery croissant with drizzled chocolate on top.

"For you, beautiful," Clint said.

I grinned. "My hero."

He sipped his drink. "So, what do you want to get up to today? You don't have any more tutoring scheduled, right?"

I shook my head. "Nope, that was my last session. I hope they're all right."

"That happens pretty often, doesn't it?"

I shrugged. "As long as I get paid, I guess."

He smiled. "I really think we should try that restaurant we saw on the other side of town. We don't have too many more nights here before we pack up again."

"We need reservations for it. You think they'll take us on such short notice?"

"I'm sure it couldn't hurt to place a call. I'd like to try and get a table up on that rooftop. The locals tell me we can see all of Rome from up there."

I smiled. "That sounds fabulous. Can you give them a call?"

"Sure thing. You know, after I chow down this croissant."

I giggled as he picked his up and shoved it into his mouth. I shook my head as I sipped my drink, watching him lick his fingers. A week and a half in Rome didn't feel like enough time. But I couldn't wait for our next stop. Naples, Italy. Where I had booked us a tour of Pompeii and a place to stay in a quaint Air B&B with a view of the ocean.

Half price, since someone cancelled last minute.

My eyes fell back out the window as Clint pulled out his phone. I heard him talking to the restaurant as I relaxed into the back of my mind. In my own thoughts. Convincing Clint to travel with me hadn't been as hard as I expected it to be. And with his stepmother already on my side of things, swaying him took almost no effort. Mom wasn't happy, of course. But I was working on letting things with her slide. As Clint kept reminding me, my mother wasn't my child. It wasn't my responsibility to take care of her.

And if she couldn't support what I needed to be happy, then she didn't deserve the same courtesy.

"Good news, beautiful. The restaurant has an opening up on their rooftop tomorrow evening."

I nodded. "Sounds like a plan."

"Which leaves our evening tonight open for our enjoyment."

I grinned. "Mmm, sounds delightful."

"Rae."

I slowly looked over at him. "Yeah?"

He held out his hand. "Come here."

He wiggled his fingers and I slipped my palm against his. I watched his grasp take over my hand as I set my drink down. I sighed heavily. He always knew when thoughts of my mother took over my mind. And as my stare found his, he nodded.

"She's going to be okay."

I sighed. "I know. I know she is."

"She hugged you tight before we left. That's a good sign."

"I don't know. I just wish--"

"Things can't be different, Rae. But they can get better. Trust me, this traveling will do you both some good."

I smiled softly. "It's already doing me a lot of good."

"I'm glad to hear that."

"Oh, that reminds me. How's the book coming along?"

He blushed. "It's fine."

"Come on, Clint. There's nothing to be embarrassed about. How's your writing? You got up pretty early this morning. Did you have a dream you wanted to jot down?"

He paused. "I wanted to catch the sunrise in order to be able to accurately describe it."

"Will I be able to read some of it soon?"

"Once I can get it edited and written down cohesively, yes."

"So, no to the immediate future."

"But yes to eventually. Gotta look on the bright side, gorgeous."

I snickered. "Well, I can't wait to read it. You've killed me with that cliffhanger you left me on."

"Patience, baby. Patience will be your friend with this."

My laptop dinged again and I furrowed my brow. I faced forward and opened my laptop before a massive smile crossed my face. I had reviews pouring in from everywhere. So many people leaving such kind things about my ability to help them learn English. Payments came through, doubling the number I had this morning. I had enough money to push through a second payment. Another dump into my bank account that would more than cover our journey to Naples twice over.

"I take it something good happened?"

I snickered. "Pay day is always good."

Clint paused. "Wait, you're getting paid again?"

"Uh huh."

"Didn't you just get paid?"

I tapped the 'enter' key before closing my laptop.

"So long as I have a certain amount of money in my account on the site, I can dump it into my bank account at any time without penalty fees. I just hit that threshold, so my second payday of the week should be in my account come tomorrow morning."

He smiled brightly. "I'm so damn proud of you."

I grinned. "I'm proud of your stepmother going after your father the way she did to get you extra money for this traveling."

He chuckled. "She's nothing if not persistent."

"How did she even go about that anyway?"

"I mean, it's pretty simple. She kept calling him until he picked up. And when he hung up on her, she called his lawyer. Essentially, he gave her the money to shut her up."

I giggled. "I take it no one knows about your book."

He shrugged. "I'm giving it time."

"Giving it time? You published the first book in your series two weeks ago, and it's already been downloaded ten thousand times."

"I mean, half of those were freebie giveaways."

"But that's still five thousand downloads at regular price."

"Are you saying I should feel bad about taking my father's money?"

She scoffed. "Hell, no. Not at all."

"What I'd like to do is make my father's money stretch before I start sending it back over to Cecilia in chunks. You know, half for me, half to help her out. Because she didn't have to give me the entire sum to travel. I would've been okay on even a third of it."

"You're a good man, Clint."

"And you're a good woman. I'm still not sure how I wound up with someone like you."

I smiled. "You throw it down good in bed."

He grinned wildly. "Whatever it takes, I guess."

I threw my head back in laughter before I closed my laptop again. When I opened my eyes, I saw a small gift bag sitting on top of it. My laughter died down as I looked at the beautiful white bag, tied shut with a pretty purple bow.

"What's this?" I asked.

Clint licked his lips. "I, uh, saw this in a window when I went up to buy the croissants. I figured you should have it, Cleaver."

My eyes flickered to his. "Cleaver, huh."

He winked. "It's cute, for a dorky girl."

"Ha. Ha. Ha."

I snatched the gift up and tugged at the bow. But when I gazed down into the small bag, I gasped. I looked up at Clint as he smiled at me, then I reached into the bag to pull it out.

It was a beautiful silver necklace with a charm dangling on it. A quill, of all things. It shone in the sunlight of Rome as tears rushed my eyes. I looked over at Clint and he got up from his chair. He came over and held out his hand, beckoning with his fingertips.

"Let me put it on you. See how it fits."

I dropped it into his palm before gathering up my hair. And as he clasped it around my neck, he trailed his fingers over my shoulders. I shivered at his touch. My eyes fluttered closed as his lips fell against my ear. He kissed me softly, chuckling as goosebumps flooded my neck. And as I licked my lips, he massaged my upper arms.

"For the budding English nerd. I guess quills can be used for doodles and such, too."

I giggled as my head fell back, but he promptly stopped me in my tracks. He cupped my cheeks from behind me and let his lips fall to mine. I slid my hand through his hair. I bent backwards, trying to press my lips deeper against his. Our tongues collided. I found myself in a completely different world. He smiled as he released my lips, neither of us caring about who might be glancing our way.

And as he gazed into my eyes, I fingered the charm around my neck.

"I love you," I whispered.

He grinned. "I love you too, Rae."

He kissed me again and my heart felt fuller than ever. The thought of all the adventures to come made me shiver with anticipation. We had our entire future ahead of us. Clint, with publishing his stories of life and love and dreams. And me with my tutoring. Which was almost grossing me a full-time traveling income. As Clint pulled back, I gazed into his eyes. I looked up into the eyes of the man I loved and knew I had made the right choice with my life. School could wait. In fact, school didn't have to happen at all. Not if I didn't want it to.

But, so long as I had him, I knew I'd always make the right decision.

So long as I had him, my rougher edges could always be buffed.

FOREVER US

1

———

RAE

I tossed the door open to Clint's apartment and drew in a deep breath. I never thought the smell of packed boxes and fresh packing tape could ever make me smile, but it did. I looked at the towers of brown cardboard stacked in the corners. For once, I could finally see the carpet of this place. I closed the door behind me and moved into the kitchen in search of a snack. And when the smell of lemon alcohol filled my nostrils, I smiled.

We were only two days away from moving.

"All right. Let's see what the fridge has for me," I murmured.

I opened the door and sighed. There wasn't much. No matter how many times I opened this refrigerator door on a daily basis, nothing seemed to change. No fun snacks appeared. My favorite soda had still run out. There was still leftover chili from two weeks ago. I shivered at the thought. The congealed mess needed to be poured into the garbage disposal.

"Don't mind if I do," I whispered.

I slipped the container out and carried it over to the sink. I held my breath as I popped the top open. Yet, somehow, that still didn't shield me from the smell.

"Oh, man," I wheezed.

I flipped on the hot water and washed it down the garbage disposal. I turned it on and reached for the soap, squeezing the green apple goodness into the disposal with it. I watched bubbles fill the sink. Both sides of it, actually. And as the bubbles started disappearing, I let out the breath I had been holding.

"Wow. Okay. Mail time," I breathed.

I took my keys and walked back out to get the mail. I needed some time for the wind to blow away the stench sitting strongly in the crook of my nose. After breathing some deep breaths of fresh air, I found my way back inside again. I hung my keys up on the hook by the door and flipped through the endless envelopes of junk, spam, and random bank statements.

Ugh. I have to call them and tell them we're paperless again.

I slipped out a couple of flyers that mentioned something about mortgage rates. Home-owning. How rates for loans were the lowest they'd been in well over a decade. And the sentiments made me smile. I knew all about that kind of stuff. The loans. The percentages. The kinds of homes people were looking for.

Then I came across an envelope I'd need.

"You're going up on the fridge," I murmured.

I walked into the kitchen and tacked the envelope onto the front of the refrigerator with a magnet. Our realtor said he'd be sending copies of all the paperwork we had signed in order to make our purchase official. And I needed to make sure I kept track of these documents. I didn't have a formal filing cabinet to put it in, so the fridge door was the next best thing.

I'll get a filing cabinet once we get moved.

My phone vibrated against my hip and I set the rest of the mail down. It was junk, anyway. Needed to be tossed with the rest of the trash bags full of stuff we had strewn around this place. I slid my phone out and smiled. Even now, every time I saw him calling I got chills on the nape of my neck. I answered the phone and put it to my ear. My body readied itself for his voice.

For the soothing, wonderful voice that had gotten me through so much as a teenager.

"Well, hi there."

He chuckled. "Hey there, beautiful. You home from work?"

"I am. Just walked in a few minutes ago. And before you ask, I finally took care of that chili. I know you must be proud."

"Proud as a papa. But I have some bad news."

I paused. "Everything okay?"

"The cover designer for my novel ran over our meeting time by about thirty minutes. I'm just now leaving."

"And you're still halfway across town."

"Yep."

"Any accidents in your way?"

"You know how it goes. One minute we're good and the next, we're delayed another thirty minutes."

I made my way into our bedroom. "Well, was it at least a productive meeting?"

"More or less. We settled on a cover, so that's a good thing."

"Should I even ask about the rest of it?"

"Let's just say the cover designer is a talker. And not always about things that matter. Ever."

I giggled. "Oh, you poor thing. Sounds like you need some Chinese."

He snickered. "We had that last night. And three times last week."

"And it sounds like you could use it again tonight. You know, before I get to packing more boxes. I need energy for that, you know."

He chuckled again. "Why don't you wait for me to get home and we can pack up those couple of boxes together?"

"That depends. Will you pick up Chinese on the way home?"

"What makes you think I wasn't already going to do that anyway?"

I kicked off my shoes. "You're perfect, you know that?"

"Eh, so I've been told."

I barked with laughter. "All right. Hopefully I'll see you sooner rather than later. Want me to go ahead and place our order so it's ready once you get there?"

"If you could do that, it would make my day."

"Consider it done, handsome. I fervently and anxiously await your arrival."

"Nice use of words. I'll have to put that in a book somewhere."

I slipped my panties down my legs. "See you soon."

He blew me a kiss. "See you soon, beautiful."

After blowing a kiss back, I hung up the phone. It took me no time at all to place an order for Chinese. Especially since we got the same thing every single time. Vegetable lo mein and crab rangoons for me; orange chicken with white rice and three egg rolls for him. They practically knew us by heart. If we walked in, the woman at the cashier knew exactly what to ring us up for. If we called and someone recognized our voice, they'd simply recite our order to make sure that was what we wanted.

We'll have to get a new Chinese place when we move.

I tossed my phone onto the bed and took off the rest of my clothes. I was ready to get comfortable. Ready to get into a nice pair of pajamas and relegate myself to another evening of Chinese, packing, and snuggling with Clint. I reached for my flannel pajama bottoms tossed over a chair in the corner and hopped myself into them before rummaging around for one of Clint's shirts. All these years later, and I *still* loved wearing them.

I didn't quite get it over my head, though, before my stomach jumped.

"What the--?"

My body contracted and I took off running, with Clint's shirt dangling around my neck as I rushed into our bathroom. I shoved the door open with my shoulder and fell to my knees in front of the toilet. And as the searing pain of my kneecaps trickled up my thighs, I vomited into the toilet.

"Holy shit," I gurgled.

I groaned over the toilet bowl. My stomach rebelled against my existence as it jumped into my chest. It was like my body hadn't digested anything from the day. And suddenly, my head began to spin. I closed my eyes, willing the nausea to go away.

Come on, I thought we were done with all this.

Unfortunately, it wasn't the first time I'd been suddenly sick. It had happened on and off for the past two weeks. I sighed as I sat down, wiping at my mouth with the back of my hand before wiping my hand off on a towel on the floor and placing it against my forehead. My neck. My cheek. Trying to see if I was running some sort of fever. Maybe I was exhausted. Burning the candle from both ends. Maybe this was my body's way of telling me to slow down. Or maybe the excitement of the move was finally getting to me.

"Or maybe not," I whispered.

I slowly opened my eyes. It wasn't possible, right? I mean, Clint and I had been careful. Very careful, in fact. I crawled over to the bathroom cabinets, opened them up and started rummaging through them. Did I have a spare pregnancy test available? Clint and I had a scare a couple of months ago. Maybe I had one of those tests left.

I didn't find one.

"Shit," I hissed.

If Clint saw me on this bathroom floor, he wouldn't stop until he knew what was wrong. So I pulled myself up, gargled with mouthwash, and forced myself back into the living room. I needed a distraction. Something to take my mind--and my stomach--off some things. Even though I told Clint I'd wait, I finished packing the box of fragiles I started last night. I wrapped up a decorative vase his stepmother had gotten me for graduation. I reached for a picture still hanging on the wall of us standing with the acceptance letter from the publishing company regarding his novel. I smiled as I ran my fingertips across the photo. I remembered that day. Clear as crystal. How excited Clint had been. How proud I was of him.

How proud I still am of him.

I placed the picture into the box and reached for the clear container at the bottom. A very unceremonious way of storing pictures. But I hadn't yet gotten actual photo albums to slip them into. I sat on the couch and smiled as I popped off the top. Pictures from our high school graduation floated around. Clint and Michael hanging all over one another. Me and Allison hugging each other tight. The four of us jumping into the air. Throwing our graduation caps around before flashing tongues and peace signs for any camera that snapped a picture of us.

Then I found our travel pictures.

"Oh, my gosh," I giggled.

I pulled out a picture of Clint posing in front of the Parthenon. Beneath it was a picture of me at the Temple of Apollo in Pompeii. There was a picture of the four of us standing in front of the Tower of Pisa. All of us smiling and hugging one another.

It would be wonderful to see everyone again after we got moved.

Especially Mom.

"Honey! I'm home!"

I giggled as I placed the pictures back in the container.

"I smell Chinese," I said.

"They also threw in a small cup of that tea they make that you like so much."

"You mean that tea that makes you heave?"

He snickered. "Yep. So, if you want any kisses now, get 'em while they're hot."

I smiled. "Don't mind if I do."

I placed the container back in the box as Clint made his way for me. He set everything down just as I stood and his arms cloaked my entire body. I felt his hands roaming down my back. Our lips collided as his hands gripped my ass, giving it a soft squeeze. I smiled against his lips and he chuckled as his tongue slid along my lips. Every time he kissed me, I felt like a teenager again. Sneaking around. On the brink of getting into trouble. Ready for action, no matter the time or place.

"Mmm, I don't know about you, but I'm starving," he murmured.

I nuzzled my nose against his. "Me too."

"And as much as I'd love to continue this little thing we've got going here, I'm going to need some energy before that happens."

"Too much to handle for you, hot stuff?"

He growled playfully. "Never."

I laughed before he captured my lips, muting my sounds. Then he picked me up and carried me into the kitchen. He sat me on the edge of the counter, his hands sliding up and down my thighs. I felt myself warming for him, gravitating to him. It had been such a long day to wrap up one of the longest weeks I'd had in a while.

And suddenly, my body wanted nothing to do with the food he'd brought home.

"You want some wine to go with this food?" Clint asked.

I paused. "Actually, I'm thinking about sipping that tea with dinner."

He quirked an eyebrow. "It's not like you to turn down wine. You feeling okay?"

"You calling me a lush, Mr. Clarke?"

"And what if I am?"

I slipped my arms around his neck. "Why, I'd take offense to it before telling you I'm simply not feeling like wine tonight."

He wiggled his eyebrows. "What are you feeling like, then?"

I grinned. "Why don't you come back this way and find out?"

His smile grew wolfish as his eyes hooked with mine. His hand migrated into my hair, fisting it in the way only he could. I sighed as he pulled my head back slowly. His tongue licked up my pulse point, making me shiver. The smell of Chinese faded into the background, replacing itself with the smell of Clint's cologne, his musk, and the scent of his breath as his lips found their way to the shell of my ear.

"I love it when you wear my clothes," he whispered.

And whatever sickness my body still held on to slipped away as his lips kissed my skin.

2

CLINTON

She tasted like mint and coffee. A smell I had attributed to her very quickly as we had grown together. Her curves had only grown thicker over the years. And my palms loved them. I slid my hands up and down her thighs, feeling her melt into me as my tongue stroked along the roof of her mouth. I'd missed her all day. I mean, I missed her every day I was away for meetings. But today had been different.

Today, I'd practically longed for her.

"Mmm, Clint."

I grunted. "Bed. Now."

She wrapped her legs around me and tightened her arms around my neck. I lifted her with ease, my muscles flexing to accommodate her. The bigger she grew, the stronger I grew, my body always morphing to take care of hers. I loved the way her hips had blossomed in college, the way her curves had thickened with the food from our travels all those years ago. Our tongues did battle as I charged us down the hallway, eager to bury myself between her legs.

Eager to make love to the woman that had changed my life.

"Oh, Clint."

I tossed her to the bed, watching with wild eyes as her body bounced.

"I've got just what I want for dinner right here," I growled.

Our clothes came off in a flurry before I pounced. I jumped onto the bed, pinning her with my body against the mattress. Our fingers threaded together. Her lips caught mine as her naked breasts pooled against my chest. I felt her curves filling the divots of my muscles as she rolled against me, stroking my cock with her wet pussy. I slid my teeth against her skin, nibbling along her breasts, feeling them bounce with every jump. She released my hands, preferring to run hers through my hair as I marked her body.

All the way down to her knees.

"Clint, please."

I slipped her legs over my shoulders. "Please what?"

I nibbled at the dollop of excess at the top of her inner thigh, watching as she gasped and jumped. My aching cock wanted nothing more than to be buried inside her, where I had found my home a very long time ago. The truth of the matter was, I didn't give a shit about this house. Or where we ended up. Or where we shared the rest of our years. I had learned a long time ago that a place wasn't a home. A structure wasn't a home. A neighborhood wasn't a home.

Rae, however, was home to me.

And no matter where we went, it would always feel like home if I had her.

"Please, please, please, please," she begged.

"God, I love that sound so much."

I lapped up her slit and watched her back arch. I took in the way her skin reddened. The way her nails raked along my scalp. I sucked her swollen clit between my lips and felt her buck with a resounding movement that almost knocked me off the edge. I chuckled as I scooted her up until her beautiful hair splayed against the pillows. I wrapped my arms around her thighs and pulled her even closer. And as my mouth opened to swallow down her offerings, my tongue flicked her clit.

Over and over.

Until she fell apart against me.

"Clint! Yes!"

I growled. "That's it. Come for me, beautiful."

"Oh, shit. Oh, shit. I'm coming. I'm coming. Clint, yes. Yes. Yes. Yes!"

She shivered and shook. I held her close to me as her hands slid down my neck. I pressed my tongue deep against her swollen nub, causing her to gasp. I smiled as her back collapsed against the mattress and nuzzled her throbbing pussy lips with my nose as her hands untangled the knots she had created.

And as I languidly kissed up her body, I readied myself.

"I love you," I murmured.

She cupped my cheeks, pulling my lips down against hers.

"I love you, too. So much," she whispered.

I lined myself up with her entrance. My gaze held her stare as she moaned with anticipation. I eased myself in, teasing her with just the tip. But it didn't take her long for her to raise her hips and engulf the whole of me.

Causing my eyes to widen.

"There we go," she moaned.

I grunted. "Fuck."

Her nails curled against my skin. "Make love to me, Clinton Clarke."

My forehead fell against hers. "Don't mind if I do, Raelynn Cleaver."

My hips rolled. Her body bucked. I lost myself in the swirling expanse of her eyes and the massaging of her wet walls. I breathed the air she afforded me and pinned her wrists above her head. Her tits jumped against me, reminding me of her growing beauty, of every curve and divot I was determined to memorize every night she let me. Her legs locked around me, welcoming me home from a long day looking at colorful creations for my next novel.

"Rae, shit."

"Clint, oh fuck. I'm so close."

"Just a bit longer. I just--yeah. Like that. Oh, shit. Oh, shit."

"Yes, yes, yes."

I pounded into her, going faster as my gut coiled tight. Rae's hands slipped from underneath mine and wrapped tightly around my neck. I buried my face into the crook of her neck, fisting the sheets as the sounds of skin slapping skin filled our bedroom. A place that held so many memories, just like this one.

I couldn't wait to make new memories in our new home.

"I'm coming! Clint!"

I growled. "Close. I'm close. Just one--more--"

With one last thrust, I felt my dick twitch, growing as my balls pulled up into my body. I sank my teeth against her neck as her nails raked down my back. Her legs fell weakly against the mattress as she quivered beneath me, her walls squeezing me tight. I growled like a wild animal, rutting against her, filling her until she pushed me out.

Then I collapsed against her, feeling her heart beating rapidly against my own.

"I love you," I murmured.

She sighed with content as our intermingled juices trickled from between her legs.

"I love you, too. So much," she whispered.

I nuzzled her shoulder. "You ready for the big day?"

She held me close. "More than ever. You?"

I nodded. "I'm ready for this transition phase to be over."

"Yeah, the boxes are becoming a bit much."

"Since when did we accumulate so much stuff?"

She snickered. "Well, we have lived in this place for going on six years now."

I paused. "Has it really been six years?"

"It really has."

I slid off to the side. "Wow."

She turned, cuddling close to me. "Yeah. I can't believe it either, sometimes."

"Oh, is your mother still coming to help us move?"

"As far as I know. I mean, she hasn't canceled or anything. What about Cecilia?"

He nodded. "Apparently, she's coming with help, too."

She gasped. "You think she's bringing that guy she's been seeing?"

"Depends. Which one are you talking about?"

She swatted at my chest and I snickered.

"I'm just kidding. I'm just kidding," I said, chuckling.

"You didn't sound like you were kidding."

I shrugged. "I mean, my stepmother does date around. We can at least admit to that."

"I think it's great. She's living her life on her terms with her own money, doing what she wants."

"In my defense, she's been that way for a while now."

"It sounds like you're concerned about it. Is this something we should be concerned about?"

I ran my fingers up and down her back. "I don't know. I guess I just don't want what happened between her and my father to somehow taint that for her. If that makes any sense."

She nodded. "It does."

"What about your mother?"

"What about her?"

"Have you heard from her lately? She still going to therapy? Still doing okay with things?"

Rae smiled. "She is. She goes through bouts where she doesn't want to go to therapy, but that's usually when she hasn't taken her medication."

"That bipolar diagnosis ended up being a godsend, didn't it?"

She sighed. "I know, I know. I didn't take it well in the beginning."

I chuckled. "You really didn't."

She swatted at me again and I scoffed.

"Hey! Cut me some slack. At least I waited until *after* the drama died down to say anything about it. That's improvement, if you ask me."

She rolled her eyes. "I think the medication she's on now is more of a godsend than the actual diagnosis. I never thought I'd get her out of bed when her therapist finally told her what she thought was up. We'll get an update in a couple of days, anyway. She said she wanted to help us with this move."

I pulled her close. "Sounds like a plan, then."

Then, my stomach let out a massive roar that took even myself by surprise. Rae barked with laughter.

"Wow," I said.

"Was that your stomach?" she asked.

I grinned. "Can you blame me? I just worked up an appetite."

She snickered. "You didn't work as hard as you think you did."

My eyes snapped to hers. "Them's fightin' words right there."

"Yeah? And what are you going to do about it?"

I rolled her over and pinned her beneath me. She giggled as I playfully glared at her, willing her sounds to stop. She coughed and sputtered, trying to swallow it all down. And as my lips moved closer to hers, I heard her giggles turn to sighs.

"You know what I think?" I asked.

She moaned softly. "What's that?"

I nuzzled her cheek with my nose as her legs spread for me. I kissed her skin softly, blazing a slow trail up to her ear. I nibbled on her earlobe. She moaned for me as her hands gripped my own. And as she rolled against me, I drew in a soft breath.

"I think it's time for dinner," I whispered.

And I moved like lightning away from the bed before she locked those soft legs around me.

Legs I'd always be weak for. No matter the time, day, or age of my own body.

3

———

RAE

"You got your coffee?" Clint asked.

I snatched up my tumbler. "Got it!"

"What about your purse?"

I lifted it. "Already in hand!"

"Your coat? It's pretty chilly out there this morning. I had to come in from the porch before I finished my coffee."

I reached for the coat rack. "Getting it now."

"Kissed your handsome boyfriend goodbye?"

I snickered. "Get out here before I'm late!"

I spun around and watched Clint come out of the bathroom. With a towel draped loosely around his waist, I wanted nothing more than to trace the lines disappearing behind it with my tongue. He padded with damp feet across the hardwood floors as I smiled at him. I clutched my coffee, slung my purse and my arm around his neck, and pressed my lips to his, tasting his minty breath.

"Now I have," I murmured.

He chuckled. "All right, all right. Come on. You're going to be late."

He swatted my ass playfully and I squealed.

"Yeah, and I wonder why that is," I said.

He winked. "You never did object."

I rolled my eyes. "Love you. Gotta go!"

"Have a good day, Rae."

I rushed down the hallway and slammed my shoulder into the door. I looked longingly at the elevator before relegating myself to the massive six-story trek. The elevator hadn't been truly fixed in months. One of the main reasons why I couldn't wait to get out of this shitty apartment complex. I'd gotten stuck in it one too many mornings as well. I mean, the last time the elevator got trapped between two floors, I didn't get to work until lunch time! What kind of fuckery was that?

Even though I heard it humming and people chattering about how it was finally fixed, the last thing I needed was to get stuck and have to rush past my boss's office in the hopes that she wouldn't realize I'd been late.

Especially on such an important day.

The publishing company I'd interned at for two years during college ended up offering me a full-time position after I graduated. In two years, I'd gone from a part-time editor to their full-time head editor with a nice salary, an office with a view, and outstanding benefits. But, just like every other job, it wasn't without its difficulties. And today was one of those.

Today I had a meeting with one of our premier authors to let him know his book was absolute shit.

Unlike what most people thought about editors, I didn't take pride in telling people that. I wanted those who sent their stuff into us to have a pleasant experience. I wanted them to walk away with something. Whether it was a contract, or feedback that truly helped them in their writing journey. Clint joked all the time that editors like me were the reason writers like him self-published. And while I knew he was being light-hearted about it, sometimes it hurt.

I didn't want people thinking that publishing houses were the 'big bad' people thought we were.

I stepped off the last stair and panted for air. I hopped around, exchanging my flats for the pair of heels I had stuffed down in my purse and stumbled out of the side door, directly into the parking lot. After slipping my heels on, I started for my car.

I need some damn coffee.

I tossed everything into the back seat and slipped behind the wheel. I cranked it up and peered out the windshield, taking in the expanse of the apartment complex. It had taken Clint and me three applications to get into this place. While it was expensive, it had been worth it. In the beginning, at least. Until that damn elevator broke. And our plumbing went bad. And our balcony had to be repaired because it started getting wobbly.

"Definitely not worth the money anymore," I said breathlessly.

I grabbed a croissant and a large iced coffee just in time. Things seemed to be moving in a positive direction as I pulled into the underground parking garage of Monarch Publishing. I drew in a deep breath, took a long pull of my coffee, and took a massive bite of my hot chocolate croissant. I relished the tastes blending together and signaling to my brain that it was time to wake up. Time to get to work. Time to get shit done.

All right. Let's go.

After wolfing down my food and sucking down half of my coffee, I grabbed my things, raced to the working elevator--thank fuck--and took it all the way up to the top floor. All the way to where my office now was. I strode by my boss's office, peeking in to see her head buried in manuscripts. I rushed by, taking my chance, and practically leapt for the front door of my office. As I quickly unlocked it, I heard someone shuffling up behind me.

"Morning, Miss Cleaver! Cutting it a bit close, aren't we?"

I cringed at the voice of my assistant. "Morning, Robyn."

I looked down the hallway and saw my boss look up before she gave me a knowing smile. I raised my coffee and she shook her head before returning back to the manuscript in her hands.

"Maybe next time, a bit softer," I said.

Robyn nodded. "Oh, yes. Of course. Sorry. So, you have that meeting in five minutes with Albert Freddington. You have a meeting scheduled with Mrs. Plumstone at ten. She wants to go over some manuscripts she just received this morning. Also, you have a lunch date with Callie and a two o'clock meeting with the rest of the staff in Mrs. Plumstone's office. And to cap off the day, Luther's retirement party. It's at four, shouldn't be more than thirty minutes. Then you're done."

I sighed. "Great. Thank you."

"Anything else you need from me today?"

A lightbulb went off. "Um, yes actually. Come inside and close the door."

"Of course."

I walked over to my desk and dropped everything on top of it. I started up my computer and pulled out my laptop, trying to get myself situated for the day. When I looked up, I found Robyn frowning at me.

"What?" I asked.

"Are you okay?"

"Yes. Yeah, of course. I just need you to run an errand for me."

"Sure. What kind?"

"The kind you don't talk about."

She nodded. "Oh, you got it. I need some things myself. Plastic insert, or cardboard?"

I blinked. "Wait, what?"

"Shi--I mean, shoot. You're a pad sort of girl, aren't you? Don't worry, I've got you covered there--"

It clicked. "Oh! No, no, no. I mean, plastic, for future reference. But I'm not on my period. Which is kind of the issue."

Her eyes widened. "Oh. Oh--oh!"

"Yeah."

"Is this… a good thing?"

I considered her question. "I'm not sure? But I can't focus. And I have this meeting in--"

"Two minutes."

"Right. Two minutes. I can't run the rest of my day like this. I need to know for sure. Do you mind picking me up a test and bringing it straight back here?"

"I don't mind at all. Want some water? Or are you just going to hold it until I get back?"

"I'll be fine. Just the test. And some gum! I ran out of gum yesterday."

"Any special kind?"

I smiled. "The cinnamon kind. The burn is very invigorating."

She turned toward the door. "All right. Cinnamon gum and a pregnancy test. I'll be back in a jif!"

She slipped out the door in a plethora of flailing colors and almost got her skirt caught in my door. Robyn was always a vibrant dresser. She'd been helping me out in some form or another since I started my part-time work at this place years ago. But my favorite part of her outfits were her glasses. She seemed to have a pair for every occasion. I'd seen her wear Christmas glasses and floral-printed ones. Rainbow, and cotton candy pink, and green ones with shamrocks on them for St. Patrick's Day. If there was anyone who could brighten anyone's day, it was my assistant.

I needed some of her brightness to carry with me for this meeting.

"Miss Cleaver?"

A man's voice filtered through my door, followed by a knock.

"Miss Cleaver, it's Albert Freddington. We have a meeting now?" he asked.

"Come in!"

I tried to push everything out of my mind as I shook the man's hand. I gestured for him to take a seat in front of my desk, but my mind was everywhere. I didn't know what this test was going to reveal to me. And even though Clint and I had talked about children, we'd talked about it as if it were years away from happening. We had things we wanted to accomplish first. Life we still wanted to experience as a couple, without distractions. Or other responsibilities. Or things to tie us down.

I mean, couldn't we at least get settled into our new place first? Maybe travel around a bit? See more of the world?

Or get married?

"Miss Cleaver."

I jumped. "Yes? Yes. Sorry. Welcome, Mr. Freddington. How's your morning been?"

"It'll be better once we can get this meeting over. I have an appointment with the cover designer for lunch."

None of this is part of the plan. "Well, that meeting is going to have to be postponed. At least, for a little bit."

He blinked. "Why?"

I pulled out his manuscript. "I made a lot of notes in the margins like you wanted me to. But I still had to attach some paper to the back."

"You had to attach paper."

"Yes."

"Why?"

"Because, while this is your third draft, it's still reading like your first. I made some notes on organiza--"

He snickered. "I'm sorry, what?"

I placed the manuscript in front of him. "It's not a bad thing. You're ten books into a solid series. Things can lag. Or get repetitive. I'm here to make sure--"

"You think it's lagging."

"It sags a little bit in the middle. Most authors have an issue with that, though. It's really not that big of a deal."

"It's a big deal to me."

I sighed. "Mr. Freddington--"

"This book is due into the hands of my audience in eight weeks. I don't have time for a rewrite!"

I blinked. "Well, we haven't established a date as to when your book is going to hit the shelves. So, unless you told your audience--"

"Of course I gave them a date. I had to! They were clamoring for it."

I sighed. "I'll get our P.R. representative on the line. That can be your lunch date for today. But for now--"

He stood from his chair. "I won't stand for this. That book doesn't need an entirely different rewrite. It's good as it is."

I stood with him. "But it could be great. That's what I'm here to help you with."

He snatched it up. "I'm going straight to your boss's office. This isn't going to happen. I'm not writing this entire thing over again!"

"It was nice seeing you, Mr. Freddington."

He flicked me off before he ripped my office door open. It slammed against the wall before he took a hard left, storming straight for my boss's office. He wouldn't get anywhere with her, though. Not once she found out that he'd fed his fans a date we didn't have. I pinched the bridge of my nose, reached for my coffee and took a massive sip.

Then I heard her voice.

"The meeting go okay?" Robyn asked.

I whipped my head up. "You already got everything?"

She walked in, closing the door. "Of course. The pharmacy's only two blocks down the road."

I strode to her and took the bag, quickly opening it up. I took out the gum and ripped it open, shoving a piece into my mouth. I needed something to keep my jaw busy. Especially since I felt so nervous. I mean, did I want this? If I was pregnant, would I feel happy?

I think I might.

"Want me to stay with you?" Robyn asked.

I sighed. "Would you? Is that too much to ask?"

"Not at all. I'll stand outside while you're taking care of things."

"Thank you. Seriously."

I turned toward the door in the corner. My own personal bathroom. Right inside my office. I drew in a deep breath before I headed in that direction, feeling Robyn hot on my heels. I had to make it quick because I knew my boss would be down here at any moment prying me with questions as to what had happened with Mr. Freddington.

"Here goes nothing," I murmured.

I made my way into the bathroom and closed the door behind me.

4

<hr>

CLINTON

The smell of fresh paint filled my nose as sweat dripped down my brow. Our new place was fantastic. It was everything Rae and I could've ever wanted out of a permanent home. A three-bedroom, ranch-style home. A two-car garage that was large enough to hold both of our cars, plus my bike. A covered back porch, a sunroom right off the master suite, and a glorious fenced-in backyard. For a house with a slice of land in Los Angeles, we had gotten it for a steal.

Mostly because the place needed a lot of work.

"She's gonna flip when she sees this, man," Mike said.

I grinned. "I know, right?"

"I mean, I wasn't sure about the whole white cabinets thing. Especially with this weird, sparkling pearly white backsplash you've got going on. But I'll be damned if it doesn't look good. And these matte black handles? Dude, it looks awesome."

"I wanted to carry the matte black around the entire house. I don't have time to get everything in order, but I've changed out all of the handles in the bathrooms and stuff . Like a little theme that's carried from room to room. I think she'll appreciate that."

"How many bedrooms does this place have again?"

I wiped at the sweat on my brow. "Three. Each of them has a bathroom, too. Which is nice."

"That's really nice. And a hell of a steal in L.A."

"You're not joking. We had to offer twenty grand above asking price for this place just to be in the running for it."

He came to stand beside me. "We've got time to give the master bathroom a second coat, if you want."

I patted his back. "Thanks for helping me with this stuff. I wouldn't have been able to get half as much done without you here."

He wrapped his arm around my shoulders. "Anything I can do to help, I will."

"Thanks, man."

"Anytime."

As we lugged the paint cans cautiously down the hallway toward the bathroom, I sighed. I couldn't wait to see her reaction once we officially moved into this place. I'd been trolling her Pinterest page in my spare time to see all the things she was favoriting. All the things that were catching her eye. And to be honest, they shocked me. Rae had always been a 'dark color' kind of person. She enjoyed dim lighting. Rich, deep colors. Palettes that had black and dark blues rather than pale yellows and pinks.

So to see her bookmarking things that had whites and pearls and soft grays?

It was a new side of her, to say the least.

"All right. These cabinets need one more coat of paint, and then we're done," I said.

Mike set up his station. "You knock out the left and I'll knock out the right?"

"Meet in the middle?"

He nodded. "Ready when you are."

There were plenty of things Rae didn't like about this house. But I'd managed to get her to see the potential it had. With a new coat of paint, a different backsplash, and a nice professional cleaning of the floors, this place had a brand new sparkle to it. Mike had helped me with a lot, too. Every time I had to meet him here, I told Rae it was because I had to work. Because I had meetings. Because I had research to do. And while it was true--mostly-- part of me felt guilty for lying to her.

I knew the little white lie would have a huge payoff once she saw this place.

But she was beginning to make mention of the fact that her weekends were feeling more lonely.

"Did you return the power washer?" Michael asked.

I nodded. "Yep. Finally. That place has odd hours of operation. Took me three tries and an endless amount of hiding it from Rae before I finally got it turned in."

"Did they charge you a late fee?"

"Not after showing them what all I had to go through in order to get the damn thing back to them."

He snickered. "Good. The carpets look nice, too."

"I've got someone coming in tonight to really shine up the hardwood and the tile before we move in. I want this place to look completely different when Rae finally sees it."

"Trust me, you've done a good job with that. Because this place was nasty when we first got our hands on it."

I sighed. "So am I going to have to ask? Or are you going to bring it up?"

He groaned. "Really? We have to do this now?"

"What the hell did you think I was going to do? Just ignore it? I know you and Allison have been going through a rough patch for a while now."

"A while? Try the past year."

"So it hasn't improved at all?"

He shrugged. "It's all right, I guess. All things considered."

"Just all right?"

I watched Mike jam his paintbrush into the can, so I did the same. We sat on the floor, feeling the cool breeze from outside filtering through the open bathroom window. I crossed my legs and settled my elbows on my knees, giving him the space he needed to gather his thoughts. I knew I'd have to practically pry this out of him.

"Come on, man. It's me, for crying out loud. Just tell me what's up," I said.

He cleared his throat. "She doesn't talk to me anymore, Clint. She's shut down. It's like I can't get through to her. Our house is so quiet *all* the time. We eat dinners and breakfasts together in silence. *All* the time. Our evenings are filled with me silently watching the news while she silently reads a book. Or flips through a magazine. Or plays on her phone."

"Well, shit. I didn't know it was that bad."

"I feel like she doesn't want to be there. Or be with me. It almost feels like she doesn't want to be with me anymore."

"Have you said any of this to her?"

He shook his head. "No."

"Why not?"

"I don't know, man. I just--I'd say we'd have to work on our communication skills. But you have to have some sort of communication in order to have something to work on. And we have none of it. How do you work on communication if there is none to work on?"

"That's fucked up."

"Yeah. It is. And that's been my life for the past year. Living with a roommate I feel like I've perpetually pissed off."

I couldn't imagine what he was going through. Rae and I had never struggled with issues like that. If anything, talking too much got us into trouble with one another. Not in a bad way. But in a blunt way. And I wasn't sure what I'd do in his shoes. I wasn't sure what I'd do if I felt like I was losing Rae. Or growing distant from her.

Well, technically…

"How did you and Rae get over that hump?" Mike asked.

"You mean, before we decided to travel for a while?"

"Yeah. When the two of you were kind of growing apart, or whatever. How did you get through it?"

I shrugged. "We talked."

He snickered. "Thanks."

I scooted closer to him. "Mike, I'm serious. If she's not talking to you, then step up. Talk to her. Tell her how you're feeling, even if she gives you nothing back."

"What if she doesn't, though?"

I shook my head. "Maybe you guys need a vacation. Some quality time together to really push hard and see if you can work your way back to each other. Rae and I got a lot of that while we were traveling that year. It really helped us out, having that time together."

"Maybe."

I paused. "Or counseling. I've heard that helps people a lot."

He frowned. "Counseling is for people who are much worse off than me and Allison."

"I wouldn't be so sure about that."

He paused. "What? You think we're worse off than I think?"

"No, Mike. I just think you two could really benefit from an unbiased party listening and peering into your relationship. That's all."

"I don't know, dude."

"Why not? If you love her, which I *know* you do, why not pull out all the stops and see if you guys can fight for this?"

"I *am* fighting, Clint."

I shrugged. "Is sitting in silence and not speaking your mind really fighting, though, Mike?"

He stared at me for a long time before he finally nodded.

"I'll consider it. How does that sound?" he asked.

I grinned. "Sounds better than sitting in silence and torturing yourself."

He snickered. "You're damn right it does."

I picked up my brush. "All right. Ready to get this done? It's the last thing we need to do before move-in day."

He picked up his brush, too. "Let's knock this out and get some food. I'm starving."

"Steaks. On me. So don't fuck it up."

"When free food is involved? I never fuck it up."

5

———

RAE

Knock, knock, knock. "Rae?"

I felt my heart hammering in my knees. "Yeah, Robyn?"

"You okay in there? You've been in the bathroom for ten minutes now."

I swallowed hard. "Okay."

I heard the doorknob jiggle. "Can you let me in?"

My mouth ran dry. I kept blinking, thinking that the test might change. Or that I might wake up. Or that I was having a stroke and would suddenly appear in the hospital. I reached toward the pregnancy test and picked it up. I held it to my face, making damn sure I didn't misinterpret any of the water marks.

But there was no mistaking it.

I'm pregnant?

"Rae. Please, let me in."

I reached for the bathroom door. "Sorry. Come on in."

I heard the door open. "I'm assuming the test is done?"

I nodded slowly. "Uh huh."

I felt Robyn work her way behind me. I looked up at the mirror and watched her eyes widen. And then the most bombastic squeal I'd ever heard fell from her lips.

"Oh! My! Gosh!"

I winced. "Yep."

"You're pregnant."

"Seems so."

"That's definitely two red lines. You're definitely pregnant."

I placed my hand over my belly button. "I guess I am."

"Well, say something! Is this good? Are you happy? Should we go celebrate?"

I blinked. "I'm pregnant."

I slowly turned around and faced my assistant. Tears percolated behind my eyes, lining them as I looked at her. I gazed down at the test again, swallowing as hard as I could. The last thing I needed was to cry all of my makeup off at work. Especially when I didn't have everything I needed to paint it back on.

"My God, I'm pregnant," I said.

Robyn wrapped her arms around me and I gave in. I cried into her shoulder, bouncing between elated and worried. Excited and panicked. I didn't know what to think. I didn't know how to feel. But as I clutched that pregnancy test with all of my might, a question rushed through my mind.

What will Clint think?

Robyn rubbed my back. "Hey, hey, hey. It's okay. Take some breaths."

I squeaked. "I'm pregnant."

She nodded. "Yes, you are. And until we can figure out what this is and how to address it, this stays between us. Okay?"

I sniffled. "At least until I tell Clint."

"Oh, of course. Definitely."

I pulled away from her grasp and felt her wiping at my tears. She started pulling tissues and makeup wipes out of her bag, and I let her clean me up. I was too tired to think about doing it myself. Besides, I was already wracking my brain with ways to break this news to Clint. Did I want to go for cute? Or memorable? Did I want to keep it a small thing between us? How long into the move did I wait before I told him? Was this something that had to be addressed tonight?

"Shit," I whispered.

"Hey, it's okay. Look at me."

Robyn gripped my arms as my eyes met hers.

"Rae, this is all going to be fine. No matter what decision you make, you know that man of yours is going to support you."

I swallowed hard. "What if he isn't ready?"

"Are you ready?"

I paused. "I don't know."

She cupped my cheeks. "Then it sounds like you need some sleep first. Sleep, food, and to lay off the coffee."

"Wait, I can't have coffee?"

She giggled. "Nope. Caffeine is a stimulant, and bad during pregnancies."

"How do you know that?"

"My sister's got five kids. I'm very familiar with pregnancy."

I swallowed hard. "What else shouldn't I be doing?"

"If you want caffeine, go for tea. But no strong caffeinated substances. No alcohol, duh. Lots of iron and folic acid. Ginger suckers for the nausea. As healthy of a diet as you can stand until you get on prenatal vitamins. Then your body can handle a couple dozen donuts or so when you're craving them badly enough."

"Oh, good Lord."

She rubbed my arms. "It's going to be fine. Just make sure you get some rest."

I sighed. "Thank you. For this. And for, you know, keeping it to yourself."

"Of course. It's our little secret. And just so you know? I'm happy for you. Clint is going to *die* with excitement once you tell him."

The rest of my workday passed in a haze. Robyn was kind enough to help put some of my makeup back on. But that was the only thing I remembered. The only reminders I had of my day were the minutes of my meetings Robyn sent to me. Thank fuck she was a detailed-oriented person. Because I remembered none of this stuff. I was too preoccupied. Too 'in my own mind' to pull myself out of it.

I can't go all week like this.

I started looking some things up online. I searched every version of 'surprise baby announcement' I could. Trying to find inspiration. Trying to swallow down my panic. Trying to convince myself that it would all be okay. Financially, we were okay. We didn't have too much debt from my degree. Our vehicles were paid off. We didn't dare touch our credit card unless it was an emergency. On that front, we were just fine.

It was everything else.

Clint and I had plans. And a baby didn't work itself into those plans until much later. Much, much later. We had agreed on being older parents. We made a pact with one another that we'd start trying once we both turned thirty. But even then, we wouldn't push it. No fertility tests or checking my ovulation. None of that stuff that made couples crazy. We made an agreement that I'd simply come off my birth control. Simple as that.

"Wait a second," I murmured.

I abandoned my internet searches and picked up my purse. I rummaged around, digging all the way to the bottom until I found it. That pale blue pouch that held my pills. I ripped it out of my purse and flipped it open. And when I saw what had happened, my jaw hit the floor.

Holy shit, I've forgotten my pills.

"Ten days?" I asked breathlessly.

I hadn't just forgotten them. I downright didn't take them. I picked up my phone and navigated to my calendar, trying to figure out why the hell it hadn't dinged at me. Alarms were the bane of my existence. I could switch them off in a heartbeat and not give them a second thought. But I synced my work with my phone calendar. So, no matter where I was or what I was doing, when that alert popped up to take my birth control, I was on it.

"Shit," I hissed.

There was no calendar notification. For the past ten days exactly, there had been no notification on my calendar. How was that possible? I'd had the same notification set for every single day for the past--

Oh, boy.

"Robyn!?"

My door whipped open. "Hey. What's up?"

"When you make one of those recurring, unending things on a calendar, is it actually unending? Or, do those kinds of things have a termination date anyway?"

"Oh. Yeah. No. 'Unending' really means 'for the next ten years.' Then you have to set it back up. Why?"

Well, fuck. "No reason. Just wondering. Thank you."

"Not a problem. Sure I can't get you anything?"

"I'm sure. Thanks."

I leaned back into my chair and ran my hand through my hair. Ten years. It had been ten years since I'd set that stupid calendar notification up on my phone. The one that followed me around everywhere. Through every phone change, every laptop change, and every work environment change.

How the hell did I not notice that?

I sighed as I turned my attention back to my search. Things weren't as bad as my mind was making them out to be. That much I knew for certain. Clint did eventually want children. Just not now. We eventually wanted to build a family together. Just not now.

What would we name our child?

I went from looking up ways to surprise Clint to searching for baby names. And I killed the back half of my day doing just that. Hell, I almost missed Luther's retirement party at the end of the day because of it. The more time passed, the more excited I grew. A baby. I was going to have a baby. With the man I loved more than anything else in this world.

I wouldn't wait to tell him.

With the pregnancy test in my purse, I stopped by a baby boutique on the way home. I found the cutest pair of white baby sneakers with pale yellow racing stripes. Very gender neutral, but completely cute in the process. I bought a small bag with some tissue paper and put the entire thing together right there at the cashier's desk. Who was just as excited as I was. I talked about the baby names I'd already come across. Most of which were for a boy. I grabbed the cutest 'you're going to be a father!' card and scribbled a little something down into it. And after slipping it into the colorful bag, the cashier rang me up.

"That'll be $32.24, Momma."

Momma.

The word brought tears of happiness to my eyes.

I was excited to talk with Clint now. I raced home with the bag taunting me from the passenger's seat. I couldn't wait to give him the gift. I knew he'd be so surprised, and so shocked, and so happy for us. I found myself lost in it all. Imagining Clint holding our baby boy. Or girl, for that matter. I saw him kissing our child's forehead. Running around with them outside. Teaching him, or her, how his motorcycle worked.

My heart leapt with delight at the thought.

I parked my car and quickly scrambled out. I slammed the door closed as the beeping of the locks chirped at me. I rushed for the stairs, taking them two by two. Not bothering to change into my flats. Which I regretted by the fourth floor when I could barely catch my breath.

"Clint!" I called out breathlessly.

I finally made it to the sixth floor and shuffled to our door.

"Clint, you home?" I asked.

Exhaustion settled into my bones. I opened the front door and dropped my purse off to the side, ready to give Clint his present. But I was greeted with absent lights and silence.

Is he really not home yet?

"Clint!" I yelled.

The only thing that echoed back at me was my own voice. I slipped my hand into my pocket and pulled out my phone.

"Hey there, babe. I'm so sorry. I'm running incredibly behind. Give me another hour and I'll be home. Okay?" he asked.

I closed the door behind me. "What's keeping you at work now? I mean, not that I'm nagging. But this has become a pretty frequent thing."

"I know, I know. But, it's almost done. I swear. Once we can get past this--"

"You know we need to finish packing up, right?"

He sighed. "I know. I promise, I'm going to finish that with you before we go to bed tonight."

"And I haven't even thought about dinner yet."

"I'll pick something up on the way home."

I suddenly felt overwhelmed. "Have you confirmed with the moving guys, too? Because tomorrow's our day and we still have the entire bathroom to pack and I don't think our office is completely packed up either, and I--"

"Rae, take a breath for me."

I rushed down the hallway and turned the corner. I gazed into his office, and what I saw frustrated the hell out of me.

"Have you not been home all day?" I asked.

He paused. "Why do you ask?"

"Your office hasn't even been touched!"

"Rae, I'm telling you. You have nothing to worry about."

"We move in less than twenty-four hours and there's not a box in your office. Not a single one."

"Which is going to be remedied when I get home."

I sighed. "Why couldn't you just--"

I pinched the bridge of my nose to try and keep myself under control.

"I know you're frustrated. And I know you feel overwhelmed right now. But I promise you, I have this more under control than it looks. Okay? Do you trust me?"

I swallowed hard. "Yeah. Yeah, I do. I trust you."

"Good. Now, get yourself a glass of wine, take a load off, and I'll be home with dinner in about an hour and a half. Sound good?"

I can't have wine. "Yeah. Yeah, sounds good."

"Okay. I'll be home soon, beautiful. You have my word."

I didn't want to unload my frustration on him, so I simply hung up. I knew it wasn't a smart move. I knew it wasn't mature. But I felt my disappointment mounting. I walked out of his office and back into the main room. I looked at the brightly-colored gift bag sitting on its side on the floor. Cast to the side, like I felt sometimes. I mean, I knew Clint was busy. I knew his self-publishing career had taken off. I knew what he had to go through in order to make it work, too. I mean, he edited his own stuff. Marketed his own stuff. Formatted his own stuff. He kept up his own website and regularly updated his blog followers. Hell, the only thing he outsourced were his book covers. And I knew if he figured out how to do that, he'd do that himself too.

But all I wanted was to spend our last night in this apartment together.

Without having to work so damn hard.

I made myself a cup of tea and sat down. The boxes loomed over me while I sat there. I hated it. I hated that those boxes were there, but Clint wasn't. I hated that these boxes were here to greet me, but he hadn't been. And I knew it was stupid. I knew I was being irrational. But that's how these things worked. Right? I came home with good news, and he was supposed to be here for it!

He hasn't been home all day, though.

What the hell had he been doing all day?

The longer I sat there, the more angry I became. I finally set down my tea and got up. I picked up a few empty boxes and made my way into his office, determined to get a jumpstart on this bull-shit. I grumbled to myself as I packed up books. I blinked back tears of agitation as I stacked file folders on top of one another and made sure everything was saved on his laptop before unplugging it.

The more I packed, the more I felt like I had been set on the backburner.

This isn't the first time this has happened.

For weeks now, Clint had been working long hours on the weekends. Going off on all these random meetings and staying away for hours. When he was usually holed up in his office, typing his head off, these past few weeks had been different. I mean, how many meetings with his cover designer did he need? How much research did he really have to do?

You don't think…?

I pushed the thought away. No. No way in hell Clint was cheating. He wasn't capable of it. But, in some ways, he was. Something else had taken priority over me and this move. Me and the life we had built together. Suddenly, spending weekends with me seemed like a chore. Coming home to me seemed to be getting later and later. Almost like he didn't want to do it.

"You're blowing this out of proportion," I murmured.

That didn't stop my mind from running away with me, though.

Which did nothing to halt my anger.

6

CLINTON

I shook my head as I slipped my key into the door. I knew I was
going to have my ass handed to me. I just knew it. It was damn
near nine o'clock, and I was just getting home with food in my
hands. Food that had grown cold, mind you. I opened the door and
braced myself. I readied myself to have to put out the energy to
make us a fresh meal this late at night.

And that energy output wouldn't touch the packing I still had
to do.

"Rae?" I called out.

"Hmm?"

I closed the door behind me. "Where are you?"

"On the couch."

I locked the door and turned the corner into the living room.
She sat there with a book in her lap, clutching a coffee mug. But it
didn't have coffee in it. I saw the string and the tab from a tea bag
fluttering over the side. Her damp hair with the smell of lavender
told me everything I needed to know.

I grinned. "Did you have your last bath in this dingy old
apartment?"

She didn't look up from her book. "Yes."

"Well, it smells good."

She nodded absentmindedly. "Thanks."

I sensed her mood and guilt seized my gut. I knew we had plans to pack together, but Mike and I had gotten on a roll. What started out as a steak lunch quickly morphed into an adventure to redo the crown molding throughout the house. And damn it, the place looked great. It was completely ready for us to move into tomorrow.

I knew Rae would understand that once she saw the place.

"So do you want to eat first? Or pack while we eat?" I asked.

She sipped her tea. "Already did it."

"Already ate?"

"No. Already packed."

I felt my face pale. "Shit. I'm so sorry, Rae."

"It's fine."

"I wanted to help you. Seriously. It's just--"

"You stayed out late. It happens."

I walked over to her. "You didn't do all of it, did you?"

She nodded. "Your office, the rest of the kitchen, and the bathroom."

I winced. "Did you happen to save what was on my laptop first?"

She snapped her book closed. "I'm not an idiot, Clint."

"I know. I know. I just--I was asking. That's all."

She finally looked up at me. "I didn't know how late you'd be. And you know I don't like leaving things to the last minute. I had to get it done to have a clear head. It is what it is. You're welcome."

The food dropped from my hands as I sat down next to her on the couch. I placed my hand on her thigh, but she didn't lean into me. Hell, she didn't even look at me. All she did was flip her book back open. I mean, she didn't even twitch!

"Look. I know I haven't been home as much these last few weeks like I said I'd be. But, there's a good reason for it, I promise."

She nodded. "And what's that?"

I paused. "I can't tell you."

She snickered. "Of course not."

"Rae, it's not like--Rae?"

She shot up from the couch and rolled her eyes. She let out a huff of a sigh before picking up her tea mug. She wiped at her thigh, like she couldn't stand the heat of my residual touch. And it was an action that made my heart sink even further into my legs. I watched her as she rounded into the kitchen. She washed out her mug before drying it off. Then her eyes hooked with mine as she picked up a piece of newspaper.

She held my stare while wrapping it up.

And it wasn't until she placed it in a box that her eyes fell away.

"Rae, come on."

She shook her head. "I'm going to bed. I'm exhausted."

I stood up. "Rae, please. Can we just talk about this?"

Her eyes filled with fire as she turned on me.

"This is our last night in this place. Don't you get that? Our very last night. We've spent years in this place together, Clint. The things these walls have seen? The things they've witnessed? The things they've heard? It's all here. And all I wanted was to spend it with you. That's it. You told me ninety minutes. An hour and a half. And look at you! Strolling in four hours later with inedible food in tow, for what? An apology? Me jumping into your arms and rejoicing that my big, strong man is finally home?"

I snickered. "You know damn good and well that's never what I'd expect of you."

"So what do you want me to do right now, Clint? Huh? Act like you aren't four hours late? Act like you're just fine? Act like you haven't been ditching me every fucking weekend for the past two months and coming home later and later than promised? I thought this was important to you, too. Just this one night."

"It is, Rae. I'm telling you, just--"

"Well, it doesn't feel like it."

Just tell her about the damn surprise. It's not worth all this.

"What if I make us a fresh dinner? I think we've got some noodles still in the pantry," I said.

"Packed that up, too. I kept enough out for coffee and toast in the morning. Help yourself," she said.

Fucking hell, she thought of everything tonight.

I fought with my mind. If I just told her, this would all go away. But then I'd ruin the surprise Mike and I had sunk endless hours into for the past eight weeks. Maybe that was for the best, though. Surprising her with it tonight. I could take her over to the house. We could pick up something on the way there and have a late dinner at our new place. Just the two of us.

And that carpet's all nice and fluffy now.

"I'm going to bed. Enjoy your night," Rae said.

I rushed for her and took her hand within mine. She paused in the hallway, but she didn't turn to face me. As odd as it was, this was one of those things I loved about Rae. Even when she couldn't stand to look at me, she always held my hand. She always let me know, with that one simple gesture, that she was still there. Still hanging on.

Even if she was upset.

"I'm not blowing you off like you think I am."

She sighed. "Where were you tonight? Because that's what it feels like you've done."

"I promise you, that's not what's happening. Look at me, Rae."

She shook her head, but I insisted.

"Please? Just for a few seconds."

She sighed as she turned to face me. And I noticed a glow about her cheeks. Her damp hair framed her gorgeous face and her skin was full of color and life. She had this aura about her that dragged me in. Every time she looked at me, she dragged me in. But something was different.

I cupped her cheek. "You have to trust me. Okay? I know I haven't been home much. I know you've sacrificed your weekend with me for something you're not sure about yet. But I promise you, with everything we are, that none of this has to do with me not wanting to be here. All right? I swear it. Give me until tomorrow morning and you'll see. Do you trust me?"

She sighed. "Does this have to do with the house?"

"You'll have to trust me."

"Clint, is something wrong?"

I cupped her face with both of my hands. "Do you. Trust me?"

She searched my eyes. "Yes. Of course I trust you."

"Then trust me on this."

"No more weekends gone."

I nodded. "You have my word."

"And no more late nights. I don't like this. I don't like how it feels and what my mind does when you're gone like that."

My lips fell against hers in a soft kiss. "I love you. And only you. Don't ever let your mind convince you of that."

Her forehead pressed against mine. "I love you, too."

With one last kiss, I released her to the bedroom. I watched her walk into the darkened expanse with the smallest limp and made a mental note to give her a massage once I crawled into bed. I just had to take a shower, brush my teeth, and get these damn clothes off me.

But first, some food.

I turned to look for the bag of cold food. Because at this point, cold food was better than no food. Something caught my eye, though. Something by the front door. It looked yellow, almost. Yellow, and white.

"What the hell?" I murmured.

I walked over to the random object on the floor and found it wasn't an object at all. Rather, it was a present. The tissue sticking out of the top was white and yellow, just like the sparkling bag. The ribbon handles felt soft against my fingertips. I picked it up, furrowing my brow as I walked back toward the hallway.

"Hey, Rae? What's this?"

And when I walked into our bathroom to show her the gift bag, I watched her eyes widen.

7

———

RAE

"Hey, Rae? What's this?"

My eyes widened as his words hit my ears. The toothbrush in my hand stopped moving as foam dripped from my lips. Where had I put that gift? I could've sworn I picked it up. I had every intention of putting it in the closet for a rainy day. That gift certainly wasn't appropriate for tonight, anyway. My eyes locked with the mirror as I watched him stand in the doorway. I saw the yellow and white sparkling bag dangle from his fingertips. My heart froze in my chest. I felt my legs go numb. Oh, no. How in the world could I have forgotten to put that away?

He grinned sheepishly. "Did you buy me a present? Is that why you wanted me home so badly?"

I shook my head and started mumbling, but I felt foam dripping onto my shirt. I wiped it away and quickly turned around, trying my best to finish up my teeth for the night. Clinton chuckled as I jammed my face beneath the faucet. I rinsed my mouth out and let my toothbrush sit at the bottom of the sink. With traces of toothpaste still sitting on my chin, I whipped back around, trying to wrack my brain for some way to pry that gift out of his hands.

And when I saw that he already had a ball of tissue paper in his hand, I panicked.

"What was that? I think you had your mouth full."

"Wait!"

He paused, his eyes staying connected with me. "Okay. Why?"

What in the world am I going to say? If he looks down, he'll see that damn test!

I wasn't ready for this. I wasn't ready for another fight tonight. Another letdown. Another emotional meltdown moment. It would be real once he saw. Once he knew. Once he acknowledged. And after tonight, I wasn't ready for it. Surprises were supposed to be picture-perfect. They were supposed to happen to happy couples with their lives pieced together in just the right fashion. And tonight wasn't one of those nights.

I needed more time.

Tomorrow. After we move tomorrow will be the perfect time.

I could even give it to him in the room I wanted to have as the nursery. Yes, that's it. I could take him down the hallway, stand him in the middle of that smaller room at the back of the house, and give him the gift then. In the afterglow of moving seemed like the perfect time. My heart was now set on it.

I just had to get that damn present out of his grip.

"Rae? You okay?"

I lunged for him. "Give me that."

He held the gift over his head. "Uh-uh-uh! No takesies backsies."

I jumped for it. "Don't. Seriously. You weren't supposed to see-
-"

"Oh, a present I wasn't supposed to get right now. I'm even more intrigued."

"Just give it back. Come on. Please?"

I jumped for it again, but he held it higher. And higher. Until I was practically climbing his body to try and get to it. He laughed as I clung to him, trying not to fall onto my ass. But when my fingertips scraped the bottom of the bag, he moved it behind his back.

Throwing me off balance.

"Clint!"

"Shit, Rae!"

We fell to the bathroom floor and I groaned in pain. I came down against my funny-bone and felt that shivering pain shoot up my arm. Tears rushed my eyes. I felt Clint's hands all over me as he tried to help me sit up. But, with his hands on me, they weren't on that present.

Now, where the hell is it?

"Rae, are you all right?"

I slapped his touch away. "I'm fine. Will you give me that gift now?"

"What's so bad about it? I don't get it."

"Will you just, for once tonight, do as I'm asking you to do!?"

Even I didn't realize how loudly I had spoken until my voice echoed off the bathroom walls. I pushed myself upright and sighed as I leaned heavily against the steady surface. I pressed the heels of my hands into my eyes. I didn't want to cry. I couldn't cry. If I cried, I'd never get out of this. I'd never have a second chance to make this the perfect moment it deserved.

The perfect moment our child deserved.

"Is this a joke?" he asked.

I shook my head. "No, it's not. I just want to give that to you at the right time. And I thought it might be tonight, but--"

"We're having a baby?"

His words snapped my eyes open and all time seemed to freeze over. Clint sat on the other end of the bathroom, with his back against the tub. His eyes were cast down into the yellow and white bag, destroying my vision of this entire announcement. I let a tear slip down my cheek. I drew in ragged breaths as he slowly reached inside. He pulled out the small pair of shoes and studied them, turning them over so his eyes could process what he was seeing.

"Is this real?" he asked.

His eyes met mine, but I couldn't move. I barely knew how to breathe.

"Rae, talk to me. Seriously."

I blinked. "Yes."

"Yes, what? It's a joke? It's real? What is it?"

I swallowed the lump in my throat as I shook my head.

"Words, Rae. I still don't know what you're shaking your head at."

I sniffled. "I'm pregnant."

I waited with baited breath for his reaction. My hands trembled as they fell into my lap. I wiped the crusted toothpaste off my face with a swipe of my chin against my shoulder, trying to buy myself some time. Maybe I could still cover this up. Maybe I could still make this a joyous occasion.

Maybe I could still salvage tonight.

Clint grinned. "You're pregnant."

I nodded. "Yes."

He moved closer to me. "We're pregnant?"

"Yes, we are."

He kept moving until he was sitting beside me. The bag was at the other end of the bathroom, the sneakers still gripped in his hand, the pregnancy test still on the floor.

"We're having a baby?" he asked softly.

The second I whimpered, his arms were around me. A sob escaped from my mouth as I leaned into him. I felt his fingers running through my hair and the strength of his arms enveloping me. I turned into his chest, burying my watery eyes against his muscles. I felt him pull me into his lap. His legs spread, accommodating me as he cradled me against him. I felt the small sneakers pressing into my back. Reminding me of just how badly this had all gone.

"You were supposed to come home on time," I said through my tears.

He peppered kisses along the top of my head. "I'm sorry. I'm so sorry. I didn't know. I should've been here. And I swear to you, it will never happen again. You have my word."

I sobbed. "I was supposed to be all sweet and pretty."

"I know. You did a great job wrapping."

I squeaked. "We were supposed to be happy!"

He held me closer. "We're going to be a family. How in the world couldn't I be happy?"

I sniffled deeply. "We were supposed to make love after you found out!"

I unleashed against his chest. I listened to him chuckle as he continued kissing every part of me he could find. He gripped my chin and tilted my head back. And when his lips found mine, my crying stopped. His tongue stroked me softly. His hand cradled the back of my head. I heard the sneakers fall to the bathroom floor as my arm slipped around his neck, holding him close as his kiss swept me away.

Like it always did.

"There we go," he murmured.

His forehead fell against my own. I felt his thumb brushing away my tears. I sniffled hard, causing him to chuckle again before our gazes met. I sighed heavily. It felt like an elephant was sitting on my chest. But when Clint smiled, all of my worries melted away.

"We're going to be a family, Rae."

I blinked. "You're not upset?"

His own eyes filled with tears. "How could I be? I'm going to have a child with the woman I love most in this world. How could I ever be upset at that?"

I snickered. "You're going to be a daddy, Clint."

He cupped my cheek. "And you're going to be the best damn mother on this planet."

8

CLINTON

I kissed her marked shoulder. "Morning."

Rae yawned. "Mmm, morning, handsome."

I kissed her cheek. "It's time to wake up. We have an hour before the moving truck will be here."

"Five more minutes?"

I chuckled. "Want me to shake you when I get out of the shower?"

She wiggled her butt. "Yes, please."

I patted it softly. "Sounds like a plan."

I planted one more kiss against the mark I'd left on her shoulder last night. Then I forced myself out of bed. If I had things my way, I'd stay in bed with my naked woman all day long. But today was a big day and I needed to be prepared. Last night had been such an emotional drain on my heart. We'd stayed up all night, making love and talking about the life blooming in her belly. She told me all about the names she already had picked out. And I was thrilled that she kept leaning toward boy names. Not that I'd mind a girl. I just thought I'd be better suited to raise a boy.

So long as they're healthy, that's all that matters.

As I showered for the last time in this old shower of ours, I thought about my dream girl still fast asleep in bed. I thought about all we had been through over the past few years. High school. Bullies. Traveling. Getting stuck in airports due to bad weather. The struggles of getting her through college and the all-nighters we'd pulled together so she could help me crank out books for my fans. We'd been through so much in our short lives. We'd seen and dealt with and fought through so damn much.

Damn it, I'm the luckiest man alive.

Suds dripped down my neck as I lathered up my hair. I closed my eyes, remembering the troubled teen I used to be. All the fire and fight with no grace. The mean, nasty attitude I used to carry around with me. The assholes I used to party with. The idiots I used to entertain. I'd been nothing but a glorified villain. A jerk with absolutely no future.

Until Rae came along.

I'd been an asshole. An instigator. And had it not been for that perfect woman lying spreadeagle in our bed right now, I'd be dead. Literally and metaphorically. I would've died in that accident had she not come after me. Had she not cared enough to come searching for me. Even when the people I considered my best friends now hadn't even come after me. Raelynn Cleaver not only saved my life, she saved my soul. She pulled me out of the bowels of hell and showed me a life worth living. She shone light into my darkness, and no matter how much it hurt my eyes, she kept shining brighter. Shining deeper.

Until I adjusted and started enjoying the warmth against my skin.

She invaded every part of me as a teenager. She came in and wrote over every part of my life I couldn't stand. And had it not been for her unwavering support, I'd be dead in a ditch.

Or dead on the side of an embankment.

As I rinsed my hair out, I smiled. Today was the day. The day I showed Rae just how much she truly meant to me. Without her, I'd be nothing. I'd be nowhere. I'd have no one. That woman changed my life. She changed the course of it the second she set her sights on me. And for that, I'd be eternally grateful. I'd spend my entire life worshipping her, if it came down to it. Anything she wanted, it'd be hers for the taking.

For the rest of our lives.

I turned the shower off and wrapped a towel around me. I wiped off the condensation on the mirror and took a good, hard look at myself. I saw my father's eyes staring back at me. I saw his stubbled jawline taunting me in the mirror. But the light behind my eyes as I recalled last night forced all of his features to the side.

"I'm going to be a father," I whispered.

Joy filled my heart. Hope filled my soul. And fear gripped my gut. A father. I was going to be a father. I'd have a child in nine months' time. And I'd be responsible for that child. I gripped the edge of the bathroom counter and closed my eyes. I'd never been much of a God person. Especially considering how I grew up. But at that moment, I needed a bit of His attention.

"I don't know if you can hear me, or if you even exist. But if you do, and you can hear me, I just have one thing I want to ask."

I opened my eyes and found my face staring back at me. Just my face. Not my father. Not my mother. Not even Cecilia.

Just me.

"Help me be the best father I can be," I whispered.

I drew in a deep breath before turning away from the sink. I walked back into the bedroom, venturing around to Rae's side. I sat on the edge of the mattress, dipped down and kissed her cheek softly. I pressed a soft one against her ear, too. And her temple. And her shoulder again.

I loved it when the marks I left behind grew darker the next morning.

"Five more minutes," she grumbled.

I smiled. "It's moving day, babe. Gotta get up."

She stretched. "So no more minutes?"

I chuckled. "No more minutes. Want me to make you some coffee?"

She sighed. "Can't have it anymore. Tea?"

I paused. "Whatever you want."

Guess I still have a lot to learn about all this.

I watched her roll over with a sleepy smile on her face and it warmed my heart. I loved waking up to this woman. But I knew I'd enjoy it even more as her stomach began to grow. I thought about all the times I'd feel it poking into my back. Or my own stomach. I thought about how my hands would be able to engulf the small bump before it outgrew even both of them. I leaned down and pressed a kiss to her lips. Her hand slid into my hair, holding me close to her. I gazed into her beautiful eyes. Eyes I hoped our child might have. Eyes that sparkled with hope, and strength, and determination.

"I love you," she said softly.

I kissed the tip of her nose. "I love you, too."

She grinned. "Do you love me enough to go get me one of those croissants from the cafe downstairs?"

"Anything for you. How about you get a shower and I'll go get breakfast. Then we can sit out on the balcony one last time together."

"That sounds perfect."

"You're perfect."

She winked. "You're coming along nicely. I'm sure you'll get there."

I chuckled. "You're a stinker, you know that?"

"I have my moments."

I captured her lips softly one last time, then I slipped away from the bed. I quickly threw some comfortable clothes on as she stretched and yawned, preparing herself for the cold trek from the bed to the shower. I snatched up my keys and headed downstairs, locking the front door behind me. And as the smells of breakfast pulled me toward the cafe next door, everything rushed through my mind at once.

Getting breakfast was a blur. I kept thinking about all the things our child would need. A crib. A changing table. Clothes. Diapers. I started calculating things in my head and running those figures through our savings account. I started thinking about the time we'd take off once she gave birth and the kind of help Rae would need. I carried breakfast mindlessly back to the apartment, head-deep in all sorts of thoughts.

Like, how could I make Rae's life easier while she was pregnant?

When did we find out the gender of our baby?

Had she set up an appointment with the doctor yet?

Holy shit, we'll have to babyproof the fuck out of our new house.

"Something smells good."

Rae sing-songed the words as she pranced down the hallway with a glow on her face that left me breathless. She took the tea from my hand and I smiled at her, watching as she blew over the small opening. She wiggled her little butt around, dancing to a song only she could hear. And as I made my way over to the kitchen counter, I started pulling out food.

"You know, you got pregnant at the perfect time," I said.

Rae sipped her tea. "How do you figure?"

I shrugged. "Now you can't help with all the heavy lifting."

She scoffed. "Hey. I'm not dead, you know. I can still work."

I shook my head at her. "Nope. You can't. Doctor's orders."

"Are you my doctor now?"

I pulled out her croissant. "I am until we find you one. Plus, you're better at telling people what to do, anyway."

"I'd take offense to that if it weren't true."

I walked her food over to her. "So, that means you can tell everyone where everything goes."

She plucked it from my hand. "Sounds like a productive day to me."

I threw my head back with laughter before we made our way out onto the balcony. We sat there one last time, watching the sun rise over the city we loved so much. I couldn't wait to share more breakfasts with her on our own back porch. In our own home. With our own food stocked in the fridge.

"I think I see the moving truck," Rae said.

I followed the pointing of her finger all the way out to the road.

"Yep. I think that's them," I said.

"You should get downstairs and wait for them. I can start making a plan as to what goes first and what we wait on."

I grinned. "Told you."

"Huh?"

I kissed her cheek softly. "Just tell us what to do, sweetheart, and let me take care of the rest."

She swatted at me playfully, but she listened. It took us just shy of two hours to get the truck loaded up with all of our boxes and furniture and bags of clothes. One of the moving guys was nice enough to drive our second car over to the new house so I could ride my bike over. I led the moving truck to where our new place was and smiled when I saw the little blue car parked by the curb.

Perfect. Things are slowly panning out.

"Hey, Clint?"

I slipped my helmet off. "Yeah?"

She pointed at the car. "Is that Michael and Allison's car?"

I grinned. "Maybe."

She narrowed her eyes. "What are you up to? I thought you said--?"

I shrugged. "I'm up to absolutely nothing."

"Clint. What did you do?"

I put down the kickstand. "Want to do the honors?"

"Clint. Tell me. Now."

I handed her the keys to our new home. "You do the honors. I insist."

She plucked the keys from my palm and rushed to the front door. I set my helmet down as the moving guys tried to get the truck backed into our driveway as best as they could. I rushed after Rae, getting behind her just as she threw open the door. And as I led her toward the kitchen, she gasped.

"Oh. My. God," she whispered.

I placed my lips against her ear. "Welcome home, beautiful."

Her hands flew to her mouth. "Oh, my God!"

And as her squeal filled the space around us, I kissed her softly on her cheek.

While silently hoping Michael and Allison could hear us in order to get their entrance right.

9

RAE

"Oh, my God!"

My hands covered my mouth as I gazed around the kitchen. The entire house, really. But especially the kitchen. The entire thing had been redone. The cabinets were a beautiful white-wash color. The matte black handles on everything looked absolutely outstanding. The soft gray tiles on the floor ushered the theme of the house into the kitchen, and they sparkled with a fresh shine. The appliances had been cleaned down. There was a completely different stove in here from the last time I saw this place. And as I turned around, my eyes fell to the carpet.

The soft gray, fluffy, freshly-cleaned carpets.

"What in the world?" I asked breathlessly.

He chuckled. "You like it?"

I shook my head. "Is this where you've been all these weeks?"

He nodded. "It is. I wanted to surprise you, Rae. That's all. We've worked so hard for this, you and I. You, especially. And I didn't think you should have to settle for anything less than what you want after everything we've been through."

She sniffled. "Oh, Clint."

His hands gripped my shoulders. "This isn't all that got done, either. All of the carpets have been cleaned."

"Seriously?"

"Mm-hmm. I ripped up all of that linoleum and replaced it

with the gray tile. The bathrooms have white cabinets with matte black handles as well. To 'carry the theme,' as you so quaintly put it."

I brushed away my tears. "I can't believe you did all of this. This is amazing. I just--I can't--it's--"

I drew in a shuddered breath as I turned back around to take in the kitchen.

"This is everything, Clint. I love you so much. I can't believe--I'm so sorry. I just--I'm the luckiest woman alive."

He turned me back around slowly. "Now you know how I feel every single day I wake up to you."

I let out a soft giggle. "Our children are going to be so lucky to have you as a father."

I cupped his cheek as tears streaked my own. No matter how much I wiped at them, they wouldn't stop coming. So I simply let them fall. Clint brought his knuckles up and wiped them away softly, only for more to replace the ones he had swept away with his rugged hands.

"Did you do all of this yourself?" I asked.

He shrugged. "I mean, I had a bit of help."

"Seriously? Only a bit? When I've been here every damn weekend for two months?"

"Hey, don't forget me. I'm the one who sent you all of that stuff from her Pinterest in the first place."

"Wait, you told me you found that stuff yourself. You were in on it, too?"

I heard their voices, but couldn't see them. I whipped my head around, trying to figure out where the hell they were. Michael and Allison's voices echoed in my ears as I continuously wiped at the small streams flooding my face and my neck.

"Where the hell are you two?" I exclaimed.

They came into the kitchen from the formal dining room with massive smiles on their faces.

"Sorry, we got turned around in the living room," Michael said.

Allison smiled. "Welcome home, beautiful."

I screamed with delight and went rushing for her. I wrapped my arms around her neck, burying my face into her shoulder. I hadn't seen her in months. Life always kept getting away from us and we always had to push back plans. Or cancel our girls' weekend. Or generally postpone due to sickness or work or life, in general.

"I've missed you so much," I whispered.

She kissed the side of my head. "This place looks fabulous. I can't wait for you to see the bedroom. They really did it up nice."

"Congratulations on the new home, man," Michael said.

I heard him and Clint shaking hands and clapping backs as I held on to Allison as tightly as I could. I knew she and Michael were struggling. I knew they had been having some serious difficulties. So I hoped they were in town for a few days. I really wanted to speak with my best friend about what I felt she needed to do. Because that conversation had been coming for quite some time now. All Allison needed to do was find a way to be vulnerable again. To open up to this man that had done nothing but support her and love her through all the difficult times they had back in college.

"We'll talk later," I whispered.

I felt her nod. "With wine, I hope."

I pulled back, smiling. "Always with wine."

I peered over my shoulder and saw Clint fiddling with something in his pocket. I furrowed my brow as the two men of my life started laughing with one another, and I saw Clint's cheeks tint a soft shade of red. Was he... blushing?

It was very rare that I saw Clint blushing.

What is he blushing over?

I sighed. "Thank you, Michael. For everything. For helping Clint and generally making sure he didn't kill himself. This place is beautiful."

Michael turned around to face me. "There's one more thing, though."

I furrowed my brow. "What is it?"

Allison giggled. "Yep. Just one small, teeny, tiny little thing."

Michael nodded. "You know, the one thing that's missing."

I snickered. "Missing? What in the world is missing right now? Everything is beyond perfect."

Allison rubbed my back. "Almost perfect, at least."

I looked over at my best friend to try and pry an answer out of her. But all she did was nod. I turned back toward the boys, and the second I did I felt tears rushing down my cheeks again. Michael had stepped off to the side by the refrigerator, where Allison quickly joined him. And there, in the doorway of the kitchen, was Clint.

Down on one knee.

With a box in his palm.

"Oh, my God," I whispered.

"Come here, beautiful," he said.

I felt myself moving, but I wasn't sure my legs were working. I felt as if I were gliding over the fresh tiles while the world faded into almost nothing. My heart seemed to be falling out of my chest and my stomach leapt into my throat. Was this happening? Was this real?

Is he really about to ask?

He took my hand in his free one as he smiled up at me. I kept wiping away at my tears, trying not to let them drip on him. And I could've sworn I saw his own eyes line with tears. I heard Allison sniffle beside me. I watched in my peripheral as Michael held her close. And my heart grew twice its size when I turned my head and saw Allison melt into him, relying on him for comfort and support and strength.

Bringing a massive smile to Michael's face.

"I didn't know what happiness looked like until you walked into my life, Cleaver."

My eyes fell back down to him as I snickered. Making him smile brighter than I'd ever seen.

"I knew only darkness before you shined your light into my eyes. And I have to admit, for a while, it hurt. It hurt to look at you and it hurt to touch you and it hurt to kiss you because I'd never experienced that kind of light before. My knee-jerk reaction was to shield it away from my eyes. Pull away from the source of my pain. But you kept coming. You kept knocking at my door. You kept fighting with that strength I admire every single fucking day, and I adjusted."

I giggled. "You make me sound like a virus."

He chuckled. "You came into my life and your light illuminated my darkness. You showed me the absolute hellscape I was living in and showed me a better way of living. A better way of existing. A better way of loving. And I want to spend the rest of my life bringing you the same light, and the same hope, and the same happiness you bring me."

"Oh, Clint."

"I want to love you like you deserve to be loved. I want to protect you the way you deserve to be protected. There's no other woman I want in my life--or for my children--but you. And everything I have is yours."

I sniffled. "I love you so much."

He stood to his feet. "I want to build our family with you under this roof. I want to bring you home after our wedding to this place. I want us to grow old here. To make memories here. To live out the rest of our days in one another's arms here."

I watched him pop open the black velvet box, only to reveal the most gorgeous ring I'd ever seen. Well, from what I could see out of the bottom of my view.

Because my eyes never left his face.

"Raelynn Anne Marie Cleaver. Will you marry me?"

I smiled brightly. "Yes!"

I threw my arms around his neck as Michael and Allison clapped. I buried my crying face into the crook of his neck and his arms cloaked my back. He swayed us side to side. I thought my heart might burst with too much happiness. I clung to his broad shoulders. He picked me up off my feet. And after swinging me around a few times in the middle of our new home, he set me back down.

Before taking my left hand within his.

"I believe this is yours, then," he said.

I sniffled and wiped at my face as he slid the beautiful, sparkling diamond ring onto my finger. I wiggled it in the sunlight streaming through the windows behind me, watching it twinkle, like Clint's eyes did every morning. I couldn't take my eyes off it. The damn thing was mesmerizing. And it wasn't until I heard Allison's voice in my ear that I lifted my head.

"I love you so much. Congratulations, Rae."

Michael patted me on the back. "You deserve it. Way to go."

I smiled. "Thank you. Both of you. Really. I love you two so much."

Allison smiled back. "We love you, too."

Clint tucked a loose strand of hair behind my ear. "Ready to tell them the news? Or do you want to wait?"

Allison paused. "There's more news?"

Michael gasped. "You're not."

Allison furrowed her brow. "What?"

I looked over at Michael. "We are."

He leapt for joy. "Holy shit, you are!"

Allison scoffed. "What are you two talking about!?"

Clint laughed. "We're pregnant, Ally."

She gasped. "Oh. My. Goodness!"

We rejoiced in the kitchen as Michael kept swinging me around. Hugs were exchanged, love was confirmed, and tears were shed. We wrapped ourselves up in a group hug before jumping up and down. Something we always did whenever we first got together after spending so much time apart.

But a rough knock at the door pulled us from our trance.

"Whoops," Clint said.

Michael chuckled. "That the movers?"

I sighed. "Guess it's time to get to work, right?"

Allison took my hand. "Not for you. You get to rest. I'll help the guys with some of the smaller things."

Michael slapped Clint's back. "Guess you knocked her up at the right time, huh?"

I furrowed my brow. "What?"

Clint grinned. "Yeah. Perfect timing, actually. I knew she wouldn't say 'no' to the ring if she had my spawn in her belly."

I slapped his chest. "You take that back, Clinton Clarke. Right now."

Allison laughed. "Ooooh, the last name. He's in the doghouse already."

Michael shook his head. "First night in the new home and you're already on the couch."

Clint smiled brightly. "You know I love you."

I rolled my eyes. "Yeah, yeah, yeah."

Another loud knock came at the door and I pushed through everyone. As I walked around the beautiful round mahogany table in the middle of the foyer, I already pictured the vases of flowers I'd decorate it with every week. I unlocked the door and opened it up, only to find a shocking revelation behind the door.

"Hey, Clint?" I called out.

"Yeah, beautiful?"

I furrowed my brow. "Didn't we only have two movers?"

"Yeah. Why?"

"Because I'm definitely looking at six. With their hands full of stuff."

Clint trotted up behind me. "Well, let them in and get to work. You're bossing everyone around, right?"

The mover grunted. "Where do you want your stuff?"

I moved to the side. "The red boxes go into the kitchen. Oh! And that bed goes all the way down to the hallway, last door on the right."

Michael walked up with Allison. "Sounds like you've already got a handle on your work."

Allison paused. "Where did the other four men come from, though?"

And right at that moment, the last mover came in. He had a red box in his hand, but there was a letter on top of the box. It had mine and Clint's name on it, so I slipped it off the top. Then I pointed the man toward the kitchen.

"Thanks," he said breathlessly.

Clint peered over my shoulder. "Who's it from?"

I opened it up. "Guess we're about to find out."

Rae and Clint,

I'm sorry I can't be there this morning. I took a slip in the shower and bruised my hip pretty badly. Don't worry, it's nothing serious. But I'll probably be at the doctor's office still by the time the movers show up. I know it's not like having me there, but I promise I'll come by with dinner since you two probably won't feel like cooking. And tell Clint not to worry. Brent's accompanying me to the doctor, so I'm not alone. I'll see you two tonight for dinner!

• Cecilia

Clint shoved his hand into his pocket. "I should give her a call."

I placed my hand against his wrist. "Brent's with her. Let him take care of her."

"I need to make sure she's okay."

I held up the letter. "She just said she is. I'm sure she'll call if it's more serious. So let's focus on what we have to do today and we'll see her tonight. All right?"

Allison piped up. "Everything okay?"

I held up the note. "Clint's stepmother took a fall. So I guess she sent four other movers to help us unload in place of her being here."

Michael shrugged. "That's pretty nice. She all right?"

I nodded. "The note says she is. Brent's with her, so…"

Allison giggled. "Oh, yeah. She's just fine, then. A woman is always fine when her man's doting on her."

I watched her shoot a look up to Michael and he smiled.

"I read you loud and clear, cutie pie," he said.

And when the two of them shared a kiss, I didn't think today could get any more perfect.

Until night fell upon us in our new home.

10

CLINTON

I flopped down into the chair out on the back patio before I felt her hands on my shoulders. The way her thumbs dug into my muscles made me moan. And before I knew it, my eyes fell shut. Feeling Rae's ministrations against my sweating muscles felt like heaven. Plus, every time I felt her ring slide against my shirt, it made me smile.

"So, what time should we expect Cecilia?" she asked.

I sighed. "I figure around the time she actually eats dinner. Which won't be until eight."

"Well, that sounds terrible. We should find a snack."

My eyes slowly opened. "What about your mother? Where did she end up today?"

She snickered. "Hell if I know. I haven't heard from her all day. I'll give her a call tomorrow if she doesn't resurface."

"You think something's wrong?"

"Actually, no."

I chuckled. "Well, if you're not concerned, then I'm not concerned."

She let her hands slide down my chest and I let out a soft growl. She pressed the smallest kiss against my cheek. One that shivered me to my core and made my body come alive. I leaned my forehead against her temple, reached back with my hand, and threaded my fingers into her hair.

The night wind softly wrapped around our bodies.

"How are the boxes looking?" I asked.

"Nice and stacked."

"Good. I don't want you unpacking without me."

She giggled. "Already getting overprotective, I see."

"That's my job. I figured you'd already gotten with that program."

She snickered. "Just making a bit of fun. Don't get all weird on me now."

Her lips fell to my neck and I groaned at the feel of her lips. Kiss after kiss, pressed against my pulse point. Causing my cock to rise to the occasion. I gripped her hair and let out a soft grunt. Her hands rumbled down my abs, stopping just shy of the button on my jeans.

"Oh, what you do to me, Rae."

She giggled. "You know, we have a tub now."

"Mmm, we do."

She lowered her voice. "With jets."

I growled. "Perfect."

"I think our celebratory bottle of alcohol-free champagne might taste better in a hot bubble bath, don't you think?"

I craned my neck to look at her. "You always have the best ideas. You know that?"

She kissed the tip of my nose. "Race ya."

"What?"

She took off laughing as she leapt back into the house. I scooted the chair out from behind me and raced into the kitchen, scooping up the bottle of champagne. Fuck glasses. We didn't need any fancy shit tonight. All I needed was her, that bath, and my hands splayed across her stomach.

A stomach that would grow over the coming months.

"Can't catch me, Clint!"

I chuckled. "Better watch those words of yours. Come here."

"Ah!"

She squealed as I picked her up, swinging her around in our bedroom. I peppered her shoulder with kisses and nips, listening to her soft sighs. Gripping the neck of the champagne bottle tightly, I nuzzled my nose against the shell of her ear and walked her into the bathroom.

"Celebrating in baby-friendly style, huh?" she asked.

I pressed my lips to her ear. "Not exactly."

My lips fell to her neck as I stripped her out of those clothes she had on. She turned around, running her fingertips along my muscles as she undressed me as well. I watched as her naked form grabbed the bottle. I ran the water in the tub, preparing it with lots of bubbles, while she struggled with the cork. She pointed it towards our bedroom and a resounding 'pop!' finally filled our ears.

Before the cork fell right at her feet.

She sighed. "Well. That was…"

I snickered. "I don't even care. This is the best day of my life. And I wouldn't want to change a thing about it."

She turned around. "You took the words right out of my mouth, big guy."

"Now, why don't you come over here and give this big guy of yours some lovin'?"

She held out her finger to me and tipped the bottle up to her lips. My eyebrows rose as she took one chug. Then, two. But, soon after that, it started spraying from her mouth.

"Rae?"

She started coughing before she lunged for the sink.

"Rae!"

She heaved into the porcelain concavity as I held her hair back.

"It's okay. I gotcha. You're all right."

She spat. "Holy shit, that stuff tastes terrible."

I paused. "Wait, you're not getting sick?"

She stood up. "Only off of that. You can have it. Ugh. That's nasty."

My eyebrows rose. "I got something to replace the flavor, if you're up for it."

She wiped her mouth off. "Is that a blowjob joke? Because if it is, it's not as good as your other ones."

I chuckled. "Get over here and kiss me, woman."

I wrapped her up in my arms and pulled her against my body. My cock pressed against the warmth of her skin, ushering me back home. I picked her up and walked her over to the tub, stepping us both in and settling us beneath the bubbles. I slid my fingers into her gloriously soft locks and gazed into her breathtaking eyes. And when my lips pressed against hers, the whole of the world stood still.

"I love you so much," she whispered.

I grinned. "I love you, too."

Her head settled against my shoulder. "You know what we should do for the nursery?"

I kissed the top of her head. "What's that?"

"Make it gender neutral."

"How so?"

"You know, yellows and pale greens and rainbows. Make it so that a boy or a girl could fit well into it."

"Those kinds of colors would go well with the scheme of the rest of the house."

"Plus, we could get started on it piece by piece while I'm still able to move. You know, instead of waiting until I'm practically swollen everywhere to do something about it."

"I mean, you're not doing any of that hard work anyway."

She scoffed. "Why can't I help out with the nursery?"

I grinned down at her. "Because you're going to be too busy growing our child, Rae. I can take care of that stuff."

She snuggled against me. "Fine. I'll just put it on my Pinterest and see what you come up with."

I smiled. "Sounds perfect to me."

She reached her foot up and turned off the water as the bubbles reached an all-time high. I mean, we were covered from head to toe, except for our faces. She giggled as they popped against her nose. My heart warmed as she kept snuggling deeper into me, wiggling herself between my legs. I didn't even care that water was sloshing out onto the freshly-tiled floors.

I was just glad to be holding the love of my life against me in a tub in our forever home.

"Our parents are going to freak. You know that, right?" she asked.

I snickered. "Your mother is going to go ballistic."

She nodded. "And Cecilia's going to practically have a stroke."

"You know we won't have to buy this child a single thing between the two of them, right?"

She looked up at me. "Yeah, and you better not fight it, either."

I kissed her forehead. "Noted."

"Good."

"It's kind of nice, having this little secret to ourselves for a while."

She pulled my hands over her stomach and I kissed the shell of her ear.

"I mean, minus Mike and Ally."

She snickered. "Yeah. They don't count."

I laughed. "All right. Fine. They don't count. You want to talk about how and when you want to tell everyone else?"

She shrugged. "Let's at least keep it to ourselves for the weekend. You know, really keep it ours. We can have them over for dinner sometime this first week once we're settled and we can tell them then."

"Sounds like a plan to me."

"I knew you'd see things my way."

"Oh, you come here, you cheeky little thing."

I tilted her head back and captured her lips. I kissed her, over and over, as she slowly turned herself around in the tub. She straddled my hips and my cock throbbed with a need to be inside her. She cupped my cheeks, pressing her luscious lips against my own. And when our tongues connected, nothing else mattered.

Nothing else ever mattered when Rae was around.

My forehead fell against hers. "So I take it you like everything?"

She scoffed. "Like it? I love it, Clint. Every single bit of it."

I smiled. "Well, that's good. Because I was thinking."

"About…?"

"We can't technically use the kitchen yet."

She blinked. "What?"

"Nope. Completely unusable."

She paused. "Why? What didn't you get done?"

"Oh, no no. Don't get me wrong. The kitchen is completely finished. It just hasn't been christened yet."

She furrowed her brow. "How the hell do you christen a kitchen, you dork?"

My gaze met hers. "Do you really want to know?"

I slid my hands up her thighs, feeling her tremble against me. Her breasts, seated tightly against my chest, puckered as my hands continued their adventure. I gripped her hips, dancing my fingers along the dip of her waist. I watched her cheeks tint that beautiful red color as I cupped the back of her head, fisting her hair to hold her there. I hovered my lips over hers as my dick toyed with her entrance. And as she gasped, I felt her nod.

"I do. I want to know, Clint."

I grinned wickedly. "How about this? I carry you out of this bathroom and put you on the kitchen counter."

"Uh huh?"

"Then, I pull up a chair and spread these delectable legs of yours."

She sighed. "Yeah?"

"And then, I put my tongue right--"

"Shut up and kiss me."

I smiled as I nuzzled my nose against hers. But when she leaned in for a kiss, I slowly backed up. She let out the most decadent whimper I'd ever heard, and it took all I had within me to not fill her right then and there. I steeled my resolve enough to gather her into my arms and stood up into the tub, balancing myself as I stepped over the edge. I walked us through the bathroom, the bedroom, down the hallway and into the kitchen.

And after setting her on the kitchen counter, I did exactly as I said I would.

I pulled up a chair and sat down between her legs.

"Clint, I--"

My lips fell to her ankle. "I love you so much."

She gasped. "I love you, too."

I kissed up her calf. "Every inch of you."

"Oh."

"Every cell of your body."

She groaned. "Fuck."

I sucked on the dollop of excess her upper thigh provided as she leaned back.

"I love you with everything I am, Raelynn."

Her hand fisted my hair. "I love you too, Clinton. So fucking much."

As my tongue touched down against her slit, I vowed to always show her. To always prove to her. To always remind her of just how much I adored her. She was my savior. My guiding light. My inspiration, and my safe place to fall. I'd never stop loving her. I'd never stop needing her. I'd never stop enjoying her.

"Clint, yes!"

I growled. "There it is."

And I sure as hell would never get tired of hearing her yell my name.

Thank you for reading THE DIAMOND IN THE ROUGH series. Don't miss my RED THORNS series, a College Bully Romance full of bad boys, motorcycles and a passionate love story. And be sure to join my email and SMS lists below to don't miss any of my future books!

Want to read an exclusive novella from Clinton's point of view? Check out CLAIMING ME.

Get an SMS alert:
Text REBEL to 77948

If you want to support me, consider leaving a review on Amazon. I'd love it!

REBEL HART

Rebel Hart is an author of Dark and Contemporary Romance novels. Check out her Dark Bully Romance series The Elites Of Weis - Jameson Prep Academy. You'll fall in love with Emmett and Ophelia's story. And don't forget to join her Readers' Group to chat with Rebel and other fans: facebook.com/groups/rebelhart

NEVER MISS A NEW RELEASE:
Follow Rebel on Amazon
Follow Rebel on Bookbub

Text REBEL to 77948 to don't miss any of her books (US only) or sign up at www.RebelHart.net to get an email alert when her next book is out.

authorrebelhart@gmail.com

CONNECT WITH REBEL HART:

ALSO BY REBEL HART

For a full list of my books go to:

www.RebelHart.net

www.ingramcontent.com/pod-product-compliance
Lightning Source LLC
Chambersburg PA
CBHW031601180726
48284CB00005B/1350